Also by Stephen Swartz

Contemporary Literary Fiction

After Ilium

Aiko

A Beautiful Chill

A Girl Called Wolf

Exchange

Fantasy & Science Fiction

The Stefan Székely Vampire Trilogy

I. A Dry Patch of Skin

II. Sunrise

III. Sunset

Epic Fantasy *With Dragons

The Dream Land Trilogy

I. Long Distance Voyager

II. Dreams of Future's Past

III. Diaspora

The Masters' Riddle

The Flu Season Saga

1. The Book of Mom

2. The Way of the Son

3. Dawn of the Daughters

4. The Book of Dad

5. The Granddaughter

THE GRANDSONS

Conclusion to the FLU SEASON Saga

[Book 6]

A Novel

Stephen Swartz

MYRDDIN PUBLISHING GROUP

UNITED STATES ✦ UNITED KINGDOM ✦ AUSTRALIA

ISBN-13: 978-1-68063-139-5

www.myrddinpublishing.com

Cover design by Iris Schaeffer

NOTE

This is a work of imagination created for entertainment purposes and is not intended to convey any medical advice or provide health care information for readers.

What characters may state on the pages is solely a product of their fictional personalities and should not to be construed as the Author's own views on any particular facts and opinions whether accepted or contested.

FLU SEASON
a pandemic saga

I.

The Book of Mom

Part 1

Journey

Part 2

Destination

II.

The Way of the Son

Part 1

Exile

Part 2

Vengeance

III.

Dawn of the Daughters

Part 1

Births

Part 2

Deaths

IV.

The Book of Dad

V.
The Granddaughter

VI.
The Grandsons

Part 1
Strangers

Part 2
Fifteen Years Earlier

Part 3
Family

TABLE OF CONTENTS

Part 1 – Strangers

  1 Stranger Comes to Town . . . 11
  2 Little Miss Gunslinger . . . 25
  3 Truths & Falsehoods . . . 39
  4 Three Sisters and a Wilderness . . . 51
  5 Marks . . . 63
  6 Badlands . . . 71
  7 A Few Words . . . 79
  8 Judgment Day . . . 89
  9 An Imperfect Posse . . . 105

Part 2 – Fifteen Years Earlier

10 The Lost Boy . . . 123
11 Initiation . . . 139
12 The Remains . . . 151
13 Morning in America . . . 161
14 Shortgrass Trail . . . 173
15 Hideout . . . 183
16 Schism . . . 195
17 The Red Devil . . . 203
18 Winterborn . . . 215
19 Standard Townsfolk . . . 225
20 The Gauntlet . . . 239
21 Mountains and Rivers without End . . . 257
22 Tourist Village . . . 275
23 Underground . . . 291
24 The Facility . . . 303

25 The Project . . . 319

26 The Council . . . 333

27 The Committee . . . 343

28 A New Protocol . . . 355

29 Forbidden Zone . . . 371

30 Battleground . . . 385

31 A Fine Hacienda . . . 401

32 The Brethren . . . 421

33 Caliph Orna . . . 437

34 The Setting Sun . . . 451

Part 3 – Family

35 Two Outlaws . . . 463

36 Three Prophets . . . 471

37 Four Horsemen . . . 483

38 Five Senses . . . 495

39 Six Months Gone By . . . 507

40 Seventh Day of the Seventh Month . . . 521

41 Eight Weeks . . . 533

42 Nine Months . . . 543

Genealogy . . . 549

Acknowledgements . . . 551

About the Author . . . 553

The Way of the Son is fraught with danger, menace at every turn, and a lot of stupid mistakes that pop up when you least can handle them.

—'Sandy' in *The Way of the Son,* an opera by Maggie Baumann, premier: 15 Tenthmonth 2155

THE GRANDSONS

PART ONE

STRANGERS

S T E P H E N S W A R T Z

1

STRANGER COMES TO TOWN

A LONE RIDER APPROACHES, emerging from the orange palette that smudges the sky, a mosaic across the horizon, as it has for months, the sun refusing to set, continuing to glow. Townsfolk feel the itchy heat, smell the fire, yet its source is too far away to be known, something from the distant east and the dirty industry set there that cries out for production or a groan of dissatisfaction at what humanity has done to this world after only a few centuries of miscalculation. We've wrought what we've sown, some like to say.

From that blazing sky, a lone hawk falls, unable to fly on, baked in the heat, wingtips fried by a flameless fire.

The rider comes on, like a dark devil delivering a message.

A black silhouette moving against the orange glow, against the dark hills, the ragged chaparral where buffalo no longer roam.

People gather at the edge of town, see the rider sitting upon a poor horse pulling a two-wheeled cart, making its ungainly pace. Nothing good comes from the east, they know. Yet rider and horse and the cart come. And people wait. They watch fearfully, like the visitor is bringing a long-craved meal in their starvation. What news is there from the bright east? What madness lies that way?

Grasslands have wilted out there, they've noticed, cacti fallen, animals which once grazed there now dead or they've run away to find better territory, as though the world has changed. Has been for years, the older ones say. They recall a time when the east did not glow day and night. No good ever comes from that direction. People feel glad to be far from that terrible land, from the savage coast.

After a smoldering eternity, the dark rider saddled upon the weary mount, lashed between the staves of the ragged cart, enters the dusty town, keeping to the same lumbering pace, having no urgency, having no need to pause and greet townsfolk who stare or the few who call questions. Is it safe? How did you survive? What's in the cart?

The rider turns the beast, aims the cart to the edge of the street, directing it to the rails set before a row of shops, chooses one, and the cart rolls to a halt.

A crowd gathers to see who this figure might be, as none have come from the east in months – none worth addressing. Stragglers with tales of flameless fire and putrid illness. Waves of death. Or fleeing criminals hoping for a break. The rare lost tax man or some ignorant seeker of opportunity, random scalawags, bold outlaws. A gunslinger or two. A foolish family believing they'll survive.

Dark in the road-rough garb, the figure glares from beneath the brim of a felt hat at the townsfolk gathered: passersby, the curious, morning shoppers, businessmen going to offices. Another cow town, the stranger seems to acknowledge, a disappointed shift of chin. They're harmless, and unarmed.

The figure, looking more to be a woman in man's clothing, lays her hand on the grip of one of two pistols set upon her hips, ready to use.

"Skinner Canyon?" asks the stranger in mild tone.

"Yes, ma'am," says an older man, wiping his moist brow, beady eyes fixed in permanent squint. His office suit is soaked with sweat. "This's the place." He gives her a long look, not approving. "What's yer bidness in town?"

Townsfolk can see the two pieces of cargo lain in the cart. There is a crudely constructed wooden box, looking like pine, large enough and in the shape to hold a laid-out man. The wood is well-smudged with dirt, grimy like it was dragged up from the earth. A coffin, they presume, nailed tightly shut. Who could be inside?

Beside the box on the flatbed lays a rolled-up tarp, a dingy green square of tent canvas, and townsfolk guess it contains a body.

The townsfolk back away when the rider dismounts the winded horse, brushing against its bare ribs, its ragged legs, as her frayed boots hit the dirt, raising a dust cloud. A figure of mean leather and filthy denim, snake-bit hat bent low, pulled down, hiding dark eyes. A lithe figure, certainly a woman, yet of what age? Strapped across her chest are two half-empty bandoleers, cousins of the silver pistols resting anxiously on each hip. Sad boots, once elegantly crafted now scuffed and in patches worn down to the last fibers, mingle with the town's dusty street. She rights herself before the crowd.

Her gnarly hands sweep dust from her chest, breeze carrying the cloud away. She lifts her grease-stained hat, pulled down tight over her head, and a bundle of black hair falls down her shoulders. It's a woman, they confirm, a few of the gathered surprised but the others suddenly afraid. Her grim face belies a hard journey across a wild landscape. She's not large but none dare approach.

Some in the crowd gasp at the sight of her. Half of them don't expect such an ornery-looking figure to be a woman. The other half know her, recognize her through the tough disguise. They've seen her face on old posters tacked up across the territory. There's one of them on the wall of the shop right behind her, been stuck there for a while, the reward no longer increasing.

With a hard glance at the gathered fools to keep them in place, she bows to the trough beside the railing, one hand on a pistol. The horse is already taking its loud, slurping drink. She takes a handful of water, splashes it over her face. A touch of her bandanna to wipe her face. Another cupped hand of water goes to her lips. Another dip of her hand and a swallow, the other hand on her gun.

Straightening, she regards the townsfolk around her, forces a grin. She's got her teeth. More people recognize her, adding to the murmurs. Is it her? Could it be? They keep their eyes on the pistols at her hips. Who is she? Why has she come? The town's had peace for years now.

Breaking through the crowd stomps a mature man, the rotund banker in his crisp black suit, thinning hair swept back. Townsfolk part for him, let him take charge.

"Trinity," the banker puffs warily, standing before her. His word sounds like a question. Like he isn't sure what to say.

She snaps a look that makes him cower.

"'Preciate ya not usin' that name," she grunts from beneath the brim of her hat. "It's Trina."

"Yes, ma'am," he stammers. "That's right: Cimarron. Forgot."

That makes the woman bristle, hand to her pistol.

"No offense, ma'am," the banker says, cowering. "I wasn't there. Heard of it, though."

She glares at him a moment. "Got business."

Folks gathered round murmur at the presence of the woman, all afraid of what she might do, what's she's known for doing: shooting anyone who displeases her. They wonder who's displeased her this time. Who lays on that cart? How will their lives be changed?

"What kind of business, might I ask?" The banker stands firm.

"Ya got any deputy here?" asks the woman in a dusty voice.

The banker gathers himself, sighs as he runs a hand through what's left of his hair, aware of the townsfolk behind him.

"We got one," he says. "Got a right good one. What should we say it's about?"

She waves at the cart.

"Got these," says the woman, standing stern at barely five-five, looking fit but weary, at the front edge of middle age yet fighting it. Clean her up, put her in a pretty dress, and she could pass for any man's happy bride, the banker must be thinking.

"He be wantin' 'em," she says.

Townsfolk aren't used to having bodies brought into town, least of all by a woman, not by *this woman* whose history gallops ahead of her, clearing a path as wide an autumn cattle drive.

"So who's it ya got there?" asks another man, stepping forward, bold beside the banker. His muscular arms and craftsman's apron lend strength to his presence.

She grins to herself, adjusts her hat, and steps around to the end of the cart. She taps on the box.

"This here's yer sheriff."

The crowd gasps, a couple of them shriek in shock. Women grow faint. He was a good man, they say, and fate has been cruel to him.

Now they know his destiny after all these years.

"This one," she indicates with a tug of the canvas roll.

Two men come forward to help unroll the tarp, turning the body over and over on the flatbed until a face is revealed. As suspected: a dirty, bloody corpse, soiled bandage wrapped around the body, an obvious belly wound, the red beard matted with mud and blood, face almost unrecognizable. Yet he is known to some of them.

"Bad Bart," someone mutters, and the others take up the name, stating their surprise and their shame. "It's Bad Bart."

The dusty woman backs away, unfettered by their reaction, and unstraps the horse from its labor, adjusting the saddle.

"You better go get Miss Maggie," says the banker to those behind him. "Her boy's come home."

+ + +

The glow in the east is the same each morning, like the sun rises as it always has. What's different is that the glow stays throughout the day, fills the eastern sky like a perpetual sunrise. It crawls painfully overhead, grins down harshly in the noontide, descends begrudgingly below the horizon in the west. What's not usual is the orange glow that remains constant in the eastern sky. The glow never wavers, doesn't grow darker, never fades into a lighter hue. It stays through the night.

Some people think it's a new star, born off the port bow, come to life in the past year, either a blessing or a curse, too soon to call. If it is a new star, it sits in the sky below the horizon so none can't see it directly, not from this western outpost. Other folks believe it's something worse, the after-effect of some catastrophe in the east – where the largest cities are, days by railway.

People everywhere have been wary of things ever since that ten-year pandemic and the decades of lawlessness more than a hundred years earlier. Some call it a plague. It disrupted the whole world, ruined a country that had stood here, made everything stop, caused people who survived it to start over. That's why it's taken so long to get back to the way things were a hundred years ago. Out here it's more primitive: horses, not motor carriages.

Folk who know things remind us of the days the earth shook, a rumbling disruption we felt underfoot even out here at Skinner Canyon. A few of them had visited a city or two in the east and knew how they were filled with factories and dangerous operations. Made sense that something had gone wrong. An explosion, perhaps. Some major destruction. And nothing remained.

"They done blowed up the place," wiry old Mr. Calhoun cried out whenever the topic arose. "The damn, dirty apes!" he would shout, seeing something the rest of us couldn't see. Nobody knew what he meant, but everyone knew he'd gone soft in the head, nursed a war wound, so we paid him no mind.

No communications from that side of the country for a while. The wires ran silent. Only a few weak, random signals that made no sense. No messages came by railway, either. In fact, all traffic was halted east of Kanza City. Disruption of the resources usually coming out to us on the railway. Mostly self-sufficient, we're used to doing things without help from the eastern cities, have been from the start of this town, counting about ten-thousand souls, but we do like getting our treats and trinkets from the east. We no longer think of sending anything eastward, however. It can only go as far as Kanza City or on to Louis.

Missy Cable, who went to college in Kanza City, first speculated it was a vast fire raging, like a forest fire only larger, fiercer. Lots of field and forest between the capital and that first mountain range, she explained. Nothing had been done to secure that wild territory following the plague. Then everybody was on their own, doing what they could to survive. As years unfolded, people began to rebuild, start over, making a new country from the remnants of the old. Almost returning to the kind of life they had before the plague.

"It's probably one of them explosions you can read about in some old books," Mr. Cruz says. He keeps a personal stash of paper books in a large trunk in his cabin, charges folks a fee to borrow them for a spell. He's read them all, he says, tells us the stories he's read of flying through outer space, monsters from other worlds, and the big boom that ends the Earth. We wonder if he's crazy. He says his

16

grandfather rode in flying wagons that dropped bombs on enemy cities a century ago.

Miss Maggie, who once was the town's school teacher, repeated stories her grandmother told her father and her father passed on to her, so we know what happened. Her grandmother was born in the seventh year of the pandemic, and lived through the lawless times and reconstruction, witnessed everything first-hand. Maggie had notebooks written by her grandmother's father that described what they experienced back in those days. Then cities were rebuilt, some better than others. The new capital was nice and clean for a while, a beacon of hope, then shifted into manufacturing which took a toll on the lives of citizens. They tried to rebel but were put down.

Even in her elder years Miss Maggie never stops talking about things her father said, or his mother's father wrote. She used to be a music writer. She lived in the capital a number of years and was the conductor of the orchestra. Her career started with forming a band for kids in this town. Later she made a singing-show called an *opera*, based on stories about life during the pandemic. She said people liked it – what turned out to be the only performance in the capital. Another performance was planned for Kanza City, but the leading singer died of an illness. Complaints of feeling sad by the opera, despite its happy ending, doomed it. We never got to see it out here but we never expected to.

"Must be God striking down the sinful," says Father James, too old to stand for a full church service, He's training a new priest to take over soon. Father James is Miss Maggie's older brother. "Lots of sin going on back east there," he rants, "good our sister left there, came home to us at last."

Thing is she brought a son home with her and nobody dared say anything about how that might've happened. She insisted the boy's father died in the capital years before. He died before she knew she was carrying his baby. Kind of a sad story. I played with that boy; we grew up together, me being a couple years older.

"That Delbert, he went to doctor school," Cory Conn insisted, "and he said it were 'nother pandemic, what they call plague, that they need to burn out. That's what we seein' every day and night."

Of all the townsfolk, only I seemed to consider his idea. I'd read in those old notebooks or heard from Miss Maggie herself that they often set fire to a place where plague was found, burned down farms, a house with an infected family inside. Maybe the plague returned and they were burning it out again. The scent of burnt flesh seemed to trickle over to us from time to time.

Missy Cable insists we're safe. Too far for cleansing fire to reach us. A friend of hers in Kanza City, hundreds of miles closer to the Glow, said they could smell the heat, feel ashes on the wind, said it smelled like burnt flesh, concrete dust, iron metal, and sappy wood all mixed together, but we didn't believe that. It couldn't happen. Nothing could destroy such a large portion of the country. She liked to remind us of her studies, like she was some kind of scientist. I had to dismiss her – but in a kind, gentleman way, because I still liked her even though I was seeing Annie in those days.

Eugene Cable is the town mayor so everyone is kind to Missy, no matter how snooty she can be. Other times she's sweet. Mother said I should be kind to everyone, no matter how other boys act. She told me how Miss Maggie took in my mother when she had no one and she became like a daughter. Then my mother married that man from the ranch, Maggie's nephew, and I was born. They raised me as best they could but life can be hard. I finally understood why they called her Jackrabbit, being a tribal woman, and why they call me Little Bear when they know damn well my name is Jacob. Boys my age and older men call me Jake. Mother explained how I got the name Baumann added on. Maggie's other brother Frank had three sons, and the oldest was Jeb and he was the one that married Jackrabbit. Right after I was born, Maggie went to the capital to do her music business and didn't come back for ten years. She brought her son, surprising everyone. His name was Bart. We played together. Then one day Bart left to join the posse led by Frank, our sheriff, going after a criminal by the name of J.C. Wells.

Today talk about the Glow is not as important as the truths we see lain out on that cart at the side of the street. If both of them are who that woman says they are, I know them. Both of them. They're my kin. And I stood there at the back of that crowd when they were finally brought home.

+ + +

"They say you come from the east, from the Glow. Wonder if you can say what it is. You know?"

Doc Baker, son of the older man who died a couple years ago – same day as my Aunt Eve – who went up to Kanza City to learn the physician trade, sits calmly behind the same desk where his father used to sit in the clinic office. I stand like the good assistant I am. I hate being called a nurse, but that's the work I do in this town.

"Not so far," says the stern woman, looking maybe thirty-five but thin and not so tall. Her hard-riding outfit makes her look tough. You don't want to cross her. "Five days' ride, figure."

Doc Baker starts to speak but she cuts him off.

"Listen, just brung 'em here fer the money," she says, and lets out a rasp of impatience. "That's all. The man in the tarp there, he said I kin get some money if I brung him and th' other to this town." She levels her dark eyes at the doc. "Be needin' a fresh horse, too."

"He told you?" asks the doc, eyebrow raised.

"Weren't dead yet, but we both knowed he gonna be dead by time we get to town. Said his mama would want 'em both."

"Yes, indeed," says the doc, sounding a lot like his father. "We've sent for her. Please wait. I'm sure she'll have questions."

She gives a nod. "Ain't one fer questions."

Her eyes shift around the clinic, as if marking items to steal, and noting the curious folks watching through the windows. She keeps a hand on the pistol at her hip.

"She'll be right along," says the doc. He gives her a lengthy look, assessing her. "You hurt at all? Need any assistance?"

"Ain't hurt," she grumbles, straightening herself in the chair. As she does, she spies me, gives me a cold stare. Maybe it's because I have a similar look as her: tan skin, black hair. I know my heritage but I have to wonder about hers. My mother was Kanza, my father plain American, pale and sandy-haired.

I stand up straight, not leaning in the doorway. I'd been looking at her and I guess she felt it. I figure she and me are the same age or close enough, both of us a bit older than Bart. But I'm too afraid of her to even say 'hello'. And she knows it.

"I really wish you'd consider setting aside your weapons. I'd feel a whole lot better," says the doc. "Nobody's gonna be coming for you. You're under truce on account of you bringing us these bodies. That qualifies. Like holding up a white flag."

"Deputy Cal's coming." I see the burly forty-ish man sauntering across the street, his pistol already drawn.

Doc jumps up, stumbles around the desk and meets the deputy at the door to the clinic. I peek out of the office at them.

"Hold up, now, Cal. We're under a truce."

"You can't be serious," Cal cries out. "You got Trina Culpepper in there?"

The doc puts his hand up. "She brought in two bodies."

"I bet she shot them herself," says Cal.

"Never shot nobody din't deserve gettin' shot," she calls from the doc's office.

I can see Doc holding back the deputy, hand on his chest, as the man strains to get past.

"Put your gun away," says Doc.

"Fine," says the deputy. "If you're vouching for her."

Once Cal's holstered his pistol, Doc steps aside.

I move against the wall as Doc and Deputy Cal enter, filling the space in the small office. Both tower over the woman who remains seated in front of the desk. Her hand fidgets over her pistol.

"Truce," says Cal. "Agreed? Till you leave town."

She gives no response but the tension in the room grows.

"Been a while," says the deputy in a dry voice, moving to the side chair and facing her.

She gives a growl. "Ain't long 'nuff."

Cal's face flashes something: satisfaction?

"Doc says you brought in two bodies." He looks out of the office. "Where are they?"

"In the back room," I say at the doc's glance.

Cal clears his voice, leans on his elbow on the corner of the desk.

"So, obvious question: who are they? Next: who shot 'em?"

With no show of emotion she speaks in a firm voice: "First is yer Sheriff. Th' other one call himself Bart."

"Bad Bart?" the deputy exclaims.

"No account o' him use any other name," she says plainly.

"Bart Baumann?" Cal seems doubtful. "Why, he's been gone for near fifteen years. Just stop in for a drink or shoot somebody, I hear. Away before anybody could identify him."

"Purdy sure he never shot nobody in this town," she says.

"But he sure did in other towns," says the deputy, "and outside of towns. You both did."

"Ain't never shot nobody din't deserve it," she repeats sternly.

"And who would deserve it? Townsfolk? Innocent customers of a bank or standing at a depot? People working farms and ranches?"

"Bullets don't know where they s'posed to go. People just get in the way."

"So next question: Who shot them? Was it you?"

Her stern façade breaks then. She snickers like she got the joke, shaking her head. "Weren't me, kin promise ya that."

"And why can you promise that?"

"Cuz that man y'all callin' Bad Bart. Ya see, me an' him, we's like what they call husband an' wife but no preacher sayin' words."

"Is that right?" the doc muses.

Her announcement strikes me in the heart. My childhood friend and this tough woman? A couple? Like being lovers?

"And the man in the box?" asks Cal.

"Yer Sheriff. He was long buried but Bart said I'll get money if I brung him back here, so I dug him up an' brung him to ya."

"But when did he die? Who shot him?"

"Weren't me."

"Bart?"

She snickers. "Hell, no." She shakes her head. "He wouldn't do it, Sheriff bein' his uncle."

"Frank Baumann," I mutter, knowing the man from when I was a child. My grandfather. He taught me how to shoot. Frank's eldest son, Jeb – a twin with Joe – was my father. But he left when I was very young. They say Jeb got tangled up with some outlaws.

Deputy Cal sits back with a loud sigh. "Poor Maggie."

"Yep, her." The woman scoots to the front of her chair, like she's ready to leave. "That's th' one s'pose to pay me."

I regard this disagreeable woman with scorn. "You know Bart's mother is our Miss Maggie, the famous music lady?"

The deputy glares at me for interrupting.

"What he means is," the doc starts, then can't finish.

"Yeah, he said," the woman speaks up. "Ain't got no tears fer any mama lost a son. Not fer no mama lost three daughters, neither. Fer no papa dying. It's how the world is. Not one o' us is to blame fer anythin' happens."

"There are some things we can sure blame people for," Cal says. "Plenty of acts that run foul of the laws."

"Ain't here t'day talkin' no *phi-lo-sophy*. Just need my money. An' a fresh horse. Then I'll be on my way, never bother y'all again, promise."

"Here she comes," I announce, seeing the woman making her way across the street, using a cane, bent a little but waving off the man who fetched her and who's offering to help her to the clinic. She's been to this clinic too often in her life and knows the way, I'm sure she's telling that man. She once was in a wheel-chair because of an injury but she recovered and put the wheel-chair aside after three years. Another two years to get rid of crutches. Now her age forces her take up a cane.

We hear the clap of the cane on the wooden landing, then the door flings open like a bigger man has punched it.

"Doc Baker!" she cries out in a thin voice but with a full force of wind behind it – like she's blowing her tuba.

The doc scrambles out to meet her.

"Thanks for coming, Maggie." He takes a breath. "Now, gotta tell you, this is gonna upset you so I want to caution you first, things you will hear. And what we come to know...about...." His voice trails off as her gaze cuts through him.

I pose in the office doorway so she can see me, giving her a smile – the sad version. Seeing me, she seems to relax. She knows I work with Doc, tells me all the time she's proud of me, especially when I take my bag out to tribal villages to treat injuries or illnesses.

"Real sorry, Miss Maggie," I tell her, imagining against my will how she will react to the news. "Guess it's both bad news and some good maybe, if you can think of it that way."

"Someone said it's about my Barty," she manages to say before a storm of emotion stops her. I haven't seen her cry since the day her cousin Eve passed.

Deputy Cal steps to the doorway and I move aside.

"We got us a situation," he says in serious tone. "You don't need to come in here. There's someone here maybe you don't wanna see. I can do the talking for you. I know what you wanna be asking her."

"Her?" asks Maggie, eyes narrowing.

We all look at each other.

"A woman's come to town," I speak up, regarding her over Cal's shoulder. "She's brought two bodies. One's in a pine box. Other's in a rolled up canvas."

"That's enough, Jake," Doc snaps at me.

"I trust Jake to tell me straight more than either of you," says Maggie, tapping her cane against the doc's leg. "Move aside."

Doc goes to his right, Cal to his left. I back into the office as Miss Maggie lumbers ahead, pausing in the doorway a heartbeat to notice who's sitting in the chair. They've never met.

The two men squeeze through the doorway as I push myself into the corner behind the desk. Maggie stands strong at the front of the desk, regarding the visitor.

"I see you need guns," says Maggie.

The woman gazes up at her but doesn't move, keeps her hands off the pistols.

"Ain't here to shoot nobody," says the woman.

"My name's Maggie. What's yours?"

After a moment: "Trina."

"I won't say it's nice to meet you. Depends why we're meeting. I suspect you got some information I might want to hear."

Trina gives a slight nod. "I do."

"Tell me, then. All of it."

Cal speaks up: "But, Miss Maggie, it could be rough—"

"I heard rough before," Maggie barks. Then, to Trina: "Talk."

"Brung the bodies to town here, as he ask me to, said I could get money for it."

Maggie purses her lips. "Who asked you?"

"The one in the tarp. He were alive then, but we both knowed he ain't gonna make it. He says: 'You take us to Skinner Canyon an' my mama'll give ya some money fer bringin' us home. What he s—"

"You mean...Bart? My son?"

You could hear Cal's head nod, creaky like a rusty doorjamb.

Doc glares at me, clears his throat as a cloud of dust blows down Main Street and the clock on the wall ticks.

"Jake, why don't you take Miss Maggie on back there, let her see the body?"

2

LITTLE MISS GUNSLINGER

I STRAIGHTEN, STEP TO THE DOOR. "This way, Grandma."

Miss Maggie adopted my mother, so it was natural for me to see her as my grandmother. Now Maggie is approaching sixty-six, her hair pure white and her gait hobbled. Mama and I lived in the same house with her and an older woman, Aunt Eve. We also lived in my mother's village for a few years until Miss Maggie returned from her career in the capital.

Now I have my own place: half of the upper floor of a boot shop two streets over from the clinic, which is on Main Street. It's owned by Roy Grant, who taught me all about stitching leather and flesh. Sometimes the saloon on the corner, Dog's Whistle, gets too loud at night for me to sleep, but this is where I hope to start a family. Then we'll get a larger place. Maggie keeps inviting me to live in her house but I need to stay near the clinic. Besides, a young man living with his grandmother isn't the kind of fellow who's attractive to prospective brides.

Maggie gives me that look she gives whenever I say something she doesn't like but she's too tired to bother fussing about it. I know what that look means. She saves her breath these days. Same look I imagine she gave to musicians when practicing in the orchestra.

"This way," I tell her, her first time visiting the back room.

I hold out my arm for her to grab and we go out the clinic to the landing then carefully step off it. I escort her around the side of the building, through the alley to the back door.

That's where the chill room is. We get enough electric coming in to keep a cooler going. It's for keeping dead bodies preserved. In the heat of summer, I let folks spend a minute inside. Years before, we didn't have the chill machine and, depending on the heat, we could only keep a body for a few days before the stink would get too strong and the body had to be put in the ground.

"I spend about half my time here," I tell her, uncomfortable with the silence.

Unlocking the door, I swing it open, help her up the steps and into the room. She shivers at the cold air. Too cold for me, too. She pulls her scarf up around her neck as I flip the switch on the wall to ignite the ceiling lamp.

Before us in the small room stands a narrow table of shiny silver metal, and on that table lays a body, and over that body lays a white sheet covering it from head to toe. I haven't had time to do everything I need to do. Basic preparation. Doc leaves those tasks to me – and it often can be hard when I know the person. For example, Eleanor Cribbage, a girl I had feelings for while we were in school together but was rejected. Years later she got a snakebite and died. I had to prepare her body for burial. I saw everything, but I felt nothing. Her family paid me but I refused.

"Somebody's got to do it, might as well be you," Doc told me.

Miss Maggie runs her hand along the edge of the metal table, a wistful look on her face like the silver metal brings back memories of the tuba she used to play.

"I haven't had time to do much," I say in a solemn voice.

She gestures to lift the sheet. I pause, then take hold of the end of it by both corners, by the head. I want to ask if she's ready, as I steady myself for her reaction.

Again I regard her; our eyes meet. She gives a nod and I lift the end of the sheet, fold it neatly down over the chest and step back.

She stares for a long time, not moving.

I have to say his face is in good condition after cleaning him up, washing away the mud and blood that had stuck there, combed out his red beard, trimmed it, brushed his red hair back, eyes closed as if in sleep. The damage is in his belly. A good stomach wound will leave you dying for days. You know you'll die but can't do anything about it but suffer up to the final moment. That was his fate.

It's shocking to look at this corpse, but I've seen worst. What's it been? Fifteen years? He looks like I'd expect him to look at the age of thirty. Got the same traits he had when we played together: red hair, broad cheeks. I recognize him. This is how the boy I knew back then would look fifteen years later – and putting on twenty-five pounds. I only wish I could've talked with him before he died.

Standing back from the end of the table, against the wall, out of the way as much as I can be, I watch Miss Maggie gaze down upon the face of her grown son. She hasn't seen him for fifteen years, but I detect no emotion on her face. Most people believed he must've died the same as his uncle who never returned with the posse. Some men told what happened, then others went to retrieve Frank's body but never found it. Didn't find Bart either. Yet Maggie refused to give up hope of him ever coming home. Now he has.

I watch Maggie studying her son's clean face, and recall the day he rode off. It was important, everyone in town knew, but it didn't feel important; more like it was a trip to pick up someone from the railway depot twelve miles away. I couldn't go with them. I knew how to ride, how to shoot, thanks to Frank but he said I should wait in town. They'd do what was necessary. Nothing for me to get involved with. Meantime I should keep busy. Plenty to do. There was Mr. Jenkins to prepare for burial. The old man died west of town and coyotes made a mess of him.

I was too busy on that day to see them off. They were after the outlaw named J.C. Wells, a notorious robber who stole from several ranchers in the area with his gang, finally adding murder to their list of crimes. Maggie told me how her son begged her to let him join the posse, thinking it would be an adventure, but I remember him saying he wanted to see justice done.

"He begged to go," Maggie mutters, then looks at me. "I told you before, didn't I?"

"Yes, ma'am." I swallow hard. "It's a sad story."

She stares down at his face but doesn't cry, doesn't whimper, like the man isn't her kin, a total stranger – but I can sense her heart is screaming in pain at the sight of her boy, now grown and labeled a bad man, feared and scorned. Has a bounty on him. Maybe some of that evil's rubbed onto her, the way townsfolk curse her for this man who has terrorized the countryside.

"He looks like his dad. Just like him," she says. "Except for the beard. While I knew him, his father never had any beard." She admires him another minute. "I think he would've looked good with a beard."

"I reckon so."

She directs me to uncover his chest. She places her hand over his heart, closes her eyes, and her lips move in silent prayer.

When her eyes open, she focuses on an ugly round mark on the side, over the ribs.

"What's this?" she asks, pointing to the blemish.

I clear my throat. "It's a bullet wound. Healed as well as it can, I guess. Probably five, six years past." I show another similar mark on the other side, older. Lucky fellow. And the usual cuts and scrapes of a hard life. An old knife wound here, there.

On his upper arm there's another mark: red outline of a heart, drawn into the skin like tribals do, with the name *Trina* in black at the center.

"That's her?" asks Maggie, poking at the tattoo.

"Yes—" and the word catches in my throat. "The woman in Doc's office."

"Must mean something."

"She said they're like husband and wife but without a wedding."

"I see," she mutters. "Like his dad and I did. Things just happen sometimes."

After keeping her eyes fixed on his face, she raises her wrinkled hand and places it over his closed eyes. Another prayer slips from her lips as her hand brushes his whiskered cheek.

"Good-bye, Barty," she whispers. "I love you. Still do. Always. I forgive you of everything. Rest in peace, my dear boy."

When she looks up she seems surprised I'm there in the room.

"Death is the greatest adventure," she says.

I move to unfold the end of the sheet, replace it over the head.

"What's his wound?" she asks in a stronger voice. "Do you know what took him?"

I have to take a breath. "Gunshot in the belly."

"Show me."

"You sure you want to see that? It isn't properly prepared yet."

"Show."

After counting heartbeats, I take the middle section of the white sheet and pull it up from her side of the table to expose his belly. The dirty bandage has been removed and the wound cleaned up. It's still a mess: loose skin unsewn, without the blood to block the view, a stark display of mangled flesh, right through to his insides. I count again, waiting for her to give a signal. When she finally gives a nod, I lower the sheet.

+ + +

I take Miss Maggie to the front of the clinic. She gives my arm a squeeze, halting us.

"Is it true?" she asks. "That woman brought them back?"

"Yes," I respond.

"She's an outlaw? Under arrest now?"

"She brought the bodies," I say. "Doc says she's under a truce."

The Culpepper sisters have been notorious for crimes committed as bad as if they were men. Better known south and west of Skinner Canyon. They all had bounties on them.

"At least Trinity's gone now," I feel the need to say, referencing the infamous hanging in Cimarron nearly three years ago. The rope hadn't been properly set so the drop didn't break her neck instantly but left her dangling until she choked out.

I shake the image away, wondering if her crimes deserved that.

"This one's Trina, the middle sister," I say.

"I want to talk with her," says Miss Maggie in a firm voice.

"You sure you want to do that?" I'm being protective. It could only make things harder for this woman in her final years.

"I want to know what happened. I want to know about my boy."

Nodding a few times, I think of how to introduce them. I have no idea how that woman and Bart carried on.

We enter the clinic, hear them already in conversation.

I help Miss Maggie take a seat in the waiting area outside doc's office, afraid of putting the two women together in the same room. Sitting on the end of the bench, I can glimpse part of the office.

Trina is bent over, elbows on knees.

"Only ever been seven or eight days east o' here, maybe ten days one time," she says. "All ever did see was same orange sky. Never heard no booms. Never seen no damage like from anythin' fallin' from the sky. Land get drier goin' east, like everythin' burned. Not just dried an' died, but like it was dissolved right outta the soil, withered away to nothin' an' ya couldn't see it ever been there, but ya know it had to been there 'fore cuz ya remember the place as a field of tall grass, like buffalo graze in. Now it's just dirt, red dirt, almost sandy, an' nothin' grow in that."

I lean over to Miss Maggie, whispering: "She's talking about the Glow. Doc was asking her before."

The woman in the office lets out a long breath, sits up adjusting her hat as though she's ready to leave.

"We come out th' east by way of Kingman. Before that up from south there, but same landscape. Heard people talkin', most gettin' on with their lives like nothin' changed, like they never seen orange sky. But I seen it. We seen it, both us. As big as the sky itself, cover the horizon eye to eye an' almost to the top of the sky."

"The zenith," Doc adds.

"But odd thing is sun still rise. Like ain't the sun makin' the sky all orange. Seen the sun blink out there on the prairie like it always do, then rise on up the sky as day draws on, right up to that zenith an' back down to th' other side o' the world. But that orange glow stay in th' east, always orange, lit up like fire but never waver like a real fire does."

"You ever smell anything? Anything on the wind?"

"We camped an' smell our fire but nothin' on the wind ever did notice. People say they smell fire blowin' from th' east but it's rare 'cause most wind blow west to east. They say it smell like death an' I kinda knew what they meanin' – not fleshy decay smell but dry, burnt smell. Like yer standin' outside one them crematoriums, ya know?"

"So what do you think is causing that glow?"

"Heck if I know." She snorts, like it amuses her. "Could be near anythin'. Best I guess it's somethin' bad happen an' maybe never know what but just lucky to be out here in the west an' not touch by it. Maybe better not ask questions. Maybe we don't wanna know."

"If it's anything dangerous, especially if it could eventually reach us, we should be prepared. Can we still breathe? What will it do to the crops and livestock?"

"My guess, it'll turn same as out past Wichita, red ground an' nothing growin' there. Yer crops gonna die, turn to dust. Livestock live a while but die soon."

Doc must've heard me shuffling in the waiting room. "Jake? That you? Come on in here."

I get up from the bench. "I've got Miss Maggie here."

Doc turns ashen, purses his lips. "Might as well get it over with. Dang it. Well then, bring her on in."

I help Miss Maggie stand, looking her in the eye but she gives no hint of her intentions. She pauses in the doorway.

The young woman turns in the chair, studies the old woman a moment, then gets up and gestures for her to take the chair.

Miss Maggie gives no indication of thanks, shuffles to the chair and drops down on it with a loud expulsion of breath.

"I used to be stuck in a chair – a wheel-chair," she says for the woman's benefit. "For three years. Then a pair of crutches. Then a cane. Got me around. For years after I needed no cane." She rattles the wooden cane against the chair. "Now a cane once more."

I take the spot behind her, my back at the doorway, hands on the back of her chair.

"You saw him?" the doc asks Maggie.

"I did."

"How'd he look to you? Jake's not quite finished preparing him for burial."

"He looks fine for burying." She half turns in the chair. "Thank you, Jake."

I pat her shoulder.

"We can schedule the funeral service for a couple days from now. Get the townsfolk together – if anybody wants to join in. Most folks, you understand, have no affection for your boy. No doubt some will want to come out to see Frank properly buried."

"I understand." She sits grim-faced, staring at Doc, then regards the woman. "Thanks for bringing them home."

The woman remains stern, unmoved.

"I need to know his circumstances," says Maggie. "How he came to be in this condition. Tell me about you and him. I won't hold anything against you if you tell me the truth." She gives the woman a hard stare. "Will you tell me the full truth?"

Trina shifts her hat on her head, gazing into Maggie's eyes, then takes off her hat. Her dark hair is matted flat. She runs a hand through it, shakes it loose, resets her eyes.

"Yeah," she says. "Yer his mama, right?"

"I'm his mother."

Miss Maggie is one of the most stubborn women I've ever met, a lot tougher than people would guess from looking at her. She had a hard life. Most people respect her even if they don't accept some of the things she's done or been accused of doing. Like a dalliance with a music salesman long ago. And that man from the capital who came looking for her that time, but Aunt Eve shot him.

"Never talk much 'bout his mama," says Trina.

Miss Maggie gathers herself. "I was born in the capital sixty-six years ago. My mother brought us out here to Skinner Canyon when I was eleven. Me and my brothers. It's where my dad's cousin lived. My dad died in the capital while saving the governor from a gang of criminals. She granted us a pass, allowed us to leave. It was a strict place. I finished growing up out here, my mother being the teacher, then me after she died."

Trina nods thoughtfully, like she's heard it before.

"I started a band for the children. It grew and became famous. I was invited to conduct orchestras in cities in the east. Not many of us musicians left after the pandemic and everything that happened after, so they were down to me: a music teacher. Got involved with the Protest Concert in the capital, helped force a change to the law to disband the musicians guild. Then they could play without fear for their lives. That got me appointed as the principal conductor, a position I held for ten years."

The doc tries to speak: "That's well-known—"

"At the start of those ten years, a boy was born to me. That's my Barty. 'Little B' when he was young. Bart to you. I reckon Bad Bart to anyone crossing his path these past years. Yet he will always be my sweet boy. Always. No matter what he's done."

"Sorry," Trina says, barely a whisper.

"I returned here, to my home, and devoted myself to composing music. Did you know he played the cornet for a while? Not long, though. He wanted more to follow his uncle, be a lawman. I couldn't persuade him to give music a longer try. He was just fifteen when he came to me begging to go on that posse his uncle got together."

"He told me," says Trina. "J.C. Wells. Dead already."

Cal speaks up: "We know—"

"I couldn't say 'no' to him. He was in such a hurry to be a man. I expected my brother, who was the sheriff, would protect him. Still, I did worry. Looked for him to return home any day, ride into town like he'd just been away driving cattle. I looked to the horizon for him month after month, a full year, until I gave up, stopped looking. My brother never returned, so I had to believe they'd met their fate together out in the wilderness."

"He got Wells," Trina says.

"He did?" asks Cal. "You saw them?"

"Bart told me."

Maggie continues: "A few men rode out that way to take a look but reported not finding any sign of them. No Frank, and no Bart. No bodies even. We had a memorial service for them anyway. My other brother, the priest here, spoke fine words over a pair of empty graves."

"Sorry," mumbles Trina. "But I brung 'em back."

"From where?" asks Cal.

The moment's pause lets everything settle.

Doc fidgets. "Well, then—"

"It's been fifteen years since he left me, went on his adventure," says Maggie. "Fifteen years not knowing if he died or if he found a way to stay alive, maybe living a new life. He had no cross words for me, so I can't believe he hated me and didn't want to come home. It was better to believe he was killed. My brother, the priest here, said it was the best way to think of him, the best way to remember my boy. My beautiful red-haired son."

I see the first hint of emotion breaking Maggie's stern façade and my heart shakes for her. She sniffles but remains composed.

"There ain't no need to be telling all that," says Cal.

"You don't need to be here," Doc reminds her.

Maggie looks up slowly, puts a finger to her eye and wipes away a tear. "I want her to know what I felt waiting for him all of these fifteen years."

"I know it's been hard," Doc says.

"I went to the capital," she continues, ignoring him, "to help the musicians with the Protest Concert. You see, they were condemned. The governor declared they could play one final concert before they'd execute the leaders. So they played – played for days, never stopping. I arrived and took over the conducting. My dear friend, my fiancé, came with me, and carried my tuba on his back. I gave speeches between the music we played. I conducted until I could raise my arms no more. But the governor's sister, disguised in the crowd, was impressed enough to call him on her tablet, let everyone in the auditorium hear them as she demanded he take back his order of execution. No more plan to rid the capital of music. I had the music sheets with me, what my grandmother's grandmother composed in the lockdowns during the pandemic. A concerto for tuba, but only the first movement had orchestra parts – composed by me, making them anew from themes in the tuba part. I called Bart on stage – my son's dad. I must've had my son starting in me already – and they passed out the parts, and we played that concerto for the first time ever in a public performance! That tuba player was Bart – Barty's dad."

Doc looked down. "Really, Miss Maggie, it isn't necessary—"

"After the concert, with the music saved, the crowd exiting the concert hall was torn apart by a truck slamming into them. Several people were killed. My Bart, too. Run over. My family's tuba, carried on his back, was smashed. That was supposed to be me, I've always believed. I should've been carrying that tuba. It should've been me who died that night. I shouldn't be here."

"Aw, geez," Cal mutters. "I never knew that part."

"After that awful day I was too distraught to finish writing the orchestra parts for the second and third movements. I couldn't ever play a tuba again. Although I was appointed as the conductor of the National Symphony, it was hard staying there in that city, seeing each day the spot where Bart died when I went to the concert hall for rehearsals and performances. Then I found that Bart had left me a beautiful gift. I grew fat yet I continued with my conducting and composing. Then he was born, looking just like his dad."

Cal starts to speak, stops himself.

"So you see how precious my boy is to me. He is a living memory of my fiancé. We pledged to marry after the Protest Concert, but he died before we could. Even so, I consider him my husband. After ten years in the capital I brought my boy back home. My home. And he thinks he's a man at fifteen, wanting to go with his uncle on a posse. I thought he would be safe."

"I'm sorry," Cal moans, and I know he means it.

"I never knew what happened to him, not for fifteen years of me looking for him each morning and each dusk. I could only pray he was safe, had some happiness in his life. If he lived. Didn't know. Too many times I believed he died. Just a feeling deep inside me. I could only wish him a decent life."

Trina straightens herself, puts her hat back on her head, tugs it into the alignment she likes. Her hands go to her hips and the doc is alert. Her hands brush her pistols, the rattle of her bandoleer the loudest sound in the room.

"I brung 'em here," she says in a clear voice, eyes on the doc.

"Thank you," says Miss Maggie, her words quivering.

Trina points out the doorway with her chin.

"Like he said. Said I should bring him an' th' other here. It were before he died, but we both knowed he gonna die on account of that wound. Ain't no way to fix it. But he wanted to be home at the end.

Said his mama woulda want it that way. So I brung him. That's all I done."

"If that's the truth," Doc speaks up, "we thank you for that."

"It's truth," she practically growls. "Him an' that box."

"The box?" asks Maggie. "You mean the coffin?"

Deputy Cal speaks up: "She says...says it's our sheriff."

"Frank?" Maggie exclaims. Her hand goes to her face.

"Buried goin' on fifteen years. Had me dig him up," says Trina.

"To bring him home?" asks the deputy.

"He wanted ever'thing settled," Trina says.

She turns to the doorway, like she's expecting someone. She has to go past Miss Maggie to exit. Assessing the path, she pauses.

"Here he is. Here's his body, like he want. Home." Her tone is abusive. "I brung him home. Him an' his uncle. He said I get paid if I do, so here I am. Here he is. Both of 'em. Now what'll ya pay me?"

Maggie turns in her chair, head tilted down.

"What do you want?" she asks.

A grin stretches across on Trina's face. "I figure five-day ride, a beat-up cart, not worth much. But the bringin' is worth a lot. Let's call it a hundred each."

"Two hundred credits?" the doc erupts.

I prepare for a fight, standing behind Miss Maggie.

"It's fair," says Maggie.

"And I be needin' a fresh horse, too." She smiles defiantly at the deputy. "Better not be any those that got the glow in 'em neither."

"I can assure you," says Deputy Cal, "we have no horses like that here. Not yet anyways."

Maggie digs in the satchel resting in her lap, produces a quartet of golden 50-notes, lifts them into the air.

Trina reaches for them but Miss Maggie snatches them back.

"First you tell me everything," she says. "All that's happened to my boy. About you and Bart. Then you'll get the money."

"And a fresh horse," Trina adds.

"And a horse."

"Miss Maggie, she don't deserve none for doing what's the right thing to do," says Deputy Cal.

"I don't care. It's settled now," says Maggie. "All I want now is to know what happened. I don't care about any money or horses or the funeral. I need to put my heart to rest. Then my weary head will be calm and I can go to my reward."

3

TRUTHS & FALSEHOODS

"AIN'T NO ASSOCIATE with no J.C. Wells – like I told ya." Trina keeps her teeth clenched responding to Deputy Cal's questions. "Never heard nobody like that."

"I'm trying to establish any connections there might be between you and him." Cal glances over at me. I lean against the wall, Doc behind his desk. "Has something to do with this man's mother. So I'm gonna dig until I get some answers."

What he says sends a storm of nerves burning down my spine. I don't want to go there. Not after I've made my peace with Mama's death. Then Deputy Cal has to bring it up again.

"Don't know no Wells," she says in her dusty voice.

Her eyes narrow at me, as though recognizing I'm the one who's causing her trouble. Then she thinks for a bit and I – maybe only me – see something flash across her face.

"Yep, 'member he told me 'bout somethin' he did. What Bart did, I mean. But ain't involve me."

"Tell us," says Cal. "Repeat his story."

She doesn't look happy, but she talks anyway. "When I come on him he was purdy lost an' roughed purdy bad, like he been in a fight or two an' wanderin' a ways in the wilderness."

"What did he tell you?" Cal demands.

"Gettin' to it."

"Go on then."

"He was in a bad way cuz he been in a fight. Now ain't no nurse or nothin' but he was just a young fella so kinda look at him soft, ya know. No danger ta me."

"What did he say? What happened to him?"

"First we fix him up. Me an' my sisters, mostly me. Dress up his wounds, give him food, some water, let him sleep. He was mighty grateful. We ask what trouble he got himself in. We din't know he's good fella or bad."

"And what did he tell you?"

"Said he was in a fight – a gunfight – with some others. 'What others?' I ask. He say 'J.C. Wells.' That don't ring no bell for me, but he say that gang's bad news. I believe him, base on how he come to look."

"Anything else? What about the gunfight?"

"Took some days 'fore he got it out o' his head, out his mouth, but he say they rode out o' Skinner Canyon – this here town – after J.C. Wells an' his gang. It were a posse he join. So I says to him: 'You's kinda young fer goin' after some outlaw gang.' No, it were Trinity said it, she bein' oldest."

"So Bart rode with the posse. We know that."

Doc sits up, preparing to speak.

"And he didn't come back," I cut in, focusing on Trina.

She grins to herself. "Yep, he din't come back. Not till now."

"So what happened?" Cal presses as Doc sits back in his chair.

"We get him back to feelin' right. We don't ask an' he don't say. We just take him in our gang, let him ride with us. Fool says we're doin' crimes an' he won't be part of. But we give 'im food anyway. He kinda cute in a porky kinda way. Don't mean he's fat, just got that red hair an' the sun shore turn 'im redder."

"Didn't he ask you to help him go home?" asks Cal.

"Not at first," says Trina. "Later he din't wanna. He wanna ride with us. Or with me – later. Just two of us."

"So you two were a couple?"

She looks down but I can see her smiling. Cal is about to speak when she looks up. "Hard to figure."

"He's been gone for fifteen years," Cal demands. "A long time for things to happen. What happened between you two?"

"Is Miss Maggie going to want to hear this?" I cut in.

Cal sits back, takes a breath. "I want to hear it first. Then we can bring her in to hear it repeated." He turns to Trina. "Now, from the beginning. You find him wandering in the wilderness...."

"In them badlands down southwest," she says. "Said he been lost fer bunch o' days. We figure a week. He was frightful worn out by then, almost dead. He got a scratch across his ribs. No breaks we kin feel, just ugly stripe from a bullet cut him in passin'. Lucky boy. But it weren't the first meetin' between him an' Wells, he said."

"I did see a scar on his ribs," I speak up. "Like a bullet burned across his skin, healed over time."

Cal sits up. "Not the first encounter?"

"He say they found Wells out past Black Mesa, come on his camp accident-like an' attack right off. Got some men. Others run off."

"What about Wells?"

Trina lowers her head like she's trying to recall the incident. "He held back. Say his uncle told him to."

"His uncle? That would be Frank – Sheriff Baumann."

"Guess so. He call 'im 'Uncle Frank'. Say the man's his mama's brother."

"That fits. Go on."

She sits a moment, staring at the wall beside me. "We ask they goin' after Wells, guess it were some good reason. Say he killt a woman – native woman. Did things to her."

"Stop!" I snap.

Cal tilts his head, indicating I should step out.

My whole body tightens. "I know what happened." Taking a big breath, I let it out slowly as everyone stares at me. "I was staying with Uncle Frank and Aunt Vera. I was supposed to help with the ranch, learn about being a cowboy. But Mama was coming to fetch me for a holiday dinner at Miss Maggie's house. They all lived there – Maggie, Eve, my mama, and me, too, when I wasn't at Frank's."

"Yep, he told me," Trina says. "So you's his buddy."

"My mama took the carriage out on the north road around town. Straight to the ranch house." I have to stop, have to take a breath.

"It's awright, Jake. You don't need to say no more." Cal regards

Trina, who looks bored. She must already know what happened.

"Did he say?" I ask her but she doesn't respond.

"It was the last straw. Last of a long line of crimes," Cal goes on. "Just had him for cattle rustling up to then. Rumors of worse acts but couldn't get charges. But that day was beyond cattle rustling and petty crimes. Frank got a posse together, rode after the Wells gang."

"Purdy torn up, he was." Trina looks around as if checking for spies. "But he shot him. Wells, I mean. Shot him dead."

Cal almost jumps up. "What? He did? Bart shot him?"

"Said he did." She glances around us. "Din't see."

Shaking his head, Cal gazes at Trina, reviewing the scene in his mind, thinking.

"Then why didn't he return with the others?" he asks at last.

"He say it were later. They already got split up."

"So where was he – Bart?" asks Cal.

"He got split from them," she responds. "That's how he could shoot Wells. Got in the wrong place during the first gunfight. Lost among the rocks out there. Say his uncle told him to hide. Tried to find his way back to the posse when the shootin' was over. Din't know who won the fight, he say. But he saw it. That's when Wells shot yer sheriff, shot him dead."

"What? Wells shot Frank?" Cal shakes his head slowly. "Damn." He looks up, his face tense. "Damn him to hell, the bastard."

"They got him, your sheriff, on his knees on the ground. He was cursin' 'em, Bart told me. Then Wells shoots the sheriff in the face an' he goes down."

Doc gasps, like he can't believe it. "No need for that."

"Not the best way to go," Cal mutters.

"Bart was hiding?" I ask her. "He saw it?"

"He say his uncle told him hang back. Say it was his mama told him to be safe cuz he just a boy."

"So Bart wasn't part of the first gunfight?"

"He say he creep through them rocks an' saw the camp between the rocks. Through a gap. He saw them shoot yer sheriff. So he got right between the rocks, he say, an' push his pistol through the gap, fire at Wells. Got him in the side, right through his gut. Hit another fella behind him, he say. So his men rush around the rocks to find him but he scramble away."

My heart is beating fast. "Wait—"

"So Bart shot Wells? Killed him?" Cal confirms.

"That's what he told me. Then he wander in them badlands for forty days, he say, hidin' from the men trackin' him. The rest of that posse still livin', they went on home, figure, back to Skinner Canyon or other place."

"I remember that," I say sadly. "How they rode into town acting so brave. People looked for the sheriff...but didn't see him."

"Cowards," Cal mutters. "Didn't even retrieve Frank's body."

"Din't know Wells got shot," Trina says. "Or yer sheriff, neither. Too scared to go back fer him. Lay there a week or more. Lookin' real bad." She meets my eyes. "So we bury him. Went over to Boys City—"

"You mean *Boise* City?" Cal checks.

"They call it Boys City." She glares at Cal. "Got a box sittin' out. All line up front of undertaker's shop, so we took one. Stold it, yep. Drag it back to our camp where the body lay out. Put him in that box, nail it shut. Dug a pit. We bury him there. Never had no plan to take 'im nowheres."

She barely got the words out when Deputy Dave runs in, pistol drawn, with two other men following him into the clinic.

"What's this all about?" shouts Doc Baker, jumping up.

"Hands off those guns," Dave demands of Trina. "Lift 'em."

Slowly she raises her hands, still sitting in the chair.

"Truce or not, she's a dangerous woman. Wanted in five towns."

"She's not hurting anyone," Doc Baker insists.

"Not yet," Dave snarls.

One of the other men, at Dave's gesture, reaches for her pistols, slides them out of the holsters.

"Any other weapons?" asks Dave. "Knives?"

She purses her lips, nods down at her boot. The men aim their guns, expecting trouble. Dave reaches down, pulls a long knife from a sleeve in her boot, hands it over.

"Any more?"

Slipping her hand inside her vest, she retrieves a small two-shot pistol, gives it up.

"More?"

She shakes her head.

"Now stand up. Real slow."

With hands raised, Trina gets up from the chair. Her eyes fall on me. Her look suggests she expects to be treated this way, has been before, and I worry she has a scheme and will try to escape – which would give the deputies an excuse to shoot her.

"Din't come here for no trouble," she says clear as day. "Just doin' what Bart want me to do, is all."

"You're under arrest," Dave announces with a nod from Cal.

+   +   +

"Doc! Doc!" shouts a youth in the street outside the clinic. "Come on quick! Mama's ready to push out the twins."

Doc jumps up, rushes to the doorway. "Already? They're not due for yet another couple of weeks." He grabs his bag and hurries off with the youth.

I turn back to the office, straighten papers that scattered.

"Doc sees them when they start their lives," I mutter. "I only see them at the end."

Heading over to the jail, I worry about the woman's treatment.

When I arrive, Miss Maggie's already there, sitting properly in a straight-back chair as a witness to everything. She tells me what I missed as I gaze at Trina, wearing a worn-out gray gown like a granny's nightgown, standing barefoot in the jail cell.

"It was awful," Maggie reports, "the way they stripped her, looking for weapons. I tried to get them to go easy. She wasn't even giving them much trouble, just cursing."

The jailers collected her clothing and boots in a bag and hung it on a wall hook in the back room. Her weapons were stored there, too, and the door locked.

Trina complained the gown stunk. Dave laughed, said it hadn't been washed since the last woman they put in the cell. Locking the door after, one jailer knocked on the iron bars as if to welcome her home. The others grumbled about her smelling bad.

"Miss Maggie," says Deputy Cal, his back to the cell, "you can go on home. It's done for now. She ain't going nowhere."

"I still wish to speak with her. Her and me. Privatcly." Maggie appears disappointed by the harsh treatment of this small woman by big men. "You did your business. Now I'll do mine."

"Go ahead," says Cal. "She ain't going nowhere."

"I'd rather not have to talk through those bars."

"Afraid that's the only way now. Until Judge Robinson gets back and can decide what to do with her."

"I thought she was under a truce. Jake said so."

I perked up at my name, always used to staying out of the way.

"Well, he don't know all the law," Cal replies.

"When's the judge returning?" asks Maggie.

"Few days." He rubs his chin. "Depends how long that trial goes on up in Cimarron. They'll get a message to him and he'll be coming down to deal with this woman."

"That could be days...weeks. I want to talk with her right now. However, I don't want to talk through those bars."

Cal wiped his brow. "Sorry. That's the only way."

He glances at the cell, receives a scowl from its guest and, feeling satisfied, strides out.

I stay with Maggie even though I have work to do. Mr. Owens, late husband of the late Miss Mavis, owner of the Bar-Q Ranch, needs to be prepared for burial beside his wife. Their six sons have been running the ranch for a while. I have to stay ready. Someone might die on any given day and have to be prepared.

Maggie stands, grabs hold of the chair she's been sitting on and pulls it across the wooden floorboards, leaving a scratch, right up to the cell. She rubs her hip, the one that got broken long ago then healed, and drops herself onto the chair with a loud exhale.

"Now then...."

Trina glares from under her dark eyebrows, a cold look.

"Ain't got nothin' more to say," she growls.

"I'm not judging you," says Maggie in a firm voice. "I just want to know about my boy. About Barty. What all he did. Everything. Start from the beginning."

"Beginning?" Trina seems surprised. "I said it already."

"Yes, you did. I want what happened next."

"Fifteen years?" She shakes her head.

"Fifteen years, yes."

Trina seems to relax a bit, maybe realizing the test will be easy. She can fake her way through it. I watch her closely.

"But it better be the truth," says Maggie.

Trina purses her lips, refuses to speak. I see her shake her head, conceding. She was almost out of here with money and a fresh horse only to be captured. That would make anyone mad.

"Miss Maggie, should I stay? You want me to stay?"

She looks at me. "You were Bart's best friend. His only friend. Don't you want to know how he got lost?"

"Yes, but...."

I'm a little afraid of what I might learn. After all, I saw his body, the wounds on him, and they told me a lot. My childhood friend lived a hard life. He survived for a while. Then he didn't.

I wanted to tell Maggie that, but instead I say: "Yes, I do."

So we sit a spell but nobody says anything.

"Nothing to say?" asks Maggie after the long silence.

More silence.

I offer to take Maggie home using the funeral wagon. On the way we talk some. I promise to let her know if Trina says anything. She thanks me, says I'm a good grandson. I thank her, adding how much I miss my mama. She pats my knee.

When I return to town I get my supper at The Five Ladies. The saloon also provides meals for prisoners. The place used to be called The Five Whores but a new owner, Jim Watanabe, wanted to make it a respectable place after wedding one of them. He changed the name.

I go to the jail with supper on a tray. It isn't much but I sneak in a small chunk of pork belly to the bowl of beans. Deputy Dave sits in the chair behind the desk, boots up, looking at a folio with drawings of ladies with their skirts flying up as they dance.

Trina sits cross-legged on the floor, displays an angry face.

"Here you go," I announce, offering the bowl through the bars.

Rather than acting snarly and refusing it, Trina gets up. She mutters a thanks and returns to her spot on the floor, bowl in hand. She tries to go slow, not wanting me to see how hungry she must be, but she eats quicker when I turn away. She slurps down the liquid and smacks her lips.

"Mighty fine?" I quiz and she almost grins. "They do a good bowl of beans over at the Five Ladies." I dare to regard her. "Oh, I don't go there much. Only for meals. They give me a deal."

Geez Louise, I'm being foolish! This woman don't care about my life. Not my poor, simple life. And she's a prisoner. You brought her supper, as agreed. That's all you have to do. Now get on home and forget her. Plenty of work to do in the morning.

"Wonder what they're gonna do with you," I mutter, loud enough that I must want her to hear. "I thought we had a truce."

"Yeah, men lie. Don't they now?" she says with a grunt.

"I'm sorry." I feel conflicted. Should I be nice to her? Or be mean? Act like she really is a criminal? All I know for sure are a bunch of tales people pass around like old money. Could be true – or not. I'm unable to decide. I've spent thirty-two years trying to find my place in this world. I don't need to be sitting in judgment of others.

"You din't lock me in," she says in a flat voice.

"For what it may be worth, I do believe you."

"Believe what?"

"All you said about Bart." I take a breath, my chest quivering. "He was my childhood friend. He was ten when he came here to Skinner Canyon with his mama. I was twelve. Just five years being friends. Then he left on that damn posse and we never saw him again. Not until you brought him home."

She gives a slow nod, thinking. "It's what he want."

"I'm also the one who has to fix him up, make him look good for the funeral. I stitched him up."

"That's yer job?" It seems to surprise her.

"I do lots of tasks for the doc. Nurse. Surgery assistant. Coroner. I actually trained as a dentist, went to school in Kanza City, but all people want done is a quick pull of a bad tooth."

"You pull teeth?" she asks, perking up.

"That's what I said. Even went to school for it."

She makes a sound deep in her throat. "Got this back tooth give me frightful pain."

My heart almost jumps against my ribs. I see it: she wants me to check her tooth and then she'll do something tricky to get away. I'd be blamed for her escape. I hold my breath a moment.

"How long?" I ask, cautiously.

"Been coming on a year now. When I bite on it."

"Could be an abscess under the tooth."

"Abscess? What's that?"

"It's an infection. Germs in a bubble of pus. It only gets worse."

"Cain't stand it right now."

"I'll see if I can get some anti-biotic drug for you. That'll kill the germs and the pus will dry up. Then check it later."

"Be mighty grateful," she says in a perfectly normal voice, like it's not a trick.

"I'll have to check with the deputy. He needs to know if I give medicine to a prisoner. Rules—"

"Bart talk about ya few times," she speaks up. "Yer name Little Bear, ain't it?"

"Yes." I give her a quizzical look. "That's my Kanza name. Jacob is my other name but everyone calls me Jake."

"Ya relations with Bart?"

"We are...cousins." I have to think. "It's strange, to be honest. My mama was adopted by Miss Maggie, but my mama married Maggie's brother's son – her nephew. Bart would truthfully be my uncle even though I'm older. So I'm half of each."

"Like me," says Trina. "Half Comanche, half Irish-something."

"That's why we look alike." I chuckle, feeling better about her. "Close enough. Not like most folks around here in Skinner Canyon."

"Kanza and Comanche are long-time enemies."

"In the old days," I counter.

"These are the old days," she offers. "Nothing changed for near a thousand years, reckon."

"A thousand years? I'd agree if you were talking about the past hundred or hundred-fifty years. That much we know. Back to the pandemic when Maggie's great-great-grandmother first left on their journey to sanctuary and everything got worse. She likes to tell me about those times. Believe me, it gets old after a while. But on she goes, always another story."

Trina is shaking her head.

"Not much bad happened out here," I say. "Back east everything was terrible. So lots of people came west. Tried to start over."

She looks up, says: "Like my pa did."

4

THREE SISTERS AND A WILDERNESS

THREE DAUGHTERS BORN into a make-shift family of a crusty old miner and the native woman he bought down in Nuevo America for a big pouch of Carolina tobacco he'd brought with him. Feeling thankful the first girl was born crying and eager to suckle, Simon Culpepper named her Trinity, though his church days were far behind him. He made some fortune, bucket by heavy bucket. The second girl they called Trina, short for Katrina, a name he'd heard people from the swampy southern coast talk about, a great storm that swept in and destroyed everything. The third daughter they gave the name Triss, a corruption of Teresa, a saint her converted mother prayed to while carrying the baby inside. Never had a boy. Ajei, his wife, offered her sister, Doba, to try for a boy but he refused her and Doba left them. Three daughters was good enough, Simon decided. They lived happy beside that mine he dug from. Until robbers came.

The band of robbers sought to take his claim, gather his gold, get rid of the whole family. Simon was just one man and when six men approached him, already tired and sore from his labor with a pick, he could only take a few swings at them. Cut into one of them, and the pick couldn't be shaken loose before another man got a knife into Simon's belly. He shook it off, pulled out the knife and stabbed into another robber. A pistol went up to the side of his head and he gave up, surrendering to the awful sight of a pair of robbers pulling his girls from the tent home they'd set up below the rocky hillside.

"Now you leave 'em be," Simon demanded.

Bleeding badly from the belly wound, Simon could barely stand as they pushed him down the path to the camp.

The man who'd called up the hill to Simon stood at the bottom wearing a wiry black beard and a hat with a gold band. He stood laughing but nobody understood the joke.

"We's here to buy your mine," said the man, leader of the gang.

"Ain't for sale," Simon grunted.

"Why, I'm offering you a good deal," said the leader, whose name we learned only later was Shane McNally. "I shall offer you for this mine – and all surrounding territory here – the princely sum of one credit. That's a full credit, no tax deducted. Which I figure is about what you pull from this mine in a week."

"It's more," Simon grimaced, wincing from the wound.

"I think not," Shane countered. "Been watching you for a week."

His men laughed: howls of wild animals, quick to demonstrate their loyalty. Three of them held onto Simon's wife and the two older girls. The youngest daughter stood dumbfounded but they didn't care about her.

"Just let us go," said Simon, keeping his eyes on his family.

"Go where?" Shane challenged. "Maybe we let you stay here. You could be our labor. We'll pay you."

"Not much I can do with a gut wound like this," Simon growled.

"That surely is the truth," said Shane, going over to the man.

"Please, just let my family go free," said Simon. "I'll work for you. Let them go. Send them to the nearest town. Figure that's Skinner Canyon."

"Skinner Canyon?" Shane laughed. "That craphouse? Been there a few times. Met a lovely gal in one of the saloons." He looked back at his men. "What was her name? Maude? Something like that. But you never remember the name of a whore."

His men laughed.

"No, it was Maureen," Shane cried out. "Now I remember."

"Let my pa go," shouted the eldest daughter, looking old enough to be interesting to the men.

"Whoa!" Shane burst out. "Who's this? One of them whores?"

"Ain't no whore," the girl growled, rising up on her knees. "Ain't never done none of that before."

The ugly pig-faced man standing behind her moved to slap her but Shane waved him off and approached the girl.

"You say you *ain't never done none* of that, huh? What kind of language is that? Too much time at a filthy mine like this instead of being in a school. You see, a proper educated lady is worth something. The other kind's only good for pleasuring a man. Seems you're the latter category."

"You leave her be," shouted Simon from where he slumped.

"Well, now," said Shane, regarding him on the ground, holding his belly. "Looks like we got a situation. Deal's on the table, mister. What's it gonna be?"

"I said I'll work for you if you let my family go." The pain was too intense for him to stand and he let out a groan. "I promise."

"That's a fine promise," said Shane, looking back at the mouthy daughter. With his eyes on her, he spoke to his men: "Seems we got a deal. We'll let 'em go and keep the worthless sonuvabitch to dig for us. And that gal, the whore, too. She don't know nothing by her own admission."

"You mean she's part of the deal?" asked one burly man.

"Like I said, for you idiots that don't ever listen, she's not worth anything but pleasuring a man."

"Please!" shouted Simon, hands over his bleeding belly. "Please don't touch her. Let her go with the others."

"In due time, mister. In due time."

Shane selected his best four men, told them to take the mouthy girl into the tent. The fifth stood guard outside. Simon and his wife pleaded to let the daughter go free but the leader of the gang only laughed, enjoying their consternation.

"Go on," he called over to the tent. "This about all the recreation you're going to get on this trip, so you had better enjoy it."

The two younger daughters could only cringe at the cries of their sister coming from the tent.

They didn't know what to do. Ajei feared for her daughters. Maybe better to sacrifice one to save the others, she must've been thinking. Simon lay mortally wounded, unable to do any more than loose his anguished moans. They had no weapons, only mining tools. The younger daughters weren't strong enough to use them.

Ajei stood, shook out her skirt and went for the shovel laying on the ground by a pile of rocks.

"Get back," called the man guarding her and the girls.

Then a man stumbled out of the tent, ripping the tent flap as he tripped, wailing like a pig, both hands pressed to his eyes. Blood ran down his face. Ajei and the girls startled.

Another man tripped out of the tent, falling on his knees, getting up but falling again as he tried to pull out something stuck in his throat, what looked like one of Ajei's hairpins, then dropped to his knees and rolled over onto his face in the dirt.

Shane stood puzzled by the unexpected sight, took steps toward the tent, halting cautiously. The man guarding the woman and girls paused in shock, asked the boss for instructions. Keep an eye on the girls, he told him.

Ajei jumped in front of Shane, blocking his way, and he swung his fist at her. She moved so he missed. She lifted the shovel, tried to strike him with it but it was too heavy for her to lift high enough. The shovel grazed his shin. He cried out, then shoved her down.

The man guarding the girls glanced back to check on them.

A third man bowled out of the tent's opening, grabbing the flap and tearing it as he collapsed there, his hand at his chest. Ajei saw two things protruding from between his ribs. Looked like scissors.

The man guarding the girls gasped, not believing that the girl in the tent could've done it. Must be some kind of witch, he thought, and got scared. Shane ordered the man to stand fast but he begged to be let free, no matter his share of the profits.

"Go on then," Shane growled at him, his eyes on the tent, "Get your ass outta here, you coward!"

Shane stood with hands on his hips, cursing. He pulled his pistol from its holster, stormed toward the tent.

Ajei leaped up, swept herself before him, knocking his legs out from under him. Shane scrambled up, turned to deal with her. He aimed his pistol, hesitating a moment. He cursed her, then slapped her aside.

He stalked toward the tent, pistol drawn.

Again Ajei leapt at him and he pushed her down. But in that instant, she managed to grab the knife from his belt. He paused to aim the pistol down at her, cursing her for making him use a bullet.

A cry from inside the tent grabbed his attention.

Rolling up on her knees behind him, Ajei drew the knife across the back of his thigh. He reached back at the pain as she sliced into his other thigh. More cursing as he dropped.

Ajei got herself up, stood over him, his face wide-eyed at his fate, as she readied herself to bring the knife down into his chest.

They startled when thirteen-year old Trinity stormed out of the tent in naked rage, hands bloody but holding a kitchen knife and a long screwdriver, both dripping blood. Her face was a mask of pure hate. She saw that Shane devil on the ground and stomped over to him, dropped herself down hard on him without pause, weapons going straight into his chest.

Ajei fell back at her daughter's attack, then got up, kept away. She called to Trinity but the girl was mad with rage and didn't hear her. She called to her younger daughters but they were stunned into silence, shaking in fear. The man guarding them had fled and Shane lay dead. Other men had died, had tried desperately to get out of the tent after the girl struck them. They never figured a girl like that would have such weapons. The man who got his eyes gouged just wandered aimlessly about the campsite, groaning and cursing as he bumped into things, tripped over rocks then got up and stumbled on, falling and getting up again, finding a trail out of the camp, crying out to his mama until he'd gone far enough they heard him no more.

The girls gathered around their mama but she assured them she wasn't hurt. They went to their papa, but in that short space of time he'd succumbed from his wound, the soil around him receiving his blood. They knelt, said prayers for him. Except Trinity. She shouted to the sky, waving her arms like a challenge to the gods to fight with her, and she wouldn't be calmed.

Ajei lifted her face to the sun, beseeched the gods to let Simon go in peace. The younger girls repeated their mama's words. Trinity wouldn't let go of her tools even days later, thinking the men might return. She regarded the blood on her body, refusing to cover herself – and Ajei dared not get close to her. Trinity stood watch as the others dug a grave for their pa.

+   +   +

Staring down at the body of the man who had torn apart their lives, Ajei and the girls didn't know that Shane McNally out of Fort Dodge and his gang of thieves had long been pursued by both local sheriffs and commissioned militia. Ever since he was a young man, McNally had run afoul of the law countless times, gathered a gang around him and their crimes increased. When they were stealing ore claims and rustling cattle they had bounties on them. Chased across the country, they'd hide here and there in the hills. They had running gun battles with pursuers, held as hostage one sheriff and traded him for a pair of their thieves. Frank Baumann called them 'bad news' and put reward posters front and center on the jailhouse wall. That was long before they rode out to get J.C. Wells.

Shane McNally, like so many of the post-pandemic generations, grew up in those bad years following the restoration of the national government, a collection of separate states put back together after a frightful civil war. It wasn't that some states had tried to break from the union but rather they vowed to go on in different ways after suffering decades of anarchy following the Great Pandemic. A mistake or a plan, an accident or a deliberate attack; either way, the result was madness: ten years of death, of hating your neighbors, fighting over scarce food and water. For some, hiding out and waiting for the plague to burn itself out. But what was left? Only scraps of lives thrown back a hundred years, with none of those conveniences required in a modern society they'd been used to having before the pandemic.

Many chose to head west where they could make a fresh start in areas the pandemic hadn't touched. In that far-away land, people from the devastated northeast and survivors of the southern coast met and mixed, making a new country: a wilderness not ruled by any government but the local sheriffs and deputies. The Old People remained, however, and had taken back their tribal lands that had been lost before the pandemic, claimed once more as their sovereign territory. So it became a strange time of settlement for the bands of ravaged people escaping from the tyrannical northeast and the poor south.

From the interior valleys of the southeast along the great rivers now dwindled to streams came the McNally family: Ma and Pa, and six boys; two babes were buried along the journey. They made their way west like many did, arrived in a survivor camp called El Reno, which had grown into a good-size town. There they made a shop for selling hardwares, the father pounding metal to suit the needs of townsfolk. In that way they gained income and community status.

One day, a boy at the school house pushed one of the McNally boys down and the eldest, Shane, took it upon himself to fight the bully, left the boy seriously wounded. When that boy went on to die, Shane's father cursed him for bringing shame on the family. The townsfolk demanded justice. Before anything could be done, Shane had ridden out of town on his own, a teen boy with no money, lost himself in the wilderness west of town, and never returned.

He was not quite a man yet he comported himself as a full-grown devil, hating the world for all it had done to him in his few lived years. But he learned life's ways, discovered how he could bend it to his will. Following his will, he did as he pleased. He found a buddy here and a friend there, and together they did as they pleased. They became what simple folks in town and village called bad men. They drank and whored, stole, fought, eventually killed. They got their names on reward posters with drawings not too good a likeness but close enough that folks could spot them if they should ever come to town or race hell-bent through a dusty village, frightening folks.

With another brother, Drake, joining Shane, they grew bolder in their callous adventures, seeking pleasures wrought of destruction. Pure iconoclasts, a frustrated sheriff called them: those who seek to destroy everything that's good and beautiful for no reason. Maybe it was the joy of seeing beauty torn asunder, seeing people cry in horror at their sacred icons being destroyed. There was a kind of joy one might garner from such destruction: when one destroyed something good and beautiful, one might presume to take the higher seat, sit among the gods, hammer out pride from vile ore. 'I become the thing I destroy' went the chant among gang members.

Their reign of destruction swept across Okala lands until they arrived in the border strip counting five territories. From the end of the Okala trail, a short ride would take you up to the Colorado highlands, west to the Nuevo America territory, south to the Tejano country, or north into the Kanza plains. There in Kanza land the town of Cimarron proved to be a delicious destination for mayhem, and the gang made incursions several times, drawing out the local lawmen. News-writers filed lurid reports of the lawlessness for their curious readers back east.

This is what we have gained, the news-writers wrote: a lawless land set by the filth of sin. God has surely cursed us and our kin for what we have done to this world so generously given to us. He sends us the plague, a ten-year pandemic that cut half of our population, and the great anarchy that followed snipped off another quarter of us. We rebuilt our world as best we could, yet tyranny overtook us, made the renewed cities into factories of misery. Only music saved us – yet for only a brief time, as people obsessed over it like a new outfit from the best clothier shop in town before their joy had to fall to the wayside for new and more powerful ways of menacing each other. A love of music failed in the end. No, it wasn't God sending us curses but we ourselves who made the land cry out and the people moan. It was by our own hands.

+ + +

The sisters stripped the dead of anything that might be useful and left the naked bodies to rot under the blazing sun. At night, the coyotes would come to dine, gathering around the pile of corpses steps from the tent. Wolves howled their pleasure. By day, vultures descended over the flesh. The girl named Trinity would shout at the coyotes and vultures, keeping them away. She kept a man's gunbelt on her slim hips, tightened to the last notch, so the pistol remained ready for use.

Without a man, they could no longer dig in the mine, nor haul the ore to town, exchanging it for a fair price. They'd be constantly on guard for criminals bent on theft or worse. Easy prey. Ajei knew some fighting skills but she was not ready to use them, didn't want to have to fight. But she had daughters: an older girl now terrorized and unable to be calm; a quiet, observant girl almost ready to fight; and a girl still in need of mothering. Yet they required food and that wasn't easy to come by in the wilderness.

Trinity, remaining a hot-head all her life, took the lead role in what remained of their family. She took her papa's rifle and hunted, got a few hares, birds, other small game. Got an antelope once that went bad in the heat before they could get many meals from it. Triss got sick and they feared she might die, spitting up everything, but she recovered. Trina would help as she could, learning a lot from her mother: what things could be gathered from trees, bushes, and the ground that could be eaten safely. Ajei settled back, unable to do much, her wound a ready excuse.

"We gotta take care of Ma," Trinity told her sisters.

They made their way to the nearest town, kept in the shadows, and when they could they grabbed food here and there. The grocer, a tall, mustached man with a long apron, caught on to them. He must've taken some pity, seeing they were girls running off after stealing, and he left out some fruit and other food for them.

Trinity continued her thieving ways, but it was Trina who grew bold, let herself get caught, and the grocer lectured her on the evils of theft. Playing the poor orphan child, she got him to give her a job: sweeping floors, picking up anything that fell, and keeping out of the way of the customers. Paid in her choice of food: fill up the handbasket.

"What a pitiful gal," the grocer was heard to say when Trina left each dusk. "Must live under a rock by the look of her."

Triss accompanied her big sister on petty crimes. More daring as time went on, and getting seen plenty, until townsfolk set a trap for them. But they got away. After that, they were well-known and had to move on to a new town. Trina didn't show up at the grocery one day and that was that. People talked about the three thieving girls, half amused yet half annoyed by them. Everyone wondered who they were, where they'd come from.

Town after town became their targets. They had schemes. It was Trina who played the poor hungry child while Trinity grabbed items and Triss stood as lookout. Little by little they began to steal other things, a curious trinket here or a useful tool there. They had guns and ammo from the men who attacked them at their mining camp.

They piled up their possessions at a camp they made outside of town, a place set among the rocky hills. Ajei remained distraught, wouldn't acknowledge the girls had fed her. In time, Ajei passed on from a lingering infection in her gut. The girls made a pyre; Ajei had shown them how to do it for their father's body. They'd burned both bodies, watching the smoke rise to the sky, off to join the Great Spirit.

Then one night, staking out a rich man's house, they bumped into other robbers, surprising him and his buddy. They drew pistols, aimed at the girls. Trina played the nice girl, got the men to relax, until Trinity could smack one man in the face and grab his gun. The other man fired at her but missed and Trinity shot him. The noise awoke the people in the house and the girls had to run off empty-handed. But they had more guns and a belt of bullets. That made their robberies grow bolder. Didn't need to be sneaky.

People got to talking about the three girls in rough clothes who would come into town and steal things at gunpoint.

Trinity saw the hats on the wall of the General Store one day, took two down, set one on Trina's head, the other on Triss. Both had flat brims, low draws, and gold satin bands. Trina's was a little big on her head but she would grow into it. She could draw the strings under her chin and know it wouldn't fly off when she rode. Triss had no complaints, smiling in delight.

"That'll be five credits for each of them," the old, bewhiskered shopkeeper announced.

Trinity turned to him, her dry lips tucked to one side as was her special trait when she felt confident. Her hand rested on her pistol.

"How much ya reckin yer life's worth?" Her narrow eyes told him a lot more.

"Oh, I'd say more than five credits," he stammered.

Trinity raised her pistol. "Then I'd say we're even. Wouldn't you say?"

The old man shook in his shoes. "Yes'am. I'd say it's right even."

"Thought so. I can count numbers," said Trinity.

"That's a right even sum, I'd say." He forced a grin. "You ladies have a nice day."

"Thank ya kindly," said Trinity as she ushered her sisters out. Then she flipped a gold coin back at the shopkeeper.

He gazed at her in awe. "For what?"

"For reminding me of my pa," she called back.

They were easily recognized by townsfolk everywhere: three female demons garbed in black leather, only their long hair telling them from men. Horses was another matter, but Trina had a way with beasts and could lead them away without making a sound.

In time they got their own posters. You didn't get a poster until you'd killed a man. More murders and your bounty grew and new posters had to be printed. When the girls collected three posters in their saddle bags, they knew they were the territory's top thieves. They only killed in defending themselves. Shoot at them and they'd shoot back, and they were more accurate. Let the girls go and you could live another day. A posse might try to pursue them once in a while when they raced out of a town with items they could gather, but they'd shoot back at anyone who followed. Some fell dead.

5

MARKS

JUDGE ROBINSON HASN'T RETURNED so Trina has to remain in the cell. I take it upon myself to look after her. Deputy Cal thinks my efforts are odd, teasing me about being sweet on her. He speaks his barbs every time I step into the jail to bring her supper.

Deputy Tom, who takes the night hours, is kind enough to me, but he likes to curse at her or tease her with bawdy jokes.

When she has to let out waste she only lets me help. We develop an awkward understanding. Maybe because we're both half-native, maybe because of the way I've treated her in the days since she came to town. We talk a while in the evenings – as much as she is willing to share.

"Now you keep a watch on her," Tom warns me when I unlock the cell, him sitting back with his boots up on the desk.

With Tom in charge in the evenings I can unlock the cell and slide in the bucket, then lock the cell door again, following the rules.

I unfold a sheet I have tucked under my arm, hold it up with both hands, my arms stretched out to shield her while she squats over the bucket. When she's done and puts her gown in place she calls "Done" and I lower the sheet. Then the protocol of unlocking the cell door and grabbing the bucket, locking the cell door, taking the bucket out to the latrine. Being a medical person I can't help being attentive to her output, noting changes like a mother might for a new baby. She is handling the beans just fine.

The third night, Tom gets impatient and steps out when it is time for her evening evacuation. Once Trina has the bucket and the cell door is locked again, he lights up his smoke and leaves. I hold up the sheet as usual but at some point, the corner of the sheet slips from my hand. A portion of the cell is visible to me.

Trina stands awkwardly with her gown not yet in place. My eyes catch sight of her belly. The sheet blocks the lamplight some but I see her. It's not any kind of sexual look but a medical one. Bart had plenty of marks on his body that showed his hard life. This woman does, too. I've seen the same kind of marks on women's bodies I've had to prepare for burial: lines radiating upward from the groin and outward from the center of the abdomen, like worms trying to crawl away.

I dare not mention it or ask Trina about them.

So I take my questions to Maggie, who at first laughs. When she sees I'm serious, however, she speaks in a clear, calm manner.

"Those are stretch marks, Jake. It means she was pregnant. She had a baby. I got them, too."

I tell her who it was I saw — not one of the cadavers I work on — and she freezes in her chair.

"You telling me that awful woman is a mother?"

"I'm just saying what I saw." We stare at each other. "But that doesn't mean she has a child now. Maybe...maybe it didn't make it. I can't imagine a woman like her tending to a child. Can't imagine her being loving in that way."

"You're suggesting she might've killed it?" asks Maggie.

"No." But now I can't be sure. "Those marks mean she had to be with child, got big enough for her belly to stretch like that. But did she give birth?"

"Why're you talking like that? 'Did she give birth?' Of course she did. None of those sophisticated procedures way out in these parts to end it, not like doctors in a city. Nothing to do but give birth."

"What I mean is...." I stop to think. "If she got pregnant and had a baby...."

"What're you thinking, Jake?"

"I'm wondering where the baby is now. How old is it?"

"I'm wondering who the father is," she speaks up, almost having to repress a laugh. "That's what I'm thinking."

"Well, she was with Bart, we know."

"You think...it could be my Barty? He's the father?"

"She doesn't seem the settling-down type. But she's been talking about her and Bart."

"You're thinking that child's hers and Barty's? Is that what you're saying?"

I regard her, feel something darkening between us.

"She could've been with anybody. Before she even met him. Even if it was Bart, no telling what happened to the baby."

The oil lamps flicker, casting shadows on the wall that move like actors in a theater play, a new act starting.

Maggie takes a big breath, her hands clasped calmly in her lap like a proper lady, and slowly lets it out.

"Long ago my cousin Faith had a baby. Her husband Raymond saw it was deformed and likely an idiot, so he wanted her to leave it out in the brush – to let it die. She obeyed him or else he would leave her. Everyone thought it was her decision, not his, and they thought the worst of her for it."

I ponder the idea, never hearing that story before. I knew about Faith only through stories. Shot by a crazy man who thought in the dark that she was Aunt Eve.

"You best get on home now," says Maggie, seeing me thinking too hard. "Tomorrow's another day."

It should be well past dark by now but the Glow keeps the sky lit enough to see the way back into town. I keep expecting it to burst, like a huge orange balloon, then the darkness will return.

"Or you can sleep here, if you want," she says. "Four bedrooms in this big house and three of them unused."

"Should I just plain ask her?" I say, regarding Maggie.

"You think she's going to be honest? A woman like her is going to be careful. She'll say what she needs to say in order to get an advantage. I would be looking out for lies."

+ + +

Deputy Cal stops rolling a fresh smoke, glares across the table at me as I take a seat. "You're in the wrong place, ain't you? This here's a saloon. You belong in the doc's office 'cross the street. A saloon's no place for discussing politics. Or about criminals."

I'm about to speak again but he continues.

"A doctor's helper gotta keep his hands clean, see."

"I finished my work for the day," I tell him, rubbing my hands together for show. "Now I need a drink."

"Work? The dead? Or...hmm. Yep." He glares at me. "You got a fancy for that woman. What a poor boy." He takes up laughing for a minute as he finishes rolling up his smoke, lights it. "She ain't your type, now is she?"

It isn't that I have any feelings for her, that Trina woman in the jail cell, but I do for my childhood friend, Bart, who took up with her. I want to know all I can about her, and about him, their life together, as much I can, to report to Maggie.

"Well, the judge be back tomorrow," says Cal, "so you can get your answers then." He takes a long draw on his tobacco.

"What's she charged with?" I stammer.

"Charged? What *isn't* she gonna be charged with? Thievery. Petty stuff, to be sure. But also murder. Quite a few, I suspect. Hard to count 'em, her being in that gang. All what they done when the three sisters rode together. Sure enough to hang her, I expect. Like they did her sister."

"But she...." I lose my nerve.

"Go on," says Cal. "Spit it out."

"But she brought the bodies back. That counts as a good deed."

"Sure, I'll give you that. But is it enough to balance out all the bad she's done?"

"But, just maybe...." I wait for Cal to cut me off but he keeps on puffing his tobacco. "Maybe she didn't really do all those things. Not anything too bad, I mean. Like it was her sister pulling her along. Or maybe...maybe she's a completely different person now. A person can change, you know. Change for the better."

"I suppose it's possible," Cal responds after a long draw and long exhale. "Judge'll be deciding anyways. He might go easy on her cuz she's a woman. Not the ringleader. Hard to say. But a stint in the penitentiary would be a decent outcome, if that's what you worry about. Women's wing. A few years, I suspect. Not too hard. She'll be out as an old woman, twenty or thirty years later, of no harm to anyone."

"There's gotta be extenuating circumstances," I say.

Cal gives me a quizzical look. "Those are some mighty big words for a half-breed like you."

I tense. "Don't call me that."

"But you are. It's fact. Don't mean any insult."

"You know I went to the dentistry college in Kanza City," I like to remind him. "No matter that I'm Sheriff Baumann's grandson, I made top marks in the classes there. No matter that my mama was Kanza. I'm the best of both of them."

"And your pa, he's got some bad in him to give you, too."

"My father started good, yes, then he got with those rough men, drunks and robbers. Haven't seen him since I was little. Yes, he's a part of me. But I am me, most of all. I make my own life."

"You have. Good on you. You're surely welcome here. Welcome to do your chores for Doc Baker."

"More than that," I challenge. "I'm a citizen of this town, of this state. No less because of who my parents are."

"Ah, you're a clever boy, ain't ya?"

"Clever?" I feel wound up, ready to explode. "Boy? You're hardly older then me. What, three years?"

"Clever for a half-breed, I mean."

A hard-edged voice booms from across the room: "Enough of that half-breed talk," the beefy owner, Mr. Watanabe, calls out, standing behind the bar. "This is a respectable establishment. Don't want any fighting here. Nor those kind of words. You can take that outside."

In this town, the saloon owner is king and even a deputy has to mind his speech. Mr. Watanabe used to be a wrestler, what they call Judo style. I smile to myself.

"Thanks," I call back, "but we were discussing a delicate matter of jurisprudence."

"Jurisprudence!" Cal laughs. "Dang college boy!"

"I only want what's fair. Bart would want it, too. I'm thinking of Maggie. We still don't know what happened to Bart the past fifteen years. They couldn't be criminals all that time. For one thing, I think she's had a child. There's marks on her belly. I saw—"

"You what?" Cal practically shrieks. Then, in a lower voice: "You got a look at her? ...Naked?"

"No, not exactly." We both take a glance around the saloon, find not many present at this afternoon hour. "I was holding up the sheet while she was using the bucket but the corner slipped loose and I...I got a glimpse."

"Glimpse of what?" He leans in, grinning. "Tell me."

"She hadn't fixed her gown yet and her belly was showing—"

"So how'd she look? Mighty fine?" Cal sits back, chuckling.

"No, she.... I mean, I saw she had marks on her belly."

"What kinda marks?" asks Cal. "Injun tattoos?"

"No, marks like after a woman has a baby. I asked Maggie and she called them 'stretch marks' – meaning she had a baby. She got her belly full and stretched out."

"Well, ain't that interesting." Now Cal is concerned. "Mighty interesting. So where's the baby? Maybe *child* by now. How long ago you figure?"

"I don't know much about that stuff," I admit. "Just guessing. She's what, about thirty-five now?"

"Well, don't that beat all?" Cal takes a long draw on his tobacco. Then, blowing out a stream, he says: "Our Bart's a papa. Miss Maggie's got a grandson."

"I'm her grandson," I say, an edge to my voice.

Cal glares at me. "Yep. Well now, however you figure. Not quite the same thing, is it? You're by way of adoption. Bart's the real deal. Her own flesh and blood. And now you're saying her son's got a baby or child out there somewhere."

"If she's a mother, I care what happens to her. And that child. I was Bart's friend. So she's my responsibility." I take a breath. "Now that he's dead."

"Jake, you ain't got no responsibility for her," says Cal, using his serious voice. "None at all."

I shake my head. "I think I do."

+ + +

Four full days since Trina rode into town with those bodies and the judge is still away. She's still making her home in that jail cell, and I talk with her twice a day, bring her supper, and hold up the sheet while she does her evening ritual, then empty the bucket out back. Better than trying to let her out and keep an eye on her while using the latrine, says Deputy Cal.

In the evenings, it's only Tom and he's happy to snooze behind the desk while I talk with Trina. This time I bring her a change of clothes from Maggie's house, leftovers from my mama's wardrobe. I add a bar of homemade soap and a towel. She acts thankful for my kindness. I feel like she is, in some ways, part of the family, being Bart's woman, so I want to be kind to her.

She washes herself using a bucket of fresh water, me holding up the sheet again. After she dries off with the towel, she pulls on the once-white dress with blue-petaled flowers on it, stands awkwardly, her bare feet marked with boot sores, and turns around once for me. I say she looks lovely, thinking of when my mama wore that dress. I remember her dancing with my pa at his pa's big house. Seeing her in that dress, I tell Trina she reminds me of my mother.

"Don'tcha be thinkin' that way," she sneers. "Ain'tcher mama."

"No, ma'am. That's not what I meant at all," I respond. "It's her dress. And she had the same color skin and hair like you. So you do kinda look like her. I don't have any pictures I can show. Except their wedding picture, but it's in a frame at home. I mean at Miss Maggie's house."

"Ain'tcher mama," she snarls.

"I know. I didn't mean anything like that. Didn't mean to offend you. Just a comment. An innocent comment. About how lovely you look in that dress. That's all."

Her face shows decisions being made. "Yeah, Bart was like that. Mush-faced and soft as a wormy apple. Specially he talkin' 'bout his mama. Always talkin' 'bout his mama."

I level my eyes at her. "Did he ever think of going back home? Of seeing his mother again?"

"At first," she says after a moment. "Yeah, he cried out fer his ma at first. At the end, too. But in between we got too busy for any o' that. Had ta ride."

"Ride where?" I ask innocently, but considering their crimes.

She goes silent but I bide my time. She's not going anywhere.

"You still yammering over there?" calls Deputy Tom from behind his picture book. I got him interested in what they had at the library and he picked up a thin book that's all pictures with some words in circles of what the people in the pictures are saying.

"It's private talk," I say.

The clock on the wall shows it's getting late. I need some sleep to do my tasks tomorrow.

"I'll tell ya," Trina speaks as I stand up. "Tell ya damn near ever'thin' I kin recall, if ya truly wanna know. But ain't a good tale."

I lean down. "I do want to know."

6

BADLANDS

IT MIGHT JUST BE A LEGEND, something to wrap up a good story, or it might be true. Doesn't matter which. Word we got was the outlaw John Claude Wells and his men met their fate at the hands of Sheriff Frank Baumann and his posse. Good riddance, we like to say. I, for one, will say it. I will say it every day the rest of my life. I'm glad he's dead.

Years after the nasty Shane McNally met his well-deserved fate at the hands of three girls, another criminal came to terrorize our lands, being open and free to raid with not many lawmen around.

The Wells family came from near Sorrow Mountain National Park but before it had that name, just other survivors of the Great Pandemic. Like so many folks before them, they managed to keep to themselves through the ten-year plague, making a go of the land until it was farmed out. By then, rival factions fought over territory that included their farm and the family chose to leave. The father was killed in the civil war that preceded the reconstruction era, so the family hated anyone associated with the restored government and all policies spewing forth from those in power. Their farm was appropriated by the government, divided into fenced camps to house people who disagreed with official policies, questioned stories they were told to believe and forced to deny the experiences they'd lived through and knew as fact.

Maggie could confirm a lot of that. Her father had gotten caught up in that strict system while living in the capital and suffered for what he knew was true. He got facts straight from his mother, Isla, who lived through it. Maggie was Skinner Canyon's teacher after her mother died. She had a card for the town's library where dozens of old books sat on shelves, free of electro. You turned paper pages yourself instead of tapping on a tablet screen. From time to time she would mention stories her father told, repeating what Isla told him. There weren't a lot of books remaining; most of them had been used as kindling by desperate survivors. Books that remained preserved events from before and during the pandemic and the years after when there wasn't any government.

Isla was Maggie's grandmother and she lived through it. Isla's father, Sandy, wrote several notebooks about the adventures he and his wife, Hannah, and baby Isla endured in the lawlessness. Sandy also wrote about how he and his mother, that tuba player and music professor, fled their chaotic city back in its worst days, seeking a safe place to wait out the pandemic. They'd tried to stay with other relatives but found them worse off, so they kept going, made their way to a coastal island where they had a vacation home.

Isla was born in the seventh year of the pandemic, as Maggie states for the record. It lasted nine to fourteen years depending on the location. Isla grew up hiding with her parents in the forest of a national park. She met a boy there from another survivor family. In time they had a daughter they named June. Maggie explains how, as a joke, they began calling her Junie, then Jamie, became Amie, then Amy, but later added back the June so everyone knew her as Amy June by the time she'd grown up and become a mother and grandmother. Maggie traveled back east to attend her funeral. That's when she met her cousin Eve and they became fast friends.

Maggie's father, Fritz, who was Isla's last child, preferred being called Frank, which was his father's name. He named his own son Frank, too: my grandfather, the Sheriff. Fritz/Frank returned north from the marshes where he grew up after being born in the national park. He worked in the capital at a broadcast station. There he met Sandra and they married. He made videos: a camera box that gathered images in real-time and you could record them as a stream of flickering pictures, show them in order like another version of life.

It was popular in the days after reconstruction when old devices were invented anew. People had no information floating in clouds or pressed into things called *thumbs* so a lot of knowledge was lost. Information whisked away. Only what was preserved on paper in books remained and they were too few. People started to read again, had to read to regain the lost knowledge. The old things were rebuilt: first came electric power on a grid system, then camera boxes, then the electro-carriages.

The government found the cameras useful – also the devices that captured sounds, especially spoken words, and saved them for later. Often the images and words spoken were used as evidence to condemn citizens for opposing the government policies. The wrong-thinking citizens were sent for rehabilitation in special camps. The re-education enabled them to return to correct thinking. For most people it was effective. For Maggie's dad, Fritz/Frank, it was only temporary. He slid back, as they say, and got in trouble again. Then he died, still believing the stories his mother told him but which were not considered the true history.

Maggie didn't know everything that happened, being only ten at the time, but her dad saved the governor, Roberta Wornall, from a gang of anarchists who captured her and took her to their hideout. He blocked a shot meant for her and he died. It was stated in the official report. The governor praised his heroism, and gave Maggie's family special status. Fritz/Frank had always insisted the governor was his big sister – probably only an illusion that stuck in his head, Maggie considered, after seeing so many posters of Big Sister in the capital, declaring *Big Sister Cares For You*. He preferred 'Big Sister Lies to You.' That situation would've driven anyone crazy.

Maggie's mother, Sandra, realizing the oppression around them in the capital, took the opportunity to escape the city with her three children. They traveled out west to live with Fritz/Frank's cousin Faith, who'd been living with her half-brother, Raymond – until he was killed in a gunfight. Faith had two sons by then, Benjamin and Clemson, neither by Raymond. It's a long story.

In fact, too many stories told by Maggie got stuck in my head. I must've been gifted some of those odd family ways from the

Baumanns. Mama, being a Kanza, was pure and true. She was called Jackie, short for Jackrabbit, and wedded to Jeb, me already on the way. Jeb was the eldest son of Maggie's older brother Frank and wife Vera. Jackie and Jeb got to scrapping and he got too mean so Mama left him, returned to her village with me because Maggie was far away in the capitol. When Maggie finally returned to Skinner Canyon ten years later, Mama and I lived with her and Aunt Eve in the new house she had built from her music money.

A lot of families were like that back then: desperate.

The Wells family got caught up in the fighting between militia from both northern and southern territories as each side struggled to reclaim territory left ungoverned during the pandemic. It started with some people wanting to restrict other people so they wouldn't catch the virus; one side demanded compliance to a set of rules while others believed in 'natural immunity' or other God-given power. In the end, forgetting the virus, they had to fight for basic resources, now that nothing was being grown or produced for the shops. Hungry people will fight hard.

To the west of the national park where Isla grew up, in those interior valleys, the Wells family made a homestead, set up a farm. Then the war spread across their land, ruined their crops, and they got caught up in the fighting. In fact, the Battle of Sycamore Ridge – after the stand of sycamores had been blown down by artillery – saw their barn used as a targeting point. The family was lucky to survive, escaping before the worst of the battle raged. The fighting made an impression on the children, made them rebels.

The Wells family made a new farm near Nash's Village, tried to produce a new generation of children only to find themselves soon at the mercy of Ken Tucker's clan. Raids and fighting along the border reduced both groups. By then, the six sons, who were not old enough for fighting, were old enough to bury their parents.

John Claude Wells and his brothers fled west, riding all the way to the Missy River that marked the end of the country as they knew it. They followed that river north to Louis, another city in ruins, as the river ran south to the ocean. They didn't fare any better there. Testing their ability to get into trouble, they had many encounters with the law or with other criminals fighting over territory. On they traveled, across the hilly back-country, but no longer seeking farmland in the abandoned country between pockets of heartbreak where survivors clung to a stream, an orchard growing wild, a stave-fence yard where they'd captured a nanny goat to provide milk for a baby who'd lost its mother.

The road running southwest from Louis was a harsh journey, the land rugged and the denizens suspicious of anyone who had horses to ride where locals might prefer to dine on the beasts. The Wells boys made it to Spring's Field, then on to Tulsa and found the town inhabited more by tribal folks than country people. The change in residents didn't disturb them; tribal people reclaimed the land, even cities, as their own during the fifty years of anarchy.

Lawlessness suited the brothers. So they took up – or, rather, continued – their thieving ways. They built up some wealth in that fashion, began trading. Trading led to buying and selling using the New Dollars the restored government began to issue. That led to a store being built along the turnpike in Broken Arrow, where they charged a toll. The brothers gained respectability, though few liked paying the toll. Don't pay the toll and they'd shoot you. The graveyard nearby grew each month.

J.C. still had wanderlust burning in his gut. He'd ride out in different directions to see what trouble he could get into, then ride back saying none existed, only the chance to steal from isolated farms and ranches, maybe take women and girls from the families trying to make a homestead with only one man working the fields or no man and the women doing the labor. He could enjoy his time with them or sell them to other men. Easy pickings, he told his brothers, trying to excite them.

Most of his brothers had settled down by then, had gotten wives and then came kids. They couldn't see continuing the vagabond life. They considered themselves folk who contributed to the good of the community. *Community*, J.C. scoffed. They had become respectable. *Respectable!* Only Jordan, the youngest brother, joined J.C. on his quest for a magical land that lay further west, hills full of gold.

+   +   +

Skinner Canyon had seen its share of bad folks trying to take what they wanted and threatening citizens. The early days were the most violent but it never stopped for long. Once Sheriff Baumann and his posse took off after J.C. Wells, everything seemed to calm down. It was as though the sheriff was a kind of sacrifice, a gift offered to the gods. Then we waited, expecting more, but years went by with little to disrupt a growing town in the rugged western land at the edge of a restored nation, the Union of American States, all fifteen of them.

Again this corner beckoned, drew fortune-seekers from the east, and more from the southern territories those unwilling to submit to the regimented society imposed by the capital. Good families came and evil men followed to prey on them. The mayor implemented rules for arriving settlers. Homesteads were marked off and sold – paid with labor and the production of crops or livestock until the mortgage was paid in full later. Other people came to live off those farm and ranch families, offering their services. Others came as bankers, setting up lending shops for settlers – which attracted men who offered themselves as money collectors. Some of them did what would be described as 'bully work' when money wasn't paid on time or wasn't the full amount. A lot of work for the right kind of ruffian walking a line near criminal acts. And not enough lawmen to keep the peace. A few lawmen got tempted with money from the bankers if they'd turn their eyes away from some things done to the citizens.

But not in Skinner Canyon, which was always a peaceful town of happy, productive citizens, protected by Sheriff Baumann and his proud deputies. He did his best to maintain order, but a few times there were confrontations with bankers and others in the money trade and their henchmen. His primary responsibility, he told them, was protecting citizens. He wasn't one to measure contracts although he could read just fine. That was the responsibility of the lawyers – and more of them were coming to town to set up offices, making sure contracts were fair. They also stood in court to argue on behalf of citizens when a contract was broken or found to be unfair. That made for lively days, full of shouting and often fights when words didn't suffice. The mayor's job was to hold the bankers in check, to make sure the deals were fair and collections on the up and up. Until the mayors began taking bribes from bankers and others who had a stake in the town's farms and ranches.

Then material riches were found in the rugged hills to the west of Skinner Canyon and the opportunity to get rich drew settlers, including Simon Culpepper bringing his wife and daughters. Assay offices opened in every good-size town. The chance to make deals with prospectors drew more undesirables to the area, seeking the easy life of robbery. Rather than staking a claim for themselves and digging it out, shifting through dirt and rock to find the elusive flake of gold or other precious minerals, they would simply rob those who did. Like what happened with Simon Culpepper.

J.C. Wells was a different kind of man. He grew up hating everything, always looking for ways to be cruel, and that tendency didn't lessen over his life but grew more refined, more sinister. Until he and his gang did the worst thing possible.

"I know that part," says Deputy Tom, sitting back at the desk.

Talking in a low voice with Trina through the bars of the cell, I don't want Tom to hear me but he does.

"Sheriff Baumann took a posse out after Wells," Tom continues, uninvited. "And now he come back home in a pine box. Long buried, I hear. But they're gonna put him under again, maybe tomorrow or next day, see him proper buried next to his wife, with good words spoken over him. And buried next to Bad Bart, who don't deserve a nice funeral for all he done."

"Shut your mouth," I snarl at him.

Tom sits straight up in the chair so fast he almost falls. "Now you listen here," he growls, then stops himself, takes a breath. "Yep, I get ya. It's personal. I know. I'm just saying it is what it is. No hard feelings, awright?"

I nod, shaking with anger. "All right. Those are the facts."

Trina meets my eyes when I look back into the cell. "That man, he hurt ya?"

"Not me," I say in a rush. "Maybe Bart told you all of that."

"He told me plenty."

"I would like to know what he said."

"It's one them long stories."

Then Tom speaks up, overhearing us despite trying to keep our voices low: "It'll all come out at trial anyway. Whole court'll know what happened. Then folks on the jury'll decide if it's better to hang her or send her up to Kanza City to the penitentiary."

I glare at Tom and he shuts up, his face rosy with amusement.

Trina grunts. "That one, he deserve ta get shot."

7

A FEW WORDS

THE SKY IS CALM, wind still asleep, grassland bowed in respect as townsfolk gather at the square of plots in the cemetery, the growing yard marked off with white picket fences like a child's playground. Now white crosses stand within its boundaries, one for each family member who came out west and never left.

Miss Maggie wears the same black dress and black boots she did for previous funerals. On her head sits a bonnet with a black veil hanging down over her face. She'd worn the same black dress for her cousin Faith's funeral years ago. Cousin Eve's funeral a couple years past. And Vera's, her brother Frank's wife, who was never the same once she realized he wasn't coming home from that posse adventure. Her other brother, the aged Father James, his arm long-crippled from a gunshot, spoke at each one of those funerals, and he arrives for today's.

I stand behind Maggie, wearing my best church clothes but the suit isn't black. I'm afraid to say anything. I remember Mama's funeral but dare not glance at her white cross.

Movement next to me makes me turn to see Frances joining me. She's my aunt; her brother Jeb is my father. She's two years older than me. Daughter of Frank and Vera, she's now married with two sons. I'm certain she won't let them join a posse.

Seems like only yesterday they rode off, eight of them, going after that outlaw gang. Frank's been laying underground for fifteen years somewhere far away, so we have to presume someone said a few words over him at the time. We will do it again for him.

"Morning, Jacob," says Frances and we exchange half-smiles.

"Morning," I respond.

"Good to see you," she says. She's dressed in black and waves her hand before her face to whisk away a fly. "Not good to be here."

I nod, searching for the right words. "I'm sorry," I say at last.

"You don't have to be. Your loss as much as ours."

The way she says 'ours' cuts into me. She's always been kind but in way that's like she's adopted a stray pup. Her brother married my mother, mostly because I was already growing inside her. Then my father got in with some bad men, started being mean until Mama left him. When I was only a little boy he rode off and we had to live in Mama's tribal village because Maggie lived in the capital. I look more like my mother than Jeb. So I wasn't closely related to Frances, it might seem to her.

"It's all of us," I mutter, eyes forward to the two wooden boxes.

Frances leans around me to speak her condolences to Maggie, who nods politely to her niece. Maggie asks about the boys; they're home on this solemn occasion. Today's event is only a polite ritual we have to get through before we can return to our ordinary lives. We've gotten used to Frank being dead.

When a person gets old and dies we can celebrate a life lived and not be so grim about it, maybe cheerfully celebrate the things they did. But if the deceased is young and life has been cut short either by illness or violence, it has to be properly mourned. It felt different with Bart as I prepared the body. I kept thinking with every stitch *Oh, what trouble have you gotten into, Bart?*

Maggie keeps her handkerchief out, lifting her veil and dabbing her eyes. I have no tears for my one-time buddy. I didn't know Bart as a grown man, couldn't remember back to days playing together as boys.

Jenny Chandler comes up behind me, takes my hand before I can notice her. I'm glad she's here but worry I'll look weak.

"You doing all right?" she speaks softly. I give a nod. "Y'all keep worrying about people that ain't here no more."

"It's my family," I say, too soft for her to hear.

She holds my hand, leaving me more certain she's sweet on me. Or I'm just another stray pup to care for.

I see Joe and his wife Hilda in the crowd. Had to take a second look, then calm my heart. He's the twin of my father, Jeb. The resemblance rattles me. And there's Jon, the younger brother. He stands with his new wife, Melissa May, after his first wife, Georgia, passed from illness. The brothers and wives pose solemnly before the coffin of their father. They barely look at Bart's.

Frances excuses herself and strides up there to join them. It's a moment for family time. Together they place their hands upon the box containing their father, the old box cleaned up from the dirt of its first burial, wood repaired. Doc Baker had me open it, check it was actually Frank inside it. Remains well-decayed, bones intact, sheriff's star still pinned to his vest, rumpled hat at his head, skull grimacing, no boots or gunbelt. Marks on his shirt showed where bullets entered. One remained loose within the rib cage, another rattled around under him. It seemed as though no one had bothered to clean him up for the first burial, just dumped him in the box and nailed it shut, dropped it into a shallow pit and covered it up.

Until that woman, Trina Culpepper, brought it here. I reported to the doc what I found and he signed the certificate.

How did she know where he was buried? I fall into a dumb mood as I think of more questions. *Did she dig him up by herself?* A man his size would be heavy for her lithe body to bear.

Mr. Clampett, our town undertaker, added a fine copper plaque to the box commemorating Frank's life as a long-time Deputy here in Skinner Canyon, then Sheriff. Father and grandfather, born in the capital, brought out west by his mother, Sandra, when he was seventeen. The younger brother James was fifteen, the baby sister Maggie barely eleven.

Sheriff Frank Baumann rests in the box on the left. His nephew Bart Baumann, bearing his unmarried mother's name, occupies the newly constructed coffin on the right. I paid Mr. Clampett for the box so Maggie wouldn't have to worry about it.

Jenny hooks her arm around mine. I welcome her, although I have no more romantic feelings for my schoolmate. We were only kids flirting. She takes her wages from the communications office on Main Street, runs a printing machine for the news-paper office. She has a prettiness that makes me look longer each time, a smile that holds my attention.

The elderly Father James makes his way slowly, carefully up the aisle between guests as a hot breeze blows past us – like God has just arrived. James leans on his cane, a young acolyte in church robe following to assist him. I see a good number of townsfolk gathered. They know James, had him speak over their kin. He's had a hard life.

After Sandra brought the children from the strict capital, James worked in the bank, where he survived three robberies in one year. In the last one he suffered a gunshot to his arm which left the arm useless. So he quit banking, went to the chapel on the hillside overlooking both the town and the canyon. He became a priest there. He's led the chapel since the old priest died. Now James is the old priest. Watching him make his way forward in such slow fashion, I wonder how many months he may have left.

I gaze away from the yard, across the chaparral, and spy a band of tribals on horses, watching our ritual from afar. I want to wave to them, my people, the tribe of my mama. But I've been raised in this settler town for too long, become one of them as my father's son yet never fully one of them.

"See those riders out there?" asks Jenny, nodding at the tribals.

"I see them," I reply quietly.

Father James stands before the box on the left, drapes a purple sash over it with the church's symbol in gold. Mr. Pinder sets up his camera, ignites a few photo-graphics for printing later on the news-paper, then moves the breadloaf-sized device and its tripod away. James grimaces, clearly disliking the photo-graphics.

"We are gathered here today," Father James begins, pauses to cough. "Gathered to commemorate our brothers, Frank Baumann and Bartholomew Baumann. Although the state of their affairs have long passed, we welcome them home to their final place of rest, a place where God has been expecting them, where He may at last grant them peace."

He pauses to clear his throat. There is dust in the air.

"Frank Baumann, lawman and father, protector of our town, has been at rest lo these many years, only recently being exhumed and brought to us for his rightful destination: his family's sacred yard. He can finally lay at peace among his kin."

Father James looks back over his shoulder at the crosses in the yard, perhaps knowing he will join them soon. A rectangle of land is reserved for him. It's an eerie moment: he seems to see something the rest of us can't.

"Beside him: Frank's nephew, Bart, who likewise departed from us, from our safe keeping, for adventures unknown, only to return in his final moment. We welcome him home nevertheless. His is a life ended too soon – or not soon enough, some folks might say. We are not here today to judge this man but to welcome him home. Even at the bottom of his life he remains our kin. He shall be judged by the Almighty at another time and place. It is not for us to do so today. Now let us pray."

Everyone bows their heads as Father James begins a prayer. I hear weeping between his slow words from the people gathered. He asks forgiveness for everything Bart's done. His voice never fails to move me, deeper and richer as he's aged, now rough but sonorous, like the Great Spirit speaks through him.

"Fine words," Jenny says and I pat her hand that's on my arm.

"Amen," says Father James.

The gathered townsfolk raise their eyes to the front of the yard.

Father James raises his good arm, makes the sign of the cross over Bart's box, repeats it over the other box. He intones a prayer for Frank. He gives a list of major events in Frank's life. We know the basic story. How the family came west after difficult lives in the capital. He felt the call of justice, became a deputy. He eventually became the sheriff. In his final act he went in pursuit of the outlaw J.C. Wells with a posse of seven. My cousin Bart, not quite sixteen, went with them.

"We commend our dear brothers to their heavenly reward and bid them restful peace." Father James places his hands one on each box and bows his head. He speaks another prayer, gets teary-eyed and wipes his face with a shaky hand. The acolyte gives him a cloth to wipe his face.

Then the men of the town take hold of the ropes on each box and carry them to their graves. Frank goes beside Vera. Bart goes next to the plot set aside for Maggie when her time comes. We gather around the open pits, Frank's first. We witness final words and the sprinkling of dirt down upon the lowered boxes.

I help Maggie step to the graveside, ready to catch her if she should falter. She keeps her fist clenched after letting go her last handful of dirt over her son's grave, and lifts her hand to her face. She raises the veil and smears the dirt across her cheeks, lets the veil fall. She seems to weaken at that moment but I'm close enough to steady her. Nobody should have to wait fifteen years to see a brother and son properly buried.

The men shovel the pile of dirt into each grave, filling them, covering the boxes, and when the mounds are tapped down, a final prayer is spoken. Townsfolk gradually depart.

Family members remain by the graves.

Jenny appears behind me, puts her hand on my shoulder. When I turn, she repeats her condolences and bids me farewell, stretches up to give my cheek a soft kiss as a dry wind blows, coaxing dust to rise and swirl. A quick hug and she turns to go.

Maggie remains fixed to her spot before the two graves, her eyes roving from one to the other. Markers have been made, the crosses hammered into the ground at the head of each mound. The white crosses bear their names. She observes unwaveringly each act, as though she must approve them.

Father James steps cautiously beside her, speaking in a voice too low for me to hear then falling silent.

Warm breeze caresses us, the Glow always there in the east like an expanded sun rising from the horizon.

When I turn to go I see her: a dark silhouette before the Glow, visible against the bright noontide.

Trina, the woman who brought them back, waits, watching. She stands up straight in her leathers like she's ready to ride, like this short visit is a side-task taking her away from more serious crimes.

A kind gesture to let her wear her preferred clothing and attend this event. I'll have to thank Deputy Cal later.

Who is she? Why would she care?

There has to be more questions, more answers. And I have a few. Like how did she know where Frank was buried. Maybe it was Bart who knew the location, who also might've arranged for his box. We can't ask him now, only her. Need to be gentle to get answers from her. Instill confidence so she will speak the truth.

I didn't expect her to show up, forced to remain in that jail cell. Even if she were free to come here, she would expect people to fear her, accuse her, hate her. She and her sisters' reign of crime had crossed the territory for years and only ending when Trinity was caught and hanged. Something must've gotten to Trina and Triss. They stopped their crimes, were never seen again. As if they settled down somewhere.

Now Trina stands at the rear of the gathering, hands together, locked in silver bracelets. Deputy Tom holds a chain that's fixed to her cuffs like she's a hound to be led. She must've begged them to let her attend the funeral of her...what? Her lover? Husband? Sad for her, any way I think of it. Not allowed any closer.

"Come on, Grandma," I say after an hour of staring down at the ground. "Let's see you home."

I gently take her arm. She goes with me, out through the graves already filling the yard, using her cane and leaning on my arm, on to her house set away from the family cemetery, the house where I lived with my mama. From the back windows of this house she can watch the yard and keep an eye on its sleeping residents.

"Are you going to be all right?" I ask, stupid question. Of course she won't be after seeing her brother and son delivered to the earth. "Do you need anything? I mean, anything I can do for you? Get you anything?"

She sniffles back tears, turns to me. "You're a fine man, Jake."

At least I don't go chasing outlaws. I never grew into that kind of man. I liked studying the natural world, full of questions – not running cattle or doing other ranch work. I got interested in plants and natural healing. Mama told me about her grandfather's healing abilities. Old Doc Baker saw my interest and helped send me to the college in Kanza City, thinking I would join him and his son.

"You've done well," says Maggie. "Money well spent. You make me proud." She sniffles, grabs her handkerchief. "Better than I can say for my own son."

For a heartbeat I wonder what she means. Was it for me to hold Bart back when he was keen to ride away? I was barely eighteen myself. I had no sway over his choices.

"Don't say that," I speak too quickly. "We don't know what all he did, what happened out there."

Inside the house, I sit with her.

She's nodding her head, thinking.

"A boy gets a spark in his head and nobody can extinguish it, nor make him use it for warming a cold night," she says, maybe more to herself than me. "He was always more of his grandfather's boy than his father's. Or his mother's. He was his own man. He made his own life, as we all do eventually."

She gives a final nod and I hear the silence in this large house. There's a piano against the wall in this sitting room. I've listened to many songs played on it. Doesn't feel any different than the day before or the weeks that have passed. Silence in a house once full of music. Ever since my mama left us, since I left, and Aunt Eve left, Maggie's lived alone. She spends her days scribbling music on paper. She tried teaching me how to read it. When she's finished with songs she sends them to her friend in Kanza City: Mr. Hill at first but now to his daughter, Priscilla, after he passed away. She prints the music and sells those papers to music groups across the country, although there are fewer of them each year.

"Will there be a trial?" asks Maggie as I help ease her into her lounging chair, aching feet free of boots and raised on the stool. She hands me her black bonnet with the veil, gesturing where I should set it.

"Trial? What for?" I ask, not wanting to answer.

"That woman."

"Trina? There's no accusations on her," I say, trying to act like I don't know anything. "Not that I've heard."

"She's kept in the jail cell, isn't she? No suspicions at all?"

"She's well-known in these parts for things best not ignored, it's true. But she's not done anything for several years. Deputy Cal said they're under a truce for her bringing them home. I think they'll let her go free."

"I see." She regards me a while. "I want to speak with her more before she leaves."

"She could've left town during the funeral. Grab Tom's pistol and shoot him, unlock the cuffs, take a horse and ride out."

Maggie stares hard at me and I know I said too much.

"She didn't though, did she?"

"No, I saw her. At the rear of the assembly."

"She has some honor in her then."

"Or...maybe love? I heard her talking about having something with Bart."

"Oh? Like that baby you talk about? That sounds like relations." She struggles to get up, changes her mind, settles back. "I should be there when they question her."

"They already asked questions. Now they're just waiting for the judge to get here."

"I got my own questions."

"Maybe there will be a trial, after all." My chest is tight, feeling the strain of my deception. "Or they'll let her go. If they honor the truce. But no telling what the judge will say."

"Then you go into town," she tells me with a stern tone. "You hurry to Deputy Cal and get him to keep her in town longer. Tell him I got questions and if she's any kind of decent person she'll stay and answer me. If she's got relations with my boy she's my kin now. And that means a thing or two. I want to know more. I need to know what my boy's done."

8

JUDGMENT DAY

JUDGE ROBINSON LOOKS UP from the papers on the desk, gazes over his spectacles, his bushy white brows threatening to cover the lenses, as he rolls a wad of phlegm over and over deep in his throat before daring to swallow it and cough out its memory.

"Should be a hanging case, Your Honor," says Deputy Cal before the judge. "Best be done speedy. Get it over with. Then folks can get back to everyday life."

But Judge Robinson waves him to be quiet.

"We gonna have us a trial," says the judge. "That much you can be sure of. Set the record straight. Until then—"

He erupts in a coughing fit. People wait, concerned. If this judge dies then we will need to send for another, maybe from as far away as Wichita, and that could take weeks. But the judge recovers, wipes his mouth with his well-used hanky.

"Well, now, it ain't no mark of the devil, least," he says, gravelly voice rattling the floorboards of the courtroom. "Though it truly is a sign of motherhood, even if it didn't last, even if it left a poor little thing alone in the desert, even if she killed the poor child far from here, we can't prove nothing. However, I do declare those marks to be enough to grant her motherhood status for purposes of this trial."

I'm glad that my short carefully written page sways the judge to grant Trina a bit of kindness.

Judge Robinson glares at Deputy Cal who straightens up.

"You take her outta that jail cell and put her in a hotel room. Put a guard there but, otherwise, she's allowed the dignity of a proper bed and private bathing."

"Yes, Your Honor," Cal responds.

Posed before the judge's desk at the head of the courtroom, Trina buttons up her shirt, tucks it into her trousers, cinches her belt.

"And get her a dress," the judge calls out. "No woman's gonna be looking like a gawldarn gunslinger in my courtroom."

"Yes, sir," says Cal.

"And get her a lawyer," the judge growls, slamming his hammer on the desk. "I ain't running no hanging court here."

We clear the room, me standing at the rear to watch everything.

Miss Maggie doesn't attend. She's a bit 'under the weather', one of her common expressions, then laughs and says all of us are under the weather. And we turned together to gaze at the Glow, as orange and unyielding as ever.

So I came to the trial alone, promising to report back to her.

"The judge said she'll be on trial for murder," I tell Maggie. "As suspected. But they got petty crimes on the list, too."

Maggie seems concerned. "Nobody stood up for her? Nobody said she came to town bringing those bodies? That's not worth a truce?"

"I figure they want to get her while they can. Ain't seen her in years so no telling when they'll get another chance."

"Now you stop with that 'ain't' nonsense. I taught you better."

"Yes, ma'am." I offer a grin, like I'm still a little boy watching my mama tend to Maggie's needs.

"So who's this murder she's accused of?" asks Maggie.

The room suddenly turns cold as I put my words together. "They read off a list of names."

"A list? How evil is that woman?" She shakes her head.

"Eleven names on the list." With a sigh I tell her five names that I can recall from the clerk's reading. They're ordinary citizens of nearby towns who were shot during the gang's thieving days, going back eight years. Three of them are known criminals so maybe they won't be counted against her.

"Eleven!" Maggie nearly shrieks. "I only expected one or two, the way tales are told of these types of criminals. Better they kill each other and leave the rest of us alone. I expect she was defending her sisters or herself. Or Barty. I could understand that."

"Possibly."

"If you're defending yourself or others then shooting is allowed. I believe such a person is required to acknowledge the shooting after, of course, to make it legal. Own up to it immediately."

She launches into the story about how Aunt Eve shot a man who came here looking to hurt Maggie. Just a misunderstanding during her visit to the capital, then the man locates her in Skinner Canyon, shows up one day at the schoolhouse with kids having band rehearsal. The man returned later when Maggie was living in the capital and shot Faith, thinking she was Eve. I wait through her telling, forgetting how many times she's told me before. Eve shot the man dead, spent a day in jail for it.

"I heard...." As I stop to think of the right words, she coughs and wipes her mouth with her handkerchief. "I've been talking with her in the evenings. At the jail. I mean, her in the cell, me outside it. She told me a lot of what she did – what she and Bart's done."

"And what's that?" Maggie demands.

I have to frown. "I'm still piecing it all together."

+   +   +

Next morning I go get Trina from the hotel. I offer to go for Deputy Tom who is taking too long in the latrine. I promise I'll watch her close. He offers me a pistol but I don't think I need it. I'm only escorting her to the courthouse where everything will be sorted out.

The guard outside her door is glad to see me, knowing he can go home and sleep. I flash the silver badge Tom gave me for the task and the guard grins.

When she opens the door, Trina stands fresh and rested, pretty like nothing I've ever seen in that white dress with the blue flowers that Mama used to wear. The dress was a gift from Maggie. Trina's put her dark hair into a pony's tail and her face shines with desert sunshine. This is how she looks in my dreams.

"Good sleep'll do it fer anyone," she says, making it sound like a complaint. Yet I have no doubt those kind of nights are few and far between for such as her.

"Yes, indeed, ma'am," I respond, trying to be a gentleman. "I'm here to take you to the courthouse. Deputy's busy and I offered."

"Mighty kind."

I extend my elbow and she gets the idea to take hold of my arm with her hand.

"No cuffs?" she asks.

"I trust you."

Then I see her bare feet below the hem of the dress.

"They ain't gimme my boots back," she grumbles at my look.

"Yeah, nobody can get far in this land without boots."

Being a prisoner, she's gotten her breakfast in her room, set the empty tray out on the hallway floor. A housekeeper comes for it as we leave. We go down the stairs, minding the hem of her dress, out through a lobby with more than a few curious guests, plus a pair of news-paper writers.

We go straight out of the hotel into the dusty street, my shoes and her bare feet immediately dirty.

The Glow can't be avoided, filling the eastern sky. The ball of sun struggles to pierce that orange curtain, as I dare glance in that direction. We've noticed it each morning for so long now we hardly shake our heads anymore. Whatever it is, it's not hurting us yet.

Crossing the street, I hear someone shouting. I look around for the voice, see Mr. Henderson in front of the courthouse, his arm pointing down the street. I look that way, see a bedraggled figure stumbling along, coming toward us.

Mr. Henderson rushes into the street, continuing to point at the stranger coming into town. "What is it?"

The figure is undistinguished, its ungainly form hard to look at. Like a corpse.

"Doc," Mr. Henderson calls to me. "Somebody's coming from out of the Glow."

I have to squint. I can make out the condition of this stranger. Decrepit, wounded, thin as bone, with strings of flesh hanging off its skeleton like paper flapping in the breeze. Yet it pushes ahead, step after anguished step, giving off a low moan.

Just as I decide I'd better get my medical bag, Deputy Cal steps in front of me, blocking my view. He holds up a shotgun and with no hesitation lets go two blasts at the horrible figure. It freezes in an upright pose for a frightful moment, then collapses, legs crumpled under, hips crashing, torso falling forward, head hitting the street.

Cal lowers the shotgun as the crowd gathers behind us, staring down the street at the dead figure.

"Gotta get 'em before they get us," Cal says, eyes on the man.

Seems to be a man, terribly wounded.

"Why you just shoot him?" I ask.

Cal half-turns to me, trying to keep an eye on the body down the street. "Some of them bring the plague. You saw him. We don't want no one like that getting close to us. Nothing you could've done for it. Ain't got no regret."

"But I could've checked on him, at least."

"Then you'll be like him," says Cal. He looks around. "I thought you were bringing that woman to the courthouse."

My head spins. Where's Trina? In the excitement, she's taken off. I spot her running in the opposite direction, the long dress flapping and hindering her run.

"Dang it," Cal curses. He takes out his pistol.

"No, don't shoot," I cry out.

Cal calls over to Deputy Tom, on duty again. "Get after her."

A few men, recognizing the escaping woman, stand before her to block her way. She stumbles before them. Chunky Tom isn't a fast runner but he catches up with her. They're afraid to grab her, lady laws being what they are. I hurry after him.

Tom grabs her arm, tries to pull her to her feet. But when she's upright, she lashes out, her bare foot kicking at his groin. He wails and gives her face a hard slap.

Deputy Cal rushes to them, cursing like he does.

She has a few more moves, swatting at Tom, laying a hand chop against his throat. Tom shakes off her attack, gets his arms around her, tries wrestling her to the ground, threatening to hog-tie her if she doesn't behave.

"Stop it!" she shrieks. "Got a babe in me."

Tom pauses, arms around her, ready to slam her to the ground.

"What? You got a baby in you?" he asks, puzzled.

Cal arrives, orders Tom to let go of her.

"She say she got a baby in her," Tom tells Cal.

Cal looks her over, cussing. "Don't see nothing."

She's got a cross look on her face, challenging them. "It's inside, don'tcha know?"

"But you ain't showing nothing."

"Yeah, but it comin'," she growls.

"I'll bet," Cal sneers.

They take her between them, grasping her arms, and lead her to the courthouse.

At the steps, I show my surprise that she tried to run off. She gives me a look, half sorry but half disdainful. I feel bad for letting that happen. She was my responsibility.

"You were focused on that terrible thing coming up the street," Cal tells me, "not the pretty thing running down the street. Shoulda been Tom doing his duty."

I agree. Trina gives me a dark look, like she expected me to help her. Her eyes make me feel like I've betrayed her. I was despicable for siding with the settlers instead of her.

As much as I want to be in the courthouse to hear what is said, it's my task to put on the protective suit and go to that body in the street. It's a hassle, but I'm the designated cleaner. We must limit any chance of infection.

I kneel down to examine the figure, holding the G-meter at three locations along the body, needle hitting the red mark each time. Cal was right to shoot first and let me ask questions after.

What once was a living human now lies in rags of flesh, bloated organs half-exposed through torn skin that's nearly thin enough to see through. As the corpse lays there, the contents of its body seep out. I throw a tarp over the mess and go to wash off as the designated team wearing similar suits come to remove the body off the street, following the protocol, and take it far away, bury it in the plot where a warning marker is set. They clean the street where the thing fell dead.

"It definitely came from the east," I tell Doc Baker. He insists on a complete report, gives me paper to write on. "Obviously in pain and disillusioned, quite mad and possibly blind. Eyes clouded over. Probably navigated by sound. Heard the church bells ringing to let people know the courthouse is open. Stumbled into town."

"And Cal shot him – *it*."

"Straightaway. While it was still fifty feet away."

"That's about the minimum distance," he says, rubbing his chin like his father did. "Lucky we have those government hazmat suits. Everybody said we didn't need them anymore since the pandemic ended." He smiles in a devious way. "So something's gone wrong out east. We all know it. Now this man finds us, seeking help, let's say. Damn puzzling."

"What help could we give? He was nothing but rags, the flesh all hanging in strings from the bones."

"That's what they're experiencing back east, I fear."

"What could do such a thing? Another pandemic?"

"I think it must be something worse. Much worse."

+   +   +

They have been listening to various witnesses for a couple hours by the time I take a seat inside the courtroom. People gather outside, too, listening to a hawker pass the words out to them. When I sit, a man is up front by the judge, talking about the state of the nation. On the chalk board they've written his name: *Mr. Darren Wallace*.

"Now when they got some power they set up their Ideal Society, which is what they called 'we rule, you obey' or what some old time philo-*sopher* calls tyranny, or like that old book people talked about like it was a government manual. *The Bible*, they called it. After decades of anarchy when we lost the western half, and all that remained was the fifteen states that held together after the war between northern and southern territories. They got a governor in the state with the most people and he ruled like it was the capital city – the capital district. The president they chose lives in that city, too. So does the governor, and someone acting as mayor of that city. But it's not confusing. It makes sense to have all three rulers in the same city, concentrate the power in one armed camp. It's no wonder they put up walls around the swanky neighborhoods. Heck, now you need permission to even enter the capital."

People are nodding in agreement, accepting how bad our nation has become, murmurs bouncing through the assembly.

"And your point being?" asks Judge Robinson wearily.

"Point being, sir, we set it up this way. Made it hard for people to get by so it ain't surprising they get to be cruel. Take matters into their own hands. Matter of survival. You don't remember everything our grandparents been through? The times of anarchy? What they are still calling the Time of Troubles – between the pandemic that lasted for ten-plus years and the war between the north and south territories another ten years. And nothing being grown or raised."

"Your point?" asked the judge.

"Point being she and her sisters just doing what they need to do to survive. Like we all trying to do. Just survive. Laws don't help an empty belly. Laws won't save us from evil men."

"Or women," someone speaks out.

Then the man sitting beside me leans over, whispers: "This one's a fool. Thinks he's a know-it-all from a city college."

I sit up straight, focus on the man in the chair up front.

"Now we're on our own," Mr. Wallace continues. "Fact is, we could be our own country. We run things out here, all on our own. Capital's far away and likely destroyed by now. We all've seen the Glow. All what's left of those northeast cities. No way we need to keep on taking orders from dead men."

"Or women," the same person speaks out.

"That Roberta Chesterfield, she was worst," adds a man behind me. "She's the one started that whole society. Should've been killed instead of her being saved."

People sitting behind me are muttering to each other about the freak that wandered into town and how Deputy Cal shot it dead. It annoys me; I'm trying to focus on the testimony at the front.

I gaze at Trina perched on the wooden chair in the front corner, a guard standing beside her. She's not cuffed and looks pretty in the dress I gave her, although there's a smudge of dirt from when the deputy tackled her in the street. She must sense my stare because she turns her head as if looking for me. Our eyes meet over the rows of curious people sitting for their entertainment. Her lips pinch, which I call a smile. She knows I'm on her side yet I don't know why. She could've done lots of terrible things. And what about Bart?

+ + +

"So Sheriff Baumann got the posse together, like we did before, all according to protocols set forth in the law." It's Deputy Mike on the stand, who rode with Frank fifteen years ago. He still winces when the bullet that's still in him touches a nerve. "Frank Baumann led it," he says, then names the seven men assigned to the posse, "and his nephew, Bart, just fifteen, went with 'em, too."

I waited through the lunch recess, unwilling to give up my seat, eager to listen to the afternoon testimony.

"There weren't no Glow in them days," Mike continues. "But it was fearsome hot. We was hotter, gotta say. Hot for justice."

"Just tell what happened," Judge Robinson grunts.

"I'm getting on it. So we ride south, out toward Guymon, then a spell west, on to Black Mesa. Where we seen the smoke rising from those rocky hills there and we suspect it's them, the J.C. Wells gang. So we slow and dismount, go on foot to sneak up on 'em."

"And Bart?" asks the judge.

"Frank told the boy to hang back, mind the horses."

"Go on."

"So Frank and us, we climb up through those rocks," and he goes on a long description of the area, the rocky outcrops, how everything looked at that dusk hour, until the judge cuts him off. "We think we got 'em surrounded, but somebody snaps a twig and they get alert. Frank was the lead, and when that gang sprung up, it was Frank they saw. Ordered him to drop his guns. I was right behind him in the rocks but weren't nothing I could do."

"Why not?" asks the judge.

"Frank said most important thing is to get Wells, so I'm staying calm like he wants. Others behind me down that trail hunker down so it's only me could help him. But weren't a thing I could do."

"Your Honor," shouts a man in a black suit, white shirt, and a trimmed black beard who stands at the front, "what does this tale have to do with my client's case?"

I recognize him as the lawyer: a stout figure who always seems to take the prosecutor role.

The judge straightens up, looking over the desk at the man who must be the lawyer assigned to defend Trina. I've seen him before when trials were held in Skinner Canyon. Mr. Duda is his name, I recall. Delbert or something. Couple years back he called me to the chair to testify what I found doing an autopsy of a criminal.

"We need to start at the beginning," Judge Robinson intones. "It started with Sheriff Baumann going on that posse after J.C. Wells, and the boy going with them, and him getting lost and meeting up with those women, and they joining together to commit crimes."

"We can establish from the testimony of the men who returned," says Mr. Duda, "what occurred at the place in question. That is not in dispute. Sheriff Baumann was taken hostage and, rather than use him for leverage or seeking a reward for his freedom, chose to shoot and kill him at the same location. An execution. We don't need to go through the details."

"There's folks here," counters Mr. Horace Hitchens, the other lawyer, a thin man with a large nose and beady eyes, thinning hair, and a pocket watch he likes to juggle as he speaks, "who don't know any of the pertinent facts of this case. Details are crucial."

Deputy Mike glances around, like he's afraid he won't get to say more. He seems to enjoy his chance to talk.

"Very well," says the judge. He turns to Deputy Mike. "So Wells shoots Baumann, who dies. What happened with the other men and especially that boy? After the sheriff was shot."

Mike perks up, given another chance to talk. "See now, Bart, he was back with the horses. After they shot the sheriff, I scramble out of there. To get the other men, ya know. Weren't being coward, just need to get the men, tell 'em what happened, make plans. I couldn't take 'em on by myself. That woulda been foolhardy, strung down that trail the way we was." He tells about how narrow and steep the trail was, complains about thorn bushes poking his arm. "I knew it weren't gonna be easy. Coulda took 'em on myself but I'd be dead too, then not able to come back to tell the tale."

"So you left the scene," asks Mr. Duda. "Made your way on back down the trail. To save yourself. Isn't that correct?"

Mike looks down. "S'pose what you said is true. But you weren't there. The Wells gang had like a dozen men and we had only eight."

"Talk about the boy," insists Mr. Hitchens.

"Bart Baumann," Mr. Duda adds. "Where was he at that time? You said he was told to mind the horses."

"Yep, he was." Mike looks up, eyes wet. "He weren't there when we get back to where the horses are. The boy's horse is there but not him. We didn't know where he gone to."

"The boy took it upon himself to go investigate," says Mr. Duda, all serious, "when he heard shots fired. Isn't that right?"

"S'pose. But we didn't give him orders but mind the horses. He shoulda been right there when we got back. He shoulda stayed there. Horses coulda run off without him there to mind 'em. Boy had no bidness on his own thing like what he did."

"So what did he do?" asks Mr. Duda, like he's set a trap.

"We can't know it. He was gone." Mike looks forlorn, appearing as a coward. "We didn't have no time to go looking for him cuz we had to do something about Frank. We need to make a plan. A plan to get that gang for what they done. But we was only eight and they know we's coming, so no surprise. We decided to go back to town and get more men, then go back after Wells and his men."

Mr. Duda is nodding his head thoughtfully, begins pacing across the front of the room.

"You left the scene to return to town. Left the sheriff dead there. Left the boy to whatever his fate was. How soon did you return?"

"It was...couple days later." Mike gets flustered. "It takes time to get men together. But we rode back to those rocks soon as we could. But, we figure it's too late. Wells gang is gone."

"The gang escaped," Mr. Duda says with a dramatic pause. "And what did you happen to find there? At their campsite."

Mike glances around the room, like he's seeking help. "What we found there...."

"Was it Frank's body?" asks Mr. Duda.

Mike shakes his head. "No, it weren't."

"What did you find?"

Mike hesitates, shifts his eyes to Mr. Hitchens.

"Go on," says Mr. Hitchens. "You can say."

"There was a body," Mike says. "Sure was. Laying there where he fell." The courtroom crowd murmurs. "But it weren't the sheriff. No, sir. Weren't no other bodies there but that one. And it weren't Frank's."

"Whose was it?" Mr. Duda demands.

"It was...." Mike takes a breath. "J.C. Wells lay dead there. Shot in the face. Right through the eye. Musta killed him instant-like, we figured."

"Any speculation who shot him?" asks Mr. Duda.

"Weren't none of us," says Mike. "Maybe one of his own men, we figure. Musta had a disagreement. Maybe about Frank. What to do. Like that, we figure."

"But no body that was Frank Baumann's. Is that correct?"

"Yessir. Only one body and it was J.C. Wells. Shot dead."

The crowd erupts in chatter that requires the judge to bang the gavel to silence them.

"None can know for certain what occurred," shouts Mr. Hitchens above the audience.

"Who then, in your estimation," Mr. Duda presses, "would've had the opportunity and motive to shoot a vicious criminal in that place, at that time?"

"Can't think of no one, sir."

"How about the boy?" Mr. Duda grins, then puts it away. "Would the boy have been able to sneak around through those rocks, get to a good spot to observe what occurred and do something in reaction? Is that possible?"

"S'pose it's possible." Mike looks worried. "But we got no proof. It's just guessing."

"And where did Frank's body go?"

"Maybe they took the body with them when they cleared out," Mike responds. "What we figure. Maybe they gonna ransom the body for the widow. That's just like him, that Wells bastard."

Mr. Duda paces a while, halts before the judge. He's clearly thinking of a good question. He turns to the man in the chair.

"How long did it take you to ride out there?" he asks Mike.

"It were three full days," Mike replies somewhat nervously. "It's how we got there when it was getting on evening."

"And when you left there to ride back?" asks Mr. Duda. "To get help, as you said. How long did it take? You must've been enraged, so you likely rode faster."

"No, sir," Mike responded, voice strained. "It take three days to ride back to town."

"And how many days for you to get another posse together? Or a search team?"

"S'pose about three days. First day was telling what happened and getting rested. Second day was getting men together. And third was seeing to our supplies."

"Three days," says Mr. Duda. "I presume it took another three days riding back to those hills."

"Yessir."

"Three days riding out there. Three days riding back. Three days in town. Then three more days returning to the hideout. What did you do then?"

"Why, we look around for Frank. And for his nephew."

"However, you didn't find either. You found only the body of J.C. Wells. Shot dead. Is that correct?"

"Yessir."

"So let me, and our fine court assembled today, get the timeline straight," says Mr. Duda. "The posse goes after Wells, finds him, he and his gang, but Frank, leader of the posse, is captured and soon shot dead. You, being right behind Frank, see it all but you back away, get the other men together for...an attack on their camp? Is that right? Instead, you – all of you – decide to return to town to gather more men—"

"But we was a full dozen men going back to the hideout. Twelve good men. And the priest, Father James. He joined because Frank's his brother, but he never used a gun before."

"Twelve men and a priest." Mr. Duda rubs his chin, pacing the room. "Sounds prophetic. The priest intended to say last rites?"

"Not sure. Just wanna come and help us."

"But you knew Frank was dead when you left then returned for him, for his body."

"Yessir."

"And you didn't find the boy, Frank's nephew, anywhere around the area. No idea where he'd gone. No body laying somewhere."

"That's right."

Mr. Duda nods slowly, adding things up.

"Thank you, Deputy Calhoun. That will be all."

"Now hold on a minute," says Mr. Hitchens, but the judge waves Mike to get up. "I have questions!"

Mr. Duda wipes his brow, gazing at those in attendance as Mike pauses a moment then steps away from the chair and quickly exits out the side door, looking embarrassed.

"Ain't no coward," Mike is heard to mutter.

Turning to Judge Robinson, Mr. Duda says: "I shall now like to call to the witness chair Mister Jacob Baumann." He stares at me. "I thought I saw him slip into the courtroom."

Caught by surprise, I startle. People near me give me hateful looks. I could be asked about my funeral preparation work, the only person who saw the bodies and could state their condition.

"He has nothing to do with this case," Mr. Hitchens argues.

"An expert witness," Mr. Duda counters.

"Expert in what?" demands Mr. Hitchens. "He's just a half-breed that stitches bodies for burial. Nothing more. And he wasn't even a part of that posse."

"He will testify on the condition of the bodies," says Mr. Duda, and the judge nods approval.

I stand, feeling all eyes on me, and make my way to the front as murmurs fill the room, setting my nerves aflame.

"State your name," says the clerk. He holds up a Bible, motions for me to put my hand on it.

"I doubt he has any god to vow to," says Mr. Hitchens. "Is this legal? We can't accept his words."

Judge Robinson waves him off, shows him a serious scowl.

"I swear to tell the truth," I speak firmly and clearly, "so help me Great Spirit who reigns over all the earth."

"Good enough?" the judge asks Mr. Hitchens, who nods.

Mr. Duda stands before me. He covers who I am and my job. He informs everyone that I'm the person who examined the bodies and prepared them for burial. Then comes the question I fear.

"Now, will you tell the court why the posse was going after J.C. Wells?"

Not expecting such a direct question, I stammer.

"I know you know," says Mr. Duda, showing patience. "You were, fifteen years ago, just seventeen. Yet Frank Baumann let Bart go on that posse but not you. Didn't think it would be good for you to go. Isn't that true? Why was that? Please tell us for the court record."

I swallow hard, but I must remain calm and speak the truth. It must be stated for the record, to make it real: "The posse went after him...after the whole gang...because they raped and murdered my mother."

9

AN IMPERFECT POSSE

EVIL COMES INTO THIS WORLD with the same ease of a dove alighting on an olive branch. Just happens. Nobody knows how or why. There's a click of something, a flick of a lever that changes everything, and no one can do anything to stop it. You have to get rid of that evil any way you can. Can't be turned back. Can't be convinced to change. No amount of treatment can correct it. And the world goes on as best it can, evil woven throughout it, forever a part of it.

Only later did I understand the point of getting me to say it. To show I have a motive behind the testimony I give – even as the only person to examine the bodies. Everything has happened because of this random evil crossing paths with an innocent woman on her way to fetch me from my grandfather's house. By most accounts a lovely day yet there was evil blocking her way.

"Frank Baumann laid in a wooden box in the ground for fifteen years," I explain soberly, addressing Mr. Duda's inquiry concerning the condition of the bodies. "After removing the remains from the box – requested by Doctor Baker for the official record – I found a pair of bullets. They fell loose in the box, given the disintegration of the corpse. Wounds caused by bullets can be detected in other ways, too. One bullet apparently struck the lower edge of the second rib, at the point where the cartilage meets the manubrium and the sternum. The cartilage there was torn, indicating the direction of the shot. A chest wound."

"Can you show us on yourself?" asks Mr. Duda.

I place a hand over my chest, press my finger to the spot where the bullet entered him.

"High up on the ribs at the breastbone," Mr. Duda confirms.

"Yes," I mutter, dropping my hand from my chest. "Missing the heart by an inch."

"And the other?" asks Mr. Duda.

"The other bullet caused a head wound." I pause, wanting that to be enough of an answer, but Mr. Duda urges me to explain more. "That bullet hit the mandible – the jawbone – on the left side, near the upper edge. Three lower teeth were displaced. Two pre-molars broken off and the first molar knocked from the jawbone. The direction of the shot and the damage caused indicates he turned his head slightly at the moment he was struck."

"Could he have been turning in reaction to the first shot?"

"I can't tell which shot came first," I say. "I guess the chest shot would've knocked him over, making the head shot impossible."

"Speculation," Mr. Hitchens cuts in, acting like I've told a lie.

I have to take breath. Mr. Duda waves me to continue.

"That bullet continued into the skull, cutting through the lower portions of the brain: the temporal lobe, mammillary body, and into the occipital lobe, where it stopped. It didn't break through the back of the skull: the occipital bone at the lambdoid suture, just above where they meet the mastoid portion – three plates of the rear skull. The markings on the inside of the skull there suggest the trajectory rising from the jaw into the back of the head. It would certainly be the cause of death whether the chest shot came first or second."

"Was anyone else seeing this?" asks Mr. Hitchens.

"Nobody asked to see it," I respond, and someone laughs even as a woman faints.

I need to take a breath, so glad that Maggie isn't present to hear my testimony.

"Take a moment." Mr. Duda stands like a stern father over me. "I know it's uncomfortable to describe, yet you did well. Clearly you know anatomy. You've studied at the college in Kanza City. I would trust you to make medical diagnoses, at least of a dead body."

"Yes – thank you," I say, feeling relieved and hoping to leave.

"Now that we have established your credibility," he starts up, "if you would, please tell us about any significant observations you may have about Frank Baumann's corpse."

I think a moment, recalling what I saw, then tell how the body appeared to have been dumped into the box without preparation, wearing the same clothing and the sheriff's star on his vest. Boots were missing. No gunbelt. Likely stolen. Mr. Duda seems interested in the clothing and asks about the condition of the shirt that hung on his skeleton.

"It was in rags," I say, then stop to think, trying to remember. "The front of his shirt had the gunshot."

"How about the back of the shirt?" Mr. Duda asks.

"The back? It was shredded."

"Shredded?"

"Hardly any of the fabric remaining."

"Shredded is not a scientific term," Mr. Hitchens blurts out.

Mr. Duda stands straight before the room. "Shredded." He nods. "As though the body was dragged over rough ground. Would that be a fair assessment?"

"I think so." My eyes close and I see him lain on the table in the chill room. "And the vest he wore. It was split in back. And the seat of his pants, too: roughed up."

"Like he was dragged over the ground." Mr. Duda gazes around the room, nodding to himself.

"None of us were there," cries Mr. Hitchens. "Speculation."

"A man too heavy for a teen boy to pick up and carry. No, a boy of fifteen would've had to drag him. It would be hard labor. But he would do it because the man was his uncle."

"Could be tribals taking the body," Mr. Hitchens loudly suggests only to get a frown from Judge Robinson.

"That seems accurate," I say. "Him dragging the body."

Mr. Duda exchanges nods with the judge, faces the audience.

"Deputy Mike has testified that the second posse, returning to the hideout, found the boy's gun. They swept the area looking for him. His horse had been left in the same place as the other horses, so the men took it back to town with them. The gun, however: a pistol of newer manufacture, a type used in the war decades past, one of those models able to bear seventeen bullets in its magazine." He nods thoughtfully. "Yes, and how many bullets were missing when it was examined? We asked Deputy Mike that question earlier, as you may recall. He stated there were two bullets missing. We presume the boy pulled the trigger of his own pistol. Pulled it twice. There's evidence of that. One of those shots hit J.C. Wells in the face, took out his eye and cut into his brain." He turns to me. "Would that be a fair presumption?"

I startle, lost for a moment as my mind formed a picture of when Bart shot the man.

"Yes, I believe so." And I swallow hard. "A bullet entering an eye socket would tend to go straight on back into the brain. But I didn't examine that body, obviously."

Mr. Duda nods as though he is pleased with my answers.

"No, you didn't. The body was, in fact, burned, the ashes buried – somewhere out west, in the far wilderness, unmarked. I heard the grave diggers unleashed their full complement of piss over the site once they'd filled it. Rumors."

I smile at that image, looking down to hide my expression.

Mr. Duda paces a moment, halts, points to the ceiling.

"No chance to recover the bullets in that body. Wells' body."

I'm nodding to myself, but when I look Mr. Duda wears a grin.

"And one final question," he says. "Were the two bullets found in the wooden box containing Sheriff Baumann's body of the same type as the bullets found in the pistol Bart Baumann dropped there at the hideout?"

That surprises me, but it suddenly makes sense.

"No – different," I speak confidently. "The bullets in the box, that were shot into the sheriff, were forty-five caliber."

"And we've heard from Deputy Mike that the bullets they found in the gun they found nearby, the pistol the boy took great pride in, carved his initials 'LB' into the handle, were nine millimeter."

"Yes," I confirm.

Bart did take a lot of pride in that pistol, passed from Maggie's great-grandfather Sandy, who used it in the war between the north and south territories. She told me his story plenty of times: Sandy alternately fought on each side – both against his will. Bart loved shooting at cans and bottles with that pistol when we were boys. He talked about how he would shoot an outlaw some day, like his Uncle Frank, the deputy, did sometimes.

"And can you tell us what those initials stood for? Was it Little Bear? Like your initials?"

I shook my head. "No, it stood for 'Little Bart'. His mama called him that. Big Bart was his father, who died before he was born."

"Yes, yes," says Mr. Duda, glancing at Mr. Hitchens as if daring him to offer a counter response. "Little Bart. Or, in the proper form, Bart Junior."

"That's him, yes," I say. "My cousin."

"So it would seem," Mr. Duda speaks a little louder, "that the boy took matters into his own hands. He not only shot Wells, thus ending the reign of criminality but he also took charge of his uncle's body, left unclaimed after three days while the posse rode back to town, three days lollygagging in town, and three days riding back better prepared. Seems this teen boy displayed an adult's sense of responsibility...where grown men did not."

Mr. Duda scans the crowd for men who ought to feel ashamed.

The crowd breaks into a clamoring that forces the judge to hit the gavel once more.

Mr. Duda turns to me. "And you examined the body of the boy?"

I nod. "His was more recent. According to the woman—"

"Let's stick with what you observed of the boy's body. The man, we should say. He'd be thirty by now. Your professional opinion on the body's condition, if you please."

"I'm more used to working on the recently deceased than a body fifteen years in the grave," I say, gaining confidence. I can still see people's eyes disbelieving me because I'm an outsider to them. But I know my craft, trust my skills, and have done a lot of study.

"Let's start with the cause of death," says Mr. Duda.

"Gunshot to the belly," I respond without hesitation.

The crowd has fallen into a deathly silence, eager to hear all the grisly details, but I give them only medical terms and so they grow impatient.

"You're certain?" Mr. Hitchens challenges.

"As most belly wounds will, it took a few days for him to die. It had to be painful. The gunshot started sepsis in his body, which was more the cause of his death. I found evidence of it when I examined the body. He likely died a few days before she arrived in town."

"She?" cries Mr. Hitchens. "You mean the defendant."

"Yes," I confirm. "She's the one that brought his body here."

"Were there other marks?" asks Mr. Duda, waving his arm to get the attention back on him. "Any other indications of violence upon the body?"

I tell about marks I found indicating knife fights and gunshots that were near misses and adequately repaired. One showed crude stitching to mend it. He'd had a rough life these past fifteen years, I testified. It sounds worse in my listing of wounds than it probably was. And he had Trina with him.

I glance over at her, sitting in that dress, on the chair at the front corner of the room. Despite Mr. Hitchens standing in the way, shuffling back and forth, I see her fighting against any reaction to what I've said about her lover. It's strange how she and I can share intimate knowledge about Bart that nobody else knows.

"The question is not who killed this boy," Mr. Hitchens starts up. "It's about this woman. About what she and her sisters have done these past fifteen years in this corner of the territory. And if she deserves punishment for their crimes. All this recounting of the posse's activities is unnecessary noise!"

"I maintain," Mr. Duda speaks up, blocking Mr. Hitchens, "that this boy, our Bart Baumann, went missing because he did his duty and saw to the burial of his uncle in that location or somewhere not too far away. With him not knowing if anyone from the posse would ever return, he did what was right, and for that he suffered fifteen years lost in the wilderness."

He didn't actually suffer much, I believe, giving a glance at Trina. Maybe at first. Fear, hunger, fatigue. He had to have used a stick to dig a shallow grave. No food or water other than what he could find out there. It was like the times Frank took the two of us camping, taught us how to live off the land, how to survive – like *his* father had told him: those stories of how our grandfather's grandfather survived the pandemic, the lawless land, and civil war.

"It seems fair," Mr. Hitchens announces like a carnival barker, "that we now hear what this woman has to say concerning the facts we present here this week."

+   +   +

People drifted out through the long afternoon. I admit getting a bit drowsy myself listening to each old deputy telling his side of things. They were all mature men in their prime fifteen years ago but now retired, three members of the posse passing already. Their memories weren't sharp. They agreed to the basic facts: Frank was killed by Wells, they rode back to town for more men, returned and didn't find Frank's body. They only found Wells body. They looked for Frank's body, looked for the boy, too, but didn't find either and returned to town, had a memorial service.

I glance at Maggie sitting in her widow black, alone against the wall toward the rear. Her face doesn't reveal emotion, as though she's not listening to the testimony. She must be there just to make folks uncomfortable; they know her story. Now everybody's curious about her boy's story: what happened to this man they came to call Bad Bart before he showed up in town dead, wrapped in a tarp.

"It ain't no lie," says Mr. Brewer, a former shopkeeper from the next town over.

Brewer's right arm below the elbow is missing. Had to cut it off after the terrible gunshot wound he sustained: shredding flesh from bone. I recall the older Doc Baker performing it as I watched. "Watch and learn, young man, watch and learn," he said, "cuz you'll need to know this procedure."

The litany of crimes has begun. A dozen men, young and old, and a couple of women get up to state their experiences confronting Bad Bart. He was quick with the trigger. Shot first, no questions later. He made a fierce outlaw, being young but angry at the world. Often seen with the trio of women. They'd ride into towns and take what they wanted. Grew into bank heists at gunpoint. They needed those notes to exchange for food and ammo. In time, they realized they could skip the notes and just take at gunpoint what they wanted.

Everyone had him pegged in their minds: that red-haired man, chunky yet fast, strong but foolhardy. Stood about six-foot. Carried a notebook with him and scribbled words in it like he was recording his crimes. If only they could find that notebook, some say, it would be evidence against him. But no evidence was needed now with him laying in the ground behind Maggie's house.

I can sense Maggie tensing at each statement of fact, each nasty insinuation, each crime described. I wish it would stop.

The only relief comes when Judge Robinson orders a recess until the next day.

I help Maggie return home but we don't speak, not a word about the testimonies. I guess we understand everything well enough. We saw a good boy go out into the world and get turned into an outlaw, only to return home dead.

"I failed him," she says once inside the house, sitting in her easy chair with her boots pulled off.

"I'm sure he failed you more," is all I can think to say.

She nods slowly, as though she's counting the hours she has left in this world.

"Are you all right now?" I ask, worried about her.

She looks up at me from her chair. "I won't do anything foolish, if that's what you're asking."

"Then I'll say goodnight."

"Goodnight, Jake."

But it isn't a good night. I don't sleep well. Dreams come upon me: I see a woman who looks like Trinity being led from a jail to the gallows by a squad of angry men. A crowd waits for the spectacle, clamoring for justice. The noose is set but it's not coiled properly so when the platform gives way she drops but the fall doesn't break her neck and end her life. Rather, she merely chokes, swinging there, arms and legs flailing. The crowd continues to taunt her. The men in charge grab at her gown, tear it off her, leaving her naked as she dangles, slowly expiring. The news-paper reporters write stories, go to call their offices over the comms. Photo-takers take their pictures, scandalous as they are, then rush to develop them. They leave her body hanging there a couple days, crows pecking at it, before they cut it down and haul it away to where they bury the unknowns and criminals. And it wasn't as though she committed heinous crimes. It wasn't like she raped and murdered an innocent woman.

I pop awake before dawn, sweating like the Glow's come down over me, sheets soaked. I decide to get myself ready for the day. No point trying to sleep only another hour. I get a breakfast of eggs and flapjacks at The Five Ladies and head over to the hotel to escort Trina to the courthouse.

Deputy Tom takes over, leads her to the chair in the corner, and the bailiff guards her. I take a seat half-way back, against the wall opposite from where Maggie likes to sit. She refuses to attend today, knowing what the day's testimony will cover.

When Judge Robinson calls the session to order, Mr. Duda has a couple men come up and describe the hanging of Trinity Culpepper and it's exactly as I saw it in my dream.

"Ain't bad as what he done, though," says Mr. Kleine, bent over and using a cane, "not as much as Bad Bart did coming later after her, after her body. But we turned him away, yessir, we did. Then we cut her down and took the body to the pauper's yard."

I recall reading about that. My eyes go to Trina sitting in the front corner. Her face is stone, staring at the far wall, likely trying to block out the words spoken. No matter what Trinity had done to deserve her fate, I doubted it was that accurate. She was the leader, yes, but the one least likely to shoot somebody. She had her own tough life, never trusted community folks, played with them and threatened them, sure, made suggestions of what she'd do to them if they didn't give her what she demanded. Yet if she shot anyone, it had to be as they rode off, townsfolks shooting at them as they fled, and the sisters would fire back, maybe hit some of them. Not like what Bart did, not the same as his predilection to shoot first.

"He done come at us, both guns drawn, and we offer to let him go and nobody gonna follow him," says Mr. Landon, his arm in a sling to this day. "No, he won't have it, just shoots us right there, at close range. Got my dang shoulder bungled up ever since." He gives the shoulder a rattle, arm laying limp in his lap. "At least like to give him a shot back, but look like it's gonna be impossible now he's done put in the ground. Good riddance."

Next is Widow Bentley, who describes the day Bad Bart came to her farm east of Cimarron looking to steal a horse, and he shot her before she could dare ask what he was doing. He'd already shot her husband as he tried to pull the horse away. She had to get the bullet pulled from her thigh and remained hobbled ever since. A day later, her husband died from his chest wound.

Mr. Wayne told his version of how Bad Bart came to his house demanding money and anything of value that could be traded to the tribals. He took most of the food in the house, too. Made him load it onto Bart's horse. Then, as he was about to ride off, Bart had looked back and shot angrily at Mr. Wayne's barking dog. But the shot hit something in the yard, a stone perhaps, and ricocheted through a glass window of the house and hit his daughter sitting at her play desk stitching a doll, which killed her.

And there was the time Bad Bart came into Dirty Dirk's in Westfield, a notorious saloon advertising the most bawdy ladies, and sauntered up to the bar demanding a stiff drink like he owned the place. Other men there didn't take a liking to the young upstart and challenged his right to be in there. So Bart spun around with his pistol aimed. A man came at him from the side, knife drawn, and they had a fight. Bart was surprisingly agile for a big man. Each of them took a good swipe across the chest. But it ended with Bart's knife cutting up the belly of the other man. "He had a look like he liked doing it," said Odel Finney, who was there that night. After the fight, Bart had the town doc stitch up the knife wound, holding a gun on him.

I could attest to seeing that dull line across his chest.

The Reynolds twins, as customers, each took a bullet allegedly from Bad Bart as he raced off after stopping in at the First Bank of New Hill for a quickly filled bag of credit notes. Jimmy recalled him laughing that he had a 'woman needing stuff' – Julia confirmed as she rubbed away the pain in her arm.

I see Trina fidget. She slowly shakes her lowered head left then right, twice. Stupid boy, she must be thinking.

Another man speaks of another incident. So do others. Random events. Nothing ill intended, most likely, just ordinary thievery, but with deadly outcomes nobody expected. The outrage grows through the afternoon and some folks suggest they go out to Miss Maggie's family cemetery and dig up the body and burn it, dump it out of town where buzzards can dine.

"Seems more proper," Mr. Hitchens professes, sauntering before the audience, "they should've hanged Bad Bart more than that Trinity woman. Yet what can be done now?"

"Bart Baumann is dead," says Mr. Duda. "He's not on trial – not today nor on any future day, although everyone is free to speculate and hate to their heart's content. This trial is about that woman."

That woman: barely five-foot and a trio of inches, a hundred-ten pounds soaking wet, about a hundred twenty-five with her leathers, boots, and gunbelt on. Even Trinity was hardly five-foot-seven.

Everyone in the room sets their eyes on Trina, perched upon the chair in the front corner with the bailiff standing tall beside her. She stares back at them, her dark eyebrows pinched, a plain face that challenges them. She looks so small to me, like a stray cat.

"However," Mr. Duda continues, "we should establish what the circumstances were so we might best understand how this woman, Trina Culpepper, could influence this innocent boy into his life of criminality."

"You're blaming her for his crimes?" Mr. Hitchens demands. "Or him for her crimes? Why, she's as guilty as him. You could hang her today and none here would mind. Now that her beau's been already dispensed with – and rightly so."

"That is not what we consider justice, may I remind you, Mister Hitchens," Judge Robinson growls. "We shall hear all of it. Every damn word. Then we will render a fair decision."

"Thank you, Your Honor," says Mr. Duda. "Let us continue—"

"The trouble started with that native woman being in the wrong place at the wrong time," Mr. Hitchens cuts in. "Everybody knows it.

If it weren't for that woman getting herself raped and cut to pieces after, we wouldn't be here today, no sir. We would be—"

"Mister Hitchens!" cries Judge Robinson.

"We would be going straight after Bad Bart, taking up his many crimes, sorting them out. Eleven shot dead because of him. That's a whole lot more serious than one old tribal woman. And she well over the age of beauty, at that. Hard to figure what Wells's gang would've seen in a plain woman like her."

+ + +

I have to go out, my stomach feeling queasy, ready to spew. Can't stand hearing about Mama. All because of J.C. Wells and his gang. They caught her on the road where they abused her and left her for dead. Old Doc Baker did the examination, confirmed her injuries, noted the indications of rape. She's buried next to Aunt Eve, next to the space reserved for Maggie.

Frank didn't take kindly to Mama or me, looking different than his family. But his wife, Vera, welcomed me and cared for me in my early years, said it was their responsibility. The eldest son, Jeb, was my father, after all, so I counted as their grandson. Vera still would say an odd phrase now and then that would slip into offense, but I knew she meant well; her acts showed she accepted me as her kin. Later, when I was old enough and already helping Old Doc Baker in the clinic, they arrange for me to go to college in Kanza City. I learned how to pull teeth and other dentistry skills. In fact, Skinner Canyon collected funds for me to return as the dentist.

A few years before I went to dentist school, Vera prodded Frank to do something about my mama. The gang had been spotted in the next town. So he got a posse together to go after J.C. Wells and his gang, hanging out toward Black Mesa. Even my cousin, Bart, joined. Frank insisted I stay behind because I was needed in town. I suspected he thought I might get too upset confronting those men and get in the way. But I could shoot as well as Bart. Maybe Frank thought I couldn't handle the violence after seeing my mama laid to rest in the ground, her face so torn, her body cut up, that the undertaker just stitched her as best he could and closed the box for the funeral.

Frank knew vengeance creates unstable actors. He could trust his posse, all men he'd ridden with previously, well-trained lawmen and a couple of good shots from the militia. Bart would stay back when they came upon the gang and wait for Frank and the posse to take care of business. Frank would watch out for Bart. It was to be an adventure he could handle, part of growing up, Maggie told us. So she gave in to Bart's insistence on going.

After the men returned to Skinner Canyon without Frank or Bart, the whole town went into mourning. I took it upon myself to spend more time with Maggie. She never cried much. Possibly she was more numb than aggrieved. She was always telling me how she met Bart's papa, a brief tryst during her visit to conduct a concert although she insisted they'd met a year earlier so it wasn't as though he was a total stranger. They planned to marry, she liked to remind me.

I ride out to the house where Mama and I used to live, arriving after dinner. I want to give Maggie time to eat in peace. As hard as it might be, I've sworn to tell her what I've learned from Trina, from our private talks.

"You come to tell me something?" asks Maggie, standing firm on the porch as I arrive, as though she sensed my visit.

I dismount, tie up my horse at the railing, and slowly go up the steps. I look her in the eyes and that moment grows into a pain we both share. We sit down on the top step, side by side. We take some time to reflect on Mama, who was Maggie's helper in the early days of her music career when Maggie was in a wheel-chair.

"I'm just checking on you," I say, "but I'll keep you informed of what they say in the court."

As Deputy Cal tells it, getting it straight from Deputies Hank Sheer of Boise City and Denny Chang of Guymon who'd gone with the posse, other lawmen had chased those three girls but lost them. Instead, they found a camp at an abandoned mine, discovered what used to be a homestead. They found men's bodies well-stripped. What remained had been gnawed by coyotes and pecked by birds. Items remained to give some identification.

"This gotta be Shane McNally," said the Sheriff who was named Darrel, Cal's boss in those days. "I'd know that face even with half the flesh eaten off. Lookit him. Just as ornery as ever, grinning up at the dang sun."

Sheriff Darrel glanced around the rocky terrain, put his hand to his brow to block the sun.

"Who coulda done this? Another gang? Heck, whoever it was, got his whole gang. Gonna need to give that bounty to whoever got 'em."

His cohort rummaged through the camp, checked the fallen tent, dug around, and came up with some answers to who might've done this awful deed. The tent was full of lady things, some with names. They found the Deed giving the name of the family staking a claim on the site. But where were they now? The only grave they noticed could be one of them.

"Ain't so awful, them being criminals," said Sheriff Darrel.

I explain what they decided, how they put up notices about that family, seeking information. It was still their land claim and one of them had to be found to maintain it.

"The women's camp," Maggie says like she's heard it before.

"But what they found there," I say, making my voice as calm as I can, "was the camp where their papa was murdered. I suspect they took their hatred and used it to kill those men. The whole McNally gang. Minus a couple that got away. That would be the blind man, Winfred Jordan. He wandered into town, you remember, saying how he had been wandering for years. Nobody believed him. I do – now."

"So that woman on trial's one of them?" asks Maggie in a solemn tone. "That entire family murdered by the McNally gang?"

"Not the entire family." I wait as Maggie contemplates it. "The girls got away. That one on trial – Trina – she's one of them."

Maggie looks at me like I've just arrived with good news.

"How's she doing? How's she handling the trial?"

"Well, her tooth isn't hurting no more," I say, my first thought at that moment.

Maggie gives me a strange look.

"And the doula, Missus Wang, confirmed she's got a child inside her," I say like I just then remembered. "She went up to her hotel room and checked her. I heard her tell Deputy Cal she's about three months along. Going to be born in the spring."

Maggie tries to hide a smile. "A new babe."

Her eyes land on the clock ticking on the mantelpiece. We listen for a while.

"I think they're trying to tie her to his crimes," I say. "Want to punish her for what he's done. Seeing how he's dead already." I realize how heartless it sounds. "That's what their strategy is. Now they got her in custody, they won't let her go."

She doesn't seem to hear me, lost in her thoughts.

I can't stand the silence. "Of course, she's got plenty of her own crimes. No reason to bring Bart into it."

Maggie turns to me, her face suddenly desperate.

"Specially she being pregnant," I say. "They sure don't wanna be locking up a pregnant woman. And if they decide to hang her, they'll wait until after the baby is born...."

The clock ticks on the mantelpiece.

"Guess we'll never know," she says after several minutes pass. She takes a long breath and pulls off her spectacles, wipes her weary eyes. "We won't ever know what happened to my boy. Wish I could. Perhaps there were a few moments he was happy. Perhaps a few. I'd be grateful to know he had some of those moments."

PART TWO

FIFTEEN YEARS EARLIER

10

THE LOST BOY

BY THE SHORE OF A POOL set among the rocky outcrops, like a pleasure garden hidden in the desert, three women sat naked after their swim. While talking about their latest adventure, their escape and hiding, what to do next, they heard pebbles tumble down off the rocky ledge above the pool, a couple of the stones going plunk in the water. They glanced up, thinking someone managed to crawl up there to watch them, and not too quiet about it.

Not covering herself, Trinity grabbed the shotgun. Triss pulled her pistol from its holster. Trina stood up confidently, the sun not yet drying her tan skin. Her eyes narrowed on the spot the latest pebble dropped from. She pointed there, urging her sisters to put the guns down.

Trina called to whoever crawled around up there: "Hey you!"

To their surprise, a gnarled hand stretched over the top of one of those red rocks, feeling along the ledge. Fingers sought a firm grasp, failed. The hand struggled, gave another try, as though too weak to pull the body along behind.

With nothing on but boots, Trina had her sisters stand watch as she climbed up the rocks. Trinity held the shotgun ready.

"It's just a boy," Trina called down.

What she found was indeed a boy – a young man, maybe, not yet an adult. Half-unconscious and wounded. His clothing hung in rags, his white skin showing through the rips, scarred and bruised, rough hands blood-stained, face scratched, barely a whisker, hair dirty –

like he'd been crawling among the rocks for days.

Trina called for Triss to help her get the boy down but even with two of them grabbing him, the boy fell hard, hit his head on another rock, winced, then lay unconscious for a while.

He startled when he opened his eyes and saw three women, now back in their leather clothing and looking tough, standing over him. His body jerked, but he had nowhere to escape, weak as he was, and lay there ready to give up.

"Ya lucky buck," said Trina with a chuckle. "That fer shore."

"How'd a boy like this get so far out here?" asked Trinity with a scoff, adjusting her gunbelt and holsters.

"Why, he look not even old as me," said Triss, grinning.

"Look like he done crawl his way over them rocks from who the heck know where," said Trina. She squatted, reaching her hand out to his brow, brushed dirt away.

"No matter where he come from we cain't bother with him," said Trinity. "Not on us."

"Cain't just leave 'im here." Trina looked up at her big sister.

The older sister frowned.

"How the hell a boy that young get himself way out here?" Triss spoke up. "Like he fall down from the sky."

"Ain't that young," said Trina.

"Whaddaya figure?" asked Trinity, giving a serious look.

Trina studied the boy's face, noting the fuzz on his upper lip and chin. "Look maybe fifteen, sixteen...."

"How old ya?" Trinity demanded. "Ya know when you's born?"

He squirmed at her aggression. "I was born in 'thirty-five."

More words mumbled, eyes closed like he refused to look at the world. They listened to his mumbling, again asked when he was born, made him repeat it, and laughed at his response.

"That ain't no boy, that a baby man," said Trinity with a laugh.

"He gonna be a full man next week or two," Triss added.

"What'll we do with 'im?" asked Trina.

"Leave him," said Trinity with a grunt. "They just grow up to be bad folk. Ever'one o' them."

"Not Pa. He weren't no bad man," said Triss.

Trina regarded her big sister. "Cain't just leave a young'un like him out here. He gonna die fer shore."

"Not our problem," said Trinity. She got serious with the middle sister. "No different us findin' a wounded dog on a trail. He maybe lookin' pretty but gonna be trouble haulin' 'round. We don't even got no horse for a boy to ride."

"He can ride with me," said Trina. "He ain't too big."

"What'sa matter with ya? Got a fancy fer 'im?" asked Trinity.

The boy had awakened enough to understand what the women were saying. Nasty coughs to clear his throat. Painful breaths, trying to rise on an elbow, gazing up at them.

"Just wanna go home," he managed to get out.

"Home?" challenged Trinity. "Now where that gonna be?"

"S-Skinner C-Canyon," he sputtered.

"Skinner Canyon?" Trinity shrieked. "That old cow town? Why, whole place smells like cow biscuits."

"Biscuits an' gravy," Triss snickered.

"How ya get way out here?" Trinity pressed. "That's nearly forty mile back. Ain't got no time to return ya there." She broke into a few devilish chuckles. "No time to return ya to yer mama."

Trina took the boy seriously. "How ya get so far out here?"

"I...." He stopped, appearing frightened.

"Go on, tell us," said Trina. "Ain't gonna hurt ya."

"Uncle Frank...he...." His eyes visited each woman, seeking an agreement not to hurt him. "He brung me out. He...."

"Yer uncle brung ya out here? What fer?"

"P-p-posse," he sputtered. "We got us a posse."

"Posse?" Trinity hadn't expected that answer. "Y'all goin' after somebody? Better not be us."

"After J.C. Wells," said the boy. "He's bad news."

"Yeah, well, lotta bad news in the world, boy. But don't know no J.C. Wells," Trinity responded coldly. "We got our own gang right here." She waved her hand at her sisters. "That one's Trina. And th' other's Triss. I'm Trinity. You better remember."

"Don't worry," Trina spoke up, "we won't hurt ya."

"Not much anyways," Trinity said with a laugh.

"Not hurt 'im? Why not?" Triss laughed. "He look hurtable."

"No – don't," Trina countered. "Just lookit 'im."

"Yer sweet on him so quick?" Trinity spit, the glob landing in the dirt close to the boy's face. "He's too wounded to be useful."

The women squabbled, calling out each other for crimes past, not showing enough guts, not enough glory, until the boy slipped into unconsciousness once more.

"He don't care 'bout none yer tales," Triss snickered.

"Lookit 'im," said Trina. "We don't take him with us he gonna die out here."

"Not our problem, I said." Trinity gave a grunt of frustration. "All kinda critters die in the desert."

"I kin take 'im. He'll be my problem," Trina answered. "When we get to Skinner Canyon, we kin leave 'im there."

"We ain't headed that way," Triss said.

Trinity had a stern look. "We leave him whatever next town is, then we're done with 'im. He kin make his own way on to Skinner Canyon."

Trina saw the boy was scared. "Hey, we ain't gonna hurt ya."

That seemed to give him some relief. More likely, she realized, his stare was aimed at her open vest, her moist chest revealed.

She laughed, buttoned the vest. "You's naughty boy, ain'tcha?"

"Stop teasing the boy," Triss snickered.

"He's ripe for teasin'," Trinity said, adding a laugh.

Trina had dropped down on a knee beside him. She held out a cup of water from the pool, offered it. Sliding her other hand under his head, she helped him sip. He seemed ravaged by the desert air, sipped loudly and frantically.

"Whoa, boy," she said. "Don'tcha choke."

"Ya shore be motherin' that boy," Trinity laughed. "He gonna be fallin' fer ya. Fall hard, reckon."

When he'd had his fill, slopping the final sips, Trina eased his head back and stared down at him.

"Ya shore do need motherin'," she said to him. Then she turned to Trinity. "Ya recall Rocky? That baby raccoon we found an' nurse to health? Then he run away?"

"Yeah, remember," said Trinity, her face softening.

"No thanks," Triss said, "none 'tall. Just run off."

Trina was studying the boy. "Ain'tcha mama. But we gonna fix y'up right an' send ya home. That's all we doin'. Get it?"

He gave a nod, his eyes still showing fear.

"Lookit this," Trina spoke up, looking him over. "He got shot."

She put her fingertip to the wound, a burned line across his side ribs, like a bullet flew by and cut his skin. She pressed gently on it.

"Hurt?" she asked. He shook his head. She pressed harder until he winced, harder still until he wailed. "You's a lucky buck."

"Ain't no buck," laughed Triss. "That a baby man."

"We need to fix it or gonna get the pus," said Trina, then glared at Triss. "Like you got that time."

"The time I got butt-shot?" She burst into laughter yet the boy wasn't amused. "Bounce right off the saddle an' nick my butt."

"And it got pus real quick."

Trina called for the iron rod stuck in the campfire.

Pulling a glove on, Trinity returned with it, carefully exchanged it with Trina who let it drop in the dirt.

"This gonna hurt," she told him, ignoring his frightened eyes.

She picked up the cool end and pressed the hot tip to the wound, only a heartbeat, and the boy howled like a mad coyote.

"That ain't no baby man," Triss snickered, "that a baby boy."

He whimpered, shaking at the pain, even after Trina poured cool water over his side, forming a pool on the ground under him.

"Ya definite one them baby boys," she told him. "But ya took it like a man. I mean the gunshot, not the iron. Ya got shot, but ya din't die. It's a good day, ain't it now?"

"Y-yes, ma'am," he got out between clenched teeth.

"No callin' *ma'am*." She gazed into his eyes. "Ain't no ma'am."

"I'm a ma'am," Trinity called and laughed hard. "He kin call me ma'am all he want."

"Ain't no more ma'am than rest us," said Trina.

Trinity kept nudging him with her boot, staring down at the boy. "Leave 'im, I say. Not our bidness." She regarded her sisters. "Boy like this gonna be full of trouble. Best be rid of 'im."

Trina called to Triss, asking for one of her shirts – of the three stuffed into her pack – and gave it to the boy. She helped cut off the ragged shirt he arrived in, ripped from his rough adventure and not worth saving. He eased up on his elbows as she removed the shirt. She poked at the sparse red hair on his chest, scratched at the hair on his head, remarking that it was red as a fox although so dirty it looked brown. The women laughed at that deception.

"Queer lookin' fella," said Trinity.

Trina studied his trousers, also torn and ragged, decided to cut off the lower legs, the dirtiest part, letting him keep the rest on. She tugged at his belt, an empty holster hanging loose on it.

"Lost yer gun, huh?"

He wasn't in a mood to be teased, merely grunted a response.

"Just wanna go home," he mumbled.

"Yep, I know. But here y'are," said Trina as Triss brought over a rag wet from the pool. "Lay still, young buck. Lemme clean ya, see how ya look after."

Trinity observed the cleaning, spitting out teasing remarks that made Trina curse back at her.

"This my boy," Trina growled. "Clean 'im up an' he'll be fine."

"Thought we's gonna drop him off nearest town an' be done with him," Trinity reminded her.

"We raise him right he can be a good partner," said Trina as she wiped the wet cloth over his face and down his chest. "He can help. Like mind the horses. Cook dinner. Carry things – after when he's got back his strength."

"Ya just be wantin' 'im for playin' fools," Triss chuckled. "Like ya bin talky-talkin' for so long. It's sad. Really sad. Don't need no man. None of us do."

"I just wanna go home," the boy moaned.

"Oh, yer goin' home soon nuff," Trina told him.

"P-please, ma'am," he sputtered, desperation in his eyes.

"Easy, boy," She rested his head in her lap, regarded his face, gazing down at his blue eyes until his mouth twisted, lips fidgeting, broke into a weak grin. "There now. Ya know yer in good hands. Saved from the desert. We gotcha. *I* gotcha. Yer mine now. Gonna fix y'up, so in return ya kin work fer me. Ya do as I say. When I think ya done nuff I let ya go. Agree?"

He gave a hesitant nod. "Thank you."

"Oh, don't thank me yet. Gonna be hard work." But she smiled and his mouth curled into a smile, a mirror image. A stupid grin. "Now, what we gonna call ya? Got a name, boy? How 'bout we call ya 'Boy'?"

"Mama calls me Barty," he spoke softly.

"What's that? Speak louder."

He grunted, cleared his throat. "My name is Bart."

"Bart? Sound like a cowboy. You a cowboy?" teased Triss.

"Bart's a good name for a boy," Trina said. "Anyways, he's mine. But you kin call him as ya like."

"Then I'ma call 'im 'Boy'," said Trinity. "Maybe Baby Boy. Yer name's Boy now. Unnerstand?"

"I'll call ya Bart," said Trina. "I'll only call ya Baby Boy if ya do wrong."

"I promise," he stammered, "won't never do wrong."

"Better not or we send ya back home to yer mama an' she deal with ya right good."

+ + +

The sisters continued their thieving ways while Bart stayed back at their camp, doing what he was told, doing what they demanded or else he feared they'd hurt him. He kept the fire going, went for wood when needed, cooked whatever they caught or killed, and generally tried to make himself useful. He worried the older sister might shoot him if he ever gave her a cross look. The younger one just laughed in a mocking tone, sometimes kicked dirt at him or spit near him to make him jump. She might be a year or two older, but skinny. If she weren't so mean to him he might like her.

The middle sister, though, being older by four or five years, saw him as a little brother at worst. She'd give him a glance sometimes that encouraged him, let him feel she'd protect him from the others. And she was, to his eyes, the best-looking of the three, though he had little more than a teen boy's hankering for a bit of affection, not daring to think of anything more. In time she might be more to him, he would ponder, but for now he had to obey them or else get some kind of punishment.

Sure, he could run away while they were doing a robbery, but he had no idea where the camp was or which direction to go. He had scraped and scrambled his way to the camp, following the scent of a campfire, but he hadn't left any breadcrumbs to find his way home. It would be just as much a struggle to find a trail and hope some settlers might come by or meet a tribal band without them giving him trouble. For now it was best to stay in the camp and do things; at least he was getting some food.

"Here, boy," cursed Trinity another time when they returned to the camp. She tossed him a brand-new shirt and trousers, a good set of cowboy clothes. He caught them in his arms before they could hit the ground. "Them's yer new get-up," she said.

Trina explained how they had gone into a town best not named, burst into a clothier demanding a good set of 'boy clothes'. The few customers there were startled by the women, Trinity raising her pistol at them. Triss stayed at the door, watching for trouble.

"You," Trina called to a man older than her, shaking in his shoes in the corner, "come here."

The man went over, quicker when she threatened to shoot. She stood close, looking him up and down. He stammered his answers to her odd questions.

"This one's about same size," she concluded.

Trina had the man spit out his measurements to the clothier in his fine suit and the clothier searched his wardrobe and pulled out a neatly folded set of shirt and trousers.

"This is the best we got," said the clothier. "Honest."

With Trinity waving her pistol around, the clothier began to cry.

"That do?" Trinity asked Trina.

"And boots," she replied.

"For a p-pair of boots y-you'll need to go down the street a bit to Mister Hardin's shop," the clothier spoke. "Finest boots in town – in the whole state, if you ask anyone—"

"Shut yer mouth," cursed Trinity.

He practically bit his tongue when he shut his mouth.

Trina scanned the shop once more, saw a man younger than the first man she accosted, waved him to come over.

The young man trudged through the displays.

"Please don't hurt me," he whimpered, looking down.

Trina stamped her boot down hard next to his, making him jerk, and took a visual measurement. "Looks right." She raised her eyes to him. "Take 'em off."

The man quickly pulled off his boots and stood barefoot on the wooden shop floor.

"W-we got s-smelling salts, if you like. Freshen them up," called the clothier.

Trina accepted and the clothier tossed a tin over. She ordered the barefoot man to pour half the salts into each boot to soak up the stink and he obeyed.

"What're you gonna do with us," asked the first man.

"We came fer clothes," said Trinity with a snarl. "Ain't it clear to yer dumb head?"

"Be calm," Trina spoke. "Don't wanna shoot nobody."

Trinity laughed and customers took a step or two back to give the women more space.

But they were quickly out the door.

"Gotcha boots," Trina announced, pulling them out of her saddle bag and tossing each to him. "Try 'em on. Betcha gotcher size."

He had to dump out the smelling salts first, then pulled them on and stood up straight, admiring them. He took a few steps this way, that way, stressed them to see how the leather responded.

"Feels good," he said with a smile. "Thanks."

"Ya better say thanks," Trinity barked at him.

"Now yer decent fer goin' to town," Trina teased him. "Get them other clothes on now."

"Go on," Trinity commanded.

"Ain't gonna spy on ya," Triss said with a giggle.

They stood before him, the older one with her arms crossed over her chest, the middle sister with arms at her sides. The youngest sister looking at him over the shoulder of the older one.

He nervously obeyed, stripping down to the nasty pair of shorts he still suffered with.

"Undershorts," snapped Trina. "We forgot undershorts."

"Yup," said Trinity.

"Ya best get a pair o' them, cuz they get dirty easy," said Triss.

"He do look fine, don't he?" said Trina. "Gotta strong body."

"Good fer workin' hard," Trinity agreed.

That incident must've been a couple months back, Bart counted, sitting on his haunches by the fire. The women also sat around the fire, chatting and chuckling as they finished the dinner he made: beans and greens boiled in a pot. Triss praised the taste, said he had a knack for kitchen work. Could be a good house boy for one of those rich families, Trinity offered.

He washed their monthly rags, hung them up to dry, and never complained. Trina would grin at him, notice how his body regained its health. He was growing into a fine boy. A fine man. Seemed he'd gained another inch or two since he arrived, growing some muscles.

They shared a knowing wink here and there.

"Come here, Boy," Trina called in the dark of one evening. It was after he'd cooked the dinner in the pot hanging over the fire, cleaned up afterwards. He washed the bowls, tidied the fire.

Bart looked up, about to wash himself after his tasks. "Huh?"

"Said come on over here," she spoke in the evening silence.

The other sisters had gone into their tent. Trina lay looking out her tent, flaps open. He saw her grinning in a strand of moonlight. Puzzled, he took a step toward her.

"Ya better getcher ass on in here, Boy, or we gonna send ya back to yer mama!"

And so he went, like a man to his doom, and there witnessed the Gates of Hell opening wide, beckoning him in.

+ + +

The middle sister held him against her, told him he needed to keep her warm as autumn slipped into winter and a blanket wasn't going to be enough there on the cold, hard ground with only a tent canvas over them. The other sisters had their own tent, taunted their sister about her boy. She didn't mind. He was growing on her.

"Now tell me how you come to be a lost boy," Trina spoke as the wind blew hard outside, shaking the tent. Snuggling, she made his arms wrapped around her. "Tighter," she demanded.

"I told you," said Bart, feeling sleepy after they'd played around.

"Tell me again," said Trina, patting his chest.

"I said it all. Ain't much more to say." But with another kiss he pushed himself to tell it again. "I joined up with the posse my uncle led and we rode on out here. Just like I said already."

"No, the other part," she insisted. "After."

He knew what she meant but he dreaded returning to that part of the story. He'd been foolish and almost died out in the wilderness alone. He couldn't tell anyone about that or they'd laugh at him. But she told him he showed courage making his way to their camp.

"Now, see, Uncle Frank, he told me to stay back when we got to J.C. Wells' camp, so I did. But it was dusk by then."

"After that."

"After I heard shooting I got worried so I go around them rocks to have a look, see if I can see their camp. Got off my horse, crawled up over them rocks. Big ones, they were. I got my pistol drawn."

She poked his chest. "Ya 'spectin' trouble?"

He never liked the way she'd prompt him, but he continued.

"Yep, cuz of the shooting. I knew something gone wrong. So I got between them rocks and could see in their camp. I saw through the gap. They got a good fire going so I could see them clear as day. And they...they got my uncle. Got him down on his knees, with Wells standing before him waving a pistol."

"Did he shoot yer uncle?" she asked, like it was her turn to say the lines. She knew the story but liked hearing him tell it.

"He was talking at him, looked right angry. But my uncle never said nothing back, just cursed at Wells a few times. He slapped my uncle's face. That was his response. But my uncle kept cursing him. That's when Wells lift his pistol and shot my uncle in the face. He kinda turned so Wells shot him in the chest and he fell over."

He had to take a breath, remembering the scene.

She lay her hand on his arm, waiting. "Then you shot that Wells fella? Din't ya?"

The boy shook his head, not wanting to remember.

"Go on now," she urged him. "Ya gotta 'member it. Part o' yer life now. Part o' who y'are. First thing ya done as a man."

He took a big breath. "I was right there looking at them through the gap in the rocks, and I raised my pistol and aimed right at him. At Wells. I calmed myself, held my gun steady like my uncle taught me and squeezed the trigger. It popped off before I expected. First shot hit him in the shoulder and he spun around so he was facing me. Don't think he saw me. But he's facing me so I fired again and bullet got him in the face, like right through his eye. Lucky shot."

She smiled at him. "You's a real gunslinger."

"Naw – ain't. Just lucky."

"But you got him! Ya did it!"

He liked how she acted excited at this part even though he'd told her a dozen times.

"If he'da lived they gonna call him One-Eye Wells for sure."

"But he died, din't he?"

"Yep. But ain't gonna bring my uncle back."

"Someday yer gonna hafta tell it to somebody."

"Don't wanna tell nobody."

"Someday yer gonna." She smiled, kind of like how his mama did when she was proud of him. "People gonna wanna know." She gazed into his blue eyes until he relaxed.

"If people gonna wanna know, then they're gonna ask why I shot him from behind those rocks. Hiding. Being sneaky. Like a coward. You gotta face the man you shoot, my uncle always said. But I was hiding like a damn coward."

"Y'ain't no coward," she said, putting her hand to his cheek. "Ya shot a bad man, an' that's a good thing. No ways anybody gonna be complainin' on ya. They gonna say yer a hero."

"But it was a cowardly act."

"Don'tcha be talkin' like that. Now what ya do after?"

"His men seen where I was shooting from and they scrambled up to chase after me. I got the hell outta there, run down through them rocks, thinking of hiding but I knew they find me, so I kept on running. Fast as I ever run, lemme tell ya. Got far from my horse and ya cain't run much in boots. When I got to open ground, I heard shots fired and I think that's when one of them got me, right across my ribs – what you fixed for me."

Again she smiled. "It's the right thing ta do fer a boy."

"I never felt it when I was hit. Only later."

"But ya lived."

"I ran on a ways, fast as I could. I got to some more rocks and I scrambled into them, found me a good place to hide, scrunching into a little cave. I waited a while. They got right close. Heard 'em talking. But I kept quiet and they moved on."

"Yer a brave boy." She gave him a hug.

"I seen I lost my pistol somewhere but I feared going back for it, looking for it. And my side was bleeding. I tore my shirt crawling through those rocks and got a boot with no heel. All I could do was try walking home, but I didn't know which way to go. Too far away. So I just rested, but then I got hungry so I looked for anything to eat but nothing out there in the wilderness."

She patted his head, tugged at the red hair. "Ya poor boy. Wish I'da bin there. Get some jerky fer ya."

"Didn't hardly feel no appetite, just thinking of Uncle Frank and what I'm gonna tell Mama. She's his sister. See, I was begging her to go with him on the posse and finally she let me. She decided I had to go cuz it's gonna make me a man. That's what she said. I talked her into letting me go. But I let her down. Uncle Frank was s'posed to watch out for me, not let me get in danger. In the end, I was watching out for him. But I failed."

He sniffled, a tear slipping from his eye.

"Aww. Hey now. Don'tcha be cryin' now." She put a finger to his cheek, wiped away the tear. "Yer doin' better. Ever' time you get ta this part ya got 'nother tear but less o' them ever' time ya tell it."

"Mama says it's awright if a man cries if someone he cares about dies. Then it's not being a sissy. When a man is weak like a woman." He regarded Trina, her dark eyes always on him. "But not you. Not like you. I know you're strong. You're a tough woman."

She grinned. "I am. Gotta be out in these parts."

"But as I was laying there thinking of what I'm gonna say to my mama when I got home. I was afraid. I shoulda done a lot more. I failed everybody."

"But ya shot that Wells fella. A wanted man. Ya get a bounty for that. Then yer a rich man."

"Don't want no bounty. Just want my uncle to still be alive."

Trina wrapped her arms tight around him. "Shore wish my pa was alive still. Shot dead a few years back, like Trinity said, back when we was little. But we cain't have things like that."

"My mama liked praying." He looked into Trina's eyes. She didn't seem to understand. "That's when you say your wishes to God. He's up there in the sky."

"Like a bird? A hawk maybe?"

"No, higher. A lot higher. Where the stars are."

She turned her head as if to gaze up to the heavens, but the tent canvas blocked the view. "Yeah.... Mama talk about a Great Spirit. She said prayers, too. In the end, din't help her."

"Sometimes you don't get what you want, my mama told me."

Trina took his face in her hands. "And what ya want now?"

"First, I wanted to go home. But I was afraid. I couldn't face my mama – or townsfolk, deputies. If I was the only one to come home they'll be calling me a coward cuz I didn't get killed."

She continued cradling his pudgy cheeks. "And now?"

"I sure don't mind helping out you and your sisters. If I can go on a ways I'll stick with you. Maybe I'll be ready to go on, find my own way soon. Never have to say nothing to my mama or the folks in Skinner Canyon."

"Oh, you's too young ta go yer own way," and she laughed.

"I ain't sure what day it is but I know I got a birthday passed by a few weeks ago. I should be a man by now."

Trina smiled, held it too long. "You's a baby man."

He tried not to let his displeasure at the name show, but his lips pinched anyway.

"Yep, maybe you's a full man after all. Now's time to be a man," she said, her voice softening as her hand slid down his body. "Think ya be better man tomorrow if we make us a pledge tonight. You and me. Me and you. We gonna stick together."

"Together?" He liked the sound of that word.

"Yep, together," she said. "An' that's gonna be forever."

11

INITIATION

TRINITY KICKED HIS BOOT, rousing him from his *siesta*.

"Here ya go, boy. Gotcher horse. Now ya kin ride with us."

Bart rubbed his eyes, took a look at the beast: a brindle mare that looked older than the sisters' horses but rideable. He'd ridden horses like everybody out west did; no electro-carriages to go on.

"Bet he don't know thing about horses," Triss teased.

"I do too," he barked back. "I had a horse before I got lost."

"Leave my boy alone," shouted Trina, going to her tent.

He went to the horse, the animal acting shy, and he spoke to it, calming the animal, putting his hand to her nose, patting withers until the horse expelled a loud breath and relaxed.

"Where'd you get her?" he asked.

"No need to know," said Trinity. "Rider's dead, so she's yers."

He glared at the older sister. Did she mean she shot the rider? Or found the horse abandoned? He dared not question her; he'd found her limits during his year of living with them. He turned to Trina, returning from her tent.

"Din't see nothin'," she said to his look.

He just nodded and walked the horse around the camp.

"I'll call her Betty."

"Betty? What a fool name," Trinity snickered.

"My mama had a horse named Betty," he said.

The horse came with a saddle, left when the rider dismounted for the last time. He saw engraved letters on the saddle: *H.B.* – the owner, he suspected. Yet he couldn't be blamed.

He mounted the horse, took her for a short ride away from the camp, down the trail to some open land, then back to camp.

"She's easy," he called to the sisters.

"Easier 'an this one?" laughed Triss with a nod to Trina.

"Now get on with yer chores," Trinity commanded.

Typical morning was Bart getting up in the cold and coaxing the fire to spark up, then preparing something to eat, heating water for the coffee. He'd scoop out the beans from a bag stolen from one town or another, pour the beans into a grinder left from the girls' camp long ago, and turn the handle until his arm got tired. Then he'd add the grounds to the hot water in the pot, stir it all up. He poured the mixture through one of their rags, keeping the grounds for another time. When three cups were ready he'd call the women.

Trina was always the last one up, having to fix herself after the nightly exercise with her boy, teaching him how to please her – which she determined by one experiment after another. She found the boy to be a good student.

"Really?" he'd ask at her tawdry suggestions. "That what you want?"

And she'd reply: "Just give a try."

When the women were up and having their meal, he'd go back to the tent and straighten up, make sure it was neat and as clean as possible given all the red dirt that blew in through the tent flaps. If necessary, he'd set aside what needed washing and while the women were off on an adventure he'd wash the sheets as best he could, get them hung up to dry in the warm sun that defied the cold of winter days. They would bring him something from their day's episode, let him know his work was appreciated. Trina most of all. She would be sure to give him a big kiss so the others saw.

"You's a good pet boy," she'd say, giving his head a pat.

He didn't dare say he hated the name. He actually liked his new position: a steady routine so he didn't have time to feel bad about all he'd done. He got food in exchange for the chores. The nightly service he provided was...well, he wasn't too sure if it was actually a chore or a reward for doing chores. He didn't mind, had never suspected such naughty things could feel so good.

Trina was strict; she wouldn't let her sisters use her pet, and he was glad of that. The thought of him laying with Trinity frightened him to softness. He might make do with Triss if asked, being closer to his age, but she'd laugh at everything, make him feel so stupid no matter what he said or did. No, it was Trina, only her and no one else he had fire in his belly for, a fire that grew day by day until he began to feel like he was the one in charge of coupling time and he could press her whenever urges came to him. She complained little, letting him have his way beneath the canvas of their tent.

"Ya do me good, Barty," she'd coo into his ear when he lay back, breathing hard. Rubbing her hands down his back as he lay over her, her nails would scratch his moist skin as she sailed off to heaven beneath his frantic pounding. The boy could go all night. Yet if she cried out, her sisters would tease her the next day.

"I try my best," he'd moan when finished. "Try my best for you, best I can, yes, ma'am."

"None o' that *ma'am* talk," she'd snarl playfully. "You's one o' us now, don'tcha know?"

"Ma'am is a word of respect," he said and she fell silent, gazing into his eyes.

And so it was four who rode into the town of two-thousand in the cold winter afternoon, the Glow not yet risen over the land in those days, and barged straightaway into the bank with guns drawn, the five customers and three clerks caught by surprise but willing after harsh words to hand over a bag of bundled credit notes, then just as quickly ride out of that town without any shots fired. Three tough-looking women in leathers and a young man waiting outside holding the horses. People recognized them in other towns they visited. They had to lay low for a while.

One day Trinity held up a bank note, waved it at him.

"Now you go get us things on this here list," Trina told Bart on behalf of Trinity.

He took the wrinkled 5-note with the red and gray flag on it. The stern face of the woman below the flag scared him a little, reminded him of his mama. She told him about how life was in the capital, the governor there like a Big Sister caring for everyone.

The older sister had drawn on the note, made pictures of things they wanted: all food items. No words written, only the drawings, so he figured maybe she never learned letters or how to write and he felt better about himself. He'd teach them if they wanted to learn.

As Trinity instructed, he was to go into one of the towns several miles away, one they hadn't stolen from, and get the things drawn on the 5-note and bring them back by a switchback route so nobody could follow him. His first test, Trina told him. She believed he was loyal, swore to her sisters that he wouldn't ride off or bring lawmen down on them.

Yet Trina knew he might run off, take his chance to return to his home, and for that she felt satisfied to set him free yet also sad that he might actually ride off never to return.

"He kin do it," she insisted but Trinity and Triss were doubtful.

"Ya gonna let yer pet go free, ain'tcha?" Trinity cursed.

"There go yer bed buddy," Triss giggled.

"Gotta be him," Trina countered. "Ever'body know us. He kin go there, get things we need, get back here and nobody suspect him fer nothin' an' we kin be eatin' again." It had been a few days, with only the burlap sack of red beans and the smaller bag of coffee beans remaining.

"I don't mind," Bart spoke up, feeling more a part of the gang.

"He don't mind," said Trina.

"I'll do it." He looked at each woman. "And I'll be coming on back here, too. I ain't got nowhere else to go. Like I told you, I'll be called a coward if I go back home."

"Ain't no coward," Trina grumbled. "You's a boy knowed nothin' at all, an' did yer best else ya be dyin' in the desert with no mama to cry out to."

"And...." His face broke into a rosy grin that made Trinity laugh. "And I like being here, being with you ladies."

"Ladies!" scoffed Trinity. "He definite hooked on you."

"Leave him be," Trina snapped. "He one o' us now."

"Don't you worry, I'm coming back, swear," he said, pressing his felt hat down on his head then mounting that brindle mare.

Bart rode and rode, passing two towns that didn't look right, a little too guarded. He made his plan, taking the name Hal Black in case anyone asked about the letters on the saddle – his mama had a friend named Hal, he recalled. He'd never met the man, but she sent the music she wrote to him.

Now he was on a horse, one that seemed reluctant to get up to a gallop for barely a quarter-mile. No need to hurry. A trip to a town for groceries was all it was. In the old days, people did it twice a week, mostly using a motor carriage with a big closet in the rear for storing what they purchased until they got home. You could still see some of the old machines rusting along broken stone roads.

Riding on, he was happy to be on the range, breathing fresh air.

He came to the next town, slowed to have a look from afar. Saw men walking its streets, got nervous. He checked his pistol, secured it in the holster on his hip.

Not that town – maybe the next one. Or the next.

He arrived in the next town and acted regular, tied up his horse there in front of the General Store. That brindle mare was easy to remember with its mottled coat. Kind of ugly, he decided.

He strode in like he'd lived there all his life, broad smile on his wide face, cheer in his voice, giving a confident "Howdy" to the clerk at the back of the store.

"What can I do you for?" responded the clerk, a tall and thin man twice Bart's age, bearing a bushy brown mustache.

"Mama sent me for some greens," he began, story worked out in advance, "and whatever else ya got that's good. She's planning a big party for kin coming to town."

"Your mama? You say lots of kin coming?" asked the man.

"I'm just doing what she told me," said Bart, his voice starting to slip. He fought to keep up the act. His hand settled on the pistol on his hip. "Being a man, I hardly know a thing or two about picking groceries." He gave a laugh.

"I see." The man regarded him suspiciously. "And your mama?"

"Uh...Maggie. Her name's Maggie. Course I call her Mama."

"Don't know any Maggie in these parts. There's that music lady over in Skinner Canyon. Used to lead the children's band."

"That ain't my mama," Bart spoke in rough tone.

Bart saw the clerk eye the holster hanging on his hip, perhaps interested in the squarish green pistol looking like models left over from the war. It was what Trina had given him, saying she found it in the wreckage of a vehicle in the desert. Similar to the gun he lost while escaping from J.C. Wells' camp.

With a dismissive smile, the clerk grabbed a wicker basket from a stack by the counterboard, started going about the store, choosing items from the bins, barrels, and shelves. He glanced back at Bart a few times, holding up a vegetable or fruit for his approval.

Bart saw apples and felt happy, suddenly missing home. With an approving nod, the clerk added them to the basket. Pears, too. And a hank of green beans and some leafy greens, peppers, and tomatoes like what his mama sliced up for dinners and demanded he eat. And golden potatoes. Two ears of corn, a box of salt, a box of sugar.

A loaf of fresh-baked brown bread still cooling on a table in the corner smelled so good he wanted to shove it into his mouth with a chunk of butter. The sign on the table stated *Courtesy of Barbara's Bakery* which was next door.

The clerk regarded Bart.

Enough for a party? he calculated. He couldn't carry too much on the back of a horse.

The bell over the door rang loudly as another customer entered, startling Bart. His hand went to his pistol. The clerk noticed.

"Morning, ma'am," the clerk called to the woman entering.

With a snicker, Bart dropped his hand. "Too many foxes getting in the chickens."

"I hear you," said the clerk, shifting his attention to the woman of about thirty and daughter of ten, dressed nicely like they lived in a fine house on a hill with a servant or two.

"If you need a good beef roast," the clerk spoke up, returning to Bart, "Mister Harding's shop down the street, he's got the best beef in town, straight from Loomis Ranch, if you don't mind me saying."

Bart gave a nod, not needing any fresh meat – might not be very fresh by the time he got back to camp, even though he really craved it. He thought of how his mama cooked it and served it sliced on a plate, sprinkled with salt and pepper, covered in a brown gravy. He was getting hungry – getting nervous, too.

He moved carefully to the cashier station, not letting his holster catch on the bins as he passed through. He felt the bundle of notes in his pocket. The women had to trust him. This was a test. Succeed and Trina would surely reward him.

"And, if you don't mind, lemme get a couple boxes of them bullets up there on the shelf," he called to the clerk. "Too many foxes to deal with, ya know."

"Which ones?" called the man, still among the vegetable bins.

"For this pistol." He reached for his gun.

"You don't know what it shoots?" asked the man, amused. He waved the woman and daughter to help themselves to what they came for, pointing to the baskets.

"I know what it shoots," Bart grumbled.

The clerk came over to him. "Let me see."

Bart lifted the pistol slowly from its holster, trying to not look as though he was ready to shoot. Uncle Frank always told him never to pick up a gun unless he was prepared to fire it.

The clerk reached for it too quickly and Bart jumped.

"Easy now. Just need to see it so I know what bullets you want." The clerk chuckled. "Guess your mama doesn't let you shoot much. Or maybe it's your pa don't let you go around with a gun."

"I'm eighteen already. That's a man, ain't it?" Bart spoke firmly. He was still seventeen, but eighteen real soon. He could pass for eighteen if he acted tough. "I'm a man now and I got a gun."

"Indeed, you do." The clerk gestured for Bart to lay the pistol on the counterboard. He hesitated but complied. "Mind if I pick it up, son? I'll need to take a closer look."

At a nod from Bart, he lifted the pistol in both hands like it was a precious gift.

"This one looks fairly new." He examined it, turning it over and over. "In good condition. Not like most of them you see these days. I heard they have special electric guns in the capital. No bullets. Just shoots some kind of red light that knocks a man down."

"Yeah, heard of them," said Bart, playing along.

The clerk kept his eyes locked on the gun. "What kind is it? Oh, I see: says it's nine-millimeter. We don't use those measurements out here. This mark: the *Sig Sauer* logo. See here? It's...." He turned to look at the shelves behind him. "We haven't got much ammo for this. They don't make a lot anymore. Nearest armory is Wichita. They make bullets there but not all kinds. Electric guns, like I said."

"Don't know how any gun could fire electric, though," said Bart, both curious and fending off any suspicions the clerk had.

"Me, neither." He faced Bart again. "They put the electric into a small box that's shoved into the gun like you load bullets into a magazine. When you pull the trigger it shoots out the electric. If it hits you then you fall over. Not dead but unable to move. That way they can take you to jail." He smiled at Bart, like a warning. "I heard if you hold down the trigger the electric keeps shooting out until you die or the electric runs out. It's kept in a box, like I said. What they call a *battery*."

Bart didn't like the clerk talking to him like he was stupid, but he knew he wasn't. Just curious. If you don't experience something then you don't know about it. Doesn't mean you're stupid.

"But how they get the electric in the battery?" he asked.

"They put it into another box called a *charger*. After some time it is full again and they put it back into the gun."

"But how they get the electric into those chargers?"

"From the terminal." The clerk blinked. "Most buildings have an electric terminal. Two or three in some rich houses. They put those chargers to the terminals."

"But where the electric come from to the terminals?"

"From the cables they strung across the land. You've seen them, haven't you?"

"I seen 'em."

"There you go."

"But where all that electric come from to go through them cables to the terminals at the houses and into them chargers?"

The clerk flashed a polite smile. "Well, they make the electric at a factory somewhere. They pour coal rocks into a big machine and it burns the rocks and that turns the spool around and that turning makes the electric."

Bart grinned like he'd gotten away with a joke.

"Gonna hafta get me one of those electric guns," said Bart. "It's already too hard to find ammo." He realized he was wasting time. "Anyways, that's what I need. Regular bullets, not any of them electric boxes."

"Awrighty," said the clerk, turning back to examine the shelves.

"Nine millimeter," Bart repeated.

"I recall," he said, facing Bart again, "there was a robbery at the armory up in Elkhart. Lost some guns and ammo."

"Don't know nothing about it," he responded, his voice firm. His ladies knew. Growing frustrated, he felt anxious to get out of there. "It's what Mama gave me. Said it used to belong to her grandpa. He was fighting during those war years. Back east. But I keep it up. Still works fine."

The clerk admired the pistol, laying it gently on the countertop.

"Yes, that's a nice looking piece you got there. The modern ones look so sleek. Don't know much about them, though. We don't have a lot of guns here, at least not those short guns."

"Mama says we gotta keep varmints away from the garden. And there's tribals sometimes, too. We live a ways out." Then he stopped himself from saying too much. *Garden? Why'd I say that if I'm here getting vegetables, dammit?*

"So with kin coming we need more than we grow," he muttered.

"I see we have one box of the nine-millimeters," said the clerk, reaching up to the shelf.

Bart felt the folded 5-note in his pocket with sketches of items to get but he didn't know if it showed bullets. Did they use the same kind? Triss liked her revolver, spinning the bullets around like she enjoyed the sound. If he only got bullets for his pistol the women might be mad. He might lose his privileges.

He looked up, studying the shelf, the boxes in a row there.

"Gimme all ya got." He scanned the shelf. "Need twenty-twos and thirty-eights, for sure. Some of those thirty-aught-six, too. Got some guns need ammo. The forty-four magnums. And those shells. Couple boxes'll do. Just to be ready for anything."

"That's quite a lot, young man," said the clerk, his lips pinched. "Got a whole army to equip?"

Sounded like a joke but Bart took him seriously.

"Just gimme one each of those," he said. "I know we'll need them sooner or later. Got lots of varmints to deal with."

The clerk glared at him. "You have money for all of this?"

"Mama gave me plenty." Then he knew it sounded wrong.

The clerk looked at him curiously. "Your mama doing awright?"

Maybe he thinks I stole this from her.

"She's fine." He decided it seemed too rough, thought of a better response. "Well, she's been ill, so it's why she sent me."

The mother over in the corner called a question and the clerk paused to reply.

"Just gimme what I asked for and I'll be on my way," said Bart and his voice started to falter.

"Fine, young man. I'll wrap them up."

The clerk took the basket of vegetables, fruit, and other items and gathered them into a paper box he unfolded. He laid a sheet of waxed paper over the top and tied it up with string.

"There you go, young man."

He turned around to retrieve the boxes of bullets off the shelf.

With his back turned, the clerk heard the click of the pistol that had been laid on the counterboard. Glancing back, he grinned sheepishly.

"I almost thought you was gonna pull a fast one on me." He gave a cautious chuckle. "Hearing a click like that. But it's all right now, ain't it? We're just doing business."

"Gimme one each of those," Bart demanded, his hand resting on the pistol sitting unstrapped in its holster.

"These are going to be a pretty penny, if you want all of them," the clerk explained as he climbed the ladder to the upper shelves.

"How much?" Bart dug in his pocket, pulled out the thick bundle of notes with the bank's strap still around them. He plunked it down on the counterboard. "This'll cover it."

Looking down, the clerk's eyes widened. "More than, I'll bet."

The mother asked another question of the clerk. Bart startled at her voice, half-turned as the clerk climbed down from the ladder to answer her. He set down five boxes on the counterboard, gave Bart a look before focusing on the woman and her daughter.

"If you finish up my sale," urged Bart, "I'll be on my way and you can deal with them folks."

That prompted a glare from the clerk.

This boy's nervous about something, Bart sensed him thinking.

He grew frustrated, hand heavy on the pistol, finger stretching down the holster, getting ready to snatch it.

"I'll be right with you, ma'am," called the clerk.

He returned his attention to Bart, looking down at the boxes set in a row on the counterboard. "Now then. Four boxes of bullets, like you wanted. And a couple boxes of shells. Will that be all?"

"The food stuff, too."

"Yes, of course. I've already tallied those."

The clerk reached over to the counting machine and pulled out a slip of paper, looked it over, and laid it on the counterboard.

Bart tried to act like he knew what he was doing. He picked up each box of ammunition in turn with one hand while his other hand remained on his pistol. He gave a quick look at each box, examining the numbers on the sides.

Feeling uncomfortable as the clerk waited for him to make up his mind, Bart decided to check his pistol.

"Something else, son?" asked the clerk impatiently.

Son! That was enough.

Bart snatched up his pistol, knowing it was fully loaded, held it straight to the clerk's face. The mother screamed from back in the corner of the store. Startled, Bart turned, the pistol's aim moving with him, landing on the mother.

"Stop right there, young man," the clerk ordered.

Bart swung his head back to the clerk, his pistol still aimed into the corner of the store where the mother and daughter cringed. His finger merged with the trigger. His eyes narrowed at the clerk—

It happened faster than he could fix it in his mind later, trying to figure out what went wrong.

He rode as fast as he could due east, not expecting to head back to the women's camp directly. Even with the jostling of the mare, he tried to think it through. Half the basket of vegetables and fruit had spilled as he left town at full gallop. But he swept the bullets and shells into a burlap bag from beside the barrel of beans, swung the bag over his shoulder as he held out his pistol.

He figured the clerk had a gun under the counterboard, the way his hand slipped down out of sight. And the mother was screaming, the daughter gathered in her arms bawling. Confusion clouded him, made him rush everything, his finger squeezing the trigger and hearing the sound of the pistol going off, not knowing what he hit. The mother stopped her screaming, the daughter crying louder. The clerk brought down a hammer on his hand on the counterboard. It hurt like dickens and he didn't hesitate a breath. The next bullet went into the clerk's chest, dropping him behind the counter.

Taking what he'd come to town for, wrapped box under his arm, burlap sack in his hand, he stormed out of the store, glad to see his horse waiting at the rail. He tried to load the package on his horse, but saw two men rushing toward him, shouting at him. Behind were other men running toward the store.

He raced up the street with men calling after him.

"Come on, Betty!" he shouted at his horse.

Then a shot trailed him, whizzed past him as he urged Betty to gallop faster than she ever had before, racing until he was well out of town. His heart never pounded so hard – a lot harder than when he shot J.C. Wells. He didn't have time to think, had to flee. Plenty of time to sort it all out in a jail cell if they caught him.

12

THE REMAINS

THE LAND STRETCHED WIDE before him like a new bed sheet, a lost world he couldn't recognize, and he rode hard for as long as he could – until his horse complained. Shortgrass and weathered dirt, patches of mud and gravel, flaking buffalo chips, an old dirt road, a few rusted vehicle hulks, dry creek winding on before him, a murky puddle here and there for the horse to slurp. A rickety iron bridge leaning to one side, old railway cars dead on the tracks. More rusty vehicles from long ago spotting the landscape, more in the distance like people had parked and walked away to die somewhere else in peace, maybe under a nice shade tree.

A once-red bent-down metal sign told him to *Stop*. So he did.

He gazed far ahead: purple hills looking like roofs of a village, dark clouds overhead deciding whether to rain, coming his way. He felt God watching him and he leaned low against his horse to hide. He cursed his mama for telling those stories. He regretted going to the chapel on the hill where his uncle was the priest. Too many sermons about guilt. He left there feeling awful every time.

Nothing else mattered now. He'd shot two people and sent them to their reward – like his mama would say. And they didn't deserve it – not like that bastard J.C. Wells did for his crimes. But Bart wasn't a criminal like him. He was a decent fellow, he insisted but the wind mocked him.

You figured you're gonna get away clean and be done with it, but I'm gonna track you the rest of your life.

"Shut up!" he cried out and slapped his thigh. He'd imagined the voice of God sounding different, not so much like his own.

He thought of his mama standing over him when he'd made a mess in the food preparation room in their unit in the capital when he was a little boy, the way she'd seemed like God staring down at him and he feared her wrath. Yet she never struck him, not even a small spank to his bottom. Instead, she picked him up, set him in her lap, and spoke softly to him. That seemed worse: made him cry in shame – shame that he disappointed her, as though the whole reason for his existence was to please her, be her perfect little boy. He knew what she wanted of him but he couldn't ever give her that: be a music person like her. Then, after moving to Skinner Canyon, he spent more time with his uncle and had a lot less interest in a musical life. He stopped playing that cornet after his mama insisted too many times that he practice more if he wanted to be good.

Dammit! He knew he couldn't blame her for what he'd done. His heart shook, rattling his whole body, as the hand hit by the clerk's hammer throbbed. Even Betty seemed to notice his displeasure and shook beneath him. His head felt hot, ready to burst. Then tears popped from his eyes without command and grew into a flood until he couldn't see clearly. The world looked like a window pane spotted with raindrops.

He eased up on the reins, let Betty slow to a walk. He wiped his eyes, turned to stare behind him, seeing if anyone pursued. But he saw no horse and rider at the farthest range of his eyes. How many miles had he ridden? Not far enough, he decided, not far enough to escape his guilt. He could never ride far enough to escape thoughts of his mama confronting him for the bad things he'd done. How would he ever explain? He could never face her again.

Then his horse tripped over a stretch of flat gray rock, cracked in dozens of places. He almost fell off but got the horse back in balance, a frantic whinny to express her fear. He paused to have a look. What a strange thing to find out in the wilderness: one of those things the metal vehicles used to go over. With a horse he didn't need to follow them, could go nearly anywhere he pleased.

He dismounted, tugged the reins for Betty to follow.

The flat stone extended for some distance, as far as he could see, straight as a razor, wide as a few wagon trails running side by side. A faint white line ran down the center, other markings on each side – faded paint. This stone road was wider and longer than most he'd seen closer to Skinner Canyon. Mama called them roads, the larger ones highways. Motor carriages rolled along them in the years before the great pandemic. Then no vehicles rolled anywhere. No more carriages were built for decades. The roads wouldn't last long without someone coming to fix them.

Thoughts of the room upstairs in his mama's house came into his head: shelving pressed against each wall filled with books his mama gathered when they closed the town library. Too old to keep, they said. She argued for preserving all of the history, technical knowledge, and arts contained in them. She reminded them in vain what happened when the power grid went down. As a child, he had to read the books, one after another. His mama insisted he learn everything he could because one day the books she'd saved would crumble to dust. Now, going on two years since he last saw her, he suddenly wanted to return, feel safe once more if only for an hour, and not be on the run.

He scanned the length of the broken stone road, recalling what he'd seen in the pages of his childhood books.

There was one book full of pictures he loved looking at. Pictures of different kinds of moving machines. He'd sounded out the words: automobile, locomotive, oceanliner, rocketship, semi-tractor-trailer, airplane, lunar lander – all magical words that no longer matched anything he could see in his daily life. He recalled a picture of an airplane, a vehicle with long side panels stretching out like bird wings. He recalled the wide road it went on before it jumped into the sky. Actually this kind of road only went far enough to launch the machine. Other pictures showed lines of vehicles in all shapes and colors rolling along a gray line much like this crumbling road. According to his mama, his great-great-grandparents, Sandy and Hannah, had a motor carriage like those, used it to escape their city when the pandemic got worse.

How long since anything used this broken road?

Some roads remained, laying like corpses of the transportation cult, crossing the landscape like dried, crumbling memories. A lot of people said it was good that vehicles were gone, saying they spewed out bad air. They required digging oil from the ground. Others said vehicles ensured their freedom: they could go anyplace they wanted. With the government finally restored, designs for vehicles were prepared. They first made vehicles called 'buses' that carried many people at once, powered by electric. Everyone praised them. He'd ridden on them in the capital when he was a boy.

Out in the western region, however, none of that existed. Sure, Skinner Canyon had put down cobblestones on the main streets to keep the dust and dirt under control. Yet the trail from town to his mama's house was still dirt – muddy in the spring and fall, icy in the winter. A few rich folks had one of those electric carriages and were happy to show them off driving down the cobblestone streets like they were ancient kings and queens – another book he recalled looking at with fascination. His mama hated them, telling of life in the capital when she was born. She was quick to remind him it was one of those vehicles that killed his papa.

Shaking his head at the flood of memories, he crouched there, let the horse wander, and let himself weep for all he'd done in his short life, all the disappointments he'd gathered, all the guilt filling him. If he were so bad, he might as well be badder. Who would care? Let God chase him down. He wouldn't be afraid any longer, wouldn't worry. He would be a man.

You're just a boy, a boy-man, a baby man. Now's time to stand up and be a man, now you've done shot folks.

Mounting the horse again, he rose in the saddle, staring down the stone road as far as he could see. Something was there, far off. Another vehicle, most likely, left for decades.

Urging his horse on, they strolled the length of the stone road, horseshoes clapping. As he got closer he saw it was huge: wreckage of some kind. He studied the gray remains, fixing it in his mind like pictures from the books he looked at in childhood. This thing was an *airplane* – but without its wings. Actually, the wings had broken off. One appeared far off to the side on the grass. The one that should've been on the other side of the airplane was torn away at its middle, that portion laying nearby. It must've crashed, he decided, and wondered how long ago it happened.

Runway. The word came to him suddenly. Roads that airplanes went down before they went into the sky. He smiled at recalling his childhood lessons. He stared at the wreckage, weathered and ugly. His mama told him about the great pandemic and everything that happened after, when airplanes stopped flying in the skies. That was a hundred years in the past. Unless the restored government invented airplanes again – but they'd have to get designs from books because everything stored up in the clouds was lost when the power grid shattered. The power grid, recalled from school lessons, was a system of electric that everybody could borrow. That was how they had lighting in the night, how they could operate machines. They invented the streaming machines and the camera technology so they could watch everyone. And electric guns. The developments made his mama flee the capital when she was a child – only to return later. He was born in the capital, if anyone might ask, and what he remembered seemed mostly good.

It's somewhere way the heck over there, a strange voice told him, making him turn and look.

He wished he could be in the capital once more. He could hide there in its tall buildings, its cozy housing units, lots of cabinets to crawl into. He could get lost in the throngs of workers going to and from their labor. He remembered his mama complaining everyone was forced to work so many hours that they had little time for leisure. Music became an indulgence. He'd grown up while his mama led the National Symphony as principal conductor. He'd loved sitting alone in the empty auditorium while she rehearsed the orchestra, waving his arms as she waved hers.

Now look at me! Just a dang fool. Tears came to his eyes again. *I shot someone! I killed someone! Two, actually.* Plus that bastard J.C. Wells. Three dead by his hand.

There was no going back, no undoing his deed. He could only go forward. He'd return to the sisters, but he'd no longer be their pet. He'd be one of them, an equal. In time, he'd be the leader of the gang.

That was the only way forward. The only direction for him to go. He had to forget his mama, put aside all she'd taught him, and dismiss the love she'd given him. Was it love? Motherly protection? She was so demanding. Yet she let him go with the posse, after all, so everything was her fault. Everything he did from this day forth he could blame her for. He would be bad, and it was his strict mama who drove him to it.

+ + +

He stepped carefully over to the wreckage, avoiding getting a boot heel caught in a crack, seeing the door on the side had been torn open, the windows in front and along the sides smashed. Metal legs with burst rubber tires lay bent outward from each side of the long tube – his memory of the transportation book slipping the word *fuselage* into his mind. Must've crashed, he decided. *Where were they going? Here?* He looked around: nothing of any interest. Just a short tower further down the stone road that could've been the place they watched airplanes arrive and depart.

An oval door in the side of the tube had been thrown open, steps extending down but not quite reaching the ground. Remains of a body lay there as if coming out from the fuselage, maybe tripping on the steps. He saw the boney roundness of the head, a hairless skull protruding out of a green uniform. Animals must've picked the body clean – and a small mouse scampered out a sleeve where a hand had curled its boney fingers into a ball.

He kicked the body away from the steps.

Nerves fired as he leaned into the open doorway. Enough light pushed through the broken windows to show him the interior. Someone had picked through whatever was there. With the door open, coyotes could come inside and have their snack. That was evident by the remains of seated passengers: bones extending from inside their limp clothing, unhappy skulls set within jacket collars, streams of hair crawling down shoulders. He thought of backing out to avoid the viruses that may have killed them; they didn't seem to have been killed by the crash. But a pair of black rats exploring the interior let him know it was safe.

His eyes landed on a large chart fixed to the curved wall in a gap with no seats. A small table was folded down there. On the table lay a mess of papers and a couple black binders with three rings to hold papers.

Maybe these folks were escaping somewhere.

You can't escape your destiny, his mama's voice seemed to speak to him, making him look around.

This is what happened to some of us: an escape from horror that came to a horrible end. He found the words coming from his mama and had to take a breath.

Ain't my destiny!

Holding his aching hand, he tumbled out the doorway, ran a few steps away and thought he might toss up whatever was still in his belly. He stopped. Scanning the wide plain, yellow grass waving in the breeze, he felt ghosts taunting him. He spun around as though they'd tapped his shoulder. He cried out, cursing them.

Dropping to the ground, breathing hard, he wondered what to do next. He worried about the sisters. They sent him to fetch food and he failed. Lost half the food he got, the other items dirty from the dusty ride. They'd be mad at him.

He called Betty over, checked the flimsy box strapped behind his saddle. He pulled out the loaf of bread, brushed off the dust, and took a bite. Beside it was the butter, half melted, and he spread it over the bread with his fingers. He sat on the ground, eating the bread pinch by pinch until the loaf was done.

Feeling better with his belly full, he got up and returned to the wreckage, climbed inside and surveyed the passengers. A curtain separated the front part from the rest of the interior. Sweeping the curtain aside, he discovered two bodies sitting upright in the seats, boney grins facing each other like they had a final kiss.

He stumbled back, fearing he'd gotten contamination. Even if they'd gotten the virus that caused the great pandemic, they likely wouldn't be flying. If they were sick when they flew, they wouldn't have gotten so sick during the flight that they'd die in their seats upon arrival. They would've gotten up, tried to leave the airplane.

This had to be their destination, a place they believed was safe.

He shuffled through the papers on the table, saw them covered mostly with numbers, a few charts and graphs similar to what his mama taught him. He tried to decipher what they meant but it was too complicated. He looked at the chart on the wall of the fuselage: a drawing of the continent. Places had been marked, lines drawn between marks. He wasn't sure what the map showed; didn't know where he was anyway. Leaning down, he scanned the brownish landscape, noting mountains drawn and rivers as blue lines. He found Kanza City on the map, tracked southwest until he located Cimarron, then continued to Skinner Canyon near the edge of the nation. Someone had drawn a red X west of Skinner Canyon.

"They were arriving here," he muttered. "What's here?"

He laughed. *Nothing's here. If I were escaping from something like that, I'd want to come to a place where there was nothing.*

The loose papers intrigued him and he studied them longer. Not much paper in Skinner Canyon, just what his mama used to write her music. The charts showed a worsening future, he decided. Lines trended down. Red marks by someone's hand – not like the tablets used in the capital. He decided to gather the papers, thinking they might be important, took them outside to stuff into a saddle bag.

Returning for a final look, he stepped into the front where those lovers sat and scanned the space for anything of interest, especially the board with all the buttons and switches below the wide window. He spied something jammed alongside the seat. He pulled it free: a book. He held it up to the window's light.

Opening the cover, he saw the curly writing on the first page. He flipped through the book, found the other pages blank, returned to the first few pages covered in words. He recognized the writing but couldn't figure it out. His mama wrote by hand all the time and he knew her style.

He was born at a certain time and place, and set on a path he never chose. His mama never failed to remind him how he fit into the greater plan of the world. Taken to this western territory, a city boy trying to play cowboy. He was only ten when his mama brought him out to Skinner Canyon, what she called her hometown. It was in

Skinner Canyon he made the switch from music boy to cowboy, preferring his uncle and cousins to his mama's world of music.

Others had it worse, he could see in the skeletons of the few who didn't make it to a safe place. He'd heard his mama's stories. She repeated them like church scripture, events and dates, names and places, as though he had to memorize them, repeat them after her. He hated that. None of those stories ever had a happy ending. Everyone died, some in awful ways.

With a final glance, he tipped his hat and mounted his horse.

13

MORNING IN AMERICA

THE SUNSET LED HIM in the right direction and he pressed on in the dark an hour more, then had to halt. Too dark for safe passage. He stopped in a small grove by a creek, tied up Betty, pulled off the saddle and made it his pillow for the night. Not bothering to make a fire, he shivered through the cold hours and awoke stiff as stone, back aching, his hammered hand swollen up and purple. He dug in the paper box from the General Store, chose a smashed tomato for his morning meal. Everything else needed to be cooked, except the apples and pears but he had to save those for the sisters.

The morning sunshine warmed him as he found his way again, turning south then west, south again and west again, until finally he saw the hills he recognized with their tall rocky outcrops. Deep in those hills was his home now. He ordered Betty to gallop until she demanded he take back his command. They agreed to walk the rest of the way, feeling calm at the sight of home.

He climbed up the old trail through the hills, winding among the pines up to the bare rocks beyond. A hawk cried, a fox scurried away, and he smiled. Home! He made it. The fresh air revived him, made him forget recent events.

His heart beat fast as he got close, urging Betty on up the path through the rocks – the same route he'd taken when escaping from that gang a couple years before. Eventually he had to dismount and lead her when the path narrowed through rocks, where water had run over time to split the hard stone into sentinels, not even as wide as that airplane fuselage, with thorny bushes that cut his arms if he brushed against them. Betty hesitated, refusing to go forward and he had to pull her on.

He broke through the last obstacle and saw the pool there in the hollow of the red rocks and lost his breath.

The camp was gone. Tents no longer there. The fire ring cold. He gazed around, puzzled, searching for the sisters. They must be hiding as a joke. They were always teasing him.

Not even a note left! Even if they didn't know how to write, they could draw a picture with an arrow to show they left. He had to think: sending him off for food...? Was it a trick to get him to leave?

They gotta be planning it, he decided, kicking at the quiet coals in the fire circle. "Need me to get going so they don't hafta say no goodbyes." He cursed under his breath, kicking the fire ring. "I ain't nothing but a baby man to them."

Sitting down on the dirty ground where the tent used to be that he shared with Trina, he shook his head, clenched his fists. But his hammered hand was too sore to clench much and he shook it to let out the pain. It was good it wasn't his shooting hand that the clerk struck with that hammer.

Bart scanned the rock walls around the pool, remembering when he first arrived, sick and starving, saved by the sisters. He worked with them as his thanks. Now they abandoned him.

He got up, stood tall, hands on hips.

"Awright now," he called out, with echoes against the rock walls returning to him, making him wait a moment, "ya got me. Ya fooled me. I know it ain't hard to do, fool that I am. So you can come out now. I know you're all hiding for sport."

His throat grew tight and his chest felt on fire. His eyes blurred, began filling with tears. He slapped his leg, demanding that he be a man. Like in that General Store when the clerk wouldn't believe he was a man. That look, and calling him 'son' and 'young man' like he had no gun. So he shot the man. It might've been an accident, he told himself, *reflexes*. No loss, he figured, one less store clerk in the world wouldn't be missed – like so many others hadn't also died but from other causes like a virus his great-grandmother lived through.

"Come on out!" he shouted, getting the echo then silence.

Turning angry, he went over to unload the items from the horse, set them out where the supplies used to be kept. Made it neat. Then he chose one of the pears and ate it, still feeling hungry after he spit out the seeds. He thought of making a fire but the flints were gone.

Evening came on, light fading early behind the rock walls, the pool dark and placid. He had nothing to make a shelter with and the air turned cold during the night. He couldn't sleep and awoke with a bellyache, his hand throbbing, his head heavy. He got up, stomped about the camp, got his blood flowing, cursed the sisters with every turn of his path.

All this for nothing, he grumbled. He was on his own again. Not as bad as before, when the sisters found him. He had a horse, and he had a gun, lots of bullets, and some food. He needed to make a fire to cook the vegetables, but he didn't have materials. And not even a pot or pan left in the camp. They cleared it out. Like they'd waited for him to go off on the errand so they could run away.

A good part of the day he looked around the hilltop, checking places they might be hiding. He thought of his choices. Now that he was an outlaw he couldn't just go into a town and settle down. They would recognize him. The red hair his papa cursed him with! Trina said the whiskers tickled her when they kissed but she didn't mind.

He made dinner of the food he brought, huddled against a bend in the rock wall that blocked the breeze. He didn't sleep well, cursed several times during the night. An owl arrived to mock him from up in a tree, forcing him to get up and shoo it off.

A cloudy morning greeted him, offering only cold wind and a hint of drizzle. He pressed into that rocky alcove to shield himself from the rain. He thought through his plans – tried to make plans.

The night was cold again but he was so exhausted he fell into a sleep that felt like death.

The next morning was better, bright sunshine glowing against the opposite rock walls. He got himself up, stretching his arms, and shaking his swollen hand. He could manage the pain. Worse than that was what he felt at being abandoned. Maybe he deserved it.

"Damn bitches!" he shouted at the rock walls.

"Hey!" an echo called back.

He looked up, squinting.

"Hey there," called a woman's voice.

He jumped up, faced the direction of the voice. Then he saw her: Trina, hiding up there right where she found him that first time.

"Hey," he called up to her, daring to smile, but she disappeared.

Maybe his eyes were tricking him. His head felt cloudy.

Then she appeared again, coming through the gap in the walls, tugging the reins of her horse, entering the camp, her usual black leather clothes and boots, twin holsters flapping against her hips, hat pulled down with the brim level with her eyes.

She stood straight before him like she was ready to draw on him, put her hands to her hips, glaring at him.

"Who ya callin' bitches?" she snarled, then broke into a grin.

He gave her a big smile but he didn't move, stood firm, waiting for her to come to him.

"You and your sisters is who," he shouted at her.

She narrowed her eyes. "Ain't no bitches."

"I don't really know what it means," he said, adding a chuckle, "just something my cousin used to say. Means a bad woman."

Trina made her way around the shore of the pool, coming up to him, going straight into an embrace, her arms sliding under his and clasping across his back. It surprised him.

"Aw, missed ya," she said, holding him tight.

He wrapped his arms around her. Just as he was starting to feel good, he broke free, stood showing his anger.

"Why y'all run off? Leaving me alone? It weren't right."

"Calm down, boy." She looked him over a moment. "Trinity said we better be movin' camp cuz lawmen gettin' too close, gonna find us. It was her made the decision."

"And you never thought about me?"

"Yeah, we did. Knew ya be coming back here. Guess she thought them lawmen get you 'stead o' us. She got 'er way of thinkin' make no sense sometime."

"I thought so. She never liked me."

Trina grinned at him. "You's a hard boy ta like."

"I ain't no boy. I'm a man." He tried to show anger but she knew him too well and his angry face melted.

She chuckled. "You sure are a man, boy."

"Stop it. Don't ever call me a boy again."

He grabbed her, held her like he feared she'd get away.

"Ya gonna hurt me?" she challenged.

"Naw, I couldn't ever hurt you. You're my woman."

"I am? Yours, huh? How ya figure? More like yer *my* man."

"Either way, we gotta stick together."

"Stick together?" She spit on the ground. "That make sense."

He smiled. Then, with a sharp breath, he grabbed her and held her within his arms.

"I'm glad you came back," he spoke into her ear.

"Couldn't never leave ya," she cooed.

Their lips pushed together. After a moment, he lifted her off the ground while keeping the kiss going, her lithe body firm in his arms, turning around and around.

"Ya shore did grow up mighty strong," she said when they broke from the kiss.

"My pa was a big man," he said, almost apologetic. "He could carry a tuba. On his back. Play it, too." He reluctantly set her down on the ground.

"An' he gots that red hair!"

He grinned, happy like he'd never been before. "Same."

"We gotta do sumpin' 'bout that. People gonna remember ya from that hair. An' yer beard that's growin' out." She put her hand to his cheek. "Ya kin scrape it off. Gonna mark ya ever' time we go into a town. Folks be sayin' that girl gang an' that red devil."

"Then I'll cut it off. I'll shave this beard too, even though it ain't much yet."

"That beard's nuff fer me to call ya man."

That made him smile brighter, made his chest puff a bit.

"Then I'll grow it more," he said proudly. "I don't care. They can know me by my red beard. They gonna fear me!"

"First we better get to the new camp," she said, putting her hand to his chest. "Lawmen's gonna be down on us purdy quick."

"Nobody knows we're here," he said, just as his lips were silenced by her fingers.

"Ain't it the truth," she spoke softly, coyly. "It's just you an' me now. So whaddaya gonna do 'bout it?"

+   +   +

Making a supper of what foods they could eat without cooking, they sat back satisfied, comparing belches.

"Ain't ready ta go back there yet," said Trina, huddled by the fire she made after scrounging kindling and using her knife and flint to spark it. "Rather stay here."

"I'm happy to be here with you, too. Just you. Not your sisters."

"Yeah, they's handfuls," she said with a chuckle.

"Should've cooked them veggies," he muttered, seeing her work.

She warmed water in a small pot from her saddle bag, enough to add leaves from plants she gathered from her travels, called it 'tea'. They took turns drinking it straight out from the pot.

"Ah, this is the life, ain't it?" Bart spoke, adding a long sigh as he lay his head back against the saddle on the ground. "Just you and me, and some hot tea."

"Gonna need more 'an that," she called to him from the edge of the pool, "if we's livin' out here a spell."

She began washing the pot in the pool, then packed things away in her saddle bags. He watched her, wondering if it was really time to go. He wanted more time alone with her.

"They gonna be wond'rin' where's she at. Thinkin' I got jumped, or worse." She kept talking, sharing the stories in her head like she never had anyone to tell them to before. Lots of incidents where they were thieving, where they held guns to folks to get them to give up whatever they had, how they stormed into this bank or that bank – yet they had to hide away where they couldn't spend the notes they stole.

"I never suspected you did so much," he called to her as she went around gathering their belongings. "Gotta admit, I was scared of you three when I first seen you. Usually, bunch of women gonna hate a man, gonna wanna get vengeance on him, on any man they come across, for whatever some particular man did to 'em sometime past. Can't blame 'em for feeling that way, doing what some do."

"Not me," she said, then paused. "Ain't had no man 'til you."

Trina was digging in his saddle bag, looking for the bullets that must've spilled out of the broken box. She found two. And a book.

"What's this?" she called to Bart.

He looked up, squinted. "Oh, I got that from the wreckage."

"What wreckage?"

"The airplane," he responded.

"Airplane? What's that?"

He frowned. "You don't know what an airplane is?" He shook his head, understanding the sisters never had any education, never saw a book growing up. He pitied her but also felt superior.

"Lotta old things laying about the world, leftover from before the pandemic. You remember hearing about that, I bet." She gave a nod. "That's one of the things that ended. See, airplane's like a *bus* – you know what a bus is? Those electric carriages that bear a dozen people at once?"

"Seen 'em in bigger towns. So airplane's like a bus?"

He laughed. "Kinda. But airplane has wings so it can go up into the sky."

"Into sky?" She seemed not to believe him. "How?"

"Well, I never did see it myself. They stopped flying before I was born. Never made any new ones, I guess. Still haven't. They lost all that information: how to make airplanes, how to make it fly."

"You mean ta tell me people got into one o' them things an' they drove into the air just like a bus do?"

"Yep, kinda like getting on a bus. But you have to put a belt on when you sit on the seat so you won't fall out. I saw the seats had belts fixed to them. That's what I saw: an airplane. Like it crashed on the road as it came back to the earth."

"It came back to earth?"

"I think they tried to touch down gently but they must've hit too hard and the wheels broke off. Wings, too. But for some reason the people in it stayed in it, with their belts on."

"It crashed. Why'd they stay in it?"

"All I can figure is they were dead by then. My mama had a lotta books and I read them, looked at pictures, all kinds of things, like airplanes. They can fly by machinery inside them. Maybe the people inside died while it was flying in the sky. Then it came down by a command – but they're already dead. That's what I figure."

"Tough them dying up in the sky an' never knowin' when they got back to the ground."

"Yeah, I guess. But they didn't feel nothing if they were already dead. I got inside and saw the bodies, just bones now. Almost ran out, scary as they look, still strapped to their seats."

"That's awful."

"So what I found was lots of papers. I put some in my bag to look at later, see what they say. But mostly numbers. Like science stuff. Too much for me. And I found that book. It's only got writing on the first pages so I figure I can write on the rest of the pages. Now I just need to get some ink pens."

"So what's it say?"

"I didn't read it. Not much anyways. Some fellow writing his last thoughts."

She stared at the first page. "What it say?"

He smiled to himself, thanked his mama, glad that she sent him to school.

"You never learned your letters and numbers?"

"No, din't." She frowned. "Mama din't know an' I was too young when Pa got killed. Maybe Trinity learn some."

"I can teach you. I went to school all eight years. Plus my mama made me read at home."

She lifted the book, keeping the pages open. "So what it say?"

He went to her, squatted beside her, gazing over her shoulder at the first page. It took a moment for his eyes to trace the curved lines that made words.

"Hold on." He kept his eyes moving over the scribbling.

"Come on," she urged, jostling him. "Read it."

"Hold on. I *am* reading it."

"But ain't hear nothin' ya sayin'."

"I'm reading it in my head first. Getting the words right."

"In yer head? How ya do that?"

"Shush." Then, with a quick breath, he read it aloud:

"I, Solomon Wise, being of sound mind and body, do hereby bequeath my entire fortune - or whatever may remain of it - to whoever can find it in these dark apocalyptic times. Try looking in Area 32. Having left my family and home for the safety of our vacation home, I beg forgiveness from all my colleagues and my patients. I hope to find a solution to our disastrous endeavors."

He paused, finger stuck on the page where he stopped reading.

"I don't know some words but you can figure 'em from the other words, what it all means."

"So what it mean?" she pressed. "What's Area Thirty-two?"

"I dunno. Some place near here. Maybe the same place they was going to when they crashed."

"And what's that 'apocalyptic times' mean, huh? Is it now?"

Taking the book in his hands, he stared down at the page, then flipped to the next page. Written there was a long list of items. Most were things you'd find in a house, personal possessions. At the bottom were numbers and the names of banks.

"So this fella, he got some things he wanna give to somebody," Trina said with a sigh. "He dead now, ya said."

"Yep, dead. Just bones in a seat. He's never gonna need any of the things he list. That's how it works: You know you're gonna die so you say who gets your things after you."

"But he din't put any names on the page."

"Just wrote 'whoever', which can be anybody. Maybe people he'd give his things to are already dead. Or else he knew none of them could get to his things, didn't know where they were put."

"Maybe it's all in that Area Thirty-two he wrote about there."

He turned to gaze into her eyes, and a grin erupted on her face.

"You think so?" he asked her.

"Seems a place to go lookin' fer what he got stashed there."

"But who knows where that place could be? Nothing around here but grass and rocks."

"Ya said there was a chart in the wreckage."

"The map?" He thought a moment. "I remember. Showed all the towns around here. All the trails between. At the top it said 'United States of America' or something like that."

"What's that?" She tilted her face up to him in that sly way she had to let him know she was playing with him. "America, I mean."

He grinned at her playfulness, then got serious. "My mama said it was the name of this land before all that bad stuff happened. Like that pandemic or plague or whatever they talk about. Seems it was a larger country back then. Went from one coast to other coast." He pointed west. "Out there somewhere."

"Nobody ever go that way," said Trina solemnly. "Only death that way. Ever'body know it."

"Just mountains. There used to be roads, broken up by now."

"Cain't go that way," she insisted, sensing his interest in it.

"Maybe they were flying over there. Maybe they didn't make it, had to stop where they did. And they were all dead."

She gave a yawn. "Guess it just a mystery."

"Yep, a mystery."

He sat back, thought about what he saw there in the wreckage. After a while he got up and dug out the papers he saved, tried to lay them out flat in a row across the ground but the breeze kept trying to rearrange them. He leaned down, nose nearly grazing the pages, studying the numbers, most in columns, a few marked with a pen.

"I think they're measurements," he said, then looked up at her.

She stood there, her clothing off her, barefoot on the soil, a hand raised to beckon him.

"Gosh," he uttered, his jaw low, mouth open.

He scrambled up.

"Getcher rags off," she cooed. "Wanna see my man."

He quickly obeyed and they entered the pool, hands clasped, and paddled about in a tight embrace.

"Hafta get more food," said Trina as they swirled in the pool.

"I rather stay here with you." His grin faded as thoughts turned serious. Decisions intruded as a moment became an entire life.

"Just you an' me? That's crazy," she said, then kissed him.

Drying themselves, they lay together under the saddle blankets snatched from Betty and Brownie, Trina's dun mare with a black mane. The horses whickered together, seemed to be friends. The man and woman likewise together took refuge in each other, soon became one.

14

SHORTGRASS TRAIL

RELAXING ON THE SHORE in the afternoon, the sun drawing back from the edge of the rocks, he turned to her. Sliding his hand down her sleek body, he leaned in for a kiss. But she took his hand and guided it between her legs. She welcomed him there. He didn't know what he was doing but it seemed such a natural thing – like they were that old couple in the book his mama read to him as a child: the first two people in the world, living their lives in a walled garden.

This rocky outpost was hardly a garden, although there were trees and brush around its rim, bushes below, some with berries, several pretty flowers, and a few of what Trina called 'tasty leaves' that his mama called 'herbs' though he dared not correct her. She'd make a tea and they'd drink from the same cup. It relaxed him and he could lay beside her, hold her, and feel that God was far away, unconcerned what they did in their privacy.

She hadn't a clue either, she said. She just felt things that drew them together, like an invisible hand pushed her upon him, made her want him, and got her to welcome him like it was something she herself wanted but without her even thinking about it. He felt the same way, like he was acting without thinking. She recalled how her pa would lay over her ma at night, the blanket covering them, and how he grunted and grunted, how her ma simply lay still until his grunting stopped.

"So's how 'bout I try on top this time?" she asked.

He confessed he never read a book telling what folks do in their privacy. His cousin Jake once told him of witnessing a saloon gal and a drunk man trying to push together out back of the saloon one night, the man standing behind her and she bending over, and how that tale got him excited in ways he hadn't expected. Had dreams of saloon gals after that.

"Well, it makes you look like a cowgirl riding a bronco," he said with a chuckle. "Yippee-ki-yay!"

"Woo-hoo!" she cried, bouncing on him like he was a horse.

They got too loud, could've drawn any close lawmen upon them, so they stopped, realizing that something happened. He dared gaze into her dark eyes as she bent forward against him. But in her eyes he saw himself and suddenly looked away.

Hiding his shame, she pulled his face back to her.

"Ain't got nothin' to feel shame for," she whispered to him. "Part o' ya bein' a man."

She inspected him, found everything to be proper.

"Ya did good," she said. "Real good. But dang it shore hurt ma legs, doin' it thatta way."

Her words had a way of soothing ill feelings and that most of all was why he loved her. He decided it was love but not the kind he felt toward his mama or any of his kin, not even the schoolgirls he felt attraction for. This was different.

"Honest, Trina," he said once they'd finished that same exercise, apologizing to no one, "in that black leather get-up you like to wear, you look like a devil woman. I kinda shiver in my boots. But then you take 'em off and I ain't never seen nothing as beautiful as you. And that includes couple times I caught sight of my mama when she was having her bath."

She giggled. "Better 'an yer ma?"

He realized what he'd said, flashed a grin, then got serious.

"I never had no thoughts of anybody like you." He proceeded to list all the attributes that made his heart soften and his body tense. She nodded at each one as though she agreed.

"I'm just born, is all." She leaned in, kissed his lips. "Ain't done nothin' to make ya fall fer me."

"That's the best part," he said. "So I had this thought...."

He slipped away for a while.

"Yeah? About what?" Trina asked to draw him back.

"Just thinking."

"What about?"

"Nothing."

"About us?"

"No.... That woman I shot dead."

He stared at her, saw in her eyes his mama scolding him, finger pointing down at him. What happened? He wasn't sure. Maybe that woman didn't die. Maybe it was only a flesh wound that would give her an interesting story to tell. His mama told interesting stories, like how her horse tripped over her and broke her hip bone, sent her to a wheel-chair for three years. He wondered why the woman in the store reminded him of his mama.

"Bart?" called Trina. "Y'awright?"

He shook himself back to the present, felt the breeze on his face, saw her stretched out beside him, risen on her elbows, her brown skin a sight equal to that garden in the big book his mama read to him. The tiniest smile on her placid face warmed him, brought him back from that dark place his mama liked to call a fox burrow.

"Go someplace?" Trina got up, went to get a cloth to wipe off. His gaze followed her, locking on the sleek brown body that moved so beautifully.

The evening grew cool and they gathered themselves, dressed again, as they boiled the last string beans. Later, still hungry, they huddled under blankets, talking of the future – the next day and the one after, how they'd get food and start their life together. Or else go on to the new camp and face Trinity who would be plenty angry for taking so long and arriving with no food to show.

In the night Bart awoke screaming, starting a coyote howling.

"Mama!" he cried out, sitting up straight. "I shot my mama!"

Trina awoke beside him, put her arm around him, head against his shoulder, saying "Easy, easy now."

He was breathing hard, sweat running down his body.

"I dreamed it was my mama I shot back there," he sputtered.

"Ain't yer mama ya shot," she spoke softly. "Just a woman got no

175

name. Got no face."

"No," he snapped, trying to push her away. "She had my mama's face. She looked just like Mama."

"Weren't yer mama, Bart. Just a woman you never knowed."

"No, it was her."

"In yer dream maybe she was. But that ain't real. Yer head makin' up stories to trick ya. A demon's after ya, is all."

He understood but remained agitated and only calmed with the paling of the eastern sky. He knew for certain that demons haunted the world, strode across the land on a hunt, whispering into the ears of guilty folks, coaxing them to come follow.

+ + +

The morning sun painting the tops of the rocks like a stairway to heaven, stretching down to the limpid pool. He was confused at first, but got the hint. He stripped down and joined her. Swimming left them giddy, in waves of delight, smooching and embracing as they spun in the water like children having no care. The sun warmed the pool by the time they pulled each other onto the shore. They lay naked on the hard soil as the sun striped their skin, the trees moving in the breeze.

Rolling against each other, skin slippery, they pressed their lips together.

"I love you," said the woman, catching her breath. Then saw his surprise. "Only heard Ma say to Pa once or twice. Don't know what it means."

He threw himself off her, lay huffing and puffing beside her but took her hand tight in his. "It means she got strong feelings for him and probably he does for her, too."

"That what I mean then. I got strong feeling fer ya."

"And I do for you."

"Then it's true thing," she whispered, gazing up at the sky.

Other than a short break to make a lunch from what remained in the General Store box, boiling it in the pot, they remained like the First People, naked and unashamed. They danced by the pool. They returned to the water, holding each other as if a baptism. On shore they mated like savages: rough then gentle then rough again to the point of exhaustion.

"We best be goin' to the new camp," she told him when he rolled off her and tried to catch his breath.

The night grew deep and they got the rest they needed to hit the trail in the morning.

The path was too worn to be overlooked by pursuing lawmen. A child could find the way to their camp through the rocks, seeing the pool where they swam, spots where they'd raised tents, where they slept, made a fire. Lawmen wouldn't find them there, however, long departed for parts unknown.

"I'll always remember that place," Bart told Trina as they rode side by side over the shortgrass range with no town in sight.

They made a meal of what foodstuffs were getting old, kept the hard vegetables in the paper box tied behind his saddle. Everything else was gone – but for the sack of bullets, neat in their boxes. Trina was proud of him, took her share of bullets to fill up her bandoleer, making sure her pistols were fully loaded in case they met trouble.

"Pair like you an' me's gonna meet a whole heap o' trouble," she called over to him as they rode. "No way around it. Trouble's gonna keep after us."

"I'll get in trouble with you," he called to her. "But only you."

An easy ride through the morning, pausing so the horses could drink from a creek. By noontide, they paused again under a grove of trees. Bart and Trina sat beneath the trees, welcoming the shade as the day grew hot. A few sips from the stream, wetting rags to wipe their faces and necks.

Riding on, the mountains rising ahead appeared higher than he ever imagined. The peaks were white. It must be snow, he decided. *Gotta be cold up there. Hope it ain't where the new camp is.*

They came upon one of those old, broken roads, the line of stone curving on toward the mountains. A few rusted hulks of vehicles, big and small, rested on the remains of the road or sat to the side. They slowed to inspect them, one after another. He reminded her of how such vehicles used to be common but when everything fell apart there wasn't any fuel to make them go. When they stopped, the people in them could only walk. Many were already infected with the virus. Like in the stories his mama told.

"Ya keep on tellin' it like ya don't never want to furgit it," Trina spoke sternly. "It's old news. Best furgit it now."

"Mama said if we forget what happened it can happen again."

"She did, did she?" She frowned at him. "Mamas say a lot."

The rusted hulks had been sitting there quite a long time, glass windows smashed, insides ravaged by the weather. At least there were no skeletons, he thought, not like in that airplane.

"Wait," Trina cried.

He looked up, followed her eyes down the stone road.

Far ahead was movement. Someone approaching. Pulling a cart. A few people, large and small. Maybe a family, he decided.

"What'll we do?" he asked Trina.

Her hand slipped down to the pistol on her hip. "Ain't lawmen, I reckon. Not with 'em pullin' a cart. Family, maybe?"

"Way out here?" he quizzed, rising in his saddle to peer ahead. "I count two adults, two children."

"Ya shore got sharp eyes," she said with a chuckle.

"That's the way we have to go, right? We can't avoid them."

She gave a nod as she squinted down the road. "Lookit."

"They're gonna arrive here. We go on. They go on. No trouble." It seemed like a question, but she didn't respond. "Just gonna let 'em pass by, right?"

"Lemme see who they are."

By then the group ahead had noticed the two riders and reacted to the same situation. What to do? This wasn't territory where laws commanded any respect. They might be only a family pulling a cart, thought Bart, but they could pull rifles out from under a canvas and shoot them, then cut them up for food. It was that kind of territory they were crossing.

He took his pistol out, held it ready as the group approached. He could see them clearly as they halted a few yards away. Two women in long skirts, blouses dark with sweat. Two kids followed, looking ten and eight. They were folks like him but they narrowed their eyes at Trina as she leaned forward on her horse.

"Morning," Bart called out, not raising his hand in greeting but keeping his pistol poised.

The women set the cart down with a huff – a vehicle just large enough to bear their meager possessions, two wooden wheels, staves riding on their shoulders as though they were mules. They brushed off collected dirt from themselves.

"Good day, sir," the younger of the two women responded.

"Long way from home, ain'tcha?" he called to them.

"Home is where we heading," the woman replied.

"That's still a long way. We come from that way."

The older woman stepped forward as if in pain, giving a tweak to her shoulders, a sharp snap of her neck.

"Might you, dear sir, have a bit of water for the young'uns?" She waved the kids to come stand in front of her.

She's playing on my feelings. Bart had seen that act before.

"Ain't got none," Trina spoke before Bart could answer.

"We have only enough to get us home," he said like an apology, "and that's a long way. But there's a creek about a mile behind us."

Trina cleared her throat, spit to the ground.

"Where ya comin' from? Where ya goin' to?" she barked.

The older woman flinched, flashed a nervous smile. "Ma'am, it's a long way we come, from a homestead near fifty mile thatta way," and she swung her arm back in the direction they'd come. "No more home since lightning struck our house and it burnt down. Pa and Papaw got burnt tryin' to put it out. We's tryin' to make next town, figure's gotta be Skinner Canyon though it's mighty far."

"That's a sad story," said Bart, leaning forward, arms crossed with the pistol still in his hand.

"Then we best be ridin' on," Trina said to him.

"Fifty miles?" asked Bart of the older woman. "There's a town out that way?"

"No, sir, not a town. Only us, a farm family," the woman replied, "only us making a homestead for three generations. We come west a hunert year ago or there'bout. Our kin was escaping the plague."

Bart let go a chuckle. "Sounds like my family."

Trina gave him a look that shut him up.

"How about you?" she asked the younger woman.

"Me? I'm her daughter," said the woman. "These my kids, Jeffery and Mindy. All I got now. My older boy, Jason, he died in the fire."

Trina regarded the woman, focused on her blouse, stained yet once a pretty garment with frilly lace down the front.

"Pretty shirt ya got," said Trina. "Lemme see it."

"See it?" the woman asked. "What for? It ain't nothing nice no more, not after all this cart pulling."

"Then ya don't mind givin' it over," said Trina in a rough voice, pulling out her pistol.

"What?" Bart snapped.

"I like it," Trina said to him. "You kin wash it later an' I look real purdy fer ya."

"But you always look pretty—"

The younger woman stared at the pistol, began unbuttoning the blouse. The top one seemed to be missing, torn off in her labor. She jerked the hem out from the waistband of her long skirt, shook it free. She slid an arm out, then the other, held the blouse up.

"Here," she said sadly. "Take it."

Bart stared at the woman's bare chest, expecting to see an undergarment like his mama wore. Instead, he had to compare this woman's creamy bosom, drooping with their weight, with what he recalled of Trina's smaller brown breasts. He smiled.

Trina urged her mount forward and snatched the blouse from the woman's hand.

"Mighty fine work, this one."

"I have another in our cart," the woman said.

"Clean?" asked Trina.

"I wore it already, but it's washed a few days ago. Lots better than that one."

"Seems so." Trina gestured for her to get the fresher blouse from the cart and they exchanged them.

Bart watched the woman put on the sweat-soaked blouse again and fix herself. She glanced at him, knowing he'd seen her chest. You could get people to do all sorts of things if you got a gun to wave at them. Trina knew how to do that. No hard words, just look tough and have a gun.

Trina held up the blouse, admiring it.

"So we're done here?" Bart asked her.

"Yep." She stuffed the blouse into her saddle bag.

"Good day to y'all," he said with a tip of his hat.

He prodded Betty onward. Trina followed on Brownie. Neither of them gave a look back at the destitute family. He thought of how they would survive. Far worse folks they could've encountered with a far worse result, too. He believed he acted fair.

The shortgrass extended to the horizon before them, a mountain range rising ahead, always seeming far away, never getting closer. Hours later they came to a dirt road leading up the hillside where a blackened skeleton of a farmhouse stood, the yard's grass a carpet of brown, no beasts behind the fences. Other houses sat nearby, like it had once been a village. But they saw feathers laying on the ground and caught in bushes, signs of a visit by tribals of one kind or another. Beside the ruins stood three crosses made of thin planks ripped from a fence.

STEPHEN SWARTZ

15

HIDEOUT

THEY MADE A CAMP at the base of the mountains, what turned out to be foothills. Twisted oaks gave them shelter. They dared make a fire to cook up the last potato, made a stew but had no meat. Bart offered to hunt for a rabbit or quail but Trina expected he'd miss and waste bullets. They needed the bullets for defense if they came upon lawmen or strangers.

"You ever decide what you're gonna do with your life?" he asked Trina as they lay together on the cold ground despite a blanket beneath them and one over them.

She grinned in the darkness. "Ain't never had no choice. Never wanna be nothin'. This what I am."

"I know what you mean. My mama wanted me to do all sorts of things I never liked doing."

"Folks get born, never ask fer it, then they expect us to do what they want us to do, no chance to decide fer ourself."

"Yeah, parents. They're the worst."

The morning was disturbed by the shaking of the ground and the noise of horses approaching, so they packed up quickly and galloped off. They knew the squad of horsemen had spied them, and taken to pursuit. Five of them, Bart saw, glancing back. He rode against his horse like Trina did, keeping his head down. Following her, they raced awkwardly over the uneven ground until they broke free and flew across the dusty plain.

A shot whizzed by Bart and he ducked lower against Betty.

Trina shouted over to him but he couldn't understand as they veered apart. He tried to turn Betty but she wouldn't move, instead slowed, and he tried to get her going but the horse was winded.

He could see the horsemen coming on hard. They looked like the posse his Uncle Frank led. He wondered if these were bandits or lawmen, and which would give him the better justice. If they caught up to him, they might shoot him for no good reason, just thinking he must be a criminal if he was found out here.

"Come on," he commanded and his horse sprung into a gallop.

He raced after Trina, heading into the hills again.

Slowing to maneuver up a steep trail through the trees, he found her waiting in the shadows.

"Who are they?" she called back to him.

"Don't know," he said, coming beside her in the shade, the trees rustling around them. "They shot at me. Never even ask questions. Couldn't've got a sight on me. They don't know if I'm friend or foe."

Trina gave a laugh. "Yer both."

They waited a while. Trina snuck down the trail on foot, spying through the trees but didn't see anyone below. She crept back up to Bart and mounted her horse.

"Look clear," she said. "Keep yer gun ready."

Riding slowly down the trail, a bird sang out, a pair of squirrels scattered off the path, and Bart smiled. He looked ahead at Trina, a woman he loved. Older than him, she was more like a sister but one who loved him, too, but in unsisterly ways. She knew a lot about the range, riding and shooting, camping and cooking, surviving. He knew a little about being a cowpoke, how to ride in a herd of cattle, make them go this way or that. Not much else he knew except for books his mama made him read, books about how wonderful the world was a hundred years before.

So why'd it come to be the way it is now? he wondered – and got a tree branch slapping him in the face.

The posse had gone, or else hid. Either way, the two galloped at a bright pace over the rough terrain, rising higher, cutting through the wooded hills. Slowing to make their way through the trees, they gazed back, found nobody following them and eased their pace. After a few miles' steady riding, they paused at a creek.

"That was close," said Trina, putting her hand up to her brow to scan the territory they'd traversed.

"Can't think who they might be," Bart spoke up, squatting.

"Ain't got nothin' ta do with that woman ya shot?"

"Maybe," he said, making a face like he didn't want to talk about it. "Or that foolish clerk."

"They track ya to the camp, I reckon."

"But we lost them."

She turned to him. "Main thing is, ya gotta check yer bullets. We ain't got a lot an' they not makin' a lot no more."

He nodded, understanding. "That clerk in the store said so."

"An' some yer gonna miss, so it's waste."

"I don't miss." He lowered his voice: "Maybe from a horse."

"Just ya take good aim, make it count."

"How much further?" he asked, anxious to change the subject.

She looked ahead, measuring the hills, glancing at the sun.

"Be there tonight," she said coldly.

They mounted up and rode on, trotting on even ground, walking up rises and down slopes.

They came upon the broken road again as it bent through the hills. Once a king's highway it was a line of rocks now unsuitable for traveling over by machine or horse. They maneuvered alongside, the way narrowing and forcing them single-file on the edge.

After a short way, the road split and a smaller line led to an old building half fallen, leaning to the side, roof slumping. All old buildings were the same way, he observed. In front of the hut stood four short pillars rising from the ground. A roof had stretched over them but it had fallen long ago, now resting on the pillars.

"What's *Chevron* mean?" Trina asked, motioning toward marks on each pillar: parallel lines like an army soldier's sleeves. Each of the pillars had tubing curling out from them like snakes sleeping on the broken stone.

"I dunno," he replied.

"Ain'tcha school boy?"

"Never saw these before." He thought of those pictures in books in his mama's house. He looked carefully at the hut. "I think this is where carriages got fuel. See, they had to stop when fuel got used up and needed more." He pointed to two pillars to the side. "Them over there give you electric and these give you gasoline. From what I read." He pointed to the hut. "You go inside there to pay."

"Nothing for horses?" she said, adding a snicker.

"Didn't ride horses back then," he said, sadness poking him. The stories his mama told about her family, going far back, played on his feelings. Suddenly he understood why she kept telling him the stories: to tie him to them, make him never forget.

"So it damn useless," Trina grumbled.

"Yep. Long ago, folks went around in those machines: carriages run by motors, not pulled by horses."

"Now don'tcha go spillin' yer tales," she snapped. "Ain't got time fer none o' that."

Pulling their horses away from drinking, they mounted and rode on as the sun began its descent into the west. The eastern sky's blue slate darkened.

"Nothing out here," Trina said as they rode. "Maybe the reason folks had that road, trying to go away to 'nother place, better place. Hope fer safe life somewhere west o' here."

"Yeah, like that Skinner fellow coming out and starting his own town by the canyon. Maybe we can start our own town."

Trina gave him a queer look.

"That's what my mama told me," he said. "She's always right."

"Dammit!" she barked. "'Nuff talk o' yer ma! I'm yer ma now."

"You ain't my ma." He tried to laugh, but he realized what she meant. "You're what? four, five years older than me? Ain't enough to be my mama. Hah! And you sure ain't my sister. But, anyways, you sure are bossy like a big sister."

"Y'ain't my brother, neither." She gave him a snarl. "Fact is, we doin' that thing ya like doin', so t'ain't no reason be treatin' me no diff'rent. That higgity-piggity jumpin' 'round ya do. That's whole lot more 'an bein' yer ma, more 'an bein' yer sister cuz neither them ever s'pose to do no squiggly-wiggly all night, what ya like doin' cuz ain't nothin' but two fools playin' 'round feelin' good 'fore sleepin' is all we doin'. So it's only you an' me now, not yer mama an' not my sisters. Just us. Unnerstand?"

He had to grin, seeing her upset over nothing. "I do understand. I sure know what you are. You're my woman. My wife."

"Ain't yer woman," she said, feigning anger. Then she broke into a grin. "Not yer wife, neither. I'm my own woman. Don't belong to nobody. You an' me, we's partners, is all. Don'tcha furgit."

+ + +

Trina led him through a narrow canyon into an area looking much like the old hideout. His hand slid over the smooth rock walls, streaked in red and brown, as Betty squeezed her rump through the gap, nervous and hesitant. Bart urged her on and they came into the arena where two tents sat and a campfire crackled. He saw the frame of what looked like the start of a hut, floor marked off with boards, one frame risen and flat boards in place, blocking the view of the interior. It wasn't much larger than one of the tents.

"I see y'all got a cabin going," said Bart. "My mama built herself a whole house. Got two floors with a staircase. Mighty fancy place. I got to watch 'em put it up when I was young."

"Ain't no need you spitting on our work," Trinity said in a gruff tone. She waved a welcome at Trina but offered only a scowl to the man she'd brought back with her.

"Wasn't spitting nothing," said Bart, dismounting. "Just saying out my thoughts."

"Yer thoughts ain't 'preciated here. Otherwise ya kin ride on out an' don't never come back," Trinity snarled.

"Leave him be," called Trina. She dismounted and tugged the horse behind her, over to the others. "He's a man now, got his own ways, an' I'm gonna bring him in my tent, no matter what y'all say 'bout 'im."

"Yer makin' big mistake, girl," Trinity growled.

"She just want him layin' top o' her," Triss said with a laugh.

"More 'an that," Trina came back. "He's a full man now."

"Shore is," Triss giggled.

Ignoring the silly sister, Bart and Trina unpacked their horses. He followed her over to the tent that was to be his. They set up their goods, then returned to deliver the paper box of the remaining vegetables to Trinity.

"It's all that's left," Bart said sadly. "I had to eat some. Had to ride hard to get away. Might've been after me."

Trinity looked up from where she squatted, fixing beans in a pot. "Who's after ya? I told ya to make shore nobody follow ya." She went for the shotgun leaning nearby against the rock wall.

"He's clean," said Trina, holding a hand up.

Trinity set the shotgun against the rock again.

"Nobody followed me," said Bart. "I took a roundabout way. I got away clean. Even though I had to shoot somebody. Or two."

"Ya what?" Trinity cried out, glancing at Trina. "Ya s'pose to get away clean. Shootin' ain't no clean getaway. They see ya?"

"It was kinda accident, see."

"They catch sight o' ya?" Trinity pressed. "Damn red hair's a mark they gonna remember."

"He's gonna shave," Trina spoke up.

"Who ya shoot?" asked Trinity.

He suddenly felt the weight of his crime. "The clerk."

"The clerk?" Trinity was alarmed. "What'd he do?"

Bart was about to tell her how the clerk didn't respect him. But that wasn't the real reason he shot him. No, it was just a random act, not even a decision, only a reflex. He never decided in his mind to squeeze the trigger. He got startled by the mother screaming and the pistol was already aimed. Then that clerk brought the hammer down.

Trinity let go a string of curse words, shaking her head. Then to Trina: "Ya brung him back here, straight to us here? Bunch o' fools. Now we gonna hafta move again."

"It's awright," Bart spoke out. "Nobody followed us. We lost 'em. Went far out east before coming back this way. And nobody followed us coming here."

"An' he found a...what's it? *Air-o-plane*," Trina cut in.

"But ya shot somebody!" Trinity was clearly mad. "Ain'tcha seen how we do it? Ya show yer guns, folks get obeying, no need ta shoot nobody. Got it?" She shook her head. "Ya had notes, didn't ya? S'posed to buy what we sent ya for. No need to flash yer gun."

"I put the damn credits on the damn counterboard," Bart said, raising his voice to match hers.

The realization hit them both at the same instant.

"Ya left the notes there? An' ya still go shootin'?"

Bart's pale face turned red. "Yep. I guess I did. I was planning to pay for everything like you told me. But things changed. The clerk got suspicious when I asked about the ammo."

"It's all yer fault," Trinity curse at Trina.

"What I do? It's him that go shootin' folks," she barked back.

Trinity was huffing, face a mask of hatred. Bart grew afraid, knowing what she was capable of. He might find himself asleep one night only to awaken with his throat slit. He heard what she did to a man she pretended to like just to get him to relax with her so she could kill him. Cut away his manly parts, according to Trina who'd laughed when she told him.

"I'm sorry," Bart said, conceding. "I knew what I was supposed to do and I did most of it. I got the foodstuff and the ammo. I was ready to pay for it good and proper. But the situation changed. It changed in a flash and I did what I had to do."

Trinity gave a nod, glanced at Trina, then returned her glare to Bart, holding her anger. "Ya got the food things. And bullets."

"He done good," Trina insisted.

"And y'all tried moving camp when I was gone," Bart said with an edge to his voice.

"I come back fer ya," said Trina.

Trinity met Bart's eyes. "We moved the camp cuz lawmen been gettin' too close, scoutin' us. Ain't got nothin' to do with you, boy."

"Easy now," said Trina, seeing him steaming at the word.

"Awright," Bart said gruffly. "I got lots to learn. I messed up. I'll do better. Next time."

"He'll do better," Trina echoed. "I teach him."

Triss broke into her snickering laughter which annoyed him.

"So," spoke Trinity in a calm voice, "you left the notes there? On the counterboard. All bundle up with the bank's ribbon.... That right?"

Bart swallowed hard. "Yep. Guess I did."

"So they gonna know what bank they from, right?"

"Uh...yep."

"So they kin figure out who robbed that bank a while back."

Bart grew paler. "Maybe. Bet they get robbed a lot."

"So now those folk know it was us robbed that bank. And we sent a stupid boy to get some food." Her voice had hardened again and he grew wary. "And he goes an' shoots the clerk."

"There was also a mother and daughter in the store," said Bart.

"Two customers?" Trinity shook her head. "Shoot 'em?"

"Only the mother. Maybe. I'm not sure if the shot hit her. It's maybe just a wound."

"Maybe?"

"But the clerk, he got it full in the chest. Up close." He raised his hand to mark the location. He showed his bruised hand. "Then dropped him like a sack of beans."

Trinity laid a highway of curses as she glared at him. Nothing Trina could do; he'd acted badly.

"We moved camp. Had to," Trinity spoke as calmly as she could, "so no way they find us. An' no thanks to you, we gotta move camp again, just when we gettin' a hut set up. Better we send ya off then us move again. Don't need no fool with us."

"If that's what you want," he offered sternly.

"No," said Trina, stepping forward.

"No?" asked Trinity, staring hard at her sister. "Yer goin' off wit' him? Is that it?"

"I want us all ta stick together," said Trina. "Bart's a good man. He'll be a good part of our gang. He can learn."

"That boy ain't good," Triss chuckled. "That baby man is bad."

"So what if Bart's bad," Trina responded. "We just as bad. He fit with us. Gonna be bad like us. It's what we do."

"Bad only lasts so long," said Trinity, eyes moving to Bart. "Ya get old sooner or later. Ya lose yer speed. Get sloppy. Get old. Ya get tired o' runnin' an' some day it ends – fast 'n' furious. Lawmen catch up witcha. Down ya go. Nothin' ya e'er did matters no more. Done. An' who're ya then? Who were ya? Nobody gonna remember – only if ya done something great, or ya done something evil, like the worse thing ever. Like that Spike Thorsen: shot up that family after they let him sleep over. Pure evil, that one. They caught 'im an' hung 'im." Her eyes narrowed at Bart. "Lot worse 'an shootin' some mother an' daughter."

"Only the mother," Bart said quietly. "And she probably only got nicked, not killed."

"Or Wayne Forrestal over in Wichita, killed that whole family. Slowly. Like he wanted to draw it out. He left 'em swinging on ropes from the ceiling, slicing off bits of flesh each day for his meal. Only one still alive when they got to them but missin' a lot of flesh. Now that one's evil, worst of 'em all."

"Dang," he muttered. "I ain't never gonna be that evil."

"No matter," said Trinity, shaking her head. "Always starts with small things ya do. Yer not evil, boy. Not yet. Yer a bad man. That's all. Yer bad at being bad. But they gotcha on a record now. Gonna be watching ya. Gonna catch ya someday. Maybe soon. Then what's yer mama gonna think o' ya?"

He smiled proudly. "She'll know me as Bad Bart."

+   +   +

Trinity squatted by the fire to finish her work, fixing the beans in a pot. She tore a few green leaves and sprinkled them in, stirred it.

"Beans-n-greens," Bart muttered at the sight, then he spoke louder: "I tried to bring ya what ya wanted, what ya wrote on that five-note. But, see, I had to rush out and some of it fell off. I got lost, so I ate some of it. And when I got back to the camp, the old one, Trina and me, we ate some. All that's left is the hard vegs but you're welcome to 'em. Got some bread, too, but I ate it. Got hungry out there. But you know what else I found?"

"He got us bullets," Trina cut in. "I loaded mine, rest's yours and shells for that shotgun, too."

Trinity almost grinned. "Boy done good." Then, after stirring the beans, "He kin go get us more."

Bart stood defiantly. "I'll go if you want, but I'll need notes."

"Cuz the fool left 'em behind," Triss snickered.

"They know him now," grumbled Trinity, stirring slowly. "That red hair anybody'll remember."

"I kin go with 'im," Trina spoke up.

"Ain't no use," Trinity said, adding a curse under her breath. She set the spoon down beside the fire. "Ever'body know us now. Why we move camp over here. Gotta start fresh. Gotta be on our own, make our own life away from ever'body."

She regarded Bart with her dark eyes. Something was different. Like she had a change of heart overnight.

"Gotta grow our own food, and hunt game," she went on. "If we wanna go on livin' – an' that's just the livin' part, ain't no kinda life really. Like what Pa did. Get up an' work, then go ta bed all achy fer a spell."

"It's a good spot for a camp," said Bart, relaxing a bit. "Secluded. Protected. I just meant it's easy to get blocked in. One fellow with a gun at the entrance to that short canyon and we're stuck here."

"Th' aim is nobody know we's here," Trinity countered.

"If you go out and do anything, somebody'll track you back here. Then they got you. All of us. Blocked in here."

"We're hidin' out fer while," said Trina. "Ain't forever."

To test his idea, he and Trina squeezed out through the canyon and rode across the shortgrass below the hills, watching flocks of birds break into the sky at their approach, dark clouds of them, saw them wing past the blue and orange clouds.

"My uncle picked a spot on a hill for his house," Bart called over to Trina, "where he can see in every direction, keep his eyes fixed on anybody coming. Course, folks can see him, too, up there on his hill."

They rode on a ways, letting the evening tease them, then rode back before the sky turned completely dark.

He offered to help with dinner but Trinity said she'd gotten used to him not being there and doing it herself. Had been since before he fell into their camp, in fact. Didn't need no man to help.

He grumbled about her being a bitch.

Triss urged him to take it back. Trina defended him. Trinity had words to say. The sisters started squabbling.

"All we got is what Pa left us," said Trina, her voice strained.

"And Ma too," Triss added.

"Everything else we got for ourself," said Trinity.

Trina laughed. "We stole it."

"But we need it so we deserve it," said Trinity.

Triss chuckled. "Shore wish we coulda stay in that town, livin' as fine young ladies."

"Hah!" Trinity snapped. "Young ladies? Of night? On beds? That what ya mean? Not like them whores, no ma'am. Ma didn't raise no whores!"

"We don't know nothing—" said Trina.

"No men woulda treat us right," said Triss.

"—Nothing but thieving."

"Them's skills," said Trinity. "Gotta find ways to use 'em that ain't criminal."

Trina smiled. "Maybe we kin get paid by some rich fella, maybe a rancher, an' do work fer him, like hassle folks owe him money."

"That shore be sum fun times," Triss laughed.

"Still think it be a whole lot better livin' in a town an' doin' somethin' normal for wages," said Trina, lowering her voice. Bart heard her but her sisters dismissed the idea. "We kin learn things. Ain't gotta be no man's wife. Just livin' our own way."

She looked up, caught him gazing at her, pinching her lips like she wanted to take back her silly words.

"Naw," said Trinity. "There ain't nothin' we know better 'an how to thieve. It's what we do. Like it's a wage job. Every week we go get us groceries. Like one of them standard families. Them that got kids."

Triss giggled at that. "With kids!"

16

SCHISM

RIDING INTO BOISE CITY once more, they weren't even inside the bank when Deputy Tanner brought his men to block them, telling them to get out of town. Trinity took exception to demands, shouting they were getting notes from their safe-box, which was their right. Tanner didn't believe them, ordered them to leave or they'd be arrested. Trina stood firm, rifle raised to her shoulder, pointing right at Tanner. Triss held a shotgun at her hip, ready to shoot. Bart had his pistols aimed at the horsemen beside Tanner.

The men rushed Trinity, knocked her down, wrestled her gun away and ripped her shirt open, shouting at them to give up or they'd shoot her right there in the street.

"Awrighty," called Bart. "Let her go."

He went toward them, acting like he would surrender, hands up but pistols grasped in them. And in a move too slick to figure out he brought his hands down in a flash, blasting away at the men that held Trinity until she could scramble to her horse. Three men lay wounded, one dead for sure by the ugly hole in his forehead. Deputy Tanner took a shot in his knee.

Bart followed the sisters, dodged a couple return shots, leapt on his horse and raced after the women.

"Again?" Trinity cursed as the other sisters waited outside town to let Bart rejoin them.

"Guess they won't be kind next time," he crowed, pulling reins as he arrived.

Bart saw the slick mess running down the side of Trina's horse, another spew from her belly, like she was sick, eating bad food.

"You awright?" he asked her.

"Yer eatin' same food as us," Trinity snarled at her.

"Gonna be awright," said Trina. "Gimme a moment."

"Ever' morn she keep spittin' up," Triss laughed.

Trinity glared at Bart. "It's yer fault. Makin' food she cain't eat."

"Maybe she gettin' sick from playin' round with that boy," Triss suggested and Trinity stared hard at her sister, then at Bart.

"Is it poison?" asked Trina, looking up from her bent position. "That stuff he gimme?"

Trinity stared hard at Bart, made him flinch.

"Hells bells!" she cursed. "Ain't no dang poison, but if'n ya get too much it'll make ya spit up fer shore. What the boy bin givin' ya ever' night. I remember Ma gettin' fat with ya, Trin'. She spittin' up ever' mornin', just like you."

"Ya mean when I's gettin' born?" asked Trina.

"Then you was born," Trinity answered.

"So that boy – that one right there, the red-haired boy – he fill ya up with poison 'til ya cain't stand it no more and out it comes," Triss explained, giggling throughout.

"Seem so," said Trinity with a catch in her voice.

Bart suddenly understood. He remembered his cousin Frances, a few weeks after her wedding day had the same illness. He heard the women calling it 'morning sickness' and chuckled at her plight and sighed in sympathy. He thought it happened when she hadn't had a good night's sleep. But he was a young boy, fresh from the capital, and didn't know about women.

"It's morning sickness," he announced.

"Ya gotta stop lettin' that boy in ya," Triss snickered.

"It's not that," Trina insisted, waving off Triss.

"The boy's right," said Trinity. "Reckon it is."

Trina tried to stand straight but she was clearly weak. "Right about what?"

Bart saw Trinity struggling to hide a grin.

"Ya got yer self sick with...with a babe comin'," she said. "Worst thing you kin be sick with. Gonna happen if yer gettin' together too much. Not shore how it goes. No time fer yer insides to breathe, fer yer body to deal with it." She shook her head. "I watched Ma goin' through the whole damn thing with you bein' born at th' end, Trin'. An' again when Triss was gettin' born."

"When I's gettin' born?" Triss gasped, like she thought she just appeared one day fully formed from a wild fruit torn open.

"Ya tellin' me I'ma gonna push out a babe like Ma done?" Trina was getting agitated. "How we s'pose ta know that? Nobody teach us nothin'."

She turned to Bart, her eyes full of desperation. He had a whole lot of sympathy for her, but he couldn't feel the change yet, the pure realization of what had occurred. Whenever there was any problem, his mama would always say: "We need to think on it."

"Sorry," he muttered, the best he could do in that moment.

Trina glared at him, her face still red from the strain. "Ya got yer book learnin', so why ya never teach me 'bout this?"

"I—I didn't know," was all he could say. "I only saw my cousin go through it, come to mind."

"Now we shore as heck need a safer camp," said Trinity sternly. "Far from folks. Baby cryin' ain't never good fer no hideout. Maybe best ya take yer man here an' go yer own way."

"No—"

"Don't need no baby givin' us away," Trinity spoke.

"But I—"

"I'll ride in her place, whatever we need to do," Bart declared.

"Awrighty," said Trinity. "We switch up. Trina is the camp girl, and this redhead fool is our other outlaw."

Bart grinned to himself, proud at being promoted. He regarded Trinity and she sensed his look, turned to him.

"Gotta thank ya fer gettin' me away from them gnarly men," she said. "You's a tricky sonuvagun, that's fer shore."

"We're all one family," he said with a humble bow of his head. "I'd come for any of you."

+ + +

The new band rode out to the northwest with a plan to get notes from the Bank of Buffalo Springs, then ride east to the village of Kerrick to buy food, liquor, and ammo. Kerrick had a good farmer's market, a fair saloon, and a poorly guarded armory. Trina stayed in the camp, doing necessary chores as best she could with her belly filling out. She worried whether Bart would return safely, chiding him before each ride to be careful – like his mama used to say when he rode over to Uncle Frank's to do cowpoke things.

Bart led the way, being taller than the sisters. He let his beard grow out, let his hair go long, and liked to flip his fingers at the long red strands as a flirty woman might, to make sure folks knew who they were dealing with.

"Hands up," shouted Bart, bursting through the double doors, a pistol in each hand. "Push 'em up high! All the way up. Lock those elbows. See if you can touch the ceiling."

Trinity and Triss marched in on either side of him, went right up to the teller row and made their demands. Caught by surprise, the tellers obeyed. At morning opening there weren't customers.

Bart's eyes snapped from one side of the lobby to the other. He spied someone ducking around the corner, went to see who it was.

"Come outta there," Bart snarled in that direction. "Come out, or when I find ya you're gonna get shot."

He glanced back at Trinity holding her gun on the teller. Triss collected bundles of paper notes in a canvas bag.

He stepped over to the side where he saw the person peek out.

It was a manager, as he expected: a short, fat man with a curly mustache and beady eyes, a rumpled brown suit and a string tie.

He ordered the man to his feet, put one pistol in its holster and used that hand to shove the man hard against the wall. He berated the older man for being a coward and the man began to whimper.

Enraged, Bart slapped the man, demanding he stop crying.

He took the manager by the flap of his suit coat and dragged him into the lobby where the tellers gasped at his rough condition.

"He's a coward," Bart announced.

When released from Bart's grip, the manager rose to his knees, a stream of tears wetting his face, begging Bart not to hurt him.

"Ain't gonna hurt no coward," Bart growled. "You're to be pitied, not shot dead. You can live with your shame the rest of your life."

"Yes, sir." the manager whimpered.

"Ain't no sir," Bart barked. He raised a pistol to the manager's head. "You can call me Bad Bart. Got it? Now say it!"

"Yes, sir, Mister Bad Bart."

"Just Bad Bart."

"Bad Bart!"

"That's better."

Trinity turned at the whiny spectacle. In that instant an alarm sounded, bells echoing against the stone walls of the lobby. She spun around to face the teller handing over bundles of notes.

"You pull that?" she demanded.

The young woman was shaking, face white. "Not me."

"I did."

An older woman came out from a side room into the teller line, her white hair in a big mop. She held up a tiny two-shot pistol, like what a lady would keep in her purse for nights out.

"You?" Trinity challenged.

"You and your thugs better clear out. Deputy's coming."

Trinity made a nasty face, hate spilling over, aimed and fired.

The woman tumbled backwards, sprawled on the floor in the narrow space. Tellers behind the barred windows screamed.

"We coulda done this th' easy way," Trinity shouted. "But some dang fool gotta try be the hero." To Triss: "Gotta go!"

Bart got the order, let his finger press the trigger and the bank manager's head tore apart. He dropped the body and rushed out.

They mounted their horses, hearing men shouting at them, running toward the bank with guns drawn. The three rode down the street, shots trailing them. One hit Triss in her calf, but she kept on riding. Another shot caught Trinity in the shoulder.

Bart turned Betty around and pulled the rifle from its sleeve, put it to his shoulder and aimed down the sights, trigger pressed, sending a bullet through the air, knocking one man off his horse. Bart fired a second shot, dropping a man on foot into the dust. More shots fired as Bart raced off, ducking against Betty, more shots whistling past him.

Back in their camp, they mended their wounds. None cried, just gritted teeth at the needle going in and the thread drawing flesh to flesh. Lucky there weren't any bullets embedded in them to dig out, Bart laughed but got no amusement from the women.

Trinity wasn't happy. "Didn't need ta go sayin' yer name. All yer boastin'. They gonna remember ya. We s'posed to be in an' out an' nobody know us."

"I want them to remember me," he spoke boldly. "Let them be afeared of me. I'm Bad Bart now."

"Yer a vain boy thinks he's a man," Trinity said.

"I'm working on my reputation. It takes time. Word'll get out. I'll be somebody everybody fears someday. Sooner than later."

"That's crazy talk," Trinity growled. "Ya get recognized an' they gonna shoot first, an' ya never get thievin' done. Ya gonna be dead straightaway. They gonna get a bounty on ya."

"I want a bounty on me," he announced. "I don't care."

"Ya better care," Trinity said. "Having a bounty means anybody kin kill ya on sight, get paid fer yer body."

"I don't mind it none. Not at all. Maybe my mama'll see me on one of those posters and she'll know I'm a man now. She'll know I'm awright the way I am. Don't need her."

"She ain't gonna be proud o' ya," Trina called out from across the camp. She finished stitching Triss's calf wound.

"Ya better care, boy," Trinity said, her tone darkening. "What ya do gonna get us killed too. Gotta be a team. Work together. Like Pa said miners do. Line o' men workin' together. Heave-ho and out it go. Not lettin' some firecracker keep blowin' up our plans."

"We still got plenty *dy-no-mite* sticks," Triss said with a snicker.

"Leave him be," Trina cried out, echoing against the rocks. "He's mine, if ya wanna punish him."

"No punishing," said Trinity, acting tough. Her eyes met Bart's and he could see she wasn't minding her words now. "Yer boy's got a lot of fire in 'im. But we don't got no time for him to heal. Gonna get us killed one day fer shore."

"I'm just like you," Bart shouted at Trinity.

"No, y'ain't," she countered.

They argued loudly until Trinity hauled off and slapped him.

The air in the camp froze. She seemed surprised she did it. Bart stepped back, glaring at her. He didn't put his hand up to his cheek, just let it sting. He could make a tight fist and lay her out with one punch, he thought, yet it wouldn't make things better.

"I'm one in charge here," Trinity spoke, though not boldly.

Her sisters waited to see what Bart would do. He stood taller, had more muscle, could easily beat her to a pulp if he wanted to although Trinity would get in plenty of punches herself. She was good with knee kicks, too.

"So you say," Bart responded, maintaining a grim face.

"You two calm down," Trina shouted. "Don't want this here baby to get bawlin' from yer fightin'."

"She's right," Triss laughed.

"Listen ta me...*Bart*," said Trinity, fighting with herself. "I'm the leader, but we kin use a man like you. We want ya to stay, be part o' this gang. Trina takes to ya, and that's good enough for me."

"Maybe I should be the one in charge," Bart declared, hands on his hips.

"Maybe you's bigger 'an me," said Trinity, "but we three been doin' this whole lot longer 'an you. We need to work together. You got the muscles an' we got the know-how."

"I think I can get on by myself," said Bart, holding his lips firm.

"That what ya want? Go on by yerself?"

"If I have to."

"Fine. Then git on outta here."

"I'll take Trina with me."

"We need her."

"I said I'm taking her."

Then Bart, hands on his hips, let one hand slip to his pistol and withdrew it from its holster, held it at his hip pointing at Trinity.

"Ya drawin' on me?" Trinity seemed surprised but also afraid for once in the time since the boy joined them. "That the first thing ya think? Is it? Well, I got nothin' to live for. Got nothin' else to do. Ya be doin' me a favor. We get born and hafta figure out what to do in this life. Then it ends, and thank the Great Spirit it ain't too long a life to suffer through. So you go on and shoot me, ya big dumb boy! Ya be doing me a favor. Do it, ya coward!"

"Bart! Don't!" cried Trina.

He stopped, waiting as his hand itched against the handle of the pistol, eager to act.

"She's my sister, Bart," cried Trina. "Please don't."

He glared at Trinity until she let out her breath. Only then did he slowly slide the pistol back into the holster.

"Better not make my sister no widow," Trinity spoke. "All I got to say on it."

He wanted to look over at Trina, to see her expression and know she approved, but he dared not take his eyes off Trinity.

"I'll take care of her. Don't you worry none," he said. "Her and whatever comes outta her. That baby."

"Be sure now that's what ya want."

He blinked. "That's what I want."

"So we're agreed?"

"Agreed on what?" said Bart, eyes narrowing at Trinity.

She took a breath. "You go yer way an' we go ours."

Bart gave a nod, glanced over at Trina. "Agreed."

17

THE RED DEVIL

GOING SEPARATE WAYS was a hard decision, Bart soon realized, having gotten used to the sisters always being around him. Splitting bundles of credit notes, even harder. They weren't good at counting but they didn't trust him to do it, thinking he would trick them.

"Gotta stash it in a safe place," he told them, regarding the four piles of paper rectangles emblazoned with the gray and red flag he saw every day in the capital. "Gotta remember where you put it or it'll be lost. But we know not to put them in a bank, don't we? They get robbed too easy."

Triss giggled at his words but the others remained quiet. He'd learned to handle her with bad jokes, like: "Why'd the family leave the city? To get away from the pandemic." With Trinity he needed to maintain his toughness. With Trina, he had to be affectionate, let her know he was always hers.

After a moment, Trina reached out, one hand holding her belly as if it needed support, and took her stack of notes and placed them beside Bart's pile.

"Ours is together," she said, her expression serious.

Bart smiled at her, then shared his smile with her sisters.

"Then it's settled," said Trinity. "Y'all kin go any day ya like."

He gave a nod, his eyes still fixed on Trina, who looked weary at that late hour, the fire burning low and the chill overcoming them. She pulled her mama's native-weave blanket around her shoulders, and looked so pretty: her pleasant face, long dark hair, and curving belly caught in the light of the fire.

Later, in their tent, he lay beside her, holding her.

"I'm gonna take care of you," he said, and she forced a smile. "I mean it. I won't leave you."

"I know."

"But we gotta do something," he said softly, like it was a secret he didn't want the other sisters to hear. "We can't be going on like we been doing. Not thieving. Even if we never get caught, never get shot, we gotta do different. Kid's gotta grow up different."

"Different? Like what?"

"I mean, we gotta turn around. Live different lives."

"Don'tcha wanna be Bad Bart an' go on devilin' ever'body from Guymon to Cimarron?"

"Can't keep it up," he said, a vague veneer of sorrow slipping into his voice for a wild life coming to an end. "Not with us being a family. We gotta be different. I guess my mama's talking's stuck in my head. Can't shake it out. I tried, believe me. Makes me wanna do something standard. I mean living like normal folks. In a town. Doing something standard every day. And that's how we get by, get some notes. And we buy things with the notes. Like our food. Things for you and things for the baby."

"An' that how our life go from then on?"

"Yeah, like that. Every day a new adventure. You and me, and this here baby." He tapped on her belly.

"Ain't shore I know how ta live standard like yer thinkin' but I'll try anythin' with you. Anythin' at all."

He looked up at the top of the tent, as though there was a gap in the canvas that allowed him to see stars up in the sky, where that Great Spirit watched him from. He felt nervous, expecting the Great Spirit might be looking back.

"If they can forgive me for all I done." He got upset and she put her hand to his cheek. "I figure if they don't know me, then we'll be fine. But I worry they'll treat you bad cuz you being a tribal woman. My mama was kind to them, but a lotta folks ain't."

"Only half," she said, placing her hand on his chest. "Pa said his family was from an island far away called Ireland."

"You're with me, so it don't matter. In Skinner Canyon, folks are more nice to tribals. But we can't go back there. Not anymore. I got a cousin there, half-Kanza. See, my mama adopted his mama long ago and then my cousin Jeb married her and they got a boy born to them. That's the one I'm talking about. Jake's his name. Funny how he's my nephew and my cousin rolled into one. That's how they count things. But they're kinder there."

"Sound like good place to live."

"But I can't go back. Not with my mama there."

"Cain't face yer ma?" She felt a tear in her eye, wiped it away with a finger, refocused on him. "Least ya got a ma still."

He couldn't respond, thinking for a while, then said: "We'll find a new place for us to live. I'll take care of you. You and this baby. Like I swore."

+ + +

Too cold for riding out of towns with a cloud of notes fluttering after them that a crowd of folks grab up to shield their escape. Snow and ice made their mad scramble dangerous. Towns were getting wary of the Bad Bart gang. The red-head devil and his demon-succubae, they were called, even mentioned by preachers in church sermons. It was tough to ride into a town without folks recognizing them and men ready to shoot them. They had to lay low again.

But you run out of what you need laying low too long.

"I'll find a town that don't know us," said Bart by the campfire.

"Ya better," Trinity said, an edge to her voice.

"She getting right sickly," said Triss, no longer giggling.

"Trina is a strong woman," said Bart. "She'll make it. Only a few more weeks of this. She'll be fine."

"Fine this, fine that. All ya ever say," Trinity responded.

"I mean it." He glared at the two sisters.

Trina was napping in the tent but it was cold no matter where they lay. All the blankets went to her. They needed more. And some medicine, Trinity advised, recalling her ma taking some during the pregnancy that was Triss. Her pa had to go into town to get it. She wrote out the name as best she could recall on a credit note, gave it to him.

"Heck, I can go into a town disguised, and nobody'll know me," said Bart.

"And keep yer guns outta sight," Trinity warned.

"I'll play it straight. I'll act cowardly so I fit in," he said.

"Take these notes and you buy some clothes for you and her," Trinity said in a gentle voice. "Act like standard folks. Be humble. Stay in a hotel for a night."

"I'll say I'm there looking at cattle."

"Be good nuff yer gettin' medicine fer yer woman. Better call her yer wife, don't furgit."

"I know what to do."

Bart rode out from the camp, with a scattering of snowflakes sprinkling the sky, dusting the treetops on the mountainside. The plain was dull brown, the grass muddy and matted, as he pressed on. A steady drizzle beat against him as he urged Betty into a trot. He pulled his hat down in front, shook his coat up on his shoulders, turned up the collar against the back of his neck, and bent lower in the saddle.

The next town was Richfield. He wouldn't be so picky. Get in and get out. Staying in a hotel would draw attention. He hadn't bothered to shave off his red beard or cut back his red hair to hide under his hat. He didn't care. Lots of reds in the world, he mused. A man's got a right to wear his hair as he likes.

He rode slowly down the main street, packed dirt, and tied up Betty in front of the greengrocer. It was winter dusk, dark at supper time, but lamps lit the street. People went out despite the chill, doing things they had to do even when night came on early. He watched them, kept the brim of his hat pulled low.

Shops were closed at that hour, he discovered. But he found the apothecary and rapped on the door's window until a light came on and a man clothed in nightshirt came out of a dark doorway at the rear of the shop, strode among the aisles of goods to the door.

"Need some medicine," Bart called through the glass. "It's for my wife. We're desperate."

"I'll let you in," said the pharmacist, "only this one time."

"Much obliged," he called through the window.

Inside, Bart was already on edge, expecting to be recognized, but the man kept the shop dark. Holding a lantern, he led Bart to the rear of the shop.

"I got a note, says what we need on it," said Bart, holding it up. "I can't read it. Maybe you can figure it out?"

That was just the right touch. Playing the ignorant country boy would work just fine. Play on the pharmacist's sympathy.

The man held the note within the lantern's light. "I can make out the words. Barely."

"My wife, she wrote it. But she's sickly."

"I see. Well, I can read it. But it's not something we got in bottles here. I'll have to mix it up. Take an hour or so, if you're planning to wait around."

"Need to get it," said Bart. "She's right sickly. Gotta get straight home with it soon as possible." He was proud of himself, making his way of talking like the sisters talked.

"I'll get right on it," said the man, turning to the shelves. He called out to Bart: "You can come back in an hour."

Outside the apothecary, Bart saw the saloon down the street, all lit up like a party, people in front laughing, smoking, and drinking to their heart's content. Like real folks, he mused. He envied them. What fun can't a boy have? But he was a man now. He took a few breaths, then sauntered over to the place.

"Whatcha here for, mister?" the first woman asked him. He gave her a once-over: frilly skirt and a sparse top crisscrossed by leather straps like she was a horse ready to be hitched to a wagon. Her full chest stuck out quite a bit, and he wondered if she was a mother. "A good time, you thinking?"

"Ain't here for nothing," he grumbled, acting mean.

"I can help take your grumpies away," she suggested, batting her eyes. Her face when seen up close did not please him. She had to be as old as his mama, but not as pretty.

"Just getting me a drink. Don't need none of your attention."

The woman frowned, spun away from him to give her attention

to another man.

Inside, he went straight to the bar, like he'd been doing it all his life when he'd only been in one a couple times with Uncle Frank as his escort. He'd only drank a cola. His uncle drank beer. So he ordered the same. Between sips of the warm beer he glanced in each direction. He didn't want anyone to catch him staring, didn't want anyone to recognize him. He'd smudged some dirt on his beard to darken it and it seemed to cover the red enough. He looked rough. The poor lighting helped hide him. Tossing down the last swallow, he thanked the barkeep, left a note on the bar.

A different, younger woman accosted him but he waved her off.

"Got a wife," he grunted like it was a punishment he endured.

"Ain't no problem," the woman called after him. "I'll be your girl friend. Talking's no problem."

He continued down the street. Pausing to regard the clock above the bank's doors, he saw he had a few minutes before collecting his medicine. He strolled down the landing, taking his time.

When it was time, he again tapped on the window and the man came out from the back room to let him in.

"All finished. Just letting it cure a bit."

"Thank you, sir." Bart put on his humble face. "We sure mighty thankful for you helping us out tonight."

"What I'm here for," the pharmacist replied as he returned to the back room.

He came out with a small brown bottle, pressing a paper label around the curve of the glass so that it stuck.

"Read the instructions carefully," said the man as he handed the opaque bottle to Bart who slipped it quickly into his coat pocket, the flap hiding his holster.

"Thanks again, sir. My wife'll be mighty glad."

He stated the charge and Bart peeled off notes from the roll he'd pulled from his trouser pocket. The pharmacist looked astounded at the roll of notes. This young man wouldn't likely have such a fortune on him, the man had to be thinking.

Bart leveled his eyes at him, saw the questions on his face.

"It's all we got," said Bart, acting humble. "It's our whole life's savings."

"I see." The man flashed a grin like an apology.

"Thank you again." Bart turned to exit.

"And give my best to your missus. I hope your child is happy and healthy."

Bart left the apothecary, waited a moment for the man to lock up, then started across the street to where Betty was tied up.

Immediately he saw a quartet of serious men approaching from the direction of his horse. He couldn't risk letting them get close, maybe recognize him. He would let them pass, then go to his horse and ride fast out of town.

Nervous, he swung himself off the landing into the alley there, taking a few deep breaths.

When he heard the men approaching, boots clucking against the wooden landing, he held his breath, waiting in the shadows for them to pass. Instead, the men paused at the corner, talking in lively voices about some plan they had.

"They'll return, no doubt," said the bass voice.

"And we gonna be ready this time," said the tenor.

"All he said was they come around first week of the month," said a baritone, who had a scratchy voice. "When all the company wages are deposited."

"Can't figure what they do with bundles of notes," said the bass.

"Kindling for a fire?" the tenor chuckled in his whiny tone.

"Must be saving up something big," offered the baritone, adding a dry cough.

The men went on discussing what they'd do and Bart recognized they must be talking about him and the sisters. They did hit banks in the first week of each month, then use the money to buy things in other towns the rest of the month.

He rested, his back against the wall of the building, hat pulled down, peering out from under the brim at whatever was lit by the street lamps. Laughter from the saloon provided the only noise but for the men talking a few steps away.

"Hey there," someone called.

Bart looked up to find a man leaning around the corner.

"You doing fine?" asked the man.

It was the tenor, Bart figured. The man was alone. His partners had sauntered off.

"Awright," Bart grumbled, trying to make clear to the man that he wasn't interested in a chat. He wore a suit and a long coat over it, like he was a business man. Definitely not a cowpoke.

"You must've overheard me and my friends talking."

"Heard ya," said Bart, his voice low. "Didn't make out no words. None of my business anyways."

"I'm glad to hear you say that, friend."

"Ain't a friend."

"Are you just passing through here? Stop for the night?"

"Stopped a while. Then moving on."

"Where you headed?"

"Up north. Plainview maybe."

"Already late. You should stay over. Richfield's got a fine hotel."

The man pointed out of the alley and Bart knew which place he meant. The hotel was across from the saloon.

"Got plans," Bart said.

"Oh, do you? Would that possibly be the saloon across the way? Be pleased to share a drink with a stranger."

"Not a drinking man," said Bart and let out a snicker.

"Well, you sure do look like a drinking man. Way you're dressed. How you carry yourself. Figured you were one of those ranch hands. Or could be one of the Colonel's gunners."

Bart looked closer at the man. "The Colonel's gunners?"

"Colonel Spaulding. He was in the big war years ago. You never heard of Brenton Spaulding? He and the men he's got, they're formed into a squadron of gunmen. Might fine shots, all of them. It is their honor to keep the Colonel safe. He's got enemies, as you can imagine. Sometimes they go out and do some work for the Colonel."

Bart studied the man. "What kind of work?"

"The usual." The man glanced behind himself, returned his gaze to Bart. "They collect payments from farmers, ranchers, sometimes the merchants. They keep order in this town and surrounding area, too. No marauders here. It's good pay."

"Ain't looking for no work."

"Then what are you in town for?"

"Passing through, I said."

"You did. You surely did. Well, I must be getting fatigued to let my mind go soft like that. So I'll bid you a good night."

"Goodnight then."

"Unless you change your mind about having a drink."

"No thanks."

"Awright then. You take care, stranger." The man glanced up at the moon, noting it didn't shine upon the stranger leaning against the building, leaving him hidden in shadow. "And if you're heading north, you should be watching out for a red-haired fellow by the name of Bad Bart. Got a red beard. Right frightful coming out of a cloud of dust on that devilish horse he rides. Ugliest beast I ever did see."

Now Bart was interested. "You seen him?"

"Few times. Lucky it was from afar." The man seemed to puff up. "Like right here in this town about six months back. That Bad Bart and his lady gang come riding in here and robbed the bank."

"Which bank's that?"

"The Bank of Wichita branch. They shot a manager. Always go for the manager. Let the women go, but never the managers."

"Why is that?" Bart inquired.

"Don't know. Maybe the manager tries to do something."

"Yeah, something."

"But we got plans," said the man. "When they come back, we're going to be ready. Me and the deputies and...."

"Those were deputies you talking with?"

"Say, stranger. You look about the same height. About six-foot or so. Same build. A well-set man. Would you mind stepping out of the shadows? Just for a second."

"Why?"

"Just like to see who I'm talking to, is all."

"Does it matter who?"

"I do like to see my conversation partner. It's a courtesy we have in proper towns like Richfield. Would you mind, stranger?"

"Rather not."

"Please, sir. I insist."

"Ain't gonna."

"I do believe you could be—"

Bart raised his hand – the one that had taken hold of the knife in the sheath strapped across his lower back – and pushed the knife into the man's belly as he took a step into the moonlight.

The man gasped, frozen in place with the knife deep in his gut.

"I do believe you have red hair."

"I do," said Bart.

"And red beard...."

"True."

"The Red Devil—"

The man slid off the blade, crumpling to the ground in the alley, a quiet thump as his head hit against an empty rain barrel.

As Bart took a step out of the alley, the man spoke – seemed to speak up, calling to him, or else it was a voice in his head.

"Am I gonna die? Is that what's happening?"

With a jerk of his head, Bart took a step back to the man, looked down at that forlorn face. Such a cowardly fellow! Why'd he have to talk to me? Dang fool. You don't talk to a red devil.

Bart knelt beside him and grabbed the man's hand, moving it roughly over the wound.

"Press here," said Bart. "Keep pressing. I'll find a doc for you."

Steps down the landing, hurrying without breaking into a run, a woman's voice called after him. He halted, thinking she'd found the man in the alley.

"Hey, mister! Yer friend is calling fer ya," she cried out.

"Looking for a doctor," he said, with a half-turn to her. She was a matron in apron and shawl, looking cross at him.

"Doc Whistler's back th' other way," she said.

"Good. Better go get him."

"But you're going the wrong way."

"I'm going my way. You wanna help that man, you go the other way and get that doc."

"Awrighty," she said. "I'll go wake him. And who should I say is helping that man?"

"Nobody. Just a stranger."

"You're a kind stranger, sir. I'll get that man some help."

He thought to say something like "Thanks" as his mama trained him, felt the word in his throat, but he didn't have time. He would be found out if he stayed any longer. Off to get Betty and ride away. He'd gotten what he came for.

"Say now, mister," that darn woman called to him. "You look a might familiar. Are you from over Skinner Canyon way?"

"Not hardly," he grumbled, stepping off the landing onto the dirt. He glanced up and down the street for anyone coming for him.

"No, sir. I'm sure ya look familiar to me. I used to live over there. Before I married Sam Taylor, the butcher here."

"I'm not from there," he said with a grunt. His hand went to his holster, felt the pistol. Getting rattled by this old woman.

"Pretty sure," she went on.

"You better go get that doc," he called out, crossing the street to his horse. He loosed the reins from the railing.

"Aren't you Maggie Baumann's boy? I know she had a boy. Gots a mess of red hair everybody talked about. Like he was a devil child, don'tcha know. But then he run off."

"Ain't him," he barked and climbed onto Betty.

He spun his horse around and galloped off down the street, into the darkness where he felt safe again.

18

WINTERBORN

BETWEEN THE CHILL IN THE AIR and the campfire's warmth, he was never so comfortable as when he slipped into the tent with Trina and held her close, felt her belly push against his, waited for a kick and see her smile at him, knowing it was real. He felt like a man, pride running through him, wanted to shout it to the world.

They had a safe camp, enough food stores to make it to spring, he figured. The deer he shot was good meat. He'd go after another next month. Trinity hung up strips of venison to dry. Triss stirred the endless stew, always hot. He would bring Trina a bowl of it, watch as she sipped it and spooned a bit of meat into her mouth. They could speak with their smiles.

Sometimes he'd forget the sisters were there and it was only him and Trina. Like they were completely alone in the world, just he and his woman and their baby. Like at the beginning of time.

"I remember my mama telling me stories when I was young," he spoke one night inside their tent. "She thought me being born was some kind of miracle. Like it was magic, and she told me about this book she read. There's a story in it about a man named Adam and his wife named Eve and what they did."

"Yeah? And what they do?" She liked when he told his stories.

"So they got in trouble and had to leave the nice place they were living in and go into the wilderness." He thought a moment. "Kinda like leaving Wichita, going into the prairie. Or down to Okala, much worse. So they had kids. Had to work hard in the new place when they could've sit back and relax before."

"But why they leave there, the easy place?"

"They got in some kind of trouble. It's a long story," he replied. "You and me are kinda like them, all I mean. Mama said they were the first man and woman in the world. That was a really long time ago. Now there's gotta be like a million people in the world – and that's after that pandemic killed half of everybody."

"Ma never taught us to read," she said. "I's too young fer it when Pa got killt. None o' us ever gone to no school, so it's mighty good they wrote it down back then."

"My mama said the story ain't about those two people really, not themselves and what they did. More like they're just symbols. Like a school lesson."

Trina gave a snort. "Symbols? Of what?"

He grinned, feeling smart. "I mean not about two people living in a forest – not like my mama's grandmother did during pandemic time – but they represent forces in the world."

"Forces? Ya mean like good and bad?"

"In a way. Like if you do bad you get sent out of the good place, have to work hard in the next place, and it ain't fun. Like me being here. I sent myself out of that place."

She regarded him warmly. "What place?"

"A place where I had peace." He gazed into her eyes. "That place where my mama could comfort me. Felt warm and safe there. No fears. No worries. Just complete...love."

She made a face. "But don't I give it now?"

"Sure you do." He took a breath. "But you ain't my mama. And I'm grateful for that. You're my woman. My partner. See, I walked out of that old place, the garden, you call it, right into wilderness – actually came all the way out here to this wild land – and found you. A new garden. This new place we got. Maybe it's hard living out here but I got you by my side. And me by you. We help each other. You're my new home."

+ + +

The Red Devil rode out in the new year wearing a ragged blanket over himself, holes cut for head and arms, bearing a rifle and eyeing any game out on the plain. There was a quartet of antelope foraging. He let Betty stroll toward them, just another beast, and he fired at the largest one, a buck. He got it in the hip, which kept the antelope from running off. Still had to follow another mile until it gave up. When he dismounted, he had to use a second bullet to the brain to end it. Then he set to work dressing it.

When he arrived with the antelope laying over the rump of his horse, he barely spoke a word before the strangest noise slapped his ears. It sounded like a wildcat. He pulled off his bloody gloves and went to the tent he shared with Trina.

"What happened?" he cried, expecting a tragedy.

Trinity came out, pushing him back. "Ya best wait a spell."

"Why? Is she awright?"

"Trina's fine. And don'tcha know? You's a papa now."

His face, set for bad news, burst into a smile. "Can I see?"

Trinity held the tent flap open and he gazed inside, saw a weary Trina with limp braids, laying with a bundle that kept wriggling in her arms. Triss sat with her, dabbing her brow with a cloth.

"Ya got a boy," Triss called to him.

"I helped Ma when Triss was born," Trinity bragged. "I knowed what to do. Got the babe pushed out an' ever'thin' tied off."

"I'm sorry I missed it," he said, "but I brought back a pronghorn for our dinner. That'll make her strong again."

"Ya wouldn'ta knowed what ta do," said Trinity.

"I think I can figure it out," he responded, keeping his eyes on his woman and son. "She just gotta push, then I catch it."

He watched Trina move the bundle to show the baby's face. The wrap slid down a bit, exposing the start of what would grow into a full head of red hair, though not as bright as his. Then, at Trinity's instruction, she put the baby to her breast and let him feed.

Bart continued to gaze in awe at his woman and their son.

The other sisters moved into the tent with Trina, all bunched up to keep the baby warm. Bart took the sisters' tent for himself but it was a cold place. All the blankets went to Trina and the baby.

A few shivering nights and he announced one morning he was going out, meaning away from the camp, and didn't say where. The sisters didn't mind. They were content to keep the tent warm for the new addition.

He saddled Betty, led her down the hillside, mounted her at the bottom and rode over the plain as a sharp wind drove snow across his face. He hunkered against her withers, wishing he had stayed at home long ago instead of going on a posse with his uncle.

He'd seen the bison herd moving across the bottomland over the past week and hoped to get one. Plenty of meat and a good hide. He found them huddled together against the cold wind, arrows of snow driven against them. He saw a mother and calf had wandered off, stood beside a frozen stream. She gave a weary call, anxious hoof pushing at the ice. Her child tried to get milk underneath her but she kept pushing it away as if saying she had none to give.

Bart dismounted, pulled the antelope hide from the saddle bag and swung it around his shoulders like a cape. He had made a wire get-up that held the horns atop his head, but he hated having to remove his hat the way the wind was blowing.

He crawled on his hands and knees what felt like a mile but likely only a hundred feet. The frozen grass made his hands stiffen, his knees ache, but he got close.

The mama regarded him, her dark eyes questioning this strange antelope. The young one tried to get milk again and she urged it away with a push of her hindleg and a grunt.

Bart aimed the rifle at the mama from his prone position, the deathly cold seeping up from the earth making his body shiver. He tried to hold the rifle steady. From this distance he shouldn't miss. But if he did, the enraged bison might trample him before he could get up and run. He had little chance of out-running the beast.

It would take at least two bullets, he figured. And the head was not the place to aim. He worked his way around to her other side, between her and the rest of the herd. He was trying to get behind her so he could shoot at the back of her head, right behind her ears, where it connected to the neck. The bullet needed to enter low, sneaking in where the bone was thinner.

Yet as soon as he got into position, the mama would turn, let go her grunts as if warning the others. He could only get a little closer before he would be found out. She already seemed suspicious of this antelope. There was no more time; he was getting too stiff to move over the frozen ground.

There. She moved. Turned. Looking back at the herd—

Her calf pounced behind her, blocking his firing line. He waited as the calf tried to claim the mama's milk. Snow drove past him, obscuring his view, but it was now or never, he decided, and let his finger go heavy against the trigger.

The calf bolted away as its mama dropped to the ground. The shot hit right where he wanted and she gave a lurch like it was a surprise, then glanced at her puzzled calf before collapsing on her front legs and rolling over.

The herd noticed. A couple bulls sauntered toward her body but the others moved away. The bulls gave a long look, then turned and rejoined the herd as though this one had always been trouble and now they were rid of her.

The calf continued to moan, let its anguish be known, refusing to join the herd, staying close to its mama. Wolves would recognize its cries and come for a feast.

It had to be done. "Better if my baby keeps warm than yours," he said in the voice of a preacher. "It's God's will."

He set to work cutting the hide from the body as both bison and wolves watched him. He called Betty over and grabbed the axe from the saddle. As a fox arrived, Bart took the axe to the hindquarters of the bison, hacking off the leg, making a mess. He wanted to take the other hindleg but he could only carry so much. The hide itself was heavy.

The herd moved further away as a pack of wolves gathered. The fox dashed away after Bart cut off a snippet of meat and tossed it. Accosted by the wolves, the calf didn't last long.

He watched the wolves leaping in to take their share of the calf, heard its wails then falling silent, and his heart cracked apart. He was sorry for the calf, but it couldn't be helped. He had to provide for his own family. He was a man, now a father. Nothing he'd done before could matter. Only the future mattered.

What had he wrought? He asked himself as he worked on the hide, scraping it while snow flittered down. The wind lessened but his cold hands shook as he drew the knife through the skin.

He kept eyeing the wolves. He glanced around for the horsemen who would come to arrest him.

"I'm sorry," he muttered as his scraping reached to the far side of the hide. "Guess I done plenty. If only they could forget all what I done. I'd stand up and be right. Take a good stand. Be standard. Then they would let me be, let me and my family start over."

He looked up from his work, scanned the plain, saw the herd had moved further away. The wolves had grown fat and now lay content. Birds swooped down for a portion. And he knelt on the cold grass, his whole body aching from his efforts. But it was the carcass of the bison mother that captured his attention. She had cared for her calf yet failed.

"I won't fail," he told himself, scraping back toward himself.

Then he stopped and sat back, his eyes set on the calf's carcass, naked and bloody, stripped to the bones. He shifted his gaze to the mama bison, then got up, stood straight, his body feeling strong, and he didn't feel the cold.

"Thank you for your sacrifice," he spoke. "We will remember you for what you've given us. I'm sorry for what I did. Maybe I saved you from a miserable death, if you were sick and the herd shunned you. It was quick, at least. Maybe a good thing. But it's a sacrifice either way."

The wolves hadn't fled but moved around him. One on the right, another to his left, two big grays in front, and one behind him. When he glared at the two in front, one of them barred its teeth, growling. Hadn't they had enough meat? Or were they insisting on the mama, too? The one behind him snarled, pacing back and forth, as a low rumble rolled threateningly through the dark skies, clouds of snow blown by the wind. The other wolf in front began to snarl.

All were on their feet, agitated, waiting for the right moment to strike. Don't show weakness, he told himself. He reached for the gun in his holster, easier to shoot at multiple targets with the pistol than the rifle. Pistol in hand, he planned which wolf would go first.

"You got the bison," he shouted at them, "so leave me alone. I'm a skinny man."

The snarling increased as another low rumble passed overhead. He assessed the situation, ready to fire the pistol.

Just as the wolves stepped closer to launch their attack, a great yellow knife of lightning stabbed the ground too close to them. The shock made the wolves scatter and left him on his knees in fear. He saw the wolves running away. He saw a fresh lightning strike. Thundersnow! A grin burst across his face. More thunder. More lightning. The wind-driven snow lessened.

Yet Bart remained on his knees. He set down the pistol, put his hands together, gazing at the overcast. Was God up there watching him? The Great Spirit looking out for him? Judging him? What had he done to deserve this fate? He knew: acting like a fool, like a madman, shooting people, stealing, robbing banks, taking what he wanted and not caring. But that was all behind him, he decided as more lightning flashed overhead.

"It ain't all luck," he mumbled, getting himself up from the cold prairie grass. "I killed again. For my family. And that damn calf was left alone." He thought of his woman and their babe, left alone while he was out in this storm getting a blanket and some meat for them. He was doing the right thing. Providing for his family. As the wolves were doing for theirs. As the herd did for themselves. Like all creatures of the earth. They did what they had to do to survive, never pondering what they did as long as it kept their family alive a little longer.

He blinked, feeling the icy wind in his face, watching lightning crackle through the clouds as it pushed away.

He bundled up the hide, struggled to carry it over his shoulder to where Betty waited. Must be a hundred pounds, he figured. She felt the weight, too, and complained. But he insisted and she obeyed as he got the hide up and over her rump and tied it down. The bison leg was also heavy but he could only carry it by the ankle, letting blood drain as he led Betty back to the camp.

It had taken him the full day, and when he arrived, tired and frozen, he let them know what he'd done. The hide would need to be cured and tied up, stretched, but it would be the best blanket for the winter.

"Now ya got food," Trinity said with a snarl, "whaddaya gonna call this one?"

He tried to squeeze into the tent once he'd shed his blood-soaked clothes. Half-naked, he reached for one of his shirts crumpled in the corner, pulled it on. He saw the frilly shirt, too, that Trina took from that family on the road, now cut up for baby cloths.

The sisters huddled under the native blanket, stripped down to share their warmth, the baby between them. He smiled at the scene, even as wind pressed hard against the canvas.

Trina let the blanket fall away so he could see his son: a tan-faced doll that didn't look real, with a smattering of reddish hair.

"Ain't so red," she laughed.

"Not black like yours, neither," he said.

"This one's 'tween us. Now what we call 'im?"

He stared at the little thing, still unable to believe it was real. A flood of thoughts swept through him. For some reason, the image of his Aunt Jackie came to him, the Kanza mother of his cousin Jake. The black hair she had, always in braids. When his mama brought him back to Skinner Canyon from the capital, he was introduced to her and Jake. Bart had never seen anyone like Jackie before, not in the capital, and he was immediately smitten. Yet he couldn't ever understand why he had the feelings he had. He was too young to be thinking that way but he always got nervous around her.

"I love you," he spoke suddenly to Trina.

Everyone fell silent, staring at him.

"Them's the words ta say," Triss laughed, breaking the silence.

He wasn't sorry for saying them, but he realized he held the image of that other woman in his mind when he said them.

"Sorry," he said, shaking his head. "But I do mean it."

"Know it," Trina responded, gazing warmly at him. "Now, we gonna call him Bart, after you?"

"Naw, I'm Bart after my father. Don't want any other Bart." His lips pursed. "This one's gonna be good. Gonna make up for all that I've done."

"Then name him," Trinity snapped. "Or we gonna call him Boy."

He thought of the names in his family, running back through the stories his mama told him.

"I'm thinking," he barked when Trinity pressed him again.

His mama never married after his father was killed in that bad accident, yet he recalled a good friend who visited often, a tall man named Isaiah. Bart had been six. He recalled his mother calling the man Izzy in a playful tone. The man would pat Bart's head when he came for a visit. When the three of them went out to a restaurant for dinner, it felt like they were a family. He never knew his real father but this man was kind to him – sure, it was most likely to get in his mother's good graces. She seemed to like him, let him sleep with her in the big bed.

"Let's call him Izzy," he announced.

The sisters questioned his choice.

"I knew a man back when I was a kid, and he was nice to me. He was kind to my mother. So maybe it's the name of a good man. It's a short name for Isaiah."

"Eye-zay-uh?" Triss quizzed, giggling. "What it mean?"

"I like it," Trina said with a big smile. "But will it fit him when he grow up lookin' like me?"

"No more, no less than you," said Bart. "He can change it later, when he's grown, if he wants to."

Something flashed in his head: a scene unfolding.

He saw himself as an old man, sitting in a cushy chair with three children standing around him. He was reading from a book set in his lap. He told the children the names of their family. All the names. Fritz Baumann, the prisoner-of-war who played the tuba, became a music professor. His son Ludwig, called Uncle Louie by his niece, Paulina, who became a professor herself. Her son by way of a liaison on a beach who was named Sandy. Then he and his cousin Hannah came together during the pandemic and had a baby named Isla. Isla met Frank when he was an old man, gave him a son named Fritz after that first one, but he preferred to go by his father's name. That

Fritz, Bart's grampa, had two sons, Frank and James, and a daughter named Maggie – Bart's mother. Another man named Bart was his father, he knew.

Now he would join the list, had the right to add names to the family history. In the vision he penned into the open book set upon his lap the name of a woman: Trina. And the baby they made who they named Isaiah Baumann – Izzy. Bart wrote the date, guessing at it: somewhere in the middle of Twelfthmonth, picking the twelfth day, at the very end of the year 2155 or thereabouts. He tried to count back to his own birthday but got confused. Close enough, he decided.

19

STANDARD TOWNSFOLK

WHEN SPRING HAD FINALLY ARRIVED, Trina took a razor to Bart's beard, shaving off his red whiskers. Got a couple nicks but he never complained. She cut short the hair on his head and his hat fit looser. A new look for a new life.

"We gonna live normal," said Trina to her sisters, much to their disappointment. "We gotta, now we's got this baby."

Trinity acted like she didn't want them to go, didn't want to give up a life of thievery, but Bart thought he saw her soften to the idea. Triss seemed confused but tended to go along with Trinity.

"Ya think ya kin live normal?" Trinity challenged, or maybe she was joking. Hard to tell these days.

Trina held the baby against her chest inside the native blanket but lifted a hand toward the rocks around their camp. "Ya think a baby gonna wanna live out here?"

"Suit yerself," Trinity said with a grunt.

"But we ain't ready yet," said Bart. "Gotta get some notes, stash them away. Clean up and act standard. Make sure nobody can recognize us. Play it standard."

"You an' yer *standard*," Trinity said, her rough tone returning.

"I mean it," he said, growing bolder. "Me and Trina's gonna live standard. In some town. Doing standard things. I'll find good work. Trina can stay home with the baby. We'll be fine. Course we won't never say a word about you two."

"Ya think she wanna stay home all day?" asked Triss, giggling.

"That's a standard life," said Bart. "Somebody's gotta stay home with the baby. For a while anyways. Till he go to school."

"School?" Triss laughed. "We ain't go no school an' we fine."

Trinity watched them, grinning.

"Just a few more tricks," he said, "then we'll be done. We'll have enough money to get started in that polite society everybody likes so much. Hah! Maybe I'll buy me a cornet. Used to play one when I was young. Izzy can learn it after me."

Trinity almost laughed, a rare thing for her. "So ya think playin' cornet's a standard thing? Meanin' standard townfolk?"

"Like I said," Bart responded, "after we get set up a bit more."

Times were hard – worse than before. More guards at the prime locations. Fewer towns they hadn't hit. Yet Bart grew bolder, happy to take risks, knowing this was the last time.

One time he rode into Griggs with Trinity and Triss, did the bank robbery the way they always did. Got credit notes handed over. Nobody got shot. They rode away.

Then they hit Eva just up the road.

And Wheeless, riding clear the other way.

Leaving Wheeless, Bart found something strange following him after he'd split from the sisters. A vehicle with no horses. Three men in it, one operating the machine and the other two sitting up high with guns aimed at him. Only the rough ground made them wait to pull off shots, the way the machine bumped and shook.

It gained on him, Betty at a full gallop. Had to be one of those motor carriages. He'd seen them in the capital but there were very few out west. Only the rich folks had them; only a few streets in the larger towns could provide smooth surfaces to roll over with their rubber wheels. Yet here came one after him!

Betty reached her limit, refused to keep on at a full run, despite Bart's urging. The machine drew close – close enough he could see the men's faces: grim and determined. Rifles raised, ready. The vehicle pulled alongside him as Betty slowed. One man shouted over at him, demanding he halt.

"You'll get a fair trial," the man shouted.

Bart looked for an escape but he saw only a line of trees ahead.

What lay behind them? As Betty slowed down, the vehicle slowed, too. The men held their rifles on him. He was caught. But he had only one bag of notes; the rest went with the sisters. He thought of his woman and his baby and his gut hurt.

As they approached the treeline, Betty got her wind back and Bart urged her on faster. The vehicle fell back, then shifted into a faster speed. Bart headed for the treeline, racing as fast as he could get Betty to go. The vehicle had to maneuver around rocks in the ground, slowing them.

Then he broke through the trees and right there before him was a gorge. A raging stream tumbled through the passage. Its rocky sides were rough, jagged. He sized it up: if Betty was game for it, he believed she could jump over it.

A glance back at the treeline made his decision. As that vehicle smased through the trees, the riflemen had to block swatting branches with arms raised, rifles lowered.

Bart pulled the reins hard and Betty snorted her displeasure at the sudden halt. He wheeled her around, backed up – as the vehicle broke through the trees, rolling straight toward the lip of the gorge. The driver saw it, cried out his fate, but it was too late.

Bart gave Betty the command and they rambled as one down to the edge and leaped over the six-foot gap. But the motor carriage roared off that rocky ledge, the front end scraping the opposite ledge before the entire vehicle dropped straight down into the narrow chasm, crumpled front end first, smashing into the quick stream. Blocking the flow, the vehicle got swamped as the men tried to climb out.

Bart didn't pause to look back but galloped away before any of them could climb to the top.

Back at the camp he told the sisters about his escape.

"Those things can out-run a horse on even ground," he said with humor in his voice, "but they sure can't leap a gorge. And that one wasn't no wider than Betty herself nose to tail."

Trina was alarmed, held him tight. "Glad yer safe."

"No way I wasn't gonna be safe," he said, but she could feel him shaking. "Just saying they got them motor carriages to chase after us now. Finding that gorge was pure luck."

Triss chuckled at the story, made shocked faces at him.

"There ain't many them kinda machines left these days," said Trinity thoughtfully. "Don't know how they get their charges. From a terminal at their fancy house?"

"Gonna run down if they out too long," said Triss. She only knew that from Bart trying to educate her on the old days, telling about life in the capital when he was a little boy.

He described the men in the motor carriage.

Trinity cursed, then explained it could've been Sam Bean who pursued Bart. The Red Devil was well-known. What hope was there if a small town bank could hire security? Larger town banks were out of reach. Bean was a marshal from up in Nebrasque territory, out of Kearney, known for taking bank robberies seriously. He'd been hired by a lot of banks in the Kanza territory.

"They ain't foolin' 'round no more," Trinity complained, shaking her head. "Hope none o' them follow ya. Took roundabout way back, didn't ya?"

"Nobody followed me," Bart replied sternly.

"Sam Bean," Trinity mused. "Still alive...."

Bart regarded her. "I don't know for sure if it was him riding in *that* motor carriage."

"Oh, that bastard's known for his damn motor carriages."

That night Trina told him about the time Trinity met a man she took a fancy to. After some play up in a room over a saloon she discovered he was a lawman. He tried to arrest her, being with her only to gain her confidence. In that attempt, she shot him with his own pistol, left a wound in his hip. It hurt to ride a horse after that.

"That's the reason he walk queer now. Hated her ever since, an' vowed to get her," said Trina. "Now he use pair of crutches when he ain't ridin' in one them motor-carriages."

"He did look right sincere about getting me," said Bart.

"Maybe th' only time she ever bin with a man," snickered Trina. "And Triss? She's pure as drivin' snow, I betcha."

They lay low for a while, happy with what they'd gotten, and he continued to plan for their new life.

One day Bart tore a blank page from the journal he got from the airplane wreckage and drew on it with a pen he snatched right off the teller's counterboard several robberies past. He tried to draw out a map from what he knew, what he'd seen inside that airplane, and riding around the territory. He drew circles for the towns. He drew lines for the roads, double lines for the rivers. Marked where bridges were, where fords were. Triangles for mountains, a line of them running north to south along the western edge of his map, and made other shapes for mesas and canyons.

The sisters were impressed.

"Now here's us," he said, using the pen to point where their camp was. "Here's the towns around us. I put an X at every town we done hit."

The sisters stared at the map. Trina's attention was pulled away by a grabby baby wanting to play.

"Don't see no towns ain't got X on 'em," said Trinity.

"Me, neither," said Triss.

Bart regarded them, feeling like a teacher. "That's right. There are none. 'Less you wanna go farther north, east, or south. Nothing but wilderness to the west. We've done something in each of them. All the close-by towns. We can't be going three days' ride and three days back for a score."

Trina had to excuse herself, Izzy getting too fussy in her arms.

"Let her be," said Trinity, studying the map he drew.

"That last time, I saw them posters outside the jail," said Bart. "One for you and one for me."

"None for me?" asked Triss showing a pitiful face.

"Mine pays better," he said, ignoring Triss.

"Yer easy to spot, all yer red hair flappin' 'round," said Trinity in a gnarly voice. "Beside, yer a man. Always pay more if ya kill a man. They afraid to shoot a woman."

"Not you," he replied, letting go half a chuckle. "Not you women. They'd hang you just as soon as lock you up."

"I shoot 'em first," Trinity snapped.

"Me, too," Triss echoed. "I's gonna shoot 'em right away."

Bart waved off the rebuttal. "If they look at a map like this one, it's gonna be easy for them to figure out that in the center of these towns we hit, there's a hideout. Right here." He put his finger down on the dot on the map that marked their camp. "Doesn't take one of them rocket scientists to figure it out. And they'll be swooping down on us right quick."

"What's them rocket science-tists?" asked Triss.

Bart glared at her. "People that know how to make rockets."

Her eyes went dull. "What's rockets?"

"They shoot up in the sky." Bart started to explain, recalling that childhood book, then gave up.

"Forget rockets," Trinity snapped. "Ain't no more noways."

"So we gotta move again?" asked Triss.

Bart frowned. "If we're gonna keep ahead of them."

"And now we got a cryin' baby to keep quiet," Trinity grumbled as noise from the tent filled the camp.

+ + +

Bart rode to the town of Clayton, which the women stormed into years before. Nobody there should know him. He was interested in signs that it would be a fine place for his family to live. Even if he had to go off to other towns to conduct his 'business', he would have this town as a refuge. Townsfolk would know him as an upstanding citizen.

He tied Betty outside the General Store and strolled down the landing with confidence and a bright smile. Fine dressed ladies and gentlemen passed by him, tipping their hats at each other. He said "Good morning" to them with a gentle drawl. They welcomed him, recognized him as not a resident of their town. Everyone knew each other, he noticed. People were gathering, heading to a white church at the end of the street. Must be Sunday, he mused.

"Be a fine sermon today," said a big man, dressed like a banker, giving him a genuine smile and a casual bob of his shoulder urging him to follow.

Bart was not a church-goer but he smiled back. One uncle was a priest in Skinner Canyon, giving his own sermons each Sunday. But

Bart grew up in the capital where everyone worked on Sundays just like other days. All they worshipped was efficiency, had a devotion to order, prayed to whoever stood at the balcony of the governor's tower during the mass gatherings to chant slogans. Love of music was winding down, his mama noticed.

So he went. Entered like a sinner, which he knew he was, sat at the rear of the long room, hat in his hands, hands in his lap. He took a swipe at his hair, hoping it wasn't too red. Trina stained it with juice from some herbs that made it darker. His beard she shaved off, said he looked better. He didn't wear his Sunday best, but no one there said a word to him. There were a few ranch hands dressed like him who took seats on benches in front of him. One turned to introduce himself, wanted to shake hands. Bart nervously shook the hand, replying that his name was Hal – after the letters on his saddle.

"Glad to have you joining us, Hal," said the cowpoke, Vic, who had sandy hair, matted by his hat, and a wispy mustache. This man seemed the same age, Bart noted. If Vic could have a bright smile on a Sunday morn, then so could he.

Eventually the preacher stepped out from a doorway. He wore a long white robe, looking like an angel to Bart. The man was balding yet bore a great white beard. Heavy-set, not fat but strong, beefy, he looked like he could go a few rounds wrestling with God.

"Dearly beloved," the preacher began, raising his thick arms as if trying to touch the arched ceiling, his wide sleeves slipping down, arm muscles displayed, "we are gathered as one today to remember our oath to the Almighty!"

Bart listened faithfully but his mind drifted off to memories he'd thought were lost. His mama taking him to the chapel on the hill where her brother preached. He was only a boy, didn't want to go but she'd insisted, offering him an iced-cream treat after if he behaved. Always the good boy! His grunt at the memory got the attention of those sitting around him.

"...even if they should come unto the Lord begging for His loving forgiveness, it shall be granted," the preacher spoke.

He imagined his mama in that chapel today, many miles from

where he sat. A different life, a different world. What would she pray for? Her son to return? Or she'd be thinking up a new song.

The preacher had words for him, it seemed. He came to believe the preacher was speaking directly to him, as though everyone had informed the man that a gunslinger was in their midst and needed some talking to. But he wasn't that kind of man, he had to insist. He was a papa now so he swore to be a good man. Yet he couldn't undo the bad he'd already done.

He stood up when the preacher called for sinners to rise. People around him stood, like a thick forest of sentinel pines sprouting from fertile ground, rising to the sun. They bowed their heads. Bart took a look in each direction.

"May each and every sinner be forgiven," the preacher spoke in his full-throated, godly voice, "and the Good Lord shall bless each one that they may go forth and commit sin no more, and commit perpetual goodness for their remaining days."

Then there was music. A woman sat at the piano machine in the front corner and her fingers moved the keys, making a whole choir of notes sound. Just like his mama did at the piano in her house. She had a piano in their unit in the capital, too. She'd tried to get him to learn to play it. But all he could do was poke his finger at one key at a time to make a sound. Enough noise and she would shout at him. No, more like *calling* to him, suggesting he put more effort into his music.

"Are you going to the dinner?" asked his new friend Vic.

Suddenly he realized the program had ended. He'd gone into his memories and missed the final "Amen".

"Dinner?" he asked Vic.

"We go share Sunday dinner," Vic explained. "All of us. Like one big family. It's out back of the church. You're welcome to join us."

He did feel a bit hungry, he had to admit. Only a meager meal in camp then a long ride to this town. But he felt nervous – like how his mama always described her dad. Bart couldn't mingle with people. They made him feel nervous; more so now that he worried about being recognized as an outlaw. Living with only his mama for so many years, then with three sisters left him fearing crowds. He might need to put a pistol in his hand to calm himself if he got agitated.

"Thanks," he said to Vic, "but I should be getting on."

"Where to?" asked the fellow.

"On to Buffalo Springs," he said, choosing a town he knew.

"That's a ride," Vic said. "Happy trails then, Hal."

They parted with another shake of hands.

Bart continued down the street, away from the church. He could hear people gathering behind the building, could smell the food. But he had to leave. Had to get away. For his own good and theirs. He'd seen enough. Clayton wouldn't be a good place to live. Not a place where everyone knew everyone.

The same as Skinner Canyon, where everyone knew he was the son of the music lady. He'd done too many bad deeds to ever return. Let her think I died out there, he decided. She could forgive him if she thought he died out in the wilderness, but never if she knew it was him that did all of those crimes mentioned in the news-papers.

She had to have seen the ugly posters tacked up at jails in every town from Clayton to Cimarron, including Skinner Canyon. There he was: a grim-faced man with bright eyes and a strong jowl hidden under a beard. In the posters his red beard was black, his face white. What he'd seen looked close enough that she might recognize him if she ever studied the poster. His worth was now measured by the numbers under his face: the bounty paid for his body, dead or alive. But if she never suspected her boy was the outlaw on the posters then she wouldn't ever bother to look, wouldn't have any concern.

No, thought Bart, it was different now. Everything changed. He was already a papa. He had a woman. He had to look after them. Being away from home five years had changed him, he was surprised to realize. Refusing all sense of duty as a teenage boy, he now accepted those responsibilities, was willing to take them up and bear them. Good time to start fresh as a normal family living a standard life. It might be dull but better that kind of life than risking a quick death every time he dared to ride into a town, leaving his family behind. Living a standard life, he could forget all he'd done that made him the highest bounty in the territory, even higher than Trinity.

+ + +

"We can't stay here," Bart told Trina as she cleaned Izzy's poop. He watched with fascination: how gentle she could be when she wasn't holding a gun. "Can't keep on like we're doing. They're gonna come down on us sooner or later. And those towns out west ain't at all good for us. Too small. Everybody knows everybody. We need to be in a big town where nobody knows us. Else we gotta live far away where ain't nobody close by at all to bother us."

Trina wrapped a clean cloth around the baby. "That gonna be far west, ya sayin'?"

"Over the line. Clear out of this nation." Bart stared at her until she looked down at Izzy again, began coo-cooing at him. "Mostly we don't wanna get recognized."

She smiled at Izzy. "So we gotta be on our own a while."

"Your sisters can do what they want, but you and me, and this baby, we gotta go our own way, find our own place to live, then *just live*. We can make it work. Ain't gonna be outlaws no more."

"Just livin' do seem whole lotta fun," she said, grinning. "Don't need to rob no bank."

Trinity heard them talking, called over: "Robbing banks's what we do. Cain't stop now."

Triss snickered at that. "She shore is right 'bout that."

Bart shook his head. "It ain't a fun time but it's the right thing to do." He pursed his lips, thinking. "We done frightful things. Can't even see why I done most of them. Just young and stupid, figure. I see it now. But I can't take them back, can't undo them. Like them folks that got shot. It was all accident. Well, most of them."

Trina tried to smile. "Ya worry too much. People die every day."

"Not because of me they don't."

"Y'only responsible for what? five? six?"

"I don't know." He had to think. "Some others got shot – maybe they lived, maybe they died." He slipped into a fog, seeing a ledger on a wall. He tried to count the marks but soon gave up.

+ + +

Bart rode into Campo alone intent on robbery, believing one last score would pay for the supplies they needed to go far, far away and live on their own, get away from the whole world. Before he could do anything, men came with guns as though expecting him and he had to ride away. Word was getting around about this gunslinger with the red hair, usually running with a trio of outlaw women.

Bart heard men talking about how they hired a famous gunman whose specialty was going after the hard-to-kill outlaws. Even Bart heard the name of László Vass, although he believed it was from a story book. Ain't no way a bounty hunter could live for a hundred years.

His mama had him read many books and at first he enjoyed it. But as she selected the books most valuable to his education, he grew tired of them. One book she had him read was about a fantastic land called Europa that existed across an ocean long before the pandemic came – or existed during the pandemic, according to his mama.

His school teacher explained what happened over there while people faced the pandemic on this side of the ocean. Over there, one nation rose to dominate the continent and the leader was a powerful yet vain man who claimed descent from a line of *vampires*. Those were a unique kind of person who lived by drinking blood, his mama explained. But she never believed those stories. Lots of books involving those kind of weird figures had been written before the pandemic but most of them were burned when people began to fear vampires showing up on this side of the ocean.

"Bart?" he heard Trina call, but he couldn't shake himself loose from his worrisome thoughts. Not even this woman could comfort him some nights.

The Empire of Europa arose as his own nation fell into civil war following the pandemic. With half the population gone, those who remained didn't know what to do, fought over how to build a new nation. Perhaps the pandemic aided them in seizing power over in Europa. The emperor was said to be one of those vampires, a man who could live for hundreds of years, so he'd accumulated vast wealth, rumored to have powers of life and death over anyone who wasn't a vampire, yet he relied on consuming blood daily from specially raised slaves. It was a frightening story. He had night terrors, so his mama dutifully tossed the books out and finished his geography lessons using what she gathered from the weekly news-paper.

This László Vass who the men mentioned was one of those kind of people, Bart understood. He didn't believe it, but that's what people said. And so what? If the man actually needed to drink blood to keep going, he could be easily controlled. Deprive the creature of blood and he'd grow weak. No threat to a fit young man like Bart. And yet, hearing that name sparked fear in him.

"There ain't no such thing," he cursed. He wished he could take a look at those books in his mama's upstairs room. But he'd run away from home, met up with those outlaw sisters, and that was that. His mama said the book police left those books because they were considered pure fantasy and no one would mistake them for being a different version of history.

"Go to sleep now," Trina muttered beside him, then kissed him and the baby.

Another day Bart rode up to Kenton to buy food for his family, plus some for the sisters.

First he needed to exchange notes for the new notes they were issuing by a proclamation from the capital. All old notes would be exchanged for the new notes on the basis of three old notes for one new note. The new notes bore the face of former President Baskins. Before he left office, he ordered new notes printed and put into circulation after the older President Templeton fell out of favor when someone discovered a receipt from a brothel. Bart had laughed as he read the news-paper report of Templeton's father purchasing for the boy his first experience with a woman at the notorious House of Delight.

Kenton, one of the last towns in the western territory, seemed as good a place as any to do the transaction. The sisters had been there a few years past but Bart hadn't, so nobody would know him. He'd act like a normal citizen of what remained of a once great nation, what they were now calling the Americus: fifteen reformed states and a western territory that ended at the mountains. Beyond the mountains, nobody knew. Hadn't had any contact for a century.

Although he felt nervous standing in line inside the bank, pistol in a holster under his coat-tail, Bart smiled like he learned they liked to see. The pretty teller – name tag: Dolly – smiled warmly at him, maybe flirting, yet Bart remained polite, even dared mention his wife. The transaction went smoothly. He feared they would know the notes he presented came from a different bank far away – notes likely marked as lost in a robbery. Dolly happily gave him a bundle of the new notes and he walked out grinning like he'd won a fight while some in the line cheered for him.

Next was the greengrocer.

He strode down the landing, boot heels clapping the wood. It was a bright, sunny day. He had to squint. No vampire would venture out on an afternoon like this. Then, his eyes blinded, he bumped into a tall man in a black suit coming out of the hotel.

"Pardon," said the man in a deep voice, righting himself.

"Excuse me," said Bart, forcing his eyes open against the light.

The man looked grim, like he'd just been digging graves for his newly dead friends. He stood neat and well-dressed like a preacher. But gaunt.

Bart continued down the street but felt the gaunt man watching him. He glanced back one time, trying to not appear suspicious, yet the man had moved out into the street to observe his direction. Bart grew nervous, wondering if he should go elsewhere, throw off his attention.

Tall and sickly pale, almost albino, in black suit and boots. Bart searched his memory. That was how vampires looked in the books he read. The gaunt man he bumped into looked like he could be a vampire. But there was no way it could be true. Not all the way out here in the western territory.

Bart shook off the dire feelings, decided to treat himself to a beer in the saloon. Entering, he affected an ornery look that put off the saucy ladies inside. He refused to banter with them. They looked tired from a long night anyway. He preferred the thin, brown woman he had back in the camp.

A bewhiskered older man tickled the keys of a piano to the side of the room as Bart ordered his beer. The Skinner Canyon brewery was always good. He wondered if the piano man knew any songs by Maggie Baumann, Bart's musical mother, and if he would play one of them. Heard of her, the man admitted, but couldn't recall a tune. Bart suggested her most famous song "Skinner Canyon Blues" but it didn't ring a bell.

"Where ya from, stranger?" asked the barkeep.

"Nowhere," Bart grumbled.

"That's a might distant place."

"Sure is."

Bart lifted the glass, put it to his lips, took a draw and set the glass down, smacking his lips – as that tall, pale man in the black suit entered and stood in the doorway. The piano player halted his playing and slunk away. The ladies scattered up the stairs to the landing, disappearing. The barkeep straightened his necktie, hand smoothing his long apron. Bart held the beer glass firmly in his non-shooting hand, the other hand dropping down to his leg.

20

THE GAUNTLET

THE TALL, PALE MAN garbed in black suit stood in the doorway, surveying the room as if searching for one particular cockroach hidden in the shadows.

"Good afternoon, Mister Vass," called the barkeep cheerily.

The man didn't respond, kept staring at the mirror behind the row of bottles on the shelf back of the bar.

Bart gave a quick look at the mirror, saw his hat poking into the frame. He could also see the doorway to the bar there in the glass. But he couldn't see the man who stood there. He narrowed his eyes at the mirror. Only a gray smudge seemed to mar the glass, like something to wipe away.

He turned and looked directly at the gaunt man: clear as day.

"What'll it be?" the barkeep asked the man.

The man shook his head once and the staring went on for several more minutes, like the man was frozen in place waiting for a charge up like the old motor-carriages needed. Maybe he had too much sun, thought Bart. Maybe those weird folks could go out in the sunlight but they had to recover in the shade for a while.

Then the man abruptly turned, exiting without word or gesture.

The barkeep gave a loud sigh of relief.

"Whew! That grim fellow always has a way of bringing trouble wherever he goes."

"What's that?" asked Bart.

"Well, you saw that sheath on his leg, didn't you?"

239

"What sheath?"

"It's black like his trousers, so it's hidden to a lot of folks. Got a long knife in it."

"No, never noticed."

"You better be noticing stuff like that. He's deadly with that tool. Heard he cut down dozens of men in battle."

"In battle? What battle?"

The barkeep informed Bart about the stranger. László Vass, the pale man in the black suit, was a famous bounty hunter. "He travels the land seeking outlaws. He always wears that long blade. Prefers it to a gun. Also uses a long rifle with a long scope. Can hit a target nearly a mile off. Trained marksman, hired to go after the toughest outlaws, the ones local sheriffs can't seem to get. Collects on a lot of bounties."

Bart kept a calm face. "Is that so?"

"He's from way over the other side of the world. What they call Europa. The Empire of – to be proper. From the capital there, a city called Budapest."

"*Buda-pest?* That's a funny name," said Bart.

"Don't go smarting off to him like that."

"I ain't afraid."

The barkeep glared at him, then slowly looked away, tending to his glasses wiping chore.

"Odd thing about him though: he requests a young woman visit him in his room each night, I heard. Up in the hotel. Young woman meaning a virgin. But we are fresh outta virgins in this here town, lemme tell you."

"Heck, saloon girls," Bart snorted.

The barkeep gave a sad laugh. "Can't just say they're virgins. He can tell. But he don't do nothing private-like with them, if you know what I mean." He leaned down against the bar. "Like, Mitzi said he just licked her neck for a while and then bit her. Bit her! It hurt at first, she said, then felt good, like she took some drug. That's what she said. Sally, too. Same story. And Trixie. But she didn't like it, said it made her feel sick. She couldn't work for three days."

Bart's head grew hot. "Sounds like one of them vampires."

"Ya think?" The barkeep grinned fearfully. "I wouldn'ta thought it, neither, but there he is. Gotta be one."

"How'd a thing like that get all the way over here?" asked Bart, straightening up.

"He just come by one day," the barkeep replied. "Here on bounty business. Word is he's on the hunt. After a murdering thief they call the Red Devil. Bank robber mostly. But he's got a dozen kills and a high bounty."

Bart was in mid-sip when the name was spoken but he played it cool, finished his sip and swallowed, set the glass down.

"Is that right?" asked Bart, lifting his hand to scratch his clean-shaven chin like he feared a red whisker might still show. It was good that Trina stained his hair, made it darker.

"He got Big Vandy. Cornered him right in the street down there in Amarillo. Drew on him right away, one shot 'tween the eyes. Dropped him like sawn timber."

"Just like that?" Bart was surprised. "No regard for laws about street shooting? What's this world coming to?"

"I guess he got a special license. Nobody complained. Anyways, Vandy's not gonna hurt nobody no more. You know he was accused of lots of *sex-u-wal* mischief. I mean women and children. Better he's gone now."

"Yes, better gone."

"But that Mister Vass. He knows where to find them, how to lay them low. All he asks for is the bounty and a virgin – that he don't even touch privately. Mighty strange."

"But how'd he come over here? They got any ships that go over the seas? How'd he decide this was the place to go?"

The barkeep leaned down again, lowered his voice. "You seem right inter'sted so I'm gonna tell ya, but ya can't pass on what I'm about to tell ya."

"Don't worry, I won't. I don't know nobody noways."

The barkeep glanced around the empty room. The piano player hadn't returned. Upstairs on the landing, a busty blond woman in a red bustier craned her head over the railing. "Gone?"

"He's gone now, Trixie."

Bart gazed up at her. She smiled flirtatiously then, with a wave of her fingers, slipped out of sight.

"You know over in Europa they got an empire ruled by a king of sorts. An emperor, they call it. Székely. Emperor Stefan Székely."

The barkeep saw Bart's eyes lingering on that landing where the woman had leaned, but at the pause he returned his attention to the barkeep.

"Used to be one of us: American. I heard he used to live down in Okala, where they got all them fields of glass, catching the sunlight, all broken now – but that was more than a hundred years ago. Left here long before the pandemic hit, made his home over there – where his family's from originally. So he returned over there, got wealthy. But he made this deal with the devil – so they say."

Bart blinked. "And what deal's that?"

"Oh, it's gotta be a story." He grinned like he was about to lie. "It was his lady. His *Beloved*. Had to save her from the same affliction he had: the vampire curse. So the story goes. So he agreed to do all kinds of evil in exchange for her being free from that curse. And he did. And she was saved. But it changed the whole dang continent. The Black Storm, they called it. Blocks the sun, turning the whole land into a vampire paradise."

"I read about that," Bart muttered. "Made skies dark through the daytime."

"That's it. But that's not all." The barkeep seemed pleased Bart knew something about it. "Like any empire, they went conquering their neighbors, expanding the empire 'til it covered most of the continent. People became fodder for the vampire class, treated like cattle, served up for their blood. Awful, awful times. But he's gone now. Székely left the palace when a mob rose up, backed by traitors seeking to bring him down. Some other vampire rules it now, but not any better. Nobody knows where Székely went."

Bart nodded, rapping his fingers on the bar. "Where could a vampire ever go?"

"Anywhere he wants," the barkeep snickered, "as long as he got a coffin of rich soil to sleep in. Eases the painful skin condition, they say. Must be an awful life."

"That ain't no life," said Bart, imagining the situation. "So what about that man who was in here just now?"

"Right," said the barkeep with another glance around the saloon. "That man, the one just come in, used to be a captain over there. In the army they had. But he didn't lead any troops. He was Székely's personal assassin – *they say*. Credited with the deaths of presidents and ministers, industry leaders, and at least one famous actress – anybody Székely wanted removed. He ruled a cult of fear, as you can imagine. So, with Székely out of power at long last, our pale friend no longer had a job. He heard about the Americus – what folks calling it now – and he found work here. Lotta outlaws to catch or kill."

Bart had to grin at the way the barkeep was making the story so mysterious. Yet he'd seen the bounty hunter himself. If anybody was a vampire it would be that gaunt man.

"Lotsa folks got those jobs 'round here," said Bart. "Why's he so damn special?"

"Special? He never sleeps. Always on the hunt. And he's deadly. He's accurate. Efficient. Quick. Never misses. Never gives up."

"Any ordinary man can do that," Bart said with a snort.

"Oh, not like him."

"He just came in here. What for?"

"Maybe he was looking for you," the barkeep said with a wink.

"I ain't no criminal." But Bart had to turn away, chose to look up to the landing where the bar girl had watched him. "Not like what that man's looking for. Hardened criminals. What man ain't never done no foolish boy tricks anyways? You grow out of it."

The barkeep shook his head. "Ain't that the truth?"

"Heck, I ain't one of them harden criminals." Bart looked at the barkeep, held the gaze as proof he was telling the truth.

"I s'pose not. He'd've shot you straightaway if he'da been aiming to get you."

"So I'm clear," said Bart, offering a snicker. He tossed down the last of the beer. "Just in town on business. Now I'll be going."

The barkeep flicked his fingers off his forehead. "Then a good day to you, sir."

+ + +

Bart strolled through the greengrocer's shop, confident that nobody recognized him. He felt safe. He acted like normal folks do though he kept a pistol in its holster under his coat. Main thing was to see if the town would be good for his family to live in. The town had a fine greengrocer like the sisters said. The ladies putting vegetables into their baskets didn't seem concerned with him, nor about that gaunt man walking the streets. Kenton could be a good town to live in. The vampire wouldn't be here long, he decided.

Yet the gaunt man wouldn't leave, kept appearing in the streets. Bart hated that. Like they were playing hide-and-seek, a game he'd learned in the capital. Now he hated the game.

He couldn't go anywhere in the town without seeing that man, a fixture like a lamp post or a caution sign. Unmoving, ever watchful, like a stone statue. Suddenly here, suddenly there. The man clearly suspected him of something, maybe marked him as the target of his efforts. He could just ride away and never see the man again, Bart thought. He'd seen enough of the town.

But what if the man somehow followed him? Tracked him back to the camp? Then his family would be in danger. He couldn't allow that. He needed to protect his family. No, it had to be settled here in this town.

With evening coming on, he dared seek a room for the night.

"One night," Bart told the stout woman at the front desk of the only hotel in town. He proudly laid a new 20-note on the counter. "I'll let you know if I need a second night."

"That'll be fine," said the woman with a rosy smile. "I'll give you your change when you're leaving."

"But no more than two nights," he confirmed.

At supper in the hotel's dining room he sat staring across at the gaunt man sitting at another table, back against the wall, a lovely mural painted there of snowy mountains and thick forests. The man ordered blood pudding, which Bart didn't find on the menu. He held up a goblet of something red, sipped it, then seemed to raise it in mock toast to Bart, who simply narrowed his eyes and didn't flinch.

He got his fare, steak and potatoes, ate it quickly, and left the dining room while the gaunt man remained, savoring another goblet of red.

Bart stepped carefully along the hallway, listening at each door. He took long sniffs, too, certain there would be something unusual wafting from a dead man's room.

He paused at number six. A funereal scent seemed to emanate from behind the door. That room was suspect. Bart's room was four, the next one. They shared a wall, he mused. From inside his room, he might be able to shoot through the wall and hit the gaunt man. Or the gaunt man might do the same.

Before Bart could enter his room, the gaunt man appeared at the top of the stairs, caught him in the hallway, stopped and stared, not advancing. The man hardly appeared surprised. Yes, only one hotel in town.

Bart didn't want the man to see which room he was going to so he stepped backwards slyly to room three, pretended to search his pocket for the key. He expected the gaunt man to proceed to his own room. Instead, the man remained at the top of the stairs, coolly studying him.

Of course, Bart's ruse wouldn't work if he didn't have the actual key, so he acted like he'd forgotten it, patting his coat. Giving up, he turned as if needing to go to the stairs. He would have to pass by him.

Where to now? Only one way up and down to the rooms.

His hand went to his pistol under his coat-tail, felt it there.

"Excuse me," called a woman, coming up behind the gaunt man. She halted, surprised he stood in her way. She was almost the twin of the stout woman at the front desk, could be sisters.

The gaunt man didn't take his eyes off Bart.

"Oh! Mister Vass, sir," the woman spoke. "I brought fresh towels just as you requested." He didn't turn to her, so she continued. "I'm so sorry about the accident. It happens. But you needn't worry about blood-stained towels. We've got plenty of towels."

Only then did the gaunt man step aside, letting the woman pass. He followed her to his room, keeping his eyes on Bart. She used her master key to enter. The gaunt man gave Bart a stern look before disappearing into the room.

Bart hurried to his rightful room, unlocking it quietly, swinging the door gently so it wouldn't creak. Giving a final glance down the hall, he took a light step inside.

The woman didn't come out although the door remained open.

Then the door swung shut.

Bart closed and locked his door, stepping lightly over to the wall they shared and put his ear against it. His hand rested over his pistol, then released the strap on the holster. He could hear a string of mumbled words, all the woman's. Then laughs like she'd received a surprise gift.

"Oh, Mister Vass," the woman said in a drawn-out cry.

The steady rumble of seduction followed, as Bart guessed. Loud panting from the woman. Grunts from the man. A bit of blood as fitting dessert for such a creature.

He didn't want to hurt the woman, an innocent housekeeper, but he wouldn't hesitate to stop that gaunt man. He continued following their movements by the sounds through the wall. His hand drew the pistol from its holster as he located them sweeping around the room. Perhaps she was trying desperately to escape as he chased her. But there were no screams from her.

Then only silence from the other room. He couldn't hear words or movement. Nothing. He waited against the wall, pistol poised.

If only she would scream, Bart thought. Then he could burst in and shoot the vampire. People would accept that as a heroic deed. But she had to scream first.

He took his pistol and rushed into the hallway, stood outside the door to number six, listening. No noise from the room slipped out to the hallway.

Bart put his hand gingerly on the door knob, recalling the gaunt man wore gloves.

Scream, lady!

He heard movement: like a body being dragged across the floor, the heels of shoes catching here and there. But no scream.

She's dead. I better go in.

He held up the pistol, ready to fire, and kicked at the door knob. The door held, so he kicked again and it broke open.

The first bullet went straight into the gaunt man's forehead as he looked up at Bart from the center of the room, the housekeeper's body hanging limp in his arms, her shoulders against his chest, the shoes indeed scraping the floor, leaving marks.

The second bullet went into the man's mouth, the only targets available the way he was holding the woman. His face was bloody, his mouth the darkest red. It was clear he'd been supping at a vein in her throat. The shot broke off a fang, continued through the back of the throat into the lower part of his skull.

But the gaunt man didn't drop, refused to collapse in death. He let the woman's body slip from his arms to the floor, leaving a bloody trail down his white shirt to his black trousers. And once she was on the floor, the gaunt man reached for the long knife at his leg and swept the blade free, holding it high as a challenge.

Bart glared at the gaunt man, this undying monster.

Two head shots and he still wants to fight?

He fired two more shots: one in the armpit and the other at the shoulder, trying to disable the arm grasping the knife. The arm dropped like a rope was cut, muscles and tendons ripped apart, yet the knife remained grasped in the gloved hand.

By then the gaunt man hung in the air, upright yet unmoving, a puppet on strings. Those eyes stared at Bart, hitting his face, causing a surge of heat – cold heat. Bart dared not look away though he wanted to avoid injury from that gaze.

Better give him one more, just to be sure.

A final shot hit the gaunt man to the left of the breastbone, right into the heart, as Bart calculated. The stories about these creatures said they could only be killed with a silver bullet. But if they were dead already, according to legend, what was the point?

He fired again at the chest of the gaunt man, frozen in place, posed like the crucifix in his uncle's chapel in Skinner Canyon. The gaunt man barely jerked when the bullet entered. The eyes dulled, dimmed, and the lids closed.

A scramble of boots up the stairs took Bart's attention from the gaunt man. Men arrived behind Bart, gasping at the scene from the open doorway. The housekeeper lay on the floor in a pool of blood, the guest also bloody, refusing to fall, a statue.

The hotel manager desperately tried to break through the bunch of on-lookers, shouting for someone to get the deputy.

"You killed him!" one of the men behind Bart erupted.

Bart remained cool. "He was attacking the woman."

"We can see that," said another man, pushing for a better look.

Bart started to back out of the room, came up against the crowd in the doorway.

"Wait for the deputy," one man told him.

"I gotta go," Bart grunted and, holding his pistol up, got them to divide and let him pass.

"He ain't even bleeding much," said a man, pointing to the gaunt man posed awkwardly in the middle of the room.

"It's all *her* blood," said another.

Suddenly the gaunt man's legs appeared to break apart at the knees and ankles. Arms bent in unnatural directions, ribs snapping apart, neck bones dissolving until the head fell forward, chin hitting chest. The whole body crumpled in one great swoosh, to everyone's astonishment, the remains forming a putrid pile of crumbly flesh and spongy bone that seemed to merge into a vile paste that, as they watched, dried into dust. A pile a housekeeper might sweep away.

People behind Bart stood in shock at the spectacle, murmuring about what they'd seen.

"He was standing right there," said one man.

"Then he just collapsed into that pile of dust," said another.

"He was attacking her," said Bart. "You can clearly see what he did to her."

They dared not enter the room. The scene was too gruesome and the pungent odor of the demise repelled them.

Bart pulled his head away from the view, forced himself into the hallway and hurried to his room. Not yet unpacked, he grabbed his bag and rushed out. He met the crowd of the curious, cut through them with his hand – "Excuse me! Excuse me!" – pistol safely back in its holster, under his coat-tail.

Before Bart could get free of the people bunched in the hallway, the deputy arrived with his men, the team bulling their way up the narrow stairs.

"He said he heard the woman screaming," one man announced to the deputy as his men forced the curious to step down the stairs to make room for them. "Took matters under his own hand, he did."

"And you can see what he done to her, the crazed wolf!"

"Sucking her blood right outta her."

"Never had no chance, poor maid."

"That man's a hero, even though he got to her too late."

Men halted Bart's departure, put him in a chair in the lobby.

+   +   +

Four strong men stood around him as the deputy, Bob Cole, spoke to Bart, asking all sorts of questions. Bart played it straight: he was a visitor looking for a good town to live in with his wife and child. He decided to stay the night because it had gotten too late to start the ride home. He saw the man in the next room take the housekeeper inside and she never came out. He heard noises.

Deputy Cole wore a thin mustache, his black hair slicked back and matted flat when he took off his hat. A younger man than Bart expected, but he seemed on his toes, going by the book. And his men seemed to respect him, so Bart took him seriously.

"Then I heard those kinda sounds like fighting," said Bart, "you know, *oomph* and *aargh*, *pow* and *bam* – sounded like she's fighting him, trying to get away."

"And she never screamed?" asked Deputy Cole. He stood with his arms crossed over his chest, silver badge showing above his arms, and a pistol low on his hip like he never needed to use it.

"I figure he had a hand over her mouth, the way he had hold of her when I barged in. She couldn't've screamed."

"So you just kicked in the door, started shooting?" asked Cole.

"I believed she was in danger," Bart responded. "And I was right. I saw them together, him holding her tight, his mouth at her throat. And all the blood—"

"Throat? Not her mouth?" asked one of his men.

"Could they have been in some kind of amorous position?" asked Cole. "Engaged in a kiss perhaps?"

"A housekeeper and a guest?" one of the men asked, amusement in his voice.

"It happens," said the hotel manager from behind the lawmen.

"They were covered in blood," Bart snapped. "That ain't the kind of kiss anybody want."

The hotel manager snickered. "Oh, there's deviants about—"

"She wasn't going up there for any love stuff," said Bart. "I saw her arrive. She brought fresh towels, said others got stained with blood. I heard them talking in the hallway. I was entering my room. He must've invited her in, then attacked her."

Deputy Cole studied Bart a moment, then looked around at each of his men. Got silent responses.

"Awright now, Mister Black – Hal," said Deputy Cole. Bart gave his fake name, matching the initials on the saddle the sisters stole for him: *H.B.* "I'm gonna need you to stay the night. We'll talk more tomorrow. Don't go nowhere. We'll get this incident adjudicated as quick as we can. It needs to be recorded. Then I think we can let you go. Act of defense, defense of others."

One of his men cleared his throat. "When we poked through the mess on the floor – after the body...*dissolved?* – found five bullets."

"One didn't stop him," said Bart. "Neither did the second. Head shots, too."

Cole remained focused. "Hard to tell now, afterwards – after that body-dissolving effect – where your shots went exactly. But you shot five times?"

"He raised his knife to strike at me so I shot at his arm. And when he was still standing but he dropped the woman, I could get a clear shot at his chest. They say—"

"Chest? At his heart? That's what you were aiming for?"

"That's the only way to kill them. A bullet straight through the heart." Bart looked up at the men guarding him. "Unless the head is cut off. That's what I read." One man gave a nod, another a grin. Bart regarded the deputy. "You didn't know that man was one of them...a *vampire?*"

"Well now, sir, that kinda talk is pure speculation," said Deputy Cole. "We treat all men the same here. Any talk of vampires is just gonna be some fool's storytelling and isn't to be believed."

"I never did believe none of that stuff, neither," said Bart. "But I did read a few books on it when I was young."

"Welp, sure is good to be young," said the deputy. "And to know how to read. Hopefully there's something for you to read up in your room. Should be a Bible to occupy your evening."

Bart wasn't happy. He knew the sisters were relying on him. But he hadn't purchased anything yet that he'd come to town for. Always getting into trouble, he cursed.

"I need to get on home," said Bart, trying to soften his voice. "Got my family waiting on me. S'posed to bring foodstuffs back."

"And they'll have to wait another day," said Cole. "Where's that, by the way? What's your business in town?"

Bart had his story ready. "I'm here for finding fair work. See if this town's a good place for my family to live."

"Well, it's a fine town. Excepting the occasional vampire."

Bart gave a chuckle, hoping to seem like a regular fellow. "Yes, I think so. But I was also supposed to purchase some foodstuffs they wanted. Gotta get home quick."

"And where's that?"

"Oh, it's...." He had to make a quick calculation, send them off in the opposite direction. "Toward Buffalo Springs."

"That's a long way from here," said the deputy, eyebrow raised.

"No other towns close that are suitable," said Bart. "I got family, like I said. Want them to be safe."

Deputy Cole smiled. "Glad to hear. Kenton's a fine town."

"Seems so." Bart thought he was about to be let free. But then the deputy stood up and stretched his back.

"I'll have one of my men stay here," said Deputy Cole, "to be sure you have everything you need."

"To make sure I don't leave?" asked Bart awkwardly.

"If you want to say that." The deputy looked at one of his men, smiled at him, back to Bart. "Anything else you need? I'll make sure they send it up."

Bart gave a nod, unhappy.

"We'll talk more in the morning," said the deputy. He patted his holster, then started away. His men followed.

Except for the one who stayed behind, a man older than Bart, sporting a yellow beard, big shoulders and beady eyes, who likely had nothing pleasant in his life so he was the one selected to guard this wayward fellow stuck in a hotel room.

"I'll get you a chair," Bart offered, stepping into his room.

He placed the chair in the hallway opposite the door and the big man plopped down on it without a word.

Bart entered his room, closed the door, and stared at his bag on the bed. He was supposed to fill it with food. He began to pace the room, stopping himself at each interval as he thought what to do.

He went to the window, which looked out the back of the hotel, saw a small garden plot below, a high fence separating it from the alley beyond. Then he remembered Betty. Couldn't leave his horse tied up and saddled all night with no food or water.

"Need to see to my horse," said Bart when he opened the door, prepared to go out.

The guard gave a grunt, disbelieving.

"She's been out there all day," said Bart. "Needs food and water."

"I go with you," said the guard, standing with stiffness. He stood more than a head taller than Bart.

With the empty sack hanging over his shoulder, Bart acted like it contained something for his horse.

He went down the stairs to the lobby, gave a wave to the clerk leaning against the desk, and on out the double doors with the giant following.

"There you are," Bart cooed, arriving beside the brindle mare. He patted her withers, speaking loud enough the giant could hear. "Need to get you down to the livery, get you some food and water." He turned to check with the giant.

No response, the hulking man standing like a mountain to block his way.

So Bart led Betty away, walking her down the street, her hooves clopping against the hard-packed dirt. Actually, he detected stone beneath the dirt in some places from years past that got covered by countless dust storms, patted down by hooves and wagon wheels.

Bart glanced back at the giant following. He saw the livery when he first arrived in town but in that moment he expected to be riding out well before dusk. Now it seemed a lifesaver: a lone gas-lamp on a darkened street. The scent of horses and manure, hay and leather. He took long draws, enjoying the smell. Like at his uncle's ranch outside Skinner Canyon.

"Let me settle her care," said Bart to the giant.

He called into the livery and an older man stepped out of a door into the barn, pushing through two horses to get to Bart.

"I see you need a horse taken care of," said the grizzled old man, wearing an apron. "Oh dear, what an ugly beast."

"She's been tied up out on the street all day," said Bart. "Needs a good meal and maybe a wash. What'll it be?"

"We're near full tonight. I can get to her soon. But ain't no stall for her. Looks old. How old's she?"

Bart wasn't sure. "I think five years when I got her. Been riding her five."

"Holding up purdy good, looks. But that brindle coat ain't much to look at."

"I don't mind," said Bart, running his hand down her neck, over her back. He saw the giant waiting by the open door, wide enough to roll a wagon through. He leaned tiredly against the wall and yawned.

Then Bart was up on top of Betty and whirling her around and leaping out the wide doorway as the giant stumbled to attention. He tried to grab Bart as he passed but failed, falling on the straw floor where balls of manure lay.

Bart galloped down the dark street, taking a look back.

The giant ran out of the livery, his shirt stained, shouting and waving his arms like an enraged monster.

Men popped out of doors on both sides of the street, saw the situation and ran for their horses. One man took a position in the middle of the street and raised a rifle to his shoulder.

Bart maneuvered Betty left and right to dodge the shots. He got her past the hotel, turned down an alley to the next street, and once free of the confining space urged her onward.

He saw a wagon before the greengrocer, flatbed full of bushels of produce being unloaded. He swung low as he passed, snatched a sack of apples from the wagon as delivery boys shouted at him. The shopkeeper came out at the noise, watched Bart race away.

Yet he wasn't free. Men from the town chased after him, he saw. They were fast, faster than Betty. Once out of town he could hide, no moon showing his path. He blended into the darkness, let Betty's brindle coat hide them.

How could they get after him so quick? Had to be a dozen men in pursuit. Like the posse he'd gone on with his uncle years before.

Bart slowed, the darkness around him complete, worrying about the unknown terrain, unable to see where they stepped. It was flat but the ground was scored with stones and he feared Betty breaking a hoof. That would end his escape quick.

"Easy," he cooed to her. "Easy, now."

He saw a mound through the darkness, myriad stars overhead glowing like the gods had tossed handfuls of fire into the sky. He led Betty toward the rise.

He still heard the horsemen making their way toward him. They had to slow down to maneuver over the rocky ground, too, as Bart tried to reach the mound ahead.

"Mister Black," came a voice slipping through the darkness like it was from another world. It might've been Deputy Cole. "Halt your horse. We mean you no harm."

He waited, huddling in a particularly dark patch of shadow.

The message was repeated, sounding closer. A gunshot crackled through the silence. Bart flinched but the shot must've gone into the air, just a warning.

"You need to return to town," the deputy's voice sailed forth. "You need to testify. That's all we want."

Bart knew that by fleeing he'd marked himself as a criminal. Why else run? But if he let them get him, it wouldn't take long for them to determine what other bad things he'd done. His whole list of crimes would come to light. He'd be wrangled, sent to Skinner

Canyon, put on trial for his crimes, and there would be his mama seeing him. He couldn't stand the thought of her seeing him being hanged. He wouldn't wish her that scene.

So he ran. Like a fool. Like a coward.

"We aren't interested in putting you in jail," the deputy called.

Not yet, thought Bart, but you will quick enough.

"Light a match, let us come to you," called the deputy. "Or else we'll have to shoot in your direction. Might hit you. Better if you come to us."

He couldn't move. But his hand could: reached for his pistol and drew it up to his face, his hand against his cheek, trying to look down the barrel, aiming at the point where the voice seemed to come from. He extended his arm and fired.

A man cried out and Bart knew he hit one of them. Now he was in big trouble. If they caught him now they'd really put him in jail and maybe a lot worse.

He wheeled Betty around and tried to gallop away, hoping the ground was free of stones. Shots trailed him but missed as his horse scrambled in fear, almost bucking him off. A couple apples popped out of the sack he'd snatched but no time to retrieve them.

He rode deeper into the night.

Gazing up at the stars, he no longer knew where he was, or which direction he should go. When he let Betty rest as he listened for pursuers, he could hear their horses behind him. Keeping the same distance. Staying back just enough. He couldn't out-run them.

He couldn't give himself up now. He had only one way to go. He had to return to the camp, had to get his woman and baby, had to escape. But he dared not lead these men to the camp.

21

MOUNTAINS AND RIVERS WITHOUT END

DAWN GAVE HIM NEW HOPE. The sunrise set his compass. He'd been riding west all night, not east. He scanned the terrain, tried to find a point he recognized. Instead, what he saw was the same band of horsemen now close enough to read their faces.

One man raised his arm, rifle in his hand. "Hoy!" he shouted.

Bart was not ready to wave back.

"Come on, Betty," he spoke, leaning down. "Now or never."

He galloped off, heading in the same direction he'd been going all night. The horsemen followed, keeping to a steady pace, as though they knew he would tire eventually and they'd get him.

Bart rode on. The posse rode after him. He slowed after a while. They slowed, too, yet kept a safe distance always near enough that he knew they were after him.

He could imagine all sorts of things they'd do if they caught him. *When* they caught him. First would be a sound beating. Then jail. Then a trial – if he was lucky – then the reading of his crimes and a march to the gallows. How many folks had he killed? He wasn't sure. More important, how many had he simply fired a shot toward and they happened to get struck down without him aiming at them or intending to kill them? Bad luck, mostly. He shot with intention to kill maybe...oh, five times before that vampire fellow, but they were people that deserved it.

Deserve it how? It was his mama's voice asking the question. So he answered her. They were being disrespectful. Disrespectful how?

In what way? Calling him a boy! He was a man now, already twenty-one. Yet folks refused to obey him when he gave a command. Like in those banks. Didn't give him his due. Foolish people that didn't need to be taking up any space in this world.

And anybody pursuing him!

+   +   +

Bart burst into the camp on foot, jerking the reins of Betty behind him, shouting: "Gotta go! Gotta go! Pack it up! Now!"

Trinity squatted by the campfire, a pot of beans cooking.

"The hell you sayin'?" she exclaimed.

"We gotta go! Right now! Get packed."

"What for?" She got up from the fire, stood defiant before him.

At the shouting, Triss came out of her tent.

"What's goin' on?" asked Trina, coming out of hers with Izzy in her arms.

"Lawmen!" Bart shouted frantically.

"Lawmen? What?" asked Trinity.

"Men are after me." He glared at Trinity. "Gotta leave. Now!"

"You brung down lawmen on us? What a damn fool y'are!"

"Ain't no damn fool," he said, his face red. "But we gotta leave."

"What happened?" asked Trina, coming up beside him with Izzy wrapped inside her blanket.

"No time," he shouted. "Gotta go!"

"Damn fool brung the law down on us," Trinity growled.

"The law?" asked Triss.

"Listen, ladies," he declared in a firm voice, "we got maybe ten minutes. Take what you can. You and Triss go south. Me and Trina, we'll go west. We'll meet up again someday."

Then Trinity slapped him across his face. "Damn fool!"

Bart became enraged. He put his hands to her shoulders, shoved her back against the rock wall. She stumbled but hit hard, remained upright. She came back at him, fists raised, but he grabbed her by the arm as her punch swung by him, missing.

"Fool or not, we gotta go. Right now! So pack what you can and let's get outta here."

Trinity got the message. Didn't say a word but turned to the fire and kicked dirt over it, left the beans in the pot. Triss was already tearing down the tent, rolling up the canvas just like Bart was doing for Trina's tent. The rolls went over the horses' rumps, other items stuffed into saddle bags or lain across the withers. But not too much that would weigh down the mounts who would need to ride hard.

Bart swung Trina into her saddle then handed Izzy up to her, together wrapped in the native blanket like a good tribal mother. Triss climbed on her horse, spun around, heading to the gap out of camp. Trinity followed her and Bart led his horse through the gap before Trina's. Once free of the rocks, they paused.

"See ya later," Bart said to Trinity.

"Only if God's got a burr up his ass," Trinity said with a snarl, and turned her horse onto the other trail going south through the woods and into a draw that led to the plain stretching to the south. That direction would lead her and Triss down to Plainview, the next town, and Caine after that. In Okala territory they'd be safe.

"Let's hope so," Bart replied, his face mean and his breath hot.

He turned away angrily, trotting down the trail beneath golden leaves. Trina followed, holding Izzy pressed against her chest, the blanket tight around the both of them.

Below the hills he could see the posse approaching: five horses kicking up dust as they galloped over the shortgrass. Only five now, he mused. They're giving up. But he had to hurry to get away before they could see him and Trina.

He led her down another trail that turned west. They should reach the bottom out of sight of the posse as the lawmen took the main trail up to the camp.

Breaking from the trees with Trina behind him, Bart spied the five horsemen. They were at a canter, looking around for him. One caught sight of them and pointed to him for the others. A whoop and a holler echoed across the plain and the posse shifted.

Bart broke into a gallop with Trina following, Izzy crying as he bounced uncomfortably against her chest.

The terrain was flat but there were breaks in the ground, small dried rivulets that could clip a horse's hoof. He dodged a few stones. He feared going too quick for Trina holding their baby so precariously. One stumble and his family would be injured.

Maybe it's better if I give up, he thought, let them go on to safety without me. I should fend off the posse while they get away. Even if I die, they will be free.

"No," he muttered as he pressed Betty onward at a steady pace. "That's not being a man. I gotta fight for them, not give up."

"Bart," called Trina, "we cain't go on."

He looked back, saw how ungainly they rode, threatening to fall off with every bounce of the saddle. They had to slow to a walk to be safe, he knew, but the five men still pursued them – and gaining.

"We can't stop now," he shouted back.

"Iz's pooing down me!"

Bart shook his head. It was impossible. Everything in the world conspired against him.

He wheeled Betty around to meet Trina. Paused side by side, he assessed the situation, seeing the posse approaching fast. He could see their eyes.

"Give it up," shouted the lead horseman.

Bart recognized him as Deputy Cole.

"You running makes you look guilty," shouted the deputy.

"Ain't guilty of nothing!" Bart shouted back.

"Then why you running?" The posse slowed, kept a fair distance yet moved toward them.

"Just don't want nobody getting confused at what I done," Bart cried out. "I did it to save that woman, nothing more."

"We just want to talk with you," the deputy continued from that safe distance. "Sort things out. You're not charged with any crime. Not yet."

"Then why y'all follow after me?"

"You left under suspicious circumstances."

"Ain't nothing s'picious about wanting to go home to my family."

"That's true." The deputy took a moment to study their horses, seeing one with a tribal woman in the saddle, holding a squirming bundle. "Those your family?"

"They're my family. Now leave us alone."

"Cain't just let you go without getting more answers about that incident."

"I think you can."

Bart took the reins from Trina and led her horse away after him. They moved slowly, not appearing to be fleeing, just an even trot away from the posse, nothing suspicious.

"Wait! Where you going?" called out the deputy.

"Going far away," Bart shouted over his shoulder. "Ain't never coming back. So y'all ain't got nothing to worry about."

He knew where the line was. It stood as a barbed wire fence that ran north to south with posts of local timber, bent and ugly but good enough to keep back cattle in the olden days. Now half of it leaned so low that most cows could step over it. And yet he knew what was beyond that fence: the wilderness.

One of the deputy's men came alongside the deputy, rifle raised to a shoulder, speaking to him.

Deputy Cole shook his head, waved him to lower the rifle. "Not worth it," he called out, loud enough for Bart to hear. "Out there, they'll be dead in a week."

+ + +

The Forbidden Zone some called it, out past tribal lands, beyond the civilized part of the world, an area not explored in over a century. Only rumors and speculation of what lay beyond. On the west side of that limp fence, the shortgrass growing sparse in the red soil, it didn't seem so forbidden.

Bart looked back from atop his horse to see if the posse had gone, couldn't detect them at the far reaches of his sight. He turned in the saddle to Trina, with Izzy tight on her chest, wrapped in that native blanket, her horse patiently facing west.

It was a sign, he decided.

No longer were they outlaws on the run. They were explorers. Somewhere out there they'd find a good place to live, try to make a homestead, and forget about vampires. Forget about lawmen, too.

"When we goin' back?" she called over to him.

"Ain't," he said with an amused snort.

"Wanna go with my sisters."

"No telling where they went. Could be anywhere by now. We'll never find them. Best we go on."

"Got lots hideouts 'tween here and Wichita. We check 'em all."

"We can't go back. Posse'll be waiting for us."

He rose in his saddle, gazing west, seeing the way the sun dared to go and decided he was just as daring.

"Whatcha think's thatta way?" asked Trina as he gazed west.

"Whole lotta nothing, reckon. Plenty for us, though. Take what we want. Live our own way." He reminded her about the map he saw in the airplane wreckage. There was an ocean over there. And cities. Only the mountains kept him from seeing them.

"Don't wanna go see no ocean," she told him sternly. "Wanna go back to my sisters."

"Well, we can't go back."

"Why cain't we?"

"Because we have left the garden."

She didn't seem to understand, but she followed as they headed west, with a hot wind blowing against them.

The land rose, the twisting road broken into loose stones, with the occasional abandoned shack leaning awkwardly near the usual pump machines Bart had seen before on his rides, the remnants of a world he never knew when motor carriages stopped to buy fuel and drive on. But to where? It seemed people had more places to go back then, and they were always going somewhere.

He put a hand to his brow, shielding the sun from his view. He couldn't see anything ahead but dry mountainsides, bare rock, and stands of conifers on the higher slopes. He wondered why that deputy thought he'd die out here. Likely nothing dangerous here but some tribals, not that they weren't to be feared. Anything else he could only imagine – and he had a big imagination thanks to the books his mama made him read.

A simple mistake in some place where viruses were made, let out to the public, catching people unawares, sickening them, taking out half the population and leaving those who remained fighting over scarce resources until everything that had stood before lay in ruins. In time, some people got together and rebuilt the cities, made a new society, took control over everyone else. A few escaped those places. Like his grampa almost did. His mama told him the story: he was a hero and that status gave him the right to leave. But he'd returned to save his children from that cruel society, including Bart's mama. They went west to a dusty cowtown.

He'd seen the capital as a boy, recalled its grandeur and its excesses. Noted the tyranny that endured, praised for an efficient society, and the way everyone was forced to behave a certain way, think alike, never complain – until his mama took him away and they arrived in Skinner Canyon. He'd read the books she put before him. He pulled others from the shelves in that room, curious about most everything. He almost forgot those years he read voraciously, absorbing all of it – while his cousin Jake kept pulling him away for kick ball or shooting at cans and bottles.

Now he was as far away from that home as he'd ever been.

The road bent through the mountains, the old stone cracked into rough blocks that challenged hooves. One bad step and a horse could be injured, lame at worst, need a new shoe at best, and he had no spares. So they kept to the side of the old road, along the grassy strip, pausing at fallen signs to read the strange words on them. *I-25* read one blue sign in the shape of a shield. He couldn't believe how many miles the sign stated to get to a city called Taos.

"Think there's people there?" Bart asked Trina, pointing to the sign as the dry wind pressed them.

"If they got some," Trina replied, "why we never seen 'em? Never come over our side of that fence."

"Maybe they're as scared of us as we are of them."

"Ain't scared o' nobody," she said with a grumble.

They rode on, Bart constantly alert for threats coming over the next hill or out from the woods on either side of the road. He wasn't sure what might attack them, but he believed other people would be the worst, wanting to take what he had, including his woman and his son. He kept the rifle ready, lain across his saddle. He told Trina to keep her pistol close as she held Izzy against her.

"Know it," she responded gruffly.

Over the next rise he spotted a creature hunched over in the grass beneath some trees. It seemed naked, and Bart wasn't sure what it could be. As he got closer the creature saw him, turned quickly on its long feet, then rose to full height. It was as tall as a man – maybe it was a man, some strange human with a vicious face and huge paws. The creature seemed to be dining on a fresh kill, some large rodent, looking like a prairie dog but larger.

At Bart's approach the creature took a stance, ready to attack.

"What is it?" he asked himself, raising the rifle.

The creature seemed half man and half...something else, like a wildcat or a wolf. Bushy facial hair, a slight mane down the back, but otherwise without any fur. The hands and feet were larger than a man's, had long claws that looked more serious than untrimmed nails. Definitely a wild animal.

When it rose to challenge Bart, he shot it with the rifle. No need to give it a chance to attack his family.

"What is it?" asked Trina as she held Izzy tight in her arms atop the horse.

"Not sure." He got off his horse, strode over to the creature.

A long rough tongue lay limply out of its mouth. He could see its huge fangs. A predator, but not a man. Not any other animal he knew. None that he had read about either. Unless....

"This here's one of them *werewolf* creatures," he announced, the business end of the rifle put to the beast's head. "Never thought they was real."

"Look more like bobcat than wolf," said Trina.

"Those spots sure do make it look that way. Like somebody bred a man with a bobcat and got the worst of both."

"An' there it is," cried Trina, worry in her voice.

"I read about things they did to folks way back when during that pandemic, trying to treat sick folks. Made mistakes, got things mixed up, made a strange combination like this one."

"It's terrible," she said, staring at the beast.

Bart poked the creature with the end of the barrel. It lay still.

"Mama told me about the vaccines, what her great-grampa wrote about. Some people just couldn't get enough of them. They'd demand every one. Took too many and got sick. Different kind of sick. Maybe they turned into creatures like that one."

She shook her head, a mask of uncertainty dulling her face as she clenched Izzy tighter.

"I'm sorry for all this," he said. "Probably a rare thing. We'll find a good place to start a homestead, I promise."

"Ain't got no tools. No seed. How ya gonna start a homestead? Got no livestock. How ya make a farm?"

"We gotta start small. I can hunt. We got a tent. We'll survive."

"Don't wanna just survive. Not like this. What of this here boy? He gonna just survive?"

"Don't worry." Bart regarded her: she appeared unconvinced. "I'll take care of you. You and him. You're my family. My first and last thoughts."

"Ya better be thinkin' how we gonna live out here as yer first an' last thought."

"I am," he said, gazing at the horizon.

They rode on but Bart continued to keep an eye out for other strange creatures that might lurk in the mountains. He thought of a few other things he saw in books. Like vampires. And the giant hairy beasts standing on two legs that some called Bigfoots. But they weren't in these dry southern regions.

Making a camp in the crook of a narrow valley, a clear brook curling through it, Bart set up a lean-to shelter using the canvas. Trina lay under it while feeding Izzy.

Bart made a fire, sat by it, stirring a pot half-full of beans.

"Now I'm not saying that fellow really was a *vampire*," said Bart as the fire burned low in the deepening darkness. He'd divided the beans between him and Trina but there wasn't much for either. "But he sure had all the traits I read about in some books. They should be thanking me for taking care of it. Not be chasing me like they were. I did the right thing. They gotta've see that."

"Ya done good," Trina said after hearing the story. She bounced the boy on her knee. "Ain't that right, Iz?"

"That posse, they just want to ask me questions. But I feared they might recognize me – heard 'em refer to the Red Devil. They'll put other crimes I done together on a long list. Then I woulda never got back to you."

"I know ya done right," said Trina, nuzzling the baby.

"Here, let me hold him a while. You get some rest."

She handed the drowsy baby to him, watched as he settled the bundle on his shoulder, pulled the blanket around them, and rocked gently. She lay beside him and slept.

+   +   +

Higher into the mountains they rode, following the broken stone as best they could, treading carefully over rickety bridges spanning gorges. Some spans still seemed strong but others looked like they could fall any moment. Forests rose thick on both sides of the road, hiding potential dangers or offering fruit. And the abandoned vehicles, rusted and broken into, some with skeletons sitting inside, tore at his heart. He recalled what his mama said about those far-off pandemic years and now he knew it was true. Back east, he'd seen how they cleaned up those remnants, made it nice again, like a pandemic never happened.

Out west, especially in this new empty zone, nobody bothered to clean anything. Maybe there wasn't anyone to take care of it. They hadn't seen another person since they rode away from that posse. It wasn't as though he wanted to meet people. He expected they'd try to trick him, get a jump on him. He didn't want to be recognized either, didn't want to be called Red Devil, or even Bad Bart. But he was ready – as long as his ammo held out.

They got to a high pass, paused at the overlook. A bent sign read "Scenic View" and he looked down upon what appeared to be a town. It was larger than any he'd seen in the western territory. Yet he couldn't detect movement down there. He watched carefully. No folks walking about, no wagons or carriages rolling on streets, no lone horseman. As though everyone had died and left the buildings standing. Or they left for a better place.

The road led to the town, he guessed. Likely they'd face danger from starving, vicious creatures, whatever remained. Better to skirt the dead town, he decided.

He didn't share his thoughts with Trina. He was in charge now. A man like him just knew what to do. And yet, weeks of riding, of camping, of being constantly on alert for wild beasts and any bad weather was starting to wear him down. And he got no comfort at night when they rested. Those days when that dust storm battered them as he held the tent canvas against the wind, then brushing off the dust after before packing up everything and riding on. He was exhausted. That day a pair of tornadoes crossed their path, striking down trees left and right, and they ducked into a ravine fearful for their lives. The dry, desert sun burning down, making Trina fold up the blanket, she growing faint and nearly falling off her horse when they'd gone too long without water. The baby crying. Trina cursing. All their complaining!

"When we goin' back?" Trina asked every night. She moaned on and on about missing her sisters and Bart grew tired of it.

"Maybe we ain't gonna go back," he'd say, trying to stay as calm as he could. No point being mean.

"Don't mind ya gettin' caught," she'd say. "Ya get out soon an' ya come back to me. But this boy now, he gonna grow up but I tell him 'bout ya."

"You do that," he'd say, voice gruff. "You tell him all that I done. You tell it true. Bad with the good. My life's a lesson for him."

She began looking at him a different way, like she was thinking of plots, and despite her being his lover he kept a knife at his side and the pistol near for anyone or any beast that might come too close during the night.

"Ain't going back," he'd mutter before blowing out the candle.

One night his words sent her into a crying spell, something he'd never seen from her before. She was always acting tough. But that was when she stood with her sisters. Now she was alone with him, this younger man who decided to act like he was the boss of her. She hated that, he could see.

He took Izzy into his arms some of the days, let her take the lead as they traveled. Yet he worried she'd be caught unaware if danger attacked them. No, it had to be him who met the attack, who had to fight and protect them. Maybe sacrifice himself so they could flee. So he insisted she take the boy and he'd go first.

Days went by, turning into weeks: every day – most of them – on horseback making their way slowly, following the broken stone road, pausing where there was a shack standing near the pumps he recognized: different names, different colors and designs. Some had water pumps that still worked. They passed rusted hulks of vehicles large and small, some with skeletons inside. One vehicle had a small seat resting on the second bench: in that child-sized seat were child-sized bones. Ran out of fuel and died. They found more wind-swept skeletons, bones gnawed clean, scattered by the road. Like those skeletons in the airplane wreckage, it looked like they'd been sick and were trying to flee from somewhere only to fall dead along the way.

Bart checked every old building they came to, rifle held ready, looking for anything that might have use, but they'd been cleaned out long ago. They'd left camp so fast they had little time to gather the food they had. Bart gave an apple from his saddle bag to Trinity and Triss when they parted. The others he shared with Trina, but now those were gone. He chewed on jerky Trinity made from the antelope he shot. Now that was gone, too.

He wanted to go hunting, find a deer and turn it into several meals and hearty snacks, but he found none as they rode along. The woods on either side of the stone road remained silent but for the eerie rustling of golden leaves. He hoped to see a herd over the next hill. They'd go a couple days with nothing to eat only to come upon some fruit trees or berry bushes. Then they'd take all they could. Izzy enjoyed grabbing them, squeezing the berries in his tiny hands. They'd make a meal then rest after eating. The next day the journey continued.

The land turned drier, with fewer trees to offer shade. None had fruit. The roads became a tricky configuration, going off in different directions, most with the signs torn down. He saw one sign like the I-25 sign he saw before and pointed to it.

"*I-forty*," he said to Trina. "Wonder what the *I*'s for?"

This new road was a twin pathway with a grass strip running down the middle. It seemed to be heading in the right direction: due west for the next town. They could ride along the grass instead of try the stone which was broken like the others. Over time, weather would wear down the stone, he understood. Changing temperatures would break it apart, cracks expanding year by year until the stone snapped apart. Hadn't been repaired in a hundred years. But horses couldn't go over broken roads like these. Hard for those old vehicles, too.

They started down the grassy middle way, Bart in the lead with Trina following. Izzy looked out from the cloth sling Trina had fashioned to carry him against her. He seemed fascinated by all the strange new sights passing by.

"Almost there," Bart would cheer.

"Almost where?" she'd growl at him.

"Somewhere else," he'd respond.

Not far from the abandoned city they skirted, where the desert met them again, they spied the pointed tops of some tribal homes. They halted, keeping a distance, studying them. Were they in use? He scanned them: a dozen of them in a line on the horizon, the late sun making them silhouettes.

Bart couldn't see people or animals around the *teepees*. If they weren't in use by anyone, he thought, then his family could stay a night or two. They needed to rest. Stopped in one place for a while, he could hunt, try to get some food.

They eased up to the line of teepees, saw a sign designating the site as "Tourist Village" – whatever that meant. He regarded Trina, who shrugged. Who were these 'tourists'? Another tribe? Be careful, there's Tourists out there, he mused. Looking around, he noted the remnants of several other buildings set along another stone road. A big square box, as big as the main street blocks in Skinner Canyon. A large sign hung at an angle on its front: Costco. Must be a tribal name, he thought, and checked with Trina. She didn't know. Next to Costco was a larger building with a sign reading Sam's Club. Club, huh? He decided it must be some kind of saloon, a place for cowpokes.

He would look closer the next day. It was already late.

He dismounted while Trina waited.

Each teepee had an open entry; no door to close. He determined they had doors at one time but they'd been removed. No one inside. He checked six teepees, found them empty but for scraps of tribal gear the last residents forgot. The buildings weren't made of animal hides, he discovered, but walls of plaster that had flaked off in many places showing a wire frame. They were sturdy, could last a hundred years.

Even if they weren't real teepees, Bart thought, they could stay overnight and be protected from the wind and the night's cold.

He unloaded the horses and they moved in.

The horses wouldn't go through the low doorway but he feared leaving them outside.

He took the horses to another teepee that had a larger entrance. The entry had been broken, torn apart, making a larger opening. Inside was strewn a lot of straw like a stable, so he kicked out the doorway more, made it large enough for the horses to squeeze through. He gathered handfuls of grass outside and took it inside for the horses to eat. Found a metal pan in a pile of junk, filled it with water from a ditch and brought it to the horses. More trash lay about, decades old, forgotten. He moved a fallen pallet over from a line of them on the ground and leaned it up against the doorway to block in the horses, then more pallets to weigh the first one down.

The plaster teepee proved a good home, the solid walls blocking the night wind. The floor wasn't earth or grass but stone. Trina laid out the blankets, made it a home, then took to feeding a fussy Izzy. The boy was always hungry.

Bart made a small fire from brush he collected, checking that the smoke rose out through the vent in the top of the teepee.

"Don't know 'bout this place," Trina spoke after a while, laying on the blanket. "This whole land with no name. Clear as day folks lived here at one time or other. Kin see what they leave behind. Wonder where they all went."

"Some died," Bart responded flatly, just to make peace. "I figure most went to some other place, where all these roads lead to."

She checked on Izzy, asleep beside her, then gazed up as though she could see the stars through the teepee's plaster walls.

"Here we are," she said, letting out a long sigh. "Ya get born, an' ya find somethin' ta do without gettin' killt or killin' some other. Ya do it fer years, whole years. An' that's yer life." She regarded Bart. "Why we here?"

"Those're questions best answered by my uncle. He's a priest in Skinner Canyon. He got all those answers."

"No, I mean us. Why we here? What this place? Why the Great Spirit show us this path?"

He regarded her. Her hand on Izzy's belly, she seemed afraid. He went over and sat beside her, put his arm around her like he always did back in the camp.

"The road led us here. Maybe it's the way we're supposed to go. Maybe there's some purpose in us coming here."

"Purpose?" She smiled sadly. "What kin it be way out here?"

"You see people used to live here. Used to be something for them to do here. They must've liked living here cuz they built a whole city here. Don't know why they all left. Or, like I said: died."

"Never lived in no city. Not a town, neither. Too many folks."

"I know. Even Skinner Canyon was getting too big for me."

He looked at her, then leaned in for a kiss.

"But we gotta keep going," he said after the kiss.

She wiped her lips. "What's ahead? Where're we goin'?"

"There's a town somewhere for us."

"Where's it, Bart? Where?"

"West." He thought a moment. "As far west as we can go in this world. Looking for a town with good people where we can live. I'll find work and you raise our boy."

"Ya think there's a town like that way out here? Seems only a land of death. Ever'one's gone. Just disappear."

"I dunno," was all he could think to say.

Later in the night Bart awoke at the sound of something outside the teepee. He grabbed the rifle, went to the entrance, peering out.

He saw something in the darkness moving between the teepees: a beast on four legs. Didn't seem like a wolf. The creature padded to the teepee where the horses lodged, letting out a kind of laughing growl. Bart stepped out with the rifle, going barefoot over the dirt, and came upon the beast.

One growl and Bart fired, catching the animal with its mouth open, ending the threat. Moving closer with rifle aimed, he saw the thing was another of those weird beasts he shot before: somewhat like a man but also a wildcat, golden-brown with brown spots.

He heard the horses whinnying in fear so he went to calm them.

"Same animal," said Bart, returning to Trina.

"Don't like this place. Got bad spirits."

He watched her a while, laying beside their baby, and his heart paused a beat as he realized all he had in this world was right here before him. What was he seeking? A place of their own? Just live each day? He would toil and ache to put food on a table for them and she would teach their son everything he needed to know to...? To what? Toil and ache after him? To labor all the days of his life? No, his son had to have a better life.

"I used to have a dream," he spoke softly to Trina, face to face on the floor of the teepee. "Mama had plans for me, but after a while I didn't want it. She told me about the capital where she grew up. A very strict place, for sure."

"Y'ain't there no more," she responded.

"I know, but she told me one time. I remember it now – thinking of us out here. She said people will accept less and less each day. It ain't hard. A little at a time. Until they know nothing but work. And obedience. A day free of work will be like a dream." He sighed. "Yeah, but those days without work were filled with patriot events we had to go to. And you better go or you get fined. You work for the day when you don't need to work. Then you get to rest. In your grave."

"Don't want no life like that," she said, putting her hand on his shoulder. "When I got a dream way back, time I's little, it was bein' a rich lady in fine clothes. Pa was gonna be rich from his digging, he like to say, sell ore for top credit. Said we soon be in a palace."

"Guess we ain't gonna be in a palace out here."

"Lucky to find a fake teepee, ain't we?"

That made him smile, and she smiled.

"We gotta stick together," he said.

"Know it."

"We only got each other."

"Know it, too."

Patting her holster, she gave a nod and closed her eyes.

22

TOURIST VILLAGE

AFTER A RESTLESS NIGHT trying not to awaken Trina, Bart got himself up, smiled at Izzy peeking out of the blanket. Going to the entrance, he saw the sky was light and thought to go check on their horses in the other teepee. He took the rifle, as was his habit now.

A mild morning, sky pale blue, the wind light, and all around him was the world: a flat plain of waving grass with jagged lines of mountains in the distance, like he was on top of the world. The line of old buildings and the flat stone yards meant for motor carriages. Yet this was not a place to set up a homestead. These teepees would be a target for anyone looking for victims.

His mind went straight to a memory of his mama perching him in her lap as she read some old notebooks her great-grandfather Sandy had written, what he called *The Way of the Son.* She said she would compose an opera based on his tough adventures during the pandemic. Mostly him taking his young wife and baby into the savage wilderness, fighting to stay alive, eventually hiding in the forest of a national park. He knew the story but didn't wish to recall it on this fine morning.

But it stayed in his mind as he glanced back at the teepee where his wife and baby slept, felt a gnawing fear in his gut that he might not be able to protect them. He had to get them to a safer place. There were no forests out here, no place to hide.

"What a fool I am," he muttered, regretting the past five years.

The horses were anxious, stirring inside their teepee, unable to be calm. He brought them more grass, patted their necks, spoke softly. Yet something kept them worried. Might be an animal like before, and he went outside, rifle in his hand.

He saw it right away: another one of those creatures that looked half man and half wildcat, tawny and spotted, pointed ears pulled back, ready to attack. It crouched fifty yards away in taller grass, watching him. No doubt it could smell the horses.

Before he could raise the rifle to his shoulder and line up the sights, a noise erupted and the beast screamed for an instant and tumbled over. The death cry was no wildcat: sounded like a woman.

Dropping to his knee, Bart glanced around. Someone else was up this morning and on the hunt.

He scrambled behind one of the piles of junk left on the ground, this one looking like the boards of a broken cart stacked up. Part of a wooden sign lay among the junk, words reading: *Navajo Village*. Bart tried reading the sign's smaller words when a voice called out.

"Helloooo!"

Bart peered over the top of the broken sign board.

"Speak English?" the person shouted from where Bart heard the blast come from. Hadn't sounded like a rifle shot, not a bullet. "Or are you Navajo?" Then: *"Diné bikéyah?"*

Bart slowly stood behind the junk, rifle still held up.

"Oh," said the figure approaching him. *"Gringo."*

The figure looked nearly as strange as the man-cats. Covered in a pale yellow garment that reached from brown boots up to a head covered with a white hood. There was a window in the front of the hood where the person peered out. In gloved hands the person held a kind of rifle that looked different than Bart's.

"Hold it right there," the person commanded, raising that rifle.

Regarding each other, the distance narrow enough to get a good look at each other, they lowered their weapons simultaneously. The person inside the suit seemed to be a man. Definitely not traveling clothes, thought Bart in his shirt and trousers. He remained wary.

"Never seen anyone out this far," spoke the man in the hood and coverall. Up close, Bart saw he also had a small pack on his back, with a tube curling around that attached to the side of the hood. The belt around his waist carried tools and devices.

"You're the first person I've seen in weeks," said Bart.

The man in the suit gave a nod. "You're the first I've seen out here in years."

"Only people I seen were nothing but dry bones."

"Yes, that's what most of them are now."

"Is it safe?" asked Bart, gesturing to the man's suit.

"Maybe." He looked right then left. "Could be. How about you?"

"I think I'm safe," Bart responded.

"You know where you're going?" asked the man.

"Not really," said Bart. "Just someplace safe."

"Then you must be lost."

Bart heard laughter from inside the hood, saw a grin on the face in the window.

"How come you wear that suit?"

"How come you aren't dead?" asked the man in the hood.

"I ain't fixing to die," said Bart.

"You aren't wearing a hood. How can you breathe this crap?"

"What crap?"

"All the crap that's in the air!" The man seemed angry.

"Seems fine to me. Smells good. Natural," said Bart, sniffing the air and looking around. Had the smell of a ranch.

"You sure? No bad effects?" The hooded man stepped closer. "You been sick recently? Any symptoms? Like the flu but worse?"

Bart shook his head. "Nothing like that, no sir. I like breathing this fresh air." He took another long draw, expelled it dramatically. "See? It's good air."

"Well, damn." The man shook his hooded head. "You do look like a healthy kind of person. Never been sick, huh?"

"Nope. Never. Wounded, yeah. But never got them illnesses."

"Never?"

"Nope."

"Well, damn."

The hooded man stared at Bart, then reached back and released a catch at the back of his head. He pulled the hood open inch by inch, breath by breath, let it fall forward to his chest, still attached to the suit. What the fallen hood revealed was a swarthy man with curly black whiskers. He grinned like he'd been caught in a trick.

"Nick," said the man, extending his gloved hand. "Nick Ramos."

Bart figured anybody out this far west wouldn't know him so he dared give his real name.

"Name's Bart." He shook hands with the man. "Bart Baumann."

"So like I said, Bart, I've never seen anyone out here for several years. And I check it nearly every week."

"Nobody?" asked Bart.

"No humans."

Bart pointed at the killed man-cat. "How about those things?"

"They don't count as people."

"What are they?"

"They are experiments gone wrong. All I'm allowed to say."

"Why's that?"

"Cuz I'm part of the problem, you might say. I live with them, the people causing the problems."

With a wave of his hand, Nick turned toward the fallen creature and Bart followed.

"You said experiments? Like what?"

Arriving at the dead beast, Nick crouched in his cumbersome suit, put his gloved hand to the chest of the beast. No heartbeat, he indicated. He gazed around for any others waiting to attack.

"What are these things?" asked Bart, keeping his rifle ready for an attack. "Ain't never seen none of these back where I come from. We got some wildcats, sure, but not near this big."

"These aren't wildcats. They're hybrids," said Nick, then saw Bart looking puzzled. "It's like if you put two things together that don't usually go together, it's a mix of both. You never know what you'll get, however. That's the experiment."

Bart stared hard at the beast. "Why would anybody do such a thing? And *how* can they?"

Nick stood, staring down at the creature. "Better get this one put away or others will come for it. They're happy to eat their own. But I sure wouldn't take a bite of them. Likely poisonous for us."

Bart went grim. "From the experiment?"

Nick held up a hand for Bart to wait, then stretched his arms, taking in a big breath. He held it, then let it out slowly.

"You're right. It is fresh air." He chuckled. "Been living a lie for years now. They always said to wear the hazmat suit when I go out. Put on the hood or I might die. Lots of viral stuff outside. Swore the air is poisonous."

"Who says that?"

Nick grimaced, like he was about to say too much.

"Scientists. I guess you could call them that. Wear white coats like uniforms. Like it means something. Still think they're gonna fix all sorts of problems. Those experiments were part of that. Try new concoctions, injecting them into cats."

Bart's face lit up. "Cats? Those? They experiment on cats?"

"Cats and people.... More specific, cats and women." Nick leaned closer as though there were others listening. "People they took from the city back there. You probably passed it getting here. Well, there weren't many by then, but whatever they found, they dragged into their *lair*." He laughed. "I call it *lair*. They call it a *bunker*. Like it's a secret hiding place that's safe from the plague they created. More like it's a safe place from the people that wanna get them for all the horrible things they've done. They're hiding from their victims."

"Victims?" Then Bart got it. "You're all covered up. Like you're thinking something is deadly out here. That'd be the virus you're talking about, right? Like that pandemic long ago? And the victims, they got that virus? Is it the same as the pandemic we had?"

Nick frowned. "Well, guess I said too much. You don't seem like a victim, though. Actually, those victims should be long dead. You know about that, huh? Lived through it or avoided it?"

Before Bart could respond, he spied movement in the corner of his eye and turned to see Trina standing outside their teepee with Izzy wriggling in her arms. She glared at him like he'd forgotten to do something. Maybe he was supposed to start a fire to warm them in the cool morning air. Yet she looked plenty warm wrapped in her native blanket.

Nick turned and saw them.

"You got others with you." He bowed his head in greeting. "It's a good sign. People surviving. People keeping up, getting by. I keep telling them there's other people somewhere out here."

"My family." Bart felt proud to say the words, watching as they came over to him. "We're looking for a new place to settle down."

"Well, this sure isn't it," said Nick. He smiled politely at Trina as she arrived. "Morning, ma'am."

"Sorry," Bart said to her. Izzy reached his little arm out to try to grab him. "I went over to check on the horses and saw one of those cat creatures. But this man shot it, so don't worry. He's from some place nearby."

"Nick Ramos," he said, pulling off his glove and extending his hand.

Shifting the baby in her arms, Trina shook it. "Glad ta meet ya."

"This is Trina," said Bart. "My wife."

She gave Bart a look. "Ya kin call me T. Like the letter."

"Awright now, T," said Nick in a cheery voice.

Bart looked puzzled, then smiled. "And this little one is our son, Isaiah, but we call him Izzy."

"Isaiah? Like in the Bible, huh?"

"Don't really know about that."

"Well, I know all the verses. They don't like the Bible down there and they're always telling me to shut up when I talk about it. But I got it memorized. Just about all of it. They keep me around because I'm the only one not afraid to go out here."

"Said ya live 'round here?" asked Trina.

"In the bunker." Nick glanced behind. "It's hidden away. About a mile that way. They like to keep it secret. Pretending it's Navajo land. But everybody knows the tribe got sick, died from the virus a while back. Or the man-cats got some of them, broke out of the pens and ran out of the bunker. Some scientists were killed. Now they're very strict with coming and going. I'm the only one they send out to check on things. Seeing if the world still exists. But I don't mind. Others are scared of going out." He gave Izzy a smile. "So where you coming from?"

Trina held up Izzy and kissed his cheek.

"The world does exist," she said. "See here? See this baby?"

Nick smiled at them, ignoring his question. "That's the first real child I've seen in years. I mean, not many people come out this far, and the ones who do are old – older than you – and they don't have babies. So good for you. You two must be healthy."

"He's nearly a year old," said Bart, beaming at Trina.

She stepped forward. "Now lemme ask ya. Got any food?"

"Food?" Nick acted like he didn't know the word. "Oh.... Well, in the bunker we take packets of what they call 'supplements'. I guess it's like food. There's really no taste to it. You get all your nutrients, of course, but it's not a tasty meal."

"We need something," she said, glancing at Bart. "Taste or no taste."

"Yeah," said Bart, looking humble. "Whatever it is that keeps us alive. We ain't had a proper meal in more than a month. Last was a deer I shot."

"Gettin' out of milk for this one," said Trina.

"That seems about right," said Nick. "Well, you almost got one of those *femo-cats*. That's what we call them. *Femo* as in female. But I don't recommend trying to eat any of them."

"Then what's there to eat that ain't poisonous?" asked Bart.

Nick grinned, thinking. "I suppose I could take you back. They might be happy to see you, get a look at you, people from the other world. I told them there's people somewhere around up here."

"Back where? Your home?" asked Bart, noting the barren land.

Nick waved his arm, smiling at Bart.

"It's home for now. Maybe forever. Hard to say." He had to think. "Like you, I came here all innocent and hopeful. Trying to get away from what was happening in my town. Plague, you know. But I got into some trouble when I got here. They rescued me. Saw I was in trouble and came out to help. I've been with them ever since. About eight years now. Not what I ever planned or expected to be doing. But here I am. Surviving. Waiting for a better day."

"So you came from somewhere else like us," Bart confirmed.

"Yeah. Up north." Nick grimaced, bad memories coming into his mind. "Anyway, I'll try to get you inside. Maybe need to have some testing first. Make sure you're safe. No virus. They do that. Even for me whenever I return from these outings."

"Whatever it takes," said Trina. "Just need food."

"What about the horses? Can't leave 'em out here."

"Bring them with you. They need to see horses still exist, too."

"They gonna be safe?" asked Trina.

"Safe as you. Maybe study them a while. More testing. They love their tests." He put his hand up to his head, scratching at his curly black hair. "I got a cart. Runs on electric. You can lead your horses after us but the lady and the baby can ride on my cart."

"A real electro-carriage?" asked Bart.

"Well, it's not too big. Not like what I drove coming down this way. Had a jeep. One of the last. But that was years ago."

He pointed to a gray squarish thing set on four thick wheels. It sat among the scrub brush fifty yards away.

"It's good for going out for a day. Used to be for playing a game. You ride along on them and hold out a stick. Try to hit a tiny ball with the stick as you go by, hope the ball rolls into a hole in the ground. They count how many times you have to swing the stick to get the ball into the hole. Fewest swings wins. But never got to play that game here. They don't like games here. Everything is serious."

Nick pointed to the vehicle: two seats in front, flatbed in back.

"Sounds fine. Thanks," said Bart.

Nick gave Bart a stern look. "You better put away your guns. I know they're crazy about guns. Probably more after that scientist went crazy being stuck inside for so long." He laughed a little. "But they dealt with him."

"I'm not giving them up." Bart regarded Trina. "I can put them out of sight. Don't wanna scare nobody."

"They have guards," said Nick. "They will check you."

Bart turned to him. "You know we need them in this wilderness. The only way to get food. I got a rabbit and I got some birds for us to eat. And that deer. Even tried to catch fish in a stream. No luck. But she's good at pulling down fruit from trees. I lift her up and she snatch 'em."

"Ain't no trees out here," Trina spoke gruffly.

"Well, there are no rabbits or birds, either," said Nick, "no fresh fruit to eat down there."

"Down there?" asked Trina.

"Yes. Underground. A whole city."

"A whole city?" Bart quizzed.

"Yes," said Nick and they had no words to reply. "So if you're ready, let's go." He gave them a welcoming wave. "I'll try. Worse that could happen is they don't let you in and you have to go on your way."

"And best?" asked Bart.

"Best is they let you in and they're curious about you, how you survived. Maybe ask you lots of questions about where you're from, what it's like there. Not likely they lock you in a cage to observe you, check if you got any viruses. They did that with a couple of humans we caught years ago. But they were completely wild. Time in the wilderness will do that to any person. Vicious and diseased. A lot different than you."

"Would they do that? Really?" asked Bart.

"Honestly, I don't know. They watched me for a while. But they were kind. Like I was their pet human. Treated me good. Now I do a job for them that none of them want to do: checking up top."

"We ain't nobody's pets," said Trina.

"I know, I know." He screwed up his face against the bright sun, scanning the hills in the distance. "Or I could go in, maybe get some packets for you, bring them out? Might have to steal them. But I want to see you two – you three – get on with no trouble."

"Thanks," said Bart. "Let's go there and give it a try."

He went back to the teepee and fetched the horses, helped them push through the opening, and took hold of their reins, speaking a few words. He walked them over to a drainage ditch.

"I wouldn't drink that if I were you," called Nick, half way to the cart with Trina and Izzy. "Could contain some run-off from the lab."

Bart pulled the horses away. Betty complained, tried to return to drinking but he jerked her reins to come along. He stowed the saddles on the rear of the cart.

"Come on now," he urged the horses.

They followed the man in the hazmat suit, hood lowered again, riding on his electro-cart across the grassless land, along a winding trail between rocks large and small, past piles of trash and remains of broken-down buildings, the refuse of a world left to rot.

The hills ahead were the reddish rock Bart was used to seeing, and remnants of the rocks lay everywhere in the form of dust their boots kicked up. The cart threw up red dust as it rolled slowly toward the red mountain.

Riding on the cart, Trina covered her and Izzy's face. Bart had to pull up his bandanna as the wind blew clouds of red grit, then tugged the horses to follow him.

Nick called over the hum of the cart's motor: "Not much further."

Trina gazed back at Bart, her face showing concern, as the cart rolled on, slow enough to allow Bart and the horses to keep up. Nick gave a wave of reassurance.

I'm sure it's safe, thought Bart. *Seems like a good man.*

Yet Trina's expression seemed to be saying *We don't know where he's taking us nor what's gonna be inside that place.*

Bart gave her a look: *You want food. I do, too.*

They continued across the dusty ground with the sticker bushes annoying the horses, to red hills crowned with bare rock that stood like castle ramparts in the books Bart read as a child.

"Don't you worry," Nick spoke as they gathered before the final leg. "No safe place west of here. I thought it's not safe here, but you proved it's safe, going around with no hazmat suit on, no hood, not even an air device. When I go out to check on things, I always dress appropriately. I still have to get decontaminated when I return. It's a rule. You will, too. They're very strict." He pulled on his hood, sealed it.

Bart gave a nod, wary of what would happen next. Trina looked desperate to get food, so he decided to trust the man in the hood.

They went down a slope, fell into the shadow of the red cliff.

At the bottom of the slope marked by cart tracks, stood a huge door of gray metal three times as high as a man and much wider than for a cart to enter.

Nick halted the cart, shut off the motor. He pulled a device from his belt, spoke into it, requesting entrance. Scrabbled words came back through the device but Bart couldn't understand them.

Bart stood tall, holding the reins of the horses, awe-struck by the huge structure before him. He noticed Trina staring back at him, giving that same look as when she questioned something he did. He never liked it, but they were a couple, had to look out for each other. Between the wilderness with nothing to eat and dangerous creatures, it was better to try this hidden world.

"I said I got guests," Nick told them. "They're coming out."

A door within the larger door opened and two figures stepped out cautiously, closing that door behind them. Both figures wore the faded yellow suits with white hoods. Both held long guns that looked like what Nick used on the man-cat.

One figure raised a hand in greeting.

"I have returned," Nick announced with dramatic flair. "Bearing with me these weary travelers."

He stood by the cart, hand waving at Trina sitting on the cart, showing what he'd found in the wilderness. Bart held the reins of Betty and Brownie well back of the cart.

"Found these people out at the Navajo Village," Nick spoke up, raising his voice through the hood. "They aren't infected, have no symptoms." He held up a rectangular device the size of his hand, taken from his belt. "They check out clean."

"What about them?" asked the guard, pointing to the two horses with his gun.

"They can go in one of the pens," Nick responded. "Like all the others. Doctor Emory will be interested."

As Nick spoke with the guards, Bart gazed at the huge door. At its center he saw a faded image: a six-sided logo. He recalled the same logo at the airplane wreckage. Inside everything was stamped with that logo: the paper folders, notebooks and binders, even the uniforms the skeletons wore. Now it was emblazoned on this door.

"What is this place?" Bart called to Nick.

He turned back to Bart. "I call it home. But you probably mean what's its official name, like the name of a town." He pointed to the hexagonal image on the door. "Probably you can't read it now, as worn away as it is, but it says *Institute of Infectious Diseases*. It's a laboratory. It's run by the gov'ment. Used to be. What's left of the gov'ment. They keep working on their own. The writing below is supposed to say *Albuquerque Station*. There's other stations around the country – if any are still in use. If you didn't know, you couldn't read it from what's left on the door. Needs repainting." He laughed. "But you needn't worry, friends." Again with the dramatic flare like he enjoyed teasing them.

"We gonna be let in?" Trina spoke in a serious tone. "Get food?"

"I told them about you. They will let you in." He pointed to the device in the guard's hand. "He called in, got permission for you. The horses, too. Gonna study them. But you have to go through the de-con procedure. Horses will get theirs, too."

"What's that?" Bart asked.

"They'll test you for viruses. Then you'll get sprayed with anti-viral stuff. And you put on fresh clothing after, probably a coverall like mine only without hood. Don't need it inside. The air is filtered."

"And they ain't gonna lock us up," Bart checked.

"Shouldn't," said Nick. "I'm vouching for you."

"That's good," said Bart, his voice failing. He coughed to clear his throat from the dust. "We ain't no outlaws, after all."

The huge metal door began to rise upward, disappearing into the rock wall. When it was high enough for them to pass through, the door stopped.

"Let's go," said Nick, waving them to follow.

He mounted the cart, started the motor, and drove into the dark space inside. Bart led the horses after the cart. The door rolled down behind them, engulfing them in darkness. Lights blinked on, a line of them overhead running down a very long corridor.

The corridor, plain gray walls and gray floor, was wide enough for a wagon with a team of horses to pass through, Bart noted. On either side were doors set at regular intervals. The corridor seemed to go deep into the mountain. Bart couldn't imagine so much space being out of sight. He couldn't see the end of it.

The horses got anxious and Bart had to calm them.

Two figures in coveralls appeared from deep down the corridor, walking up to them.

"We'll take them now," said one to Bart. He hated to let loose the reins, but Nick gave a nod.

"Take care with the saddles," Bart cautioned. "It's all we got."

"It's awright," said Nick. "They'll get food and water, the same as you. I mean, they get horse food and you get people food. I mean the nutrient packs. Hah, maybe you'd prefer some hay."

Bart tried to appreciate his humor but he was worried about the horses. He'd relied on them for so much: dangerous escapes, a long arduous journey, never complaining much. Betty was a gift from Trinity, after all, by way of someone named H.B. He watched the men lead the horses down the spotless corridor and hoped there wouldn't be any manure droppings.

"This way," Nick directed, leading them to one door.

He put his hand up to a keypad on the wall beside the door and the keypad glowed. He typed in a code. The door slid open without a sound. He waved his guests inside.

"First let's get decontaminated," said Nick like a tour guide.

Bart saw a square space surrounded by clear walls, like windows of glass but these were not glass but some other material. He tapped on them, scratched at them, left no marks.

Inside that space, wider than a man standing with outstretched arms, a person in coveralls and hood was scrubbing the floor with a long device that had a green-glowing tip that was put down to the floor. The man straightened up and stepped out as they arrived.

"Do what I do," said Nick, then to Trina: "Be sure to cover the baby's face when they spray."

Bart and Trina watched Nick unzip his coveralls, slide them on down his body. He wore nothing under the suit.

They regarded each other. Nick wasn't shy.

"Come on," said Nick with a chuckle. "It's protocol. You have to do it. Especially if you want food."

Bart and Trina hesitated, then followed, stripping off their dirty clothing cautiously. As they disrobed, they exchanged Izzy back and forth between them. Trina gave Bart a glance, unsure how far to go. Nick was completely naked. But Trina didn't like anyone seeing her. Nick seemed amused by their hesitation. Bart said they had to, so she shed her final item, the ragged cloth between her legs, and stood embarrassed with Izzy in her arms. Off with the diaper cloth, too, Nick instructed.

Following Nick, they tossed their discarded clothing into a bin outside of the transparent walls of the chamber, the diaper in a trash container.

Bart saw a man in coveralls approach the bin that held his and Trina's clothing. The man first swung a wand over the bin. Beeps. Then a red light flashed at the tip of the wand.

"Weaponry detected," a voice announced from above.

"Wait," Bart cried. "We come from the wilderness. We need those for protection out there."

"It's okay," said Nick. "They detect the discharges of weapons. It picks up the residue. Same for my gun. They'll keep them safe until you leave."

The cart with the bin was rolled away.

"Got to make sure everything is decontaminated," Nick assured them. "Can't let bad germs in here. Required before anything else. Can't go anywhere without being checked. You can see why I don't like to go out too often: have to go through this hassle every time when I return." He laughed again like it was all a joke.

The adults stood naked in the de-con chamber as a series of beeps and buzzes provided a concert. Izzy looked with amazement, curious at the lights that flashed around them, reached for them.

"Arms up," a voice overhead called out.

They raised their arms. Trina kept one arm around Izzy.

"Spread feet," the voice instructed and they obeyed.

Bart couldn't help but look at Nick, a thinner man than what he'd suspected while wearing the hazmat suit. He saw Nick getting an eyeful of Trina, even with Izzy blocking some of the view. She wouldn't look at Nick, kept her attention on Izzy. Bart caught on and moved between them, blocking Nick's view.

"Now what?" asked Bart, seeing Trina's distraught face.

"Almost finished. Next is the decontamination spray. Close your eyes and pinch your nose. Keep your mouth closed."

The warning noises that sounded startled Bart. Before he could ask another question the spray hit them from all angles. They were quickly soaked in a blue liquid. It foamed on their skin. Nick indicated how they should be sure the foam got to every part of the body, then use their hands to wash themselves. Then came the rinse cycle.

After the spray ceased, a bright red light came on overhead and soon the chamber heated up, drying them. By then Izzy was crying, afraid of all the lights and noises. Trina cooed to him.

To Bart, it felt good to be clean once more. He looked at Trina. She looked good to him, like after they'd swam in that pool by their first camp, when they'd lain together. He felt something happening below, then felt Trina's hand on his belly to remind him they were being observed.

Nick smiled at them. "Now let's see about getting some food."

STEPHEN SWARTZ

23

UNDERGROUND

"LOOKS LIKE YOUR HAIR is actually red," said Nick with a grin. "That is a unique DNA. They'll want to test you."

The de-con washing had removed the dirt and dust from his hair that made it look brown. His whiskers had grown out, too. And hair on his chest and elsewhere was just as red. Trina smiled at the reveal. The Red Devil.

"Ain't my fault," Bart grumbled as he pulled on the robe he was given, a fresh white cloth that went over his head and fell down to his ankles. He slid his feet into a pair of slippers, feeling awkward at the sight of his toes sticking out. Not a manly style.

He regarded Trina, looking like a goddess in her white robe, her hair in a pony's tail, her feet in slippers. She held Izzy, now in fresh diaper cloth with a small jacket matching their robes. They could be a royal family, thought Bart, like one of those myths.

"This way," Nick directed. He wore a clean gray coverall, had yellow marks on the shoulders, yellow stripes down the legs. On his feet were more substantial shoes, something he could wear outside without hurting his feet.

They left the dressing room, Nick in front, and went down a new corridor, turning this way and that way, every corridor looking the same: gray on gray. Everywhere was so clean. Bart grew wary at being stopped and captured, kept his hands ready to fight.

Finally they came to a door, just as ordinary as all the others.

"They said bring you here," said Nick.

Bart was completely lost, couldn't find his way back if he needed to. He began to panic but fought to keep his fear under control. He wished he had his guns, and wondered where they took their possessions, and if they'd get them back.

"Ya gettin' us some food?" Trina prodded Nick.

"Please wait here," he said, and frowned. "Now you're here, I won't be seeing you for a while. Maybe later. Got work to do. Make a report of my outing. I'll mention you. I told them you need food. They will bring it to you. Some of our scientists will be joining you. They will ask questions."

"Questions?" Bart demanded. "What if I got questions?"

"You can ask them." Nick grinned. "What questions you got?"

"I dunno. Maybe, uh, what does 'Costco' mean. I saw it on a sign out by them teepees. Is it a Navajo word?"

"Oh, that. It means 'mercantile'; a place to exchange goods, like a trading post. Or a general store."

"Oh. But it looked 'out of business', as they say."

"That's correct. Been that way decades. Any other questions?"

"Questions about what?" asked Bart.

"Anything." Nick waited patiently.

"How far is it to the ocean?"

"Ocean?" Nick seemed surprised. "Oh, it's got to be hundreds of miles from here. Anything else?"

Bart couldn't think of any more questions.

"I imagine they will ask about you and your life on the outside," Nick proceeded. "They want to know what it's like out there. What's been happening. Anything I tell them isn't enough because I'm only around this area. Feel free to tell them all you want."

"My whole story?" Bart gave a wry grin.

"They'll let you talk, believe me."

"What they know already?" asked Trina, bouncing Izzy.

"They know a lot, or think they do, but there's some things they can know only by talking with people who've been there. Like where you came from." Nick wiped away a smile. "You can forgive them of their old ideas, their old ways. They still think everything is the same as it was a hundred years ago. More like a hundred-fifty/sixty years, back when the Great Pandemic struck the nation."

He grinned at Izzy in Trina's arms and the baby grabbed for him, made him laugh. Trina looked wary, didn't want anyone to get near the baby. Bart laughed and Trina gave him one of her looks.

"Nice meeting you," said Nick, with a wave goodbye.

He closed the door behind as he left. The metallic click of a lock sounded, seemed to linger in the room.

Bart's attention stayed on the sound. He considered testing the door knob. He knew they were locked in this gray room, as large – or as *small* – as one of the cells in his uncle's jail.

There were two metal chairs in the room and Trina sat on one right away, kept Izzy in her lap. Bart chose to stand, soon began to pace the small room.

"What's this place?" asked Trina, watching Bart. "Don't like it none. Not at all."

"I like it," he said, looking up at the corners of the room, seeing a device up there, pointing down. Looked like it could be one of those camera things that captures images, but this one was much smaller than the ones he'd seen in the capital. He was careful what he said, just like his mama had cautioned him. "Nice and clean in here. It's like a whole town down here. Like this room is one house. I'm sure they'll give us a bigger space."

"Cain't see no sky from here," she grumbled and Izzy took on her mood, got fussy.

"I know, but I s'pose we can go outside any time we want."

"They make ya wear them suits, an' make ya strip when ya return. Don't like neither."

"But it's clean here. Not like outside." He waved his hand at the floor, up at the ceiling, remembering dusty carpets in his mama's house – what had been his house, too, in Skinner Canyon – how he had to help with the cleaning: roll the carpets up, carry them out, unroll, then beat them with a stick to shake off the dust, then roll them up and take them into the house, and unroll them – darn near every Saturday morning. "This place is damn near spotless."

"Don't wanna live no hole in the ground. Ain't no rabbit."

"We ain't staying in this room forever," he countered. It had to be only a waiting room. Then they would be led to a new place where they would live. He considered what he would do here to earn his way.

"Ya gotta think o' safety," Trina spoke, lowering her voice.

Bart saw how Izzy was being grabby and annoying her, so he took the baby from her, smiling at him, and bounced the baby in his arms to distract him.

"Izzy don't mind it here," said Bart.

Trina glared at him. "Ya make us leave our camp. Ya make us go over land nobody want. We almost get killed twice or more. Then ya believe this stranger, let 'im take us into strange place."

"It's not strange," he insisted. "It's...*modern.*"

"We's trapped in here," she growled. "They kin just barge in an' kill us, feed us to their animals. They kin take Izzy for experiments. They kin take me for anythin' they wanna do to me."

"None of that's gonna happen." He believed it for three seconds. Then he felt a spark in his head and understood his mistakes once more. "This ain't a place to stay for long. Just a few days' rest. Then we go on."

"An' where's that?" Her eyebrows were pinched.

"West." He regarded her, felt her anger. "More west. As far as we can go. My uncle says they got an ocean out there, bigger than all the land. Gotta be people out that way. They're gonna be fishing in that ocean, I bet."

"Ya wanna go see other people?" She shook her head.

"People means *society*." He felt a dramatic speech being written in his head. "A place where we can survive. I'll work for food for us. You raise our son. We can be happy any place if we're together. It'll be good. I promise."

"Don't like ya makin' choices fer me. Got five more years on this world than you, maybe got more experience than you."

"Four and a half," he countered and saw her grow more angry.

"Soon as we get food, we gotta get outta here."

"It'll be awright. I promise."

"You promise? You trust anybody smilin' at you. But ain't gonna risk us or this baby bein' samples fer them science-tists."

"They ain't gonna do experiments on us. We're real folks. They'll treat us right. Where'd you get stupid ideas like that?"

She was about to argue back, give him a real piece of her mind, when the door lock clicked and the door opened.

Through the doorway stepped a middle-aged man, skin darker than Trina's, straight black hair like hers, wearing a white coat over white shirt and tan trousers. He carried a tablet that looked like what everyone in the capital used. Behind the man came two other men, younger than the first but dressed similarly, carrying a pair of small devices like what Nick had on his belt outside.

"Hey," Bart spoke warily.

He watched them carefully, moving back beside Trina.

The dark man smiled. The other two seemed unconcerned.

"Welcome," said the dark man, as one of the other men took the empty chair and moved it by the door for the dark man to sit on. "I am Doctor Rajneesh." He smiled, waited for a response, got none. "I have come to see you because you are new here. It is our standard procedure."

Bart exhaled. "I like standard."

"*Ffft!*" went Trina.

"We like to gather information about our new arrivals," Dr. Rajneesh continued. "Besides asking you some questions, these assistants will check the three of you and gather medical data for our records. Data we collect will help us formulate appropriate remedies for any abnormalities we find now or in the future. Not only for you but for all of humanity."

Bart gave Trina a cheerful look, as if saying *See? We came to the right place.* She continued to frown so Bart handed Izzy back to her.

Dr. Rajneesh focused on the baby. He seemed to be restraining a look of glee at the infant, but Bart could see he was surprised at the sight, the man almost giddy.

"First, let's check this little one, if you don't mind. Let's see how the infant's health is. Then we can proceed with the two of you."

Trina sat Izzy on her knee, held him straight as the doctor came close. Izzy looked at the doctor, puzzled by a new face, and turned to gaze back at his mama.

"It's awright now," Bart told Izzy.

Rajneesh took a device from his coat's side pocket, adjusted it a moment, and moved it slowly up and down in front of Izzy, then moved the device behind his head and down his back. A green light flashed as he moved the device, then suddenly changed to red.

He stopped, regarded one of the assistants who held the tablet, and gave the device to the man who inserted the bottom end into the slot on the side of the tablet. More beeps followed. Bart could see numbers spilling down the screen.

They waited as the doctor regarded Trina.

"You are South Asian?" he asked her with a hopeful grin.

"Ain't South anythin'," she replied curtly.

"Excuse me then."

"She's half Comanche," Bart spoke up. "Other part's Irish."

"Ah, I see." He accepted the tablet back from his assistant and tapped on the screen. "I will make a note of that."

"I'm all white," said Bart, then ran a hand through his red hair. "Some kind or other. Our whole family is from an old country."

"We can compare your DNA to our database," said the doctor.

"D-N-A? What's that?" asked Bart.

Rajneesh paused to read information on the tablet, nodding.

"He is a little undernourished, but that is not concerning. It's to be expected given your travels. But generally in good health. We can provide adequate nutrition."

"So what's this D-N-A you said?"

"Next we will test for pathogens," the doctor continued. "We will do the same for the two of you."

"What's D-N-A?" Bart insisted.

Rajneesh handed the tablet to his assistant, folded his hands over his knee, as though ready to instruct a child.

"DNA is the abbreviation for *deoxyribonucleic acid*," the doctor spoke. "It is the name given to the hereditary material in humans and other organisms. Every cell in the body has the same DNA as every other cell. Most of this DNA is located in the cell's nucleus, but a small amount of DNA can also be found in the mitochondria."

"Hold on now," Bart cut in. "So it's stuff that's inside us. Inside everybody's body. So why you talking about it?"

"It is the essence of what a person is, you might say. Your DNA is you, not someone else. And yet parents share their DNA with the children they have. Your baby is half you and half the mother."

"Ain't no illness," said Trina, frowning.

"No, it is not. Merely a code for the replication of cells. A kind of blueprint for making new cells. You need not worry about DNA. We only mention it in describing your genetic heritage." He turned to his assistant, spoke some science jargon, then faced Bart and Trina once more. "It should be interesting to analyze your child's DNA in light of your different heritages."

"Listen here, doc," said Bart. "We made this baby, no matter DNA, and he's a good little feller. Gonna grow up right."

"Of course he is," Rajneesh responded. "We are scientists and so we are interested in the how and why of things. It's our interest. Nothing unusual. Nothing nefarious, I assure you."

"Nefarious, huh?" Bart acted like he understood the word.

"Not at all," said Rajneesh. "Now, let's have a look at you two."

+   +   +

Like poor little Izzy, his parents were also undernourished. Bart knew that. He'd seen in the decon chamber how much thinner they were. He could see it in Trina's face each day, too, and noticed how they both lost weight over the weeks of travel. He tried his best. He kept believing a town must exist out west where they would find food. He just never expected it to be underground.

They found themselves in a new room, laying on high benches.

"I remember one time when I was a little boy and the doctor put a needle in my arm," said Bart to Trina, as they lay on the benches, which had padded surfaces and small pillows for their heads. Very comfortable after being on a horse for weeks. He could lay there for hours. "That's how they gave you medicine back then."

"It isn't medicine," said the blond woman in the white coat and slacks. "This is an IV. To give you needed nutrients. We are trying to restore your health."

"But it hurt," Trina said. "And don't taste nothin'.'"

"It's entering your body far away from your taste buds," said the woman who'd introduced herself as a doctor. A *pedio-tri-shun*, she called it. They were all doctors in this underground town. This woman, looking a little older than Trina but shorter, had a curvy body and spoke like a school teacher.

In that first room, Dr. Rajneesh had waved his humming device up and down each of them, beeps sounding at intervals. Then he'd inserted the device into the side of the tablet and read the screen as information appeared there. He seemed impressed they were in good health other than needing nutrition.

"A simple lifestyle," he calmly summarized. "Yet likely exposure to viral elements present in the environment."

He ordered treatment for them and sent them to this woman.

Meanwhile, Izzy was carried off by a grim-looking woman with short-cropped red hair by the name of Erin. Seeing Bart's red hair, her look lingered, a grin almost appeared. Dr. Rajneesh told them the baby would be further examined for possible health issues.

"When we get 'im back?" asked Trina, trying hard to be polite, as though her baby's well-being depended on her demeanor.

"When we complete your examination, we will take you to him," said Marina – Doctor Kvashenaya ("You can call me Doctor K, if you like."). She flashed a reassuring smile just like she was taught.

"He's gonna be fine, ain't he?" asked Bart.

"Yes, of course," said Dr. K, showing that curious smile.

Trina lay awkwardly on the padded bench, not comfortable in the loose gown she was given.

"When we gettin' our things back?" she demanded.

Bart joined in: "Need to keep some of our stuff with us."

"Do not worry," said Dr. K cheerfully. "You will have everything you need provided to you. In this facility you do not need the sort of things you might require on the outside."

That didn't satisfy Bart. "So when we leave, we'll get everything back, ain't that right?"

Dr. K flashed her smile. "I am surprised you wish to leave...."

Her words hung in the air.

"Someday," said Bart after a moment.

"Ain't gonna be here forever," Trina said. "Got places to go."

Dr. K chuckled politely. "Forever? Some of us have been here all of our lives and we are doing quite well, safe from the horrors of the outer world. A few of us were actually born here. One of them is Doctor Farnsworth, for example. And me."

Bart grimaced. "But we can leave when we wanna, right?"

Another taut smile. "I believe that to be true. I cannot, however, imagine what circumstances might prompt you to want to leave this sanctuary. You have seen the outer world. You survived it as well as you could. There is no indication how much longer you may have been able to exist out there."

Bart shot a glance at Trina, saw her frowning.

"What do you mean exist out there? Everything's fine. Looks normal—"

"It all *standard*," Trina mocked.

"We just needed to find enough food, but seems there's plenty to hunt, but our bullets is kinda limited, ya know."

Dr. K sat up straight on the examination stool, hands in her lap. "That is not my area of expertise. Others have better knowledge of the dangerous elements out there. I only report what I have been told to report. You two are lucky to find us."

"Right lucky, yes ma'am," Trina said, pushing. "The bag of food pills ain't taste like nothin' an' not too fillin' neither."

Dr. K smiled at Trina's response, much like a teacher amused by a child's tantrum.

"We have a few guests here. Perhaps you can meet them in time. Everyone is a working member of the staff. Each of us has an important job to perform. Not everyone who resides here is a doctor or a scientist. We can assign you jobs. That way, you can contribute to the facility. 'Earn your keep' as our older residents say."

"I ain't afraid of work," said Bart boldly.

"How long ya bin here?" Trina quizzed.

"Me?" Dr. K gave a little laugh. "All my life."

"Y'ain't never been out there?" asked Bart.

Dr. K pursed her lips, thinking. Then she took a deep breath and spoke. "Our parents brought us here at a catastrophic time. In fact, you are the first outsiders to visit in.... It must be four or five years. *And* the first to arrive with a child. We thought conception was impossible due to the effects of the virus or the vaccine, or both. So it is crucial for us to study you, and your child, in order to prepare better treatments."

Bart's face grew tense. "So we're like experiments, huh?"

"Not in so many words," Dr. K replied. "However, I am certain you wish to help us, to help all of humanity. If we can find the secret of how you survived in the outer world, we may be able to find the right treatment to enable us to inhabit the surface."

"Ain't no secret," Trina muttered. "We's born there an' then we done our livin' just fine."

"You don't understand," Bart spoke up. "We come from a land of towns full of people like us, and everybody's doing good, like she said. We ain't no freaks wandering around. We come from *towns* – just don't like 'em no more. Thought we'd find a new town. But here we are. Under the darn ground."

"Yes, a new town." Dr. K grinned like she knew a secret. "This is your new town." She smiled more sincerely at Bart, then at Trina. "And everyone here needs to have a purpose."

Bart looked down, saw his toes sticking out of the slippers, made them wiggle. Nails needed trimming.

"Well, ma'am, I got nothing to do for a job. What I know ain't exactly what y'all need down here. But I'm willing to work. I can do whatever you want. I'll do another man's chores, whatever you got. I s'pose that's fair for the time we're down here. And we get food, ain't that right?"

"You will receive nutrition at regular intervals, yes," said Dr. K.

Trina picked up Bart's cue. "Ain't got no skills neither. Unless takin' care o' babies is one. But ya know I got skills too, tho' never did wanna get 'em. Just shootin' guns – but someone died."

Bart glared at her, wishing she hadn't mentioned the shooting.

"We aim to start fresh," said Bart. "Lead good standard lives."

Dr. K stared in disbelief. "I see."

"Standard, like he say," Trina added.

Bart turned to Trina. "You're a mama now. You ain't gotta work for nobody. I'll work for us. You keep the kid learning and growing up strong."

"That is so touching," said Dr. K, lifting a finger to wipe her eye. "I have no children myself, nor am I partnered with anyone. I have only read about such arrangements. I know it must begin with love. Not the chemical infusion but the more emotional clues. There was a book I recall, titled *Romeo and Juliet*, I think it was. It outlined the courtship protocols."

Bart grinned sheepishly. "Ain't read that one. How's it end?"

"I never got to the end of it." She flashed a frown. "Too intense. I had awful feelings, so I recommended that it be removed."

24

THE FACILITY

A DAILY SCHEDULE WAS MADE and someone in the gray/yellow uniform would come get them, escort them around the corridors, escort them back to their quarters afterwards. Their quarters consisted of a small room with "everything you need": two slim beds with hard mattresses, a crib, a desk and chair, a cabinet for storing their gowns and slippers, a bin for diapers. A round lamp set in the ceiling they could turn on and off from a switch on the wall. On the ceiling hidden behind a dark bubble was a device Bart suspected was a camera. He never could get a clear answer, always "It's for your safety."

Bart assumed he would he given a job, once all the testing was completed. Then he could 'earn credits'. He was told there was no need for credits in the facility as their needs were automatically addressed. There were a few items for purchase in the pretend store, made available so guests could feel like they were living in a real town. He appreciated that and planned to get something nice for Trina, something pretty, and a toy for Izzy. Already the boy was sitting up and babbling.

Thus far he'd only gone around to different rooms, sat to answer questions or stood to be examined. He had to pull off his robe, let them look at him, even the female doctors who seemed pleasantly surprised at the red hair he had, took samples. He felt special, a rare specimen, so he didn't mind the tests and usually didn't mind their questions. They asked in detail about his life before arriving at the facility, working backwards.

"I remember most days going with Mama," he said when asked about life in the capital, "to the concert hall for rehearsals. If they weren't rehearsing, she would work in her office. She would play a *piano* and write music on paper. Or she would meet with people. Make schedules. Plan concerts. I recall she had to tell one musician she was no longer needed and that woman cried and cried, but it had to be done, she told me later. The woman played too many wrong notes."

"And how did that scene make you feel?" asked Dr. Campbell, white coat pulled over his gray/yellow coverall. "Seeing your mother act harshly toward another person?"

"I didn't feel nothing. I was a little boy. Everything was new."

"Did you think poorly of your mother? Based on her treatment of that musician?"

"Listen, doc. I don't know why I remembered that. I shouldn't've told you. Just popped into my head."

"Thoughts do not 'pop' into one's head. It must be significant."

"I guess I saw my mama being mean to someone. Maybe it was the first time I saw her do that, I dunno."

"Good. You are understanding. Let us continue."

"Not sure what I'm supposed to understand. Just a childhood memory, is all."

"Let's talk more about your mother. Especially your relationship with her during your boyhood."

On it went, day after day, digging up memories he'd thought buried. But the doctor pulled them out, made him feel ashamed or wishing he hadn't said or done a lot of things. He hated his mother. He loved her. He couldn't make sense of half the things this doctor exposed but he didn't like it.

Other days he was taken to another doctor who asked questions about what he knew of the pandemic and government response. That was Dr. Sung, a small, wiry fellow bundled in his white doctor coat, looking like a thumb with his bald head. Bart gave answers as best he could, reminding the doctor he'd been only a boy and it was decades after the last pandemic victims died. That led to him divulging his family history.

He told what he'd learned from his mama, what she told him of her dad, what *he'd* said about *his* mother, Isla. She suffered a terrible life. She was born in the forest of a national park, lived among a group of survivalists who shared wives. Then the group was broken up. First, the men were marched off to war, forced to fight for one side or the other. Isla's dad fought for each side, was a prisoner. Then marauders came, took the women and girls away, sold them in the north as concubines to make babies for northern families who were sterile from the vaccines.

"What makes you say that?" the doc questioned, eyes wide.

"Ain't no scientist," said Bart. "Just repeating what I was told. My great-granny Isla lived through it. I never read nothing. She told what happened to her and her sisters and daughters from her direct experience. It was a terrible time, my mama said."

"Ah, direct experience. What they used to call 'lived truth'." The doctor made notes on his tablet. "We have learned to discount most claims of ordinary citizens. We understand how faulty the mind can be, especially under trauma. People imagine all sorts of things, see them in ways that are not comparable to the factual truth."

"No, she really lived it, had them experiences. I believe her."

"That is all very well, Bart. You are a member of her family. You follow the family narrative flawlessly."

"It's true." Bart tried to hold back his anger like he was taught by Doctor Gayle. The doctor determined he had 'anger issues' to deal with. "Don't matter if you believe her or I believe her, because it actually happened. Everything actually happened."

More notes on the tablet.

"You don't need to write everything down, do you?" Bart asked.

"It is important to make a record." The doctor looked up from the tablet. "Half this facility is filled with records of everything. For the day we can go out again and start to rebuild."

"Rebuild what? They rebuilt it already. Well, at least over in the east, the capital first of all. In fact, my mama said they built it as an Ideal Society. Only thing was, it didn't work. Was too strict, so the people rebelled."

"Interesting. You say a new city was built in the east?"

Bart shook his head. It seemed hopeless. If only he'd brought a couple books with him from his mama's library. Hand those books to these folks and say "Here, read this." Then he could be finished with all this nonsense.

At the end of his day he was escorted home to his room. He was beginning to know the route but it seemed the escort took him a different way each time, probably trying to confuse him. But he still recognized some corridor intersections as they got closer to their *apartment.* Sometimes he would arrive first and sit waiting for his family. Or, other days, Trina would already be there playing with Izzy.

"So what'd they ask you about?" he would quiz Trina, who seldom would be in a good mood after a day of 'testing'. They liked to probe her and prod her, interested in her *fertility* – her ability to produce healthy *offspring.* Like she was a prize heifer on his uncle's ranch. She had to endure the examinations in order to get Izzy back from the child's nurse.

"They askin' same questions, just diff'rent ways," she said.

"I'm sorry, T. Real sorry," Bart said, acting honest. He tried to go for a hug but she turned away.

"They keep lookin' over Iz, like he ripe fruit, like they waitin' fer somethin', don't know what. An' keep checkin' my bleedin' cycle."

"But you bleed regular. Every month."

Bart eased up to her. After a moment she'd give up, hold out an arm to accept him, cradling Izzy in her other arm.

"At least the horses are doing good," he said, parting. "The animal doc said they're getting back to good health now. He said it's a shame they're both mares or they could breed."

Trina seemed shocked. "They always talk 'bout breedin'."

"I told him Betty is old, too old for breeding. But you know what he said? He said she can still breed even being older. They don't get barren at a certain age like women do."

"Is that so?" Trina grinned like she heard a joke.

"Yeah, he said she can birth all her life but they'll usually die before they reach what he calls *meno-pausing.* He said after around thirteen years they taper off so after twenty years not likely to get a foal. Few horses live past twenty anyways, specially if ridden hard."

Trina wasn't impressed. "They shore inner'sted in breedin'."

"Figures. You ain't seen no kids here. I haven't. No wonder they take such interest in Izzy. He's a miracle to them."

"He's our miracle, don't ya furgit." She handed the baby to him.

"You have a good day?" he asked Izzy, cradling him.

Trina smiled at their play. "They got a kind o' machine baby for him to play with but it scares him."

"A mechanical baby?" He seemed surprised.

"Look like a baby but ain't. Call it *ro-bot*."

Bart juggled Izzy for a while, making his son giggle.

"I got a meeting tomorrow. Gonna assign me a job. Then I'll be getting credits. We can save up and when we get out we'll be able to buy some land and start a farm."

"Ya know somebody got land fer sale?"

"Maybe somewhere," he said, thinking. "Maybe it's a farm that's already started."

Trina gave him a smirk. "Like ya know 'bout farmin'."

"We gotta do something. Can't stay down here rest of our lives. Hah! But they think we will."

He got serious and Trina took Izzy back into her arms.

"They've been down here for generations," said Bart. "Came here during the Great Pandemic, trying to hide from it. That's what I gather from what all they told me. But they're still thinking it's dangerous outside. That's why they're checking us so damn much. Find out how we survived." He chuckled. "They never get no word from anyplace east. Got no idea what's happened. I try to tell them what my mama said, like about her dad and his mama, and older family, but they don't believe me."

"Let 'em think what they wanna," Trina said. "Ain't gonna let us go noways."

"Yes, they will. I got them to promise. We stay a while – they can check us all they want – and then we go. They'll be glad to be rid of us. They can go on with their experiments as they like."

"They ain't gonna let us go!" Her look was intense. "Not just like that, ain't so easy. We just 'speriments to them. Don'tcha see? You, me, and Iz. They testin' us, seein' if they kin make themselves like us, so they kin survive when they go up top."

"I told them everything's fine outside."

Trina shook her head. "But they ain't believe ya."

Bart tried to hug her. "I have to make them believe everything is fine out there. I'll show them."

+ + +

On the way to his day's tasks, Bart turned a corner in the corridor and nearly crashed into a man in gray/yellow coveralls coming from the other direction. Both stood back in shock, then laughed.

"There's my pioneer fellow," cried Nick. "Mister Go-West-Young-Man! Haven't seen you for how many weeks? What's it been now? Four months? Time sure flies when you're underground, can't see the sun and moon or the stars. I guess they've gotten you through all the in-take protocols by now. How you doing?"

Bart remained surprised but seeing an old friend helped him let down his guard. "Yeah, done with all that. Gave me a job."

"I don't get down here in the guest quarters too often."

"I don't get upstairs much either." Bart gave a wry grin, pointed to the orange X on the front of his coverall which limited his access. A larger X shown on his back. "They assigned me some tasks to do so I can earn credits."

"Earn credits?" Nick chuckled. "That's just to make outsiders feel like they live in a normal place. I mean, what can you buy? You get everything free. It's given to you: food, medical care. Even your entertainment, if you want anything. But nobody ever wants it. Their entertainment is always working on their projects: Save The World Up Top. They've been at work on it since they first hid here. Hiding from the people they harmed."

"I know what you mean," said Bart, lowering his voice. "But I like getting credits. I can count them up."

Nick remained cheery. "So how you been?"

"Mostly fine. Getting used to being here."

"And the missus? The baby?"

"Oh, she's fine. Still ornery, but that's normal for her. They got her doing laundry with other women. She really hates it. They tease her, call her names. But she won't let me say nothing."

Nick frowned at that news. "And how's your son?"

Bart had to grin. "Izzy's happy. He likes his nurse. They play learning games. It's protocol. And he gets checked every week by the staff, seeing if he's growing right."

"Good to hear," said Nick.

"Both of them – and me, too – we get enough nutrition. Not sure what's in the food packets, but they say we're healthy."

Nick gave a nod. "Your body will adjust to the food packets."

"Seems to be working. Ain't got sick."

"They're careful about not letting anyone become ill down here. Anything could spread quickly through this facility."

"Yeah, I can see that." Bart grimaced. "I almost got in trouble for not washing my hands for long enough. After I handled some waste. That's my job now. Collect the waste from offices and take it to the disposal unit. It ain't hard."

"So you have something to do," Nick said with amusement. "To keep you out of trouble, huh?"

"I got in trouble, actually. They suspended my credits for a day."

Nick frowned. "Really? What did you do?"

"I didn't wash my hands long enough, like I said. I complained about the shortfall and they took another day's credits away. They said I'd have to learn the protocols. I took their damn tests, got good scores. I know what they want us to do."

"They can be strict. I told you." Nick shook his head.

"My supervisor even threatened to keep me from my family. Like I was some kind of outlaw. Who keeps a man away from his family? It's like something they do over in the capital. It makes me wanna leave here even more. Just waiting 'til we can leave this damn place."

With glances up and down the corridor, Nick lowered his voice: "How'd you like to go up top, get outside for a little while? Get some *fresh* air, if it's not poisoned like they say it is. I got another ground check coming up. Could use a partner out there."

Bart brightened. "That's great. I wanna go."

"Then I'll get you assigned to me."

+ + +

Bart felt like one of them at last, wearing the gray hazmat suit with hood. He looked out through its window and breathed in air through the device on his back. He felt special beside Nick, the long guns hanging on their shoulders as the great door opened.

"Welcome to paradise," Nick quipped, raising his electro-gun in salute to the great outdoors.

Bart had an electro-gun, too. They'd met at the designated time in the designated corridor on level twelve and Nick introduced him to the armory. He'd been surprised that such a place existed in the facility; he'd only asked to take his main pistol, the Sig Sauer, out with him, but it was locked away. His other pistol and the rifle, too. Said they were still being examined even after six months. They were *relics*, they said.

Nick showed him the electro-guns, the rifles that fired bolts of electric instead of bullets. Saved on cartridges, Bart had to agree. Nick had to give up his Browning Creedmore rifle when they took him in so he knew how Bart felt. The rifle had lain across the rear window of his vehicle, what he called a *jeep*. They pulled his vehicle inside, too, parked it in a *garage*.

Nick used the electro-gun to bring down the femo-cat – what he called *hell-cats* – when they first met. The long guns had a battery pack that slipped into a space similar to a magazine, powered the weapon which otherwise was operated like any rifle: you aim and pull the trigger. Instead of a bullet shooting out the barrel, a bolt of electric would fly out and strike the target with a flash.

"I thought it'd look more like lightning," Bart said. "Like the crackle of lightning in the sky, all them fingers going everywhere."

"Not like that," Nick responded. "You get hit with that much electric and you go stiff, can't move. Fall over dead if you get enough of it. It has three settings. The lowest just stuns. The next is to kill. The highest setting will melt everything, clean up the kill."

"Then you run down the battery. How long that take?"

"Depending on how much you fire, could last all day or a few days. You go full power, like you're in a fire fight in war time, and it will run out fast, need to be replaced with a fresh battery. Shove in a new one and keep on firing."

Bart had to admire the new weapon, sleek and beautiful in its innocent grayness. He recalled mention of electric guns used in the capital, but he couldn't remember how he heard of it. Could be his mama saying how her father died while saving the governor and got shot by one of the electric guns accidentally, police mistaking him for one of the kidnappers. Maybe that was how he knew.

Outside, the weather was dark and stormy, the ominous clouds boiling over the barren landscape, looking more like a desert than when they first came to the facility. Now horrible heat tried to burn through their suits. Bart could smell the dryness even through his plastic hood.

He regarded Nick beside him, gazing far off for any danger.

"Can we get these hoods off now?" asked Bart. "You know ain't poisonous out here."

"Wait a while," said Nick. "They can watch us from the tower."

"Tower?" Bart had the urge to look back but didn't.

"Not really a tower. If you go up the main elevator to level two, you can switch to the ladder up to an observation room. Looks over the entire valley. Been up there a few times. Just little windows. You couldn't detect them from below, the way they're hidden by the overhang at the top of the mountain."

Bart had a greater urge to look. "They were watching you – all of us – before?"

"No. When we first met, we were too far out. Maybe they could see us if they cared to look, maybe use a telescope. But it's just me, nothing too exciting."

Nick waved Bart on. They followed a trail of previous tire marks, grumbling how it would led strangers straight to the door. It needed to be swept, made invisible. They'd do that on the way back.

"So what did you do before you headed out west?" asked Nick as they strode over the plain of scrub grass and bushes tumbling by, like the land hadn't seen rain in years.

"I got born then I grew up. Then I run away from home and met these sisters," Bart said to summarize. "That's one of them back in the facility. She took a liking to me and, well, you can purdy much figure the rest."

"That's nice. She seems like a nice lady."

"She is. Most times."

"No, I mean what did you do? Like for occupation."

"Occupation? Not a whole lot." He glanced at Nick, deciding whether to trust him. Out in these rugged parts nobody knew him, wouldn't have heard of his exploits. He could come clean. Or maybe it would be better to lie. Lie again and again to cover his tracks, trying to make a new life for himself and his family.

"No, tell me. I'm curious. Besides we got all day."

"Riding for hire," Bart lied. "Doing ranch work. That's about all I'm good at. Riding and shooting. Keeping varmints away."

Nick gave him a serious look. "So you could be good in a security position in the facility."

"Well, I don't really expect to stay here for a long time. Kinda wanna keep going, see what's out there. That's our plan. I heard there's a big ocean way out there. Kinda wanna see it."

"There isn't anything out there," Nick retorted, almost angry.

"Nothing? The world don't end right here," Bart came back.

"We've done surveys. Used flying cameras. We've seen what's out there, farther than where you want to go. It's nothing but barren land and death. They still think the air is poisonous."

They paused to check how far from the facility they'd gone, then Nick gave a signal to remove the hoods. They took deep breaths.

"But I'm more convinced that whatever made the air poisonous managed to kill everyone west of here. And every*thing*. Even those hell-cats struggle to find food, usually gnawing on carrion. You may notice how the bison no longer range this far west."

"I noticed. But I figured they didn't much like the dry land. Not their kind of vegetation to munch on."

"Partly right." Nick paused, scanning the land ahead. "Those scientists. You got the in-take briefing. You know they were born in the facility, so all they know is what's been passed down to them from their parents – and grandparents – some of them also born in the facility."

"Why'd they come out here and dig a big ol' facility under the ground like that one?"

"It was already built," said Nick, checking each direction. "Made for whatever might happen someday. Planning ahead. When they had that big pandemic going around, some of them came out here. What I was told was that they were hiding."

Bart screwed up his face. "Hiding? What for?"

"Not what for, what *from*. The virus, of course. Save themselves and their families. But also from the people, all the people who got sick from the virus – or from the vaccines that didn't work like they were supposed to. I heard them talk about the 'riot days' when their grandparents' labs were threatened then overrun. Scientists killed for the crime of destroying society. Those in the facility believed the people were mad from an infection, a horde of crazed maniacs. I'm inclined to believe they exaggerated the situation."

"Yeah, I heard some of that from my mama." Bart let out a sigh. "She made me read stories her great-grandfather wrote about those times. Said I should know our family history. Purdy awful stuff."

Then Bart recalled something interesting and shared it without thinking it through.

"Years ago, I was riding over in the territory east of here, and I came upon the wreck of one of those airplanes. And it—"

"Airplane?" Nick seemed interested.

"Yeah. I know what those are because I saw them in a book. But it was wrecked, like I said. The wings broken off. But I got inside it and it was full of all kinds of papers – documents, notebooks, maps, charts, even somebody's diary. And bodies. They were real old, just skeletons, a few still strapped in their seats."

"That's too bad." Nick was looking around for hell-cats.

"I happened to see inside the *fuselage*," and he was proud to use the word, "everything got the same symbol as what's on the door to the facility."

Nick stopped, looked back at Bart. "What...?" He shook his head.

"Are you saying there was an airplane with the same logo as the facility? And it crashed?"

"It was sitting on one of those run-away roads. Like they tried to set it down there but it hit hard, broke the wings off."

Nick stared at him. "The same logo? The hexagon?"

"Exactly the same." Bart smiled, amused by Nick's reaction.

But his partner on this hunt paused to think. "When was that?"

"Oh, about four years ago, I reckon. But it was sitting there for a long, long time before I saw it."

"Yes, of course." Nick kept thinking. "I've heard some down there talking about their missing colleagues. The ones who didn't make it." He regarded Bart. "Where was it?"

"Not sure exactly, but way out east. More east than my home in the east."

"By a town? Airports usually are near towns."

"Nope. This run-away was in the middle of nowhere. Nearest town maybe was Skinner Canyon."

Nick had never heard of Skinner Canyon. He heard of Wichita, so Bart said it was west of there.

"Maybe you should tell the council," Nick said after a while.

"Think they wanna know?"

Nick grimaced. "Naw, maybe not. What can they do now?"

He pulled a device off his belt, pushed a button on it. A whirring noise arose far behind them. Bart turned to see a cloud of dust, and out of that cloud came an electro-cart, rolling on its own.

Nick halted it beside them. Bart grinned in surprise. They could make a machine come to them by pushing a button on something no bigger than his hand.

"After you," he said, waving at Bart.

Bart stared at the cart, amazed, thinking back to that day when he led Betty and Brownie into the facility. So innocent! They never knew what fate awaited them. He regained his anger. The examinations, then the butchering. The two mares that couldn't mate were deemed useless by someone on the council and were handed over to the food processing department for disposal. He had no doubt everyone in the facility got a sample of horse meat. He and

Trina ate some before they knew about the council's decision.

"Still don't like what they did to our horses," said Bart.

"I would've kept them," said Nick, "but that's just me."

They climbed on the cart and rode it over to the teepees at the Navajo Village. Nick said it was a place where people would come to play at being tribals for a few days and nights, part of what they called *vacation*. There were other such places across the landscape.

Bart had to look inside, recalling how his family had suffered that cold night. Now it was spring with a storm overhead. Sprits of rain dotted their suits.

"You know," said Bart, "these ain't real teepees. Not being made of whatever this material is. The real ones are made of bison hides. My wife, she knows. She comes from a real tribal village."

Nick didn't know about bison hides or tribal customs, so Bart educated him about the woman his mama adopted as her daughter. Then that woman got killed and Bart felt duty-bound to go on the posse after her killers.

"That's a sad story," said Nick.

Nick launched into his own sad story, talking about how people fought each other – people in the city Bart skirted with his family, believing it was too dangerous to enter. Nick told him how he'd witnessed people killing each other over food, some holding back a child from a gang of hungry people. "We'll take your kid and let the rest of you go," he said, imitating the predator's evil voice. That was the reason there was nobody there now.

"But the virus killed a lot of them," Nick continued. "Vaccines killed even more, some within a few days of taking it. A bad batch, they said. Or it was deliberate. Nobody could prove it either way. Tough being a cop back then. Terrible time trying to keep order."

Bart was curious now. "Deliberate? Who would do that?"

"A lot of people – scientists, politicians – who thought they were helping but didn't in the end. Who thought they were gods and just didn't care about regular people. They could stay in power if people were sick and dying."

He paused and Bart thought he saw a tear on Nick's cheek.

"They put an end to the rioting, all right. Sent a firestorm. Hit the city with whatever they had. A lot of cities, the bigger ones, got the same response. You dare ask for help, you get bombed. Problem solved. Complain? Want to fight back? You get bombed. Seems they were consolidating power, focusing on saving the cities in the east and destroying the cities out here."

"I saw the capital," Bart spoke but his voice was shallow.

"The ones that remained killed each other out of hate, out of the need to blame each other. Then they killed over food until only a few people were left, but those that lay destitute prayed for death. Most died of starvation. Or possibly died from drinking water that turned bad. Plenty of diseases to ravage weakened bodies, whatever – you name it. But look at that city today, there's nothing there. Old buildings. Mostly the ones with the big M on them, under those arches where people used to gather for sharing food, but no people anymore. It's a haunted place now."

He shook his head a while. Bart put his hand up and patted the man's shoulder.

"Come on," said Bart. "We got a job to do."

They spotted five hell-cats the rest of the day, two feeding on a third. Nick took out one cat and Bart another one. The first time he fired the electro-gun, he almost burnt the whole hell-cat in one flame. Nick told him to lower the power. They examined the beasts, took readings, entered the information into the tablet from Nick's backpack.

"They're still active," he announced. "We're seeing how long they live. See how the radiation affects them." He gazed up into the sky then around the landscape. "It's low now."

"What's that?" asked Bart.

Nick explained about radiation, how the area had high readings for years. Bart nodded thoughtfully, trying to understand. He couldn't see or feel anything, so Nick explained further.

Bart nodded politely. "So you can die from stuff you can't even see or smell, much less feel. That's queer."

"We better get back now," said Nick. "Don't want to absorb too much of it." He gave a wave to his hazmat suit.

On the way back, Bart thought to ask Nick again about what he did before coming to the facility.

    Nick grinned sheepishly. "Me? I used to be a cop."

S TEPHEN S WARTZ

25

THE PROJECT

THE STORK-LOOKING DOCTOR had a serious expression on his pale face – almost smug, thought Bart as he and Trina sat on metal chairs in front of the desk. The doctor stared at each of them in turn, perhaps deciding what to say, as though he needed to simplify the ideas for these uneducated service workers.

"I'm gonna be late for my shift," Bart said politely, flexing his hands. Trina reached over, took his hand.

"No need to concern yourself with that," said Dr. Farnsworth. He brushed his hand over the logo on the front of his lab coat, an image of a pink, grinning baby's face. "I will give you a pass card. Show it to your supervisor."

"So why we here?" asked Trina with a hint of anger. She wore her white laundry uniform which wasn't too comfortable. But Bart liked his clean gray/yellow coverall.

The doctor sat behind the desk in the official white coat they all wore. If you were any kind of scientist (*Doctor* this or that) you wore a white coat. He glanced at the tablet on the desktop, tapped on the tablet, looked up at them.

"I see you have been with us for just over a year now," he said with a smile that made Trina's eyebrows clench. "You two joined us having a unique set of traits. In fact, when we examined both of you and the infant, we were pleasantly surprised to discover a lot of positive factors. Namely, your ability to survive outside the facility without any protective measures."

"We just come west on our own," Trina muttered.

"No idea we needed protective measures," Bart added.

"Certainly. And yet our examination of you – the required check prior to admittance to the facility – provided some interesting data. We only allowed you to join us after we confirmed you had no ill effects from prolonged exposure to exterior elements."

"What traits you talking about?" asked Bart.

"As you may have considered," said Dr. Farnsworth, "we remain in this facility for two primary reasons: first is our need to continue developing effective intercedents for the problems we may yet face outdoors. And second—"

"Gonna hafta talk normal for us dumb folks," Trina said, elbow jabbing Bart's ribs. He took her hand.

"And the second is to keep us – those who have survived the ravages of an insane world – keep all of us safe within this highly secure and medically safe facility. In short, we are doing crucial research for the good of humanity: research and development which we must do – you've heard Doctor Crane speak, haven't you? – in order for us to preserve humanity or else we shall cease to exist."

"Cease to exist?" Trina screwed her face. "Lotsa folks out east o' here y'ain't never seen."

Bart chuckled nervously. "So they say."

"Now, because it has already been a year...." He stared straight at Trina, making her sit up. "...Reproductive Engineering reports no sign of maternal development, we must insist that you attempt pregnancy. Our observations do not detect regular efforts in that direction. You two are the best choices for continuing the species."

"Wait, what?" Bart blurted. "You watching us?" He glared at the doctor. "In our private room?"

"Yes, but it's for your safety." The doctor grinned like he knew exactly what he'd seen. "Everyone is monitored."

"Well, they gave us single beds," Bart muttered.

"What he sayin'?" Trina tilted her head to Bart.

"Your genes show a remarkable ability to survive intact from the deadly elements outside. In short, you have survived. Thus, we have studied you, examined your gene samples, in order to try and determine how you have survived. Now we need for you to replicate those genes to see if we can expand our survivability rate, as well."

"Now ya talkin' plain fool talk," said Trina, frowning.

"You're saying you want us to have another baby?" Bart smiled. He hadn't been in the mood to be with her since they'd arrived. Maybe something in the food packets they got that tamped down on his desire. He'd lay beside her, touching her, but nothing happened. He grew frustrated and eventually gave up. Now it was months since they last bothered with it.

"What's these *genes* ya keep talkin' 'bout?" asked Trina.

"Yes, of course. You understand *D-N-A*, correct? The gene is one element of DNA. Rather like a piece of a puzzle. Each gene carries a lot of information about you and your family before you. When you have a baby, that baby has some of the genes from the mother and from the father. They combine to make a new human. How they mix is what makes you unique among other babies."

"Yeah, I get it," said Bart, feeling like the doctor was speaking down to him. "Our son has traits of both of us, but he sure does look more like her than me."

"It's more than the outward appearance," said Dr. Farnsworth. "What and how the baby thinks, what they are interested in, what skills they develop – so many more traits than simply hair and eye and skin colors."

"He got it," Trina responded.

"Now that we understand genes, let's continue." Dr. Farnsworth checked the tablet again. "I'm expecting Doctor K to join us."

Right then a knock got the doctor up from behind the desk. He opened the door to welcome the woman in the lab coat, her blond hair rolled into a bun, stretching her face tight.

"Good morning," she spoke to Trina with a taut smile, knowing her from previous meetings.

"Morn, Doctor K," Trina replied.

"Doctor Kvashenaya is here to explain about the protocol for new offspring."

"Offspring," Trina snickered. "Shore didn't spring outta me. Had a good time pushin' him out with my sisters helpin'. About split me open, lemme tell ya."

Dr. Farnsworth grimaced. No doubt he couldn't understand how a simple woman like Trina could have the good genes they craved, thought Bart. But she was smart. And their son, Izzy, was the best of them both.

"We would like you to produce a new baby," Dr. K spoke after several minutes babbling about saving the world, "and see how the gene expression continues with different variables."

"You lost me," said Bart.

"We would like you to have another baby," said Dr. K, giving an awkward grin, first to Trina then Bart, measuring their responses. "You two are, by standard measurement, the most fertile subjects of anyone in the facility."

"Standard," Bart chuckled to himself, then regarded Doctor K. "I gotta say, I ain't had an urge for none of that since we came here. There something in the food? Something that turn off my wanting to make some hay with my wife?"

"A side-effect of the nutrition protocol," Dr. Farnsworth replied. "We must keep strict control of our population. We have limited resources. We produce our own food – the packets you are familiar with – so we limit who reproduces."

Dr. K continued the explanation: "The real issue is that actually not many of us *can* reproduce. This is an unfortunate result of the various protocols we have been through over the years. The genes do not override the poisonous elements of our environment."

"But you don't never go outside," said Bart. "I know a lot of you were born in here and never been outside, so you don't know if you could survive or not."

Dr. Farnsworth stood up, letting his height take command of the room. "Nevertheless, we determined that the best opportunity to isolate the genes which may provide extensive immunity to the poisonous elements outside is for you to have another baby."

"Babies," Dr. K added.

"For comparison," Dr. Farnsworth added.

"Whaddaya mean?" asked Trina. "Ain't gonna be pushin' out no slew of kids no time soon."

Dr. Farnsworth sat on the corner of the desk, hands folded in his lap, the practiced reassuring smile stuck on his face.

"What we want – what we would like you to commit to – is..." Dr. K folded her arms over her chest. "...to attempt pregnancy. To have a baby. We accept it might take a few cycles. Our records show that Trina will begin her next cycle tomorrow."

Trina shot a look at Bart, then to Dr. K. "How ya know that?"

"We want you to conceive in the natural way. Without medical assistance. Any effort we might perform in the lab to assist you or help the process might throw off our protocol. We wouldn't know if the changes we would see are the results of what we did in the lab or what the genes are doing for themselves. Do you understand?"

"Yeah, I get it," said Bart, grinning awkwardly. "You want us to get together, have some fun." He chewed his lip. "But you gotta stop the stuff that's slowing me down."

"We have already ordered a change to your food ration," said Dr. Farnsworth. He smiled at Doctor K.

"Now, the protocol is for each of you to attempt pregnancy—"

"Each of us?" Bart cut in.

"Yes, each of you," Dr. K replied. "Attempting pregnancy with a different partner. In this way we can better determine how the gene expression expands by examining a new infant with a mix of genes different from your son's presentation."

"Wait a second," Bart spoke. "You want us to get pregnant but with somebody else?" He turned to Trina: she looked horrified.

"Ain't gonna lay down wit' no stranger," she blurted out.

"We know what we have with your son. Now we wish to see how a different mix produces immunity genes."

"There ain't no immunity genes," Bart growled. "We are normal people with normal genes, and there ain't no poison out there on the outside. Mixing babies ain't gonna fix nothing."

"Ain't gonna lay down wit' nobody but my husband," Trina said.

"We could extract your eggs and sperm and introduce them in a lab dish," Dr. Farnsworth explained, looking evil. "It is preferable if the pregnancy occurs naturally. No lab intervention. As Doctor K has stated. Our aim is to make the procedure as natural as possible so as not to introduce any new variables to the experiment."

"Experiments!" Bart erupted. "We ain't nobody's breeding cows."

"We wish to make the experience as pleasant as possible," Dr. K spoke, holding out her hands as if keeping back a flood of questions. "The other fertile residents of the facility are...well, myself, for one." She had a different look when Bart met her eyes. "The other is...."

"Better not be you, Farnsworth," Trina barked.

The doctor chuckled. "Oh, no. I'm well past suitable age."

Dr. K continued: "We have chosen Doctor Rajneesh."

Trina exploded at that name: the man who kept showing up when she ended her shift in the laundry, always saying his flirty words to her, suggesting she should be nicer to him.

She told Bart some of the encounters she'd had with the man she liked to call "Rat-Nest". Always flirting, making suggestions, causing her to feel uncomfortable. He'd almost touched her a few times, hand hovering over her rear. She was ready to punch him. He laughed at her consternation, seemed to enjoy it. Bart got angry hearing her stories, wanted to do something. But they recognized the difficulty of violence in the facility. Nobody could get away with anything, not with the cameras watching every inch of the place.

"Ain't gonna go wit' that fella," Trina growled.

"Perhaps another on the list...." Dr. K scanned the tablet screen. "We have two others who we determined to be valid candidates for matching with you, given your genetic heritage and theirs."

"And who's them?" Trina asked to Bart's alarm.

"You ain't gonna do it, are you?" His face grew red.

"You get to be with her," she countered, pointing to Dr. K. "And she's lot prettier 'an me, so good for you. Better 'an ya deserve."

"Naw, you're prettier than anyone," said Bart.

"Yeah," Trina responded, letting out an impatient sigh. "Bart, ya know yer my man. But this here adventure ya brung me on, it ain't my favorite thing. Ya puttin' us in whole heap o' danger. Now we got us a safe place. Ain't too nice a place but it's safe."

She seemed to be acting for the doctors, Bart noticed.

"Maybe we better do what they want so we kin keep livin' here with no troubles. Don't wanna go up top, anyway. Get torn to pieces by them hell-cats. You go do your thing, whatever they wantcha ta do. Have a good time. An' I do mine. You an' me, we still gonna love each other."

It was a perfect performance, Bart decided, fighting the urge to grin. He bit his tongue to stay focused.

"Then you accept?" Dr. K asked Bart.

He looked down. "If she's fine with it, I guess so."

It wasn't as though Doctor K was unattractive, Bart admitted. She had a certain something about her, plus the blond hair. She was older than him and, from what he could see when she slipped off her scientist coat, had a curvy body unlike Trina's slim figure. But he couldn't get excited about Dr. K. She scared him.

"Perfect," said Dr. K, then turned to Trina. "And your partner?"

"I'm gonna take the one farthest from that Rajneesh fella. I told him ain't gonna be with him if he was the last man in the world."

Dr. K checked the tablet in her hands. "Then that would be the second-best candidate: Nick Ramos, our Chief Groundskeeper."

+ + +

They argued down one corridor to the next, following the way back to their apartment. Bart demanded she refuse but Trina insisted it had to be done so they could stay in the safety of the underground. Bart explained it wasn't safe, no telling what they'd demand next. They should leave and continue to that ocean he heard about. He thought she'd been acting in the meeting but she wasn't.

Their disagreement got so loud in the corridor that Izzy, held in Trina's arms, became fussy, then started bawling. A perky KT came out of her office to confront them before it could get any worse. The KT ("Kindness Technician") immediately started running down her list of calming techniques. Bart followed her commands. Trina smirked at the woman, instead focused on getting Izzy to relax.

"Awright now," Bart said, taking deep breaths.

"Breathe.... Breathe...," said the KT woman.

"Already breathed," Trina grumbled when the woman urged her to follow the protocol. Tempers weren't allowed in the facility. They might lead to fighting which would lead to...something much worse, like what happened to people in the cities, killing each other.

"We're awright," Bart insisted and the KT gave a smile and let them go, adding a goodbye wave to a teary Izzy.

They had talked themselves out by the time they arrived at the apartment. The rest of the "day" remained silent. They only spoke to Izzy, who seemed to understood his role as moderator. He'd reach for one or the other parent and offer his grin.

"You sure?" asked Bart at the evening sleep time.

"Ain't no other way," Trina replied.

Bart let out a long breath, like he'd been saving it all day.

One final night together, squeezing together on the single bed, Izzy asleep on the other bed instead of the crib but cooing to himself in the dark, grabbing at his toes like they were stars in the sky.

"He gonna be fine, let 'im be," Trina whispered to Bart.

"How about us?" he asked.

She rolled against him, put her hands to his rough cheeks, sure they were face to face in the dark – lights off at curfew.

"We gotta," she said. "If we gonna keep on here."

"We can leave."

"Go where?" She shook her head, their noses bumping. "We ain't got nothin' now. No horses, no guns, no food. Ain't gonna be able to survive out there."

"We will find a way."

"Yer 'find-a-way' foolery. Ain't nothin' to find out there."

"You've been out there? I have. We can make it. What's over the next ridge? Over those mountains? Gotta be a place somewhere we can live, where we can make a normal life."

"They say ain't nothin' but death. Go more west, ya die."

"They're wrong. They—"

She kissed his lips to shut him up.

"Cain't put 'em off no longer," she said. "Else they gonna force us to do it. Or sumpin' worse."

"But...but not with that man," Bart grumbled. "Not him."

"Because he's yer friend? Ya rather it be some mean ol' man? A dirty man? Some fella get too much fun outta it?"

"No, I don't want anybody. Only me."

"Ya got me. We got us a baby. It worked. Ain't no different layin' with someone else. Just don't know how to do it with no fella ain't been with before."

"Then don't," he said.

"Cain't just lay with no stranger."

"You lay down with me awright."

"Yeah, did." She gave a wistful chuckle. "You's shore an odd one, but ya growed on me. Took near a year, but seen ya had promise so give ya chance. Thought maybe kin have some fun witcha."

"Only now it ain't for fun. It's for science. It's for making deals. I know they'll let us go once they get their new babies to study. Babies with the good genes. With the immunities. They can grow up and go outside and survive."

"That's their plan." Trina brushed his cheek with her hand, her fingers playing with his whiskers. "You said it's safe up top."

"They don't know it. They don't *believe* it. They're scared."

"Then we doin' it fer nothin' – cuz ain't gonna matter none in the end o' things. Them babies ain't gonna do nothin' fer 'em."

"Give them something to study for another generation, figure."

Trina laughed. "They do love 'speriments."

"By then we'll be free. We can leave. They promised to let us."

"Give 'em some babies an' they gotta let us go."

She caressed his chest, snuggling cheek to cheek.

"We gonna do it? One last go?" She gave his cheek a peck and slid her hand down from his chest. "I'ma gettin' a mood."

"They gave me new food packets. F series. I think it's working."

She put her hand down below, felt a difference.

"Yep, shore do." She kissed him. "They changed my food, too."

"I'm supposed to save it. For the experiment."

She let out a long sigh. "Yeah, that dang 'speriment."

"It'll be over soon," he said, letting out a long sigh.

Trina gave a grunt, disappointed. "I'ma gonna be right on fire by then. Ya best take yer turn now. I'ma be bleedin' tomorrow."

+   +   +

327

Dr. K had the red pass key for what she called the 'love room', which had a special piece of furniture for a couple to enjoy the process. Once inside, Bart noted the smell, something both pungent and strangely inviting. Dr. K pressed buttons on a keypad set in the wall and the lights adjusted, became purple and shone dimly, a new scent filled the room, and the special bed began to vibrate.

"This was common in the older days," she told him, waving her hand at the sudden projection of images on the wall, like streaming he'd seen in the capital. "We did research to replicate this venue as exactly as possible. Couples would go to a special place designated for conducting sexual activity. Every town had these places. They would occupy the room usually for one hour and if they had not successfully completed their activity when the time expired they had to leave anyway. Such disappointment, you can imagine. That is how a population can drop. Therefore, everything was provided in the room to assist them in completing the act. Notice the imagery on the wall. They demonstrate the steps."

Bart looked: a muscular, hairy man lay upon a bed hugging and kissing a pretty, buxom blond woman, both naked. Then they moved so he lay atop her, face to face. They seemed to enjoy what they were doing and, moreover, they knew what to do, like they were following the protocol Dr. K outlined for Bart. He wondered how he and Trina looked to the facility's camera.

The image on the wall switched to a close view of their genitals getting acquainted.

"Is it not marvelous?" asked Dr. K, watching it.

"Well, I never did look at it that way. I mean not that angle."

"This imagery was commonly available to incite reproduction in the olden days. Even as overall fertility began to fall off sharply."

"I heard of that," said Bart, daring to look at the wall. "People in the north couldn't have babies, not after the pandemic, so they hired women from the south to help 'em out."

"Remember the protocol," said Dr. K, giving a smile. "These are the steps we should follow for maximum success."

"I recall." But he wasn't happy, kept thinking of Trina. "I'm only doing this so they let us leave."

"First, we must come together and hold each other," said Dr. K, ignoring his remark. "An embrace. It should be a minimum of three minutes. That is what is recommended."

"Yeah, I know. You got it down to a science thing."

"This is important," she said coldly.

"Yes, ma'am, Doctor K."

He let her come to him, stand against him. Her chest bumped his. Their arms remained at their sides. She seemed to be thinking of the next step, then instructed him to put his arms around her and she did the same around him. That step didn't seem to achieve quite the result she expected.

"Hmm," she sighed.

"I think we gotta not be wearing clothes. Look at the stream."

They turned to watch for a moment.

"Yes," she said. "That must be it: being nude."

"Maybe I should call you by your name? Not Doctor K? Seems a bit formal for this sort of thing."

"Yes. A good idea. My name is Marina. You may call me Marina. Or perhaps we can use the pet names. Like 'sweetheart' or 'honey'. What do you think?"

"I don't mind. I like 'sweetheart'."

"Then I shall call you *Sweetheart*."

"And I guess I'll call you *Honey*."

"Wonderful!"

"I think we're s'pose to take off each other's clothes. Like in that stream there. They made it like a game."

"Precisely. Like a game. But a serious game. You may begin."

"Thank you, Honey."

"I like that, Sweetheart."

He reached for her white coat, slipping it from her shoulders. A tug of her sleeves. A toss of the coat to the special bed, humming along as it gently shook. His hand went to the zipper at the front of her white shirt and pulled it slowly downward.

"I like your attention to detail, Sweetheart."

"It's the only way to get it off," he said plainly. "Unless you want me to just rip it off you. But I figure you don't want a torn shirt."

"Yes, Sweetheart, you are correct. How wonderful you are!"

Once he'd released the zipper and the shirt lay open, he pulled the hem of the blouse out of her slacks. In the next step, her hands went to the zipper on his coverall, pulling the zipper down until his chest and belly were exposed.

"Ooo. Ahh," she said mechanically.

Trina was never so simple in her actions. She took him, took all she wanted, made him give himself to her. But that was in the early days. Now he had to beg her for a few minutes of loving.

At Marina's instruction, he lifted the blouse off her shoulders, the sleeves sliding after. Her bosom wasn't the size of the woman on the stream but she was a lot larger than Trina.

A moment to observe the two lovers on the wall.

"We should kiss now," said Marina, and moved against him.

They stared at each other, perhaps waiting for the other one to make the first move. Marina stood shorter than him – shorter than Trina, in fact. The doctor had slipped off her shoes, which had heels raising her up. With bare feet, she had to stretch up to put her arms around his shoulders, trying to reach his lips. But not enough.

Bart used his strong arms to lift her, hands grasping her waist. Their lips finally met. Then he had to set her down when his arms grew tired.

"Yes, Sweetheart," she said, breathlessly.

"That weren't much of a kiss. Kinda like mama and son."

"I agree. We should try again." She watched as the lovers on the wall kissed. "Like them."

"But they're not kissing face to face," Bart noted.

"Oh," said Marina. "I see that now. They are...reversed."

"I guess that's for later," said Bart with an awkward snicker.

"Let us continue. We must remove the remaining clothing and look at each other's body for six minutes. Touching is allowed. We must avoid touching genitalia during this period. That will serve to heighten desire, according to the manual."

"You really never done this before, huh?" He felt sympathy. "It is strange first time, gotta confess, not knowing what to do. Me and

Trina didn't know nothing. Both of us. Just figured it out, whatever felt good. You know?"

Marina appeared confused. Or hesitant to continue.

"What's the matter?" asked Bart, genuinely concerned.

"I volunteered for this experiment," she spoke, switching back to her doctor persona. "I saw I was eligible. I never had any thought to create a child. Not until I saw you and Trina and your baby. What a beautiful baby!"

"That did it, huh?" He smiled at her.

"Possibly." She hugged Bart and he swung his arms around her. "Now that I have this opportunity to not only satisfy the weird urge within me to be a mother – I am already thirty-two – but also assist in the completion of a necessary experiment to help us survive in this horrible world."

"Well, I'm going on twenty-four, figure. Lost count." He grinned. "And it ain't so horrible out there. It's kinda nice. Lots of fresh air. And sunshine."

"Oh, don't make me laugh! The air is poisonous. The sunlight would burn us. We would die without proper protection."

He started to rebut, then caught himself. "So they say."

Still holding him in her arms, she looked up at him. "You say we should do whatever makes us feel good?"

"Like it's the first time. Like nobody knows nothing."

"I studied for this. I prepared all the assists. Yet it isn't working as expected." She glared at him. "Do you not like me? Don't find me attractive? Not in a way that excites you?"

Bart tried to offer an honest smile, then began playing with the coverall's zipper, teasing it lower. It caught some of his red hair and he cried out as they were ripped from his skin.

She laughed at the mishap.

"Gotta say, ma'am, I still see you as Doctor K, which ain't much to get excited about. Just being honest."

"I see. I am too formal. Is that it?"

"I don't mean to insult you. You are a purdy woman."

"Yes. Thank you. I suppose you are correct: we previously acted in certain roles which are not easily dismissed. Not even a kiss can get us to shift into new modes. Not even the disrobing."

"That's part of it."

She pursed her lips, thinking.

"Perhaps we should simply undress ourselves. Not make a game of it. Then observe each other. We can get right to it. The physical part. Ignore the talking and affection steps. I will help you achieve the proper stance. I will put us into the best position for conception. Today is the best day for it. The ovulation is strong in me today."

"Awrighty."

He tried again to smile, failed, feeling pressured. He didn't want to do it. But he felt compelled seeing her completely unclothed, bare from head to toes, his eyes taking in all of her as she stood so unassuming, so undesirable. Like an art statue.

"Usually I get on top of her and she don't mind it that way. But sometimes she likes to be on top of me, you know? Like she's riding a horse. She gets going, bouncing up and down, like she's on a mean bronco. And that sure gets it done. Either way is good."

"Then let us try the position you suggest."

"But that paper you gave me, it said that position ain't the best for getting a baby. It said me on top's the best way."

She smiled, a blush coming upon her face. "Then that is what we should do. And I shall be happy to welcome an auburn-haired baby."

26

THE COUNCIL

FOLLOWING PROTOCOL, they made their way up to the central lecture hall, a theater of a hundred seats – although twice as many people would try to squeeze in – all to hear the regularly scheduled pronouncements of Doctor Lester Crane, head of the Council, who acted as head of the entire facility. The venerable virologist was one of the oldest of them, Bart heard, and the white-haired man, still tall and vital with piercing gray eyes, looked the part wearing his crisp white lab coat rather than the gray/yellow coveralls.

Bart sat beside Dr. Hunt, a thin man looking the same age as Dr. Crane but pale and balding, marked low on the fertility list. He greeted Bart with a standard smile but they didn't speak more as the council members filed in and took their seats at the front of the room. People in the audience fell silent as Dr. Crane rose ominously from his seat to go to the podium.

Seeing the man posed there, Bart thought of his mama standing before the orchestra in the capital when he was a little boy. Strange feelings rushed through him. He thought he heard music – coming from somewhere behind him, as if an orchestra was rehearsing in another room. He listened, tried to identify the music.

Dvořák, he suddenly knew. Antonín Dvořák, a music man from a hundred years before the pandemic. He came from an old country just like the tuba boy his mama talked about. The man visited this nation then composed a symphony telling of his experiences, used folk songs as themes, called the symphony 'From the New World" –

like the previous world had been destroyed and they were lucky to be able to build again. His mama conducted that symphony in the capital to great applause.

Applause broke him from his memory as people around him rose to appreciate Dr. Crane's good words, encouraging them. Bart got up but at that moment they sat again. He hurried to drop into his seat and got a grin from Dr. Hunt.

Dr. Crane likely repeated his admonitions against the dastardly people outside, who'd destroyed the world, forcing all of them to live underground until they could produce a hardy generation able to survive the harsh environment 'up top'. The same points he always made. He railed again about too many people in the past consuming valuable resources, taking more than their fair share, not caring about others – but they would care very soon. In fact, they had taken in a few stragglers, helped them adapt to a life underground, to become useful members of the facility worthy of their food packets.

Bart felt everyone staring at him. They knew him for what he was: an outlander, a denizen of the poison zone they had taken in and healed. Now he was fit, ready to assist in their experiments to find the right genes for immunity. He grinned, embarrassed.

"Millions were removed from the natural cycle via the virus," Dr. Crane continued, "not to mention the vaccination schedule. The inoculation protocols that were adopted did prove successful for the most part. A good start in returning the Earth to a reasonable ratio of human to other lifeforms. In this way we might cleanse and renew the earth and free Life to continue unabated, to blossom and flourish, with us poor dumb meat-bodies hiding among the foliage, taking a fruit from here or there, yet never again dominating, never again destroying."

People clapped at that, his standard thesis. Bart thought it odd they would vow to work so hard to return to the surface when they already declared they'd caused the problems, that they'd been the destroyers. On the other hand, Bart had been up top. He'd seen how everything actually was and felt no ill effect. Was he truly immune from something or was he simply a normal man and these people were crazy?

"However," Dr. Crane was speaking, "we must acknowledge that the methods may have worked too well. Even the randomly assigned air burst on particularly hostile populations worked too well. Free of the diseased and the belligerent, we find ourselves underpopulated. Not enough people to safely and securely reacquire the surface. Not without adapting genetic material which provides immunity against the harms presented up top."

The audience had quieted to listen to the serious parts.

Bart looked around, noting the red caps with white balls at the ends of the pointy crowns which many in the audience wore. On the walls tiny red and green lights had been strung out from corner to corner. A design in the shape of a fir tree had been painted on the back wall. A large drawing of a plump old man in a red suit with a long white beard stood beside the tree, holding boxes wrapped in red and green paper.

He recalled a similar display in winter back in Skinner Canyon, thought the fat man was called Old Nick. Usually had eight deer with him. His mama had given him a gift, said it was from the fat man in the red suit. Inside the wrappings was his Aunt Eve's cornet. He wasn't happy. Giving gifts in the winter hadn't been the custom in the capital.

He snapped back, made sure he sat properly, had the same look on his face as everyone else: like he was mesmerized by their grand leader's oratory.

Before the meeting could finish – and everyone join together in a boisterous singing of songs (always the same ones, as though they were required just like in the capital), then quaffing down thimbles of elixir meant to boost their immunity – Dr. Crane called everyone.

"Our newest resident, support staff Mister Bart Baumann, and our Doctor Marina Kvashenaya, who graciously volunteered for the special immunity project, have succeeded. I'm very pleased to announce that it has been confirmed that she is carrying a viable, living embryo. Well done, Doctor K! And congratulations to you, Bart, for achieving this important success in the very first trial."

+ + +

Another excursion to check the environmental conditions and count hell-cats and whatever other oddities released from the facility: dog-hares, rat-birds, snake-mice, and moth-bats. A hippo-horse had come into view the previous outing, pushing its weight through the sage, munching contentedly. Nick told him they tried a giraffe-elk but Bart didn't know what a giraffe was. He had to wonder why they kept trying to mix animals together. None of them looked good. He worried how they tasted as food, if that was their goal: making them for the day they left the facility.

Nick stared at the sky, assessing the weather. "Not too bad."

A herd of clouds sauntered by, as big as bison, letting curious sunbeams peep between them, striping the dry land in shadow and light. The air was warm for the season but they declined to switch on the air units for their hazmat suits.

They had driven the cart out to the usual perimeter, halted and eased off the hoods. They took long breaths as they planned the day. Nick looked over his tablet, checked the map on the screen, tapped it a few times, set it in his pack again as Bart prepared the electro-guns, checking the battery packs. When he looked up, he saw the plaster teepees off in the distance. He hated seeing them, reminding him of the freedom he once had.

Not much to say on these excursions. The routine was the same. They each knew what to do. Take readings. Count hell-cats. The air was dry and dusty, so conversation was kept to only a word or two and more came as hand gestures.

Nick waved them onward, electro-gun in his hand.

They counted hell-cats in the distance. Four of them altogether, lazing like a lion pride. Nick thought one appeared a bit larger than the others. He had to take a closer look.

Jogging toward the quartet of the tawny cats, Nick dropped to a knee, gun poised, studying them. Their hides were spotted although faint against the fur.

"I swear," he mumbled, looking through the telescope.

He raised his electro-gun, paused to adjust the distance setting, and aimed at the fat one. *Sizzle* went the electric energy beam at the cat. It lurched into the air as if trying to dodge the bolt, then fell on its side as the others bounded away.

Nick waved Bart to follow and they marched across the scrub to the downed beast.

"I don't mean to say I knew it," Nick spoke, taking a knee by the fatally wounded animal, "but I knew it. Somehow."

"What's the matter?" asked Bart, standing behind him.

They wore hazmat suits, including gloves, so Nick could feel the cat's body safely, poking and probing. It was still alive but barely, still shaking with energy from the blast. He felt the cat's belly, much larger than the others.

"Dang it." He glanced back at Bart. "It's happened."

"What's happened?" asked Bart, head up, keeping watch.

Nick's eyes were fixed on something in the distance. The other three cats had halted, stood defiantly watching the two men.

"One of those hell-cats has turned. Changed into a male. I heard it happening with some amphibians and other animals. If there's no males around, one of the females will become the male."

"You joking?" Bart was genuinely surprised. He knew they tried that in the capital before he was born. The government had forced some boys to become girls, saying there were too many men in the city. But that was done using drugs and surgery. Uncle James had almost been one of them.

"This cat is pregnant. I can feel her belly's grown."

Bart stood guard. "Not what they expected, huh?"

"Not hardly. They never wanted them to reproduce so they made only females. The cloning procedure only produces females."

"Like you said...."

Bart watched the distant hell-cats, the three beasts watching the humans. He kept his electro-gun ready, kept checking behind him, too.

"And the lion shall lie down with the lamb," Nick spoke, his tone dark. "That's in Isaiah. The Bible book."

"It is?" Bart was puzzled, then wondered if Isaiah actually was a good name for his son.

"The cow and the bear shall graze; their young shall lie down together; and the lion shall eat straw like the ox." Nick regarded him. "That's in Isaiah, too. The animals acting opposite of what they should. It sinful. But they don't care."

Bart thought of a comment worth sharing, was about to speak it when Nick gave a grunt.

"Dang reports," he cursed. "This isn't going to be good. Maybe we should forget we found this. They'll want samples to analyze. And you and me, we'll have to go through extra decon." He went on complaining. They would need to endure more steps since they were in direct contact with an animal. They'd get a special injection, too. "Can't wait for someone else to take over this task. I'm about done with this shit. You can have it if you want it. Wish I could just get in my jeep and drive the hell out of here."

Have it if I want it....

Bart thought of that first time in the decon chamber, the three of them disrobing, getting sprayed down, washing themselves. He saw how Nick looked at Trina. He saw how muscular his body was. He noticed how Trina tried to turn away to hide herself from his lustful eyes. But were they truly lustful? Or merely curious?

Nick told him on one of their earlier excursions how the facility people saved him and that was the reason he stayed. Saved from what? A band of savages had chased him across the desert on fast vehicles they built from old parts, fueled by corn oil or something. They'd caught him and dragged him from his vehicle, threatened to kill and eat him. If they had, Bart wouldn't be here with him.

"I'm glad you don't mind me being in that experiment with your wife," Nick was saying as Bart came out of his thoughts. "It's all to save humanity, right?" He chuckled. "If only we could convince them there's nothing's poisonous out here."

Yet Bart couldn't respond. He thought he muttered a "yeah" like he usually did but he hadn't. Words caught in his throat.

A vision of Trina laying against Nick filled his head. He could imagine them on the bed together. He tried to believe she had acted unwilling, made it too much trouble for him so he'd given up. More likely, she'd given in, seeing the opportunity to try a new man and maybe enjoy it. They never talked about the immunity experiment when they were together in their apartment.

Images flashed through his head of how Nick gazed at her in the decon chamber. The images melted into images of them on a bed, legs entwined, kissing. Purely his imagination. He stared at Nick's face as he looked out across the plain, focusing on his lips. Trina had put her lips to his, Bart had no doubt. How did that feel? Did she like it?

"I know it didn't take the first time," Nick continued as he ran his fingers over the hell-cat carcass, "but we'll get it next month for sure. Or the following month. Or the next. No hurry, right? Not as far as I'm concerned. They can have their little experiment. I don't mind at all. Happy to help out. However long it takes." He paused as if replaying a memory. "Yeah, been a while. Been eight years since I lost my wife."

He was definitely acting smug now, Bart decided.

"She can be kind of tough," he went on. "I get it now. But she can also be...how should I say? Loving? Tender? ...I mean, you treat her right and she'll come around. You know? Hell, course you know! She's got a narrow gap, so to speak, that you gotta hit just right – between treating her kinda rough, forceful even, make her obey, and treating her gently like a lamb. It's a fine line."

Treat her kinda rough, make her obey....

Bart didn't actually want Nick to tell him. It was too much.

"We worked it out, found the right way. Now she's easy, goes for it like she's a hungry little hell-cat. She's into it, on board with the protocol. Likes it. Maybe she wasn't getting a good loving before. Hard to say." And he laughed like it was a joke, just teasing him.

Wasn't getting good loving before....

The man glanced back at Bart, grinning. He was a stranger. Yet he continued to grin like he was having fun deliberately razzing him. The only one in the facility he could call a friend, and yet....

"I mean, requiring three deposits over a twelve-hour period, two consecutive days, is manageable. Damn near wore me out. Hell, I could do more. One of them's bound to hit." Then Nick startled. "What am I saying? You know it already. Congrats!"

One of them is bound to hit....

Not even praise for his success with Dr. K could dissuade Bart from hating this man.

Bart's thoughts returned to the decon chamber, recalling how Nick appeared naked, how well-formed his body was, quite fit. Trina had to like that. He grew tense.

"I could do more. Yes, a lot more," said Nick, showing the same grin, "but they have their protocol. To be honest, I enjoyed it. Been a while for me, like I said. God bless experiments."

Bart felt strange sensations run through him. He couldn't relax.

"We'll get it next time," said Nick, sounding like a boast. "Then I'll be sad to have the whole damn thing end."

The whole thing end....

Odd sensations: tentacles of energy wriggling down his arm. His hands tightened around the electro-gun. He gave the battery a pat, making sure it had seated fully, tapped the charge button on top, saw the red light come on indicating it was charged.

Nick kept on complimenting Trina's attributes, describing each favored body part – up until he heard the crackling hum of the gun.

He turned to Bart. "What're you doing?"

Nick stood slowly, giving a quick look down at the dead hell-cat, then putting his attention back on Bart.

Bart pointed with his chin as he raised the gun to his shoulder.

"Cats," he announced.

Nick turned, saw the trio of hell-cats approaching, padding at a slow pace over the scrub, coming for their fallen mate.

Before Nick could pull his gun up to his shoulder and aim, the bolt of energy hit him under the shoulder as he twisted around, the blast going into his armpit. The knife of energy bore through his chest and exited the opposite side where it dissipated in the air, leaving blue lightning crackling then blinking out.

Nick glared at Bart with his eyes wide, giving a look of surprise then of understanding. His body collapsed beside the dead hell-cat.

Bart quickly stepped away, backward to keep his eyes on the trio of cats. He kept the gun to his shoulder.

The hell-cats gathered around the man sprawled there. One cat, having an unsettling face of a scornful woman but having a jawline extended to accommodate a full set of sharp teeth, put a paw to the man's shoulder, claws scratching away the hazmat suit until flesh appeared, then took a bite. Approving, she let out a cry to the others and the three of them began dining. They clawed the suit away and snipped bits of flesh from the body, then lay casually chewing while they stared at Bart.

He watched, hating the sight of the mess they were making, but he didn't care about Nick, who had been his friend – up until he wasn't.

Filled with rage, Bart switched the electro-gun to maximum and blasted the whole bunch, merging the two cats with Nick's head and shoulders, cooking it all into a stew of flesh and bone – as the third cat bounded away.

When he finished, he stood amazed how the three bodies merged as one, each extending off in different directions like spokes on a wagon wheel. In that moment, he felt his body relax, tension suddenly gone, and he breathed deeply the blood-scented air.

What to do? How to explain this?

He grew frantic a dozen breaths after he felt stress evaporate. It returned with a vengeance. He sweat in his suit, so he scrambled to zip it down, jerk the suit free, push it down his legs, standing in the 'base support garment' they issued to him. The suit bunched around his ankles, held by his boots, wouldn't allow him to run if a hell-cat returned. He let the breeze dry him and pulled the suit on once more, set the hood, adjusting it so he could see through the window.

Next he grabbed Nick's gun, still clenched in his outstretched hand, as well as the battery packs on his belt, left untouched by the hell-cats, and took them over to the teepee where he and Trina had slept that one night more than a year before. He stashed the extra batteries there.

Me and Trina. Only us. He kept repeating the thought.

Then he rushed to the cart, started the motor, turned the cart around, and sped back to the facility with his story set.

He drove up to the big door, acting frantic, waving his arms and shouting through his suit to the guards that a terrible emergency had occurred and he needed help. He needed witnesses for his story. Someone had to see the evidence.

The guards, even after checking with their supervisor, would not go out with him. They were ordered to stay by the door. They were not authorized to go further. Bart insisted. He described what happened, putting on a drama. He could still shoot, could kill a man, he knew, but he could also lie like the devil himself.

"Return to the site," said a guard, relaying the message from the supervisor. "Capture images using the camera on your hood."

Camera on my hood? Bart panicked. *There's a camera embedded in the hood of the suit?* He tried to remember if he'd ever seen it. No, he couldn't recall. He reached up and felt around.

"I don't think mine is on. I didn't know I had it," said Bart.

"Capture images," said the guard, passing the instructions. "All angles. Then return immediately."

Bart drove the cart back to the scene of the crime, in no hurry. He got off the cart, stood regarding the scene, disgusted by it.

He snatched the device off his belt that he knew for certain was a camera and pointed it at the conglomeration of the three bodies, two clearly hell-cats, one a human in blood-stained hazmat suit. He held up the device, pressed the button, moved around the mess, repeating the image capture.

Then he returned, entered the facility, went to the decon room while others cleaned the cart and transferred images he collected. He thought of that first time in the decon chamber, seeing again the three of them together. He remembered how much he hated it. But he smiled this time, then tried to hide it from the cameras.

27

THE COMMITTEE

BART STRODE INTO THE APARTMENT like a conquering hero as soon as he finished the decon procedure. He found Trina inside, went straight to her, wrapping his arms around her, held her tight. She felt good in his arms and he never wanted to let her go.

"Y'awright?" she asked, puzzled by his behavior.

She tapped his arm and he released her, but he set his hand on her shoulder to direct her to sit on the bed. Side by side, he gazed at her tense face, waiting for a smile. She never looked happy even when she was, he knew. Instead, he could only see the ghostly face of Nick Ramos hovering there and had to close his eyes.

"Sumpin' wrong?" asked Trina. She leaned into him as her hand went to his stubbly cheek. "Ya growin' yer beard again?"

His mouth tightened. "Something happened."

"What?" She looked seriously at him.

"Never mind what," he said. "We need to get prepared to leave here. Right now."

"It's time?" She seemed surprised. But he always took things too far, always being dramatic. "We just got Izzy's check done. Listen to this: Doctor K, she was holdin' him up on the table, him naked as day he born, an' he lets go his mornin' fountain right at her. But she never got mad, just let him pee straight on her shirt. Said it soak up the pee. When he got done with peein' she wiped him clean an' went to the next room to get a new shirt. Kinda funny."

"That has nothing to do with it," said Bart to cut off her laughs.

"Nothin' do with what?" Trina smiled warmly at him. "It's early still, I know, but din't see no growin' belly on Doctor K yet – if you's wonderin'."

"I'm not wondering." He got up rough as a bear, fire in his head, hand to his forehead, pacing the small room. "Gotta get our things together. We need to go. Soon. Have to get out while we can."

"Now, Bart? We got no horses. How we going'? Got no guns. How we gonna survive out there?"

"There's carts," he said, thinking hard, remembering what he'd seen. Nick told him about the vehicle he arrived in, saying it was one of the last ones they made before the factory closed. "There's a big one, too, what they call *jeep*. He calls it his *Grand Cherokee*. Like the tribe. But he ain't Cherokee. Got a big flatbed, too, so it'll carry lots of supplies. I saw it down in the transportation bay, what they call *garage*. We can use that."

"Still workin'? One them gas carriages?" She sounded doubtful, frowned at him. He was always telling stories. "Where they get that gas-o-line? Gonna use it up sometime or other an' then we gonna be walkin' rest the way."

"No, it has...uh...." He thought of how to describe it. "Got these panels on the top catch the sunshine. Got a machine that converts the sunshine into electric. Nick told me, explained it. He used to drive it everywhere, like Denver City to Grand Junction. Then he drove it down here. Said got two-hundred-thousand miles on it."

"Two-hundred-thousand miles? Is the world that big?"

"I guess he might've run in circles."

"Did ya tell Nick we's leavin'?" she asked and Bart saw her perk up, like she expected Nick to join them. "What he say 'bout it?"

"He doesn't know," Bart said quickly. "But it's time to go."

"Ya know how to make that jeep thing go?"

"It's just like the carts. I know how to make it go, don't worry. It will carry more supplies—"

"Ya got more supplies?" she asked suspiciously.

"I know where everything's kept. Everything we need. I can put it away. Hide it. Then when we go, I'll put everything on the jeep and away we get."

"An' nobody gonna see ya? They got cameras ever' damn place." She glanced at the one in the corner of the apartment.

Bart noticed her glance, played along: "No, we can't leave. What a joke. I was *joking*. It's too dangerous out there. But I...I really had you going for a moment, didn't I?" He chuckled stupidly.

Trina forced a laugh. "Yeah, so me an' Doctor K, we was talkin' about my *fertility*, since ain't 'got lucky' yet – like she says. She was sayin' this here facility's got forty-eight men in it marked with good fertility. What she call *sperm count*. An', huh, *motility*, think she called it. It's how they know who's gonna be papas an' who ain't got no chance. Folks born in here got lowest. Except a few that're what she call *anomalies*." She regarded him. "So if it don't work out with Nick, they got others to do it."

Bart was deep in thought and only pretending to listen.

"Don'tcha want me to have another baby?" she purred.

He looked at her and she had to reset herself.

"You got lucky, Bart. So I asked Doctor K why there's no kids in the facility. She says they only can make a couple babies each year. An' two or three people die each year, too. Old age. Bodies wearin' out. That's like a hundred years of bein' alive. Doctor Crane, she said, he's a hundred-six. Can you believe it? Looks only seventy. So they try puttin' that DNA stuff in a pan an' mix it up together then grow it into a baby, but never works right. They gotta kill 'em. *Non-viable*, she call it."

Bart glared at her, wishing she would shut up so he could think.

But she continued: "She was sayin' there's another facility far west o' here they talk to somedays. Over a *radio*. Same kinda place as this one. Seem they all go under the ground to get away from the virus long ago. Ain't none o' them ever check up top again."

Bart shook his head in frustration.

"They all went to underground bunkers," Bart shouted, words straight from Nick, "to escape the mobs wanting to kill them for what they did. Making the virus. Making the vaccines that were worse than the virus. For tricking everyone, for destroying lives, for making people die!"

Trina tensed at his sudden outburst.

"Folks born down here ain't never been up top, don't know 'bout nothin' what's outside."

Bart's face grew red. "Three generations hiding out."

Trina regarded him, used to him showing his emotions. "Y'ain't a good boy today, is ya?"

He snapped a look at her. "What? What're you saying?"

Trina cringed. "Ain't sayin' nothin'. Y'ain't neither. What's goin' on with ya, Bart? Yer scarin' Iz."

Catching his rage, he sucked air, trying to relax. He glanced at the other bed, saw Izzy sitting up watching them.

"See?" Trina pointed at Izzy. "Yer son don't like yer shoutin'."

Bart took a deep breath, let it out slowly, yet he couldn't calm himself. "Purdy soon they gonna find out what happened and they'll wanna do something. I don't know what the answer is. We need to play it straight. Lemme gather supplies we need. I got access now, being a groundskeeper. When the time's right, we'll go."

"Find out what?" Her eyebrows pinched together.

"What happened out there."

She got serious again, searching his face for clues. "Ya scarin' me. We got lotta things goin' on here. Cain't be shakin' up all them things. Second trial is scheduled for eighteen days from now."

That reference yanked him back to the present situation, filling him with anger. He'd almost forgotten the damn trials.

"Then we have eighteen days to get ready to leave."

"No," Trina snapped like he was a pesky bug. "Cain't do nothin'. Not 'til their 'speriment's done."

Bart stood firm, staring at her. "It is done." His voice darkened. "Trial's done."

"Done? How ya figure? Just cuz ya got yer baby comin'? That it? Heck, I'm still under protocol."

"Because...." He bit his lip, fighting back the urge to grin. That wouldn't be the best expression although it was how he really felt: his plan was good. "Because your partner in the protocol has died."

"What?" She jumped to her feet. "Nick's dead? How?"

Bart noted how Trina reacted: like she wanted the man. Not like she felt relief at not having to continue the trials. Not like it was a hell-cat that was killed and nothing to be concerned with.

He realized then he had a chance to practice his story, to get it straight for the Committee that would call for him, question him thoroughly. First, he needed to conjure the proper mood: something sorrowful but with a twinge of horror added.

"One of them *femo*-cats got him," he spoke clearly like he was in front of a judge. "I tried to warn him it was coming up behind him, but it was too late. Cat leaped on him. So I fired the electro-gun at the cat. A second cat arrived from the other direction. I was scared and backed away. I kept firing at the cats, eventually killed them. But he was already dead by then. But I was so scared I just kept firing until the battery pack run out. By then it was all a mess, the three bodies fused together."

Faked emotions overwhelmed him and he wiped his eyes.

Trina embraced him, patted his back.

"He was yer best friend in this whole place."

"Yeah, he was," Bart whimpered as best he could.

"Poor man," she added, sniffling back tears.

He thought she meant him, but maybe she referred to Nick.

"Yeah." He waited a moment. "What a poor man."

+   +   +

What just happened? How did I get here? What am I supposed to do? So many thoughts banged through Bart's head as he sat nervously waiting for the Committee to call him in. He counted the years gone by, bad things he'd done, found the list long. Most of all he thought of his mama sitting alone in her big house, nothing but a piano to comfort her. She'd wonder about him, where he was. She'd think he ran away, got in trouble, felt too ashamed to return home, and she'd be right. Or she'd think he was dead – and he might as well be dead for the trouble he'd caused in his young life.

"Come in," said Dr. Jenkins, wearing the white coat, taller than Bart, balding, white mustache on his face and snowy whiskers on his chin, thin lips not smiling.

Bart entered the room like a pupil sent to see the schoolmaster.

He saw the half-dozen men and two women seated around the long table. The Council Chamber, the room was called. The place where rules were made, decisions enforced. When they first arrived, Trina was summoned to present Izzy to the Council, proof of her fertility, suggesting that life could continue up top. They were amazed.

No welcome this time, Bart noticed, as he met each face around the table. None smiled. Serious business this time.

"Tell us what happened," said Dr. Jenkins, the usually talkative Dr. Crane sitting beside him and motioning to begin.

They went out as usual, saw a quartet of the femo-cats and Nick shot one he thought looked *deformed*. That word was a good choice, Bart thought. The three other cats charged and Nick couldn't react in time. Bart stood behind him but Nick was in his shooting lane. The first cat bowled Nick over, attacking him. Bart fired at the first cat, knocked it down. The other two cats paused, challenging him. He saw Nick wasn't moving, saw blood gushing out of his wounds, presumed he was already dead. So Bart shot one cat and the others ran away. Two cats dead, one on top of Nick, the other fallen beside him. Bart tried to take out the charging cats but the electro-gun took too long to recharge. He did the best he could, he *confessed*, but it wasn't good enough.

"We appreciate your efforts to save our colleague, Nick Ramos," said Dr. Jenkins. "Accidents happen from time to time. How it must have frightened you to be in that dangerous situation." He glanced around the table, saw others nodding. "I have no doubt few of us would have remained calm at rushing femo-cats as you exhibited."

Dr. Sung stood and went over to the wall where a screen came on showing the images captured with his camera after going back to the site. Bart pointed out relevant details. They marveled at the way the three bodies had fused together into a single entity. A few members agreed that the electro-guns needed to be modified to fire quicker. Dr. Lee asked if the 'three-body problem' could be brought into the facility for closer examination.

"That might be unwise," Dr. Jenkins responded. "Too much risk of contamination."

"I will authorize a team to go up top," Dr. Crane spoke, a slap of his hand on the table. "They can better determine what should be done with the...uh...the remains." He looked around the table, saw nods of agreement. "In charge of this expedition, I assign our brave groundskeeper. You are hereby promoted to Chief Groundskeeper, Mister Baumann, to replace our friend Nick Ramos, who was the unfortunate victim of the cruelty of our world. I believe he had no relations in the facility we need to contact."

Dr. Yancey raised her hand. Her short bob made Bart think she might be a man at first glance. She worked in the clinic with Dr. K and assisted with his examination prior to the first trial. It had been a thorough examination and he felt embarrassed seeing her again and looked away.

"Nick Ramos," she spoke, then paused a moment out of respect, "was selected for our immunity response experiment. The first trial failed. The second trial is already scheduled. Given Mister Ramos' untimely demise, we should start the protocol again for Subject Two. With a new partner assigned."

Bart tensed hearing that idea. He shot an angry look at her but his frantic eyes did nothing to stop her.

"Next on the list is...Doctor Rajneesh," said Dr. Yancey, reading from her tablet. "His readings match well with those of the subject."

No, not him, Bart thought. *Anybody but that one.*

"I authorize the start of a new trial," Dr. Crane announced.

"The subject's cycle has been calculated to begin in sixteen days," said Dr. Yancey. "I will inform Doctor Rajneesh."

"Permissible," Dr. Jenkins confirmed. "That's time enough for a memorial service. Then we shall be able to return to our usual business of saving the world."

"Enough of those unproductive consumers," said Dr. Crane. He looked up to see the others giving their attention to him, so he went on: "Always needed to eliminate a facility member in order to keep our population a reasonable size, given our resources. Now we need not choose someone from the removal list. Nick's extraordinary death – his sacrifice – will save another life and equilibrium is thus restored."

"Well said," Dr. Jenkins offered.

He put his hands together before his face and the others around the table followed. He spoke a solemn prayer that had Bart forming tears. They seemed to be real tears, not something he forced just for dramatic effect. Sometimes he could fool himself.

+ + +

Bart knew the way now, a lot of the ways, in fact. Memorized which passages to take, which turns. He found himself at the room where the supplies were stored. He had the code from Nick, even before the Committee entrusted him with it, and typed the numbers into the keypad on the wall by the door.

Inside, the lights clicked on at his entrance.

Bart immediately looked for cameras. He turned his back to the one he saw. He took out the tablet Nick used, tapped to get the inventory list, each item with its location. He went up and down the aisles checking the items he would take when they left.

Everything he wanted was there and he grinned. He couldn't set them aside just yet. That would look suspicious. He'd gather them before leaving. He'd need the trolley to ferry items into the garage where he would load them in the back of the jeep.

He regarded the metal plate on the rear of the vehicle, a line of mountains drawn there with the word *Colorado* and some numbers, Even back then, he considered, the government was keeping tabs on everybody, marking each vehicle like cattle on a ranch. Life was a lot better now; don't need tags except in the facility where everything had to be triple-approved.

Taking time to sit in the green machine on previous days, he got familiar with the controls. He looked through a book he found in a storage space beside the control panel. He found a paper picture stuck inside the book: Nick and his family. Wife looking pretty with her curly blond hair, and three kids maybe 12, 9, and 7, all boys, the two older sons looking like the mother, younger one like Nick.

He studied them. How had they died? Nick never told him, only saying they didn't make it to this valley where the people from the facility offered him refuge. Had to be either sickness from the virus or else struck down by violence from mobs made crazy by the errant vaccines. He remained surprised how many years back that was.

What year was it? Early in the last century, was all he recalled.

He stared at the shelving before him.

The lights blinked off suddenly, not sensing movement as he slipped into his memories. He clapped his hands to bring the lights on again.

With his checklist complete, he returned to the apartment, found Trina with her shirt off, nursing Izzy. As she held the boy with one arm, she grasped a book in her other hand. He recognized it as the diary he took from the airplane wreckage. Seeing him, she looked up and asked him the meaning of some words she tried to read.

"It's about the pandemic that happened long time ago," he said, voice weary. He was pleased with her reading lessons.

Sitting on the bed beside Trina, he poked a finger at Izzy's belly and the boy giggled, swatted at Bart's finger.

"I thought he's taking food packets now."

"He did. Didn't like it. So I'm givin' him what he want."

"I'll check with the clinic, see if they can adjust his solid food."

"You kin try but they ain't the best fer listenin'."

Bart's face remained serious, thinking through his plans. Trina handed Izzy to him. "Here. Take yer boy. Be a papa."

He gathered the wriggling baby in his arms, saw his son's silly grin and couldn't help but smile back. The boy made noises with his mouth, almost sounded like words. Izzy was ready for play but Bart held him against his chest, only letting his son tug on his beard, as Trina went on reading, sounding out the words as he'd taught her.

"They were flying that airplane to somewhere out here. Maybe this facility." He reminded her about the hexagon symbol on the door to the facility being the same as inside the airplane's cabin. "Guess they had trouble and had to stop there, not reaching their destination here. But they crashed."

"What a sad story," she said, staring at the page.

"Never saw a running way anywhere around here. Not in all the excursions we did. But the logo is the same."

"On ev'ry uniform." She tapped her chest where the logo would be on her work shirt. "Like they wanna mark everybody. Nick said it was the 'mark of a beast'. Ain't no hell-cat, fer shore."

Bart knew what she meant: how they were put into functions, made to serve the needs of the facility. No free-loaders – although they'd been given time to adjust before being assigned a job.

"Asked 'em when they gonna let us go," she spoke, taking Izzy back, putting him against her shoulder. "They laugh like I's jokin'. Well, s'pose I was jokin' an' played it like I was. Like ya say to do."

He grinned at her. "What did they say?"

"Same as always: 'You must stay here. World outside's poison. Only safe inside. But if you stay down here', they keep sayin' then 'We implore you to help us.' Help how? I ask 'em. 'Help us find the genes that give us immunity.' That's what they said."

Bart liked how she imitated the way the staff spoke.

"They said: 'If you refuse, then some on the Council suggest you should be forced to obey. It's a matter of survival.' Forced, they said. So I give in. You did too. Give 'em what they want. Cuz I wanna live, need a place to live, for me an' my boy – an' my foolovaman. They wanna 'nother babe to look at, so I'm game."

She patted Izzy's back until he let out a burp, then let him fall asleep on her shoulder.

"It's price o' freedom," she said.

"Yeah." Bart forced a quick smile. "They keep saying 'You can't survive out there. The hell-cats'll get you, and you with a little boy to protect. It's foolish to think of going out. You better stay here, underground. Where it's been safe for a hundred years. And maybe for a hundred more, the way they think."

"...'So ya better help us with our 'speriment to find them genes fer th' immunity ya gots.'" She tried to laugh, then broke into tears.

"What happened?" he asked, turning serious again.

"Nobody told ya?"

He shook his head, prepared for anything.

"That committee, they wanna make me obey. They's gonna force me to...what's that word they used? *comply*? That it? Said it's necessary, important, matter of survival – and never any mind what I wanna do or not do, an' how it's my body so it's my decision. But they wanna force me – again! With that Rat-Nest this time."

Bart shook his head. "It won't happen." He took her hand. "Your next cycle is a couple weeks off, they told me. We'll be gone by then. I'm working on it. Got it all planned. We're getting out of here."

28

A New Protocol

THE SHORT MAN in his wrinkled gray coverall had a worried look as Bart stood before him, taller and stronger than the older clerk. Bart acted mean as best he could, trying to scare the man.

"Jerry," he spoke in a deep voice, as deep as he could make it. "I see you're thinking of saying something to somebody."

"No, I'm not." Jerry had shifty eyes. "Really, I'm not."

"I'm Chief Groundskeeper now." He held up the tablet, showed it to him. "This is what they authorized. An overnight excursion this time. Checking *femo*-cats at night. See how they're getting on. But you wouldn't know about none of that."

"*F-femo*-cats?" Jerry stuttered nervously. "No, sir."

"The woman/cat hybrids they tried to make – *did* make. And put up top to see how they fare. Them *femo*-cats. Some call 'em hell-cats, because they are. Straight outta Hell, lemme tell ya. Rip you apart in a Kanza City minute."

"I heard that name," said Jerry.

"Gonna need the big cart this time, what they call a *jeep*, to take more supplies outside. Look on the tablet: it's authorized."

Bart smiled to himself, happy at how he was able to convince the right people that not only would it be good to check their nocturnal habits, no matter how dangerous confronting them in the darkness might be, but that the jeep would provide good security. The cart he and Nick used had no top but the jeep did. They could stay inside it overnight and be safe.

"Are you authorized to operate the jeep?" asked Jerry, his voice shaking, then half-cringed awaiting Bart's response.

"Yes, I'm authorized. Look at the screen," he said with an angry face. "So you do what I say. You get everything together, see, what's on the list. Got it?"

"Yessir, Mister Baumann."

"Chief Groundskeeper Baumann."

"Yessir."

"And if you don't.... If you say anything to anybody.... Might just mention a thing or to about what you been doing."

"Me? I didn't do nothing." The man looked worried, which made Bart feel more important. He remembered how it felt to have a pistol at his hip, how it gave him power.

The weapons kept in the armory seemed more for studying than shooting. He saw a few he'd never seen before and some he couldn't imagine how they might work. But he'd snatched back his greenish Sig Sauer pistol from the glass case and swept all the ammo for it he could find from drawers of a cabinet into a cloth bag.

"I saw you," said Bart, grinning like he knew the score. "Clear as day. Day up top. Bright sunshine and blue skies clear."

"I don't know what you're referring to," said Jerry.

"You don't? Hmm." Bart rubbed his chin. "That other clerk. The girl. Works with you. Suzie? Is that her name? Two of you getting too familiar...?" Bart didn't actually believe the woman would see anything in Jerry, but he enjoyed taunting him.

"We never did nothing. Nothing at all. Strictly professional."

"Maybe so." Bart grinned something evil. "Or maybe not. Don't matter much at all. I can say you did and then they'll be asking you questions. Asking her questions, too. You don't want the Committee asking her questions, do you?"

The man cowered, squeezed a tear out of his eye.

"Well, do you?" Bart pressed. "Or do you feel lucky?"

Jerry shook his head, ready to cry.

"Good. Right answer."

"But I really never did nothing inappropriate. She'll confirm my behavior was proper."

"Maybe she will, maybe she won't. Hard to tell. Maybe better to not have to ask her, you think?"

Jerry gave a defeated nod.

"Now you get those supplies gathered up and ready to go on the next excursion up top. Need the jeep this time. Going farther out, be staying overnight. Lots of hell-cats to take down. So you load up the battery packs for the electro-guns. Need three guns. Me and couple others authorized to use electro-guns. Got it?"

The little man was on the verge of peeing his pants. "I got it."

"You're a good man, Jerry." Bart put his hand roughly upon the man's shoulder, let him think they were buddies. "You do good and you'll get rewards. How's that sound? How about a trophy hell-cat? One with a purdy face, not too many fangs? That make you happy?"

+   +   +

Doctor K gave him that look she had: a little tilt to the side, a pinch of her lips to the same side, her eyes just a little more narrowed, and he knew he was in trouble again.

"You do not need to continually visit me," she spoke from behind her desk, looking serious, blonde hair in a tight bun, white coat on. The tablet on the desk before her blinked as data streamed down its screen. "The process operates automatically. There is no reason for you to check on me every day."

"But I like to look," said Bart, then caught himself. "I mean, see if you're showing yet. It's what dads do."

"It is long process. You will grow tired of waiting."

"Well, you're kinda special to me. You got my baby in you."

"I know this. Yet, as you must remind yourself, it is experiment, not for a family. There is nothing more you are responsible for. You may go about your daily tasks like a normal facility member."

She waved her hand at him as if shoveling him away.

He frowned at that. She showed her annoyed face, like he was a little boy who'd misbehaved but was too cute to spank.

"All right," she said in a huff, standing behind the desk.

Holding her white coat open, she unzipped her shirt down to the waist, let him stare at her bare belly – which showed no growth since the last time he looked.

"I guess not," Bart muttered. "Still looks purdy, though."

She fixed her shirt and coat, lips pursed, nodding to the door.

He didn't move, didn't take the hint to leave.

"I was born here, as you know." She sat down behind her desk. "My grandfather was one of the scientists. He came from the east, what city I do not know. Like others in his field, he believed he could save everyone from the pandemic spreading around the world. They had to lock themselves in this facility to be safe to do their work. He met my grandmother here, another scientist. After a lengthy application process, they were granted couplehood by the Council. For them it was a natural event, not an experiment. No protocols. Then, after a generation, I was born to the son they had and a woman from another family of scientists. They were also born in the facility. I have lived here all of my life. I never have been up top. And I have no reason to."

He perked up. "Would you like to?"

"Like to what?"

"Go up top. Go outside. Breathe some fresh air."

"Oh, it's impossible. The air is poisonous."

"Really, it ain't." He grinned like he'd revealed the secret map to a treasure, unafraid that his suggestion was heresy.

As expected, she again ran down the list of concerns with going outside, and he countered each one with what he'd observed while actually outside. He had direct experience, something she seemed to accept as valid data.

"I will remain here," she said to stop the argument. "The baby–"

"Our baby."

"The *subject* of the experiment will remain here. This baby shall grow and develop under the watchful eyes and caring hands of myself and a staff of pediatric specialists. We shall gather data constantly and continue to determine the best course for the subject as it comes into adulthood. A model human. The goal is—"

"Helluva life," Bart said with a grunt.

"Listen to me, Bart."

He liked when she got serious, made him obey.

"I get your goal is make some kind of machine baby, then make it into a man that can go into the poisonous lands, do things for the facility. I read the protocol documents."

She seemed disturbed he'd read them and now maybe knew too much. Coming around from behind the desk, she prepared to confront him, this young man who thought he was so mature.

He welcomed her advance, standing before him.

"There is nothing more for you to do here. Nothing between you and me," she stated coolly. "You are free to go."

He stood tall, looking down at her.

"About that...." He wasn't sure where he was going with his idea but it would let him stay a little longer with Dr. K.

"About what?" She shook her head. "You should go now."

Instead, he grunted, cleared his throat. "No other way to say it but to say it: we sinned. You and me. We did something against all natural laws." He heard his Uncle James the priest talking in his head. "We did a sacred thing that weren't a right thing to do, not the way we did. Hurt my wife, it did. Forcing her that way. She hates the project. Only did it to stay in good graces with the Council. I did it for the same reason. If we're gonna stay here, safe below ground, we have to obey. But I can't deny you being in the project did kinda sway me, gotta say."

"How can it be a sin to create a baby?" she quizzed him.

He frowned. "The way we did it."

A winsome smile flashed upon her face. "Bart, you are not a bad man for doing this."

"You and me ain't the only sinning I done," he said, affecting the character of a forlorn boy seeking comfort. "I sinned plenty before I got here. A little more won't matter. Whatever I gotta do. Now that they made me Chief Groundskeeper, I can do things. I can protect the facility." He wasn't sure if his act was convincing, but he went on anyway. "It's my job now to go up top and keep an eye on how things are doing out there. I'll do what I need to do."

His words left her puzzled.

"That is a fine speech, Bart. I hope you like your assignment and are good at the tasks."

"I will be. I got them skills."

"But you are still young. It is like what I read in some stories in the library, called 'hot head', common for young men."

"I ain't so young anymore."

"You are younger than me," she spoke boldly. "You are younger than Trina. You are by definition still a young man. Young and immature, although fit physically. A good specimen."

The same saw cut into him once more. He raised his hand to slap her, caught himself, holding back so the tips of his fingers grazed her cheek so lightly she may have wondered if there was an air vent she hadn't noticed before.

"Sorry," he muttered, stepping back. "But I ain't no young man. I been hearing that all my life, hate it."

"You don't want to hurt me," she said firmly, putting her hand to her cheek. "You may hurt your son inside me."

His face was red. "I have a son. This one will be a girl. A purdy li'l girl. Looking like you, all blond and such."

"No, Bart." She stared at him, almost daring him to try to slap her again. "This one will be male."

That made him smile and she again was puzzled. She took a big breath, released it, and waved him toward the door.

He shook his head. "I'll go, let you get on with your work, but I'm gonna keep an eye on you. I'll protect you and our son. I can promise you that. No matter what."

+   +   +

At least Trina understood him. You share a tent over a cold winter and you really get to know someone. Know they can handle a baby. They can find food. Make you feel like a man. And got your back no matter what crime you do. And Bart was about to do a big crime. Maybe have to kill in order for them to escape. He stoked himself for the fight that was coming.

When he held her in his arms and she shed tears, he got weak, wanted nothing more than to lay beside her and moan for past days when they could ride the range and the sky would never end. That wouldn't do for the effort needed for what he'd planned. Had to get tough again, like he was storming into a bank, his pistols drawn, shouting at the tellers to put bundles of notes in the bag—

"But is that love?" she was saying when Bart started to listen. "What is love anyways?"

He felt her warmth against him, drew in her dusky scent, knew he could never leave her, would always protect her, her and their son. They were his entire world, bigger than the facility, bigger than the plains and mountains they'd crossed.

"It's a sense you have when someone close to you acts in a good way, shows he cares for you, will protect you."

Trina nudged him, rolling on her side to face him. "So it's like being a guard? ...Or a housekeeper?"

"No, there must be more: a feeling of connection."

"Connection," she said like it was a dream. "And protection."

"Yeah, I protect you. Always have." He didn't think she believed him, gave him that look of hers, pinching her eyebrows together.

"Did ya? Did ya really? Then why we go in this place?"

"It seemed a good place first time we went in. We needed a place to rest. And they gave us food."

"Ain't now. Not for more 'an a year. We's prisoners."

"I'm fixing it. Don't worry."

"Got plenty worry about, Bart. Y'ain't one of 'em. Gimme a gun an' I take care myself. Me and Iz. Ya know I can."

"I know you can. But it's my job. It's a man's job to protect his family. And I did – I have."

"Did ya?"

Now she was challenging him.

"I killed for you," he said, his voice hard-edged. "In the territory. And here. This place."

Trina sat up suddenly, startling him.

"You killed? Here?" She gasped, figuring things. "Was it Nick?"

Bart wasn't interested in that conversation but he accepted that he owed her an answer.

"Had to. He...he was talking bad about you. I couldn't stand it."

He recalled that day. "He got attacked by a hell-cat. He was in pain. Bleeding. So I ended it for him. See, the cat attacked him so I shot at it just as it got to him, so he got hit same as the cat. That's how the electro-gun shoots. Anyway, he probably wouldn't've lived if I'da brought him back."

"That ain't killin' fer me. That's killin' fer you."

"But I did it for you."

She dropped back on the bed. "And you call that love?"

"Ain't it?" He exhaled loudly. "I got rid of a problem."

"Problem for you? Or for me?"

"I think for both of us."

"But it's done already. There's nothing more now."

"That's right. Nothing more." He took a breath, let it out. "When we go, we're gonna start over. I hope you will think of us again. You and me."

"Hope ya will too," Trina responded.

He lay thinking through his plan, looking for problems, coming up with solutions, getting everything ready.

Most important was the vehicle: what they called *jeep*. The dark green machine had a roof, had two rows of seating that could accommodate five people, and had a long flatbed with a shell over it. Plenty of space for supplies. Running along the top of the shell were panels, explained Lou Bradley, the vehicle mechanic who had little to do in the facility. The panels collected sunshine and turned it into electric to power the vehicle. No liquid fuel was needed – not that any existed.

Being in the garage away from sunlight for so long, however, the jeep needed to be charged. Had to get authorization to plug it into the facility's power grid, reassigning the electric distribution from a little used lab over to the garage. Bart was getting good at using the tablet to make the underground world how he wanted it. He enlisted Bradley into his scheme, getting the jeep ready for the excursion in exchange for the promise of souvenirs from up top.

"Gonna be a tough one," said Bart, feigning worry. "Checking on them hell-cats in the dark. But gotta be done."

Next were supplies that Jerry was putting together. Everything needed for camping, although Bart said he intended to sleep in the vehicle for safety, but just in case.... He needed to be able to set up a full campsite that would sustain him for weeks. This excursion would be the farthest anyone from the facility had ever ventured, he told Jerry. What a daring mission! Needed lots of supplies. Jugs of water, bottles of everything. Boxes and bags of food packets and medicine. And ammo. Lots of ammo, although he told Jerry he didn't intend using so much. He'd rely first on the electro-guns. But if something went wrong and he was forced to remain up top, then he would find himself under attack by hell-cats or worse. Wolf-bears might come, he told Jerry and watched the man's eyes grow wide. Bart hadn't heard of those being the facility's experiments but the mere mention of them worked on Jerry.

"The people down here," Bart spoke to Jerry, "probably never had any attacks, so they won't know what to do. Probably run around like chickens. You know what chicken is?"

Jerry cut in, telling about a time when someone from outside tried to break into the facility but couldn't breach the heavy door so eventually gave up and went away. No shots were fired.

"That's great," Bart sneered. "Now, when I'm leaving, I—"

"When *we're* leaving," Jerry corrected.

"Yeah, when we're leaving, everything's gotta be in the jeep, the motor charged up. I got Lou Bradley preparing the jeep."

"I'll be ready," said Jerry enthusiastically.

"Just an ordinary excursion," Bart reminded him. "Only thing is it'll be overnight. Better not say anything in case something goes wrong, awright?"

Jerry nodded at each point. "I'll be ready."

+ + +

Bart roused Trina in the dark of the room. "Time to go."

Her grunt said *Now? It's the middle of the night*. But three seconds later she was fully awake, had gotten up and dressed, then gathered Izzy and his bag. Her bag had been ready for a week.

They stepped from the apartment into a dimly lit corridor, Bart not caring if there might be a sensor somewhere that noticed a door opening during curfew time. If anyone didn't like it, he had his pistol back again to settle any discussion.

With a glance at Trina, a confirming nod from her, he led the way down the corridor, to the stairwell, up the stairs, up more, another corridor, more stairs, going up to ground level. He had it mapped in his head. Izzy remained asleep in Trina's arms as they stepped quickly but lightly. She complained about medicine Bart gave Izzy so he would sleep through this.

They stepped through a set of double doors, arriving in the wide corridor where the decon chamber was, just inside the entrance bay. The door stood tall before them like an unmovable mountain.

"Now what?" asked Trina, keeping her voice low.

Bart looked up the tunnel to the bay, saw something in the dark that pleased him, and grinned.

"This boy's gettin' heavy," she said.

Bart waved her over to the door marked *Suits*. He followed and put a code into the keypad on the wall. The door opened. Inside, he indicated with a tilt of his head.

"Get in a suit," he told her. "You're a small. Then put Iz in the backpack. Put him on your back. Or front."

He didn't like the look she gave, but she followed instructions. She hung the pack on her front so Izzy was against her chest. Maybe he could hear her heartbeat through the suit.

Bart pulled on a fresh suit. His usual suit had gotten too much blood on it, was destroyed in the facility furnace. The blood would draw the attention of any hell-cats. He gave Trina a smile before he lowered the hood over his head, his eyes finding her again through the hood's window.

As Bart exited the hazmat suit room, lights were blinking on in the bay. He saw a few guards coming on duty for the morning shift. They had to go into the room to pull on hazmat suits for whenever the door might be opened. Had to be ready.

Bart panicked; he and Trina were a few minutes late. He swept ahead of the guards, pulling out Trina in her suit, bearing the pack on her chest. The guards halted at the sight of the two of them. One guard seemed amused by Bart's actions, the other looked confused. *Who are these two?* he seemed to be thinking.

"New guy," said Bart to their stares. "Had to give instruction."

The amused guard nodded, the other remained suspicious. They knew Bart, the only one who went outside.

He ushered Trina with Izzy over to where the jeep sat in the bay, like a shiny new wagon with prancing steeds. Had to admire it, how clean it was, like it had never been driven before. Lou Bradley had cleaned up the green vehicle nicely. Now Bart had to remember everything Bradley taught him.

As he approached the machine, the guards took notice. *What's this doing here?* they might've been wondering.

"Today's excursion," Bart announced boldly, acting as though the guards should know his schedule.

He was pleased Bradley got the vehicle in place with no trouble. It was moved overnight, already loaded with everything he would need for a trip outside. Could've been too many questions using the larger vehicle, but a few taps on Nick's tablet, using his passcodes, took care of that.

The guards would check the schedule, see an excursion was planned, and know they had to open the door. It only took the push of a button to raise the door, but their protocol for limiting the poisons from outside had to be followed.

Curious guards coming on duty dared gaze over at the beautiful machine while acting like they were going through daily tasks.

"Get in," Bart told Trina, opening the door behind the driver's seat: a second row with a padded bench. He helped her climb up and in, then thought it might look odd to the guards and dropped his hand from her hip. She nearly fell backward into his arms, but he managed to apply his hand again for the final push.

First-timers, he indicated with a shrug and flex of his hands.

The guards didn't mind. Doing a thankless job, he mused. They stared at the vehicle in the bay, wondering why it was delivered there. A couple guards in hazmat suits strolled over to have a look, discussing its attributes through their hood windows. One of them asked Bart a question.

STEPHEN SWARTZ

He put his hand to his head, gesturing he couldn't hear, and the guard spoke louder.

"It's authorized," Bart shouted back through the hood's window.

"Who else?" asked the guard, pointing inside the jeep.

Before Bart could give the response he'd prepared, the guard turned at the approach of a new figure coming into the bay from the tunnel, draped in a hazmat suit clearly too big for him.

Gotta be that Jerry, thought Bart.

"Who's going with you?" asked the guard. His hazmat suit bore a red tag indicating he was the one in charge: Door Manager, name of Cooley.

Bart regarded the ungainly figure coming into the bay and tried to laugh for the sake of the guards. They turned and saw the short person arriving.

"It's Lou Bradley," said Bart, meaning the person already inside the jeep who was actually Trina. But Cooley appeared to think he meant the person arriving. Bart hoped none of them actually knew Bradley, knew he was taller than the one already in the jeep.

"Not authorized," said Cooley, not even checking information on a tablet. "Not trained for outside situations."

"Mechanic. In case the vehicle has trouble. Besides, how do you think he gets training for outside situations? If he don't go outside?"

Bart waved Jerry over to the jeep, acting like everything was approved. Had to trust that Jerry got what he wanted/needed into the jeep already, loaded in the back under the shell. No time to check if it was done right. Might look suspicious. Guards would wonder about the supplies.

"I did as you wanted," the tinny voice cut through the window of the hood and Bart cringed, wanting him to shut up.

Waving him over, Bart swung his arm around the man like they were old friends. "He's authorized, too."

Cooley shook his head. "Don't think so." He looked around for a tablet to check the records. The other guard went to the side of the bay where a work table stood, grabbed the tablet laying there.

Bart opened the same door of the jeep as for Trina, motioned for the man to climb up. He was shorter than Trina and had trouble, so

Bart gave him a hard shove and he tumbled inside the cabin.

"This is Jerry. He's helping us," said Bart. "He's coming with us as his reward."

"Hi," said Jerry with a wave.

Trina didn't care. As long as there was space in the jeep.

"Mechanic Bradley is not authorized," called the guard from the side of the bay, walking back toward the jeep, tablet in hand. "I'm sure that other one isn't authorized either."

Bart sucked air, felt his chest tighten. He thought he'd planned for everything. He could talk his way around these guards. They all knew him, knew about the excursions, considered him a legend, a tough man who didn't mind the dangers outside. He was a hunter. As Chief Groundskeeper he carried a lot of authority, yet he was still subject to every damn protocol the facility had. But the weight on his hip reminded him of other options.

"Listen," said Bart, acting annoyed, "it's right there. Boxes are checked. That means authorized. A longer expedition means more personnel. Got a mechanic and a back-up gamekeeper."

"Neither of them are authorized for excursions," said Cooley in his gruff voice. He stood before Bart with the tablet held up.

"They are," said Bart firmly.

"I don't think so," Cooley challenged.

"Lemme see that." Bart grabbed the tablet, tapped a few times to bring up the right menu and select his choice – all just an act.

"Wait a minute," said another guard, motioning for Jerry to get out of the vehicle.

"I'm checking right now," said Bart. He held the tablet level in one hand as he reached for his pistol with the other hand. Drawing the gun from its holster, he hid it under the tablet.

"I didn't see any authorization," Cooley repeated.

"Are you saying I'm lying?" Bart growled.

Cooley grinned through the window of his hood. "You can go out, but not them."

"I need my assistants." Bart shook his head. "Them hell-cats don't care how many of us there are."

"I can't let you take unauthorized people outside."

"Got the authorization right here," said Bart, lifting the tablet enough that Cooley could see the pistol. "See? You see it right here, don't you? My authorization."

"Wait!" Cooley's exclamation got everyone's attention. "What are you doing?"

Before Bart could act, Cooley sprang toward the side of the bay, reaching the control panel on the wall.

"Call Security," Cooley shouted to the other guards.

"No need for that," Bart called to him. "Just open the door."

"Can't do that," said Cooley.

"You'll be setting back femo-cat studies by years, you don't open this door."

Cooley turned to a guard. "Get Doctor Crane on the comm."

"You don't want to wake an old man at this hour," said the guard. "They can cut your food packets."

Pushing his fears down inside his hazmat suit, Bart climbed into the driver's side of the jeep and plopped himself down on the seat. He knew the steps to operate a vehicle like this one. Bradley showed him, made him spend hours learning how to operate it. But was the jeep charged fully as he asked Bradley?

Only one way to find out.

He pushed the start button and the engine whirred to life and a deep hum filling the bay.

Guards were waving their hands to stop him. Protocol said not to start a vehicle motor until the door was opened.

Bart lowered the window of the door, leaned out. With hand raised, he aimed the pistol at Cooley standing at the control panel. He could see the man's fearful eyes through the hood window.

"You push that button right now and get this door up," shouted Bart, "or else I'm gonna have to shoot you right between your butt cheeks. Now do it!"

Cooley hesitated, glancing around at other guards. Two of them took off running up the tunnel.

Bart fired – intentionally low. The bullet flew between Cooley's knees, cutting one leg of the hazmat suit as it continued to the wall behind him. Cooley jerked at the shot, then glared back angrily. A finger went to the green button, pushed it.

The large door began rolling up and with it the usual warning alarms: be careful, stay alert. Not the warning that one of their own was stealing a jeep and heading out with unauthorized passengers. That alarm came next as Cooley's hand fell flat against the big red button: *Intruder Alert*. That would bring a security team.

A new shrieking noise filled the bay. Guards covered their ears, hands pressed to the sides of their hoods. They never expected this kind of emergency. Never planned for it. Didn't know what to do but hope the Chief Groundskeeper would return. Then they could ask their questions.

29

FORBIDDEN ZONE

THE BIG GREEN JEEP roared over the dry, caked ground, kicking up red dust, running full speed for a mile before slowing. Bart liked how it felt riding the mechanical beast. He could run over anything that got in his way, especially with the bars on the front mowing them down. A look at the control panel showed him the battery was fully charged and the sun panels on top were picking up some light already. The turning-wheel in his hands felt better than the pair of leather reins, the cushy seat better than a hard saddle. He grinned back at Trina and Izzy in the front mirror.

"Can we take off the hoods?" asked Trina, sitting behind Bart and holding Izzy in her lap.

"We better not," Jerry offered. He was busy staring out the side windows at everything he'd never seen before. "We're safe from the poisonous air as long as we stay in this vehicle."

"Stop that talk," Bart cursed from the driver's seat.

Jerry started his rebuttal, saying what scientists in the facility had been saying since the day he was born there.

Shaking his head, Bart slowed the vehicle, came to a stop by the Navajo Village teepees. Once the vehicle was halted, he shut off the engine and climbed out in anger, boots smacking the dirt, slammed the door closed.

He made a big show of it: ripping off the hood, pausing only to look for what might be the notorious camera and putting his finger over it to leave a smudge, then tossed the hood aside.

"What're you doing?" Jerry demanded from inside the vehicle.

Bart unzipped the hazmat suit down to his groin and pushed it down to his ankles. Wearing his usual garb underneath the gray coverall, he leaned against the vehicle and pulled off his boots, slipped the hazmat suit off his feet and stood barefoot.

"You know he's crazy, don't you?" said Jerry cautiously to Trina.

"He know what he doin'," she said with a weary sigh.

When Bart looked at them through the vehicle's side window, Trina appeared alarmed. Jerry was deeply concerned.

"He's holding his breath," said Jerry. "Gotta be holding it."

Bart took a big breath, sucking in all the air he could take into his lungs and then slowly sent it out, waving his arms as if to make the exhale go up into the sky.

"He actin' crazy," Trina grumbled. "That fer shore."

"If he gets sick, what're we going to do?" Jerry wondered.

Trina gave him one of her looks: *Who's we?*

"Come on out, Jerry." Bart waved his arms. "No poisonous air. Believe me. Get a breath of it. It's wonderful!"

Jerry hesitated, took time to adjust his hood. Bart kept urging him and Trina reached across to unlock the side door, gave it a push open. Jerry about had a fit, trying to grab the door handle to pull it closed but Trina managed to shove him enough that the little man tumbled out, falling on his shoulder against the red dirt.

"Welcome to the wilderness, Jerry," Bart sang happily. "You can take off the hood." He studied the man in the oversized suit. "You don't even have the air filter turned on. You're breathing the air straight from out here."

Jerry scrambled to reach back for the air filter control.

"Forget it. Just pull your hood off," Bart insisted. "Here. Lemme help you."

As Bart worked to release the straps and shake the hood off the man's head, he glanced into the vehicle, saw Trina with her hood off, holding up Izzy so he could see through the closed window what his papa was doing. Bart grinned at his son, held up his hand in greeting and saw the boy also hold his hand to the window.

"There you go, Jerry," Bart said with a snort. "Now you're fit for the wilderness. Just another lifeform, what they call. Everything is equal out here. Live and let live, like they say. Or die because another thing is hungry and you're dinner. Only dinner they got."

"You mean the femo-cats?" Jerry was shaking.

"Femo-cats, whatever they got roaming around. Hard to tell. I've seen so many weird creatures they tried to make, then released to see what they'd do, see if they'd survive. Like they had an idea to put a new animal kingdom up top for when you all would come outta there and be human again."

Jerry stared at him, an admiring look in his eyes. He breathed the air and it didn't hurt. Didn't make him sick. His nose took it in and didn't feel itching or burning, like he'd been told.

"Don't it feel good?" said Bart, taking in another big breath.

Jerry accompanied him to the first teepee where Bart stored supplies from previous excursions. He had Jerry move rocks away from the entrance then lift the pallets away. Everything inside looked untouched: electro-gun and battery packs. Food packets. Jugs of water. Extra clothing. Bart had snuck them out whenever he went out with Nick, including the last time. He'd taken Nick's boots, same size as Bart's, and put them in the rear of the vehicle, found a space to stuff them in, and closed the rear door of the shell.

"Thanks for your help, Jerry." Bart stood grinning at the man.

"Certainly, Mister Baumann."

The sun was rising over the plain. Mountains in the distance still purple, behind them the mountain containing the facility as red as always. He pointed to the mountain, seeing the rough trail back to the door marked by tire tracks.

"I'd say you got a mile to hike," said Bart. He pulled the radio device off his belt, handed it to Jerry.

"What do you mean?" Then Jerry figured it out. "I'm not coming with you?"

"Naw, Jerry," said Bart, looking down at the man. "You're not up to it. You're a fraidy cat. That's the kind of cats them hell-cats like to dine on. Can't be looking out for you every minute. We gotta move fast. This is a family trip."

"What're you saying?" asked Jerry fearfully.

"I'm saying you got your trip outside. Up top, as they say. It was a good run, Jerry. And thanks for your help. But you better get on back before you get into any trouble."

"Trouble?" Jerry was frantic. "They're gonna punish me bad if I go back now."

"Listen, Jerry: You tell 'em I made you help me – ain't a lie, you know. I made you help me, so you're innocent. You were tricked, Jerry. They gotta be sympathetic."

"But how I get back there?"

"You walk, Jerry."

Bart scanned the landscape, didn't see anything suspicious, but he knew it wouldn't take long for any hell-cats in the area to spot or sniff meat.

"Listen, Jerry. You better get going. It's about a mile, I figure. It won't get easier the longer you take. If you're up to it, I'd run. At least jog. You'll get there faster."

"You want me to run back? I can't do that."

"You better. Can't stay out here much longer," said Bart with a hint of amusement. "Get on that radio, Jerry. Let 'em know you're heading back. Say you tried to stop me but couldn't. They'll be nice to you. Sure of it."

Jerry, about to cry, gave one last pleading look, realized Bart was serious. He turned to go. He took off in a run, as best he could on his short legs. That didn't last long and he slowed to a jog. The jog didn't last, as Bart watched him receding into the dust of the plain. The man dropped to a walk.

Then Bart saw them: hell-cats. A pair of them sprang up on their legs at the sight of fresh meat, emerging from the scrub grass like smoke from fire.

"Better run, Jerry!" Bart shouted.

The man took off as fast as he could.

"Yer a mean man," Trina cursed from the open window.

Keeping his eyes on Jerry, Bart responded: "Sometimes it takes a mean man to get things done."

With a final glance at Jerry, he went to the rear of the vehicle, opened the shell door, grabbed not the electro-gun but the old rifle he'd brought with them before, stolen back from the armory. He checked it was loaded properly, then closed the shell and stood several feet behind the vehicle, gazing down the trail at Jerry running as fast as he could.

One hell-cat had approached from the right, padding toward the man, not yet ready to spring for the kill. He saw another cat on the left, the killer role as they worked in tandem.

Bart put the rifle to his shoulder, glad he had it. The electro-guns didn't have range, fifty feet or so. He aimed down the barrel, along the sights, put the cat on the left squarely on the peg, and fired. The hell-cat nearly burst into a cloud of tawny fur. The cat on the right assessed the situation, decided it wasn't about to let this meal go free, and sprang toward Jerry, who stumbled and fell in his frantic rush home.

Bart aligned the sights again and fired, taking down the cat with a couple leaps to spare.

Jerry got up, brushing himself off, and gave a pitiful wave back at Bart, then started running once more.

Bart returned to the vehicle, checked the safety was on, and handed the rifle through the window to Trina. She leaned it against the inside of the jeep.

"Now he's got a good story to tell," said Bart, climbing into the driver's seat.

"Yer still a mean man," Trina grumbled. "Ya know?"

+   +   +

Trina shifted in her seat having moving to the front with Izzy. She faced Bart as he operated the jeep, his eyes set on the road. Must be a dozen miles further they'd gone over the open plain.

"Where we goin'?" she asked.

Bart stared straight ahead, watching the road ahead, glancing to each side for any dangers that might be coming at them. There were no roads to drive on, the lengths of pavement long ago broken and not safe for rubber tires or horse hooves. He took to the side patches of grass and dirt, slowing as necessary to navigate uneven ground.

The jeep lurched, mounting bumps and sinking into dips, jolting them back and forth.

Trina complained again.

"West," is all he said for the third time.

Trina had enough of it. Izzy wasn't happy either, whimpering from the shaking of the vehicle.

"You go to all this trouble, maybe get us in bunch more trouble, to go where?" She glared at him across the seat. "West? More west than where we been? What's west of west?" She shook her head a while. "Ya know what, Bart? I wanna go east. Back to my sisters. That's where I wanna go. Should be safe there now. Ever'body furgit us. Been couple years. We kin make yer homestead there in the east. Close to yer mama."

He gave a nod, just to let her know he was listening, but he was focused on maneuvering the jeep over the uneven ground. It was a rough lesson he was learning, but he hadn't crashed yet. Good that his was the only vehicle on this lonely road – which wasn't even a road. No time to be bothered by a woman's complaints.

"You wanna go right, turn this circular handle to the right," he said, expecting her to pay attention. "Wanna go left, turn it left. And below here is the foot levers. See, you also use your feet, like spurs against the loins of a horse. One you push down to go and the other to slow and stop. Got it? May need to operate this someday."

"Yeah, I got it," Trina snarled. "Ain't so dumb."

He also had to worry how well the vehicle performed. Bradley told him the jeep could go 300 miles when fully charged and driving at moderate speed over level terrain. Those conditions weren't what Bart faced. The panels covering the shell would keep it charged, Bradley told him, depending on the amount of sunshine. If it did run down to nothing and it was night, he'd be stuck until sunrise and a few hours of collecting sunshine. He had to keep aware of the battery and its usage.

Looking at the gauge on the control panel again for signs of the electric running down, Bart realized Trina had spoken.

"I wanna see what's out there," he replied. "Go as far as we can. Maybe see an ocean."

"Now what's an ocean gonna do?"

"I never seen no ocean before."

"Me neither, but don't mean I need to."

Bart smiled at that, feisty as ever, kept his eyes looking ahead. "Lots we'll see. Izzy, too. He's gonna learn about this world we got. Maybe he'll have a house by the ocean, go catching fish, have a happy life, fall for a woman like his mama."

Trina wasn't impressed. "This ain't the life I want. Don't wanna go west. Wanna go back to my sisters. Now we got free of the damn scientists. All this trouble an' ya wanna go on a fool's errand."

"No telling where your sisters are now or how we can find them. More dangers going back east than west. There's nothing to the west but empty land. You heard 'em in the facility. Ain't nothing 'til we get to that ocean way out west. Just mountains and desert. Lotsa space where we can start a homestead."

"You an' yer damn homestead!"

"Isn't that our goal? We gotta stick together. We're a family."

"Family? Ain't belong to ya." Her face seemed to darken when he glanced at her. "I'm goin' with you cuz I wanna. But ain't gonna wanna all the time. Me an' Iz. We kin go on our own. If we gotta. He depend on me more 'an you."

"You're not going on your own nowhere," he barked.

The jeep hit a bump, shook them out of their seats.

Bart decided they'd better stop. Check that the wheels were still in good condition. He was full of worries about this machine.

He slowed the vehicle as they approached a curve in the broken pavement, a good stand of pines on the side. He studied the trees, watching for beasts waiting for a meal.

He checked the control panel before shutting off the engine.

"Well?" Trina cursed. "What now?"

"Taking a rest." He took a loud breath. "I'll check on the wheels, make sure they're doing good. Helluva lot better 'an worrying about horse's hooves."

"Yeah," she called, "but they done wrong with Brownie and yer Betty. Ain't the right thing to do fer 'em."

He got out, stretched, nodding to her. Never did learn what

happened to their saddles, which were worth something.

He strode to the rear of the vehicle, opened the shell door to grab a food packet. He dug in the box, pulling out one then another as he read the content labels and dismissed them until he found one he liked. He grabbed another, noticing a bad smell.

Movement of the canvas that covered their gear stopped him. He paused, watching the bundle against the right side. It moved again. Bart thought a little critter must've crawled inside while he had the shell door open before.

Holding the food packets under his other arm, he pulled out his pistol from the holster on his hip, in case the critter was something dangerous. But the bundle sat up and the canvas fell away.

"The hell?" Bart gasped, dropping the food packets.

The last thing he ever expected to see in this jeep – worse than Jerry somehow returning. The person regarding him from beneath the end of the canvas gave a quick smile that melted into a frown. They both accepted how awkward the situation was.

"I am sorry," said Doctor K, sitting up, blond hair tussled.

"Trina," Bart called out, staring at the woman who carried his baby. She had no business being in the back of the jeep. And yet he had some feelings that made him put away his anger.

Trina got out, came to him at the rear of the jeep, and saw Dr. K there. She gave Trina an innocent wave.

"Look who I found," said Bart, not amused.

"Yeah," was all Trina said. She wasn't amused.

Bart turned to her, puzzled. "*Yeah?* You know about this?" Trina shook her head. "You say anything to her about our plan?"

"Just we wanna go home, not keep livin' in the facility, is all."

"Do not blame her," Dr. K spoke up, pushing the canvas off. "It was my decision. She didn't say anything to me."

"Then how?" Bart snarled. "How did you just happen to hide out in the very vehicle we were gonna take?"

She was thinking of a good answer as they stared at her.

"You may not want to believe," she spoke after a moment, "but I knew from what you said."

"What I said?" Bart's face tightened.

Trina gave a laugh. "She read between yer lines."

"So you figured what we was doing, that it?" Bart seemed angry so Trina put her hand on his shoulder. "I thought you didn't wanna go outside, didn't wanna breathe no poisonous air."

Dr. K shook her head, sat up more to get comfortable.

"I studied the reports. I read the data. They were wrong, all the colleagues in the facility. I saw it clearly one night – what counts as night underground. They have lied to us for generations. They told lies at the beginning and every year after."

"I coulda told you that, but you didn't listen," Bart said gruffly.

"I did my own research, not rely on what others said, no matter the truth. Funding for research tends to redirect the conclusions to whatever those funding it want. Doesn't mean it's correct. Wrong results are ignored. No funding for you if you don't produce the conclusions they want. My grandfather dealt with that system. I looked at the readings you and Nick took. The data. It did not add up. Nothing toxic. Yet, most importantly—"

Bart had a scowl, kicked at the dirt. "So you believe me now. That's great. Then you wanted to go on a trip, huh?"

"Not that reason." She blushed. "Mostly I wanted to go with you because of this." She patted her belly. "This baby should be with his father. Not be a subject in a laboratory."

+ + +

There wasn't any point in arguing over how she got into the rear of the jeep or why. The woman was here now, here in this wilderness. And pregnant. No way Bart would make her run home. He did like seeing her again, but he was careful to not let Trina see him glimpse toward the buxom blond woman. Could be a lot of trouble. Trina seemed to understand everything, maybe too much, Bart saw and began to suspect the women had planned it.

The bumpy ride had worked well on the hidden woman. They unloaded the gear from the back of the jeep, stacking everything on the ground and cleaned the inside of pee the woman had let go. Also the mess of her throwing up fluids from an empty stomach.

Dr. K kept apologizing for causing trouble but Bart waved her off as he cleaned, saying nothing.

"It is rather hot up top," said Dr. K – Marina to colleagues. She urged Bart and Trina to call her by her first name. Izzy, too. She held up the little boy to watch his parents cleaning the rear of the jeep, bouncing him like she knew what to do. "I never would believe such heat if I did not feel it for myself."

"You like that direct experience, don't ya?" Bart snarled.

Trina nudged him to be nice.

"Thought I heard something rattling back here," he said, trying to lighten the mood. "Good thing the back area's separate from the front cabin or we'd all be choking from the stink."

Trina gave him that look: *Be nice.*

"So hot," said Marina, wiping her throat with a clean rag. "More than being close to the boiler room in the facility."

"No more talk of the *facility*," Bart grumbled.

He glanced at Marina, saw how she watched Trina work: scrub wet cloth over the flatbed, her thin brown arms flexing, showing muscles. Trina had removed the hazmat suit, stood in only a pair of short pants that left her legs bare and a thin sleeveless shirt that left her arms free. Sweat darkened the front and back of the shirt, ran down her arms and legs.

"That should do it," Bart announced, standing back. "Let it dry a while and we'll reload it."

He looked away as Marina followed Trina's cue, stripping down to a similar outfit as Trina, pulling garments from a bag she'd kept with her when they unloaded the rear of the jeep. Marina's pale skin wouldn't last long under this sun, thought Bart. Same as his: the curse of a red devil.

He stared at both women as they shared complaints about life in the facility.

"That Rat-Nest keep on askin' if I'm Indian," Trina was saying. "Kept tellin' him wrong Indian. I'm a tribal woman, told him, but he cain't never figure out what it is."

"But he is a good colleague," Marina countered.

"Yeah, but that one, he too old fer yer project, they said."

"It was a poor plan. They only wished to preserve everything for the future when humanity could come out and rebuild civilization." Marina ignored Bart's guffaw at the idea. "It's to preserve ethnic diversity, they claimed. Diversity is always a major condition, they said. However, it was not possible to perpetuate this idea given membership in the facility. They had to be practical and tried to simply match light skin with light skin, dark with dark. That's the reason Doctor Rajneesh was assigned to you."

"That's dumb," Bart exclaimed.

"I agree." Marina regarded Trina, Izzy in her arms again. "Not very scientific for people calling themselves scientists. But third and fourth generation by now, so I can only guess how their ideals disintegrated over the decades."

"Ever'body go crazy in th' end," said Trina.

"Well, ladies," Bart spoke up, "we're free of them now. Time to find a good place to rebuild civilization." He looked over the women. "A right fine start, yessir. Two fine ladies with two good boys. We can make a whole village."

Trina gave a smirk, shot a glance at Marina. "All this boy want is to be layin' close 'til he gets all his sins outta him. You be careful 'round him."

Marina didn't know whether to smile or stay serious. "Yes, I will be careful."

"I ain't gonna do nothing," Bart growled. "Stop that talk."

A crackle of static echoed from the front cabin and Bart stopped loading the rear to listen.

"What's that?" he said, tilting his head. Then he went around to the driver's door, listened again. Something on the control panel was making a noise, like a radio device was turned on.

"Sounds like a comm signal," said Marina. "There is a comm link in this machine. For an emergency. You can call for help back to the facility."

"Back to the facility? Dammit. I don't want no contact with the facility. How do I turn it off?"

"I'm not sure it can be turned off."

"*Attention. Attention.*" A baritone voice coming from the control panel: poor quality, crackling. *"Driver of vehicle, return to facility."* The message repeated. *"Return immediately. Further unauthorized use of vehicle will result in additional penalties."*

"But my use is authorized." He thought of grabbing Nick's tablet to show her. "Just not taking Trina and Iz, or going so far away. And not planning on returning." He tried to laugh, had to cough out some dust.

"How far we from 'em?" asked Trina.

Bart wiped his mouth. "I dunno. About twenty miles."

Marina cleared her throat. "Perhaps...." She waited for Bart to give her his attention. "Perhaps they have a tracking device on this vehicle. It was standard equipment in the days of countless vehicles being on the roads. I read about such things."

"Tracker?" Bart's face tensed. "Figures. So they know where we are. What can they do? They gonna come out here and get us?"

"Ain't their way," said Trina.

"Hazmat suits and hoods, they can."

"They...." Marina paused.

Bart studied her. "Out with it. Whatever you got in your head."

"They could send flying machines."

"Flying machines? Like airplanes?"

"Not the same, but flying. Small machines, about the size of your hand or maybe larger, like the size of these wheels. They can fly out to places not too far away."

"Not too far? How far's that?" He smiled at Trina. "We just keep going until we're outta range. Then they can't track us."

"I don't know how far the tracker devices reach—"

"How can we find it? I'm just gonna rip it out."

"I wouldn't know. Could be stuck in any place on this vehicle and you would only find it if you took it all apart."

"Can't do that. Just have to keep going. Gotta go too far for them to follow us."

"I've heard," Marina spoke up, "that they have several systems for monitoring machines like this. Or monitoring facility members." She lowered her head. "I know about these methods because I have used them. For a lot of scientific uses...for what they call *nanobots.*

'Nano' means very tiny. 'Bot' is short for 'robot', which is a thinking machine. Like a computer. Same as the tablets we use."

Bart stood with a serious expression, hands on his hips.

"Being so small – too small to see with your unaided eyes – they can be placed nearly anywhere, places a person would never notice. On your clothing, in your hair, or swallowed with food. You would never suspect it was there, couldn't see it with your eyes, only by using a microscope."

"A microscope?" asked Bart.

"It's like a telescope. But a microscope shows very small things."

"I never seen that," said Bart.

"They can put a nanobot anywhere," Marina continued. "A mote of dust on your clothing could be a nanobot. Some are small enough to flow through your body in the bloodstream. And because they are a computer essentially, they can communicate with a management system. They can be controlled by someone outside of your body. The controller could make it do things, from attack the host in some way, physically assault the body, or even – this is what I read in reports – can detonate a small explosive. Small, yes, but if it were in a critical location it would have devastating consequences."

"What's this about bombs in bodies?" Trina demanded, growing afraid and leaning into Bart.

Bart's voice had an edge. "She's saying they can track us, know where we are, and send out some flying bombs to get us. So we gotta get outta here, go far enough west they can't reach us."

"That what ya think?" Trina checked with Marina.

"I cannot think of a better solution. We may have nanobots in us already. On our clothing. Inside our bodies. Certainly this vehicle. It is only a matter of time before they find us. Before they decide to eliminate us from this forbidden zone."

"Forbidden zone?" asked Trina, screwing her face up.

"This entire area, as far as we have monitored from the facility, we refer to as the Forbidden Zone. We consider it to be poisonous. Humans will die if not wearing protective garments."

"Well, damn," Bart grumbled. "We should be dead by now."

Trina frowned. "But we know everything's fine."

He looked up, thinking a bird was winging its way overhead. He followed it as it circled, coming lower.

Marina looked up, too. "Like that one. It could be what is called a *bird*. Or it could be one of their *drones*, the flying machines that can see and can deliver explosives."

"Dammit," Bart grunted, going to the rear of the jeep and pulling out the electro-gun. He checked the battery, aimed into the sky. He located the flying thing. It didn't look like any of the birds he knew around Skinner Canyon. Not a real bird, he decided, and fired the gun at the thing, saw it explode in a flash of blue light.

"That was not a bird," said Marina.

"Damn sure it weren't," Bart confirmed.

"I worry they will always follow us, monitor us," said Marina, a fearful disturbance in her voice. "They will never let us go."

30

BATTLEGROUND

TRINA AND MARINA, thought Bart, as he let a grin spread across his face. The only good thing about this escape. Nothing they could do about the trackers. So he joked about their names, on and on, as he drove the jeep over the grassy strip along the broken pavement. The women were not amused.

"Come on, it's funny," he insisted. "Tri-na and Ma-ri-na. Like you two are sisters."

They drove on in silence after that, each woman gazing out a side window at the passing landscape: the dry scrubland, red dirt, mountains ahead, blue skies with gray clouds gathering, a dull sun sneering at them. Crossroads tempted them yet Bart insisted they stay with this main road, although it wasn't much of a road, not used in decades. Rusted wrecks here and there, vehicles that stopped along the way, scattered bones beside some of them or inside them.

The road led them to yet another town: desolate, ruined, like it had been struck by fire, the people dispersed like ashes on the wind. More towns, more crossroads with fuel stations, food shops, a cabin here and there offering trinkets and art, or fishing bait. Like everyone just got up and left, like they'd suffered some catastrophe that made them want to leave. Something sudden. Pandemic wasn't like that, Bart decided.

He could feel the differences between riding a horse, with the air enveloping him, giving constant attention to surroundings, to the ground the horse trod – and the way he could easily slip into a monotony operating this machine, locked inside, forcing himself to look out the windows constantly for dangers. He could easily fall asleep as he held the circular handle, he realized and shook himself to alertness. Maybe he needed to halt and rest.

The women were chatting over the seatback, Trina in the front turned to Marina in the second row, holding Izzy in her lap. The blond woman liked playing with his son, as though she were testing him, seeing how he'd react to whatever she said or did, everything noted for some future report. He didn't mind; Trina was too quiet with the boy, like she was waiting for him to grow up and take care of himself.

There were straps to hold them in their seats and Bart thought it best to use them in case the road became rough. He didn't apply the strap on his own seat, however, thinking he might have to jump out quickly to take care of something, like shooting beasts that got in the way.

"...so they came over in the era of *Glasnost* and *Perestroika*, for university positions," Marina was telling Trina as Bart operated the jeep. "After Yeltsin, I think it was. Or Gorbachev, the last Czar. Went to research laboratories. Microbiology. Virology. Those kinds of studies. Always got funding for special projects. As long as they provided the results those funding the research wanted. Then one day everything changed. They couldn't return home. Perhaps they didn't want to return."

Bart tried not to listen. He didn't want to know too much. Not the way his mama told him more than he wanted. She insisted he had to know what his family line had done over the past hundred years, like it mattered at all. She told him he was next, hinting that he had to do something noteworthy so he would be remembered. Like his mama did composing that *opera*, he cursed, the tune of the overture coming into his head, making him hum it – and getting Trina's attention.

Seeing it was nothing, Trina returned to the conversation with Marina. Now that the stern doctor had become more of a *standard* woman, Trina liked her. He heard the friendship in her voice, the two acting like best buddies. What had they planned? The question kept nagging him. He kept thinking about it, looking for signs of a conspiracy, but his thoughts were interrupted with every bump and dip as they rolled along.

They slept inside the vehicle, too tired to set up a camp. They would leave early, just as soon as the sunrise hit the panels on the top of the shell. Dinner consisted of food packets and water from a jug. Bart counted their rations and considered how the addition of Marina impacted them.

"What ya gonna call him?" Trina asked Marina.

Bart snickered, hearing them discussing his second baby like he wasn't in the jeep, couldn't hear them.

"I should name him after my father," Marina responded.

"How about after my father?" Bart spoke up.

"Yer already name after yer pa," said Trina.

Marina waved her hand, halting a fight before it could start.

"We can give him both names. You see, in my culture we give a baby two names: first name, whatever we like, and a second name from the father."

"How's it?" asked Trina, ignoring Bart's scowl.

"Let's say this boy is named Michael. His patronymic would be ...what is it? Bartholomew? So...hmm, Bartholo*vich*? Hmm...I don't think it is good, sorry to say."

"He only needs two names," said Bart. "What we give him, and what my family gives him. Bart Baumann."

"You said no more Barts," Trina grumbled.

"Then what do you like?" he asked roughly.

Trina thought for a moment. A smile swept over her face then departed as if ashamed. She looked at Bart and he could read her expression like a page in a book. He knew he wasn't going to like the answer and he knew she knew he wouldn't.

"We should give him the name Nick."

"Ah!" Marina gasped. "From your project partner."

"He's more 'an a project partner," Trina said softly, lowering her eyes. "We never did get no success anyway. He died in a terrible way an' we feel bad about it. So he can live on this way."

She regarded Bart, face half-lit in the glow of the light inside the jeep.

He didn't like the idea but he understood. They were using Nick's vehicle. His tablet, his electro-gun. He recalled that family picture he'd found. A record of something that used to be.

He pursed his lips, said: "Sure."

At that, Trina leaned over and kissed him.

"Well, at least that boy'll have your blond hair," he said with a chuckle, gazing at Marina in the backseat.

"Or red," she spoke after a moment. "Like yours."

+   +   +

Another day, another set of miles: slow going, working the jeep over the harsh landscape of hardpack dirt and loose rocks, steep grades, sharp curves, bypassing old bridges that had collapsed, fording streams, ever watchful of dangers from nature and beast. Bart remained patient and often spoke to the machine like he did with his horse, urging her ahead when the way looked impossible.

"See, you push this button and the numbers'll show zero. Then it counts the miles as you go," he told Trina, stopping at nightfall. He was always trying to get her ready to operate the jeep should they need her to.

"So how many them miles we gone?" she asked with a smirk.

"It ain't an easy road," he responded. "We covered about...." He did the math in his head. "About sixty miles, and point two. Shows it right there."

"So how far we from the facility by now?"

Again he calculated, like his mama made him drill each day.

"One hundred forty-five miles and point eight."

"That far nuff to be away from them drones an' trackers an' bad intentions?" asked Trina, glancing at Marina.

She wasn't paying attention, playing with Izzy, getting him to babble his words as she held him.

"Should be enough," Bart answered.

"How much more we gotta go?"

"Until we see an ocean."

Trina sneered. "You an' yer damn ocean."

"I gotta see it."

Trina cursed and Bart held her. This time she let him.

"I doubt they will stop trying," Marina called. "Only with a greater distance can we be free of the signal."

Bart and Trina stepped to the rear of the jeep. The shell door was raised, the food packets spread on the tailgate, dinner finished.

Marina handed a fussy Izzy to Trina. Poop time. Trina handed him to Bart with a big grin.

"Yer turn, Papa," she said with a laugh.

"That's your task," he grumbled. "I'm the protector. I'll guard you while you take care of it."

"Gimme a gun an' I take care the guardin', don'tcha know?" She glared at him. "Gimme a gun an' I shoot my way outta that facility. Ya take Iz and I clear the way fer us. Coulda, ya know."

"I know," he said, then accepted his son, began the procedure.

"That boy, he's a good pa," Trina said to Marina. "Most times."

They watched Bart wrapping up Izzy as neatly as if he were a holiday gift, enraptured like it was the best show in town.

"You make a good family," said Marina with a hint of sadness.

Bart sat Izzy up on the tailgate, admiring his work.

"You're a little man now," he said to his son, "but someday you'll be a big man, carry a gun and defend yourself and others."

"Now don'tcha be talkin' that way to 'im," Trina warned. "Let 'im be a baby while longer."

"He ain't a baby no more," said Bart, admiring Izzy. "He can stand if you hold his hand. I seen him take two steps the other day. Be riding a horse soon enough. And he talks up a storm, just can't understand what he's saying."

"Aunt Marina kin teach 'im how to talk," said Trina.

Marina beamed, then offered her insights on child development but the parents were too tired to give attention.

Before returning to the vehicle for the night, they hugged each other. A ritual started over the days they'd been together. Trina hugged Bart, Bart hugged Marina, Marina hugged Trina. Each of them gave Izzy a kiss. Bart remarked on their family and instead of

Trina sneering at his comment, she smiled and gave him an extra long hug.

"Ever'thin' gonna be awright," she whispered into his ear.

Another day, more miles.

They passed through a forest, pausing by a stream. The sunny afternoon drew them out of the jeep for a chance to wash and relax. They had no timetable. Nowhere they had to be.

The air was cool in the mountains, the trees changing colors, rustling with the breeze as Bart and Trina stripped down on the rocky shore, throwing their clothes into a pile and splashing in the water while Marina sat on the shore with Izzy.

Bart pulled Trina down into the stream. They shivered while wrapped in each other's arms, kissing like they hadn't for weeks. When he glanced at the shore, he saw how Marina watched them.

"Come on in," he called. "Bring Izzy. Everybody needs a wash."

"Oh, I can't do that," she called back.

"Don't be proud," Bart cried. "Everybody stinks after a while."

Eventually he led Trina out of the stream, stepping naked on the shore like they were back in the old camp, taking a towel to rub down each other, shaking hair loose.

"Your turn," Trina said to Marina.

"Don't be afraid," said Bart. "I seen ya already. And you and T are both ladies."

A little more urging and Marina finally stood and undressed, left her clothes on the shore and ran into the stream, tripping on rocks and splashing in awkwardly. Bart watched Marina in the stream: her pale skin, her buxom figure, recalling the project. She wasn't showing any sign of a growing belly.

"There you go," cried Bart as Marina emerged from the stream, shaking water off herself and smiling.

She strode up the rocky beach, arm across her chest, the other hand covering below. She sat on the towel beside Bart. He gave a quick look to her belly.

"See? Got nothing," he laughed.

"It take some time," Trina responded.

Marina understood their reference, put her hand over her belly and gave it a rub. "You will see it grow."

Bart looked at more than her belly. Trina noticed.

"Y'all right now?" she asked him and he knew what she meant.

He tried looking at the stream, then watched Izzy crawling over the stones on the shore, happy under warm sunshine.

"Ain't no poison air out here," said Bart as he lay back, bringing his arm up to shield his eyes from the sun.

Later, after they had driven further and found a good place to pause for the night, Bart and Trina found each other on the side of the vehicle in the darkness. They came together, Trina pushed hard up against the side of the jeep, Bart behind her, grunting. He saw Marina watching them through the window, her face unimpressed, her look clinical. As they finished, Bart trying to catch his breath, he saw her smile. He took that as approval.

"You're too good to me," he whispered as they smooched.

"Well now, ya do take a spell to get use to, gotta say. But once ya broken in, ya ride jus' fine."

+   +   +

They'd barely finished breakfast – Bart was counting the remaining food packets, using the tablet to check inventory, marking off what had been used – when static crackled in the front of the jeep.

"Turn off that tablet," Marina cried out. She went to him, ready to slap it out of his hands but he turned sharply away. "They can track us through the tablet."

He pushed the button to shut it off, gave her an apologetic look.

She took the tablet from his hands.

"Where do you think all that data comes from?" she asked him sternly – just as his mama would do when he did something bad. He hated the feeling that cut through him.

Before he could reply, thinking of something sarcastic perhaps, a loud beeping echoed from inside the jeep. They went to the open door on the driver's side. Trina joined them from the rear of the jeep, carrying Izzy.

"*Attention. Attention,*" the weak voice announced.

"I need to find that wire and rip it outta there," Bart cursed.

"*We have questioned your accomplice, Jerry Hopkins,*" the tinny voice sounded.

"He didn't do nothing!" Bart shouted at the console.

"He did," said Trina, standing behind him.

"But we can't go back to save him," said Bart in a low voice. "Not now. We're too far away."

"And they would never let you leave again," Marina spoke up.

"Can they hear me?" he asked Marina.

She gave a nod and he leaned toward the console.

"Hey, you criminals! We are outta there. Ain't coming back. But you can let Jerry go. He didn't do nothing. I tricked him. He's easy to fool, if you never figured it out. He's innocent. I used him. I'm not gonna say anything more."

He turned to Marina. "How do I shut this off?"

"Can't."

Bart took Marina by the arm, walked her away from the jeep.

"The signal reaches this far," he said, keeping his voice low, "but can you hear it's weaker now? So then maybe we *can* go far enough it won't be tracking us."

"And don't turn on the tablet again, either. Links back to the facility."

"Is there a way to disable the link and just let it work alone?"

"No, because it needs the link to access the operating system and get whatever data you call for."

"Can't do without the jeep, but I can forget the tablet. Not use it. But it showed maps of this area."

"You should remove the communications interface and the base microchip inside. But it won't work then."

"At least it won't track us."

"Until then, they could...." She glanced around as though they were still in the facility where cameras watched everything. "They can shut off the motor if we are within range of the electricity grid. Or in range of a drone they send up."

"I can shoot those down."

"Before it hits you and explodes?"

Bart looked up, scanned the sky for anything looking like a bird or not like a bird, but the sky was clear, dark clouds in the distance. In the near range he saw puffs of smoke – recognized them as the trailing dust of horses. They'd passed a herd of wild mustangs days before and he thought it was the same herd galloping toward them.

Then he caught sight of men on the horses.

"We better pack and get outta here," he said, pointing ahead.

"What is it?" cried Marina, following him to put things away.

"Trina, guns!"

Over the hills before them, from the direction they'd planned to go, came a frightful sight. Emerging out of a stand of pines not a quarter mile away rode fifteen horsemen in blue uniforms, wearing tan hats, and bearing long guns.

Bart got a quick look, captured all the detail he needed, rushing everyone into the jeep, motor started. He noted the power level, enough to get out of there.

He pushed the jeep ahead, slowly until they cleared the rock patch and returned to the long roadway. The horsemen came out of the forest on the right, surprised to see the vehicle departing. A few shouted at them.

Bart could see more clearly their clothing: dark blue coats with gold buttons, red sashes, black boots. He'd seen those uniforms when he was a boy in Skinner Canyon when Mexi soldiers came north tracking bandits.

"Those are militia," said Bart, struggling to maneuver the jeep along the broken road. He couldn't go any faster over the uneven terrain. "Don't know what they're here for, but it wouldn't be good for them to catch us."

Trina had her pistol, had the rifle ready. Marina sat back in awe of the woman's prowess with weapons. The electro-gun was up front with Bart. He'd already pressed the charging button and heard the weapon humming.

"Maybe they're not after us," he shouted back to the women, "but I'm guessing they'll be mighty interested now they seen us."

"What can I do?" asked Marina.

"You keep down and hold Izzy," said Trina, locking and loading.

Trina scrambled up between the front seats and took her spot next to Bart, rifle ready.

"No need to waste bullets," he said.

"Know it," she snapped at him.

The jeep bumped over rocks and tilted right then left, making a path through the forest, coming too close to one pine tree or another one, slamming bushes. Bart checked the mirror that showed the view behind the vehicle, saw horsemen following but not gaining ground. They had to go slow as well with the pavement broken.

A shot rang over the jeep as it hit a berm, threatened to turn over as Bart frantically held the turning handle. He righted the jeep, pushed his foot on the go lever, felt the machine lurch forward with greater power. Once stable, he looked back over his shoulder, out through the shell's rear window as best he could with supplies stacked there, and saw the horsemen had stopped.

Out of the forest on the opposite side of the roadway came more horsemen, maybe twenty of them, but wearing flowing white robes, plus guns. The two groups rushed together like two ocean storms, clashing horse to horse at first, then separating. Some men fell off, others dismounted and took up firing positions among the trees, leaving the horses to flee. The noise of battle filled the woods as Bart drove the jeep onward, maneuvering through the forest.

He lowered the window beside him to listen to the fighting.

"Them's two bad bands," Trina said, looking back by way of the side mirror. "Way out here an' just wanna kill each other."

"Must be over food," said Bart. "But I seen a whole herd of deer a few miles back."

"Who are they?" asked Marina, sitting up in the back seat.

"Look like Mexi militia," Bart replied, and told about his uncle working with some that came north not realizing they'd entered the Americus. "They were chasing *banditos*. My uncle helped them and they left."

"We aren't in Mexico, are we?" asked Marina.

"No. I'm sure of it." He snickered. "But there ain't no borders out here. Not west of the facility. It's all open land, free for anyone that takes it. Or fights over it. But I'll tell you one thing...."

He gripped the turning handle, struggling to maneuver the jeep over a rough patch of ground.

"Yeah, what's that," Trina asked.

"Your facility folks believed nobody lived out here. Well, there ya go: two bands of soldiers. They live out here. Breathing the air just fine. See?"

"Need to be careful," said Trina, wiping her pistol. "Gotta watch out. We ain't alone in this here wilderness."

From the time they left the facility they hadn't encountered any people. Not many animals either. Without people doing things, animals should've returned, forests grow up, the land returning to wilderness. Bart worried what they would do when the food packets were gone. He expected to hunt, as he did before, but other than hybrid creatures around the facility, he wondered what there was that might be safe to eat. Out farther here, he was glad to see deer and other forest critters, antelope on the grasslands.

He considered the two groups fighting each other: those in blue uniforms and the ones in white robes. He didn't know a thing about them, who they could be or what they might be fighting over. But it was enough to avoid both groups. He asked Marina what she might know and she only repeated her belief that no life existed west of the facility.

"The blues look like soldiers," said Bart, keeping watch behind them as they paused in the forest. "The others, I dunno. White isn't a fighting color. And long robes ain't good for fightin' neither."

"But they got horses," Trina spoke up. "Maybe we kin get some."

"We have this green jeep," he retorted. "Better 'an horses."

Satisfied they were safe from the battle, Bart started the vehicle and they moved on.

Miles ahead they came to open ground, crossing a plateau among the mountains, as high as Bart had ever been. The roadway was nothing but dirt, pavement broken so much that it had become little more than a bare patch of ground. From the ridge, they could see far to the north, see a vast red desert. In the far distance stood isolated stone towers they at first mistook for cities.

"Just skinny mountains," Bart assessed.

The ridge widened, became more of a plateau. Along the road lots filled with rows of white wooden stakes stretched. Hundreds of them on each side. Like so many people had died they needed to clear this land for a cemetery and put them in the ground in a neat pattern by rank and file.

Bart slowed the vehicle to take a look.

"Maybe they fought some battle already."

"They ain't got none of that old virus," said Trina. "Maybe got a virus for killing each other."

The road continued on for many miles, cemeteries on both sides, until Bart stopped looking, stopped counting.

"Seem a dead place," said Trina. "Not what I want."

"Me, neither," said Bart.

"Ain't yer homestead, fer shore."

"Why do they do this?" asked Marina, shocked at the site.

"We bury dead bodies," said Bart plainly, "up top."

"Each marker is a dead body?" asked Marina.

Bart gave a nod. "I count thousands."

What was ahead? Now he worried about his decisions. He didn't want to put his family in danger. But he was only one man. He had weapons but he was only one – plus Trina. He could rely on her. She knew what to do. But they didn't want to fight anyone.

Leaving the mountain of graves and descending to a valley, they came upon a fresh battleground. Corpses lay under the hot sun, half stripped, maybe a hundred bodies. Bart noted the same two groups: blue uniforms and white robes.

He paused the vehicle and got out, no longer fearing them.

"How about these?" he said, kneeling beside a man his own size.

The uniform was clean, not bloody; a head shot took him. He began pulling off the trousers; someone had taken the boots. Then the uniform coat and white shirt; they could be washed.

Trina got the idea and went in search of a man of her size. She found one several yards away, waved back to Bart.

Marina had come out of the vehicle, leading Izzy by the hand.

"You're taking dead men's clothing?" she called.

Bart looked up at her. "I ain't wearing these coveralls forever."

She seemed in shock by his barbarism, couldn't speak. But Izzy, who didn't know better, stood by her, hugging her leg.

"There are your parents," she said, then looked down at the boy, "stealing from the dead."

Trina gathered several of the white robes some of the dead wore, rolled them up for washing later.

Pilfered clothing hanging over his arm, Bart stood, stretched.

"I won't be wearing any of those," Marina said.

"This here's a new world," he said. "You best get used to it. Ain't gonna be pretty. Or comfortable." He chuckled, happy to see how she squirmed. "Ain't what you expected, is it?"

Marina shook her head and rushed back to the vehicle with Izzy in her arms, telling him not to look.

Bart watched her, disappointed. The outer world was a different place than down inside the facility where life was ordered and safe. She had to get used to being unsafe.

He spotted movement and saw a body up against a dead horse, the soldier's arm flinching, repeatedly clicking a pistol that had no more bullets, aiming at a ghost.

"Here's one alive," Bart called over to Trina, seeing her bearing an armful of the white robes.

She came over, meeting him beside the fallen soldier.

"This one look like Nick," she said, staring down.

The man, older than Bart, had a scraggily black beard and dark eyes, squinting up at the bright sunlight. Trina stepped to block the sun and a faint smile appeared on the man's face. His hand held his guts in, uniform coat soaked in blood. The dirty trousers were not affected, Bart saw, knowing this man wouldn't make it.

The soldier spoke in a raspy voice, spitting words Bart couldn't understand. He reached for Bart with a bloody hand.

"*Ayúdame. Puedes ayudarme?*"

Bart knelt beside him. "What happened? Who are you?"

He didn't understand, continued: "*En todas partes nos hostigan, matan a cualquiera que no sea de su credo.*"

"What's he saying?" Bart asked Trina.

"Sound like them banditos way o' talkin'."

"These ain't banditos. They're soldiers. Mexi soldiers." He gazed down at the soldier. "You a Mexi soldier?"

"Mexi...? *Sí.*"

Another voice called out several bodies away. Bart regarded the man, a wounded soldier splayed on the ground, waiting for the end. Going over and checking on him, Bart saw a chest wound he knew would be fatal.

"He say 'Harass us, kill anyone not their creed'."

"Who?" asked Bart.

"*Los hijos de Mahoma. Los fantasmas del este,*" said the man and seemed to almost pass out.

Nodding, Bart turned to Trina who squatted by the soldier with the belly wound. "Got any idea what he's saying?" Then to the man: "Can't understand a word you're saying."

"Sons of Mohammed," the man got out with a painful grunt.

"Never heard of 'em," said Bart. "Not my fight anyways."

"We...fight...them...." The man moaned in pain.

Bart was sizing up the man, believing he was the same size, the trousers useable. Boots, too.

"You ain't gonna make it," he told the soldier. "That's clear as day. It awright if I claim your trousers? Your boots, too? You won't be needing them too soon now."

The soldier grimaced, sucked a breath. He stared up at Bart, his dark eyes cutting into his soul.

"*Toma lo que necesites. Estaré en el cielo.*" Then, grasping at the sleeve of Bart's coverall, spoke more: "Take it. I go to heaven."

"Well, awrighty," said Bart. He began to slip off the man's boots, then waited through a series of gasps, trying to be respectful. After the man expired, Bart pulled off the trousers, inspecting them for blood. "Nice pants. Wherever you're from, they do good work."

Trina waited for him at the jeep, white sheets in a bundle on the tailgate.

"You figure out what he sayin'?" She put her hand to her brow, shielding her eyes from the sunshine.

Bart looked at the bundle of white robes. "Says there's some folks wearing white robes – like them there you got   fighting with them.

Done 'em purdy good, look like. Maybe better not be taking white robes. Maybe get us in trouble."

"It's just linen," said Trina with a scowl. "Iz need diapers."

Marina had words to say, complaining about life on the road. It was all beyond her imagination. She never expected to come upon a battleground. What an awful place!

"The dead don't have much to say," Bart reminded her.

He and Trina returned to the field to grab rifles that looked in good condition and any bandoleers with bullets. Later he discovered the bullets wouldn't fit his rifle, but they could be useful in the Mexi rifles. He would need to train Marina to shoot.

31

A Fine Hacienda

"IT IS A HORRIBLE WORLD!" cried Marina. She kept repeating her phrase until Bart shoved a bowl of beans into her hands. He'd cooked it over the campfire. She took it, startled back to reality.

Trina watched him sit again and start spooning his own bowl.

"So there's other people," said Bart after a few mouthfuls of the beans, munching loudly. "Thought there would be, must be. But we never saw nobody. Not 'til the facility."

"It was Nick," Trina spoke. "We saw him first – the first person we seen for weeks." She held Izzy in her lap, gave him her breast, more for comfort than food. Bart would wince seeing her chew up whatever they had to eat then push it from her mouth into the boy's mouth.

"Out this far," Bart continued, keeping his voice low in the quiet of the evening, camped beside the jeep, "figured we'd be the only ones. All alone. I could hunt and you could start a little garden. And we just live – a simple life – and be happy."

"So much death!" Marina cried out again. Her bowl was empty.

"Now we know there's other folks. Not standard folks maybe we could hope to find, form a community, but we got soldiers and got fanatics, and they're fighting each other. Not the kinda neighbors we want."

"Ain't after us," Trina said.

"Seems like they don't want nobody in the way," said Bart. "We need to keep going. Need to get as far away from them as we can.

Have to find a place to hide away." He glared at Trina, feeding Izzy from her mouth again. "Not like that camp in the rocks."

Trina smacked her lips. "It was a good camp."

"I never believed there could be so much death," Marina spoke as she wiped tears from her face. "Everyone was right."

"This ain't so bad," Bart almost laughed. "Me and T been in lots worse situations. Had to shoot our way outta some."

Marina looked further shocked, shook her head in disbelief.

"Ya kin blame him fer all it," said Trina.

"I have read the records of older civilizations," Marina said more calmly. "They rise and become corrupt. They fall into ruin. Always it ends with people who have worked together killing each other like they have became strangers."

"That's how it's done," Bart said with a grin.

"Ain't gonna hide no more," Trina said. "Tired of it."

"We got enough guns now to hold off a troop if we have to," said Bart with a big grin. He admired the rifles the Mexi soldiers used but there was a limit on the bullets they collected. "If we keep going, go far enough, maybe we get to another land where neither of them are. Then we can start a homestead."

Marina sat up straight, stared at him. "I wish I could go back."

"What do you mean?" asked Bart. "Can't do that."

"This is not what I expected," she said. "I want to go back."

Trina scoffed. "Bin tellin' him that fer couple years now, but this one he never listen."

"We're going to a better place," Bart declared. "Lots better than where we been. Maybe got an ocean. You'll see."

"Him an' his damn ocean," said Trina.

+ + +

The fire crackled, burning down to embers as they huddled around it, wrapped in blankets. Beyond the circle the air was frosty. Dinner was a rabbit Bart practically roasted with a blast from the electro-gun. Trina skinned it, cut it up for the pot and it was mighty tasty. Marina remained shocked how easily they killed.

"That ain't nothing," Bart laughed and told the story of killing a *vampire* in that hotel, with Trina *tsk*ing him every sentence. "No, T. I swear it was a vampire." He explained his reasoning, listing traits as Marina sat enraptured by the story.

"Then he rides into camp like a bat outta hell screaming 'Gotta go!'" Trina spoke up, half-smiling. "Three months later and we find Nick in the desert by them fake teepees. An' he took us to yer damn facility. Then we left yer damn facility. Now we's here." She looked out through the dark wood. "But don't know where here is."

Marina was getting some of her calmness back. Smiling at their stories, she held Izzy on her shoulder, the boy drifting to sleep, then laid him on the ground, one end of a blanket turned over him.

"Poor boy," she cooed. "The day's worn him out."

Bart jumped up, the electro-gun in hand, and Trina and Marina looked in the same direction he stared.

Out of the darkness beyond the fire's light approached a ghostly figure. Maybe it was one of those fanatics in white robes, thought Bart. Hard to tell.

"Stop," Bart ordered, raising the electro-gun. He had to stare a bit harder at the figure. Was it even real? Could it be a loose cloth caught in the bushes?

The figure halted, then proceeded after a moment.

"Said halt," Bart snarled. "Come any closer I'ma gonna shoot you." But he wasn't yet certain it was a person.

Marina was whimpering, frightened again. Trina stood, got her pistol in hand and checked behind them.

"Others over here," she called.

Bart snapped his head around: more ghostly figures floating through the trees toward the campfire. A dozen of them, gray in the firelight.

"Looks like we got a situation," Bart said in a firm voice. He ordered Marina to get in the jeep, lock the doors.

"What're they?" Trina asked.

"Don't know," he answered. "But ain't no standard folks."

He let go a blast from the electro-gun at the figure before him, heard the scream – clearly a person – and saw it drop, lost in the darkness.

Behind him, Trina held up her pistol and the ghouls paused.

"Ain't standard folk." She hesitated firing her pistol, bullets too precious to waste.

Bart turned to her, stood beside her with the electro-gun raised.

"Get on now," he called to the apparitions.

Yet they hovered among the dark trees, like angels with white robes swaying in the cold night air.

"I said go on," he snarled louder.

None of them moved. So he let go a blast of the electro-gun, the blue lightning crackling, illuminating the group. To his horror, they cringed, like they were afraid of the light. They gathered around the one that was struck, that fell to the ground, and began *eating it*.

"The hell?" Bart gasped.

Trina got a stick from the campfire, returned and held it up. In the light they saw mostly naked people, some in rags that probably had been the white robes those fanatics wore. They had grisly faces, skin worn down to bone, arms and legs nothing more than sticks. And they began to howl.

"I think they're calling others," said Bart.

Trina turned to the jeep. "Gotta get outta here."

They backed from the campfire. Trina knocked on the window for Marina to let them in. The doors unlocked with a click.

Bart stood his ground as Trina climbed into the vehicle, settled at the window with her pistol ready.

"Look!" she called to Bart.

He saw more of the ghostly figures approaching from the same side of the camp as that first one he shot. Maybe a dozen more gathered. Plus the dozen on the opposite side of the jeep.

"The hell're these things?" Bart shouted, backed up to the jeep. He reached back, opened the driver's door while keeping his eyes on the collection of ghosts coming toward the vehicle.

Slipping inside, he pushed the start button for the motor, felt it turn on, its faint hum now a comforting noise that let him know they could escape.

He looked over at Trina, his partner in crime and other things, then checked in back, saw Marina huddled fearful against the seat, afraid to look outside.

"Where's Iz?" asked Bart.

The women looked around the cabin, under the seats, nothing.

Bart opened the door, jumped out and rushed to the campfire, a final glow from embers the only light in the forest. He found the boy asleep on the blanket on the ground.

He swept the boy into his arms as the creatures broke into the campsite, the ring of specters moaning words that made no sense. They might be begging for food, he imagined. But he wasn't food for them. Neither was his son.

One got close, grabbed at him. Bart slapped the arm away, saw it fall to the ground, broken off from the shoulder.

He hurried into the jeep with Izzy waking up and fussing. Motor still on, doors locked. Headlights on. Foot to the go lever and away they charged, bulling through the forest, knocking down figures in their way, avoiding tree trunks, bushes slapping the sides of the jeep, then sliding down a slope to freedom.

+   +   +

The road is long, Bart thought again and again as they traveled. He finally felt comfortable maneuvering the vehicle over open ground. He pushed it, got it up to a high speed as they rolled over hardpack dirt, nothing to either side but the far horizons. In each direction he saw mesas, buttes, stacks, and chimneys cutting into the sky: the last images of ancient lands he would remember. Can't make a good homestead out here, he knew. No wonder people left.

He barely spoke to Marina for a week and Trina remained cool to her, too, despite her repeatedly saying "I'm sorry, really I am." Yet he couldn't accept that she laid the boy on the ground and when he shouted for her to get into the jeep that she saved only herself. He tried to believe maybe she assumed Trina looked after the boy. She hadn't been thinking, had only the one thought. She never had training in danger in the facility.

"Ain't them what's called *zom-bows*?" Trina pondered.

"Zombies, you mean?" Bart offered. "That's just in old books. All made-up stories. Ain't real."

"But was they dead or was they not?"

He didn't answer, wishing to forget the whole episode.

When they had to stop for a while to let the battery charge up in the never-ending sunshine, he leaned back against the jeep, hand to his brow and gazed at the desert. He wondered if a catastrophe fell upon the land, as dry and dead as it was. Couldn't be just a lack of rain for years. Nobody lived out here. No animals, either. Or it could be a divine strike for evils long committed, he considered, hearing the dramatic voice of his uncle the priest: "Sin too much and God'll strike you down!" Had the people here sinned so much, and now they were gone?

Another week of travel, trying to go this way or that, finding a way across the rugged land whenever bridges were out or the road too broken. Spend a whole day just going a couple miles over rough terrain. A single day spent finding a way to cross a stream. Bart felt exhausted. They made camp in the wide-open plain where he could see anybody coming from a mile away.

With a few days of rest, they welcomed Marina back. Trina pressed Bart to be nice; she was carrying his baby, after all.

Sometimes Trina would come to him, bearing their wriggling boy full of curiosity, and they'd stand together as a family, with the red sunset beaming on them, the hot breeze calling them. *You sure you want to come this way?* the wind seemed to ask Bart. Can't be here, he'd answer. And Trina would grin like she could hear his thoughts, and lay her head on his big shoulder with Izzy squeezed between them, complaining it was too snug. And Bart would wrap his arms around them, hold them tight, and remind himself that they were his entire world. He'd protect them, *had to* protect them, against anything they encountered. His hand would slip down to his hip, checking that his pistol was there, ready for action.

Then Marina would speak up, breaking him from his dream.

"Lookit her," spoke Trina from within the circle of Bart's strong arms. "She shore showin' now."

Marina heard them, straightened up, grinned. Her belly indeed had a bow to it. "It is only a matter of time."

"Naw, she's just eating too many food packets," said Bart.

"Ain't none us eatin' too many food packets," Trina came back.

"We get off this desert, I'll hunt something," he said.

He stared at Marina, her hands to her back, stretching out her belly, a pose he grew to adore.

Trina broke from his arms, taking Izzy away.

"You go on lookin'," she said, eyebrows pinched. "I know ya like lookin'. Ya get it stuck in yer head. But I be around."

Bart raised his hands as if asking what she was talking about.

"It is not much to show," said Marina, puzzled by Trina.

"Still, it looks darn purdy," said Bart. "I remember when T was fat like that. Belly bumping me all the night."

Trina smiled at him with her lips tight.

Marina invited him to kneel and rub his hand over her belly, put his ear to it and listen for anything the baby might say. At a whim, she placed her hand atop his head, ran her fingers through his hair. Like his mama used to do. It felt good but after a moment, he stood, feeling strange.

"Didn't hear nothing," he said coolly.

The road was long and rough, he understood, then turned to the jeep, pretending to check on something.

The road ahead was a dirt track, bumpy in places, putting up a lot of dust, but mostly smooth and Bart could speed up, let the jeep gallop along. They let the windows down, enjoyed the rushing wind, but the dust got to be too much. They came to several crossroads but stayed true. Heading west.

They'd long ago left the road marked I-40 when they came to a fallen bridge and couldn't cross. The twin roadway and its pair of bridges had collapsed into the stream below. Bart scampered down the slope to study the stream, looking for a ford. But it ran too fast and was likely too deep to cross.

So they turned north along a small road which became a gravel path, then came to more turns on smaller roads, passing abandoned ranches like what his uncle had in Skinner Canyon. Trees thinned, became a plain then a desert. They rolled along, marveling at the stark vastness of the world around them. Marina remarked on one feature or another every minute – things she'd only seen in pictures at the facility and couldn't believe existed. Bart dared counter with stories from Skinner Canyon, what he'd learned from his mama's library.

That made Bart sullen, gripping the turning wheel tighter as his mind slipped back. Flashes of selected moments lined up for review, wanting him to assess his role in them: the robberies, the shootings, the kills. He thought he'd left all that behind, as if no one was looking for him any longer. He had a new life. Heading to a new life. And what he'd done before would be forgotten – or else forgiven, time being what it was.

They came to more mountains, started up a road that had no end and without the tablet to show him maps he could only guess they were going west. Bart called back for an update. Marina was in the second row tinkering with the tablet again, had the panel open and was poking at the machinery inside it as Trina watched her over the seatback.

"Da-ba," said Izzy, pointing at the device.

"That is correct," said Marina, not looking up from her work.

"This boy's first word is 'tablet'?" Trina laughed. "Not even 'ma' or 'pa'. That don't stand to be good."

The road wound sharply and Bart slowed suddenly. He still had to stare out the side window at the steep cliffs they passed, the river far below. No place to stop on this narrow track. He worried they'd come to an end and have to turn around and double back to find a better road.

Then the road straightened, leveled out to a bridge crossing over a wide gap – sheer walls of stone stretching down to the churning river below. The huge wall had cracks in its face large enough for water to surge through like great fountains, draining the lake above. The road continued along the top of the wall. Bart hurried them across it, fearing the wall might break.

"What's this place?" asked Trina, hanging out the side window to see everything. "Gotta be older 'an sin."

Bart looked in the rear view mirror. "Got that fixed yet? Really need to see a map."

"Hold on. Almost ready," Marina responded. "I only saw it done once before." A few minutes more digging at the circuitry. "There. I think. Now it should work without the tracker being able to detect where we are. I hope it retains information from earlier connections so it should not need to contact the facility's computer."

"Not only tinkers with babes, she can tinker with machines," said Bart, chuckling.

He heard the hum of the tablet powering up as the jeep left the road along the wall and started down a slope, becoming sharp turns again and forcing him to focus on guiding the vehicle.

"This map shows there is a large lake above this river. The name of the lake is Mead," Marina called up to Bart. "This wall is actually a dam called Hoover."

Bart turned off the winding road onto a narrower one that he thought would follow the shore of the lake. He was right: glimpses of the lake's blue sheen filled them with joy. He found a good spot to pull over for a longer look.

"Ain't an ocean," Bart said, giving a phony sigh. He pointed out to the far shore, holding Izzy up to have a look. "But it's the biggest water I ever did see."

"Now ain't that sumpin'" said Trina, hands on hips, gazing out over the lake.

"Big as a whole territory," said Bart.

Marina brought the tablet to them, the map on the screen. The part of the lake they saw was only a small section, with more to the north and east out of sight from this overlook. Bart studied the map. He saw roads leading to a city, noticed the grid of streets.

"There's a city just west of here," Bart called to Trina.

She took Izzy, telling him about the lake and naming fish that might be swimming in it. He tried repeating after her.

Bart remembered his first view of that city near the facility and grew wary. He studied the map to find a way around this new city.

"Not sure about going there," he said.

"You think it's like th' other one?" Trina asked, coming to him after handing Izzy over to Marina.

They studied the screen together, almost cheek to cheek.

"We can go around it," he said. "Only gonna be trouble if we go in it. Maybe there's more of them ghost people."

"Don't wanna find any o' them," Trina said.

Marina heard them. "I think this area may be where the other facility is located. I heard they were experimenting on something else than our facility. Something went wrong there."

"Something? Like what?" he demanded, being reminded of the incident.

"Perhaps what you saw in the forest back there... They were...." She looked down shamefully. "They might have been the scientists from that facility. They became infected, I recall from a report, and they left the facility to wonder the land."

Trina stared at her, eyes wide. "What happened to them?"

"They were testing a new vaccine. For the pandemic virus. Got it wrong. Turned them into...into what we saw that night."

"Don't want none o' them," Trina grumbled.

"Then we definitely wanna go around it," Bart responded.

Not far from the lookout they rose into the mountains again. The lesser roads remained in better condition than the I-roads, he noticed. He was happy to stay on the smaller roads even though he had no idea where they would lead. This road, however, took them up to a ridge where they could look down over the city.

Stopping for a few days here and there along the way, enough to set up a campsite and rest, and the days of steady travel, the pauses by streams or that one day Bart went hunting and got a rabbit, the week they hid in an abandoned garage at a fuel station along the road as a pesky drone flew overhead, and the mornings when Trina boiled tea on the tailgate and had it ready for him when he got out of the front seat—

Fifty-seven days and four-hundred-odd miles going further west had delivered them within sight of a burnt city. A vast spread of streets set in a loose pattern. The sign stating how much further it was to the city gave its name as La Vega. Two letters had faded and he wasn't sure what they might be.

"This is the biggest city I ever did see," Bart spoke, scanning the place from the ridge. They'd passed south of the city, driving by it without stopping, and turned north.

"Must be million people livin' down there," said Trina.

Marina took a solemn gaze. "Used to be living."

They looked closer.

As far as they could see from the ridge, looking north and south, stretched what remained of a large city. It consisted of burnt lots, crumbling streets, fallen or flattened buildings, piles of rumble, treeless, smelling awful. Smelling like death – like burnt corpses. A few buildings still managed to stand tall like monuments. Bart pointed out a pyramid that still stood. Marina thought a structure like that must be home to the fanatics they encountered at the battleground.

A vile wind introduced itself, bringing the pungent odor of death up from the valley. Welcome, welcome, the wind seemed to moan. All are welcome here in my deathly embrace.

Trina turned away, covering her nose and mouth. Marina did the same, and held a hand over Izzy's face.

"This what ya want?" Trina snarled at Bart. "This yer safe place where ya gonna make yer homestead?"

"No," he snapped. "I never expected this. S'posed to be farmland out here. Farmland and forest. Good place to raise a family."

"Well, ain't."

+ + +

Another city of the dead. Bart pondered what happened to them as he maneuvered the jeep away from the city, winding through old streets and crumbling roads that lay far from the city. After a long day of skirting debris and backtracking when a bridge was out, or where towers and electric wire poles had fallen to block their way, they eventually saw the city was behind them.

Those roads took them up into hills west of the city, through a patch of trees, and into ranchland. They rolled onto a ridge where the air was cool. It seemed like a different world there above the desert. Along the road he saw rows of small homes, homes set together sharing walls, surrounded by trees, and homes set upon wheels like a family could live in traveling. It appeared to be a fine village, a place to visit and relax. Yet Bart saw no people. Not even a scavenger or a decrepit ghost. They got to big yards and fancy houses that sat silent along the winding road, some bigger than his mama's house in Skinner Canyon.

No people came out to see who was passing by in a jeep.

"Where's ever'body?" asked Trina, staring out her window.

"Perhaps they caught the virus and died," Marina offered.

Bart looked at her. "No bodies laying about."

"They left for a safer place," Marina came back.

"Ain't no safer place," Trina joined in.

"Quiet!" Bart snapped. "Listen for noises coming from any folks. Keep your guns ready."

Down the road they went, scanning houses on either side, seeing no signs of life. It felt odd the way the afternoon was bright with the sun shining through the trees and the crisp mountain air refreshing them. And no one else wanted to enjoy this?

Bart spied a small barn ahead. Along the narrow road were pole fences marking off pastures. The drive along this road seemed like a visit to heaven: nice houses and shade trees, fresh air and flowers. Down the road they slowly rolled, cautious yet feeling as happy as back in the territory riding the range free as they please.

He reached for Trina's hand and they shared a smile.

"There!" Trina cried out.

Bart stopped the vehicle, stared across Trina out her window.

A grayish horse with a long, dark mane blithely munched on a patch of yellow grass while a reddish-brown horse with black mane pranced over to the fence as if glad to see humans again.

They got out of the jeep, waving, and the horses came up to the fence, unafraid.

Bart patted the gray horse's nose. Trina welcomed the brown one with soft words. Marina stood back, holding Izzy.

"Musta been just foals last time anybody stopped for them," said Trina, giving the road and the yard around it a good look.

"Nobody living here," said Bart.

They offered pleasantries for animals that must've been captive a long time. Bart noted the fence was high, but if they'd thought about it they could've tried jumping it. Maybe the grass was tasty. Lucky they weren't killed and eaten already. He turned to scan the area, wary once more.

"So these are horses," said Marina timidly. She carried Izzy in her arms, took him up to the fence, hesitating a moment, then stood against the rail. "Do you see them, Iz? Real horses." She regarded Bart. "They are real, aren't they?"

"As real as I've seen in a couple years." He grinned. "But that jeep is a better way to get across a bunch of land. But I wouldn't mind riding a horse a spell. Bring back some of them good ol' days we had."

"Good ol' days?" Trina chided. "We's riding hard to get away from ever'body in them days. Now we's *standard* folk."

"Get away?" asked Marina as she tried to dodge Izzy's hand. He reached for the horses as though they were only toys.

"Yep, shore did," Trina answered. "Betcha never did know. We was bank robbers in them years past. Shore was. Then we got too many scares an' gotta ride off to a damn sunset."

Marina frowned, turned to glare at Bart as if she doubted Trina.

"Like she said," Bart responded, then listed some of the towns they'd hit. He and Trina laughed at her consternation.

"I can believe that," she said coldly. "The way you stole from the dead soldiers. Like you have no morals."

"Morals?" Bart laughed.

"We got needs," Trina responded gruffly. "Dead don't."

"That was a full month ago," Bart spoke. "They're all in heaven by now, or else some other place."

Marina was ready to say more but Trina nudged him, pointing to a barn far back of the pasture.

Bart agreed to explore. He drove them onward slowly until they found a way through the fenced pasture and up a gravel road to the barn, a big red building with faded paint. It wasn't too bad for the years it must've seen with no repairs. The roof stood firm, but slats were missing, hay in disarray inside, stalls needing swept out. A dead horse, mostly decomposed, laying in a back stall needed to be dealt with.

Behind the barn stood a fair-sized house, all one level, looking in good condition other than needing new paint. Nothing obvious that might need repair. Maybe someone still lived in it.

Bart studied the house through a gap in the boards forming the barn's wall. He watched for several minutes, didn't see movement. Maybe nobody lived there now.

"Ya think it's abandon?" asked Trina.

"Might be."

Marina held her nose against the stink in the barn, held Izzy to her chest for the same reason. Then she couldn't stand it any longer and stepped outside the same way they'd entered.

The horses had followed them, stood blocking the way. Marina gasped – getting Bart's attention. He rushed out with pistol drawn but laughed at the sight. Little Miss Facility was scared of horses!

The house wasn't large. Had weathered a lot of years but had good construction. A few windows cracked, some paneling missing on the exterior. A door was off its hinges. Shingles off the roof. Some bricks askew high on the chimney. Going around to the front, the stairs to the front porch creaked as they stepped up. Bart peered in the front window.

"Hello?" he called, keeping his pistol ready.

No response. He listened for any sounds inside.

"Anybody live here?"

Still no reply. Trina urged him ahead.

He swung the screen door open, tested the wooden door, found the lock already busted.

"We ain't the first to visit," he said in a quiet voice.

Inside it was clear the main room had been lived in, seeing the way the furniture was pushed around and torn up, cushion stuffing tossed about the room – like someone wanted to deliberately make a mess. Strange writing marked the walls.

"Could be tribal marks," Trina offered.

Bart waved Marina and Izzy to come on in.

"Ain't so bad," Trina said. "Better 'an a tent in a canyon."

She shared a grin with Bart.

"Kinda like the house in my dreams," he said with a smile.

They heard a gasp from Marina, saw she'd wandered away.

"The hell?" Bart snapped, then went to her. Trina followed.

In the back bedroom they found a pair of skeletons prone on the bed, sheet and blanket covering them but for their bare skulls and boney arms. The figures faced each other, arms around each other. Except for one arm stretched out, pointing off the bed. On the floor lay a revolver which that skeleton likely had used. The sheets were blood-stained although long-dried and well-faded now.

The end of the world, thought Bart, and the couple chose to leave it before it left them. No telling how old the couple might've been. A framed picture on the nightstand showed a handsome pair, smiling together, likely grandparents.

"Ain't sleepin' in here," said Trina.

"I'll clear it out. Put down new sheets. It'll be fine," said Bart.

He'd seen a ditch out back of the barn, like a hog trough that had dried up, decided it would be a good place to start a cemetery.

"This yer homestead?" Trina prodded him.

"As good as any we maybe find," he replied. He listed the good features of the place. Mostly isolation. Nobody knew they were there. Whoever broke in earlier wouldn't likely return if they had reason to leave before. He sighed, smiling at the women. "This is it. Our new home."

"Yer pa's gone crazy," Trina called to Izzy, noticing he was gone.

Rushing back to the main room, they saw the boy toddling over the ragged oval rug there. He'd found something stuck in it.

Marina grabbed him, snatched away whatever he'd picked up to taste and gently scolded him.

"Izzy thinks it's home now," she said.

"Shore gotta lotta cleanin' to do," Trina said with a sigh.

"I'll guard you while you ladies clean it up," Bart suggested.

"You the man, ain'tcha?" asked Trina. "Got lots o' heavy liftin' to do. I'ma guard y'all."

They both turned to Marina, the fat one.

"We all gotta work," said Bart. "But keep watch."

They agreed. Clean the house. Fix what needed fixing. He found

415

tools in cabinets, cleaning products in closets. He wasn't surprised he remembered what his uncle taught him about fixing things. He felt a knack for it. Better if Uncle Frank encouraged him instead of criticizing him for every little thing he did wrong.

He saw the house had plenty of electric terminals, lots of lamps and small machines in the kitchen but, as expected, no electric coming to the terminals. No water came from the faucets in the kitchen or bathroom, either, but there was a pump in the yard behind the house that seemed to work. Better to boil the water.

At the rear of the pasture, over a knoll, a brook ran. They could take water from it. And in the front of the pasture a pond had been dug to gather rain water. The horses drank from it. He knew gathering water from these sources would be an everyday task. All part of living on a homestead.

Out back Marina found a garden long untended. She offered to clear it out, having spent required time working in the facility's hydroponic department in her youth. What had grown wild might be edible, she noted. Seeds stolen from the facility could be planted.

The woodlands opposite the fenced pasture offered a chance for hunting – as long as no hybrid beasts roamed there. They'd seen deer on their travels. Various birds and other critters, too. And, if necessary, there were two horses available.

After a few weeks, they realized they had a real homestead.

As the winter came upon them, the house held together against strong winds, sealed them inside against the cold. Bart took an axe he found in the barn and chopped wood to keep the fireplace blazing in the main room. They huddled there, ate and slept there.

Bart went out and shot a deer, one of many that pranced by the homestead, and they enjoyed a holiday feast. They had taken over the whole house by then, so Bart and Trina had the larger bedroom with Izzy sleeping in a basket they made into his bed. Marina took the smaller bedroom, decorating it from the things she found in the closets and drawers of a chest.

Bart and Trina stood on the back porch one spring morning to watch the sunrise, the pink and orange stretching over the brown valley of the city of death, and realized they were happy. Marina joined them, carrying a still-sleeping Izzy.

And it was in that house that Izzy's half-brother was born in the back bedroom, with Trina helping because she knew what to do but Bart assisted as best he could, snapping at Trina's commands, right up to the moment when the baby showed with a final big push. She cleaned off the baby and, wrapped in a towel and crying loudly, handed the bundle to Bart.

"Here that son o' yers," said Trina. "Remember, ya gonna name him 'Nick'."

"Nicholas," Marina corrected. "It is a great name."

"Nicholas Baumann," Bart mumbled, thinking it over.

He admired his baby son: peachy skin and head of reddish blond fuzz. He kissed the boy's forehead and the boy cried louder.

"You must be his father," Marina tried to laugh, laying soaked in sweat on the bed. "He knows you."

He wasn't sure what she meant, hadn't ever been mean to Izzy, and wouldn't be mean to this boy either, no matter that he had the name of a man who died back there outside the facility. Didn't look like that man anyway. No, this baby had an even split of Bart's and Marina's traits it was clear to see.

He returned the baby to Marina and she set the baby to nursing as he watched intently, struck by the precious sight.

Trina cleaned up the bed, returned to Bart's side. Together they gazed down on the newest member of their family.

"Ya done good," Trina teased him.

"I did most of it," Marina said in a weak voice. "I know now why women in the facility prefer growing a baby in the laboratory rather than inside a womb. These wombs aren't made for it. Too fragile."

"You did good, too," Bart told her, then leaned down and kissed her brow, lingered over her.

Rising up from that kiss, Bart felt confused. He saw there not a woman from the facility but his own mama. He saw her laying on a bed with tiny Bart cradled in her arms. He wasn't sure he actually remembered the moment or he only conjured the image in his mind, but he felt everything – suddenly, like getting a hot poker in the gut. This was real: this baby, this woman, proof that life existed in this terrible land. And he was part of it.

He was Maggie's son, which made Izzy her grandson. And then another grandson named Nicky. His mama adopted that Kanza girl before Bart was born, and that girl married Jeb, and had a son named Jacob. Jake was Maggie's grandson, too.

"Bart?" Trina called to him, seeing him lost in thought.

He broke out of his moment, smirking oddly at her, then smiled warmly at Marina.

"Nothing," he said, feeling embarrassed.

He considered what his mama might be thinking all this time, a few years past that last look she'd had of him that morning. She stood raising a hand in farewell, but he was too much of a man to wave back. Couldn't let the posse think he was a mama's boy, no sir. But if she could see him now: two women in his life, and two sons – two grandsons for her. He knew she'd adore them. It would be worth going back, he mused, just to see his mama's expression at seeing these grandsons.

+　+　+

Bart stood on the front porch, his son's tiny hand in his, the toddler looking up at him with a big smile.

"Izzy," he said, gazing down at the boy.

"Pa-pa," the boy muttered.

Surprised, Bart picked up his son, held him face to face. "What did you say?"

"He said 'papa'," Trina told him from across the porch. "Ain'tcha list'nin'?" She sat there cutting up the white robes for diapers.

"Sure I'm listening. Just didn't expect it."

She didn't look up from her work. "Why don'tcha go inside, see yer other son. I watch Iz."

"Awright, I will," he said gruffly.

In the small bedroom Marina sat in a chair beside the bed as she folded clothes taken off the drying line outside. She regarded him as though she was annoyed.

"Just come to see my other son," he said from the doorway.

"You can come in. You can't really see him from the doorway."

He stepped quietly into the room as though not wanting to awaken the baby. He stood over the make-shift crib that Izzy used and looked down.

Flat on his back in the crib was Nicky, pale faced with a head of reddish hair growing out. When Bart looked, the baby appeared to focus on him with bright blue eyes.

"You can pick him up if you like," said Marina. "But be careful."

"Course I'm gonna be careful," he growled.

He scooped up the bundle as he'd seen the women do and put the baby up to his shoulder, like he'd seen them do. Pat the back gently. Get the burp out. But he didn't need burping now. Instead, he let the sweet smell of baby engorge his nostrils, felt the warm chubby body, thinking back to when he was the same size and his mama held him. And when he settled his baby son into his strong cradling arms he felt power surge through him.

"So you're Nicky," he spoke in a low voice, like he was trying to keep his words secret from Marina. But she heard them.

The baby grinned at him, peach face and reddish hair not yet long enough to comb. He could see the baby had the same jawline and broad face of his father. Same as Bart's own father.

"My son." He thought what more to say. "Named after.... Heck, after that man from the facility. You never knew him. You're my son. But you carry his name. It's like you're him, reborn kinda."

He couldn't stop his thoughts from piling up, flooding him.

"Did you say something?" asked Marina.

He broke free of his thoughts. "Just thinking. Of Nick. Back at the facility. What happened to him."

"Yes, it was sad what happened," she said, folding a gown.

"It was my fault," he blurted out, emotions leaking. "I should've shot those cats sooner. It happened so fast.... I never meant to.... It was an accident."

"What?" Now she was giving attention.

"Never mind." He took a breath. "It's just strange my son has his name. But, heck, I said it was awright. Now every day I call him it's like I'm calling that other Nick."

She regarded him. "He's Nicholas Bartholovich, remember."

"Yep, guess he is." He grinned down at his son. "So you be sure to remember," he told the baby. "I'm gonna teach you everything. What all you need to know. You're gonna be a fine man someday. Big as me. Strong as me. Unless you go taking after your mama. She ain't so tall. But she purdy. You take good care of her, awright? And your brother, Izzy. Just like he's gonna take care of you."

32

THE BRETHREN

THE SUMMER BROUGHT SUNSHINE and with it the heat, rare rain storms passing by to water the garden out back of the house. Marina spent her days there, tending to every leaf. By autumn they gathered plenty of vegetables. Bart went hunting as autumn snuck upon them, got a couple deer, had venison stew and made jerky.

He spent his summer days trying to get the horses in the corral used to him, seeing him as a friend so he could ride them but they remained wary, wouldn't let him ride them after he threw a blanket over them and rope around their necks. There weren't any saddles, anyway. He gave up. Someday they would become food.

When Trina wasn't playing with the boys, she often walked the property with rifle in hand. She openly thought of her sisters, had to wonder what they'd be doing. Bart suggested they'd be robbing banks same as always. She missed that life. Bart didn't, he had to admit. This was the life he wanted: a fine *hacienda* and a family. So he stood guard throughout the days and he was the first to rise in the night if things didn't sound right.

Through the winter, they kept to the main room, huddling in front of the fireplace. Always kept a pot of water boiling for tea and an open box of whatever flowers they'd gathered drying nearby. Afternoons, when the sun shone through the windows and warmed the room, they let the boys crawl around on the oval rug. They'd play their little games, getting to know each other and becoming friends.

"He yer brother," Trina would tell one, then the other. "Ya know

421

what brother mean? It mean yer related. So ya play nice together, hear me? You two gotta take care each other."

"Buh-duh," Izzy would say, pointing at Nicky.

"Can you say 'bro-ther'?" Marina prodded him.

"Buh-duh," the boy repeated.

Marina remained tired, napped a lot, but she went out for fresh air each day. She would stand on the back porch, wrapped in a blanket, gazing down the slope to the horizon or study the garden plot while making plans. She grew sad.

"I will be all right," Marina would assure them. "It is a process. I have read about it. Step by step returning to normal."

Trina found sewing materials in the small bedroom. She found a machine for sewing, but didn't know how to work it. Had a terminal for an electric wire but no electric came to the house. Good enough using scissors to cut the white robes she'd collected, use needle and thread to stitch gowns for her and Marina. Smaller pieces of the linen she made into diapers.

"Ma taught me," said Trina to Bart's odd looks. "She made us clothes. I helped. Pa taught Trinity how to sort rocks. Find the good ones. Triss didn't do nothin'. Too young then."

Bart got a new shirt to add to the soldier coats, shirts, trousers, and boots he'd taken. He liked wearing the smart blue captain's coat with its golden epaulets and gold buttons, proud to wear it with no shirt on underneath it in hot weather.

He'd stand guard, his self-professed duty, watching the area for anyone who might come to the house. It was a tempting target, especially in the winter. Plenty of other houses to break into along the road. Anyone finding a refuge like this would be willing to kill to get shelter and maybe food. So he marched the boundaries of the property each day, unless snow fell too heavy, with rifle on his shoulder and pistol on his hip. He never saw any trouble. Maybe they were too high up, too far for anyone to venture this way. He saw deer in the woods and took down a doe. Only used one bullet, then had to run after it and when it finally gave up used a knife. Never saw any hell-cats, only a beige panther one time sneaking through the woods. He let it go sneaking on by, waved farewell.

One day Bart came into the house, cold and tired from his guard rounds, stripped off his clothes and went to the bathroom where he heard water splashing in the basin, saw steam filling the room.

Marina was having a bath, he discovered, surprising each other: she laying back in the basin, he standing there about to step into the bath. Without words, he got down on his knees beside the basin, began scooping hot water over her. She sat up, breasts against her knees. He took a cloth, scrubbed her shoulders and back, moving her long blond hair out of the way.

"You must be cold," she said, noticing his cherry-red flesh from being outdoors. "Come join me."

With a grin, he climbed into the basin and some water splashed out, made a puddle on the floor. The awkward position forced them face to face and in that moment they kissed. Then hands went to other places—

Izzy toddled into the room, giggling at the sight of two grown-ups trying to share a bath and making a mess.

"Go on back, Iz," Bart told him. "I'll play with you later."

Marina laughed, the first he'd heard from her since the birth.

"Yes, you should go away for a while, but we love you, Izzy," she called to the boy.

"Ba-ba," he said, pointing to the basin. Before either adult could do anything to stop him, he climbed into the bath with them, with a fresh spilling of water across the floor.

That alarming act forced Bart to get up and save his son from drowning, then step out to grab a towel, slipping and falling to the floor. He got up, hand rubbing his hip, and tended to the mess.

Trina rushed to the room, Nicky in her arms, stopping when she saw it was adults who caused the mess. She leaned in the doorway.

"You two gettin' in trouble again?" She smirked like a knowing mother. "Ain't got food enough for another babe."

"Sorry," Bart managed to say, looking confused.

She stared hard at him. "Ya be needin' somethin', ya come to me. Ya hearin' me?"

He got the message.

The bed started squeaking through the nights. Afternoons, too.

No matter if a toddler came to watch or if Marina brought in Nicky. When Trina said she was fine now, finally had enough of Bart, she let him go to Marina because she was a friend. More than a friend, she suggested with a wink that puzzled Bart.

"Ain't gettin' no babe, anyways," Trina moaned.

Those women, always talking when he wasn't around!

"Y'ain't that dumb, is ya?" Trina teased him. "Ain't no big plan. I knowed ya got a babe inside that woman. If we gonna get out, ain't gonna leave that babe there. That be crazy."

"You mean you planned for her to come with us?" asked Bart. He lay back on the bed after they'd spent time together, listening to the boys playing in the main room with Marina. "I thought maybe you might've, but I couldn't be sure."

"Ain't no big *con-spir-a-cy*." She laughed and he felt bad.

"Well, I'm glad she came along. Just never figured how she coulda known. How she put herself in the jeep with nobody seeing."

"Ain't never told her what to do. Never said go hide in the jeep. Didn't even know where was a jeep in the whole facility, not 'til you took me to it."

"Then why'd you do it?" He was serious now, feeling Trina had tricked him.

She looked at him straight. "Cuz she got yer son in her."

"And you cared about that?"

"Listen, Bart." She started to take his face in her hands, didn't. "You an' me, we know what they's doin' in there. I got same deal as you. Just ain't got no babe fer it. Both us gotta do things we didn't wanna. Maybe you wanna...with her. I get it. She got the kinda body a man crave, all curvy, lots to grab hold on. I see ya, way ya lookin' at her. And maybe she got some rights to ya now."

"I'm sorry, Trina," he said, feeling his eyes becoming wet. But he had to stop that. "I'll be more careful. I won't do anything you don't want me to do."

"Ain't 'bout that," she said with a smirk. Her finger wiped a tear on his cheek. "Ya wanna be kissin' her, an' anythin' more ya wanna do, ya may as well take yer son an' go on yer own way. Ain't dealin' with none o' that."

"No, it's not like that. She was telling me about the baby, and I got carried away. Got excited. I felt something. Love, I guess it was. So I kissed her. I mean, she's part of our family."

"Yeah, maybe. She's part of yer family, not mine. I got no tie to her 'cept you. Maybe it's good. My man's son done come outta her so I got connection with him, reckon. But her.... Ya wanna keep with her then ya gotta decide who ya wanna be with. If ya wanna be with me then only one rule an' that's ya be with me, only me, no matter what ya gonna feel fer her."

"You're my wife – the woman I want as my wife on account of all what we done together, past and present. I'm gonna show you all my love. But I gotta show her love. She's mother of my son, too."

Trina gave him a nod and he thought the matter was settled.

"Ya hearin' me? What I sayin'?"

"Yes, I did. You are my woman. She is...another woman. But we gotta treat her right if we're gonna survive here. We gotta be one family. You understand that, don't you?"

She got up from the bed, reached for the white linen gown she'd stitched together in her size. A heavy green robe left hanging in the closet she pulled on next.

"Ya better get yer clothes on," she told him sternly. "Play time is done now."

Marina had heard most of the argument and met his eyes when he entered the main room, wearing old clothes the former owner had put away in a chest's drawers. They were a small on Bart. He stared at Marina, then took a seat on the chair he repaired.

Trina came in and sat on the floor before the fireplace, adjusting Izzy's diaper, with Nicky rolling happily on the floor.

The clock on the mantelpiece continued to tick.

+ + +

Bart would take the jeep, when it was charged up under a steady sun, and drive it down the gravel road to the very end of the ridge. Any further would send him tumbling off a sharp incline. Breaks in the trees let him gaze out over the plain. He thought he could see the distant remains of La Vega. He wondered if ghosts roamed its streets, howling for justice. He worried those ghosts might detect him, a living being, and come for him and his family.

One night he got up, padded to the kitchen for a drink of water from the pitcher and stopped suddenly, seeing a ghostly figure in his way. He couldn't identify the figure: maybe it was someone from this house wanting to talk. Maybe someone from his past, someone he'd killed. Maybe his mama had died and was coming to say good-bye. It shook him for a while and he never left the bedroom at night again unless he heard some noises.

Then he would drive the jeep back the other direction, past the house, and up into higher areas the way those roads went just to see what was there. More houses, abandoned, worse condition than the one where they lived. He counted themselves lucky; the old couple had taken care of their place. Finding a few things he could use in some of the houses and barns, he considered who had lived in them. Rich people lived up here, poor families down below. Yet rich people who could afford fine houses up here where the air was cool and fresh, above the harsh desert, didn't last much longer than the poor people below.

One of those times when he stared out across the desert below, he thought about the facility and their breeding project. The world needed people. They thought they were the only people left. So a program had to be established, and he participated in it. His sons would replace him and Trina in the greater scheme. But what about Marina? No child to replace her. And like the two female horses the facility couldn't mate, the two male horses left in the yard couldn't produce a new horse either. Two sons couldn't either. Had to have a daughter. Had to try again. But that would take a miracle. Then everything would get complicated, but first things first. It would be a start to saving the world.

They made a calendar, drew it on the wall in the main room with colored markers they found in the desk. They figured which day it must be, called it Friday. And on Friday nights, Trina would send him to the side bedroom with Marina. In the mornings, Trina would send in Izzy. The boy would bound into the room, climb onto the bed and jump on his pa until he got up.

"Pa! Get up! Pa! Get up!" the boy would cry, half-laughing.

"Ya get yer foolin' done awright?" Trina would ask him when he came out of that room, and he'd grin at her.

Other nights he slept next to Trina whether or not she felt in a mood for having him rolling atop her and doing their business.

It was one of those kind of mornings that Bart awoke suddenly at Trina's call: "Bart! Guns!"

He stumbled naked out of Marina's bed, grabbing the first thing he could which was Marina's white linen gown. He wrapped it around his waist, tied the sleeves like a belt, and took the rifle to the front porch where he found Trina pointing at a stranger coming onto the property. She had a pistol in her hand.

She'd gone out on the front porch to gaze at the trees budding in the yard, the sun warming the ridge, and saw the man standing at the edge of the property, out by the road. Marina grabbed the boys and one of the old Mexi rifles Bart taught her to shoot, took them to the back bedroom.

"Hold it right there," Bart called out, the electro-gun in his hand, charged up. The white gown wrapped around his hips was slipping loose as he stood barefoot on the porch.

"Ah," the man spoke. "*Habla inglés*. You speak English."

"Course I do," Bart snapped. "This here's the Americus."

The man appeared quite old with a ruddy face, snow-white hair, balding in front but long in the back and upon his shoulders, with a long, white beard hanging down from his face. He wore a white robe similar to Bart's 'skirt' and stood barefoot on the stone path to the house. He held onto a walking stick as tall as his shoulder, leaning against it as he waited.

"Are you of the Brethren?" he called up the stone walk.

Bart thought the man sounded strange, like one of the scientists in the facility, a certain rare air about him like he was smarter than everyone else.

"Ain't none of that," Bart answered curtly.

"I couldn't be sure," said the man. "Most who wear the white are speakers of Spanish."

"Wear the white?" asked Bart, then realized the connection and gestured at his 'skirt'. "This ain't my normal clothes. Just grabbed a woman's gown, being in a rush."

"Ah," said the man and he chuckled. "I beg your pardon."

Bart kept his eyes on the man, the first person to visit them at this house in the year and a half they'd lived there.

"He do anything?"

"Just standin' there, is all." She'd moved to the end of the porch as Bart arrived, her bank robbing instincts kicking in, clearing the shooting lane for him and setting up a crossfire position.

The man took a step forward, leaned on his walking stick.

"State your business," said Bart.

"I have no business."

"Then why're you here?"

"I am a traveler. I am weary and hungry. This is the only house on this ridge with people living in it. I wondered if—"

"Ain't got nothing to spare," Bart said.

"I do not ask for much."

Trina spoke to Bart: "Ask who's he, where's he from."

"Who are you? Where you from?" Bart called out.

The man bowed his head a moment. He gestured at the house.

"You have a fine *hacienda*. Where I come from we have no idea about owning property. Or owning people." He took a step forward. "Owning anything – not even a walking stick or a poor cloth wrap. It is anathema to our beliefs."

"Yeah, I get you're a poor fool out on his luck," Bart said. He was about to say more, realized in this depopulated world another person was actually a rare thing.

"Not quite a fool. And never without luck."

Bart spoke in a low voice to Trina: "Go get a food packet."

"Y'all right here?" she checked. He gave her a nod and she went inside the house, returned with a brown packet. "Shore 'bout this?"

He'd been saving the last five packets for an emergency such as if they had to run, but he suddenly felt kind.

Trina tossed the packet out to the man. It fell at his feet.

"There. Take it and go. It's all we can spare," Bart called.

"I thank you." He bent over to retrieve the packet, looking at it like he didn't believe it actually contained food. He studied the outer wrapper, traced the label's words. He stood up, packet in his hand. "This is from the facility? Which facility?"

"You know about that?" Now Bart was curious. Maybe this old man had escaped from a facility like he and the women had.

"I know of it." The man seemed to get emotional. "I met a man and woman from one of them. A year ago. They were quite mad."

"He bluffin'," said Trina.

Bart watched the man. "Got any weapons on you?"

The man shook his head. "A stick and this gown is all I own. I don't actually own them, only borrow them from the Brethren."

Bart shook his head. "Who's this Brethren fellow?"

"Watch him," cautioned Trina, resuming her firing position.

"I am not a violent being," the man called to them. "I am only on a trek. I seek the Enlightened One. One of three. I wish to meet one of them before I die, and that day is coming closer with every step I dare to take."

Bart waved him to sit. "Eat your meal. We'll get you water."

Marina had come to the front door, peeping out at the scene. "Is he a madman? We were told about them up top. The poisons change them into monsters."

"Think he's normal mad," said Bart, keeping eyes fixed on the man. "Not a poison-turned-him-mad kinda fellow."

"Be careful," said Marina.

He felt her breath on the back of his neck, sensed her hands on his hips and wanted to turn to her.

"Go on back inside," he said. "Keep watch out the back."

"I have no notes to pay for your kindness," the man called out.

"It ain't kindness if you gotta pay for it. Eat now."

He called into the house for Marina to bring a cup of water.

"Notes mean nothing," Bart said. "Even getting some for the work you do don't mean anything nowdays. No shops for buying things. We're on our own out here. Just a family of survivors of whatever evil they done back east. We have to hunt and try to grow some food. And when bullets run out there ain't no more to buy."

He was glad he had the electro-gun which could be charged and recharged. Until the battery packs got old.

"Send 'im away," Trina said, "else I'ma shoot 'im."

"You ain't shooting nobody," Bart snarled.

He dared set the electro-gun leaning against the porch rail and hitched up the white gown tighter on his hips as Trina snuck a look.

"Seems harmless," she accepted. "But could carry sickness."

"So we'll stay back," Bart responded.

"Better just shoot 'im. He's ready fer death anyways, he says."

"Then somebody, likely it's me, gonna hafta dig a grave for him. I prefer he walk off and die some other place."

"Yer call," she said.

Bart cleared his throat. "Tell me about this Brethren fellow you said before. Who is he?"

The man smiled like he'd been asked the winning question.

"The Brethren is not one man. It is all of us who believe. Believe what? you might wonder. There is much to tell if you wish to learn and be amazed. You may well choose to join us."

"Naw, got my life here already," said Bart.

"The Brethren is like a whole nation, but a spiritual nation. We share the same ideals. We treat each other as brothers. You may see us wearing the white robes of purity. As do I. Yet I am not pure. Rather, I seek purity as my sacred goal. My destination. One day, and I hope it is before my natural death, I will find that ultimate purity, the purity that allows me to enter the gate of Heaven."

"Now he talkin' fable," Trina said with a grunt.

The man continued telling his story.

"Yeah, we saw some fighting last year," Bart spoke. "Was one of them groups in white robes like yours. Others were wearing blue uniforms like they were soldiers."

"The Mexi army. We know them well – although I have not been a fighter. I became a Brethren after I passed fighting age. They did not want me. But still I follow them."

"I didn't think this was Mexi territory here," said Bart. "Should be part of the Americus. Prolly nobody's territory by now."

"The kingdom has claimed large areas of this land, including the ridge where you now live. I am surprised you have not been overrun."

Bart perked up. "They got a king?"

"Yes, His Majesty José Martinez *y* Hidalgo, who, sadly, is not a believer. So he sends his army after us where we congregate."

"The Mexi army is your enemy?"

"All who do not believe as we do we consider our enemies. Yet we prefer to convince others to join us rather than fight them. That is our way."

Bart picked up the electro-gun, pretended to examine it. "So how about if we don't believe none of that?"

The man smiled warmly. "You are innocents, because you were kind to a stranger. I would beg the Brethren to excuse you."

"Excuse us? That sounds mighty fair." Bart was smiling like he only meant it as a joke.

"He just a crazy fella," Trina muttered.

"He's a church man," Bart corrected. thinking of the times his mama got him dressed in his little suit and tie, same as when she took him to the concert hall. The concert hall was her church. Later she took him to the church in Skinner Canyon.

"Don't listen to him," Trina cautioned.

"It take you a long time get this far," said Bart with a chuckle. "Take you plenty more to get where you're going."

"He one o' them churchmen. Don't let 'im preach at ya."

The man slowly and with effort lowered himself into a cross-leg sitting position, loudly expelling his breath.

"This feels much better than putting all my weight – my body's weight and the weight of my sins – upon these old legs. I thank you for allowing me to sit in your yard. I pray I do not disturb any of the creatures of the grass or soil."

"I'm sure none of them care," Bart said.

"He gonna start up preachin'" Trina grumbled.

"No, ma'am, I do not preach," said the man as he picked up the food packet. "I am not worthy of speaking for the Brethren."

Marina returned with a cup of water. Bart gestured to take the cup to him.

"Is it safe? Will you guard me?" she asked Bart.

"He ain't gonna do nothing."

She stepped carefully down the steps, slowly down the walk, and halted a few steps in front of the man. Bart could see her wrinkling her nose. She set down the cup on the stone walk and hurried back to the porch.

"We should not use that cup again," said Marina, making a face.

"Ya better stay with them boys," said Trina, and Marina slipped inside. Then to the man sitting on the walkway: "Ya came fer some food. Ya got it. Now ya kin be on yer way."

"Let him eat in peace," Bart spoke to her.

"What about my peace? Ain't got no peace lessin' he be gone."

"I shall depart soon, I assure you," the man spoke. "The journey is long and I dare not pause any more than health requires."

Bart was interested, however, gestured for the man to approach the porch. He came up the walk to the steps, where Bart raised his hand to halt. He detected the odor of a long-journeying soul in need of washing. Good thing the breeze blew the other direction.

"I heard nuff," said Trina, starting for the door. "Just come out to take a look at them there trees. They buddin'. Gonna get some pears soon. An' them bushes over there gonna get some raz'berries. But y'all wouldn't care nothin' 'bout 'em."

She stepped inside with a heavy foot, let the door slam shut.

Bart grinned after her, shared his amusement.

"So what's this brethren thing you're talking about? Is it like the folks in the facility?"

"Oh, no. Not at all." The man tore open the packet, looked inside. "I can tell you they did not begin in an underground city. It is a story full of amazing events. Three brothers came from this very land where we repose today. They departed a life of wealth and pleasure where they were safe from the plague that consumed everyone north and east of here. These brothers traveled far to the east, further east. Over an ocean, in fact—"

"Another ocean!" Bart practically shrieked. "I'm just trying to get a look at one of them oceans. There's an ocean west of here."

"Oceans surround this land," the man said, raising his hand like he was pointing to them. "All lands. The Brothers crossed the ocean.

And found enlightenment. They returned here to share all they learned. It is a simple story. Yet what they learned astounded many. The people wished to know more. The Brothers told all, then began to say much more which they believed came direct from The Most High, the Most Gracious, the Most Merciful. People knew then that the brothers were messengers of The Most High and gave them great reverence."

"Who were these brothers?" asked Bart.

"Not *were*, for they live among us in this present age. I speak of the Brothers Perez, May Peace Be Upon Their Names."

"Brothers Perez? Never heard of them."

"Please be respectful. May Peace Be Upon Their Names."

Bart gave a nod. "Sure."

The man smiled cheerfully. "Juan. Luis. Manuel. The Brothers Perez. They have brought to us the wisdom from the east."

"Well now, I grew up in the capital – it's over in the east – and they had a lot of wisdom there. Got some big buildings packed full of all the wisdom anybody ever want. You couldn't read it all in your whole lifetime."

As Bart talked about the capital, the man took a slow bite of the pasty substance squeezed from the pouch, then made a face like he thought it was awful but swallowed it anyway.

"So what do you call yourself?" asked Bart.

The man almost choked as he swallowed the paste, cleared his throat, and barely got out a word: "Jesús."

"*Hay-soos*?" Bart pinched his lips. "Awright now, *Hay-soos*."

The man coughed. "I am known now by the name the Brethren gave to me: Idris. It means 'teacher'. I was known as Jesús Alvarez before I joined the Brethren. You see, I was a teacher of the Old School. A master of language and literature, keeper of the written history, you may say. Until I met them. Until I heard them speak and I became convinced to follow them."

"So you got took, huh?" Bart was grinning like he expected Jesús to know he was teasing. But as Idris, his Brethren name, the man no doubt had less humor in him.

"The Brothers Perez brought enlightenment to our destitute and unholy land. They told of what awaited each person after death. And that hint of glory convinced an evil population to repent and live as seekers of purity."

"Seekers of purity, hmm? Like ain't got no sexual relations?"

"It is allowed between a man and his lawful wife."

"Sure do got lots of rules," said Bart. He glanced back into the house, checking for ears. "Here it's just whatever I say. The women do the work – cooking and cleaning, minding the kids, and some good bedding, naturally – and I sit back and watch them. 'Course I go hunting, bring us food. And they tend the garden."

"As a family must," said Jesús.

The breeze shifted and Bart caught more of the man's earthy fragrance. He pinched his nose.

"Maybe you wanna get refreshed. There's a pond out in the field over there. You can help yourself to a good bath. Or I can fetch some water from the well and do it proper. You can go in that barn there. I'll bring you some water and soap."

Jesús seemed surprised. "I certainly do not wish to offend. Your offer is gracious, indeed. However, I have sworn not to bathe until I reach my destination."

"And where's that?"

"Heaven."

"Don't think people gonna last that long." Bart chuckled. "You gotta give the people a chance."

Bart urged him to wash and finally he relented.

He brought a bucket of water from the well and hung it up in the barn on a hook in an overhead beam. The man could pull it down over himself, let the water fall, then rub the soap over his body, letting down more water to rinse off. Bart wouldn't use that cake of soap after the man used it, and sent it straight to the waste heap back of the barn.

Jesús seemed grateful although he continued to complain about breaking his rule. Bart brought him a fresh white robe they'd taken off the battleground, one Bart had worn a few times before but had been washed before he gave it to the man and gladly burned his old, stinky robe.

"Just tell folks you been blessed," said Bart, helping the wobbly man pull on a new robe, noting marks of abuse on his body. Likely someone had taken a cane to his back and bottom.

"I thank you wholly and completely," said Jesús. "You are indeed a servant of The Most High, May Peace Be Upon His Name."

"Well, do what I can, given the circumstances and all. But I ain't nobody's servant."

The man kept looking at the jeep which Bart parked in the barn, keeping it out of sight as much as possible, but he never said a word, never asked questions about it. In the barn, the panels couldn't recharge but he made sure to take it out on the ridge for a few hours every week when the sun was shining. Bart knew it was important to keep the jeep charged up in case they had to flee.

They returned to the front porch, went on talking. Bart had a lot of questions; half of them just to push the old man, testing him for entertainment, something different than those women, and half because he really wanted to know about things.

Trina got tired of waiting for him to send the old man away. She came out to check on them after the man washed, made sure Bart kept the electro-gun close, then retreated inside. She returned with his favorite blue coat from the battleground, had Bart put it on, to the chagrin of Jesús.

"Go on," said Bart.

33

CALIPH ORNA

THE MAN CALLED JESÚS stayed with them for several months. He slept in the barn. Trina remained wary of him, always carried her pistol. He apologized whenever he encountered her. He shared what food was offered, as meager as it was: a stew of deer fat and grains Trina gathered from the woods. To Bart it was like he was back in school: getting himself up and ready for another lesson from the teacher, sitting for hours as tales were told.

Like the story of how Jesús was born in a town called Altadena over on the coast, how the town burned down, was always burning down. In fact, all the towns along the coast had burned. The desert winds would blow down the mountains and there would be no rain. He lost members of his large family with every fire that came. Yet they always rebuilt in nearly the same place, often using scraps of the burnt house, and got poorer and poorer.

Otherwise, in his childhood Jesús and his brothers – they called him Jesse in those days – would race down to the shore and splash in the surf. They'd take long boards out into the ocean to ride on waves that rolled in to the beach.

"You can do that?" Bart questioned, excited at the images Jesús presented of life beside an ocean.

"Yes," Jesús replied, "but that wasn't hardly enough to make it a good place to live. Life is not solely about what pleasures you find."

"It still sounds like a place I wanna live," said Bart. He glanced back into the house, windows open to the warm breeze. "Me and my family. Yeah, we could find a house, something as good as this one, and live there care-free, and life would be great."

"I don't know how great it would be. You could have to rebuild your house every year. And there would be others wishing to live in your house. Kick you out. There would be trouble. Violence. Death."

"I seen all that before," Bart mugged.

"It is much worse than what you may have seen. I will not list all the ways I saw people die. It is not a pleasant story."

"But you said you heard some brothers talking and that got you to start your walking...."

"Yes, I heard the Brothers speak. I learned of another way to live and I chose it." He described all the work he did there in the town of Altadena, and other towns nearby: Holy Wood, Burn-Banks, Griffith Park, Angel City, Pasadena, and others along the coast that fronted the Mexi border. He helped build houses. He set up schools where schools had burnt down, taught kids. But still he had no direction. He wandered.

Then the fighting began. When the Mexi army rode north to try and claim the land, he and others fought back, became the enemy. He fought the best he could but got captured, held in a prison where they tortured him and others. Bart had seen the marks on his body, couldn't imagine what that pain felt like. When Jesús was let out of the prison he'd found his direction. Heard of the Brothers Perez there and wanted to learn more.

"Now I have been walking for seven years," said Jesús, "and not always in a straight line. The road winds, takes you where it wants you to go, not where you think it ought to take you. And you go. You see all the road wants you to see. You make sense of things. Things begin to make sense to you. You understand. You continue walking that road because it is the only road available. It is your road. Your personal road."

"Ah, I get it," said Bart, adding a chuckle. "You talking...what're them called? Metaphors? Like the meaning of the story. Lessons. I like them kind of stories." He told about his mama and how she got him to read books then quizzed him.

"Yes, the road is the road. No matter where you go, there is the road to lead you on your journey. You only need to stay on it. Never go off the road or you will become lost and could possibly never be able to return to your road."

"I get it." Bart sat in contemplation. "I'm on my road right now. I got it in my head to go west, gotta see a ocean. I got that idea from some books I looked in, saw pictures of a ocean, had to go see it for myself. Then we got in some trouble."

"You left the road," said Jesús with a raised white eyebrow.

"Sure did, dang it."

"You must find that road again. And when you do, stay on it, for it will lead you to your destiny."

"Destiny, huh?" He thought more, resting his chin on his hand, arm bent from the elbow, looking like a mirror image of Jesús, this wizened wiseman, follower of some brothers that lived somewhere. "Tell me more about this Orna place you're from. Maybe I wanna see it for myself anyways."

"Oh, you would not wish to see it. It is by now a horrible place. A place of death. Nothing lives there now."

"Sure, it gots fires but people rebuild, don't they?"

"If enough fires come then nothing can be rebuilt. There will be no people to rebuild anything. Those who survive will flee."

"The ocean was my destination – what you call destiny."

"Why would you go there? To see the ocean? Are you a fish?"

"Ain't no fish—"

Marina stood in the doorway, Izzy squirming in her arms.

"Trina says it is your turn to take care of him. We have work to do. Here." She sat the boy's feet down on the porch. He was already wound up, ready to play.

Izzy flopped into Bart's lap, made him groan, started wiggling.

"Easy now, boy. We are having us a history lesson."

Jesús smiled at Izzy. "He is a good looking boy. Brown like me. He clearly takes after his mother. And yet he is also you, Bart. He will grow into a fine man. I am sure of it. All you need to do is show him the road, make certain he follows it faithfully."

"Well, that might be a bit tough to do—" Izzy squirmed in Bart's arms. "Hold on now, Iz! Seeing how he's my boy and I got so far off

439

my own road."

"There is time for you. You are yet a young man. There is much time remaining for you to find the road you lost and return to it. Then you continue walking it. Walking to the end."

"And what if my road leads me to that ocean?"

Jesús remained fixated on Izzy, the two of them playing a kind of smiling/frowning game, imitating expressions.

"How do I know that's not my road?" asked Bart.

The wiseman broke from the game. "You do not want to go there. Orna is a place of destruction, of decadence, of death."

"But you said it was a caliphate," Bart countered, drawing from earlier lessons. "That's a safe place, ain't it?"

"A caliphate is ruled by a Caliph. Laws are made, enforced, and all must submit to them. It is the reason that land is called Caliph Orna. It is a place of laws." He waved his arm to the side. "Not like here. Not like in this vast territory."

"So it's just another *state*, like they got back east," said Bart.

"A caliphate," said Jesús, "in the Arabic language *khilāfah*, is the office of a ranking member of the Brethren. It is a religious seat, not a political office. There is no choosing by the people. One must be of the sacred line to be appointed Caliph. That is different from the states of which you speak."

"But they still gonna let people visit. Maybe live there?"

"You will need to join them, become one of the Brethren, or else they will likely kill you. Kill your whole family. Or, perhaps worse, take you as slaves. The women sent to a harem. They will become slaves of high-ranking men. Your sons will be raised to fight for the Brethren. They will be trained hard. I have heard that a holy war is coming. It is all they preach: the need to conquer all lands, and make everyone subject to the Brethren, or else die."

"Does seem right harsh," said Bart. "No, wouldn't want that."

"Thus, I urge you not to go there. I *beg* you to not go there. You are a good man, with a good family. That direction is not your road. I wish you a pleasant and joyful life. You will not find that life if you take the road to Caliph Orna."

+ + +

Bart lay with Trina at night, holding each other in the dark. He'd tried telling her what the wiseman said, but Trina wasn't accepting it. He switched to just caressing her, saying the words he knew she liked to hear.

"If I'm believing him, there ain't no reason to go on there," he whispered into her ear.

"Awright here," she whispered back. "Kinda lonesome but we's livin' just fine. Garden's coming in."

They heard steps in the hallway. Marina was making her way to the bathroom. They listened as she bent over the bucket and spit up, gaging and coughing, then swishing water from the jug and spitting it out.

"And yer gal's coming in, too," Trina said.

"Didn't mean to do that," said Bart.

"It gonna happen, ya play 'round like ya done."

"Maybe we gonna get a girl this time."

"Maybe." She put her hand to his cheek. "Reckon just too old for baby making. Reason we ain't got nothin'."

"You ain't old."

That wasn't the topic he wanted to discuss.

"Jesús says we might be forced to join them brothers and their way of living if we go to Caliph Orna. Or worse."

"Ain't wantin' nothin' worse." She nudged his shoulder. "Ya be talkin' too long with that fella. He remind ya o' yer pa?"

Bart grunted. "I never knew my dad. He died before I was born. I told you." He pressed on: "He's telling about the coast, over by the ocean. Orna's the name. It's a Caliphate, like I said." He was happy to explain the meaning, sensed Trina shaking her head. "So anyways...I'm purdy much agreed with him it ain't no place for us. But I'm sure gonna miss seeing an ocean."

"Yer damn ocean!" She patted his belly. "Ya know? Sometimes I wanna sit under that pear tree out front an' look out an' see all what we got. Wonder about things. I feel things never feel before. Gotta wonder how I fit here, or anywhere."

"Yeah," he said. "You done got off your road. Me, too."

"Miss my sisters a whole lot. Really wanna go back with them. Ya hearin' me?"

He let out a long sigh. "Yeah. Me, too. I sit down and think my thoughts – all the stuff the old man said – as the world goes on, not giving a flying flag about us. I mean, is this it for us? All we meant to do? We found us a homestead and move in. Now we just grow food and play in bed and get more kids, and that's all what there is?" He chuckled but it turned painful. "I kinda miss robbing banks. Got a thrill to it, cain't deny."

"Yep, so do I." Her cheek brushed his, felt a rough beard. About time for her to shave it. "Y'ever think 'bout how the world go by? Like how the sun come up an' it go down an' come up again next day? What make it do that? Is the Great Spirit pushin' it like that?"

"Well, I read some books my mama gave me, full of science and stuff like that. It's real complicated."

"Science stuff? Like how the sun come up an' go down?"

"Kinda. About how everything works. And why. Marina knows about that stuff. She's real smart."

"Knows stuff, huh? Yeah. Like how a little foolin' 'round make a whole baby?"

He held her tight, understanding. "S'pose."

"Don't got no disagreeable feelin's fer her. She's like a sister. But diff'rent. Smarter 'an Trinity. Whole lot smarter 'an Triss. I know ya like her. Ya like foolin' 'round with her. I kin see it: them curves of hers draw a man in."

"She's good to have around. Helps out. And she's a doctor for kids, remember."

"If we ain't gonna go no place by no ocean, then what'll we do? Stay here? Just live? And she gonna keep having babies?"

"S'pose." He let out a long breath. "S'pose it's my road. Where I gotta keep going. It's our road, too. You and me gotta stay on the same road."

+   +   +

Orna had once been a paradise, the old man said with sadness in his voice. So much of a paradise that people came from other countries to live there. It became full and the people began fighting among themselves. Then the fires came. The storms from the ocean. Then a plague came from the east, from over the mountains, as if some people brought it. Even without knowing it they brought it within them and many people caught it, became ill, and died. Even more died from the medicine provided. Much hatred in those days, suspicions of everyone, and survival instinct.

"That recalls what I read," said Marina, "in the library at the facility. I couldn't determine if it was true. Limited resources. Only resources which supported their preferred history were available. That is what I learned. Education was strict. The Great Pandemic – what we call a plague – at first it was a small thing which scientists developed into a major contagion. Deliberate enhancement, reports said. Making the virus more deadly, possibly to use against an enemy. However, it seemed the enemy was us, our own citizens, a kind of population reduction plan. I've heard some scientists in the facility talk about that plan, agreeing there were too many people in the world for the resources we had."

"It is what it is," Jesús spoke, with a gesture from his hand, one of the fingers missing. "What is important today is what we will do tomorrow. That is all. Yesterday is gone."

Bart sat back on the porch listening. He had heard stories from his mama but hesitated sharing them. She spoke of her father and his mother, what they endured in those awful decades hiding from the infected, from law officers, from other people. Encounters with marauders and militia was enough to ruin the family. He regretted they had to go through it. He could imagine his great-grandmother being born in a hole in the ground, a hiding place in the middle of a forest, and compared it to the clean room in the facility.

"This one will likely be a female," Marina announced, bringing Bart out of his thoughts. She rubbed her hand over her belly.

"It is said that daughters are good to have," spoke Jesús.

He admired Marina, although she let herself look less pretty by then. He told Bart she reminded him of a girl he knew in Altadena.

Working together in the garden, the old man showed her how to grow plants from seeds taken from the facility, the special hybrids for harsh climates, and they came up on schedule: tomatoes, lettuce, peas, peppers, onions, and potatoes. There lay a trio of melons, too, stretching on a vine across the ground.

"We lived in a place called Skinner Canyon, me and my mama," said Bart, though he'd told some of it before. He pointed in Trina's direction. "I met up with her and her sisters after going out on a posse. But I never did return."

"That is sad," said Jesús, putting his hands together as if blessing him. "That must be the source of your pain."

"My pain?" Bart screwed his face up. "Ain't nothing to it. I met Trina and her sisters and that was my new life. Ain't looked back."

"Haven't you?"

"Then they arrived at the facility," spoke Marina, joining in the storytelling. "We found they had immunity. Our scientists wished to learn more about their unique genes."

"That ain't nothing nobody needs to know about," Bart said.

"It is how I met them," said Marina.

"You do have a pain," said Jesús. "Deep inside you."

Bart was used to stopping and thinking through something that had been said, as if searching for the truth of an idea, weighing it.

"Your road is the path which leads you to the answers you seek," said Jesús.

"Answers to what?"

"To the source of your pain."

Bart's face reddened. "Ain't got no pain, I said."

"I believe if you think on it you will see it is true. The pain is deep inside. It continues to grow. It will continue to grow until it attempts to break out. Then you will become a monster. You will act with violence. Because you cannot stop yourself."

"Well, we're doing awright. We come out this way looking for a good homestead. And we found one. Right here. And we got us to living here like a standard family. That was always our goal: to be a standard family so people respect us."

"An' forget past deeds," Trina called out through the open door to the main room. Bart looked back at her.

"Things ain't what they seem though." Bart shook his head. "We did things we ain't exactly proud of."

"They used to be bank robbers," said Marina and Bart gave her a nasty look. "She told me."

"Well, it's true," Bart said with a nod. "We done things that ain't proper. Tried to go straight. Couldn't. We got caught one too many times and we fled out this way. That's the story. We ain't no more bank robbers. We are standard folks now."

Jesús held his lips tight throughout, waiting for Bart to finish.

"You wish to be settlers, I think. And you have done well here. I see a wonderful opportunity for you. And yet, I do not believe it was luck that brought you to this well-standing house with a barn and two horses. It must be more, a higher power, that led you to this spot on all the earth. As I was led here and met you."

"Well, we did use one of those G-P-S things for some maps. That showed this road up to this ridge. Then we seen this house. We seen the horses first. T saw them. We rode horses west from that territory but lost them at the facility. They made them into food."

"An' weren't no good," Trina called out the door.

"They didn't tell us 'til after," Bart added.

Jesús waved his hand to silence them.

"I believe you were led here by The Most High, May Peace Be Upon His Name. This is the garden you have been assigned. You must tend it, grow what you can, and harvest the full load. Year after year. Only here can you find peace." He stared at Bart. "And yet, can you truly find peace in another family's home?"

"What're you saying?" asked Bart.

"I believe you must return to your real home. Only there—"

"Real home?"

"—can you find peace. Only there will you be able to live as the standard family you wish to be. Only by returning to your home can you right the wrongs you left. Only then can you be at peace."

"But we done shot and killed folks." Bart wiped his eyes. "Didn't mean to. Just felt mean. Ornery. Didn't hate nobody, just they got in my way. Ain't my fault, most cases." He looked up. "But I done good, too. I killed a bounty hunter who was a *vampire*, got him when he murdered a hotel maid. That was a good thing I done."

"Then he come ridin' back shoutin' for us to pack up an' ride off," Trina called out, then appeared in the doorway, Nicky in her arms and Izzy standing by her knee. "Helluva day."

"I'm sorry," Bart muttered, not looking at Trina.

Jesús dipped his chin a few times as if praying.

"There is the kind of sorry which covers the slip of an act which most men would overlook. There is another sorry which you must pay back, stroke for stroke. Which is yours?"

"Cain't bring back none of them that died."

"You could still offer something. To the widows? The children left behind? People you may not even know who were influenced by your acts. He who stands unforgiving stands unforgiven. Even those who dare to walk across the sky must step carefully. You are young still as the sky-walkers go."

Izzy went to his pa, patted his leg. "Pa! Play! Pa! Play!"

"Not now, Iz. Lemme talk some more."

Izzy seemed sad, swung his hand hard at his pa's leg. Marina called him out, grabbed him and pulled him into her lap.

"You be kind," she spoke in his ear. "Not every hour is playtime. Some hours are for thinking." She kissed his cheek.

Jesús grinned at the boy. "This is how you learn: a mother's careful words and a gentle kiss."

Bart thought of his mama, trying to recall some kind words and a gentle kiss. She'd gotten strict as he grew older. She focused on her music business, not even asking him what he'd been doing or where he'd been once he returned home, just kept on plunking those keys on that piano then scribbling notes on paper.

"I understand now," said Bart, breaking from his thoughts.

"What do you understand?" asked Jesús.

"I know what I gotta do." Bart looked at Trina in the doorway, forced a grin. "This ain't our home. Gotta go back to our real home. We gotta set things right."

"Wanna see my sisters again," said Trina.

"I will turn myself in to the sheriff, whoever it is now, ask for some forgiveness, hope they go easy on me. But even if they don't, I'll feel better inside me. Then I can see the way ahead. See the road I'm on. And walk it to the end."

"I am pleased to hear you say it," said Jesús. "Otherwise, I know a settlement I can recommend for you. They are similar to you and your family. People who have fled unhappy lives and found peace in a new community. I passed there before arriving here. There are many such communities across the land. They will grow, grow and eventually meet and build new nations. It is all part of the plan of The Most High, May Peace Be Upon His Name."

+ + +

Bart would get up every morning ready for tasks, had a list of them to do, with Trina adding to it some evenings. He kept busy and his mind relaxed, forgot things he'd done in his past. That made him a better father. He played with the boys, chased them in the yard, a monster roaring at the little demons. The boys shrieked with joy and the women could sit on the porch with their sewing tasks, enjoying the show. Then he'd wash for supper. The women would serve whatever he'd shot and cut up plus whatever they brought in from the garden, mostly stew but sometimes they'd grill the meat. And he was satisfied with his life, told the women he was and got thanks in return, sometimes got a hug or kiss.

"There ain't nothing better 'an being here," he'd say with a belch after supper. "It's a wonderful life. Love being here with my women and my boys. We got us a great family. Better 'an standard."

The women would hold the sons, admiring them.

And the old man named Jesús, who the Brethren had renamed Idris, stood looking like a grandfather. He'd dispense wisdom when an opportunity arose, would say it out in his rich voice like God speaking from behind a cloud. Bart would stop and listen, give attention, but whether he took it to heart or not was a matter of his mood, what tasks needed doing, and how he'd slept.

"These women appreciate you being here, help look after things while I'm working," Bart told him and saw the old man smile. He smiled less and less as the months turned over.

"I have never wished to disrupt a family's life," he said.

"You're not." Bart grinned. "This here family life includes you. Wouldn't be standard without a grampa."

Bart would launch into recollections of his grandfather – a man his mama said had died while saving the governor back in the capital long ago. He never got to know that grandfather.

Trina objected, said he looked at Marina in odd ways, took long breaths when she was near.

"But he ain't done nothing," said Bart. "Works in the garden."

"See him gawkin' at Marina, ain't no grandfather way."

"Well, she's getting big. It's a sight for poor eyes. I mean, I look at her, too."

"Yeah, but you's the papa, so ain't no trouble."

Bart had a talk with Jesús and his ruddy face darkened. He bowed his head, muttered how his weakness was looking where he shouldn't. A judge's daughter caught his eye once, back in his Altadena days, and he got whipped for it. They threatened to poke out an eye for that sin, but he promised to leave and never return. And he hadn't returned.

"I should be on my way," Jesús would say every few days, "leave your family in peace. Continue on my road."

"How you know when your road ends?" Bart would tease.

"It will come to an end when I no longer breathe."

Bart would insist he stay longer. The garden was growing and he had knowledge to share.

"At least stay through harvest," said Bart. "But then it's already autumn and winter'll be coming. Don't wanna be on the road during those winter weeks. That would be the death of you."

Jesús said he wasn't afraid of death; he'd met old Mr. Death plenty of times and they'd made a deal. He knew when his time was up and that time was soon.

They took care of the horses. Bart sought materials to make a saddle but didn't find good leather pieces on the property. It seemed the horses didn't want to be ridden anyway. Both horses whinnied and snorted at him straddling their backs, would snip at his arms and legs when he was close enough although he tried to be friendly.

"It could be better to let them run free," Jesús suggested. "They may find mares to run with out there. There is no reason to keep them in this corral if they won't let you ride them."

One hot afternoon in late summer, Bart had just been tossed off the gray horse once more, landing hard on his back, smashing a manure ball under him, when they heard the call.

Trina shouted for them to come. Marina was pushing the new baby out.

Bart pulled off his soiled shirt, hurried to wash off, then rushed into the house.

"It's done," Trina snarled at him, eyebrows pinched. "You're too late to be any help."

Marina smiled up at him, rosy faced. She hadn't smiled for most of the past two months as her condition pained her.

"I will name this girl Mila, after my mother."

He knelt beside the bed and gazed at her, caressed her hand.

"We got a girl." He almost couldn't spit out the words.

The little thing had only thin blond fuzz on her head, a flushed face, clenched her hands as if angry. Trina wrapped her in a towel.

"Ain't much to look at now but she gonna be fine one day."

Bart gazed down. "Somebody gonna make her a wife."

"If she wanna."

"At least she won't know about bank robbing." Bart mumbled.

"Oh, please don't," Marina called from the bed.

They stayed together in that room all night, the baby crying, the mother nursing. Trina kept the boys with her in the back bedroom, told them they had a sister and to treat her kindly. Izzy had to have a look, seemed to approve, and told Nicky about the new baby.

In the morning, Bart went to find Jesús, wanting to deliver the news. He called out, got no response. He went around the property, calling out, then thought the old man might've felt he was one too many now and left. He'd been hinting for weeks.

Finally he found the old man leaning back in a stall in the barn, not still asleep at noon but sleeping forever.

He stared down at Jesús, wanting to tell him about the birth, as though the man would want to know, would be happy for him. But he'd left before Bart could express pride at his third baby. He spoke some words anyway.

Maybe it was the old man's destiny to travel this way, to come upon this ridge and find this house where a family needed advice. Especially this young man named Bart, so lost and not realizing it. He thought he was finally happy, but maybe it was a dream he'd soon awaken from. Maybe the old man had come for a reason.

34

THE SETTING SUN

BART SMILED AT TRINA as the afternoon sun illuminated her linen dress. "I can see clean through that cloth."

Trina blushed, as much as she could, her tan face seldom ever showing emotion. She knew what he meant. Under-clothing wasn't easy to come by. If the weather wasn't cold she'd stretch out what she had.

"Ain't got nothin' to hide," she said.

"Seen it before," he said with a snort.

She went to him, grinning. "Ain't too skinny fer ya?"

He wrapped his arms around her and they kissed.

"Ma an' pa kissin'," Izzy snickered to his brother. Nicky giggled, sitting up on the blanket beside him.

"Ain't never 'spected no life like this one we got here," she said, regarding the boys. "Like gettin' them pair of sons."

"We got a good life," he confirmed.

Bart had driven them in the jeep to the end of the ridge where there was a good view north across the plain. You could see enough to the west from there, too, could get a good view of the sunset, and that's what they waited for, having finished eating their dinner and packed things into the jeep.

He was happy to let the panels on top get sunshine and charge. Already it wasn't charging fully, took longer to get the maximum, but they hardly used it these days.

"Don't mind kissing your mama," Bart said to the boys, holding

Trina in his big arms. He leaned in for a smooch but Trina playfully turned away, acted like she was held captive. The boys laughed.

"Ma, don'tcha like Pa's kisses?" asked Izzy, silly boy standing as tall as his father's knee.

"Like 'em plenty," she replied. "Specially at night."

He wore his favorite blue coat, taken off a dead Mexi captain. It had fancy gold epaulets, tassels rippling as he'd strut up and down the walk. But the days were warm now so he didn't wear any shirt, left the coat hanging open in the warm air, showing the red hair on his chest. The blue trousers with yellow stripes were tight and had ripped a few times. He liked them so Trina was happy to repair them.

Leaning back against the jeep, he told her more about the life of Jesús. She listened patiently. He sure liked to talk, but she didn't mind time spent with him, seeing how he'd grown into a fine man and a good father.

He gazed at the sunset. "Them three brothers, Jesús said, they went east – way over the ocean, found themselves a lot of wisdom someplace there."

"Y'ain't plannin' on goin' nowhere over there, is ya?"

"Naw. But I keep thinking about all the things I done. I mean what I done wrong. Then we gotta run. And here we are, living a mighty fine life after all. Like something sent us here. Like maybe it was God showing me the way. Just don't think we deserve all this good fortune."

"Here we is," she sighed. "Great Spirit or naw. So we deserve it."

He told her more about things Jesús said and she chuckled.

"He like yer grampa, ain't he?"

Bart stared through the trees beside where they'd stopped, liked how the orange light cut through them. Back at the house it was the same: every sunset came through the woods in bright beams and lit up the front porch, burned through the windows, warming the main room. Plenty of light for him to scribble in that diary book from the airplane wreck, making a list of what he'd done each day so he could leave it for his sons.

"Yeah, reckon," he said. "I think of my grampa sometimes. He had lots of trouble in his life but he did do one good thing. He saved the governor. That one thing made his whole life worth living."

Trina hugged him, laying her head against his broad chest, and the boys snickered again.

"Guess we better head back," he said after a few minutes. "She's gonna wonder where we gone to. Hope she'll be feeling better."

They'd left Marina and baby Mila at the house, the mother not feeling well, the same as after she birthed Nicky. The baby would need nursing before they returned. She said she didn't mind. She'd seen sunsets before on the screens in the facility.

Bart got everyone into the jeep, Trina beside him up front, boys in the back seat. He started the motor, turned the vehicle around to head back down the gravel road to the house, a mile and a quarter, he figured.

Just as he got to the big curve in the road where he had to slow to make the turn, his boot hit the stop lever and the jeep lurched to a halt. Trina fell forward, started complaining about him stopping too suddenly.

"Soldiers," he said, looking ahead with enough trees to block their view of the jeep. Thankfully the electric motor had a low hum or they would hear the vehicle approaching.

He narrowed his eyes, focusing on movement through the trees. Maybe a dozen soldiers in blue coats gathered in front of the house. He cursed under his breath.

"What should we do?" asked Trina, trying to see ahead.

Bart flashed back to when Jesús was still alive and they worked in the yard one day. A quartet of soldiers had marched up the road, stopped to greet them, asked about the horses. Jesús hid behind the front door, afraid of the soldiers, but he spoke words for Bart to say. They wanted to take the horses, needed them for army use. Bart spoke the best Spanish he could with Jesús telling him what to say, explaining the horses couldn't be ridden, too wild.

The soldiers were convinced and left, but Jesús worried others would come by. If the soldiers had seen him wearing the white robe of the Brethren, they might've killed him and all of Bart's family, too, for hiding him. Then Jesús died.

The winter came and they struggled through it, keeping a fire going and the stew pot full, adding to it whenever they got more food from hunting or foraging.

Now they welcomed spring, the air warm and fresh – with a platoon of soldiers in blue coats milling before the house.

"Got to get to the house," he told Trina, giving a serious look. "Remember what I showed you? About operating this here vehicle? Someday you might hafta work it? Now's that time."

"What?" she exclaimed.

"You see that lever down there on the right?" He pointed to his feet. "That's the 'go' lever. The other one's the 'stop' lever, but you don't wanna stop this time. You wanna push down on the go lever, all the way to the floor. Smash it hard. When you go, don't let up off the lever 'til after you get through all of them. Got it?"

She gave a nod, her face stern. "Through them?"

"If they come this way, you run right through 'em. Keep going."

Her face tensed. "I hear ya."

"I'll work my way around through the woods, come up behind the house and get Marina and the baby." He reached back for the electro-gun. He already carried his pistol on his hip anytime he was out of the house. "Meet you on the other side."

A kiss and he climbed out of the jeep, closing the door quietly. Trina got into the driver's seat, put her feet down on the levers, curled her hands around the turning wheel.

"Boys," she called to the back seat, "wantcha get on down there on the floor. Iz, wantcha hug yer brother tight as ya kin an' don't let go. Ya hearin' me?"

Bart scrambled through the brush, branches smacking him as he hurried, a few leaving marks across his chest. Approaching the rear of the house, he decided to pull off the blue coat. The soldiers might accuse him of killing a captain if they saw him wearing it. Still wore the blue trousers but the yellow stripes had long been torn off.

He arrived at the back stoop, spied soldiers inside the house, grabbing at everything like they were in a museum then putting items back in place. Some soldiers were in the side bedroom where Marina and the baby were. He heard the bed slamming against the wall, her screaming and knew it was going to be terrible.

The electro-gun wouldn't be good indoors, but it sure was good for mowing down a whole lot of problems. He had his pistol, too, but the soldiers had rifles.

He entered through the back door, the electro-gun charged on the run to the house. It hummed like a hot machine, ready to unload its energy beam. The pistol slapped against his hip.

As Bart came through the back door, soldiers had taken hold of Marina by her arms and were dragging her up the hallway to the main room, her white gown torn apart. She kicked at them until one soldier slapped her leg, shouting at her in their language. He could guess the meaning as the soldiers laughed.

They didn't stop but pulled her awkwardly by her arms out the front door and on to the porch, throwing her down as they called to their leader, announcing what they'd found.

Bart could only follow them through the house to the front porch, electro-gun held ready to launch.

The leader of the group stood regally at the end of the walk, his platoon huddled behind him. He appeared an older man, gray hair falling from under his cap. He had a white holster on one hip, sabre on the other side. Maybe he was another captain. Learning about the army ways from Jesús, Bart thought maybe he could reason with this man and settle everything instead of killing each other.

At that instant the spear of doubt stabbed him: he stood alone against this platoon, trying to save this woman and himself and protect his other woman and kids from these battle-crazed men. What would Jesús do? He would pray, get the soldiers to feel guilty, sad for what they'd done. But that wouldn't do for Bart, who felt a fire burning from his gut into his head.

Hand sweating against the grip on the electro-gun, he came out on the porch behind the soldiers holding Marina. They'd thrown her down on the porch, stood over her.

"*Hola!*" Bart shouted.

The soldiers spun around, surprised to see him there holding an odd-looking weapon. Was it a weapon? They seemed confused, stood back, moving to either side of the porch so this stranger, probably the owner of the house and the husband of this woman they found, could clearly see their captain.

"*Buenos días*," the captain called up the walk to Bart. "*Creíamos que esta casa estaba abandonada, como las demás. Vinimos por los caballos.*" He laughed for his men. "*Y por las mujeres que tienes.*"

Bart only understood something about his house and his wife.

Seeing his confusion, the captain tried again: "*Inglés?*"

"Yeah, I unnerstand English. This here's English land."

Bart held the electro-gun firm, showing it to the captain, the hot hum of the maximum setting filling the porch.

"Is not English land now, my friend," the captain spoke. His men acted as though they understood his English. "Thus we inspect each property. We noticed smoke from your chimney."

Bart cursed himself. He'd thought of that, but after a year with no trouble, he believed nobody was close enough to bother or care who lived up on this ridge.

"Bart, *please*," Marina cried desperately from the porch floor.

"Is this your property?" the captain called to him.

Bart turned from Marina, regarded the captain. "It is now. Don't need to answer you. You ain't no tax collector. You might be in the wrong territory anyways. Better get on your way."

"We are not in the wrong territory, my friend," said the captain. "We control all land from Mojave in the west to Tejas in the east. As far north as *El Gran Cañón*. This mountain ridge, too."

"Well, we live here now. We keep to ourselves, and ain't hurting nobody. So you can be on your way. I promise I won't say nothing how you treated my wife. Just keep on moving along."

The captain gave a regal guffaw and his men enjoyed it.

"You're an officer," Bart spoke in a serious tone. "I thought you were gentlemen. Like sheriffs. You respect civilians. You protect women and children, treat them right. Ain't that in y'all's oath, what you pledge?"

The captain flashed a knowing look, a call back to his oath, then refixed his previous expression.

"*Sí...sí.* That may be an idea you got from old books. Fanciful tales. However, it is not for us today. Now we must take on important tasks. What reward we may get from doing the tasks is whatever we may find that entertains us."

Bart continued to hold the electro-gun at his hip as if aiming at the captain. "Entertain you?"

"We have been long on the march and have needs," the captain declared, raising his chin at the woman on the porch. "That one will do for my men. Those have earned it."

Marina rose up on one arm, screamed: "They killed my baby!"

Bart startled, half-turned to see her, and the men on the porch rushed at him.

His finger pressed down on the button, sending the blue energy burst at the men to his right, cutting them in half at the waist, each half falling. He spun to his left, shot them the same, let their body parts drop, fluids spilling out.

The captain gasped, his men falling back in awe.

"There's more of this if you don't depart," Bart shouted.

"You must be from one of those *facilities*," the captain uttered. "I heard a few members escaped."

"We ain't from no facility," Bart snarled. "Now get outta here!" He waited for signs they were going to depart. "Go on now."

The captain pointed at something behind Bart but he refused to look, thinking it was a trick.

"You have set your house ablaze," the captain called out.

Bart looked, saw the energy beam had broken the window glass and lit the curtains in the main room. As the curtains fell, flames spread over the carpet.

Marina gasped at the conflagration, crying out for Mila, like she wanted him to save her baby.

Bart stopped, confused, not knowing what to do.

He charged into the house, went to the side bedroom to rescue Mila. But he saw Marina was correct: the way they killed his baby daughter punched him in the gut. Couldn't be saved. Already dead. Enraged, he realized he'd left Marina on the porch.

Rushing back to the porch, Bart saw the soldiers had dragged Marina into the yard. A soldier was atop her, pawing at her while the others formed a circle around them, cheering and crowing.

The captain stood aside, grinning at the spectacle. He gave Bart a glance, a nod of satisfaction like everything was settled.

"We will leave," the captain called, "when my men are satisfied. Your wife is paying the tax. Now go save your house. If you can."

The main room was ablaze, flames lighting the yard.

Confused and overwhelmed, Bart swung the electro-gun around at the men huddled over Marina and unleashed holy hell: using full power the men caught fire, bursting into bits of flesh and bone.

Frightened soldiers backed into the road – as the jeep driven by Trina slammed into them, mowing them down. The jeep continued on, then slowed and turned, came back up the road at full speed to hit the ones who tried to get up. Soldiers with mangled bodies moaned as the dead bodies spread over the road and across the grass of the yard.

Bart looked at what he'd done, saw the mess he'd made. He fell to his knees before the body of Marina, caught up in the storm of his wrath. Two soldiers laying over her were melted and fused with her body.

He heard gunshots, spun around to see the last of the blue coats fall. The jeep waited in the road.

"Came when I saw fire," Trina shouted, holstering her pistols.

Bart remained stunned, resting the electro-gun at his side as the fused mess steamed before him.

The house was completely ablaze, flames reaching the roof.

As evening came on all they could do was stand by the jeep and watch their homestead dreams become ash. By dawn only a smoking hulk remained, the stone chimney that had given them away the only thing standing.

In the raging calamity, the horses got spooked. The gray horse finally made the leap, cleared the fence and galloped down the road. The black horse, after circling the corral a few times, also mounted the fence and raced free.

As dawn arrived, Bart stepped carefully through the rubble, his eyes peeled for anything of value that wasn't damaged. He pulled out a few items from the back bedroom like clothes kept safe in the closet. The ice box, unable to operate with no electric coming to the house, held some food. He took what there was, packed it up, put it in the back of the jeep. He saw the boys crying, their unhappy faces pressed up against the jeep's window, staring at the first terrible memory they'd keep in their heads for the rest of their lives.

Bart found the charred remains of Mila, his precious daughter who he should've saved, might've saved if he hadn't gone off to a picnic. He wrapped the blackened thing in a white towel, carried it outside, dug a grave straightaway and spoke words.

Trina came to him. She leaned against him, put her arm around him. He heard her weeping. He'd never heard her cry before. Hearing her let him release all he had: a torrent of tears and howls of pain.

Then he dug the grave for Marina next to little Mila's. He had to cut her body free from those of the soldiers who died with her.

"I know ya love her," said Trina as they knelt beside the mound. "I know she love ya, too."

He wiped his face, turned to her. "Sometimes love ain't enough."

She didn't know what he meant, but he knew. Things happen no matter how much you love someone. Love ain't no shield. He had to have known something would happen when he left them alone.

When the electro-gun failed, battery out, Trina leaped from the vehicle with pistols blazing, shooting the soldiers who charged him. In the end he couldn't even save himself, needed her help. Nobody would know that, just him, and it hurt. Everything hurt. He would leave this place, this place of sorrow, site of his humiliation.

Giving a final look the following morning, the air gray with fog, they drove silently away, down from that ridge to the desert below, and headed east.

Part Three

Family

35

Two Outlaws

I REMEMBER THAT WEEK, now three years past. All the talk in town was about the pair of outlaws who stormed into Cimarron and robbed the First Bank of the West, racing out of town before anyone could see which way they went. All anyone could say for certain was they looked like women.

Sitting in the current trial, it all comes back to me.

I knew who they meant, the way people talked. Deputy Cal kept teasing me, like I was too busy with my medical tasks to pay attention to lawmen's problems.

Cal would call out: "Jake, you know who I'm talking about, don't you?" Sometimes he'd give me a wink.

I'd pretend to not know just to listen to him try to explain.

"Them two sisters. Two of the three of them. Still running their crimes across the territory. Don't know what coulda happened to the third sister. Ain't seen her for a while. Run off, I suspect. Maybe died some dirty place, bleeding out. Lotsa snakes out wherever they hole up. Died somewhere. Who knows? Accident? Or maybe tribals got to her. Who knows? Maybe one of them made her a wife."

He laughed, thinking I would feel shame at the talk of tribals capturing her and wedding her to a warrior, her being in the teepee taking care of babies instead of robbing banks. He liked that idea.

"But not those other sisters, no sirree. They're going as hard as before. We gotta try 'n' get 'em. Sheriff Ray sent down the order."

It was a turning point. Lawmen finally had to get serious, being a larger bank getting robbed. They tracked down the gang after six months – found their camp, at least. Eventually they captured the eldest sister, the one named Trinity, off a citizen's tip. She came to town dressed up as a wholesome matron, acted the part, purchased groceries with stolen notes. The others got away to parts unknown. Trinity had a quick trial – some say too quick – and was sentenced to be hanged until death for her crimes.

Things have been quiet the past three years.

Back then Cal's pronouncement meant little to me. The most I'd be involved was performing examinations on bodies, then preparing them for burial.

That memory popped into my head as I sit in the jailhouse with Cal, waiting for this trial to resume.

"But she came back," I say, my words ringing like a chapel bell tolling, leaving a silence in the room after.

"Sure did," says Cal, smug behind the desk. "Anyways, she's gonna have to be on the stand saying everything. Then we'll know what kinda trouble she's gotten in over the years nobody seen her."

"I only wanna know what happened to my cousin."

After taking my lunch at the Five Ladies, I return to the court and get a good seat before Judge Robinson enters and we stand. The chairs along the side of the room are occupied by several old men, deputies all, ready to tell stories about what they witnessed. Looks like anyone who's ever had a run-in with the sisters has come to report it, putting away their shame at having been bested by young women.

First up is Winfred Jordan, who looks like he's crawled out of a grave to be here on this day. The old man still wears patches over his eyes. He feels for the witness chair, gets help sitting.

"I still say I done nothing. Nothing wrong," he says in a crackly voice. "She attacked me."

"Who do you mean?" asks the judge.

"That one."

"He can't see," Mr. Hitchens, the prosecutor, reminds the judge.

"State your name for the court," the judge orders Trina.

She stands before her chair in the front corner of the room, small between her guards, and speaks: "Trina Culpepper."

Her voice sounds weak, strained, like she hasn't slept well. The judge orders her to state her name once more, louder.

"Her sister," Mr. Jordan corrects. "She's one done it to me," and he raises his hand to point to his eyes.

"Why did you call this man," asks Mr. Duda, "if it was Trinity who wounded him?"

"They're all in it together," says Mr. Hitchens, pointing harshly at Trina.

"In it? In *what?*" cries Mr. Duda. "They were young girls. They were attacked. Were they supposed to not defend themselves?"

"This witness speaks to the unnatural violence perpetrated on those men," says Mr. Hitchens, "regardless of the men's intentions. In short, once violent, unnaturally so, likely to always be violent."

"But you've already handed down Trinity's sentence," says Mr. Duda, and gets some applause. The crowd is glad she's gone.

"Proceed," the judge commands.

Mr. Jordan clears his throat. "Yeah, us boys was gonna have our way with her, like the boss told us to. But soon as we got in that tent of hers, she attacked me. Attacked all of us. But I was first. Got all kinds of sharp objects in that tent, you can be sure. Sewing stuff. I was supposed to be first – break her open, like my buddy said – we drew straws, see. But I never did. Never got no chance. I didn't do nothing to her. Never got to. Soon as I lay on her I get her fingers in my eyes. I cry out and slap her. But then I feel something sharp go straight in my eyes. Not her fingers but something like needles. I mean big, long needles. I pulled them out but couldn't see what they were. Couldn't see nothing. I was blind already. Could've been some of the needles womenfolk use for knitting. Maybe got in my brain. Don't know, just feel mighty crazy these years gone by. I can't think. Couldn't do nothing but run out. Didn't know where I was going, just screaming, and I didn't care how I sounded. Had to get away. Ran straight out, tripped over a rock, I guess it must've been. Couldn't see nothing. Where's a blind man to go? I just tried to find my way. Bumping into rocks, stumbling over them damn rocks, and always keep picking myself up and going on. Took me a year to find my way to a town but the doc there couldn't do nothing for me. My eyes were gone."

The court is silent and I hear at least one woman weeping.

"Let the record show," Mr. Hitchens speaks, "the girl attacked him prior to him performing any criminal act on her—"

"A matter of seconds!" Mr. Duda erupts.

Mr. Hitchens grins at his opponent. "Nine-tenths of the law is a matter of seconds, sir."

+   +   +

The Way of the Son is not an easy one, Bart recognized, keeping his foot heavy on the go lever. The plain they crossed lay mostly flat and if they hit a bump he didn't care.

"Where ya headin' so fast?" the woman beside him kept asking, getting angrier each time. The boys in the back cried in fear and she told them to stay calm while he snapped at them to be quiet.

Afternoon turned to evening and the power ran low, as fast as he was pushing it. He had to stop until morning. Then rain came. Hail pounded the vehicle. He heard cracks on the panels on the shell and feared the worst. Thunder crackled through the night and the boys shrieked.

He dared command the boys to shut up and Trina cursed him for his behavior.

Rain continued through the next day. A steady downpour forced them to stay inside the vehicle. Trina had to slip Izzy through the window behind the back seat, into the rear space under the shell, to retrieve the last food packets. She handed over one packet to Bart, his favorite among the choices, but he slapped it to the floor.

"Hell's wrong witcha?" she growled, then crawled roughly to the back seat to have dinner with the boys.

Bart didn't care. He stared out the front window, searching for a familiar sight, trying to guess where they were. He took a different route going east, not wishing to pass by the facility again or have to skirt the hell-cats. He wanted to stay north of the line the Mexi captain said was the border, but he wasn't sure where it might be.

No sign of Mexi soldiers.

The images stayed with him, haunted him. The bodies mangled and burnt. Body parts strewn. He had to wrench an arm from the grill on the front of the vehicle, leaving two fingers which fell out once they hit enough bumps. And that mound he made over the shallow grave of Marina. He thought of the beautiful woman with a pure heart who never should've been born in the facility, kept inside all her life, then get out only to step into the maw of death. A horrible death! And poor Mila, who never deserved cruelty. How could humans be so cruel to a baby?

He knew he was becoming a madman, as evil and crazed as any he'd encountered. In a world left naked and barren, what evil would a man do to survive? Forget food and water. Forget shelter and the weapons to get food and protect a shelter. What about his sanity? If he was to survive – and, in a second thought, protect his family, the only thing he could offer the world of the future – what more could he do but find a place where they would be protected, near good food sources, good water, and just live?

His days would be occupied writing everything that happened to them, saving it as history for his sons to bear. Between hunting, fishing, gathering what was edible from field and forest, tending a garden, he'd teach his sons how to live, how to survive, how to be good men, better husbands and fathers than him. He understood what his ancestor had scribbled in those notebooks kept in a glass case in his mama's house, protecting their pages from the dusty Skinner Canyon environment.

Another day and night stuck inside the vehicle, anger growing in the tight space. Food packets finished.

Stench filled the cabin and Bart cursed at his sons.

He'd managed to hold his waste, so they could too. Trina cursed back at him. The boys cried.

At least the rain did some good. Trina hung the diapers out, clamped in the closed windows, and let the rain wash them clean.

Fighting with himself, Bart turned to Trina sitting in back.

"I know what you're thinking, so just say it. It's my fault. It's *all* my fault. I did everything wrong. Everything happened too fast.

Couldn't figure it out in time. I know it, so just say it. I got Marina killed. Got the house to burn down, too. I did that. So just say it and get it out."

Trina sat back, her face plain and unaffected.

"Ya done said it yerself."

He felt his eyes fill with tears, could no longer hold them back.

"Go on," she said.

But he couldn't cry. He couldn't let his sons see him.

"Ya said it true," she told him. "Hell if I coulda done any better. Did what I could: mow down them soldiers. Shot others goin' after ya. They deserve it. People deserve things done to 'em. Maybe they don't never know it but if they got time to think on it they maybe unnerstand what they done an' what they get fer it."

He wiped his eyes, tried to hide them from his sons.

"Ain't it what yer grampa Jesús said? 'What's done is done'?"

"He didn't mean it in that way," Bart muttered. "What's done is done *for a reason*."

"What reason?" She waited, listened to his sniffles. "Some card game ya be playin'? Dice? Somebody keepin' score? How ya know what's done? Ain't nothin' done for some kinda score, don'tcha know? Ever'thin's like...like stars. Just happen. Ain't no plan to it." She took a long breath. "Look at what ya got. More 'an ya ever did think ya get. Ain't it true?"

He gave slight nod.

The rain gradually let up, sun breaking through the cloud cover. Bart saw the indicators on the console. Hours of sunshine needed to start the vehicle and keep going. He got out, stretched and sucked in big gulps of fresh air, expelled them loudly. The boys laughed.

He took a dump a few yards from the vehicle, returned.

"Pa done poopy," Izzy announced.

"Shore did," Trina said, unamused. "Got it all out."

+ + +

A woman as old as Maggie took the witness chair to complain about the time the sisters rode through town shooting at anyone crossing their path, got four members of her family, laying them low in the dusty street.

"And now I ask you," Mr. Duda begins, "did you see Miss Trina Culpepper do any of the shooting?" He points stiffly to the woman in the chair in the front corner of the room. "Can you be certain it was this one?"

The woman demures, pinched lips quivering. "I cain't see she's same as that one."

"Possibly it was Trinity, the older sister?"

"Could've been," she says.

"So not Trina."

"Oh, they all look the same to me."

Then a man takes the chair, tells of the day the sisters rode into his town – or they were leaving town – anyway, they trampled his wife as she crossed the street, left her for dead. Oh, but she did live – yet her injuries left her to suffer a miserable life in a hospice.

"Can you be certain it was this one who struck down your wife?" asks Mr. Duda. "This woman right over there in the corner?"

"Well, no. Can't tell. They all look alike," says the man.

Then a man in farmer's coveralls sits in the chair and recounts the night his dog was shot. "I heard they's in the area so musta been them, one of 'em. Who gonna shoot an old hound dog anyways? That a purtic'lar kinda nasty."

More witnesses, more tales of violence.

After the trial ends for the day, I hear Deputy Cal snicker to the jailer: "We need to get that one in a noose and in the ground soon as we can. Then we can go back to protecting the town from those Glow ghouls."

"You don't know that she's done anything," I speak up.

Cal gives me a look like he wants to punch me.

"Jake," says Cal in his dismissive twang, "the woman's guilty by what they call *association*. It's a law term. She's part of the crime, even if she never pulls a trigger. She's just as guilty, no matter how much you got a hankering for her."

"I do not have a *hankering* for her," I insist.

"Don't she look a lot like your mama?" Cal's grinning again.

"I suppose she does. A little. Maybe."

"A little," and he breaks into laughter. "About same age as your mama, too, when she was...was, uh, struck down."

"It's been five years at least since anybody's seen her," I come back. "She has to have reformed in that time."

Cal laughs. "Ain't it kinda like one of them cancers? Hides in the body for years, then comes raging one day when you're all tied up in knots over something. Ain't that the truth?"

"Cancer can hide in the body for years before developing into a serious condition, yes."

"This is your cancer, boy."

"How so?"

"She come back right now just to cause you pain. Pain you done thought was put away years ago."

36

THREE PROPHETS

TWO MONTHS OF SLOW TRAVEL, finding back roads that took them east, going around bridges fallen and pavement too broken to roll over, too many detours, then often cutting across open desert or grassy plains under threatening skies or smudging the edge of night until too dangerous to go on. Days parked by a grove of trees, the vehicle under the full sun to charge the panels while they lazed in the shade counting out nuts and berries from a previous stop.

And the time he took the rifle out into deep woods and returned the next day with a hindquarter of venison for them, making a fire and slicing off strips to dip into the boiled pot full of herbs gathered by the boys. Trina would open her shirt and offer her milk to Nicky, letting him fall into sleep against her shoulder. Izzy lay his head in her lap. Bart sat alone, back against a tree trunk, watching them, wondering who these people were and where they came from, what different lives he might have if he'd turned this way instead of that way, said yes instead of no, refused an invitation to adventure, or looked the other way instead of insisting he knew what to do.

They would drive on, day after day, some long and other days cut short as they had to make it over rugged terrain or avoid any town or village that appeared along the way, pausing at a few roadside huts where vehicles once could buy fuel. There he'd stroll about, like he had memories to fix, wanted to tack them to a spot deep in his head and carry them forever.

He glanced over at Trina, who stared out the side window as if she were headed to prison.

The road was bumpy, shaking them up and down inside the jeep but they'd gotten used to it, hardly paid attention to the terrain. But the evening was deepening and it was time to stop for the night. The lights on the front were dimming.

"Stop!" Trina suddenly cried out. "Stop! *Stoooop!*"

Bart slammed his foot on the stop lever and the vehicle lurched to a halt, everyone thrown forward then jolted back. He reacted to her scream more than anything he saw ahead.

"What?" he shouted, wrenching his hands off the turning wheel and shaking the nerves out of them.

"Look!" she shouted, pointing.

He stared out the front window, lights dim, the darkness nearly complete, and saw the lake spreading before them.

"Ya payin' 'tention?" she cursed.

He'd almost driven them into a lake in the dark. Sitting back, he took deep breaths.

"Ya crazy?" She shook her head. "Ya tryna kill us? What the matter witcha?"

Bart could only think maybe it would be better if he went away, keep to himself. Then he wouldn't be responsible any longer. Then he could go make his mistakes and nobody would care. For the moment he hated them.

She stared at him and he turned away.

"Better we stop for the night," she said with a huff. "I kin do the drivin' tomorrow."

He got out of the jeep, slammed the door as hard as he could and stormed around the rear of the vehicle to her side. She'd gotten out by then. The boys were glued to the windows, watching.

They faced off.

"I know ya hurtin'," Trina spoke firmly. "Ain't no reason to be actin' crazy tho'. Yeah? Puttin' us in danger."

"We weren't in danger!" he shouted, fists to his hips.

"Look at the jeep!"

In the darkness he had come to the edge of the water. A muddy grade allowed the vehicle to slowly slide down into the lake. He saw movement, which was quickening.

"Get 'em out!" Trina screamed.

Bart grabbed at her door handle, found it locked. He pulled out his pistol, shot at the window twice to break it, punched it out and cut his forearm. He reached in and unlocked the door, opened it and scrambled in for the boys. He handed Nicky out first, then grabbed Izzy who could climb out on his own. Bart pushed the seatback down and took the bags and tossed them out behind him.

He jumped free and rushed to the rear of the vehicle while it continued to slide into the dark water. He opened the shell's door and started sweeping out all the bags and boxes and jugs they'd put there, all of it falling on the muddy ground, with one jug rolling down into the water. He grabbed the jug, pulled it back, and stepped higher up the grade.

He had to bent over, catching his breath.

"We awright," said Trina, with Nicky in her arms. Izzy held on to her leg as she stood up the slope from the vehicle.

Bart shook his head. Too much for one day. For one trip. A trip to nowhere. Where was he headed? He hadn't a clue.

"Just 'bout drown us," Trina said, voice strained as though she wanted to shout it but was holding back.

Bart stared at the vehicle that had taken them so far. The jeep had slid far enough that water was spilling into the front of the cabin through the busted window. He cursed at his misfortune – at his stupid acts. Everything was his fault.

"Stupid thing weren't even charging to half," he grumbled. "You saw how we had to stop, let the sun charge them panels. Getting to be every day now."

"Look like they ain't chargin' up no more," she said plainly, but he heard it as a joke, like she was teasing him.

He turned to her. "Ain't my fault. Getting dark. And no map to check since the tablet burned up in the house."

"Shoulda stop earlier," she said, again plainly, but he heard her accusing him of being stupid.

"It was running fine," he countered.

"Ya bin runnin' it day an' night for weeks now."

One too many things being said, he counted, and felt his insides catching fire. "You can shut up now."

She set Nicky down on dry ground, in a patch of grass, told Izzy to watch him and the boy stood stiff like a guard in the facility.

"Gonna get the rest us killt actin' crazy like y'are," she said.

"I said you can shut up now!"

At that, she slapped him right across his cheek. It startled him, but in the same instant, his hand curled into a fist and he punched her straight in the mouth.

"Like you're so perfect!" he raged.

He saw her lip bleeding and suddenly felt bad, looked down.

"Sorry about that."

She drew her pistol, raised it. When he looked up again, the end of the barrel hovered an inch from his forehead, aiming between his eyes. She had it cocked, ready to fire.

"You drawing on me?" he said, half surprised and half amused – or feigning amusement. She couldn't mean it.

"I am."

She held the pistol up to his face.

"I said I'm sorry," but he didn't seem to mean it.

"Ya never did hit me b'fore," she spoke, her voice tightly coiled. "Y'ever hit me again I'll shoot ya straightaway. Ya hearin' me? Don't mind makin' these boys got no pa. Not at all, if need be."

Bart held up his hands, surrendering. "I believe you. I'm sorry. Never happen again, promise."

He waited for her to lower the pistol.

"I swear it."

+ + +

Rotund Bernard Song squeezes into the witness chair, sits with a loud spurt of gas, frowns a moment, folds his hands in his lap. Mr. Hitchens asks the same questions.

"Me and the family was sitting down to dinner. It was a Sunday evening, I recall. Said our prayers. We had a nice ham shank with sweet taters, corn and biscuits. The missus made a fine dinner—"

"Please tell us what happened after your dinner, Mister Song," Mr. Hitchens cuts in.

"Well, we heard some noise outside. Went to look and I could see someone messing with the horses, out at the corral. Now, we don't need to bother with much, being so far out. Nobody come our way. But that night, someone was trying to get our horses. I look out the window and seen him clear as day with the moon shining down. A man – one fellow with beard and long hair – going after Mabel, one of our mares. We use her for breeding, see, and she was with foal, though 'twas early."

"Go on," says Mr. Hitchens. "Tell us about the man."

"Well, I could see it was a man. But I could see there was others standing out further, past the corral. Like they was watching him steal our horse. Couldn't make out much. I says to myself: 'Could be trouble'. So I grab my shotgun, get ready to confront the man."

"So you couldn't see him clearly?" asks Mr. Duda.

"Not then, but later I did. Got a right fair look at the man."

"And how did he look?" asks Mr. Hitchens.

"He got a red beard. Red hair down to his shoulders. Scared my missus half to death when the moonlight showed him. He growled at us. Actually growled. Like a bear. Looked like a big red bear. Broad shoulders, thick body – almost took him for a bear. Like the way them science folks playing God made all them creatures that wander the western territory. Thought he's one of them. But it was a man, I knew soon enough."

"And how did you?"

"He pulled a gun on me. I stepped out on the back stoop and he raised a pistol, pointed it at me."

"Did he say anything?"

"Sure, he said he needed a horse. Two, if I can spare. Spare, he said, like he's just borrowing them. Had a good voice, sounded kind, but it was still thieving. So I told him no, can't spare any, not my best broodmare least of all."

"Did he take your horse?"

"No, he...." The man breaks down, takes a moment to wipe his eyes. "In the end he took my mare. Before that, see, my missus come to the door behind me. Right behind me. Could feel her breath on the back of my neck. I knew she was there but it happened so fast I didn't have no chance to tell her to get back."

"What happened?"

"That man, he aimed at me. I said he should go on his way. He said he wouldn't unless he took a horse with him. I ask: Where you going you need a horse? Well, I can tell you, we live so far out from Skinner Canyon that anybody'd need a horse to get there. So I ask him if he's going to Skinner Canyon. I say I'm fixing to go to town the next day on errands if he don't mind waiting overnight. He can sleep in the barn, I said."

"And then what happened?"

"Well, sir, he said no, he needed the horse that night. He spit on the ground then, like he hated the name of the place and he weren't going to Skinner Canyon."

"And?"

"Then he fired on us. Shot right at me. But the bullet hit my missus standing behind me. Got her in the face. See, she's just tall enough to stand above my shoulder. She dropped to the floor behind me." He sniffles back tears. "When I turned to her – I squatted down like folks do – she's bleeding hard from out her eye. And it weren't nothing I could do then. She didn't say nothing."

"Did he take your horse?"

"I tried to tend to my missus, sir. The kids were screaming. My head got cloudy. I pick up my shotgun and just fire in his direction, not seeing him clearly. Didn't wanna hurt my own horse, but he was leading her away. I shot at him. And he...he shot back."

"And?"

"He got my eldest: my daughter May. She came to help her ma, got a bullet in her chest. My sons come running but I shout at them to stay back. I go out after him, holding up my shotgun, aiming at him. I see him take a saddle off the rail by the barn, swing it on Mabel and cinch her up, then swing up into the saddle like he knew how to ride, and whirled her around. Well, I didn't wanna hit my horse, but he still had his pistol ready, pointed at me."

"Did he shoot at you?"

"Sure did." Mr. Song weeps as he takes off his coat, rolls up his sleeve to show the damage to his arm. A line of stitches brought the ripped flesh together. The crowd in the room can see the metal brace on his elbow. "This what he done to me, to my arm. Shot went right up my arm like a knife and busted out my elbow. Can't use no more for nothing."

"I'm sorry to hear that," says Mr. Hitchens, feigning sympathy. "You said this man, bearing a red beard and having red hair, had others waiting nearby?"

"Yeah, them. I couldn't see too sharp even with the moonlight coming over them, but I guess it was a woman and couple of kids. I could see them standing with some bags, like they were on a trip to somewhere."

"You're certain it was a woman and two children?"

"That's what I guess. Had to be a woman. And the kids, one up to her knee, the other shorter. She was wearing a dress. Or a robe like those Slammers you see from time to time near the border."

"Slammers?" asks Mr. Duda incredulously.

"Them folks that obey the three prophets. Up from Mexi. Perez brothers. Juan, Luis, and Manuel. Went east for their learning, came back to preach to their kind down south in Tejas. You see more of them down where our homestead is. Reason we had to move away from there, move into town. We ain't gonna deal with no more trouble. Not with it being just me and my sons."

Mr. Duda clears his throat. "Could the man stealing your mare be one of those Slammers?"

"Oh no. He was wearing standard Western wear. Definitely not a Slammer. They're worse down in Tejas. Some settling down in Okala, too. Better we get some militia together for the day they come up here. And they're coming, awright – like a swarm of locust – preaching their strict way of living. Lotsa rules. Killing anyone that don't follow their ways."

"That is noteworthy," Judge Robinson speaks. "However, please stick to the trial topic."

"We are establishing the whereabouts of this woman," says Mr. Hitchens, giving a nod in Trina's direction, "about four years ago, and her connection to the Red Devil, also known as Bad Bart."

"I heard of him," Mr. Song says. "I couldn't know if it was him that night or not. But whoever it was that killed my missus and my daughter, the fellow needs to be hanged by the neck until dead. And I won't mind doing the lever pulling, neither."

Mr. Duda says: "And the woman with him that night?"

"She didn't do nothing. Stood right there. Out by the road."

"Nothing?"

"Nope."

Mr. Duda lets out a long sigh, then looks down at his papers.

"No more questions, Your Honor," says Mr. Duda.

"Well," Mr. Song starts up suddenly, "she did go with him when he rode past her. They went out a ways, and he climbed down and put her up in the saddle. Saw them in the moonlight. Handed up one of those kids, led the horse away, looking like Joseph leading Mary and Baby Jesus off to Bethlehem. With the other kid walking with him. Ain't seen none of them since. Just went off into the night. Like holy ghosts."

+   +   +

Trina spoke roughly at him: "Ain't gotta do that." He refused to look at her. "Now ya just get lawmen comin' after us."

"We needed a horse. Only farm we seen in days," said Bart.

"Shoulda just offered some notes."

"We ain't got no notes. They burned in that fire."

"Got some fold up in my pocket right now. But ya never ask me nothin'. Just gotta do yer own way."

"Listen: I got us a horse. You're riding easy now."

"Don't care none about ridin' easy. Just wanna stop fer a spell an' rest some."

"You're the one riding. Why you need rest?"

"Bin good while since rode a horse. My bottom's sore."

In the gray air they spied a stand of trees rising ahead, one of a few on this open plain, and headed for it.

Under the trees, Trina handed Nicky down to him, the little boy squealing with fear, then she dismounted. The boys moaned they were hungry. She dug in the pack they tied to the saddle, found the last of the venison jerky. She wiped dirt off it and broke it in half, gave a piece to each son.

"You two be grateful now," she said when they complained. "Yer pa shot that deer so you kin eat somethin' today."

She continued to stand, stretching from time to time, breathing the cool morning air. They'd been traveling all night, ever since he stole the horse in the evening. They followed the road, mostly of dirt and gravel, easy on the hooves.

"Ya din't hafta shoot nobody," she said to break the silence.

"He shot at me, so I shot back."

"I think ya got the woman standin' behind him."

"What woman?"

"Standing right behind him. You missed him, got her."

He seemed confused, shook his head. "Naw.... That true?"

"Saw her drop to the floor behind him. An' ya shore did shoot the girl come to help her."

"What girl?"

"You dint see 'em? Ya blind?"

"No, I'm not blind. But it was dark. I was trying to get a horse, dammit, not count who all was in the damn house. And I did get us a horse. Better if we had two but one's a start. We can get by. Need to find a carriage."

After the jeep slipped into the lake, the hot battery beneath the cabin sizzled and steamed as it hit the water.

Hiking away from the lake over muddy ground, they looked for a road across the wide plain, flat as a window pane. Nothing to fix their location although he could guess which river it was.

In the light of dawn, Bart saw that the lake was actually a river swollen with flood. Water had breached its banks. The long rain they'd suffered had washed downstream. He stood watching the roof of the vehicle surrounded by water, despondent at his fate. Life wasn't fair, he cursed under his breath and Izzy asked his ma what his pa said.

"Jus' personal words," she told the boy. "Ain't nothin' ya need to remember."

The muddy shoreline wouldn't hold the jeep for long. Bart could only watch it slip into the water inch by inch. The electro-gun was saved but he hadn't retrieved the last two batteries. Now they were underwater. Showing the weapon's battery down to ten percent, he decided to use what power remained to start a fire, to let Trina put some food together in a pot. Then he tossed the weapon out into the swollen river.

They'd been walking for days, carrying the few things they could salvage. Izzy rode on Bart's back, grabbed hold of his pa: bare feet digging into his belly, hands clasped around his neck, hanging on. Trina cut a strip from the bottom of her dress, fashioned it into a sling and hung it around her neck and shoulder to carry little Nicky against her chest. Both hands of each adult held onto a bag. A rifle slung from Bart's shoulder. Pistols on hips.

He found he had taken a few pellets in the back of his shoulder from the farmer's shotgun and Trina had to dig them out, stitch him up. The wound ached and left him resting for a couple days before he swore he could go on.

"Go on where?" she challenged him.

"We're on a road, ain't we? Roads go somewhere, don't they?"

Three days of walking and they came upon a crossroad. The road they'd been walking was dirt and gravel but the crossing road had been stone once upon a time but now cracked and broken, with large holes here and there. He knew what had once been the better road would lead them to a town, so they turned and continued along the broken stone road.

Bart grumbled how this road must've been when it was new and people had motor carriages to ride over it. The boys liked their pa's stories of fantastic machines from days gone by. He told them about airplanes and rockets, drawing from his childhood books, but the boys couldn't believe him. He told them things were better in the old days.

"There," called Bart. He pointed ahead to a road sign, bent down to one side. "See? Fifty miles to Boise City."

"Boise City?" She wasn't happy. "They know us there. Ya forget?

We done a couple banks there."

"Years ago," he said. "Nobody remembers us now." He smiled at the boys. "We got us a family. We're going as standard folks. Fit right in."

"Ain't no standard folks," she snapped back. "We's outcasts an' outlaws. Nothin' more."

He ignored her as he recognized a row of low hills to the north, could place themselves on the map in his head. He wasn't so sure of going to Boise City, but he knew the land now and could make decisions where to go. Definitely not Skinner Canyon, which would be to the north.

He let the horse graze a while as he studied the horizon.

"Maybe we should head to the old camp."

37

Four Horsemen

SITTING IN THE COURT ROOM, I remember another day, going on two and a half years by now: Christmas. A dusting of snow had fallen overnight, stayed through the day. I gazed out the window of Doc's office. Nobody was out, everybody having some place to take supper. Missy brought me a plate from her family's dinner, wished me a good holiday. Doc had a sick child to look after so I offered to stay with the boy. I talked a while with Missy, hoping she'd stay longer but she had to excuse herself.

As I watched her walk away down the landing, something else caught my eyes.

Horsemen rode slowly down the snow-swept street, riding four abreast. I couldn't make out who they might be the way their hat brims were pulled low but they looked determined. Dressed in black leather with big, flapping coats, they seemed like angels – a quartet of dark angels swooping into Skinner Canyon on a solemn mission. I watched as they reined up outside the Five Ladies down the street. Two dismounted. Another fiddled with a hank of rope.

Next thing I know, the two figures that entered the saloon were bringing a man out of the saloon. Actually, the older, bearded man that exited with them seemed to come out willingly, laughing like something was a joke. Then a noose was thrown over his head and the rope jerked tight from atop her horse and he fell to the street. They made him run after the horse but he fell, tried to get up but was dragged further.

I thought to run to the jailhouse to alert the deputy.

But I didn't. I feared the four horsemen might see me and shoot. So I only watched out the window as they dragged that man away, straight down the street, smudging the snow, him clenching at his throat, unable to call out.

After they'd gone, I ran over and told Deputy Rayne what I'd seen. Four horsemen: one with hair dark as coal, one with brown hair that was almost black, one with auburn hair, the last with a blond pony-tail.

"So...four women. Is that what you saw, Jake?" the lawyer, Mr. Cobb, had asked me at the trial of Trinity Culpepper half a year after that day.

"Yes, I think so. Four women," I said. "Definitely women."

"And we now know who they were," said Mr. Cobb. "First among the criminals is Trinity Culpepper. And her sister known as Triss. The other two joined later, it seems, got into crimes. We haven't as yet counted any murders they're associated with. We can dismiss Miss Bonnie Sutton of Texhoma, safely returned to her worrywart husband. And Miss Lulu Willoughby, too young for such misdeeds, has been returned to her family unharmed, with a few unfortunate misadventures she best forget."

Mr. Cobb had turned to Judge Young with a whimsical grin.

"At this time, we have no clue as to the whereabouts of the third Culpepper sister named Katrina – commonly known as Trina. We believe she must've been one of them because.... Well, Your Honor, we've seen those three riding together for several years...."

I snap back to the present trial, feeling like I've spent most of my adult years in this courtroom either testifying about the bodies I've examined or listening to testimony from witnesses too horrible to mention.

I had to miss the previous day's court proceedings to help Doc deliver a baby – if you could've called it that – from a straggler family that found their way into town from the east. They had the red scaly skin. We had to wear special suits to deal with the case. The woman insisted her baby was coming, so we lay her down and prepared. What she delivered looked less human than a clump of human parts, too deformed to call it boy or girl. More like a brown pod: arms and legs fused to the body. Its eyes opened, looked at me, and I had to turn away. The father said it was like others he'd seen born in the camps back east and he didn't feel ashamed, just lucky the mother got it out of her without killing her. Everyone was sick back east, he said.

Settling into my seat at the side of the court room, I watch an old man saunter up the aisle, leaning heavy on one crutch. This one is older than dirt, bringing a fair amount of it with him, a trail of dust following him up the aisle. He waves off help from the guard. I can't help but notice the man is missing a leg and an arm from the same side, his left, so his use of the crutch is awkward. He makes it to the witness chair, throws himself down with a thankful exhale. His right hand adjusts his collar, straightens his coat.

"Russell 'Rusty' Collins," Mr. Hitchens announces.

Murmuring erupts through the courtroom. Most people know the man's name if not his appearance.

Mr. Hitchens takes a moment, then addresses the man: "You've had dealings with these women, have you not?"

The man gives a curt nod, face remaining grim, mouth tight.

"Please tell us how you came to know these women at question." Mr. Hitchens keeps his voice soft, sympathetic.

The crusty old man coughs hard, has something to spit out, so the bailiff brings a spittoon over for him.

He starts to speak, stops, waves his hand as if asking for some time, then gives a nod that he's ready.

"Well, see, them and me – me and my boys – we got us a kinda game going between them and us. They like robbing banks, stealing cattle, such. So do me and my boys. We got into whatcha might call a *com-pe-ti-tion*, see. Them women steal stuff, then we steal it from them. It was a game for us, but they natural didn't take a liking to it. So some of the times they stole from us. Back and forth, see. They take from us, we take from them."

He grins at the judge but Judge Robinson shows no sympathy for the man, so he continues.

"They was some fine looking women, lemme tell ya." He grins to himself, thinking of them. "Thought we might work together, get a big score, see."

He checks with the judge, gets no reaction.

"Anyways, we didn't. Didn't do nothing."

That seems to satisfy the judge.

"You freely admit to previous crimes," says Mr. Hitchens to help speed things along. "You already have been tried and convicted of them. You sit here today as a witness, to give your testimony. We shouldn't judge you again for those crimes for which you have already received punishment."

"Punishment," Mr. Collins laughs, looks where his missing arm should be, only the shoulder joint remaining with a tied-off sleeve. His leg is similarly garbed: pant leg rolled up and pinned at his hip.

"Will you tell us how you came to lose your arm?" Mr. Hitchens asks. "And your leg."

Mr. Collins sits nonplussed, hand scratching at his uneven gray beard, like he tried to shave with one hand. Sitting in that chair, he knows why he is here. He must feel proud to tell the world his sad tale. At that moment, I recognize him: the man lured out of the Five Ladies and dragged by the rope that winter day.

"Well, like I said: we was playing a game: take and get taken." He inhales a long breath. "One day they didn't like us riding up on them, me and my boys, to take what they stole. Right angry with us, but we got the jump on them. That older one, she stewed and steamed, so I poked fun at her. That's the one named Trinity, the mean one. She got mouthy so I got my boys to pull her down from her horse, put her flat on the ground. She was kicking up a storm, see, so my boys held her down. I decide it's time to teach the bitch a lesson she never forget—"

The court roars with hatred for this man and Judge Robinson slams down the gavel. The judge cautions Mr. Hitchens to temper the testimony of his witness.

"Please keep your testimony as kind as possible," Mr. Hitchens says to Mr. Collins.

"Well, it ain't a kind story, as you know. Only one way to tell it. I'm gonna tell it straight out and then you can slap my wrist – my other wrist."

"Stick to the facts," Mr. Hitchens demands. "No descriptions."

"No description? But it all description. She got bitchy and we got her on the ground to make a lesson. I told my boys to turn her over, face down in the dirt, and they stood on her hands so she couldn't fight back. So I get behind her and I jerk her britches on down, got a good sight of them glorious buttocks and I showed her who's boss in this territory. I got on her and pushed myself in and she cursing me the whole time, and when I'm done told her there's more of that if she and her girly gang don't go somewhere else to do their criminal activities. So then, few months later—"

"You confess to sexual congress?" asks Mr. Hitchens.

"What's that?" Mr. Collins asks.

"You forced sex on her," Mr. Hitchens explains.

"Not on her. *In* her," says Mr. Collins. "It was covered in my trial. I said it already."

"And you were convicted of the crime?"

"There was witnesses." He looks over the court room crowd as if checking whether those people might be present. "It was one of my own sons turn me in. Got me arrested. That was after I got torn apart anyway. Deputy ask me what I did to make her treat me that way. So I told them. It came out, every bit of what I done to her. But that ain't the real crime, like you said. That ain't why I'm here today. You want me to tell what happened after, ain't that right?"

Mr. Hitchens mugs. "Yes, indeed. Go on."

"About six months later. Christmas Day. Never forget that day, no sir. Me and my boys was taking our holiday dinner in peace at the Five Ladies, see. She and her gang come to town. Trinity's who I mean. She and her sis barge into the saloon where me and my boys's having our dinner right peaceful-like. They pull guns on us. We play it cool, make a joke or two. Like how's she feeling? Does she gotta to ride side-saddle now? Them kinda jokes. She says to me: 'Came to see how you're doing'. Just like that. Friendly. Kinda took me by surprise."

Mr. Hitchens lifts a hand to pause him. "Who said?"

"That Trinity woman. Her that I got myself into that time."

"Go on. Use names."

"I tell her – Trinity – we're all doing fine, kinda sing-songy, and I laugh. But she shows me a mean face."

"What did she say to you then?"

"She ask what we doing later, like she's got plans for us. Maybe it's the big heist I been thinking of us doing." He turns awkwardly to the judge. "But we didn't do nothing."

"Then what happened?" Mr. Hitchens insists.

"I say to her me and my boys ain't going nowhere on account of being a holiday. I tell her go away but she gets mad – more mad – holds up her pistol, aims at the table in the corner where my boys are playing cards. And she fires at the table, knocks all the cards and chips and notes off the table into a big pile we gotta sort out later. Got my boys riled up, ready to shoot back. But I stand up straight and wave my hands at them – both hands, see – get them calmed down. I say to her 'What do you want?' Playing nice. And you know what she says? She says 'I want you.' Just like that. Soft voice like them ladies upstairs say. 'I want you.' Sound real sweet."

"She invited you somewhere?" asks Mr. Hitchens, leading the witness.

"Seem so," says Mr. Collins with a grin. "She says 'Let's do it again.' So I figure, enough time to think it over, maybe she does wanna do it again. Figure she's a type likes it rough. So I'm ready even though I only got half my holiday meal in my belly."

He stops suddenly, as if the feelings he had that day rushed back to him.

"Sorry. So.... Yeah. So I go on outside with her and her sis, and there's her gang, like I expect. One throws a noose over my head right off, jerks it tight, pulls me away behind her horse. They drag me down the street by that noose, right through the snow, and out of town, out to the chaparral, till there's no sight of town."

"Is this when you lost your arm and leg?" asks Mr. Hitchens as if he already knows the answer, turning to the audience.

"Yeah, so they get me on the ground and I ain't got no weapon, got it away from me when they noosed me. I figure they gonna beat me senseless to get back at me. But they got other ideas. That one with red hair, she held the rope tight while the others put ropes on my legs and my arms. I mean, they tried to do all four but one slipped loose, and one they didn't finish before I got up and tried to run. But they got on their horses quick and rode them in different directions. Two ropes failed, see. But other two didn't. And there I go, dragged across the ground while my arm goes one way and my leg goes other way. I'm bleeding out both but she puts a torch to them. One named Triss. You can probably still hear me screaming holy hell out that way, echoing forever."

"Trinity's gang tried to draw and quarter you?" Mr. Hitchens wants to confirm. "For what you did to Trinity. Is that correct?"

"Seem so. Never did say it clearly." Then he frowns.

"Yes?" asks Mr. Hitchens. "Is there more?"

"Well, see, after they fired my stumps, she gives my crotch a hard kick and that hurt the worst. I thought she's gonna shoot it away, but she only kicked me. Still's black and blue. Can't hardly pee with no pain—"

"You identified Trinity and her sister Triss," Mr. Hitchens says.

"They said if it wasn't for being so cold that day and me all froze up, I woulda bled out and died."

"Yes, fortunate," Mr. Hitchens continues. "Now, you said there were two other women. Was one of them Trina Culpepper, who sits in this court here today?"

He turns awkwardly, looks to the corner of the room, squints a while, then shakes his head.

"Not her. Wasn't one of them."

"Are you certain?" asks Mr. Duda, standing. "Take a closer look at her."

Mr. Collins turns again in his chair, stares at Trina. "They all look same to me. Except that blond on the roan."

"You acknowledge Trina was *not* one of them on that day when you were maimed. Correct?" asks Mr. Duda.

"There was Trinity, and the stupid sister, the redhead, and the blond. Like those four horsemen at the end of the world. Coming for me. Riding me down. Devil women. Still get night sweats if they come in my dreams. Never get a good night no more. But I got my punishment, like you was saying."

"And do you have animosity for them now?" asks Mr. Hitchens.

"Animosity? You mean hate? No sir. I'm at peace with all that. I live in the house for cripple folks, get my meals fixed for me, pretty girl to wash me, get to think of my final days."

"The court convicted you of the crime of sexual battery," said Mr. Hitchens, "but you spent no jail time. You paid no fine. Judge Young simply let you go free?"

"Well, he did do a whole lotta talking and, gotta admit, I didn't listen to all of it, just the part at the end when he told me I was free to go. Said I suffered enough. Like how could he measure that? See, I figure he understood I already paid for that crime fair enough. I paid with an arm and a leg. And that ain't no joke."

Mr. Hitchens grimaces. "No one is laughing, Mister Collins."

"So I went to see her hung. Had to take a look. Glad to be there. Front row. See her all twisting around, like laundry on a windy day. And she still looked mighty fine: those glorious buttocks of hers, and her chest, too. It was a handful. Couple handfuls, lemme tell ya. I was thinking: 'Bet I'm only one there who....' What's that word? *Congress?* 'Only one ever went to congress with her'."

"Mister Collins!" Judge Robinson shouts. "That's enough!"

+   +   +

Bart carried little Nicky against his chest, riding in the sling Trina made, walking alongside the broodmare who was happy to stroll at a leisurely pace if she had to walk at all. Trina sat atop the mare with Izzy squeezed between her belly and the saddlehorn, he often complaining. Mile after long mile, as though there were none to count but only a path that would never end.

And the clouds darkened or blew past, sun shining down hard, glaring like angels, mocking them, or dust came rolling in torrents around them, forcing them to shelter, faces against the mare's heft, or the wind cutting through them despite the meager clothing they wore. And the snow coming down, light at first, then piling up to ankles, and the camp they had to make too simple to protect them.

The boys fussed and cried, but Trina kept them as calm as she could. Bart sat under the tarp and brooded like an old man without any legs. He had a dream like that: being a man with no legs trying to run away from something terrible. He awoke screaming. Trina tried to soothe him, with Izzy questioning his pa's night cries. But she kept her eyes serious, always scanning the horizon for anything familiar, hoping for home, but not finding any landmarks after weeks of this walking, walking, walking.

They came upon an ancient road, once a stone path that steel sheep ran along. Now it lay broken, chunks of stone too rough for a horse to trod. Trina dismounted, led the mare across the obstacle as Bart guided the boys. She mounted again on the opposite side and continued over the prairie, the land flat as a sheet of paper, the sky above as wide as the world.

It was there that Trina, riding atop the reluctant mare, spied movement on the horizon.

"Riders," she called to Bart.

Brushing the snow dust off his sleeve, he put his hand up to his brow, scanned ahead.

"There," she directed.

He saw them: four horsemen, one after the other, galloping fast. In a flash he calculated they would meet. This road they were on cut across the road the horsemen were traveling. Fifty yards ahead, he measured. Better to hide, but there wasn't any place to hide on this flat plain with grass withered and snow laying everywhere.

"Better get ready," he said, meaning the guns.

A quick look around: a lonely tree far ahead, a crumpled barn to the left across a barren field, a bunch of trees beside it. That could be a good hideout. A line of rusted railway cars sitting forlornly on the tracks further away, grass grown up around them. Too far.

He pointed to the old barn, told Trina to head for it.

"Trinity!" she cried out instead.

Bart cautioned that her sister wouldn't likely be riding by on a random road this cold, snowy afternoon.

"No, it's her!" Trina practically laughed. "I know that rider."

She shouted again and the lead rider looked in the direction of the shout, pulled reins. A hand rose to slow the other horsemen.

"You sure?" Bart squinted at them, couldn't make out nothing.

"I know my sisters," Trina said.

"I just as soon meet my mama again than be with your sisters."

The four horsemen turned and came toward Bart and Trina, at a slow pace, still wary. Then the lead rider gave a big nod and wave of her hand, urged her mount to speed ahead.

They arrived in a cloud of snow dust, halting in a storm before the mare who balked at the arrival.

"Dammit, girl," said Trinity, jumping off her horse. She threw off her coat and wrapped it around Trina as they hugged. "Couldn't see ya. Ya look like some straggler from the east." She held Trina at arm's length to have a good look. "But is you!"

Trina tried to smile, but a tear fell down her cheek.

"Aw, what's a matter now?" asked Trinity, then glared at Bart. "That man been messing with ya? Cain't believe ya still with that poor boy."

"I ain't messing with her," Bart growled. He'd lowered Nicky to the ground but the boy stayed close, hugging his leg.

"Lookit ya," Trinity cried out. "Another kid."

"Yep," was all Trina said.

They danced together in their joy, and Trinity introduced Trina to the gang, the new members: Bonnie and Lulu.

"Don't I know you?" asked Bart of the blond woman.

"Ain't seen ya before," said Lulu gruffly.

"When we was kids," Bart pressed. "Willow-something. When my mama brought me out west here from the capital. She made me say hello to some girls my age."

"Oooh, yeeeah," said Lulu. "I remember now. You had really red hair back then. Not so much now. So how's yer mama these days?"

Bart blanched, stiffened. "Ain't seen her for years."

"Oh, yeah," said Lulu as the sisters chatted excitedly. "They been talking about you. For a while now. Folks said you were dead. Said you went on a posse and got shot dead."

"Got shot," he said, smiling from ear to ear. "Didn't get dead."

"Hey, boy!" Trina barked. "Gotcher woman right here."

Bart grinned. "That's my woman, yup. Trina and me got a son. That other boy there is extra. But he's mine."

"Well, I'm not interested in a man anyways," said Lulu. "Just saying 'hey' like they do in social circles. My sister – remember Andrea? She got married and it's a whole lotta trouble. Her and that no-good husband always scrapping."

Bart had to grin at that news, taking him back to when he first arrived in Skinner Canyon.

"I never woulda thought you be taking up outlaw life," he said. He thumbed back at Trinity. "Running with her gonna get you in a heap of trouble. I know about that. Sure do."

"Mother is soooo strict," said Lulu excitedly. "Fixing me up with 'eligible' cowpokes. I hated that. I can ride better than any of them. Shoot better, too. But Mother wants a proper daughter...."

"Just gotta find a good man," said Bart. "See them boys? Well, they're mine. I'm good at making sons, just sayin'."

"Damn you!" Trinity shouted at him. "Leave her be."

"We just took care of some business back near town," said Lulu with an awkward chuckle. "Up that road is Skinner Canyon. That where you heading?"

Bonnie, the redhead, chimed in with her account of it. A mean old man who had tricked them too many times got his payback, and they laughed at the story. Bonnie made disparaging remarks about the man, then stared hard at Bart.

"I ain't do none of that stuff," he said like his mama scolded him. "I'm a good man. You ask Trina."

But they didn't ask her.

"Where ya head?" Trinity asked her instead.

Before Trina could speak, Bart answered:

"Thinking to try the old camp. Up in the hills. But I know it's far from here. Guess we was lost."

"That place got messed up," said Triss. "Got lotsa snakes there now. Everywhere. Counted fifty of 'em."

"We got a new place," said Trinity, narrowing her eyes, deciding to trust him. "Down south a ways. Old farmstead. People think it's abandoned. But we make it home."

Trina started to tell her about the house on the ridge, but Bart said to save it for later. Plenty of time for stories. They needed to get to shelter as the wind was picking up, the boys shivering.

Trina agreed, and the four horsemen led the way: Trinity, then Triss with Izzy riding with her, Trina on the broodmare with Nicky in his sling against her chest. Bonnie wouldn't let Bart join her, but Lulu managed to fit Bart on her horse, joking they were lovers. The horse balked at the extra weight.

38

FIVE SENSES

MR. DUDA GETS UP and hands a piece of paper he's been writing on over to Judge Robinson, then turns valiantly to the crowded court room, waits a moment for the murmuring to cease.

"My esteemed colleague, Mister Hitchens, has assailed all of you with a plethora of witnesses, a fair number of them of questionable reputation, yet each brought in to tell their stories. You have *heard* of crimes alleged, some convictions, and lurid descriptions of events at which my client, Miss Trina Culpepper, was never present or if present never acted in a criminal manner. Indeed, you have *seen* an unsavory assortment of characters ramble up the aisle to gain your sympathy. You *felt* their misery. You could *taste* the anguish in their voices like bile spit up into the back of their throats, even *smelled* the fear that clings to their garments like old sweat. Yet you have not, I am certain, been able to place the defendant at the scene of a crime, much less as a perpetrator of such crimes."

Mr. Duda turns to gaze at Trina, sitting on the hard chair in the front corner of the room between two tall guards. She wears the flower-print dress I gave her. She looks pretty although she never smiles, lets her plain tan face and dark brown hair make the case for her: being a half-breed, she must be guilty. Guilty of something to most in the room.

Judge Robinson speaks next, aiming his words at Mr. Hitchens.

"It seems you have been unable to connect this woman to the other women's crimes. Although she may have been present or been a member of that gang, no one here has testified to seeing her shoot anyone. However, as a member of such a group, she is affiliated with the crimes committed by the group, such as robbery and thieving, even to murders. For that association she may yet deserve a certain degree of punishment."

But the judge shakes his head, thinking a moment. Coming to a conclusion, he turns to speak to Trina.

"Miss Culpepper, where have you been these past years?"

She doesn't know what to do, then decides to stand. The guards shuffle into new positions on either side of their short hostage.

Then she looks the judge straight in the eyes and speaks calmly in her naturally soft voice.

"We rode out west. Saw some things. Found a place to make a homestead."

She seems to be thinking of more worth saying when the judge continues.

"Why then did you return?"

She takes a breath. "Things got hard. Got dangerous." She tells about what she's seen along the way. She tells of an underground city full of science people planning for a new world. But they had to escape. They? Who's that? So she says she was with Bad Bart, the Red Devil. Just standard folks trying to make a life for themselves. But life underground wasn't anything she wanted to write home about, nobody to write to anyway.

They escaped in a motor carriage that got its power from the sunshine through boards on the top of it.

"She's clearly a liar," cries Mr. Hitchens. "Nobody's seen a motor carriage for decades. No more fuel for them."

"Got power from sunshine," she repeats. "Rode back here in one. Most of the way. 'Til got cloudy and power run down to nothing. Then we crashed, had to walk the rest of the way."

"But why did you decide to return?" the judge asks again.

"We got us a homestead. Nice house, abandoned like the rest. Nobody living out that way, far west. Over the mountains, in the desert. Towns left empty. Cities lookin' like they got a bomb hit 'em. Thousands dead. People in the underground city said the air was poison but we breathe it just fine. But they got weird animals they put together in their laboratories, like a hell-cat, lookin' like a panther but with a face of a woman. Killed a few. Not good to eat, anyhow."

She tells of the Mexi army moving north, of the cult of the folks in Orna. What's that? Caliph Orna, out by the coast. By an ocean. Bart wanted to see it but an old man in white robe who came by looking for food told him there wasn't anything worth seeing there. It was all destroyed. Then Mexi soldiers attacked the homestead, the house burned down, and they had to flee. It was a long, hard trip returning to this territory.

Her story is told in simple words but the court remains silent during it, everyone straining to hear her small voice.

Mr. Hitchens stands to argue against her. "Nobody? There are no people out there? I find that hard to believe. Should be at least some tribals wandering about. Not in that wide open land? Gone, you say? Gone to other territories, or else died? Then where are the bodies? Let's say wild animals ate them. The bones should remain. If they died of the plague, bones would also remain. Where are the bodies?"

"Please, Mister Hitchens," the judge calls, "constrain yourself."

"But she has only fabulous tales to tell. Nothing more. Playing on the heart strings of the court. These are not facts."

Judge Robinson glares at him. "All these stories your witnesses have told are just that: stories. Not facts."

Apparently frustrated, Mr. Hitchens turns to Trina. "Nobody? There are no people anywhere?"

Trina, surprised by his attack, freezes. She shakes her head.

"Nobody?" he accuses her. "Where did they all go?"

"Don't know. Gone. Ain't gotta answer no question shout at me."

"This is a court of law," says the judge. "You must answer all questions put to you."

"Nothing there out west – west o' them mountains. Not tribals. Maybe survivor or two gettin' by on scraps an' luck. Most it's Mexi soldiers patrollin' the roads. Them an' any Slammers they meet, get into fightin'."

"Slammers, again!" cries Mr. Hitchens. "What are those?"

"They's folks wear white robes, white headdresses, be prayin' to different gods. Met one o' them, said they follow three brothers. The Perez Brothers. Brought religion back from the far east somewhere an' it spread across that territory out west. Y'all best be on lookout fer 'em. They comin'."

Mr. Hitchens glances at the judge, then at Trina. "How about you? Did you convert? Are you one of them?"

"Ain't done nothin' like that."

Mr. Hitchens stands stiffly, asserts his authority. "And to whom do you pray?"

"Ain't pray to nobody. Don't listen, no ways. Got some wishes but none o' them hear me."

A few chuckles from the audience. The Judge rises a bit, staring them to silence, sits again.

"Where would everyone go?" Mr. Hitchens ponders. "You say whole cities emptied. Left to crumble. How could that happen?"

"Don't know," says Trina, repressing a yawn, just waiting for it to end. "Maybe somebody don't want no folks around."

"Somebody?" asks Mr. Hitchens. "Who? Our government? Why would they want that? No people to run things, to make things we need, everyday things. To sit in offices or stand in factories. Why would our government want to get rid of people?" A thought comes to him. "It isn't like before, with the plague a century ago. Not like that. Releasing a virus that killed half the population...."

"Ain't got no ideas 'bout that. Just sayin' what I seen. Nobody was livin' out that way. Don't know why. But they gone."

"Are you saying that the government – our fine government – deliberately eliminated hundreds of thousands of people from the cities west of the mountains?"

"I's sayin' din't see nobody west o' them mountains. None at all. A few Mexi soldiers, a few Slammers is all. An' a hundred science folks livin' underground in a city they made." She grins a moment. "They thinkin' nobody livin' up top because air was poison. Kinda surprise we show up an' ain't dead. Had to live with 'em a year an' half b'fore we escaped. Drove right off in one them electro jeep things like I said b'fore—"

THE GRANDSONS

"More fanciful tales!" cries Mr. Hitchens. "*Jeep?* What's that?"

Mr. Duda sits smugly as his opponent rages.

"What they call that machine," Trina replies firmly. "Figure it's made by Cherokee tribe. They name it *Grand Cherokee*. But it done ended, stopped after while. All th' electric used up."

"There are no Cherokee out west," Mr. Hitchens declares. "None this side of Okala territory."

Trina clears her throat. "Don't care if a plague killt ever'body out west. Not back east, neither. Folks in that underground city sayin' mostly truth. Said folks over the ocean there sent rockets to the cities on th' east side, blew up them cities. Said folks in them east cities sent rockets back over to them, too, so it's done now. No more cities. Not east o' them Apple-chan mountains. None o' them folks complainin' 'bout ever'thin'. But them rocket systems run down, nobody left to push buttons, so more rockets blow up but don't fly up to the sky. They spread the death through the cities of the plain over there on the coast. Prolly what y'all bin seein', what y'all call the Glow. Just them cities on fire."

The gossipy court crowd falls silent. The judge turns to her. Mr. Hitchens drops his hands to his sides and Mr. Duda sits up in his chair. Trina looks out over the audience, her eyes settling on the far wall where hung a portrait of President Grumman.

"Don't care if a plague took out ever'one in th' east," she says, promptly resuming her seat. "Don't make a hill o' beans fer me."

The room remains silent.

"That may be the best we can do," says Judge Robinson in his weary voice. "Most reasonable explanation I've yet heard. However, it is not a part of this trial. I think we have heard enough."

Mr. Duda has a smile on his face but tries to hide it.

"Very well, Your Honor," says Mr. Hitchens.

The judge regards Mr. Duda, who gives a firm nod.

Leaning forward, Judge Robinson surveys the people in the court room as though gaining their consensus. He glances down at those papers before him, then looks over at Trina.

With that official look, the guards urge her to stand again.

"Given all we have heard," Judge Robinson begins, "I can see

499

nothing that would warrant a conviction sufficient to order you to a sentence in a penitentiary. However, there appears to be enough to tie you to an assortment of crimes perpetrated by your sisters and others in their outlaw gang. For any of those matters, of which we may never know for certain, there must be a ruling."

He shakes his head, glancing again at the papers before him.

"I will sentence you to a probation of five years," he speaks out in a clear voice over the court's chattering. "The conditions will be set and if you should break any of them, any at all, Miss Culpepper, I shall have no choice but to order you to the penitentiary with these five years to commence from the start. Do you understand what I'm saying, Miss Culpepper?"

Trina purses her lips, then: "I unnerstand ya. Ain't gonna do no crimes here anyways." She pauses, thinking, regards the audience. "Doctor Jake says I gotta baby to take care of."

I sit up sharply as eyes turn to me. *What did she say?*

"You're with child?" asks the judge, eyebrows raised.

The court crowd's murmuring rises. I see Cal shake his head, not believing it. Or maybe he regrets not telling the judge.

"Doctor Jake said it." A small smile appears. "Oh, he ain't the papa. Just he told me it's likely cuz me spittin' up every morn."

"Then who, may we ask, is the father?" asks the judge. "Or do you know for certain?"

A grin plays on her face. "Don't really matter now, do it?"

Mr. Duda jumps up. "What she means is—"

The judge waves him to sit. "I suppose it doesn't. We welcome all new members to our community. It's difficult enough in these dark times keeping a community growing, to find those who can conceive at all, then birth a new life that may one day improve our lot. We are thankful for each of them."

He studies her a moment. The court studies her, measuring her figure, calculating if it could be true.

"I ask about the father," the judge continues, "only to ascertain that the union was consensual."

"It was," she answers, her face plain as ever. "It surely was."

Judge Robinson looks down at his papers one last time, reads for a minute, then regards Trina. It must be a list of questions.

"One final question: Do you know who shot Bad Bart?"

The court murmurs; this is what they want to know.

"Don't know," she replies with no hesitation. "Maybe a band of tribals. Thinkin' he take me fer a slave, wanna set me free. Hard to say fer shore. I was ridin' to meet up with 'im."

The judge seems puzzled. "You found him already dead?"

Her eyebrows slide together, her head tilts a bit, thinking. But I recognize the signs of a lie about to be told. She's concocting words that will sound truthful.

"He was...." She acts like she's upset by the memory, but I don't believe her. "Yep, shot already. Wounded but alive. Said it's best if I bring him to town. Let him get buried where his mama can pray over him. Told me might as well dig up his uncle an' bring him, too. Let 'em get put in the ground side by side. That's what he told me an' it's what I done. Then I get put in this trial. Ain't got my reward yet, an' a fresh horse, neither."

+ + +

The house Trinity led them to was half broken down, roof slumping, so they had to bend down to go in through a side door, into a room empty but for some blankets and a few sacks of things they stole. Someone lit a candle, set the holder on the bare wooden floor. No fireplace or somebody might notice.

The women gathered around the candle, sitting on the floor, too eagerly chatting about their adventures.

Bart let them talk, unconcerned what they said. Women always did that. The boys stayed with him, outside of the circle.

"This house is a dump," said Bart after a while, looking around the room. It was worse than the house they found on the ridge. He knew he wouldn't be comfortable here.

"We ain't princesses, boy. Don't need no fancy castle," Trinity said to him. "Anyways, it's only for a while. Nobody look for us here. We can stay the winter. Then we'll find another place. Maybe go south and east. Over by Woodward. That's where Triss's lover boy lives."

"He ain't my lover boy," Triss snickered.

"Maybe we can get jobs working for Mister Clayborne again," red-haired Bonnie spoke up.

"And what's that?" asked Trina.

"It ain't much," said Trinity. "He hires us to collect fees farmers owe him. We get a cut of what we take."

"It's enough to get by," said Lulu, looking at Bart.

"Least it ain't no criminal act," Triss laughed.

They continued to talk about crimes they'd committed during the years he and Trina were away. The list was impressive. Good enough for a bounty being put on Trinity.

"And that bastard Collins," said Bonnie. "That there's gonna get you raised again."

"Don't care for no bounty," Trinity responded. "He deserved all what he got, no question."

They talked on about the crime they'd committed right before meeting up with them on the road. He saw the bloody gloves Trinity pulled off, tossed in the corner. He listened to their talk, endured the insults, their hatred of men. He didn't want his boys to grow up with that talk in their heads, so he looked around for another room to go to but the ceiling had sunk so low he had to crawl to move around anywhere.

After a while, Trinity got up, went to a cabinet in the next room, what looked like a kitchen, and returned with some food laid on a plate, set the plate on the floor, and the women grabbed at it. Just jerky and some beans in a sauce. They ate with their fingers, licked them off. None was offered to Bart and the boys.

"This here's women's space," Trinity announced when she spied him looking forlorn in the shadowy corner. "Men go outside, out to the barn."

He was getting angry, hating this situation. Trina would glance at him once in a while to make sure he was still there. She told her sister to leave him be, that he was one of the good men. That only made the women roar with laughter.

"Pa," Izzy spoke with a tug of Bart's shirt, saving him from any further anger. "Nicky go poopy."

He called Trina, but she told him he could take care of it. They still had a few cloths left in the bag they'd been carrying forever.

Taking Nicky out to the barn, Bart studied the stars overhead. He cleaned his son's bottom, wrapped a fresh cloth around him. He slipped the boy back inside the shirt that served as his uniform.

Inside the barn, which had an even lower hanging roof than the house, he discovered a hutch of mice. This wasn't going to be a place to sleep. It wouldn't be the 'men's space' they told him it was. This was only the start of what he expected would get worse day by day now that the sisters were back together again.

Crawling over the nasty straw, he found the coil of rope, half blood-stained. He saw what looked like bits of flesh on it, sheered off by the roughness of the rope. Bonnie had tossed the rope into the open doorway as the women went to the house. Just what crime had they committed before the big reunion on the road?

He took the boys into the house but he paused in the doorway, listening to the women talking.

"He likes the blonds. That I know," Trina said. "There's a blond woman in that underground city. She's Nicky's mama. See, they was doin' 'speriments. Had to do it, Bart and her. Me, too. Made us. But me an' my partner, we didn't get no success."

"What happened to her?" asked Lulu. "You didn't bring her with you? Sure, I can understand. Kinda awkward."

"We tried," said Trina, then her voice ran dry. She swallowed a few times. "She got killt in the fire. That was the house we had out west there. Up on a ridge. It was kinda—"

"Oh, that's horrible," said Bonnie.

"Sad," said Lulu, shaking her head.

Trina recovered. "So if he ever come at ya, ya tell me."

"I can handle myself," Lulu said with a snort.

"If it come to it," Trinity said, "I'll let you pull the rope."

Bart guessed she meant Trina. But he wouldn't ever.... Maybe, if she acted bad, he might get rough with her. He could imagine it. But he didn't want that. He only wanted to get them away from these bad women. He had to take Trina away to where they could have a good home, live a standard life.

"Took care of some business," Trinity was saying when he broke away from his thoughts. "That man weren't playing fair. Now he for sure know the game. Know what we do to men like him. Take an arm and a leg." She burst into laughter the others quickly shared.

Bart had to speak up. "You what?"

"Took off his arm and leg," Trinity repeated in a flat voice.

"*What?*" he demanded. "How can you be so...so cruel?"

"Cruel?" Trinity asked. Her face appeared to redden in the glow of the candle. "When d'you get so soft, boy? Thought you's one of us. We did crimes together. And I'll say you did fair at it."

Trina waved her to stop. "Out west things are different."

"Ain't so different," said Trinity. "Men against women. Women against men. And that one sure had it coming."

"Still got some civil'zation out west," said Trina, and Bart felt proud of her for speaking up. "Bart did good. Most times."

"But you said you lived underground," said Bonnie.

"That's true," Trina said. "It was a nice place, clean and safe. But too strict. And Bart, he got with that science woman."

"Those experiments you said before?" asked Bonnie.

"Yeah, all scientist-like," said Trina, sadness in her voice. "Seem all them scientist folk like is their 'speriments. But she push out that boy over there. Now we take care o' him."

That stopped the chatter and they turned to gaze at Nicky, the boy with the blond curls.

"He is kinda cute," said Lulu.

"Underground, hmm?" Trinity quizzed. "Kinda make sense. But I heard them kinda women turn a man soft. Easy life. No hard work to keep 'em fit and ready. Science men are like that, too."

"Ready for what?" Bart asked.

Trinity laughed. "Ready for taking care them babies."

Bart burned with anger as Izzy hung on his shoulder and Nicky sat in his lap. This was supposed to be for the women. But he dared not let out his thoughts to Trinity. Better to let her go on – and when they were outside, when the time was right, they could have it out, settle it once and for all who was stronger, no matter that Trinity was older. He could beat her in a fight, he was certain. And there was always his pistol. Could be an accident. Look like an accident anyway.

In the days that followed, Bart kept to himself. He made plans for leaving. If he had to, he would ride off on the broodmare with his sons, leave Trina behind if she refused to go with them. He had no idea where he would go, but if he rode far enough there would be a town where nobody knew him. Settle in with Trina, if she joined them. Then he'd find standard work and get paid notes, put them in a bank and hope no gang robbed it.

Trinity kept after him, though, prodding him with her words, or giving him a push or a pat to let him know he was only a pet. He hated it but kept calm, stayed silent. Time would heal the wounds, he knew. Trina would see how her sister treated him and soon she'd have to decide who to go with. He felt sure she would join him and their sons over Trinity. Triss didn't hardly matter, always taking Trinity's side. He'd let her stay with Trinity, no loss, but she could come with them if she wanted to.

One day, as winter hinted at spring, the sun bright overhead, snow mostly melted except where shade covered it along the barn, Trinity pushed him again: gave his shoulder a pat, but it was more of a shove, like a get-outta-my-way kind of push.

Bart spun around with his face taut and red. Trinity laughed at that display.

"Stop!" Trina shouted at them from across the yard.

Bart had made a fist, cursing under his breath.

"What ya got to say, boy?" Trinity teased.

Bart shoved her back, put both hands to her chest and heaved her so she stumbled and fell on her bottom.

"Whoa," she said, picking herself up and brushing off her pants.

Bart held his stance, fists up for a fight.

"Ya gonna fight a woman?" She took a fighting stance. "That what *your mama* taught you?"

He swung at her, caught her arm. Trinity punched back, landed on his jaw. He shook it off and swung at her again, hit her breast, saw that it hurt. She recovered and punched at his belly, landed, and he bent over. She punched upward, hit his jaw, stretched him out.

He got up, checking his jaw, determined to go on. But then he dropped to a knee, breathing hard. He stood up slowly, arms at his sides, shaking his hands against his hips.

"That's some man ya got there, Trin'. Can't beat a woman."

"I gave up...." Bart fought to catch his breath. "*Because* you're a woman. Ain't s'posed to hurt women. And I never did. Not 'til now. Cuz you deserve a beating."

He thought Trina would come to him, praise him for stopping or curse him for fighting her sister. But she continued her work.

Later, when he tried to lay beside her on the floor in that fallen house, she wouldn't let him snuggle with her. He thought she must not want her sisters to see her give in to him. Didn't matter. Once the snows melted and the muddy roads dried up they were out of this place.

"Why didn't you take my side?" he asked in a whisper.

"Ya need me to take yer side?" Trina questioned.

"It would be good."

"Yeah, would." And she said no more.

39

Six Months Gone By

I CATCH UP TO TRINA as she's led to the hotel where she's been staying for the trial. Thinking she's free now, I wonder why she has an escort. I call her name and she halts at the landing, the guards pausing with her.

She looks at me as though she's trying to remember my name, which hurts a little after all I've done for her.

"Jake," I say to ease her mind. "Or Jacob. Jacob Baumann. The dentist. And other odd jobs."

Then she grins, thinking what to say, then: "Thanks, Jake."

I want to sweep her into my arms, being so glad that awful trial, a circus at best, is finally over and she is free. But she isn't a woman to show affection easily. She rarely smiles.

"You're going back to your room?" I ask, a dumb thing to say but I'm flustered, want to say something.

"Gotta pick up my things," she says. "Gotta clear out. Give the room to some payin' guest."

"Yes, I suppose that's true."

"Gonna move to the jailhouse for tonight."

"The jail? They can't make you stay in the jail."

"Not in no cell," she says. "Lay on a bench. Ain't so bad."

Then I have a brilliant idea: "Why don't you stay with me?" That sounds too bold and her guards chuckle. "I mean, you can stay at my place and I'll stay over in the clinic. I can sleep there. I'm over there half the nights anyway. You'll be more comfortable in my room."

"That sound kinda good. Sleepin' in a proper place."

"The toilet is out back, however."

She grimaces like it's a deal-breaker. "Gotta get up to that room right now, ya don't mind, use that toilet in the room one last go, if ya don't mind."

I blanche. "Oh, yes. Certainly. Pardons. Sorry."

"Nothin' to be sorry for," she says with a grin I can't read.

"Well, you come over the jailhouse whenever you're ready and I'll take you to my place. Or...you probably need some supper first."

"See ya there," she says, then points to the clock on the church tower at the end of the street, "when that there short arrow point to the V-I and the long arrow point to the X-I-I."

I hurry back to my place to clean it, put away old clothes, take a cloth to the surfaces, then change the sheet on the bed. Never had a woman visit me here. It's always been too embarrassing for a guest. I have to get a better place. But this isn't like that, I remind myself. I am doing a good deed. That's all.

Deputy Cal's got some choice words for me when I show up at the jailhouse to meet Trina. He says he thinks she did it. Did what? Shot Bad Bart, he says. But I'm not concerned with that at all. He's just digging at me. Besides, Bart's dead after fifteen years of being away and already presumed dead, going on that posse to hunt down my mother's killers. And Trina reminds me of my mother with her dark hair and tan skin. About the same age my Mama was, too.

I'm in fresh clothes, my best outfit short of the medical suit that impresses patients. Just a good deed, I remind myself.

Then she arrives, wearing a different dress, something dark and matronly and she looks ten years older than me. Perhaps that's for the best. We aren't that way, of course, can't get into that kind of relationship.

"Jake," she says like a greeting.

"Ready to go?" I ask. Of course, she's ready. Dumb. But I wave her out of the jailhouse. I carry her bag, not too heavy.

I take Trina over to the Canyon Diner, but we see Mr. Duda and Mr. Hitchens having a toast, saying better luck next time.

After offering a few unsatisfactory suggestions, we go back to the hotel, sheepishly, the best place to get a meal that's not in a saloon. The men in the Five Ladies wouldn't ever let us eat in peace. They would curse at her and tease me.

"Back for more, eh?" says the hotel owner's grown daughter like she suspects something is up between Trina and me.

"Just supper," I say.

We sit in the dining room and our dinners eventually arrive: a couple of t-bone steaks with fried potatoes and greens. She eats with enthusiasm, like she hasn't had much the past few weeks. I'm happy she enjoys the food. I try to be polite, let her eat in silence. But I do ask a few questions just so I don't seem dull. A glass of beer helps me sound less nervous.

"What will you do now?" I ask between bites.

She looks up at me, chewing, her mouth moving wildly, not like proper ladies do. She spits out some gristle.

"Dunno," she gets out, continues chewing.

"I mean, you came to town to deliver...those packages." I choose my words carefully. "You must've had plans for after that. I mean, for when you left town. Where were you planning to go?"

She sits back, tongue running over her teeth.

"If you don't want to talk about it, I'll understand."

"Ain't nothin' to unnerstand," she says. "Goin' home, is all." Then, after a minute: "Back to where I come from."

"You have a house there?" I ask stupidly.

"Not my house, but yeah."

"Oh, so you live with someone." Now I worry, wonder what kind of arrangements she may have. I thought she was with Bart. Maybe she's married to someone else.

"Yeah, My sister." She grins like it's been a secret for a while and she's glad to let it out. "Gotta get back to my boys."

"Your boys?"

"My sons."

"Sons? With Bart?"

"One is. Th' other ain't. I mean, he's Bart's but ain't mine."

I'm not sure what to think. There must be a long story behind it. She kept it hidden all through the trial.

"So you'll return to them. That's good. I wish you a safe journey."

"Not too safe," she says with more breath. "Judge says I cain't leave the county or they gonna arrest me again, like he said they would, put me in that there penitentiary."

"So that place is outside the county? May I ask where?"

"They staying with my sister and.... She got this man she likes to fool 'round with. But she care for my boys. Need to go back soon as I can. She gonna worry."

"Can she bring them here? Your boys?"

"If she know to do it. How anybody gonna tell her?"

I have to nod, feeling awkward. Maybe I could go there and bring her boys back here. It's a thought.

"Well, I could go get them for you, if you want. Happy to."

She seems struck at first, then shakes her head. "Don't want 'em here. Not with them men knowin' they mine."

"Yes, I see. It could be difficult for them. And for you. This town is getting worse every year."

"Ya shore don't wanna get wrap up with them folks, Jake. Triss can be kinda rough. And stupid, too. Real stupid sometime. You's a kindly kinda fella. Better not let them know about ya."

"I can handle myself. I grew up with Bart, after all. Learned to ride and shoot with him. Yes, I haven't been shooting much the past fifteen years. Not much riding either. I never have to go far. Maybe over to a farm somewhere to treat a wounded cowpoke."

"Ya shore are a good man, Jake," she says, sounding like Maggie. She offers a vague smile, but it's likely only the play of the chandelier lights overhead.

"Thanks," I mutter. Then I think of something clearly wrong to say, but I go ahead and say it anyway: "It's truly sad what happened to your sister."

"Sister?" she asks, eyes narrowed.

"I mean Trinity. It wasn't fair what happened to her."

+   +   +

The mare had lain quiet for so long Bart thought she must've died, but then the foal appeared. Over the next hours the mare pushed, with Bart helping direct the hooves of the newborn, and out came the foal into the straw of the corral's open hut. The barn was too dirty, but the weather had turned warm as spring arrived.

"You got any names in mind?" he asked Trina as a joke.

"She looks a might unhappy," she responded.

"Like your sister?" Bart teased, but Trina gave him the look that always set him in his place. No joking about Trinity.

"Call her Marina, if ya like," said Trina at last.

He shook his head. "Not like we'll be here when she grows up."

"Where we goin'?"

"Away from here, that's for sure."

"Ain't fer shore," she countered.

"Need to be on our own. Live on our own terms."

She didn't respond, keeping at her stitching.

Later, Trinity and the other women rode back, cheering their latest take. They chattered about how stupid the folks were, how easy the score. They showed things they took besides bank notes. It was becoming a weekly routine now that winter ended.

One of those raids, the women grabbed some clothing, presented it to Trina when they returned. New leather pants and a vest, black shirt like the men wear. Trina put them on immediately and posed, got their admiration. Trina showed her outfit to Bart who tried to be happy for her. He missed seeing her in a dress, looking pretty and motherly.

"Here, boy," shouted Trinity, off her horse and storming into the house. "Get these washed up."

He almost didn't catch the gloves and a shirt she tossed at him.

"I ain't your maid," he shouted back.

"Make yerself useful, boy," she said, going into the house.

That was all he did, just like back in their first camp among the rocks, when they found him wounded and weak. They let him help around the camp. He cooked and cleaned for them. And they let him grow up, become a man who robbed and raided with them. He got a reputation riding with them: the Red Devil.

Now it was like he'd gone back ten years, doing the same things.

He hated it. He hated more how Trinity treated him, like he hadn't been the man, leading a family across the wilderness, making sons, and shooting anyone that tried to harm them. He stewed after her remark, anger boiling inside. Have to get out of here, he decided.

Another day he heard one of the women humming a tune. He crawled into the main room, found it was Lulu sitting on the floor as she mended holes in her stockings. They'd run thin at the heels the way she wore her boots.

"What's that?" he asked her, then noticed Izzy behind him, with Nicky crawling like a frisky pup.

"Don't know," she said, continuing her sewing. "Just some song I know. Heard it a lot when I was growing up." She paused the needle to think about it. "You know it?"

"Sounds like a song my mama made up." He was curious more than disturbed at hearing it. "Do more."

She hummed the tune again. "You know it?"

"My mama wrote music," he said, his voice sad. "It was like her job. And when I was real little she conducted the orchestra in the capital."

"In the capital?" Lulu smiled big, impressed. "It's true? Then she must be famous."

"S'pose. But that song.... It's from her *opera*. One she started working on after we moved out here."

"Opera? What's that?"

He tried to explain but gave up. A bunch of songs that together tell a story was the best he could do.

"She called it *The Way of the Son*, said it was based on what her great-great-grandfather wrote down in a notebook or two all about their adventures during the Great Pandemic, like finding a forest to hide in."

"I bet it's a good story," she said, smiling at him.

"Yep." He looked inward, found his mama's face there, mouth forming words meant to soothe him. He heard a new tune playing, but it wasn't Lulu's humming. It was the full orchestra, right there in his head.

"Hey, y'okay?" she interrupted.

He broke out of his trance, shaking his head. Damn memories always sticking to you. Can't never wash them away.

"You ever see your mama?" she asked, looking down like she had no right to ask such a question. "She's still living, you know. Right in that big house. Does she know you're back?"

He chewed his lip. "Ain't back. Prolly thinks I'm dead. Like all them do. But don'tcha go telling her."

"Folks don't think you the same as the Red Devil?"

"Guess not. I was only fifteen when I left. And nobody found me so they all think I died out there."

"But ya didn't." She chuckled. "Won't she be surprised you show up some morning, huh?"

"Don't matter. It's her business, not mine." He brooded a while, wondering how it would be if he did show up at his mama's house. She might faint dead away seeing him grown up. That made him grin. "You know she tried to get me to play my aunt's cornet?"

"Yeah, I know. I remember hearing you playing it. You can hear that thing for miles. Need a couple more miles between our houses, ain't that right?"

They laughed at that. "Kinda wish I had it here. Something to do when I'm stuck here doing all the women's work."

"Ain't women's work," said Lulu, turning harsh. "It's just work."

"Sorry. But I'm a man, ya know. I should be riding with them on their scores. Like I did before."

"Trinity says you'll get recognized. People know you. That red hair, red beard ya got. They got posters of you everywhere. You and Trina. I think you must be famous – what they call *notorious*. You go in town and they gonna see you and lock you up."

"Don't they know Trinity and Triss?" he asked, finding a fox hole to probe. "No bounty posters for them?"

"Oh, they got 'em. Trinity's got a high number. Gonna draw lots of bounty hunters."

"Then how they keep getting away with their scores?"

"They got their tricks." She sat up suddenly, smiling right at him. "They dress up in old lady clothes, and nobody know them that way. Go in and get what they want. I mean at shops. Not banks."

"Ah," he gasped. That explained the dresses and shawls he was always asked to wash. He never saw them wearing the clothes around the farm. They were like Sunday clothes. Nobody gonna think these old ladies would rob a bank.

When he went to do his tasks, he noted the blood stains on the shirt. He thought of what Trinity told Trina after the score. Triss lay her down and fixed a scrape she got from a bullet brushing her side. It bled as they rode back. But no way to scrub out blood stains with only rough lye soap.

He complained again about not being allowed to join them.

"Got yer face on posters at jails in three towns," Trinity said. "Trina, too. Got bounties on both ya. They remember ya. Either o' ya get seen, they gonna lock y'all up."

Bart had to complain more. He offered to shave off his red beard, color his hair – even shave it off, too. Anything to get to ride into a town and snatch notes like they did in the old days.

But he and Trinity came to a head every time, ready to fight.

"Settle down, you two!" Trina would have to shout.

Most days were full of fuming and muttered curses between the two of them. Bart insisted he and Trina and the boys had to leave, and spring was as good a time for travel as any season. Getting into summer would make them face dust storms and tornadoes, plus the unbearable heat.

When Triss rode off again, saying she was headed to her second home, the homestead where her *beau* lived, Bart thought of sending Trina and the boys with her. Triss refused. It was her trip, her time to be with her beau, a man named Riley who was a decent farmer. He'd lost his wife to illness but kept up the farm hoping to meet another woman willing to be his wife. Triss met him in town, had some fun, and she went back with him to the farm. He was a lonely man but fair and handsome, she told them. Triss could see herself as his woman, though she knew nothing about being a farmer's wife. It was mostly pure lust and in these desperate times that was good enough. She always returned with a big grin on her face. Trinity teased her, kept pushing her.

Like Trinity did to Bart.

He found those gloves again, stuffed behind the pile of clothes he had to wash. The gloves with the blood stains. Never did get any explanation. Robberies didn't usually cause blood to get on gloves, so it had to be something else. He thought back to the first time he saw them, when they met again after five years apart. The women were returning from some crime, quite pleased with themselves.

"What did they do?" he asked Trina who shook her head.

"Never said," she told him but he could see the lie on her face.

"They must've told *you*," he insisted. "You're their sister."

She wouldn't say anything.

So he rode into the nearest town, beard shaved off, acting like a poor cowpoke looking for work. People seemed happy there, unafraid of everything he'd suffered through. Robberies? None to speak of. A few teen boys getting into mischief. But that's standard. Bank looks secure. Ain't had a robbery in six years. Good to hear. Cowpoke's gotta have a place to put his wages, don't you know? The posters outside the jail didn't impress him. The unfair likeness of Trinity made him smile. She was worth something, more than him.

"Find what yer lookin' fer?" Trina quizzed him upon his return.

"Just needed to get us some foods." He made sure to stop by the greengrocer before he left town, making his trip legitimate.

"You got a big dinner planned?" asked Lulu.

Bonnie was happy to let him do the cooking. Trinity gave a grunt. As long as the food was good.

He set out cutting and slicing, putting everything in a pot. Hung it over the fire he made outside, let it cook. He stirred the mixture and made a plan. He could get free. Just ride off one day. He would take his family to the farm where Triss went, just for a spell. Then he would find his own farm to start living on, grow their own food, raise animals, and be happy. But first his problems had to end.

"They got that fella and they drug him outta town," said one old man sitting in front of a saloon in the town Bart visited. "Took him way out and they pull off his arm and leg, left him, rode off. Worst thing I ever did hear. Gotta be a reward for anybody capture them."

+ + +

I have to smile at the way she looks at me across the dinner table. She acts interested in what I'm saying, not like she has to play nice because I've helped her through that trial. She tells me I'm a good man. And it doesn't hurt that we both are half-tribal.

"Purpose?" I continue my rant. "Everyone who's ever walked this earth was born without their permission. No one asks us. Yet here we are, thrown into some existence we never wanted, with questions demanding answers. Some day you have to find your purpose in life. Others say you're free to do as you please. Enjoy your life. Do as you like. It isn't going to last too long anyway. So those people take and take more. They do as they please with no regard for others. They indulge in pleasures and they kill as they desire. In that way they believe they've found the path through their existence, a way to use up the precious days and years they've been given."

"Yeah, gotcher point," she says and I believe her.

"Criminals act in their own self-interest. The pleasure principle I mentioned before. Never think of doing anything for other people. It is the main cause of disharmony in the world. Of chaos. Look at all the leaders of the world, what they've done to us. Dominated us. Used us for their personal schemes. It's documented in the books being published these days. Take just one example: the Glow."

"Ain't nothin' but a long sunset," she says. "End of the world."

"No, it isn't."

I want to pull out the news-paper page folded in my coat pocket, but that would make me look desperate. What governments around the world did during the past hundred years or so doesn't matter to her, I'm sure. It didn't matter to me growing up, but the more I read now about what happened, the angrier I get.

"There was a rider," I say, "bringing news from the east. He had a script of a stream from President Byrne." I reach into my pocket, then halt. Now I seem odd. From memory, I continue: "Says 'We are weak. They thought we were vulnerable. We had to fight back.' The way the president was taken to a hospital and the vice-president on holiday – perfect time to see if those old rockets would still launch. And they did. Barely. Crashed down not far from their launch bases.

Made a big mess, as you can imagine."

"That's the Glow yer talkin' 'bout. Told y'all. What them folks in that underground city said."

"I know. So I did more research."

She smiles, like my words won't mean a thing to her.

"It was us doing it to ourselves," I say, letting my alarm show. But it happened months ago. "They tried to send those rockets with their bombs over the ocean to other countries, but they didn't rise. They fell down where they launched from. Imagine huge explosions. Fire filling the sky. Destroying everything on the ground. Up and down the coast. Each of those cities. Gone. The people burned up. A few of the survivors crossing the mountains and coming this way. We've had a few. All damaged in horrific ways. Better off dead than go on suffering."

"Never did hear none o' that," she says, starts poking at the slice of pie with her fork. I guess she's had enough of my doom talk.

"I understand how it can be upsetting."

She gives me a weak smile, like she wants to be nice but it isn't easy for her.

"They took my leathers," she says, and I'm strangely glad she's changed the subject of our conversation. "Said they ain't proper for a woman to wear. Men's clothes, they said."

"I might agree. You sure looked pretty in that dress my mama used to wear. But I also agree you should wear what you want. And they never should've taken the clothes you rode in with."

"When they pay my reward," she goes on, "gonna get me a new set. You know a good shop in this town?"

I have to frown. "Maybe they won't pay you."

"But there's a bounty on him. The one they call Bad Bart."

"But he's your...husband, isn't he?"

"Don't mean they ain't gotta pay no bounty to who brung him in. I brung him in. Gotta pay me." She gives me a stern look. "And a fresh horse. Don't mind buyin' a horse with that bounty. Know a fair dealer?"

I'm a dentist officially, but I also handle the dead bodies that are in our town. I take care of medical things as Dr. Baker's assistant. I don't know about anything else, apparently. I try to talk as though I do but it falls flat.

"I'll help you in any way I can," I summarize. "You can stay as long as you like in my place. I'll keep sleeping in the clinic. We can work out everything. Don't worry."

"Ain't worried 'bout nothin' but my reward money. Get that an' ain't never gotta do nothin' no more. Just live free, raise my boys."

"Maybe I can talk with Deputy Cal about it. He'll know how it's paid out. Probably has to go through the Court, get approved, then a withdrawal made from a bank. Not sure. Never knew anybody who was owed a bounty reward."

"Ain't never turned in no bounty b'fore neither," she says.

"But...." I stop myself, not sure if I should ask her.

"What?"

"You still have a poster up in the jailhouse. There's a bounty on *you*. Not sure if it's still valid. I'll check with Cal."

"Ya gonna turn me in? Lotsa men try before. They failed."

"I can believe that." I lean to the side, slip a peek at her hip. No holster. "They took your guns, too. Didn't they?"

"Yeah, I'm completely unarmed. If ya got mischief on yer mind."

But I don't. Not for her. She's maybe three years older than me. Past her prime, as they say in the bride catalogues. The cheaper ones. My interest in her is only because Bart loved her.

"I want to help. For Bart's sake. That's all I can promise you. Anything more.... Well, that's up to nature and a wink from God."

The moment of silence that follows is God inhaling, thinking of a good response. That Jacob Baumann again! *Geez Louise!*

"I have two boys," Trina says like a thunderclap breaking out of that overcast silence.

Already knowing she has a baby in her, I can't reconcile the idea she puts forth.

"They livin' with my sister, like I told ya." She keeps her voice low like she's telling a secret. Can't blame her. People gossip hard in this town. "One's a son I look after. For Bart. His son. Other one's me an' Bart's boy. We got together one night—"

"I know how it's done," I cut in, offering a grin.

She frowns. "If ya thinkin' thoughts like what Bart done, gotta warn ya. I got two sons. Third on th' way. Also Bart's. But it were like accident. It were before he died. But he never got to hear me say he's coming. Din't know fer myself when he died."

"I believe you."

"Ain't offerin' nothin' – just advice. Ya don't know me, not like ya think ya do. 'Preciate yer help, shore, but cain't do nothin' fer ya as thanks. Y'unnerstand?"

"That's not at all what I was thinking." I'm sure my face turns pale at her suggestion. I like her, and I think I should help her, but not for any kind of payment. Not like that.

"Gotta go my own way." She looks out the entrance to the dining room. "Gotta get back to my boys. That's my life now. That's my *existence*, don'tcha know?"

My heart beats fast and I draw in a slow breath to calm myself.

"What are their names?" I ask.

"Boy we got from him and me is Izzy. Bart's idea."

"I thought he would chose Bart as his son's name."

"It's Isaiah, but not from a Bible book. He said he got the name from a man his ma used to see back in the capital. Then he stopped seeing her. But he was kind to Barty."

I smile to myself. "And your other son?"

She pinches her lips. "It's long story. That underground facility I told about? It was there. We live in it for more 'an a year. Had to join their 'speriment. He got that son that way. Being with a lady name of Marina. So that boy's name is Nicky. Nicholas, to be official. I chose the name. Was the name of my partner in the 'speriment. But he died. I think Bart killed him. Purdy shore of it."

Shaking my head is all I can do, imagining what adventures my cousin lived through only to die so close to home years later.

I look up, regard her. "I wish I could meet them."

"None of them look like Barty. Izzy look like me, fer most part. An' Nicky look like his ma, blond and white. You never gonna think they're his boys. But they are. Ya kin see Bart in the eyes, ya look real close. Bet Miss Maggie'll know 'em. She be right proud o' them. They the grandsons, ain't they?"

"Yes, they are," I add to complete the conversation. "Like me."

40

Seventh Day of the Seventh Month

ON THE SUNNY MORNING OF JULY 1 of that year was Trinity Culpepper arrested as she stepped from Mel's Greengrocery. She was wearing a dark matron's dress, a widow's shawl, and a common bonnet that shaded her face well enough that she must've thought no one in town would recognize her. The jailers soon discovered under that dress she wore trousers and riding boots, bore a holster with pistol and had a sheath with a long knife. Stripped and put in a prison gown, she sat behind bars until a trial could be arranged. She had to wait through the Fourth of Seven celebration, with the kids' band marching down the street, playing songs. After that, Judge Young rode into town to administer the trial, with local lawyer, Horace "Corn" Cobb, acting as prosecutor and Mr. Cobb's law clerk taking the defense attorney role.

Two days of testimony, none from Trinity, and Judge Young hit the gavel on the desk to end it. Sentenced to hang until death for her crimes, which included several killings, she sat again in that jail cell for three days as the gallows was built.

When the morning came, folks from neighboring towns gathered to watch the spectacle. She was led out to the gallows, up the steps, noose put around her neck and set, then dropped through the door. The rope wasn't fixed properly, didn't snap her neck, so she actually strangled to death, spinning and twisting beneath the platform. A couple men from the jail tore off her gown, leaving her to die naked. After the doctor confirmed she was dead, they cut her body down and hauled it to the graveyard for unnamed and criminals outside of town, tossed her body in a pit that already hosted a few bodies. A shovel of lime was tossed over her body.

Bonnie and Lulu saw the arrest from outside the store, couldn't do anything to help her, being dressed like proper country gals also. If they acted, they would be found out and arrested, too. Panicked, they raced out of town, took short-cuts back to the farm, screaming at Bart as they arrived,

"What?" he shouted back, wiping his hands from cleaning. "Slow down. Say it out."

"They got her," Bonnie cried. "Took her to jail. They gonna put her on trial—"

"Trial for all her crimes," Lulu spoke frantically.

"Who?' he asked.

"Trinity! That who!" the women shouted.

Trina came out at the noise, asking what happened. The women dismounted and told the story again.

"They coming this way," Bonnie said, voice frantic. "You better get away while you can."

"Whatcha talkin' 'bout? Ain't goin' nowheres. Nobody know we even here."

"They do know," Lulu said. "They just a mile behind us."

"Team of riders followed us when we rode off," said Bonnie.

"Dang fools," Bart grunted. "You never come straight back here, don't you know?"

"We thought better to warn you," Bonnie said.

"Now what?" Trina asked Bart.

"You sure?" he asked the women.

"They coming fast," Bonnie replied, still breathing hard. "Here. You better take the horses. Better ride hard."

"What about you?" asked Trina.

"We're just pennies. Ain't gonna do much with us. We never killed nobody."

"They'll give us a good talking to, send us home," said Lulu.

"But you two," said Bonnie, looking back over her shoulder and across the field at the road, "got bounties. You got big posters with big numbers on them. They gonna getcha for certain."

"Yeah," said Lulu. "Better get outta here."

Trina gave him that look: a decision already made but checking that he was prepared to obey her. "Yeah, awright."

"Where we going?" asked Bart.

"Best go find my other sister," Trina answered.

They gathered a few items, took the boys, and mounted the two horses. Izzy rode with Bart, Nicky with Trina. They trotted down the path, past the corral with the mare and her foal. On out to the road and turned east. Clouds boiled overhead: just another pretty summer day, the sun not yet a gift of the devil.

+   +   +

Trina can't stay for long, I know. She has to get back to her sons, wherever they are. She said they live with her sister, but I've no idea where that might be, or if she's only inventing a story. I want to help her, but I don't know how. Thinking I need the advice of a kind old woman, I go to Maggie.

"I know you were glad to stay away from the trial." I sit in the comfy chair for guests. "It's good you did. So many awful stories from forlorn folks with tales to tell. I can't tell you how many sounded made up. None of them were much about Bart. They were trying to tie Trina to him, anyway. But none of them could. In the end Judge Robinson had to set her free."

"They have a way of sorting out what's truth, if you hear enough versions of it," says Maggie in her slow, patient way. "Seems it's all for naught. My Barty's in the ground. His uncle, too. And that's the end of it. Now I can rest in peace, knowing the end of their story. I only wish I knew how Barty met his end."

I start to give an answer, then stop, deciding to think on it more. How much do I actually know for certain? I review those few moments talking with Trina, collecting bits of information each time, assessing whether she could've been fibbing. She seems like the type to make up things just to get by.

"Would you like to talk with her?" I ask Maggie.

She nods thoughtfully. "Might be good. If the woman is willing to meet with me. I fear she's gotten a bad impression before. She's scared of me now. Tell her I promise not to be cross with her, no matter what she says. I will hear her out. Then I'll know. I just want to know."

Before I can leave the house, she returns to the piano.

"What's that?" I ask, pausing in the doorway.

"Oh, some tune I've been toying with," she says, staring forward at the paper propped on the piano. She pauses to pick up her pen and draw some music notes on the paper. She plays more notes. "If I finish it, I'll give it to Barty. He can sing it in Heaven."

It takes some talking to but I finally get Trina to agree to come and speak with Maggie. Now that I know she has a son with Bart, and another son by a different woman, Maggie will want to hear about her grandsons. I promise to tell no one else.

After an awkward greeting, Maggie gestures for her to take the guest chair. I pull out the bench by the piano. The room is full of the nervous energy that buzzes like bees, waiting to see who's the first to be stung. Looks like it will be me.

"I'm glad you two can talk," I say, clasping my hands as I sit on the piano bench. I half-turn to the keyboard. "Maggie's been writing a song for Bart."

Trina seems curious. Maggie waves me off. She's not in the mood to play the song.

"The judge gave her a probation," I say. "But she can't leave the county. Five years for the probation. So she needs a place to live for that time. Also, there's—"

"She's welcome here," says Maggie without hesitation.

Trina looks at her like it must be a trick. "Maybe ya don't want me 'round, after ya hear what I got to say."

"What could you say that would make me not welcome you?" Maggie lets a weak smile show. "If you're my Barty's lady, I should welcome you."

"She is his lady," I say, eager to push this meeting into happier territory. "You see, she has two sons. They live with her sister. She can't go back to them now because of the probation. If she's caught

524

leaving the county, they will put her in the penitentiary."

Maggie nods, thinking of a solution. "Can you get them and bring them here?"

The question is directed at me. "I suggested that. But—"

"He don't know the way," Trina speaks up. "Kinda hard to say it. An' my sis don't know him, likely gonna shoot him if he come too close. It gotta be me get 'em."

Maggie doesn't panic, smiles warmly. "Tell me about them."

"Not much to tell," Trina responds. "They just boys. Rough an' tumble boys, don'tcha know. Always rollin' 'round, playin', fightin'. Older one's named Izzy. It's short for Isaiah. The other boy's Nicky. Short for Nicholas. Izzy's 'round seven now, reckon. Nicky's five. They a handful, fer shore."

"What a delight," Maggie cheers. "Tell me more about the boys. I want to know everything about my grandsons."

Trina goes into a long account of the boys' lives, from the time and place they were conceived, to the days they were born, what adventures they've had since. She tells her about their quirks, their likes and dislikes. She throws in anecdotes that makes Maggie chuckle. It's a talk like any mother-in-law and daughter-in-law in the world might have.

I sit in rapt attention, happy for the two of them.

"I wish I could see them," says Maggie. "If you had one of those camera boxes, a picture of them could be made. At least I could look at them, see them as they are now. I can imagine them growing up, being boys, playing and carousing, and getting to be men."

I sit up on the piano bench, ready to add to the conversation, but with the wrong words at the wrong time.

"And she's got another child," I say.

"I recall you asking about that," says Maggie, and Trina freezes. "You wanted to know about her stretch marks, as I recall."

Trina shoots me a hard glance that almost hurts.

"It's not a secret," I tell Trina. "The world will know soon enough in...what? seven months? Is that it?"

Trina lowers her gaze, stares at her new boots, the cuffs of her new trousers tucked into them, just as she likes. It's only her dark hair woven into two long braids that keeps her from looking like just another cowpoke back from a trail ride.

"Yeah, gonna see it soon," she says, resigned.

"Another grandchild!" Maggie is pleased, gets herself up, steps across the carpet to Trina, gestures her to get up. When she stands, Maggie wraps her arms around the woman, pats her back. "Thank you for loving my boy. For giving me grandsons."

They hold the embrace. Trina, grinning, lets a tear roll down her cheek. She seems like a new person when Maggie returns to her chair.

"Yes, out you come," I say, ruining the perfect silence, "the day you discover you're meant to do things. A traumatic introduction to a hostile world you never ask for. All you know is your mother, the eternal other who holds you, protects you, feeds you — even when you don't yet know what that sensation of hunger is."

The women stare at me, like I'm a raving lunatic.

"There's something to it," says Maggie from her chair. "They all come out neutral, their slates blank, and every day something gets written on that slate. What will it be? Good things? Bad?" She turns to me. "That Raymond — Isla's child. He was a bad sort. And Fritz, my dad, had his own problems. Some of us haven't had good lives. I know mine could've been better. But we try. We do try."

"Yes, we do, Grandma," I say.

She regards Trina. "Now we have another chance at good lives. Those boys will grow up, I hope, to be exemplary men. Men who will make our nation great again."

Trina nods. "Yeah, good chance."

"But can good come from bad?" I toss into the discussion.

Maggie turns sullen. The clock on the mantle slowly ticks.

"How did Barty die?" asks Maggie out of that silence. "I know he was shot in the belly, but what I want to know is how he came to be shot. What happened that led him into that situation? Can you tell me? Do you know?"

Trina gives a nod, is about to speak when I clear my throat. She pauses, regards me, checking whether I will interrupt her.

"After my sister got hanged—" Her voice is quiet but firm. "—we had to run, me an' Bart. They got bounties on us, see. Ain't no good come if him an' me get caught up with that, so we run. Ride to my other sister's place, where she lay up with a fella she took up with. Got the boys with us. She don't like it we come to her place, but we tell her what happened an' she let us stay there."

"I can well imagine," Maggie says, and urges her on.

"We got us honest work, ma'am. Got hired by a Mister Leland Clayborne. He owns frightful lot of farms in the territory down in Okala. We got hired to collect rent from farmers. We gotta be rough if they not payin'. That's the job. We done it two years, put some notes in a box for later. Bart, he wanna go standard. Always sayin' it his dream."

"It's a lovely dream," says Maggie.

"Some days it get rough, like I said. That's the job. For me, I can talk a wife into payin' but Bart, he does the talkin' if a man."

She gives me a look which I can only interpret as a warning that she is about to say a lie and for me not to let on.

"One them days, farmer don't take kindly to us, gets in a fight with Bart. Pulls a gun on that farmer. An' the farmer shoot Bart straightaway. Never even talk it out."

She pauses to let Maggie wipe her eyes.

"Rush him away, take a cart from the farm, try to get to town, find a doc. But Bart, he say he ain't gonna make it. Belly wound last fer days. He know, an' I know. He gonna die, no way to stop it. He says take him home...so his mama kin bury him."

Maggie is sobbing now.

"Bart tell me to dig up his uncle. I know where. He wants both brung to town. So I do it. I do it cuz he my man, an' never want him in pain. So I brung him to Skinner Canyon, jus' like he want, but he dead when we get here. Now ya know the rest o' the story, ma'am. Never want no bad things happen to him. Ain't no Bad Bart, like folk call him, no ma'am. A bit foolish sometimes, ya know, but most times a good man."

I go to Maggie, pat her back as she weeps.

"Thank you," she gets out. "Thank you for telling me."

Trina sits back, breathing hard, and I guess she felt the stress of telling a lie. Maybe it's the truth. Who am I to judge? At least her story helps Maggie tie the loose ends of her son's adventurous life. Maybe that's all that matters.

Maggie dries her tears, sits back. "Family is measured by births and funerals. We make lists, fill in dates. We look over the pages from time to time, making sense of our family – judging. Each mark on the page is a measure of time's passage, of deeds done, or opportunities missed. Memories made."

She waves a hand at the nearby shelving, indicating the stack of notebooks proudly displayed.

"Like my great-great-grandfather did when he wrote everything in those notebooks. He had to make a record of events back during the pandemic, and the ugly events that followed. I've managed to compose an opera to keep that history alive. People don't want to be reminded of those dark times."

"Grandma, they weren't dark times," I say.

"They were," she counters, her voice strident. "Much worse than today. Even with the Glow coming at us, it was worse back then." She looks over to Trina. "Now we have some new lives that can fix all of that – all that we have ruined. The grandsons will do that, I pray. Won't they?"

+   +   +

Bart and Trina rode out on a typical day, stopping at the office to get the assignment, then out to the farm to collect the overdue fee. Normal work. The farmer hated them visiting but he knew he owed. He tried to talk his way into paying half and the rest next time. The market hadn't been good lately so he didn't make the cost, couldn't pay the full amount. Trina played the nice role, let Bart be the mean one. They got half the fee, threatened him if he didn't come up with the rest of it by the next week.

"Shoulda press harder," Trina chastised Bart as they rode away.

"Yeah," he responded. "Now we gotta come back and rattle him some more, maybe shoot out his knee. Word'll get around and then they pay up quick." He looked back over his shoulder at the farm.

"He got things he can sell. Even that old cart is worth something."

Trina grinned at him. "Maybe we can get his old bed, not hafta sleep on no floor – tho' it were right good that way."

She smiled at the way he lay over her, with Izzy asking if Pa was going to sleep on top of Ma. Bart had to shoo him away. It had been a while, with all the hassles of life crowding them, too busy to find peace with each other for a single night. They could hear Triss and her man having their play time most nights.

"Think he sell it?" asked Bart. "But we need a wagon to haul a dang bed."

"He got that cart," she told him.

Riding along, Bart got to talking about their other capers, back when they were young. Those sure were exciting times. Trina had to agree. But then they had to run, had to escape west. They fell silent as they let the horses slow.

Then he spoke up again, said he thought Trinity's plan to go into town dressed like an old woman was stupid. Better to ride into town with guns blazing. Like in the old days. Nobody going to get in their way. He chuckled at the memory.

Trina glared at him, feeling insulted, and complained.

"She should've known she'd get caught," he said with a laugh. Finally he felt he could laugh at the elder sister, already gone from their lives. "Heck, even I could see the bulge of her pistol under that dress. Not to say she couldn't've done it, course. Those lawmen saw it, I bet. Didn't need to look for a cross on the bonnet."

Trina regarded him, riding side by side. "Whatcha mean?"

"The bonnet she wore. Part of her old woman act."

She drew her horse to a halt. "What about the bonnet?"

He halted his horse. Good time for a rest anyway. There was a creek curling nearby. He wiped his brow from the hot sun.

"There's a cross on the back of that bonnet. You never noticed?"

"Ain't no cross on that bonnet," she countered.

"Sure there was."

Taking his cue to rest, she dismounted, tugged the reins to lead her horse over to the creek. A stand of trees blocked some of the sun. Bart climbed off and followed.

"Tell me about the bonnet," Trina demanded.

"What? I didn't say nothing about no bonnet." Then he smiled to himself, amused at the scheme. "It was a dumb idea, is all."

She looked cross at him. "What did you say?"

"Didn't say nothing." He turned serious, seeing her look, and set his eyes on hers. "Just she gonna look suspicious in that get-up of hers. Bonnet ain't gonna give her away. Nobody gonna look at it."

"What'd ya do?" she challenged.

"I didn't do nothing. Didn't say nothing to nobody. I told you."

"Ya said there's cross on the back o' the bonnet. Mean sumpin'?"

"Cross means it's a church thing."

"Ya tell anybody look for a bonnet with a cross on the back?"

"They all got crosses on the back."

"No, they don't!"

"You looked at a lot of bonnets? Have you?"

"How they know she gonna be wearin' a bonnet got cross on the back? How anybody gonna know? Ya say sumpin' to anybody?"

"I didn't say nothing. Just thinking aloud. Just to myself. 'What an odd thing to see a cross on the back of a widow's bonnet.' That's all. Just like that. And that's all I said."

"That's what ya said? Who was near ya?"

"Why, nobody." He had to think. "Nobody that matter. Maybe a kid or some old man buying snuff. I dunno."

"Ya talkin' that way an' people list'ning to ya? Dang fool!"

"Weren't no fool. Just talking to myself. Laughing about it. Just thought it was funny the way she dresses herself up that way. Like a poor widow. It's funny."

"An' nobody laugh with ya?"

"Maybe. Don't remember."

"Ya said she gonna be wearin' a bonnet with a cross on the back. An' people hear ya say it. That true?"

"Maybe." He stared at her: his woman, mother of his sons – and only then felt her disappointment in him. "It didn't mean nothing."

"Ya let 'em know who to get, din't ya?"

"What're you talking about? I didn't do nothing like that."

"Ya set up my sister is what ya did!"

"No, I didn't!"

Then her pistol was out, arm raised, pointing right at him.

"Wait! I can explain. They's listening to me, is all. They—"

"Ya got my sister hanged! That's what ya done!"

41

EIGHT WEEKS

TRINA FELL TO HER KNEES beside Bart. He moaned as she leaned over him, bracing herself on one arm. Her other hand went to his face, settled against his cheek. He'd fallen back, arms thrown past his head. His face a mask of desperation, his jaw clenched, teeth biting hard, eyes closed tight.

"Dammit!" she shrieked, as surprised as he was.

She saw what she'd done. The shot tore into his belly, ripped a path through his guts, the only good thing being it hit his spine in a way he wouldn't feel any pain below there.

"What's h-happening to me?"

She checked his body, daring to touch where blood pooled on his shirt, red rivulets running down the side. She didn't know what to do. She looked around, gazed at the far horizon. No doctor less than half a day's ride.

"Ya made me do it, damn you!"

He stared up at a royal blue sky, fluffy clouds drifting by like a funeral march led by children, happy the bad man was dead.

"Oh God! Oh Mama!" He grabbed his belly with both hands, as if holding in the damage. "Help me! Mama! *Maaamaaa!*"

Trina bent low over him, face to face, staring into his eyes.

"Sorry." She sniffled, but a tear dropped on his face.

Tears kept filling her eyes, falling to his face as he continued to call out for his mama.

"Real sorry.... Din't mean to."

"Take me home," he begged after his cries went unanswered. "I gotta get home. Please.... I want my mama."

She could only watch him suffering.

"Ain't gonna make it," she said plainly. "Wound like that kill ya in two, three days. No way to mend it."

"Gotta go back." He gasped for breath. "Can't die out here."

She tried to smile – for him – to ease his pain a bit.

"This the best place. Calm here. Nobody come lookin' fer ya—"

"I want my mama." His voice grew weak. "Mama...."

"Yer gonna be dead b'fore we get anyplace."

He grabbed her arm. "She'll give you money. Take me home and she'll pay you. She'll want me buried near her. With my family."

She tilted her head. "That right?"

"You gotta dig up my uncle, too. Take him home. Please. You'll get more money. You quit that collection work. Just take care of the boys.... All you gotta do."

Her hand brushed his forehead as she watched him struggling.

"That pine box an' you? How much ya think I get?"

He sucked air, hand tight around her arm. "Be enough you and the boys can live a standard life for a long time. Promise."

"Think so?"

She sat up, leaning back with her hands on the ground, as their horses grazed nearby. She watched the clouds drift, felt the hot sun cut through the tree branches. It was a peaceful scene.

She recalled a moment in that first camp, snuggling in the tent.

"I read something," he'd told her, acting proud.

"One o' them books?" she'd asked, half teasing.

"A kind of book. I think it's called a 'notebook' actually."

"So a book."

"My great-great-grandfather wrote it, however long ago it may have been. During the Great Pandemic they all talk about."

"Ya read it?"

"Tried to, but the way he drew out them words, it's hard to read. None of it made any sense. So I figure I can just make it up—"

She regarded him, his pained eyes open, searching for grace.

She began to think of what she'd say. She knew she would need to say something, returning without Bart.

First to the boys: "Yer Pa, he had one o' them accidents."

Next to Triss: "I learned he set up Trinity."

Finally to Bart's poor mama, the kindly old piano player in the big house: "That angry farmer pull a gun on him."

He called out to her: "Don't let me die alone."

Time stood still, like that orange blaze in the eastern sky that started several months back.

"Y'ain't gonna die alone."

She studied his face: red whiskers grown out, broad cheeks she had kissed. She brushed his red hair, leaned down and put her lips to his mouth.

+ + +

Dressed like she's heading to church, Miss Maggie brings the beef roast on a large platter, sets it down in the center of the table, as I carry in bowls of potatoes and string beans. The buns she made are on the table. Trina has already bitten into one, claiming she is too hungry to wait.

"So then I got that farmer's cart, hitch my horse to it, an' rode off," she says to continue her story as dinner comes to an end.

"Let me help," I say to Maggie, getting up from the table.

"I dug up that box, too, an' me an' Triss heft it on the cart. Then I brung him here. It were lots o' trouble. I deserve my money. Bart said I get some fer bringin' him back here."

Hearing her words from the kitchen as I slice the pie, I cringe. No idea what expression Maggie must have hearing them. I put the slices of pie on two plates, bring them out to the table, set down one to each of them. I turn to go back for my plate.

"I'm not feeling much like dessert," says Maggie. A smile flashes across her face, enough to be polite. "Dinner was a lot for a change. I usually don't cook for guests."

"Guess I should visit more often," I say, offering a chuckle as I take Maggie's slice of pie for myself.

"Ya shore is a kindly lady," says Trina. She seems grateful. This is what she calls a standard life, I suppose. Living in a fine house with clean sheets on a soft bed, and Sunday dinner with guests. She says it's what Bart wanted.

Maggie looks uncomfortable, says "Thank you" all the same. She glances at me. "Jake tells me you want to return to your sister's home. What will you do there? The same line of work as before?"

Trina sets down her fork, swallows the forkful of pie, clears her mouth. "Ain't figure to keep on it, now that Bart's gone."

"Do you have other skills?" asks Maggie.

Trina smiles to herself. "Ma showed me how to sew cloths. Been mendin' the boys' diapers, stitchin' rips in Bart's clothes. Not much call fer it, women knowin' how to do it fer themselves an' all."

"There's no set of skills that should be dismissed," says Maggie. "Any skill you have is something people will pay you to do for them. People tend to be lazy. They will happily pay someone else to do the work than do it themselves, even if they know how. Besides, with no government agents collecting taxes, we get no services now. We are on our own. We must learn how to survive. Even a fine house like this won't last forever. A garden will turn fallow. Livestock die and aren't replaced. And, as you said of Bart: bullets will come to an end with no more being made. Then," and she looks at me, "it is for us to fashion a bow and some arrows, isn't it?"

"I haven't used a bow and arrows in years," I tell her, grinning.

My, how the time has flown! I yawn as an excuse to leave.

The evening is already dark and I must return to town. Trina will stay in this house, in an upstairs bedroom. Maggie has taken over the spare room on the ground floor, no longer willing to climb the stairs even with a cane to steady herself.

I bid a good night to Trina and step outside. Maggie follows to be polite, seeing the guest off.

But she takes my arm, slides her hand down to grasp my hand. A tight grip that gets my attention.

"I want to say to you, Jake, a couple things in private."

"Yes? What's that?"

She regards me, looking up to my face as I gaze down.

"You are the only one I have left in my life. All the others are gone. So I've written a document that says this house is yours after I'm gone. All I ask is to please take care of everything in it. I mean for you to pass them down to the grandsons."

"But it's her that has the boys. And she's going to have the other baby soon enough. I don't have any ties to her."

"Then you need to stay close to her. After you pass on – and I pray it is a very long time – you need to give everything to those boys, although they likely will be grown men by then. Tell them why these things are important. They're family history. Nothing is more important than remembering where we came from, and what those before us struggled through, how their lives made us who we are. You tell them that. Doesn't matter what's put on the pages, it's what happened. It's the written truth."

"Should I write something about how Bart met his end? Is that what you intend?"

"You could." She pats my back, then gives me a big hug. "I leave that to you."

"Awright, Grandma."

I ride back, get into my little place, and get ready to sleep. But I can't help thinking of something Trina said in telling her story over dinner.

She previously said that farmer shot Bart. Tonight she said – or I *thought* she said – she had to go back to that farm to get the cart. I suppose it could be a slip of the tongue, being distracted while she ate. Or she simply couldn't keep her lie straight. Maybe the details don't matter. The deed is done. Maggie was fine with whatever she said. Maggie only wanted the whole story to end, for her son's fate to be resolved. But I grow suspicious.

I check with Deputy Cal the next day, ask about money coming Trina's way. He jokes again, keeps at it until I leave. I go over to the Court, ask the clerk about compensation. I say it was promised but the clerk tells me plainly there wasn't any note, no confession to prove anything she said. If Bart told her to collect on his bounty, it was only between them.

"But a bounty is paid to whoever brings in the outlaw," I try to explain. "Dead or alive. Doesn't matter if she made a deal with the outlaw before he dies, does it?"

"Perhaps, Doctor Jake," says the clerk, "might have something to do with her being an outlaw herself. She has her own bounty."

"She was acquitted of wrong-doing in court. She's free."

"I don't make the rules. Or enforce the laws."

"There shouldn't be any bounty on her. As long as she stays in the county for five years without any infractions. That's what the judge said."

The clerk glances both ways, leans forward. "You might hear of some men not accepting her acquittal. They mean to enforce their own judgment. They're planning something."

"Something? Like what?"

"Something like what the elder sister got."

"They wouldn't do that. She's been set free."

"Some folks don't think it was a fair verdict. They aim to handle it themselves."

I step away from the desk as a trio of men in suits enter and proceed to offices down the corridor.

"Does Deputy Cal know?"

The clerk grins. "He's the leader of them, don't you know?"

+   +   +

Maggie doesn't mind Trina staying in the big house with her. They seem to find a good balance, helping each other. A wild girl learning to be civilized. Maggie having something new to occupy her days. I'm glad to see that. Maggie isn't getting any younger, as they say. I worry about her. If only Trina didn't need to go get her sons – or let me bring them to her here.

I suggest she write a letter. I will deliver it to the postal office. The letter will arrive and Triss will know what happened and follow the request to bring the boys. But Trina refuses. I wonder if she's embarrassed not knowing how to write. Or she doesn't want me to know the address. Lots of ways around all of that, but she insists she go back to them. I wonder if her plan is to go and never return. To get away from us. None of them know what's happened, why Trina's been away so long. Or where Bart is.

I guess the kind of life she's lived doesn't allow her much room for trusting people. That's sad. But she can trust me, to a fault. I've bent over backwards for her, with no thought of joining her in a romantic relationship. Best I can do is be her friend. To be honest, I have a fantasy, but I've acted only for Bart's sake. I owe him that. It is a feature of our civilized existence. Most of us try to be good, to do good things, hoping for the best outcome, yet we often fail.

But I won't fail this time.

Maggie waits inside, peering out from behind curtains, trying to see the road in the growing darkness. If they are coming, they may carry torches to light their way. Or they could arrive like ghosts in the night, ready to string her up.

Getting the latest word from Maggie – no sight of them – I step out back, go to the shed where Trina is tending to my horse.

I've broken my vow to obey the laws. Maggie says it's necessary sometimes to obey the greater good more than whatever some man wrote long ago, calling it a law and saying everybody must obey it. So we agree to send her away, let her go free. No bounty money for her, but at least she does get a fresh horse: mine. I'll take Maggie's chestnut Morgan, the gelding that pulls her carriage.

I leave a lamp burning in the sitting room, its glow lighting the front porch. Unsure what to do, I wait.

Tired of waiting for trouble, I go check on Trina.

"I packed some food in the box behind you," I call.

The Glow in the east smudges the night sky as she mounts the horse, gray in the moonlight, colored by the Glow.

She will ride east, yet not so far that her skin starts prickling, not far enough that her eyes will glaze over, and certainly not to the point where her insides boil and her flesh sheers off like paper. I trust she knows where that line is and won't cross it. A lot of good territory remains west of that line.

I can hear the lawmen coming, their horses' hooves striking the hardpack ground in steady rhythm – like Maggie is calling timpani to bang a march for trumpets and trombones.

"You have to go now," I tell Trina. She's on my horse, a strong mount. "Get going. They're coming."

"Come with me," she says. "They gonna get ya fer helpin' me."

"I don't care. I can delay them. Enough to let you get away."

"They gonna lock y'up in jail."

"Don't worry about me," I respond. "I can handle them."

"Come with me." Then, surprisingly: "I need ya."

Maybe she does need me. I can imagine all kinds of possibilities. But my first duty is to stall those lawmen coming for her. Let them get distracted. Give her time to escape. I'm sending her back to her sons, and bidding her a happy life.

"You have to get away." I look for the approaching horsemen.

"Come find me," she calls back as the horse starts to trot away. "At the crossroads in Guymon. Greengrocer on the corner. Go south from there an' I meet ya."

"Go on!" I shout.

She urges the horse onward.

The lawmen's horses pound dirt, gathering in the front yard.

But she is gone, racing away from behind the house. Soon only a silhouette against the Glow, like the day she arrived pulling a cart.

I try not to look, don't want to give any clue to the lawmen.

They stand five abreast on their mounts in front of the house as Maggie steps away from the window.

"You in there, Miss Maggie?" calls out Deputy Cal from atop his steed. "Need to speak with your guest."

"What guest?" I ask, coming around the side of the house.

"You know who," Cal mugs.

"No, I don't," I say firmly. "I'm the only guest here."

"Where is she?" demands Cal.

"I haven't seen her," I say, stepping up to the porch.

Cal grins. "No?"

"No, I haven't. Not since yesterday morning."

"Yesterday morn?"

"I awoke and she was gone."

"Gone, huh?" He tries to hide a smile that threatens to break across his face. "Guess she must not've loved you after all."

"Guess not." I hold my composure. "Stole my horse."

"Poor boy," says Cal. "Got used by a wanton woman. Happens to simple fellows."

His men chuckle beside him but I have my script to follow.

"Always being fooled," Cal continues. "One way or the other. A loser at love. Ain't that right?"

It hurts. But I don't care. I did what was right. I let her go. She is heading to where her sons live. They will be reunited, the family of my cousin Bart together once more. He'd be glad for it. He would thank me. And she will give him one more child in a few months.

"Better arrest this man," says Cal. "Helping a fugitive escape."

Two of his men dismount, one with a pair of metal bracelets for me to wear. He clinks them together.

"There's no need for that," I speak up, going into my act. "She betrayed me, too. Played me right nasty. I'm as puzzled as anyone. I hope you can catch her. She's got a whole lot of explaining to do."

"Damn right she does," says Cal, then waves his men onto their horses. "Leave him. He ain't going nowhere."

"I think she's heading west," I say, pointing. "She kept talking about her old camp. Up in those rocky hills past Boise City. Out toward Black Mesa. Where they first found Bart after that posse."

Deputy Cal gives a nod and his team charges off, leaving a cloud of dust for me to choke on as they head west.

And I, foolish boy that I am, return to the house and pack a bag. Clothes and food. Water and ammo. I get Maggie's horse saddled with little disagreement, not used to being ridden.

"You're a good man, Jacob Little Bear," says Maggie in a warm voice, coming out to see me off. "I'm proud of you."

She gives me a black case with silver locks to take with me.

"If you get a chance, see that my grandsons learn to play this."

"What is it?"

"It's your Aunt Eve's cornet."

I smile. Bart tried but failed. I'll pass it down to his sons.

"I know you have to go after her. Don't you worry about me. I will be quite all right." She tries to smile. "Write if you can. Tell me how my grandsons are doing."

Giving her a big hug, she feels so frail.

"I will," I tell her, "I surely will, Grandma."

With a look at the house, I realize I might never see it again. I might never hear Maggie playing the piano. Yet I realize I have everything locked in my head. It will always be there.

42

NINE MONTHS

MAYBE IT ISN'T A STORY to end so soon, like most tales tend to. More to tell if you got some time. Skip it if you don't.

I caught up with Trina south of Guymon, where she said she'd be. I found her sitting under a hawthorn tree, horse grazing nearby. She'd taken off her hat and was braiding her hair. She'd waited half a day and seemed glad to see me. Maybe a little surprised. She said she was afraid I wouldn't come after her. But I said, maybe too boldly, that I couldn't *not* come after her.

"Come're," she called when she mounted her horse.

Pulling our horses close, we leaned out to each other and had our first kiss. Something strange yet delicious. Parting, we grinned, like we now had a secret.

We continued to the town where her sister Triss lived – which I shouldn't name.

Her boys rushed out into the yard to greet their mother, and she practically dove off the saddle to welcome them into her arms. Lots of kisses, excited chatter about how much they missed each other. Out of the house stepped Triss, her belly round beneath an apron. She hugged her sister. A giant of a man stood tall in the doorway and I guessed he was the husband.

I dismounted, led our horses to the barn. I could hear the sisters weeping behind me as I took care of the horses. Trina was telling them about Bart. Telling the boys why their papa wouldn't ever be coming home.

"He got shot," she said, "an' couldn't get him to a doc in time."

Izzy tried to stay strong but broke into sobs. Nicky cried easily. Trina hugged them, tried to soothe their sorrow with words.

"Had to bury him up north. But a preacher said some fine words over him. So he'll be watchin' ya from above. Right up there."

"Pa's gone?" cried Izzy, refusing to believe her. "Never got to say goodbye. Or I love 'im."

"I want Pa," Nicky sobbed.

She never told them *how* he got shot. My heart clenched into a fist, wouldn't let go. I stayed in the barn longer, not wanting to get the full effect of the boys' sorrow just yet when I'd finally managed to contain it within myself.

I came out after a while and Trina stood up beside the boys.

"See this man right here," she told them, "he's yer pa's cousin or sumpin. I picked him up at the General Store fer ya, but he weren't cheap. He kin be yer pa from now on. So you be good to him, an' ya mind what he say."

"He our new pa?" asked Izzy, unsure whether to smile.

Nicky was more welcoming. "Howdy, mister."

"You can call me Jake," I said, giving the boys a kind wave.

"Ya call him Pa," Trina corrected. "An' ya mind him."

Triss stepped over to me, held out her hand to shake. "S'pose yer in this family now. Ain't easy. Good luck to ya. Yer welcome at our dinner table."

I thanked her, shook her hand. Then she took Trina inside. I had to believe she'd tell the whole story to her sister: everything that happened since she left on an ordinary collection that morning with Bart. I wanted to know what happened to him since the sisters first found him. Maybe there are some things we shouldn't know. It's better that way.

"Did Ma really get ya from a store?" asked Izzy, studying me. It would become a joke in the family for many years.

I stayed outside with the boys. Izzy looked about seven, Nicky maybe five. We took time to get to know each other. They told me their games (tag mostly), how Aunt Triss cooked (badly), and what they hoped to do as grown men (be cowboys). They liked the stories I told about pulling teeth. They laughed when I tried to make it sound awful, acting like a patient in pain, grabbing my jaw.

Then Triss called us inside. Nicky took my hand, kept hold of it as we went into the house. Dinner was ready. It wasn't too bad.

+   +   +

Time is supposed to heal all our wounds. I did my best to be a good man, a friend to Trina and the boys. I helped deliver that next baby of hers and Bart's: another son. She asked me to choose the name. I thought a while; nothing fit this one.

"We kin name him Simon. If bein' awright," she said. "After Pa. He's long time off this world."

"Then this boy is Simon Bartholomew Baumann." I smiled down at the wrinkly baby. "He will do great things someday."

Finished with feeding, I held him: a boy with his mama's dark brown almost black hair but his father's blue eyes, a living memory of their last union before Bart died.

I kept thinking of that day, imagining it like I was writing out a story for a news-paper. I wasn't there; I could only rely on Trina's account which seemed to shift a little each time the incident was mentioned. I never was certain which version might be the truth. In that one way I distrusted her and made sure she didn't carry a gun around me.

Other than that suspicion that lingered, we had a pleasant life together, living in the farm house with Triss and that man she took as her husband, Riley Fairchild, and all the kids.

As boys will be, Izzy and Nicky were quite curious exploring the world, making up games. They and little brother Simon grew up but always found new ways to get into mischief. They learned a lot that way. I taught the boys how to read and write – all the kids, in fact, making a small but serious class. Riley taught the kids about arithmetics and farming.

I opened an office in town and set up a clinic. Not many teeth to work on but I handled other minor problems, too: providing first-aid, setting broken bones, tending to burns, general advice, writing scripts for the apothecary. I liked coming to the clinic, seeing those golden words emblazoned across the window: *Dr. Jacob Baumann, Dentistry & General Medicine.*

Trina got a sewing business started, took in clothes to mend. She hired a couple women to help and they got more work. Had to buy sewing machines. She set up her sewing shop across the street from the clinic, calling it *Mendy's.* "Come here to get all your rips *mend*ed." It's a joke Triss thought up.

We lived as a family, though we never did go to a church for a ceremony. We found a better way to prove our love for each other: we had our own child, a son. This one definitely looked like a Kanza-Comanche boy. We loved him like the others. We named him Jasper and he eventually went to the dentistry school up in Kanza City. He worked with me, then followed after me in the business, took it over. We added his name to the window when I retired.

Triss gave birth to a daughter from her big belly that day I first arrived. She and Riley named her Ruth. Actually, she was one of a set of twins but the second didn't survive. Another daughter was born the following year, named Rachel. No boys for them.

As the years turned over, I kept catching Trina gazing down the street, out past the town to where the wheat fields began, as if she hoped to see Bart racing by on his horse. Then she'd smile – for her it was more a pinch of her lips – then return her attention to me. I never saw anything.

In time, as Trina and I let our hair turn gray, our four sons met and married fine ladies from nearby towns: Isaiah and Iris, Nicky and Evaline, Simon and Priscilla. Only Jasper and his bride, Mary Sue, stayed in our town. The daughters of Triss and Riley married well, too: Ruth with Tyler, Rachel with Matthew. Those husbands worked the farm with Riley. After some time, Trina and I collected fifteen grandchildren. One day we gathered in front of my dentistry clinic and had a photo-graph fellow set up a camera box to capture an image of us: the entire family. I wanted to save it for our history book: *The Baumann Family: A Portrait.*

It was Mariam, eldest daughter of Isaiah and Iris (with Rebecca and Sarah being the younger daughters; Leroy, their only son), who started the project. At first it was for school but she kept going with it even after graduation. She collected all the news-paper clips and pictures she could find. She asked questions of me, wrote down my answers. I did my best to recall what Maggie had told me about her father and her grandmother Isla. Mariam asked questions of many people who happened to know us – some people couldn't believe we 'brown ones' were actually the same family. Yet we were all related; that was the point of her project. One family. She put it together in a manuscript – had a few snips of Maggie's music pages included, too. Mariam sent it to a publisher in Kanza City but never heard from them. Maybe it's still there, hidden on a cluttered desk. Maybe it was lost on the Express. The railway service became unreliable as the years went by, then ceased.

I kept expecting to make a trip to Skinner Canyon, planned for it a few times. I wanted to bring our four sons and let Maggie hug them, but there was always something to do that needed my or our sons' attention as they grew older. I wrote letters, sent them to her. It started when Nicky joined the militia and they were sent south to fight Slammers. Maggie sent letters back. In each one, she would complain how the town was falling further into disrepute. No more kids' band. A new deputy. Another saloon. Then, after receiving no letters for a while, I learned that Maggie had died. It was written in our town's news-paper, a favorable story about the famous music lady who started a kids' band, then rose to be principal conductor of the National Symphony in the capital for ten years. She adopted an orphaned Kanza girl and she married Maggie's nephew. They had a son named Jacob. Her own son, Bart, didn't survive her.

To me, she was always Grandma. When I got older, I called her Maggie, as she insisted, or Miss Maggie when in town.

Long after, with our sons grown and working hard, raising their own families, we took a trip north in a fine carriage, Trina and me, up to Skinner Canyon. No one there bothered us. Maybe they didn't recognize us. We rolled past the jailhouse, the hotel, the clinic, the Five Ladies (renamed *Five Floozies*), and that house at the edge of town where Maggie had lived. It was for sale.

She told me she'd leave it to me in her Will, yet I was situated in our town. So I consented to its sale. First, I wanted to collect anything Maggie might've wanted me to save. That proved to be quite a lot. Including her piano, which required us to hire a wagon and driver to haul it home. Our grandchildren would be delighted. I liked having music in the house. Hearing music in that house had made me feel at home. Our sons gave the cornet a try but without a teacher, they didn't learn much. However, one of the grandsons, Ricky, found it one day and liked it, played it often. He would make up songs just like Maggie did.

We went to the cemetery by where their old cabin had burnt down many years before. The family plot remained, started before that fire. I stared at the markers. I read the names. Here was Aunt Eve. I could remember her well. Her sister Faith. And *her* husband Raymond, killed in a gunfight. Here lay Bart's Uncle Frank, the sheriff, who I called Grandfather although he didn't really like it. And my mother: Jackie, short for Jackrabbit, who Maggie adopted. Then Jackie was murdered, instigating that infamous posse so long ago. Trina hugged me as tears slipped out. We regarded the marker for Maggie's other brother, James, the priest. We stood at Bart's grave, there beside Maggie's. I hugged Trina as her eyes grew wet. I knew she really did love him. Then we knelt at Maggie's site and I mouthed a prayer, wishing her a peaceful repose.

We watched the stars come up over the yard, the same stars all of our ancestors had seen, the same stars our future kin would see. Everything finally made sense.

And then we rode home.

GENEALOGY

Grandma Hannah's Line:

Sandy Baumann = Hannah Whistler
Isla

Frank =   (& Sandy = Lorraine, Frank's wife's twin)
Cherie   Polly

Trey (drifter) =
Iris

Sven (drifter) =
Jenny

Ajamu (preacher) =
Ellie

Big Joe =
Raymond

Sandy (return) =
Allie

Isla's Line:

LJ (Big Joe's son) = Isla
Amy June

Lionel Chesterfield =
Bobbie & Abe

(brothel guest) =
(Lily, died in infancy)

Ajamu =
(miscarriage)

Frank (after Isla returns to national park) =
Fritz (Frank Jr.)

Fritz's Line:

Frank Sr. = Isla

    Fritz *(Frank Jr.)* = Sandra   [Book 4: *The Book of Dad*]

     Frank III = Vera

Jackie (Kanza) = **Jeb**   & Joe (twins) =
Jon =
Frances =

James (priest)

Maggie =   [Book 5: *The Granddaughter*]

Jackie (adopted) = **Jeb**

Jacob Little Bear

= Bart Tuttle

Bart Jr. = *Trina Culpepper*
Isaiah (Izzy)

= Marina Kvanshenaya
Nicholas (Nicky)

= *Trina Culpepper*
Simon

Trina Culpepper = **Jacob Little Bear**
Jasper

Maggie's grandsons are Jacob and Izzy, Nick, Simon,
as well as great-grandson Jasper.

ACKNOWLEDGMENTS

Writing a novel requires various influences to come together in random fashion to initiate the story idea and propel the writing forward.

The *Flu Season* trilogy began with a deliberate thought-experiment based on the film *A Boy and His Dog* (1975), a sardonic adventure set in an odd post-apocalyptic landscape, based on Harlan Ellison's short story. I gave my novel the working title "A Boy and his Mom and her tuba". However, I couldn't work on it as the SARS-CoV-2 ("covid-19") pandemic worsened. Only when the crisis was coming to an end did I find a way to start *The Book of Mom*.

I wanted to focus not on those initial days we all experienced, when everything was immediate and real, but further into the future, when the worst we experienced had gotten worse still, say, six years into the future. Book 2 *The Way of the Son* continues the story through another year of the post-pandemic experience. Everything is irrevocably broken and the only way forward is to rebuild from scratch.

In Book 3 *Dawn of the Daughters*, the rebuilding begins but our family isn't aware of it for a while. When they enter the new society, they find it being rebuilt in horrible fashion. Book 4, *The Book of Dad*, shows us the beginning of a society heading into tyranny. But in Book 5, *The Granddaughter*, family members escape the tyranny of the capital for a kinder, gentler chapter.

I always select music that helps me create the appropriate emotive soundscape for writing sessions. The aural support unlocks my muse. I found the ideal soundtrack in the following music: Westerns scored by Ennio Morricone; recent songs by country/blues singers Larkin Poe, The Sweeplings, The Band Perry, as well as Marty Robbins' ballads. Scott Buckley's music continued to serve me well.

Special thanks goes forever to those who worked the front lines during the pandemic, some of whom lost their lives alongside their patients. Our gratitude is immeasurable.

S T E P H E N   S W A R T Z

ABOUT THE AUTHOR

Stephen Swartz is the author of twenty novels, including this current volume, as well as several short stories in anthologies and literary journals. He has also published scholarly articles and a Ph.D. dissertation on the role of identity in student composition. He has taught English at several colleges and universities over a thirty-year career. While teaching English courses at a university in Oklahoma during the past decade, Swartz realized his ambition to publish his previously written novels. Thanks to the notoriety of the Amazon Breakthrough Novel Award competition, the first of them, *After Ilium*, was published – followed quickly by the sci-fi tome *The Dream Land* and the anti-romance *A Beautiful Chill*.

Prior to graduate school and earning an M.A. (English) and M.F.A. (Creative Writing), Swartz lived in Japan for five years where he taught English at the middle school and high school levels. His experiences there helped inspire him to write his novel *Aiko*. Swartz taught summer courses at a university in Beijing, China in recent years. His wide travels and interest in cultures and languages has propelled his fiction into explorations of situations where the main character is often a stranger in a strange land and must find ways to adapt – much as he has done during a lifetime and career of various excursions.

He borrows from those experiences for the *Flu Season* series.